Léonie

Léonie

Elizabeth Adler

VILLARD BOOKS · NEW YORK 1985

Library of Congress Cataloging in Publication Data
Adler, Elizabeth.
Léonie.
I. Title.
PR6051.D56L4   1985   823'.914   85-40175
ISBN 0-394-54700-4

Manufactured in the United States of America
9   8   7   6   5   4   3   2
First American Edition

For my mother and father with love

BOOK
1

❧

1890-1893

❧ 1 ❧

THE NIGHT was still and moonlit, edged with ice. A thin frost lined the trees with white and tipped each furrow and hedgerow with new, cold beauty. In the distance the lights of a village twinkled fitfully and the smoke of burning applewood spiraled from low, country-cottage chimneys. The train wound its way through the night, shattering the rural stillness with a sudden shrill whistle that was echoed mockingly by some hunting barn owl.

Paul Bernard leaned back in the warmth and comfort of his compartment, sighing as they slowed down yet again. It had been a long journey. He'd missed the Paris express and had been faced with the choice of waiting three hours for the next, or taking the local, which crawled its way across the Normandy countryside toward the city. The bleak provincial station had offered few comforts, so he had taken the slow train and now he was regretting it. He checked his round gold pocket watch once again and smiled ruefully. A mere fifteen minutes had passed since he'd last checked. Peering out of the window he could see only himself reflected against the darkness—a tall, dark-haired man, in his early thirties, with nice, steady brown eyes. He smiled at his reflection, a prosperous man, a man of good taste. A tired man! His image disappeared from the window as they pulled into yet another dimly lit country station. Doors slammed, mail and milk were loaded, the guard chatted interminably with the stationmaster—would this journey never end?

In a hiss of steam the train pulled slowly from the platform. At last! The door crashed back suddenly and a battered bag flew past him into the compartment followed by a brimming straw basket and then the hurtling figure of a girl. The whirl of brown woolen skirts and tumbling blond hair picked herself up from the floor where she had landed and examined her knees carefully. A trickle of blood seeped through the twin holes in the thick woolen stockings that drooped around her thin ankles and she stared at them in dismay.

"Oh, I can't," she wailed despairingly, "I just can't."

"Can't what?" asked Paul, smiling.

"I can't go to Paris with holes in my stockings—what will people think?"

Paul bent to pick up her basket, recapturing the apples that were rolling around the compartment and stuffing them next to the country sausage and the hunk of bread. "I don't think," he said, handing her the basket politely, "that people will see your knees—normally, that is."

She dropped her skirt hurriedly, smoothing it down, and settled primly on the edge of the seat opposite him. The color rose in her cheeks and she bit her lip, embarrassed.

Paul eyed her with amusement; the girls he knew never blushed. Picking up his newspaper he pretended to read, giving her time to compose herself. There was no doubt that she was in the wrong part of the train—she should, judging by her appearance, be in second class. She was leaning back against the cushions, eyes closed, and the flickering light in the carriage cast shadows beneath the long sloping cheekbones, emphasizing the taut smoothness of her peach-colored skin. He lowered his paper, taking advantage of her closed eyes to inspect her. She was very young—perhaps sixteen. A country girl, shrouded in layers of ill-fitting garments, but there was something about her that was really quite extraordinary. Or perhaps "exotic" was a better word to describe her. Such a mass of wonderful hair, tawny blond, spilling all over the place, and there was no hiding the length of those legs, even in the thick stockings and the dreadful country shoes. He shuddered fastidiously at the sight of her clumsy, mud-covered, thick-soled shoes and tried to visualize the same feet in silk stockings and elegant high-heeled slippers. Beneath the rough, ill-cut clothes, the mud, and the country manner there lurked a beauty. It didn't jump out and grab you, but it could, given the right circumstances. He felt sure of it—and he was a connoisseur. Women were his business.

Why, he wondered, was she going to Paris? He smiled. Why else would a young, country girl go to Paris if not to do "something," to become "somebody." They all thought that in Paris anything must be possible. He stared out of the window, seeing her reflected there, and considered what to do about her.

I've done it, thought Léonie, her heart still thudding in her chest from a combination of fear, excitement, and the last-minute dash to the station. I've finally done it! Her fingers curled around the thin bundle of notes in her pocket. She didn't need to count them, she knew exactly how much was there. It was all she possessed in the world, saved from her wages as a kitchen helper and waitress at the café in Masarde. Of course, she'd get a better job right away in Paris; after all, she was educated, wasn't she? The old Curé had taught her himself for three whole years—of course, that was before her mother died. After that there'd been no time for books and learning, she had to earn her living. But it was the books that had done it.

Without them she might never have known that anything existed beyond life in the small village where she was born—even Masarde had seemed like a grand town at first. She might have thought that everybody lived like that. Now she knew better; out there lay the real world, where everything waited for you—exciting people, wonderful parties, music, romance, laughter—she'd find it all, she just knew she would. That's why she left.

When she was a little girl and her mother was still alive she had listened wide-eyed to the tales about her father, how he traveled the world with the circus—"from France to Russia," he had claimed, though oddly enough her mother had met him when the little circus came to Masarde, the bareback rider, bronzed and virile in spangled white tights, muscles rippling under the lights. He was Egyptian, tawny-eyed and commanding, and Emilie had fallen head over heels for him. "You're like him," she'd told Léonie, "you have his eyes, his profile . . . ah, if only you'd known him." But she never had, he'd gone back to the circus a week after she was born. Oh, he had promised Emilie he'd be back, promised they would be married, and her mother had kept her hopes until the day she died.

Léonie pressed her eyes more tightly shut. She didn't want to think about that, either. She'd been to the frozen cemetery today, with its bleak little stone slab looking too small to blanket her pretty mother. Of course she told her what she was going to do, standing there with the icy wind whipping her hair into knots, stinging her eyes so that the tears she fought against froze on her cheeks. And she waited for some kind of answer, some sign of approval—but there was none. She was alone. She must make her own way in life. She would do it in Paris.

The train braked and slowed down, jolting her from her uneasy sleep. Her eyes flew open, catching those of the man sitting opposite, and their glances locked. "Oh." She sat up and smoothed her hair, confused. "Is this Paris?"

"Not yet, we still have half an hour to go. But you've slept most of the way." The strange beauty blushed again, gazing at him with those enormous eyes. There was something about the slant of the cheekbones and the curve of the jaw, the tiny ears. It was a flamboyant face, he decided; it didn't hide under plump pink flesh, it flaunted its angles and hollows proudly. Yes, she could be a beauty, if she knew how.

There was a tap on the door and the ticket collector held out his hand impatiently while she fished her ticket from her pocket. "You should be in second class," he said officiously. "You don't belong in here and you've traveled all the way from Masarde in this compartment. You'll have to pay extra."

"I'm sorry," she stammered. "I didn't know."

The collector thrust out his hand threateningly. "Don't give me that story, you'd better pay up right now."

Paul Bernard folded some notes in a discreet palm. "The young lady is with me."

The conductor backed away with a sly smile. "Sorry, sir . . . I didn't realize. . . ."

Paul leaned forward and handed the girl his card. "I hope you will allow me the privilege of helping you? I could see that it might have caused you a problem."

Paul Bernard, she read to herself. Director, Music Hall Cabaret, place Royale, Paris. He was so smart, so sophisticated; he must think her just a silly country girl! "You're very kind, Monsieur Bernard," she said miserably, "I'll pay you back, of course."

"What takes you to Paris?" he asked, putting a match to his cigar and settling back in his seat.

"I had to get away." The words came tumbling out with a suddenness that surprised her. "I couldn't stand it any longer. . . ." She wished she'd never said that; what must he think of her now?

"And what sort of job will you get in Paris? Do you know anyone there?"

"No, monsieur." Her eyes reflected her fear but she lifted her chin confidently. "But I'm sure I'll get a job as a waitress. I have experience."

"Here." He wrote briskly on the back of his card. "This is the address of a decent boardinghouse. Tell Madame Artois I sent you, and if you are interested, I have a job for you."

Léonie clutched the card hopefully. "A job, monsieur?"

"There's always room for a girl like you in the Music Hall."

What could he mean, a girl like her? And what could she do in a music hall? She glanced at him suspiciously. "But I can't sing and I can't dance. . . ." Her muddy feet loomed larger than ever; surely he must be mocking her!

He smiled. "There'll always be room in the cabaret for a girl as beautiful as you."

Beautiful! Now she knew he was crazy—or worse! She recalled the whispered conversations about the girls of the Paris streets and peered at him warily from under her lashes. He didn't look so bad though, quite kind really. But she didn't trust him.

The train wound its way slowly through the outskirts of Paris and into the Gare du Nord. As it jolted to a halt she had the door open in a flash, leaping to the platform, bags clutched in her hands. She turned, remembering the money. "I shall send you your money as soon as I can, monsieur, and thank you."

"But wait, wait a minute . . ." He held up his hand as she turned to go. Can I offer you a lift? After all you don't know Paris."

"No . . . oh, no. . . ."

She was off, running down the platform, apples spilling from her basket, blond hair flying. He watched her push her way through the crowd at the barrier and disappear into the nighttime streets of Paris. "I wonder," he said to himself as he walked slowly toward the exit, "I just wonder what will become of her."

❧ 2 ❦

MADAME ARTOIS was a large, square battleship of a woman who ran her boardinghouse with a mixture of firmness and good humor and a definite rule of women only. She'd had too much trouble from the men in the old days, they were always making a play for first one girl and then another; the jealousies had been terrible. Hers was a respectable house, she made sure of that, but she was fond of "her girls": the young ladies of the music halls and cabarets around town. Madame had been an artiste herself: a long time ago she had sung on most of the stages in Paris, and now she took a vicarious pleasure in monitoring the careers and romantic entanglements of "her girls."

Madame was also a woman who knew what she wanted from life, and what she wanted at this moment was a kitchen helper. The last one had left that morning—gone home to nurse her sick mother—leaving Madame stranded and the cook furious, refusing to prepare dinner unless she had someone to do the vegetables and the dishes. Léonie had appeared on her doorstep like a gift from the gods. "You're lucky," she told her. "It's not easy to get work in Paris, but I can offer you the job and it includes room and board." The relief on the girl's face was so evident that Madame wondered, for a moment, what the girl would have done had she said no. She obviously had come to Paris, as they all did, with no money and no prospects—and no idea of what she was going to do once she got there. At that age, Madame thought with a sigh for the irresponsibility of youth, just getting there seemed to be an end in itself.

"Thank you, madame, I'll start right away." Léonie took off her coat hurriedly, before Madame Artois could change her mind. Piling the dishes in the sink, she thrust her cold hands into the hot, soapy water, feeling her fingers come back to life. She had never thought that doing dishes would make her so happy!

The tiny room under the eaves was clean and warm, the narrow iron bed beneath its piled eiderdowns comfortable, and with her meager possessions unpacked the room became her own. Her two dresses hung in the closet, her darned woolen stockings and serviceable underwear lay neatly folded in the chest of drawers, and on top were arranged her half-dozen books and the dolls. Not dolls really, just small, oddly carved statues, but they had been all she had had to play with as a child, and they had belonged to her father. She ran her fingers over the decorative symbols carved around the base. She supposed they were Egyptian, but she wasn't sure, though the cat certainly didn't look like the farm cats she knew. It was slender and sleek and aristocratic with a small triangular face and slanting eyes. She had loved that cat so much as a child. And the other doll, a lioness or a woman. A bit of both, really, a lioness's head on a woman's body. She had always thought her very beautiful. She wondered for the thousandth time if the symbols meant anything, and if so, what?

She sighed with satisfaction as she surveyed her new home. Last night that icy miserable room by the station had cost her exactly half the total she had allotted for the entire week, and she had been shocked and frightened by the expense. Really, it was all thanks to the man on the train; after all, he was the one who'd sent her here. She would repay him as soon as possible. But here she was, one day in Paris and she already had a job; what more could she want?

Patience, she thought just three months later, leaning her elbows on the windowsill of her tiny room at the very top of the tall thin house on the boulevard des Artistes. I must be patient. She gazed down at the busy streets and squares of Paris spread out below her as if for some exciting game, one that she couldn't wait to play. But how? What were the rules? What was the magic ingredient, she wondered, that made you "belong" in Paris? It was a scary city, scary and glamorous. The streets were full of cafés and bistros, theaters and cabarets, gambling halls and shops; and the people on the streets looked as though they did exciting things, they were artists and actresses and writers and rich, rich people. And kitchen helpers!

Sighing regretfully, she pulled on her hat and ran down the seven flights of stairs to the kitchen to pick up the little parcel of lunch she had prepared the night before. It was Sunday afternoon and she was free, and she intended to spend it as she usually did, exploring the city.

She headed toward the Bois de Boulogne, lingering on streets lined with grand houses, peering through their railings to catch a glimpse of the magnificent marble interiors until the glaring eye of a concierge sent her on her way. The crowded café at the corner of the place Saint-Georges looked gay and cheerful. She hovered in front of it, too afraid to go in alone and too thrifty anyway to spend the money. Everyone seemed to be with someone else; was it her imagination or did they all seem to know one another? A couple emerged from the back of the café and strolled along the street, arms linked, chatting intimately, his head bent toward her while she smiled up at him. She was so elegant, thought Léonie, following them, admiring her smart dress and tiny-heeled shoes. Lured by their warmth, their intimacy, she pressed closer, longing to be a part of it, eavesdropping shamelessly on their conversation until they stopped suddenly and stared at her. Embarrassed, she turned away.

She sat on a bench in the Bois and ate her sandwiches, feeding the little city birds who crowded around, watching the magnificent horses and riders as they trotted past, remembering the farm horses she had loved to ride in her home village. The Bois was full of surprises: there was a circus. She paused in front of the poster and ran her finger down the list of performers, her heart beating a little faster, wondering if maybe her father's name might be there. But, of course, it wasn't. And there was an outdoor dance hall! She had discovered it on her first Sunday and it lured her back every week, not that she ever went in—she watched from a distance, listening to the music as it drifted over the grass, catching glimpses of the dancers and the girls, like herself, flirting with young men at the tables beneath the trees. How did it feel, she wondered, to flirt with a man? She sighed with frustration as she turned from the scene. Patience, she told herself, I must be patient. One day I'll be part of it all.

There was no doubt that she was lonely, but Sunday evenings more than compensated for her solitary Sunday afternoons. That was when all the girls were at home, when they didn't rush off to the theater but instead lazed around, gossiping. The whole house seemed different on Sunday, relaxed and easy. Léonie basked in the other girls' attention. She was allowed to linger on the fringes of the group, listening to their talk of their latest romances, and about the stars of the cabarets. It was the best time of the week, and they treated her like their little sister.

"We must do something about Léonie," said Loulou, sipping her brandy and spreading herself more comfortably over the big plush sofa in the salon. It was another boring Sunday evening and Léonie had just brought in their afterdinner coffee. She paused in surprise.

"What do you mean, Loulou?"

"Well, look at you. You're really not bad-looking under all that hair and those awful clothes." Loulou put a finger under Léonie's chin and tilted her face up toward the light. "Yes, in fact you're very pretty. Don't you think so, Bella?"

Bella inspected Léonie. "I wish I had skin like that," she said enviously. "You'll never need to use powder, though a little rouge, here, just under the cheekbones, would show up your eyes more."

Jolie came to stand beside Bella. "And the hair . . . look, it needs to be swept up on top like this." She took a handful of Léonie's hair and held it above the girl's head, demonstrating how it might look.

"But it won't stay," protested Léonie. "It never does, no matter how many pins I stick in it."

"My dear, that will be part of its charm." Bella smiled wickedly. "A little 'tumbled' . . . a little 'unkempt' . . . yes, it would be a very charming look for you. A nice contrast to the innocence."

"Now, you girls, be careful with Léonie," warned Madame Artois. "She's not going on the stage and I don't want her to look 'common.' "

"Madame Artois," said Loulou indignantly, "are you saying that we look common?"

"Of course not, but you look like stage girls and Léonie's not that. I don't mind you helping her to look better, heaven knows she needs it, but take care with her." Madame Artois liked Léonie. She didn't want them spoiling her and making her too sophisticated—she'd seen too many young girls end up as weary women, old before their time, worn down by too many years in the chorus, too much drink—and too many men!

"Bella, get the makeup box and a hairbrush," instructed Loulou. "We're going to transform Léonie."

"Sit down here, Cinderella," said Loulou, offering her a chocolate from the large box given her by her latest admirer. She was a tall, fleshy girl with a wide crimson mouth and an easy laugh, and she was popular in the cabaret, well known for her audacious songs. She was more than a little "risqué," yet she looked wholesome, a perverse combination that was very attractive. And she was generous—she liked Léonie, felt sorry for her, really, she supposed. They all did; she was like the kid sister they had left behind at home, or maybe the innocent they had once been. Loulou applied the rouge with a light hand, sweeping it across the cheekbones, adding a touch on the chin, a little on the temples. Bella studied the result carefully and then added a slick of gleaming bronze along the curve of Léonie's eyelids while Jolie wielded the hairbrush relentlessly, pulling her hair up and back until Léonie howled in protest. "Beauty is painful," misquoted Jolie severely. "But it's always worth it!" she added with a laugh.

"There, Madame Artois, what do you think?" asked Loulou as they stood back to admire their handiwork.

It was extraordinary how different Léonie looked, thought Madame Artois. "I think it's a little flashy," she said finally.

"Flashy! It's discreet—a nun could get away with that makeup."

"A nun would not want to, my dear. However, you do look very pretty, Léonie." Léonie put up a tentative hand to feel her hair.

"You see, it's already coming down," she protested.

"No, no, Léonie, that's the way it should be," Jolie reassured her. "It's meant to tumble a little."

"Why don't you take a look in the mirror," suggested Loulou.

"No, not yet, wait a minute." Bella sped up the stairs, returning a few minutes later carrying a woolen dress in a soft apricot color, high-necked and deceptively demure. "Here, this might fit you," she offered. "It never suited me, but it's just the right color for you."

"Oh, Bella!" Léonie was overwhelmed. "Do you really mean it?"

"Of course," said Bella, pleased that Léonie liked it so much. "It should fit you quite well, although it may be a bit big on the bosom . . . and, of course, it's going to be a bit short."

"Hurry, Léonie, try it on," said Jolie impatiently.

They helped her off with her layers of clothing until she stood in her woolen chemise and drawers, shrinking from embarrassment under their collective gaze.

"You know, you have a good shape," said Loulou, "it's just hidden under all those layers of wool!"

Bella lowered the dress over Léonie's head, careful not to disturb her hair, and buttoned it up the back, swinging her around to inspect the result.

Léonie faced them anxiously, hoping that she looked all right—their silence was unnerving.

Finally Loulou raised her glass in a toast. "I salute you, Léonie," she said. "You are beautiful. And I have the feeling that after tonight, you will be a different person."

It was the second time someone had called her beautiful. Could it be true, or was Loulou joking, too? Léonie walked across the salon and stared in the gilded mirror that covered one wall. She looked just the same, or did she? The new hairdo emphasized the firm line of her jaw, baring her pretty ears and cascading down her back. The rouge hollowed out her cheeks. Her eyes looked larger, their amber gleam deepened by the color of the dress, but it was just her, still her own face. But the dress was wonderful! Even though it was too big, it seemed to cling in the proper places, making her look taller, curvier, pinching in prettily at her waist. Yes, it made her look quite different. She didn't mind that it was a little short, it was the most beautiful dress she had ever owned.

"She's like a young cat, who doesn't yet know how to use her claws," Bella murmured into Loulou's ear.

Madame Artois watched in silence. The unkempt child who had shown up on her doorstep had taken on a new dimension. Paul Bernard had seen her allure right away, of course; that's why he had helped her. And, of course, he was right.

Léonie peered closer in the mirror, her excitement growing. Yes, she did look better, pretty even. She swirled in the dress straining to see how it looked at the back, patted her upswept hair, ran a finger along her cheek to see if the pink came off. "Oh, thank you, thank you all," she said at last, tears falling down her cheeks and spoiling the rouge. "You're all so nice, so good to me."

"Nonsense." They laughed. "It was fun. And you'll never be the same again, Léonie!"

"Well, what do you think, Madame Artois?" she asked, posing before her.

"I think," sighed Madame Artois, "that I'll have to find myself a new kitchen helper, and we'll have to find you a better job. Tomorrow I'll speak to Madame Serrat at the lingerie shop on rue Montalivet. I heard she was looking for an assistant and you'd probably do as well as anybody else."

"*Really?* Really, Madame Artois?" Léonie couldn't believe it. "Oh, thank you, thank you." She threw her arms around Madame Artois and kissed her, and then she kissed Loulou, Bella, and Jolie. "I'll never forget this night," she promised.

Léonie's interview at Madame Serrat's was the most important topic of conversation among the girls that week. They were determined that she should get the job. "Although I don't know what you're worrying about, Léonie," said Loulou. "I could get you into the cabaret in a minute."

Léonie laughed at her words. Of course it wasn't true, and besides, the idea of the cabaret was frightening. Madame Artois had said that she would enjoy working at Serrat and there would be prospects for promotion to a proper salesgirl if she did well. Meanwhile, any spare moment they had the girls helped her. Jolie taught her how to do her hair herself, though more demurely, this time wrapping it into a smooth blond chignon, and they had added a band of deeper bronze velvet to the hem of the dress to make it longer, and a matching velvet collar. The shoes were a problem—none of the girls had any to fit her and obviously she couldn't wear her old ones. Finally, Madame Artois took her to the store and she bought a pair of neat black shoes with small heels, like the ones she had seen the other girls wearing, though she was shocked by the price. "Look upon it as an investment, my dear," advised Madame Artois. "Those shoes will put your feet on the proper road to success." Bella and Jolie made her practice walking in the unaccustomed heels so she wouldn't trip, and she was surprised how elegant they made her feel. For the first time in her life she wasn't ashamed of the size of her feet. Madame Artois gave her a pair of fine cotton lisle stockings as a good-luck gift and Loulou presented her with a small gilt brooch with a pretty amber stone in its center. "It's not worth anything," she said, dismissing Léonie's thanks, "but it suits the dress."

Léonie left the house early on Saturday morning wearing her new dress and Madame Artois's second-best brown wool cape with the tiny fur collar. Her interview was at nine-thirty and at nine-fifteen she paced the rue Montalivet anxiously, passing the shop for the tenth time, becoming more nervous with every minute. She hadn't realized that Serrat would be so intimidatingly smart. The tall windows were lined with rose velvet and a rose-striped awning, inscribed with the name Serrat in deeper pink letters, formed a protective half-moon across the curved marble steps. As she watched, a young boy emerged to sweep the pink carpet that led to the glass-paneled door. He added a final polish to the gleaming brass doorplate then disappeared inside. It must be almost nine-thirty now, she thought, approaching the shop nervously and following him through the door.

A bell tinkled gracefully as she closed the door behind her and stood for a moment gasping at her surroundings. She was in a pink velvet box, the walls and ceiling padded in rose velvet and buttoned with satin. Crystal chandeliers illuminated long glass tables, empty but for a huge bowl of white swansdown scarves and lace collars, silk ribbons and mother-of-pearl buckles. Along one wall was arranged a series of lacy robes, swirling at their hems with feathers or bands of silk and satin, in peach, oyster, lilac, and pistachio, with all the mouth-watering delicacy of sugared almonds. Léonie sighed with pleasure. She wanted to touch them, to hold the smooth satin against her cheek, to drape the silk across her body.

A tall woman came from the back of the shop, smiling. "Yes, madame," she asked, "may I—" She stopped short, taken aback by the sight of Léonie. "What do you want?" she asked abruptly, her voice accelerating from the practiced obsequiousness of the assistant to shrill irritation. What was this girl doing here, bringing the dust of the streets onto their pale carpet?

"Excuse me, but are you Madame Serrat? I have an appointment at nine-thirty. About the job, you see."

"The job! Then what are you doing in here? Don't you know better than to use the customers' entrance? Anyway, Madame Serrat is busy at the moment." She looked down her nose at Léonie. "You'd better leave right now before any clients arrive . . . they don't want to see your sort in here."

"Then where should I go?" Léonie asked desperately, edging toward the door.

"Around the back, of course, and through the alley, you silly girl."

Léonie's palms were sweating with fright as she let herself out the door, and she paused to rub their mark off the glossy handle with her sleeve. She caught the woman's eye on her through the glass panels and fled down the street, searching for the alley. She must have missed it and time was passing. Oh, dear, she would be late! She would lose her chance at the job; how would she ever be able to tell them back at the boardinghouse? Oh, thank God, there was the alley. She spotted it, snaking narrowly between the buildings, and ran through, searching for Serrat's back entrance. The boy she had seen earlier sat at the top of a short flight of stone steps eating a bun and dropping crumbs down the front of his satin suit. He had changed from his normal clothes into the splendid costume of an Indian prince and his turban sat next to him on the steps, the osprey feather pinned by a jewel to its front, quivering in the morning breeze. His nut-brown skin gleamed next to the pink satin and his black eyes smiled at her. Léonie had never seen anything like him in her life.

He laughed at her surprised face. "Don't worry," he said, "it's just Madame Serrat's idea of what a smart page boy should wear in Paris. I'm the parcels boy here, I open doors for the customers, pass around the coffee and the drinks, deliver the packages. Madame Serrat saw a picture somewhere of a little blackamoor serving boy, so that's me!"

"But don't you mind?" she asked, fascinated by him.

"No, it's a job, but maybe when I'm older I will." He looked about fourteen but Léonie didn't want to seem rude and ask him his age.

"I'm supposed to see Madame Serrat at nine-thirty," she said, remembering suddenly why she was there.

"Then you're late, but don't worry, she's busy right now. The silks man just showed up from Milan and he'll be at least another half hour. You can go in and wait, if you like."

"Would you mind if I sat here with you?" Léonie didn't care to be alone in there for half an hour—that angry woman might throw her out again.

He could see she was nervous. "How come you're late if you're seeing Madame Serrat about a job? I would have thought you'd be early."

"Oh, but I was. I went to the front door and some woman sent me away . . . she said I should have known better than to go in there!"

"That'll be Marianne." He offered her a crumbling bun from the paper bag by his side. "She's a real terror. Scares all the girls."

"But why?" Léonie munched her bun thoughtfully.

"Don't know. Some women are like that, I suppose. You'll have to watch out for her, she's bound to be jealous of anyone as pretty as you."

Léonie beamed at him. He had called her pretty! "What's your name?" she asked.

"Maroc."

"Maroc? That's all?"

"That's it. I was born in Morocco. My father brought me to Paris when I was a little kid, four or five years old or something, and then he disappeared. I was brought up by the nuns at the orphanage and somehow I was always known as Le Maroc—the Moroccan one. It stuck and I quite like it."

They had a lot in common. They were both young, and both alone in Paris.

"It's time for you to go in." He put on his outrageous turban and grinned at her from beneath the feather. "Good luck. I hope you get the job."

"Thank you." She followed him up the steps and through the dingy passage, feeling better. "You know, Maroc," she said as he left her at Madame Serrat's door, "you're my first real friend in Paris."

"I'm glad." He smiled.

She squared her shoulders, took a deep breath, and knocked on the pink door.

Five minutes later she emerged onto the rue Montalivet as the new assistant salesgirl at Serrat. That whole new rose velvet, peach silk, and oyster satin world of luxury was hers.

"Léonie!" called Marianne in an exasperated voice. "Where are Madame Jourdan's parcels? Surely they must be ready by now!"

Léonie tied the last ribbon hurriedly. It had only been five minutes and there were three large parcels. First she had to fold the garments carefully and then wrap each one separately. "I'm sorry, mademoiselle, here they are."

"That's simply not good enough," cried Marianne. The attention of the entire shop focused suddenly on Léonie. "Forgive me, madame"—she turned to her surprised customer with a confiding smile—"the girl will redo them." She tugged at a ribbon. "Look, it's already coming undone!"

Standing to attention behind Madame Serrat's vast pink padded chair, Maroc watched sympathetically. Marianne really had it in for Léonie; she picked on her endlessly, making her life miserable, and she seemed to make a point of doing it when Madame Serrat was in the salon. "What *is* the matter with the girl, Marianne?" asked Madame Serrat. "She seems terribly slow."

"She's careless, madame, just careless." Marianne was all apologetic smiles. "I'll finish the parcels myself."

"Come here, Léonie," commanded Madame Serrat. She inspected the girl standing in front of her. She was shabby but neat and attractive in an odd sort of way, though her hair was a mess! "How long have you been with us now?"

"Four months, madame."

"Four months, eh? Long enough to know how to tie a parcel I should have thought! You must do better."

"But madame, it's just that . . ." Her eyes met Maroc's over the top of

Madame's chair and he frowned warningly. "I'll try to do better, madame."

"And do something about that hair . . . tie it back. We can't have it flying all over the place like that."

The salesgirls watched sympathetically, powerless to do anything. It was useless to complain to Madame Serrat—Marianne was her right hand and she would hear nothing bad about her.

Blushing from such a public humiliation, Léonie returned to her task of tidying the long glass-fronted cabinets. Marianne was the one flaw in her happiness at Serrat. Why, oh, *why* did she pick on her so? Heaven knows she was dong her best. Besides, there had been nothing wrong with those parcels. She folded the sets of satin chemises and knickers and smoothed the pleated lawn nightdresses, arranging the rosettes and ribbons neatly at the front and returning them carefully to their drawers. Many of the garments were custom-made, but they always had a large stock of beautiful ready-made things. Gentlemen liked to come in and buy presents for their lovers. She opened the top drawer and peeked at the sexy corsets in daring black and slithery red satin, crisscrossed with enticing ribbons, and wondered for the hundredth time *who* wore them, and *where?*

"Léonie." Maroc slipped a folded piece of paper into her hand. "It's from the gentleman with Mademoiselle Gloriette," he whispered. "He was watching when Marianne caused that scene." Gloriette, the new star of the Carnavalet Cabaret, always had her lover of the moment in attendance when she shopped.

Hiding behind the cabinet, Léonie opened the note and scanned it quickly. "Don't worry," he had written, "she's only jealous because you are so very pretty. May I take you out to supper some evening to make up for it?" She looked up in surprise; he was watching her—a tall, good-looking young man with curly blond hair and an air of confidence—standing behind Mademoiselle Gloriette, who was busy choosing fabrics for her new gowns. He smiled and raised his eyebrows inquiringly and she turned away in embarrassment, feeling the blush rise up her face annoyingly—it always gave her away!

She turned back to her cabinets, her heart pounding with excitement. A man had written *her* a note, asked to take *her* out to supper! Of course she wouldn't dream of going, but what a story for Loulou, Bella, and Jolie; she couldn't wait for the day to be over so she could rush home to tell them; it was so *thrilling!* She heard Gloriette say good-bye and then the bell as the door closed; she turned quickly to peek at them through the window.

"Léonie! Hand me that note!" Marianne's voice was low and menacing. She thrust out her hand. "Give it to me!" Léonie looked around in panic for some escape—the other girls busied themselves at their counters pretending not to notice and Maroc had disappeared to eat his lunch in his usual place on the back steps in the alley.

"What note?" Her voice trembled and she backed away, keeping her hand with the note behind her.

"The one from Mademoiselle Gloriette's young man. I saw him writing it and smiling at you behind her back."

"I don't know what you're talking about," lied Léonie. She was *not* going to give her that note, she knew she would use it to get her sacked. Forgive me God for the lie, she prayed, but I *can't* lose my job.

Marianne took her arm and wrenched it forward. The note was in the other hand and Léonie leaned back against the cabinet and pushed it through the slit in the middle drawer. Marianne's grip was hurting her and she held out her other, empty hand. "You see, I have nothing."

Marianne glared at her silently for a moment. "I *know* you were flirting with him and I *know* there was a note. I'll tell you now, Léonie, that if I catch you again you'll be dismissed instantly. I won't have girls like you pushing yourselves forward in the salon with the customers! Stay in the background where you belong."

"But I wasn't—"

"Don't answer me back—and of course you were! I've seen the men looking at you, flaunting yourself around with all that hair tumbling down over your eyes. Get it cut if you want to keep your job!"

She returned to her cubicle near the door and Léonie could see her at her desk, sipping tea. Marianne was white with rage, her hands trembling so that the tea slopped over the side of the cup.

Putting her fingers down the front of the drawer, Léonie retrieved the note and tucked it up her sleeve. Slipping out through the back door, she ran down the dingy passage to join Maroc in the alley.

The tears pushed at her eyelids as she sat down beside him, refusing the enormous sandwich he offered, spilling out the story of Marianne's attack.

"Don't cry, Léonie," he said sympathetically, "she's not worth it, she's just jealous of you. I'll bet that in all these years at Serrat no one has ever written her a note asking to take her out. Don't let her make you cry, please!"

"I'm crying because I'm so angry! It's so *unfair*. I know the parcels were tied properly . . . and I never even looked at that man until he sent me the note . . . and it's not just today, Maroc! She's always picking on me. Oh, what shall I do? There's no way to please her. I'm not pushing myself forward. *I'm* the one who should be jealous of *her*. If I had *her* job, I'd be the happiest woman in Paris."

"Would you? I wonder." He offered her a twist of paper containing two melting chocolates. "Here, these are for you. They're Madame Serrat's best truffles from Tanrades. I thought they might cheer you up."

"Oh, Maroc, you are so sweet." She leaned over and kissed him and he grinned at her happily.

"Well, are you going to meet him?"

She was shocked. "Of course not."

He threw the crumbs to the waiting pigeons. "I had to give you the note, but I hoped you wouldn't go. Don't waste yourself on men like that—they're no good." Their glances met, and she could see he was serious. "Life has a lot more to offer someone like you, Léonie, you're different, special."

He sounded so wise, so grown up. "How do you know so much for a fourteen-year-old?"

"I've lived on the streets all my life." He shrugged. "I know about things . . . more than you do."

Her wrist hurt where Marianne had gripped it and she rubbed it thoughtfully, thinking about that young man—it was exciting that he had wanted to see her. Cheering up, she began to eat Maroc's sandwich. "I'm going to try to keep out of her way in the future, and I'll tie my hair even tighter. I'll even chop it off if it means keeping my job."

"Please don't cut off your hair." He put up his hand and touched it gently. "It's wonderful . . . like a great tawny mane. I can't imagine you without it."

She sighed as they walked down the passage, back toward the salon. "I won't, Maroc—unless I have to."

Carolina Montalva swept into Serrat in search of white lace stockings, groaning as Marianne bustled forward with a pleased smile. "Oh, God," she said to the young man with her, "it's that old battle-ax. I'd hoped to avoid her."

"Mademoiselle Montalva." Marianne smiled. "How nice to see you."

Carolina—Caro to her friends—waved her away with an arrogant hand. "No need to bother with me, Marianne, I'm only here for some stockings. I don't need to take up your time chatting . . . this child will do, she can serve me." She sat down on the chair in front of the counter and Léonie turned from the cabinet in surprise. "*Me,* madame?"

"Yes, of course you. I'd like to see some white lace stockings."

Léonie glanced helplessly at Marianne, who glared back at her. Mademoiselle Montalva was one of their best customers; she always bought lavishly, ordering everything by the dozen and in every color. She nodded her head. "You know where to find them, Léonie. Please see that Mademoiselle Montalva has everything she wants." She turned to Maroc. "A glass of champagne for mademoiselle, please, Maroc." She retreated to her cubicle, watching from the doorway as Léonie brought out the tray of stockings and began to unfold them for her customer. "There are three different patterns of lace, madame."

Caro smiled at her. What an unexpected little beauty to find in Serrat! She glanced at Alphonse—as she had thought, he had noticed, too. "And which style do *you* think is the prettiest?" she asked.

"*Me,* madame?"

Caro laughed. "Yes, *you* again—which one is the prettiest?"

"Well, I've always liked this one the most, it's so delicate."

"Then I'll take those—make it half a dozen pairs—and if you have them in black I'll take six of those, too."

"Yes, madame." Léonie ran eagerly to the desk to make up the parcel—her first sale! She glanced at Mademoiselle Montalva. She was so beautiful, such wonderful smooth black hair swept back, Spanish-style, into a knot on her neck, the black eyebrows like wings over immense dark eyes. And so chic. That ruby-colored jacket and skirt looked soft and expensive. And her shoes, exactly the same color as her suit—and so *tiny!* Maroc said that her lover was very aristocratic and very, very rich. He looked nice, not too tall and not particularly aristocratic-looking, she thought, but nice. He caught her glance and winked at her, and she looked down hurriedly, fearful that Marianne would accuse her again of pushing herself forward. She finished the parcel and returned to the counter, handing it to Mademoiselle Montalva.

"Thank you, my dear, for your advice," Caro said, smiling, as she took Alphonse's arm and walked to the door. "By the way, what's your name?"

"It's Léonie, madame." She could feel Marianne behind her, watching.

"Léonie." She studied the girl. "How very suitable. I must remember to ask for you the next time I come in, Léonie." Ignoring Marianne, she walked down the marble stairs and disappeared with Alphonse onto the street.

Marianne returned to her desk, speechless, and Léonie retreated back behind the counter. She felt elated. After all, if Mademoiselle Montalva wanted her to assist her next time, that meant she was one step closer to becoming a salesgirl! And she had done well, even Marianne couldn't deny that.

❧ 3 ❧

GILLES, DUC DE COURMONT, glanced at the sky as he emerged from the Elysée Palace. There was no doubt it was going to snow. There was a yellowish cast to the lowering clouds and an edge to the wind that cut through his jacket; he should have worn a coat, but it was too early for this kind of weather. It was the sort you might expect in January, not October. Hunching his shoulders against the chill, he strode purposefully down the rue de Rivoli toward the offices of the European Iron and Steel Company and the third meeting of the day. It was still only ten o'clock and he had already met with two gentlemen from Germany about the joint expansion of the railway links with Russia and had breakfasted with a cabinet minister who had informed him, in confidence, that there was a suggestion that he was to be offered the ambassadorship to the Court of St. James's in London. Of course, he wouldn't accept. He had no wish to be stuck in London when his true interests lay in America—damn it, they should have given him Washington! He had already set up his contacts with the new automobile companies there, he could have combined the two perfectly. Who, he wondered, had been against it? He made a mental note to have François Verronet check on it—Verronet had contacts within the palace, he would soon know who it was that didn't want him in Washington. Of course, he had his suspicions, and he'd bet even money on the minister with whom he had just had breakfast. He'd also have Verronet check on *his* business affairs in America; if the minister was up to something, there was no doubt that he would want his own man in there. No one crossed Gilles de Courmont and got away with it.

The men sitting around the oval table sprang to their feet as he came into the room. He had kept them waiting twenty minutes and they were busy men, but not only was Gilles, Duc de Courmont, president of the European Iron and Steel Company, he was the incisive business brain that had promoted its success to one of the most powerful industrial empires in Europe. Gilles made no apology but got straight down to business. "Very well, gentlemen, the situation is this. The Grunewald Steel Company is in bad financial shape. As you know, it's family-owned and the younger members took charge three years ago on the death of its founder. It's not so bad that it couldn't be saved by installing firm management, but it can also be made worse by wrong advice." He glanced at the report in his hand, prepared for him by Verronet. There was nothing he didn't know about the company, not a secret or a single detail of their financial situation. He turned to a second report—the intimate details of Carl Grunewald's life: his marriage, his children, his women, his losses at the casino and at the racetracks of Europe, and the amounts of his borrowings from the company. There was a younger brother who was fighting to keep the company together, but Carl was doing an excellent job of dissipating the capital.

"Young Grunewald is a distant relative of my wife's," he continued. "I happened to meet him—not quite by chance," he added with a smile, "in Baden-Baden a week or two ago. He confided some of his business problems to me and I offered to send him one of my men to advise him. I also promised to see what I could do to organize financial aid for the company—a loan, perhaps, from the Agence de Credit de Paris." He smiled. The Agence de Credit de Paris was another of his companies. "Olivier," he said, turning to the man on his left, "you are the best man for the job. In three months' time they will be unable to pay the installments on their loan. In four months they will be desperate. I want you to leave next week. You know how to deal with the result." He was smiling as he put the reports back on the table. "I estimate that it will take us no longer than five months to take over the Grunewald Steel Company."

It would be satisfying, he thought, to see his old rival finally succumb to his superior power, thanks to the worthless son. You couldn't trust anyone in this world, least of all your children. He'd make sure to leave his estate so tied up that Gérard and Armand would never be able to destroy what he had built. The European Iron and Steel Company, with its vast foundries and sprawling factories churning out machines, girders, railway lines, and weapons suitable for any war anywhere in the world—he never discriminated or took sides—would be his monument. He had more than added to the wealth left him by his father, his investments had been wise, he'd spread the tentacles of the de Courmont property holdings from Amiens to Aix and eastward into the Ruhr. No one could ever topple his empire. The next to tremble would be Krummer—he'd always hated the old man. It was his steel that had formed the weapons that had brought France to her knees in 1870, and that defeat was not something any Frenchman would ever forget.

With a curt nod he strode from the room, leaving his executives standing nervously, each eagerly hoping to catch his eye, to glean a rare nod of recognition, a sign of approval. There was none. Gilles was already lost in his thoughts, planning his next moves, into his next game.

The automobile, that new toy of a newly mechanized world, had claimed his interest in a way he had never experienced before. All this—the steel companies, the property interests, the diplomatic receptions, the political maneuverings—was like a series of exercises that he performed, keeping himself on his toes, one step ahead of the competition, beating companies at their own game, pulling contracts like trophies from under their noses. But the cars dazzled him with their mechanical beauty, the passion of their potential power. It was still only the beginning, but he, Gilles de Courmont, would be the man who would take France from its elaborate barouches and pony carts, its horse-drawn cabs and sporty fiacres into sleek, smooth steel more beautiful than the most desirable woman and powered with engines stronger than a dozen horses.

He lunched alone, as he usually did unless there was business to be done, at a side table by the window in the large dining room at the Ritz. They all knew him there, knew exactly what he wanted—an omelette *fines herbes* and a green salad. He always ate the same thing for the same reason all his shirts were white and all his suits were dark gray: it saved wasting time on trivialities. When you had to make as many major decisions in a day as he did, the minor ones, such as what to eat or what to wear, became an irritant. But he always took time to choose a wine, always red, always an excellent vintage—and he always drank exactly one glass.

Caro Montalva watched him from her vantage point just two tables behind his. She could see only his back, but it was an unmistakable back—broad-shouldered under the immaculately tailored jacket, his dark hair curling crisply over his powerful neck. There was no doubt that Gilles de Courmont was a very attractive man, and a sensual one—she'd be willing to bet that he would be a marvelous lover, he certainly had the right body. Pity he was such a cold bastard! He had women, plenty of women—she knew several of them—but he never seemed to have an intimate relationship with anyone, even his wife. Or especially his wife. It was common knowledge that theirs was an alliance, rather than a love match. Marie-France de Courmont's family was even older than his, and his marriage was just another business deal. But still, a man as powerful as the Duc de Courmont was always intriguing. The combination of power and great wealth had their own lure for a woman, and he could be charming and amusing when he wanted. She had seen women devastated by a smile from him, or some small attention—he had a trick of making them believe for a while that perhaps they could be the one whose charm and femininity could break through that ruthless, icy barrier. Then, of course, he would discard them, coldly and abruptly.

"He's very attractive, isn't he?" said her friend Gabrielle with a smile.

"I was just trying to decide if he was or not."

"And?"

"It's yes—and no. Yes physically, he is . . . look at those thighs, Gabrielle! Have you ever seen that man ride a horse! It makes you wonder what it might be like . . ."

Gabrielle threw back her head and laughed. "Caro, other women might think these things, but you are the only one I know who says them!"

Caro smiled demurely. "On the other hand he is so cold." She stared at his back. "I think he could be quite frightening. Alphonse says that he is probably the richest man in France—and one of the most powerful. Yet you can come in here almost any day and find him lunching alone, never with a friend."

"If you're feeling sorry for him, why don't you invite him to your party next week?"

"No one feels sorry for Gilles de Courmont. But you're right. I shall invite him to my party." The waiter hastened to pull back her chair as she stood to walk over to his table.

"Gilles," she said with a smile.

He sprang to his feet. "Caro, how nice to see you. How is Alphonse?" He took her hand and kissed it. "Would you care for some lunch . . . a glass of wine?"

"No, thank you, Gilles, I only came over to invite you to my party . . . it's to be next Thursday to celebrate my birthday."

"I couldn't refuse an invitation like that." He looked into her eyes. Caro Montalva was a very beautiful woman. He wondered if she might be interested. He knew she lived with Alphonse de Bergerac, but that wouldn't stop him.

"I know you don't like parties," said Caro, tilting her head and flirting a little. She always flirted, it was part of her nature, and it drove Alphonse crazy.

"Not usually, I admit. But yours are always special!"

"Then I shall expect you. About nine o'clock? Alphonse will be delighted to see you." She waved a cool farewell and returned to her table.

"Well?" asked Gabrielle.

"Of course he said he will come, but now I wish I hadn't asked him."

"Why on earth not?"

"I don't know." She shivered. "I just have a strange feeling that you don't meddle with lives like his. He says all the right words, but you feel he's thinking of something else. Oh, well"—she shrugged—"it could be fun."

De Courmont left the Ritz and walked over to Boucherons, the jewelers on the rue de Rivoli. The manager hurried forward to greet him, anxious to please his important client. "I need two things, Maurice," he said. "Something small and pretty for a lady's birthday, and something large and obvious for another lady."

"Of course, sir. I understand." It was a request he'd heard before and he knew what was required. He held out a bracelet, a strip of diamonds, three rows banded together with baguettes and a ruby clasp. "How about this, sir, for the other lady?"

He glanced at it. "That's fine. Deliver it for me, will you, to this address." He took out a card and wrote briefly on the back. There might never be any tender farewells, but no woman could accuse him of being ungenerous.

"And this, sir, for the birthday?"

"Sapphires? Yes, very suitable." The brooch was discreet, a pleasant gift. "I'll take it with me."

"Of course, sir." The man bowed him to the door and he continued on his way. A quick fitting at his tailor's and then back to the office—there were still the reports to read on that railway deal.

It was almost ten when Gilles finally turned into the courtyard of his mansion on the Ile Saint-Louis. Despite the cold, he had walked from his office, preoccupied with his thoughts. He strode up the steps without bothering to look to see if the door were open, he knew it would be. The liveried footman closed it behind him. "Good evening, sir." The butler took his wet jacket, there was a spattering of snow in the air.

"Is madame at home, Bennett?" This was one of the few houses in Paris with an English butler, a vanity of his wife's, not his. In his personal life he was an austere man.

"Madame la Duchesse has retired to her room, sir."

"Thank you, Bennett. I shan't need anything further, then."

"Very well, sir. Goodnight, sir."

Gilles was always courteous and thoughtful with his servants and they liked working for him. He walked through the immense hall that soared two stories high, climbing the marble stairway, unheeding of the cherubs and blue skies in the frescoes above him, crossing the first-floor hall into his study. The great house had a different kind of chill than the wintry cold outdoors; there was a bleakness despite its blazing fires and rich rooms. Shivering slightly, Gilles poured himself a glass of whiskey from the decanter that waited with a single crystal glass on the silver tray. He never brought anyone in here. It was his room, even his wife was banished from it. He gulped the brandy, grimacing as it hit his throat, enjoying the aromatic flavor. A fire burned in the grate and his big leather chair was pulled up close to it, but he wandered over to the window and stood, glass in hand, gazing moodily across the lamplit courtyard to the river. After a while he put down his glass, and pulling loose his necktie, he walked across the room and opened the door to a connecting bedroom. It contained a shelf of books, a chair, a chest; it was bleak but for the fur rug thrown across the narrow bed, one touch of sensuality in a spartan world. He was thirty-six years old and he was a lonely man.

The weather had taken on an unseasonable chill for October and the epidemic of colds and flu swept through the shop and workrooms at Serrat, daily reducing the staff as more and more retreated to their beds, until by Monday only Léonie and Madame Serrat were left to hold the fort. The sky hung gray and threatening over the city as Léonie arrived for work, and at one o'clock the snow began to fall, covering the streets with a thin white film. "We'll not have many customers today, thank goodness," said Madame Serrat, who was not feeling too well herself. "You'll have to cope, Léonie." She retreated to her office and Léonie savored the delight of being alone in the salon. She wandered around flicking the dust from the counters with a little feather duster, straightening the racks and praying that someone would come in and order ten nightdresses or a dozen sets of lingerie so that she might have the pleasure of acting as head salesgirl, if only for one day. But no one did and she was bored.

She opened a drawer and looked at the red silk stockings; they were so beautiful. She touched them lightly with one finger, feeling their smoothness, longing for a pair. She had a little money saved, but it was only a little. No, the stockings were horribly expensive—and, anyway, where would she go to wear them?

She began to parcel up the order Mademoiselle Montalva had placed earlier that week. As usual she had bought lavishly, ordering dozens of sets of lingerie and gowns in deep glowing colors. "I'm not meant for pastels," Léonie remembered her saying, although she had never again had the opportunity to serve her. Marianne had seen to that! She packed the sapphire blue panne velvet robe carefully and the matching slippers, adding them to the growing pile and thinking about Carolina Montalva. The salon always seemed different when she came in, it was suddenly lighthearted and full of laughter. She was so easy and charming, chatting with the girls as if they were friends, leaving a little afterglow of pleasure behind her. Maroc had told Léonie that it was rumored that mademoiselle was the daughter of a Spanish count, but because she had behaved badly the family had cast her out. Could that be true?

By three o'clock the snow lay thick on the ground. "You'd better leave early, Léonie," said Madame Serrat, emerging from her room looking pale and ill. "You can deliver the Montalva order on your way home."

"Me, Madame Serrat . . . go to Mademoiselle Montalva's?" Her voice was squeaky with excitement.

"You'd better take a cab, I don't want those parcels getting wet. Here's some money, tip the man ten percent and bring me the change tomorrow. And take care with those things. If you drop them in the snow, they'll be ruined."

"Oh, I won't, I won't drop them. I'll take such good care. Thank you, Madame Serrat, for trusting me."

Léonie threw on her coat, gathered up the parcels, and stood shivering in the street, waiting impatiently for a cab. Three things, she thought, three exciting events. I shall ride in a cab for the first time; I'm being trusted with an important job; and I'm going to see Carolina Montalva's home. She jumped up and down with excitement and to warm her feet. She could barely believe her luck. If the others didn't have flu, she would still be dusting the shelves and Maroc would have had this job.

She climbed into the cab, giving the address importantly, and sat back to enjoy the ride, peering out at the streets she knew so well on foot; somehow they seemed smaller and more intimate seen frame by frame from the cab's windows. What would the apartment be like? Would she be able to go in, or would the concierge just keep her standing on the step?

"Here we are, mademoiselle."

Léonie collected her parcels and climbed gingerly out onto the pavement. Her feet sank into snow that came up to her ankles, and she stared in dismay at her shoes, two black sodden lumps half-hidden by slush. She trudged on through the courtyard, leaving a little track behind her, and rang the bell at the imposing front door, staring at it nervously. It was a very grand building, just like the ones she used to peer into so longingly on her Sunday walks.

"Yes, what do you want?" The concierge was irritable. "You should have gone to the back with those deliveries. Well, as you're here now and it's snowing, you may as well go up. Mademoiselle Montalva is on the first floor."

What a bit of luck; she was going to get inside. The concierge could have taken the parcels from her, but he was too lazy to go up the stairs himself. He'd already gone back to his newspaper and his cup of coffee.

The marble staircase swept grandly up to the first floor and a red carpet flowed down the center. It looked soft and thick and shiny brass rails held it in place on each tread. Léonie looked at her shoes and back at the carpet and then walked up the stairs keeping to the narrow marble bit at the side, careful not to mar its perfection with her wet feet.

She faced the grand double doors with a smile—this was it at last.

The door was flung open from inside and someone crashed into her, sending her parcels flying.

"Sorry . . . I'm so sorry." The young man's eyes met hers with a smile. "Are you all right?"

"Oh, yes—it's just the parcels—I wasn't supposed to drop them."

He laughed. "Well, it's too late! Here, I'll get them. Caro?" he called. "There's a very pretty girl here to see you."

"Oh!" Léonie blushed in confusion and he laughed again. "It's the truth," he whispered.

Carolina looked at her in surprise, a young beauty in a worn brown coat and wet shoes, dripping melting snow onto her lovely rug. It was the girl from Serrat. "Don't tell me they sent you out with my order on a day like this!" she said indignantly.

"Madame Serrat said that you needed it today, mademoiselle."

Caro heaved a sigh of exasperation at Madame Serrat's stupidity. "You poor girl, you must be frozen—look how wet your feet are."

"Oh, dear . . . oh, I'm so sorry, look what I've done." Léonie stared with an anguished face at the spreading damp stain on the beautiful rug. "I'll leave at once, mademoiselle. I'm so sorry." She pulled off her shoes and clutched them in her hand. If Madame Serrat hears about this, she thought dejectedly, I'll never be trusted again. Oh, why do things always seem to go wrong for me?

It was so easy to read her face that Caro laughed.

"Don't worry about the rug, it'll dry. And you're certainly not leaving until we've got *you* dried out. Poor girl. We'll get you some hot chocolate and then we'll unpack the parcels and see if everything is there."

"Can I come, too?" the young man asked hopefully.

"No, Robert, you may not. I've already said good-bye to you. Léonie— it is Léonie, isn't it?" She nodded in reply, pleased the lady had remembered her name! "Léonie and I have work to do. Follow me, Léonie."

Léonie padded after her, curling her stockinged toes into the softness of the rugs and sticking out a furtive finger to touch the aquamarine wall to see if it were really silk. Imagine, she marveled, having silk on your walls! She peeked into the main salon as they passed, amazed by the opulence of its spindly gilt chairs and deep sapphire sofas, and another salon with an enormous ebony grand piano and golden stands holding music and more rows of those little gilt chairs and chandeliers that were lit on this dark afternoon even though no one was sitting in the rooms.

Caro's small sitting room seemed filled with the luxurious spring scent of hothouse hyacinths and a deep chaise lounge, piled with lacy pillows, was pulled close to the crackling log fire. It was the most delightful room Léonie had ever seen. Curtains of stiff apricot silk, swagged and tied with enormous bows, framed the snow piled high against the windows and still falling steadily, coldly, freezing as it landed. But inside it was another world, a beautiful, friendly, warm, rich world.

A maid brought hot chocolate and some small cakes, setting the tray down on the low table by the fire. "Sit here, Léonie," invited Caro. "Have your chocolate first and get warm. We'll unpack the parcels later."

Léonie sat on the edge of one of the coral velvet chairs, as she sipped her drink, barely believing that she was here, watching Mademoiselle Montalva as she sat at her desk writing a note. She must remember it all, so that tonight when she was in bed she could recall all the details, all the colors and the textures and the way it smelled—heaven must surely be like this room.

Caro could see the girl reflected in the mirror above the tulipwood desk; the color was coming back into her cheeks and her damp hair was drying, lifting with a floating energy to curl in tendrils about her face. How very attractive she was; she was wasted working at Serrat!

Léonie finished the chocolate and began to unpack the parcels for Mademoiselle Montalva to see, arranging the fragile garments carefully, the dozen sets of chemises and knickers in sapphire, amethyst, and topaz, embroidered minutely at the hem with her monogram, "CM"—and *no* lace. Caro *never* wore lace on her underwear. Léonie smoothed the creases from robes of panne velvet as blue-black as summer midnight and as deeply aquamarine as a tropical sea, and set beside them their matching satin slippers with their puffs of swansdown and delicate heels. She glanced down at her own feet and sighed; maybe they, too, would look small and delicate if she had shoes like that.

Caro pushed aside the robes carelessly, settling herself on the chaise. "Well, Léonie, how do you like working at Serrat?"

"Oh, I love it, Mademoiselle Montalva; it's the loveliest place in Paris! Or at least"—Léonie glanced around the room—"I thought it was until I came here."

"Tell me about yourself," commanded Caro, intrigued. It was late, and she would have no more visitors on an afternoon like this. Léonie was a welcome diversion.

"There's not much to tell. I come from a village in Normandy and now I'm here, working in the salon."

"And why did you leave Normandy? Why did you come to Paris? And why Serrat? Come on, Léonie," she said, laughing, "tell me *everything.*"

Caro coaxed the story out of her, smoothing over the rough parts, holding Léonie's hand sympathetically when she told tearfully of her mother's death and how at the age of thirteen she had been left completely alone and had gone to work at the café. You poor child, she thought, you poor, lonely little thing. The words tumbled out in a torrent as Léonie confided to this beautiful stranger her dreams of having a marvelous job where she would "belong."

"What do you mean, 'belong'?"

"It's just that I don't really belong anywhere. I'm always on the outside looking in—everyone in Paris 'belongs.' Do you understand what I mean? How do you 'belong,' mademoiselle? What do you have to do to become a part of it all?"

Caro stared at her in surprise, hearing an echo of her own youthful longings when she had been trapped in the rigid Spanish household, yearning to escape to a world where there was romance and love and passion. It was the same feeling that she had had then, that *life* was taking place somewhere else. Her heart went out to the girl. She had been just as simple and innocent as this, once, long ago. She glanced at the girl's face and sighed—it was expectant, waiting for her reply as though she had some magic formula. "How old are you, Léonie?"

"I'm sixteen, mademoiselle, I shall be seventeen next month."

"I'm twenty-four—not that much older than you. I'm not sure how it happens—belonging—just one day you feel that it has happened and you've grown up. Maybe it's when you first fall in love, or suddenly get a good job, or it's spring and the world falls magically into place for you ... it'll happen, though, I'm sure of that. Do you have friends, Léonie?"

"I have Maroc, my friend from Serrat. And Loulou, Bella, and Jolie at Madame Artois's—but they are busy at the cabaret most of the time, and so I usually only see them on Sunday evenings."

So she was virtually friendless, too. Oh, how could she help her? What should she do? What should she tell her? Caro stared out of the window into the gloom. The street lamps were a pale flickering blur in the swirling flakes and the snow had piled in thick drifts in the courtyard. The street was deserted, even the café on the corner had closed. "I'm afraid you'll never get home in this, Léonie," she said, an idea forming in her mind. "It's my fault, I shouldn't have kept you talking." She smiled at her. "But since you are here, you'll stay the night with me—you can be *my* friend and keep me company. We shall have supper together and I'll tell you my story." She laughed gaily. "After all, it's only fair: you told me yours. We'll have supper together by the fire, it'll be fun."

Fun! Léonie couldn't believe it. Is this really happening to me—Léonie Bahri—she asked herself, following the maid into the rose room. The rose room! The bed was a vast, pillowed, fluffy dais, lacy and beribboned. She tested it with her hand and then sat on it, bouncing gently up and down; she wanted to burrow into its pillows and soft blankets as warmly pink as summer roses. She noticed the door on the opposite wall and ran to open it. A vast white porcelain tub encased in mahogany sat in the center of the room and she gazed in awe at its splayed brass feet and complicated matching brass taps. It was the first real bathtub she had ever seen—all her bathing had been done in small clammy gray zinc tubs filled from pots of water heated over a stove. You climbed in and sat with your knees under your chin and washed yourself as quickly as possible, but this tub, this looked big enough to wallow in. Tentatively, she felt the cold porcelain, running a finger along the taps. "I'll run your bath for you, mademoiselle," said the maid bustling into the room.

"Oh, no, no, I'll do it myself," she protested, turning the gold taps, hot water gushing into the tub. After all, she was hardly a guest here, she was here only because she was trapped by the storm.

"Madame sent this for you to wear." The maid arranged the bronze velvet robe on a chair and placed the slippers next to it, with a doubtful glance at Léonie's feet. "Is there anything else, mademoiselle?" she inquired.

Léonie stared at her in astonishment. What else could there be?

"Oh, no. No, thank you."

She stripped off her clothes, casting aside the prickly wool chemise and drawers, and stood naked in the warm steamy room gazing at her reflection in the mirrored wall opposite. She only possessed a tiny square mirror; this was the first time she had seen herself naked, all at once, not just in sections. She gazed curiously at her reflection, running her hands over her high round breasts, along the deep smooth line of her waist and the long slope of her thighs, fingering the curled tuft of blond hair. With a shiver she turned to the tub. An enormous bowl of blue-green crystals tempted her and she sniffed them. Tossing an experimental handful into the water, she smiled as the heat released their fragrance. Léonie lay back, stretching her legs, arching her back, soothed by the hot water and smoothed by the oil from the crystals. The sponge was enormous, soft and squishy, and she lathered it with a vast cake of perfumed soap until it foamed. She rubbed it slowly across her breasts, pushing it lightly, around and around until her nipples swelled pink and firm. Filled with a new kind of excitement she stood up and began to soap herself, watching herself, a stranger in a steam-clouded mirror—head flung back, trembling. With a sudden wild cry she flung herself back into the water, rolling around and around in it like a dolphin, laughing out loud.

Caro handed Léonie a fluted glass and watched as she took her first sip of champagne. The bronze robe suited Léonie's peachy skin, and her cheeks were flushed from the bath. Her bare feet peeked prettily from beneath the hem and, as she drank, her toes curled into the softness of the carpet; the girl was enjoying herself.

"It's wonderful," said Léonie. "This whole day is wonderful, mademoiselle." She rested her head against the cushions, her eyes dreamy, her body relaxed. Caro stared at her curiously. This was a different girl from the nervous frozen child who had come through her door only a few hours before. There were no labels of poverty on her now. In her robe and with her golden hair drying in front of the fire she could be anyone—she was a girl just like herself. "You must call me Caro," she said, "everyone does."

A small table had been set up in front of the fire and the heavy curtains were drawn, shutting out the blizzard and the silent streets. Caro watched Léonie eat, enjoying the sight of someone so obviously relishing her food. Afterward they sat on the rug together in front of the fire and she peeled the peaches specially grown for her in the enormous hothouses at Alphonse's country estate. They dunked fleshy slivers of fruit in their champagne, giggling as they licked their winy juices. They were isolated by the storm, forced into an immediate intimacy, trapped together with no men around— "Like schoolgirls," said Caro, laughing.

"Please tell me," begged Léonie, sitting cross-legged on the rug, the sumptuous velvet robe wrapped around her, a glass of champagne in her hand. She felt elated, all her senses were alive, her body was drifting on a sea of champagne bubbles.

"Tell you what?"

"Your story . . . Caro," she added, pleased to be allowed to use her name.

"My story . . . ahh." Caro's lovely face looked suddenly wistful. "It was a fairy story, Léonie . . . for a while. My home was in Spain. I suppose if being loved means being 'spoiled,' then I was a spoiled child. My father was handsome and my mother young and beautiful. I remember how I used to wait, for what seemed ages, every morning until she awoke and I was allowed in. She'd be lying there in that great old bed, tiny, dark-haired, always in something pale and lacy and always holding out her arms for me, laughing as I'd run across the room and hurl myself into them. Papa would hear us and put his head around his dressing room door, laughing, too, as he saw me covering her face with kisses. And then it was his turn to be kissed and he'd swing me up in the air so that I could reach his face—sometimes I'd have to smooth away the soapy foam where he was shaving and sometimes he'd hold my hand over his long-bladed razor and allow me to 'help' him shave. And afterward I'd receive a little dab of his cologne behind my ears. Then we'd both go and sit on Mama's bed and nibble at her breakfast. I remember sneaking a finger into the little dish of delicious peach preserves and giving it to Papa to lick. They were both so young, so beautiful—and so very much in love. I know now how selfish lovers can be and I suppose I was lucky that they let me share that love.

"As the elder son, my father had inherited a title and everything that went with it, a castle, townhouses, estates. And Mama was rich, young, and beautiful. They were truly the golden couple on whom the gods smiled. But one day the smiling stopped. They had left to spend a weekend at the country house of some friends, it was November, the weather was foggy, the roads icy. . . . There was an accident. . . ."

Caro's face reflected the pain of twenty years ago and Léonie turned her eyes away, not wanting to intrude.

"No one told me," whispered Caro, "that was the worst thing. I suppose they wanted to shield me from the pain. The servants who were my friends went around red-eyed, bursting into tears when they looked at me, the curtains were drawn, mirrors draped in black; there was whispering. I couldn't understand it. Then suddenly the house was full of relatives, lawyers, priests . . . and everyone in black. My father's brother, who now inherited the title, explained finally what had happened. He said that they had gone to a better place and were happy there. He took me to see them. They were lying side by side in coffins lined in white satin, they looked so lovely—just the way they always looked—but they didn't hold out their arms to me. I was five years old and they had gone forever. And so had all the loving, the spoiling, and the sharing. I, who had been the center of their universe, was to live with my uncle and aunt and their eleven-year-old son."

Caro took a sip of her wine and sighed deeply. "It wouldn't have been so bad if it weren't for my aunt. Of course, looking back I realize that she and my mother could never have been friends. Aunt Macarene was a plain woman who'd done well to marry the second son of a good family. She was strong and domineering and uncle was an academic man, lost in his world of ancient manuscripts and texts in Latin and Greek. Aunt Macarene ran his life and now she ran mine. From silks and muslins and colored ribbons woven through my hair by my mother's loving fingers, I now wore blue serge and a white pinafore and stout shoes. My hair was brushed back so tightly into its braid that I could feel it pulling my scalp. I had meals in the schoolroom and was kept in the nursery at night so as not to disturb uncle, or so she said. I think I must have cried for years and years—every night my pillow would be soaked." Her eyes met Léonie's in understanding. "I was so lonely, Léonie—like you. My cousin was older, away at school, uninterested in my misery. Uncle had inherited the estates, but it had been my mother's money that had kept up the houses so beautifully, that had paid all those servants, bought all the extra extravagant pleasures, and I had inherited it all. I suppose my aunt coveted it for her son—what good were estates and titles without money? Gradually she managed to deprive me of everything I was used to and had loved: my mother's little dogs were no longer there, my pony was sold, lessons were long and dull—there was nothing to open up my mind, to excite the imagination or curiosity. It was no use appealing to my uncle—he was often away giving lectures on his favorite classical heroes, and besides, he wouldn't have understood. 'Your aunt takes care of all that,' was all the response I ever got. I had to wait until I was sixteen to shock him into action. He had just emerged from his study as I was crossing the hall and, still lost in his translation from the French, he spoke to me in

French. When I couldn't reply, he was stunned. He engaged a French tutor for me at once."

Caro leaned forward, smiling at Léonie. "I rarely had the opportunity to meet boys my own age, let alone attractive young Frenchmen of twenty, with dangerous eyes. And I'd never met anyone who found me attractive!" She laughed, remembering. "I was clasped in my one and only embrace when my aunt walked in."

Léonie drew in her breath sharply, caught up in the agony of that moment.

"Of course"—Caro shrugged—"that was the end for both of us. He was gone and my aunt demanded banishment for me, too—and not just from Barcelona, but from Spain! A convent in Paris was my destination. I lasted a few months within those demanding gray walls and then I escaped—it wasn't difficult—they didn't expect girls to run away. I was alone in Paris in my convent gray. I went straight to the Paris branch of my mother's bankers, where I knew I had money, but Aunt Macarene had managed over the years to have the funds transferred to their own Spanish bank. She had been clever. As executors she and my uncle claimed that it had been used to pay off monstrous debts accumulated by my parents' extravagant life-style, and that it had been used for my benefit. Very little was left for me. But—Alphonse was that banker."

"You fell in love," breathed Léonie, still spellbound.

Caro smiled. "Within a year he brought me back to the joyful world I had missed. I had pretty clothes again, my hair was unbound at last. I heard music, I read books, I went to the theater. I drank champagne, Léonie—and I made love. Alphonse loved me."

"And you are in love with him?" Léonie wanted the fairy story to be complete, with Caro a radiant bride on the arm of her charming groom—a happy ending.

"Perhaps, perhaps I am." Caro smiled. "We've been lovers for seven years now, and every week he asks me to marry him. I always say no, and still he asks."

"But why? Why won't you marry him?"

Caro laughed. "I like it the way it is, I don't want to change things by getting married. I like being the unconventional Caro Montalva—and maybe that's part of my attraction for Alphonse. Wouldn't it be foolish of me to spoil it?"

Léonie smiled too. "You're so clever, Caro. How do you know all these things?"

She shrugged. "When you're close to someone, it's easy to know what they like, what they want. And Alphonse takes such good care of me. His family have been bankers for nearly two hundred years and he is very, very rich. He bought me this apartment, settled an income on me, made investments on my behalf. It's important when you are in my position to make sure that you are properly taken care of like this, there's no room for financial insecurity. You are not a wife, and men are easily attracted by a new and pretty face. I know lots of women who have been discarded and been left with nothing, back where they began."

"But not you," cried Léonie, "not by Alphonse!" Caro was so beautiful, she must be irresistible to any man. Everyone must adore her, she thought. I do.

The fire had burned low and Caro glanced at the gilt clock on the mantle. "Let's look at the storm," she said, taking Léonie's hand. They peered through the cold glass at the sparkling white coat that had transformed the trees in the courtyard into alabaster columns, turning branches into fairy fingers. For once Paris was quiet, there wasn't a sound, and the only movement was the flickering of the street lamps.

Flinging open the window they leaned out, brushing the snow from the sill with frozen hands, their laughter muffled by the carpet of snow. "Oh, it's a magical night," cried Léonie, floating on champagne and freezing air. "Gods and goddesses have changed the world tonight—and now they've changed me. I'll never be the same again."

Caro leaned over and kissed her. "You have magic, too, Léonie Bahri, and one day you'll belong. I know it."

Cocooned in the vast bed, in sheets of smooth linen and soft woolen blankets, Léonie embroidered Caro's story with details. Would any of these things happen to her? How could they? Where would she meet a man who might fall madly in love with her? Not at Serrat—and not on those lonely walks in the Bois, and certainly not at Madame Artois's! She clutched the pillow in her arms, holding it close, longing for someone who would hold her, dreaming of someone saying, "I love you, Léonie."

A maid brought breakfast to her in bed, served on a pretty white tray with pots of preserves and honey and brioches still warm from the oven that she dunked hungrily into the big bowl of coffee.

But all too soon it was time to face reality, and she climbed reluctantly from the bed, dressing slowly in her woolen underwear. She watched her everyday self returning in the mirror as she dragged her frock over her head and pushed her feet into the black shoes that only a few months ago she had thought were so smart. Last night had been a dream, she thought sadly, a warm, wonderful dream of friendship and fun, just another glimpse of a world where once again she didn't belong.

With a final glance in the mirror, she went in search of the maid.

"Madame is awake"—she was informed—"and wishes to see you before you go."

Caro was alone in a big four-poster bed, its curtains partially drawn. "Léonie," she called, patting the bed beside her, "come here. I hope you slept well?"

"Oh, yes . . . but I wish I hadn't because I didn't want to miss a single moment."

Caro laughed. "Now that we're friends, I'm not about to lose you so soon. I'm giving a party on Thursday, why don't you come? Please do, Léonie, it'll be fun."

"A party?" She could feel her spirits rising.

"You must come, I insist! Nine o'clock then, on Thursday?"

Léonie brimmed with happiness, she wasn't to lose this world just yet! She kissed Caro on the cheek. "Oh, thank you, Caro, of course I'll come."

Gangs of workmen were clearing the pavements as Léonie trudged along, slipping on icy patches, splashed by passing traffic and oblivious to it all. She was floating again on champagne bubbles. . . . Thursday . . . the day after tomorrow. Oh, God. She stopped in the middle of the road, frozen in horror by a terrible realization. What would she *wear?*

⤜ 4 ⤛

"THERE'S NO TIME to make anything," said Loulou, "so that's out. Bella, you're the nearest in size, what do you have that might do?" They sifted through the contents of Bella's wardrobe, making Léonie try on the red velvet and deciding that it made her skin sallow, and then the black lace, which was too old. Nothing was suitable, and the girls had been Léonie's only hope. She wouldn't be able to go, she knew it. How *could* she, without a proper dress? "Wait a minute," said Loulou, "I think I've got the answer. Put on your coat, Léonie, we're going to the theater."

At any other time Léonie would have found the novelty of being backstage at the cabaret exciting, but her whole being was absorbed by her problem: she must find something to wear. She paused for a moment to peer across the footlights from the side of the stage, breathing in the smell of dust and paint from the ornate backdrop, then hastily followed Loulou and Bella down the dingy corridor into a long room stacked with rails of costumes. Loulou sorted through them rapidly, searching for the one she wanted. "Gloriette used it in the party scene a few months ago, Bella," she said, her voice muffled as she thrust the tightly packed garments along the rails. "The gold one."

"Do you mean this?" Bella held up a shiny little dress of gold satin.

"Try it on," urged Loulou, "I know it will suit you."

Hurriedly Léonie unbuttoned her dress and wriggled into the golden costume. It was a bit low on her bosom and her chemise stuck out incongruously over the top, but it nipped in at her waist, swirling in a flurry of tiny points at the hem. The long sleeves formed matching points at her wrists, and the low neckline peaked in little stiffened points just under her ears.

"As usual it's too short," said Bella, exasperated.

Léonie glanced down at the skirt floating around her calves. "Oh, Loulou," she said despairingly, "what shall we do?"

Loulou examined the dress; there was no way to add another band of fabric to the bottom that would not be too obvious. There was only one alternative. "If you can't change it, then you must make an advantage of it," she announced firmly. "You'll need stockings, Léonie—silk ones—and shoes . . . you'll emphasize the shortness as though it was meant to be that way!"

Léonie stared at her doubtfully. Could she be right? She remembered the silk stockings at Serrat, but shoes were expensive. Loulou read her thoughts. "We'll go to Hector," she said. "He makes the shoes for all the shows and they'll be cheaper than the usual shops."

Bella hid the dress under her coat as they sneaked giggling past the concierge at the stage door and made their way through the slippery streets to Hector. It was a gloomy little shop, smelling of leather and polish, and Léonie's hopes fell—how could they find anything suitable in here? An old man came to the counter. "Hello, Loulou, Bella," he said cheerfully. "What can I do for you ladies?" They were frequent customers, as were all the girls in the cabarets.

"Our friend needs some shoes—gold ones—and not too expensive, please," stated Bella firmly.

"Not too expensive, eh?" Hector had a twinkle in his eye. The girls always said the same thing. How did they expect him to make money? But they were so charming! He looked at Léonie's feet, measuring with a practiced eye. "Mmm, larger than usual," he said. "I've not much to choose from in gold . . . in fact, this is all I have." He set the pair of little gold boots on the counter and they stared at them. They were narrow and shiny and soft, ankle high with laces up the back, and prancy little heels and two golden dangling tassels.

"Try them," Bella urged, as Léonie eyed them dubiously.

Léonie eased the delicate boots over her clumsy woolen stockings and tied the laces with their little tassels. She stood up and walked around, testing them; the prancy little heels made her feel like a circus pony.

"Perfect," said Loulou. "With the right stockings they'll look wonderful. She'll take them, Hector—if the price is right!"

Thursday seemed interminable, and Léonie counted the hours until six o'clock, when she would be free. Maroc was in on the adventure, and he watched her with concern as she paced the salon. She was so young, so unwise . . . he hoped she would be all right.

On the dot of six, clutching her new silk stockings, she flew home to the waiting girls, and sat uncomplaining as they tugged and teased her hair until it stood out in a golden cloud, like that of the girls in Renaissance paintings. Jolie touched a little bronze to her eyelids, a hint of peach shadow under her cheekbones, a faint glitter of gold dust along her slender shoulder blades. They forbade her to wear a chemise and Léonie pulled the dress nervously over her naked breasts, and Bella fastened the tiny buttons up the back. Loulou had lent her the proper frilly garters and at last she smoothed the red silk stockings along her legs, thrilled by their silkiness and guilty about their expense. She laced up her gold boots, tying a neat little bow so that the tassels swung at the back, and walked stiffly across the room allowing the girls to look her over.

"It's *no good,* Léonie," cried Loulou in despair, "you *must* stand up, pull back your shoulders, lift your rib cage. You can't hide your breasts with rounded shoulders, just look what it does to the dress! Damn it, girl, you have the body for it, flaunt it a little—like this." She stalked across the room, head high, chin tilted arrogantly, strutting elegantly on her high heels, and Léonie tried to copy her, lifting herself taller, shoulders back and down. Loulou was right, it wasn't a dress to be worn cautiously, it needed confidence. She only hoped she would have it.

Rupert von Hollensmark almost didn't go to Caro's party. It had been a hell of a day. He'd arrived back from Munich at eight o'clock that night and it was bitterly cold with the threat of more snow in the air. He had been tired and hungry and wanted nothing more than a glass of whiskey and a bite to eat. The journey to see Puschi was really a chore, though it was always good to see her. He wasn't in love with her, but she was nice and she was also fun—if he had to marry, then it might as well be to Puschi. Her father had the Krummer millions and his father had the title, and Puschi *was* madly in love with him. He would take good care of her, once they were married—they were such good friends.

With a sigh of relief, he stripped off his clothes and climbed into the tub, floating away the fatigue in the hot steamy water, sipping his whiskey. He was feeling better already, maybe he would go after all. Caro's parties were always fun.

The courtyard was already crowded with people and carriages as Rupert paid off the cab, pushing back his blond hair with an impatient hand as the wind blasted around the corner. God, it was cold tonight. Ducking his head against the gale, he strode across the courtyard to the house just as the most amazing girl disappeared up the steps in front of him, flashing a glimpse of the longest red silk legs and the strangest little gold boots. Rupert followed the legs; he *had* to see who she was.

"Rupert!"

"Oh, damn," he groaned as a pretty girl in a blue dress waylaid him at the door. Now he'd miss her!

Gilles de Courmont knew he shouldn't have come. These parties were always the same, the same faces, the same chatter—the same women. He leaned against the long window watching the scene moodily, wondering if he should bother to stay—perhaps he'd just make some excuse to Caro and leave, he had the new designs of the automobile engines to look over.... *Who* was that girl? She'd just walked in the door on the longest legs, wearing the most bizarre outfit, and was staring around nervously, obviously feeling very much out of place. Would she or wouldn't she turn and run? She was certainly different, not quite a beauty, but there was something about her. Something quite irresistible. Something that pulled him toward her.

Damn that man, staring at her! Léonie wanted to cry, to turn and run. She shrank into a corner, looking desperately for Caro. All the guests seemed to know each other very well. Oh dear, she should never have come. There was so much noise, music and talk and laughter. She glanced again at the man by the window. He was still watching her, a faint smile on his lips. He knows I don't belong, she thought miserably. "Flaunt it a little"—Loulou's words came back to her clearly. She *wouldn't* be beaten, this was her big chance! Tilting her chin arrogantly, she straightened her back, pulled down her shoulders, and strode into the room on strong red silk legs and prancy circus pony boots.

"Léonie," cried Caro, stunned by the girl's appearance—the hair, the shiny dress, the legs, the boots. But the odd thing was that once you got over the shock, Léonie looked wonderful, a shiny golden being from some other world. She kissed her warmly and introduced her to Alphonse. "You look marvelous. Everyone," she said to the guests watching in fascinated silence, "this is Léonie."

The instant focus of their silent attention, Léonie dropped her gaze nervously, then, remembering Loulou's admonition, she lifted her chin and stared back, challengingly.

"Of course, I remember you," said Alphonse. "Yours is not a face anyone forgets easily."

Léonie hoped it was a compliment. She was still unsure about her dress—none of the other women's dresses were as short, or as shiny.

"May I get you some champagne, Léonie?" a dark young man asked eagerly.

She sighed with relief and began to relax a little, maybe she might even enjoy the party after all. Glancing around, she again caught the eye of the man by the window and hurriedly turned away, peeking at him from under her lashes a moment later. He came closer and stood by the table drinking a glass of champagne. No one else spoke to him. He was as alone as she. But he looked sinister, surrounded by his pool of silence, and she turned hurriedly to the buzz of conversation and laughter that flowed around her. He was oddly attractive, she thought, feeling an unfamiliar flutter in her stomach.

"Léonie," said Caro, "I'd like you to meet Rupert von Hollensmark. We're lucky to have him here, he just got back from Munich this evening."

Léonie gazed upward into the deep blueness of his eyes and it was as though the stars had fallen from the heavens. She felt the pressure of his touch, the harsh texture of his fingers, the warmth of his breath as he bowed over her hand. Surely he could feel her shaking, it was a tremor—a volcano—Vesuvius. She was erupting with new emotions. Rupert was smiling at her. "I saw you before," he said. "We arrived at the same moment. I wanted to speak to you then but at parties like this it's difficult to get through the crowds."

She wanted him to continue speaking so she could just listen. His voice was deep with the faintest of accents. His thick blond hair fell over his eyes so beautifully that she wanted to touch it. Léonie realized suddenly that he was waiting for her to say something, but she couldn't speak and she gazed at him, her eyes wide with panic. Oh, God, she thought, here is the man of my dreams and I don't know what to say to him.

Rupert made it easy for her. "Supper is being served in the next room," he said, taking her by the arm and leading her away. "You must be hungry by now—I know I am."

They were the most romantic words Léonie had ever heard.

"Oh, Alphonse," said Caro, watching them go. "What have I done now?"

* * *

The buffet table brimmed with extravagances. A cornucopia carved from ice spilled green and purple sugar-glazed grapes onto an enormous silver platter piled high with long-stemmed strawberries and scattered with fresh roses so their scents mingled tantalizingly. Silver bowls held figs and peaches fresh from Alphonse's wonderful hothouses in the country. There were tiny quails stuffed with truffles perched on circles of basil-scented toast, and crystal glasses filled with mellow Clos Lafite, poured by a white-gloved butler. There were elaborate confections in pastry, creamy things, perfumed things, tiny exquisite chocolatey things—it was a buffet designed to titillate the senses, and Caro's guests crowded around, ready to sample it all.

Léonie couldn't eat. Rupert tried to tempt her with the truffles. "What am I going to do with you?" he cried in despair. "You don't talk to me, you don't eat . . . are you a goddess not to need food and conversation?"

"The truth is," she whispered, "I'm scared."

"Scared? Of what?"

"Of this," she waved her arm at the crowded room. "They all know each other, they all belong."

"You belong"—Rupert took her hand possessively—"and you're with me." He picked up the fork and offered her a morsel. "And now you must eat; I'm afraid you'll disappear unless I know you're mortal like the rest of us."

She was lovely, so innocent, he thought. She was like a young animal; no matter what she did, how she moved, she had her own charming grace. How had he lived before he met her? He was absorbed in her eyes, the pinkness of her mouth as she opened it to receive the strawberry he offered. His hand trembled and he longed to touch her. Could he be in love with a girl who barely spoke to him, whom he'd known for only a few moments? Oh, yes. Oh, yes, he could.

Caro watched them anxiously from across the room. She was aware of Rupert's family commitments, and like a fool she'd introduced him to Léonie. Looking at them now, their blond heads together, sitting so close at that tiny table that their legs touched—even from this distance, she could feel the vibrations. Léonie was too vulnerable and Rupert was no good for her; she had to do something about it.

"Rupert," said Alphonse, "I believe Caro has someone she'd like you to meet." Rupert was irritated by the interruption, but too polite to snub his hostess. "Of course." He looked into Léonie's eyes. "Will I see you later?"

"Oh, yes," she said. "Please."

Alphonse took her arm. "Let me introduce you to some people, Léonie." He smiled. "Rupert has been monopolizing you."

Gilles de Courmont kissed Caro's hand. "I haven't enjoyed a party so much for years," he told her as he said good-bye. He made his way toward Alphonse, and Caro stared after him in surprise. He certainly hadn't looked as though he was enjoying himself.

He moved toward his prey. "Gilles." Alphonse was surprised; de Courmont usually didn't make a point of asking to be introduced. "This is Mademoiselle Léonie Bahri."

She *was* beautiful, perfect. Léonie blushed under his intense gaze; tension crackled between them as he gripped her hand. It was strangely exciting, and it left her feeling breathless, shaky.

"I came to thank you for your hospitality," he said to Alphonse, "but I'm afraid I must leave. I'm off to London first thing in the morning." He bowed to Léonie. "I'm happy to have met you, Mademoiselle Léonie." Their eyes met again, briefly. She licked her lips nervously.

"Does he ever smile?" she whispered to Alphonse as de Courmont walked away.

"Yes," Alphonse replied, "when he's winning."

Rupert fretted impatiently next to the girl in the blue dress. Caro had asked him specifically to look after her and he had no choice but to do so. They were surrounded now by a crowd of young people, but it was late, and the party was beginning to thin out. Where was Léonie? He couldn't see her anywhere. Damn it, how could Caro do this to him!

De Courmont signaled to Verronet, his personal assistant, who was waiting by the door.

"Find out *who* she is," murmured de Courmont to Verronet. "I need to know where she comes from, where she lives, what she does . . . what she needs. . . ."

Verronet knew what he meant. He'd done it all before. It wasn't the Duc de Courmont's way to compete openly with other men, either in business or in his private affairs. His was a more devious, more subtly binding approach. He would find out what a person needed—money, fame, sexual perversions—and then he would use the knowledge to undermine his adversaries, to put them in a more vulnerable position, ready for him to make his move. His adversaries didn't stand a chance—and he always treated women as adversaries. It was never a matter of love with de Courmont. He knew everyone had a price. And he loved the challenge best of all.

Léonie accepted her old brown wool coat from the butler and walked slowly down the marble stairs into the freezing night. She didn't feel the cold, she didn't feel anything. All the elation had left her. Rupert had deserted her for the girl in blue—all he had said, all she had felt had meant nothing. Had he just been flirting with her? Was that what flirting was? She had lingered for half an hour alone in the cloakroom telling herself that if he didn't talk to her this time when she walked past, she would leave. He hadn't even noticed her. *No one* had noticed her as she left. She'd looked around for the tall man with the piercing gaze, but then she remembered he had left earlier. Perhaps he'd been meeting some exciting and beautiful woman, taking her to supper and then back to his apartment—and his bed. She shivered. He looked that sort of man, older, experienced—a little frightening. The sound of music and laughter drifted into the night. It was a long way home through the frozen streets.

"Léonie!" She swung around, her face lighting up with a ray of hope. "Léonie, it's me, Maroc." He stood on the sidewalk holding open the door of a cab. "I thought you might not have enough money to get home, so I got Lanson to come here and wait with me. . . . It's all right," he added. "He's a friend of mine. I often take his cab from Serrat when I have to deliver things, I sometimes do him a favor and he helps me."

"Oh, Maroc." She was torn between being glad to see him and wishing he had been Rupert. "How kind you are. I don't know what I'd do without you."

Maroc had been worried about her all evening, and looking at her now he knew he had had good reason. She didn't look like a girl who'd been to a wonderful party; in fact, he thought she might cry. "Are you all right?" he asked anxiously.

"Yes, Maroc, I'm all right, I'm just tired, that's all." Léonie leaned back against the cushions as the carriage clopped its way home from her first party in Paris, holding hands with Maroc.

"But you *must* remember," cried Bella. It was three o'clock in the morning and they had rushed home, longing to hear about the party, whom Léonie had met, what had happened, and now she didn't remember!

"What did you eat?" asked Jolie practically. "Let's begin with that."

"Truffles," she said, "and strawberries, I think."

"*Truffles,*" groaned Loulou, rolling on the bed in mock agony, "I'd *never* forget a truffle! And strawberries when there's snow on the ground—you *must* remember."

Léonie sat up in bed, looking pale and tired. She'd forgotten to wash the rouge from her cheeks and it looked blotchy and unreal against her skin, and the golden eyeshadow had smudged.

"There's more to this than meets the eye," said Bella intuitively, "and I suspect it's a man."

"A man!" They looked at her expectantly, waiting. "Come on now, Léonie, no secrets." Loulou laughed.

"Oh," wailed Léonie tearfully. "Oh, Loulou. His name's Rupert and I'm in love with him."

They stared at one another in astonishment and then back at Léonie, the tears streaming down her face. "Oh, my God," said Loulou slowly.

The sky was blue and innocent of snow, pretending to be summer as Léonie raced through the streets toward Serrat. She skidded round the corner of the alley and arrived gasping at the back entrance, leaping up the steps two at a time and throwing off her coat as she raced down the passage to the salon. Marianne was waiting for her.

"It's half past nine, Léonie. We thought you weren't coming." Her voice was silky.

"I apologize for being late, Marianne." Léonie was penitent, head bowed, eyes downcast.

"And why are you late?"

"I don't know, Marianne."

"You don't know why you're late?"

"It's just that I slept late. I . . . I didn't feel very well last night."

Marianne pounced triumphantly. "That's not what I heard," she said. "I heard you were at a party."

How could she know? Léonie glanced at Maroc questioningly and he shrugged. "It was after the party," she said, "that I didn't feel well."

"It's just not good enough, Léonie." Marianne walked toward her cubicle. "You'd better come with me, and close the door behind you." The salesgirls watched them apprehensively. "As well as being late," said Marianne, "there's the other matter."

"What other matter?"

"The red silk stockings."

Léonie stared at her. What did she mean? "I understand that you took some red silk stockings yesterday"—Marianne's eyes bored into her—"without paying for them."

"But of course I paid for them! It was all the money I had."

"Then you'll have a receipt?"

A receipt? She had no receipt, why would she write out a receipt for herself? Too late, she realized what Marianne was getting at. "I must ask you for the money, Léonie—now!"

"But I told you I paid for them yesterday. I didn't bother with a receipt, I didn't think it would be necessary, but I put the money in the till, I swear to you."

"I have no record of any such money and the till balanced with the number and price of items sold yesterday." Marianne sat back in her chair, waiting. "I'm afraid that I must ask you to leave, Léonie. Right away. I shall not do anything about the stockings—you're a young girl and I would not like to prosecute you for theft, but I can't tolerate it in this establishment. You may get your coat and go."

Léonie stared at her in desperation. "I'll pay," she promised. "I'll pay again."

"With what?" asked Marianne, holding open the door. "I want you out at once, and please don't come back here again."

Too stunned even for tears, Léonie put on her coat and walked out into the alley. Maroc was waiting on the steps; he could see from her face that something was terribly wrong. "Léonie, what happened?"

"She said I stole the stockings, Maroc," said Léonie wearily. "I thought she was going to lecture me for being late, but then she said I had taken them and not paid."

"What?" He was used to Marianne's petty attitude and her constant picking on the girls, but this was something new. Why had she done this to Léonie? It was more than simple jealousy. He had a sudden thought. He'd been at the shop early that morning, hoping Léonie might come in early and that he could speak to her before opening time, but only Marianne was there. She had been deep in conversation with a youngish man who looked vaguely familiar. He hadn't been able to place him at the time, but now seeing Léonie had triggered his memory. He'd seen the man standing near Léonie in the courtyard last night. He had been at the party! Maroc remembered more: money had changed hands that morning. He had seen Marianne putting it into her pocket and he had thought it was just an early customer, ordering some present for his lover of the previous night, but now he wondered.

They talked it over endlessly but could come up with no answers. Léonie couldn't think of any man she'd noticed at the party who fit Maroc's description, and anyway, why would anyone pay to have her dismissed? No, Maroc must be mistaken. It was just Marianne, she had wanted to be rid of her and had seen an opportunity to get her way. And what was she to do now? She was too ashamed to tell Caro she had been accused of stealing and dismissed. Besides, Caro was to leave Paris today and would be gone for weeks.

"You must ask Loulou to help," said Maroc at last. "Maybe she can get you a job in the cabaret."

"In the cabaret! Oh, I couldn't do that, Maroc."

"Maybe backstage—as a maid, or a dresser?" he suggested.

Léonie needed a job desperately. She had spent all of her small savings, intended for sensible winter shoes, on the gold boots and the red silk stockings. The week had started so perfectly, and now she was in a worse position than when she had first come to Paris. She had fallen in love with a man who had only been flirting with her, and she had lost her job.

The manager of the Cabaret Internationale was used to girls, all types of girls, from the flashy ones to the innocent, and he stared approvingly at Léonie, liking what he saw. Of course, she'd have to buck up a little and put a bit more spark into it, but with that body and those legs she didn't have to sing or dance. Put her in a leotard and feathers and the customers would be happy; they paid to see as much flesh as possible and this was excellent flesh. "Being a showgirl is like being part of the scenery," he told her. "You simply stand on stage in a gorgeous costume and let the audience look at you."

Léonie's skin crawled at the thought. "What sort of costume?" she asked suspiciously.

"The same sort all the other girls wear—don't worry about it, it'll cover all the necessary parts." Monsieur Briac laughed crudely. "Anyway, they've seen it all before. Now, can you ride a horse?"

"Yes, I can ride."

"Tell you what, Léonie." He leaned across the desk and smiled. "Why not start out as a showgirl? We've got a new act we're putting together on a circus theme. If you work out I'll give you a part in that—sort of a bareback rider. What do you say?"

A bareback rider in a circus. Like her father. Somehow the idea was comforting; it couldn't be too bad if she were riding the horses. She brightened up. "Yes, I'd like that, Monsieur Briac."

"Then you can start next week. Have Loulou take you to get fitted for the costumes and come back in the afternoon with the other girls."

Rupert raced up the steps, past the grumbling concierge, and knocked on Caro's door. It was answered by the butler. "I'm afraid madame is not here, sir," he said courteously. "She left with Monsieur Alphonse for the country early this morning."

Rupert was taken aback. He had come to ask Caro for Léonie's address—he simply *had* to see her. "Where in the country?" he demanded.

"It's the Château du Clanard, sir, at Rambouillet, but I'm afraid they were going on from there to London."

"London!" Rupert stared at him aghast. "I must catch them!" He dashed off down the stairs. He was supposed to be at a meeting at the Krummer office this afternoon, but the hell with it. He *must* find Léonie.

* * *

Verronet waited while Monsieur le Duc read his report. It was very brief. There was little to know about the girl and it had been a simple job to find out. It had taken him a week but he knew everything. "Is this all?" asked de Courmont, looking up with a frown.

"Yes, sir. Remember she's very young, not yet seventeen. I did as you asked, sir, and she no longer works at Serrat."

"I know, I know." He threw the papers on the desk impatiently. "And now she's at the Cabaret Internationale."

"Opening on Tuesday, sir."

De Courmont glared at him. There had been no indication of what the girl wanted, needed. He'd thought that she would be more vulnerable after she had lost her job. Well, he'd have to wait until Tuesday and then he'd go to the cabaret to see her. There was no hurry.

⪍ 5 ⪐

"THERE'S NO REASON to be this nervous," said Bella, adjusting the sweeping scarlet plumes in Léonie's hair.

"It's just stage fright," comforted Loulou. "We all get it—especially before a new show. All you have to remember is to stand the way you were shown and throw back your cape at the right moment."

Léonie clutched the blue velvet cape closer, huddling miserably on her wooden chair in front of the mirror. Other showgirls dashed in and out in various stages of undress and she averted her eyes modestly from their nonchalantly displayed nakedness. She wondered how long it took before you got so used to other people seeing you without your clothes on that you didn't even notice anymore.

"Now, stand up and we'll practice one more time," said Loulou patiently.

Léonie stood obediently, shoulders and feathers drooping. "Oh, Léonie," wailed Loulou, "pull yourself together. How badly do you need this job?"

Léonie straightened up. "I need it."

"Right, then work for it. Now, remember I once told you that you had the right body and that you should flaunt it, well, now's the time to do just

46

that. One foot in front of the other, that's right . . . now! Back with the cape, head up, and smile!"

There was a spontaneous round of applause and laughter as Léonie obediently flung back her head and smiled, posing in her red, white, and blue leotard, sparkling with sequins. Her legs in their wobbly high heels and flesh-colored tights looked even longer, and the leotard fit snugly, exposing half moons of her bottom. "Bravo," cried Loulou, "that's more like it. You look stunning!"

"You see, it's not so bad." Bella hugged her sympathetically. "It's just the first time that's the worst."

"On stage, please." The boy popped his head around the door. "Five minutes to curtain."

The plumes on Léonie's head trembled prettily as she began to shake; only five minutes.

Rupert headed purposefully down the rue Montalivet toward Serrat. At last Caro had returned and he knew where Léonie worked. God knows what she must think of him, he wouldn't blame her if she never spoke to him again. She must have thought he didn't care—but he did. Oh, he did, so much! "SERRAT," there it was. He leapt up the steps. The place was full of women and he hesitated by the door, embarrassed to be the only man in this fancy feminine lingerie shop.

"Sir, may I help you?" A tall thin woman smiled at him. "A present for a lady, is it?"

"Er, no. The fact is I'm looking for Léonie Bahri. I was told she worked here."

The smile was wiped from the woman's face so fast that he wondered what he had said wrong. "Mademoiselle Bahri no longer works here."

"She no longer works here?" Rupert repeated in dismay. "Then, where is she?"

"I'm afraid I've no idea. Serrat has no further interest in Mademoiselle Bahri," she added loftily.

"But you must have her home address."

"We never give out the addresses of our employees, sir, even after they have left us."

"You don't understand"—he put an urgent hand on her arm—"I *must* see her. I was told that you would know where she was."

"I'm afraid you were misinformed. And now, if you'll excuse me, I have a customer."

Rupert lingered by the door. The woman *must* know where she lived. How could he find out? He walked back down the steps and into the street, turning to look again at the shop as though he might see her suddenly there.

"Sir, sir. . . ." Maroc ran toward him, panting. "Excuse me, sir, I work at Serrat. I heard just you now, asking Marianne about Léonie. I know where she is."

"You *know?*"

"Yes, sir. She's a friend of mine." Rupert stared at him. This strange boy in his satin suit and plumed turban was a friend of Léonie's? Maroc stared back hoping he'd done the right thing, remembering how sad Léonie had been since the party.

"Can you take me to her, now?"

"Not now, I have to get back to the shop, but I can give you her address."

Rupert wrote it quickly on the back of a card. "Madame Artois, 59 boulevard des Artistes."

"Maroc," he said, offering his hand, "you're *my* friend now as well as Léonie's."

The Cabaret Internationale was much larger than Gilles de Courmont had expected and more brightly lit, and he decided to stand at the back of the stalls rather than take a seat in the auditorium—you never knew who might be here and he preferred anonymity. The garish rococo theater was a plush establishment, with a proscenium arch garlanded with cherubs and flowers in a complexity of plasterwork that spread gilded tendrils over the adjoining boxes and balconies. The red velvet seats were beginning to fill with a noisy audience—mostly young men having a night "out on the town," here to see the girls—and the bar on the mezzanine was doing a roaring trade as they rushed to get in a last drink before the curtains rose. He found himself automatically estimating the cost and overhead of running such a place, calculating the turnover—it was a risky setup, he decided rapidly, heavy outgoings, a fickle public. The owner must have had a lucky run to keep the place looking so well and to bring in the crowds. But it wouldn't take much, a couple of bad months, to be out of business. The orchestra filed into the pit and there was a general flurry as people rushed at the last moment to their seats. Gilles waited until the orchestra sprang into a rousing overture and then made his way to the now empty bar in search of a whiskey.

"You're missing the beginning, sir," the barman said, handing him a drink.

"Yes."

"It's a pretty good show, sir, but I expect you've heard Loulou before. I always think myself she's better than Gloriette."

"Really." His voice was cool, noncommittal. "I heard that there are some new girls this time."

"Showgirls, yes . . . they'll be on in the second act, sir, in the Parade of Nations scene." He leaned confidingly across the bar. "You should see the legs on those girls, sir," he said with a wink, "and the tits—in those costumes you can practically see it all."

De Courmont tossed back his drink and walked away, suddenly irritated with the man; he paced the darkened area behind the stalls, not bothering to watch the action on stage until he heard the announcement for the Parade of Nations. The orchestra plunged into a rousing Cossack tune and the curtains drew back to reveal a troupe of leaping Russian dancers. Two girls, wearing enormous Cossack hats, high white leather boots, and daringly brief white satin shorts, stood on a catwalk jutting from the stage. Their minute satin boleros gave tantalizing glimpses of fleshy curves, bringing spontaneous applause from the noisy audience, who whistled their approval as the girls raised their arms over their heads in a statuesque pose as the music came to a rousing finale. Gilles stared at the spectacle in amazement; it was so awful that it was almost fascinating. Two black girls, barbaric in beads and bangles, and a new set of dancers performed a mock tribal dance to African rhythms as the girls swung their beads and their hips erotically. Gilles turned away, pacing impatiently as the act continued through Japan, India, and other unidentifiable subcontinents, until at last they came to the finale, La Belle France.

Léonie stood center stage, plumed head bent, hidden from neck to toe in her blue velvet cape while the dancers marched and sang patriotically around her. Gradually, as the music rose to a crescendo, she lifted her head and gazed out at her audience, remote and unsmiling. She was beautiful and proud and the audience watched in silence. The music approached its climax as Léonie stepped forward and flung back her cape, radiating a smile, a glittering vision in red, white, and blue sequins. Despite the ridiculous charade, de Courmont caught his breath. His eyes were riveted on her, an extraordinary symbol of France, as she raised both arms above her head and spread her legs in a pose of victory and triumph, casting her cape to the ground, delivering her smile—and herself—to the audience.

They loved her. They whistled and shouted, wanting to see more, and as the curtain came down he turned away, their lewd, raucous comments echoing in his ears.

He strode down the street and back across town, too tense to look for a cab, and besides, he needed to walk. He knew how he had felt looking at Léonie just now, and he knew that every other man in that theater had felt the same way. God knows how she had done it: for an innocent sixteen-year-old girl, she projected sex across that stage as none of the other girls had—those legs spread so arrogantly. He quickened his pace angrily. Of course, that was the quality he had sensed the other night at the party; under the innocence was a bubbling energy, a force just waiting to be unleashed. He turned into the courtyard of the de Courmont mansion and stalked angrily through the halls to his study, slamming the door behind him, reaching for the whiskey waiting on a silver tray.

Throwing himself into the big green leather chair, he thought about Léonie. Oh, he wanted her all right—every man in that theater had wanted her—but it was more than that, there was something else about her, something familiar. There was a memory lurking somewhere. He sighed impatiently. Of course, he could go to her, invite her out to dinner, give her presents, but that was all too obvious: he'd be buying her and she'd know it, and he had the feeling she couldn't be bought. No, there was a better way than that, a much better game to be played. He sat for a long time in the big leather chair, sipping his whiskey and thinking.

"Léonie," Bella dashed up the last flight of stairs gasping for breath. "Léonie!"

"What is it, Bella?" She stuck her head out from her door. "What's wrong?"

"You've got a visitor, a man! A *gorgeous* man! A blond-haired, blue-eyed man. A Rupert von Hollensmark!"

It couldn't be him, could it? He didn't know where she lived.

"He's waiting for you in the salon. Madame Artois showed him in there herself. Oh, Léonie"—she hugged her excitedly—"he's lovely. He's the one, isn't he? The one from the party . . . the one you fell in love with?"

Léonie nodded slowly.

"Then hurry, change into your other dress, brush your hair, put on some perfume. Oh, *hurry*, Léonie, he's waiting. Your Rupert is waiting!" Bella was thrilled that at last something was going right for Léonie; she'd seen her crying the night of the party, and though it might only be first-love despair—a sixteen-year-old's romantic despair, as Loulou had pointed out—still, Bella could remember the first time she'd fallen in love, and how desperate it was and how marvelous it was—usually both at the same time. "Come on," she said. "I'll help you." She brushed Léonie's hair and lent her some perfume and held her hand as they walked sedately down the stairs together. "Now, don't look too eager," she cautioned on the second flight. "Be a little aloof, a little distant. Make him think there's a line of other men just waiting to take you out."

He was there, standing in Madame Artois's salon, and he was just as she remembered him, his eyes were just as blue, his hair exactly as blond— and the world turned cartwheels just like before. "Oh, Rupert," she said, forgetting Bella's advice, "I thought I'd never see you again."

Bella sighed in exasperation as Rupert took Léonie's hands in his and they gazed into each other's eyes, and then he put his arms around her. Closing the door softly behind her, Bella walked back up the stairs, sighing as she went. "The fool," she said quietly under her breath, "the silly little fool."

The Café Anglaise was *their* place. They met there every night for supper and every night Rupert waited impatiently, wondering *why* she would insist on being so late. But he forgot everything when she appeared in the doorway, her lovely face anxious until she spotted him, and then the delicious melting smile, the amber eyes gleaming her happiness as he came toward her and took her hand, leading her to their special banquette in the corner, away from the crowd and prying eyes, where he could hold her hand and sneak a kiss without being observed. He was crazy about her, she was the most beautiful girl he had ever known. And she was sweet, oh, so sweet. And innocent. There was no doubt about that. She was completely honest, without guile of any sort, but she was mysterious. When she wasn't with him, he didn't know what she did—I have commitments, she said vaguely. He thought perhaps it was her family, that she might have to take care of them and didn't want him to know. He didn't inquire too closely, all he wanted was to be with her. He wanted to be with her forever. He closed his mind to thoughts of Puschi and his family—all that existed right now was Léonie.

She was wearing a new dress! It was blue, the blue of the Mediterranean in summer, and he could just imagine her swimming in warm seas, her long, tawny hair floating behind her—of course, that was it! The perfect place, the old whitewashed inn at Cap Ferrat. He would take her there.

"I'm so late," Léonie said apologetically. It was sinful to waste a precious moment away from him, but the show had run late tonight. The cabaret was another world, one she didn't want him to know about. What would he think of her if he knew, if he saw how she was on stage, how she flaunted herself to the audience? She shuddered.

"What's the matter, darling, are you cold?" He was solicitous, wrapping his arm around her.

"No, no." She laughed. "I'm not cold. I'm just happy."

He filled her glass with champagne. They drank only champagne—to match the color of her hair. "I've had a wonderful idea," he told her, "but I'll save it until after you've eaten."

"No, now, please tell me now." She kissed his fingers, clasped around her own.

"Later," he teased. "First you must eat your supper like a good girl."

Gilles de Courmont watched from his table by the window. He was there almost every night, discreetly hidden behind the decorative little trees and palms. And Verronet waited outside to follow them; so far he had always taken her home. Admittedly, they did drive around in a cab for a long time, but still, he hadn't taken her to his apartment yet. Gilles sipped the excellent Lafite without noticing, ignoring the food in front of him. He hadn't reckoned on Rupert von Hollensmark. Without realizing that there was a game to be played, he had lost. But only the first round. A waiting game usually proved to be more profitable in the end. He considered his next moves.

"Do sit down," Caro sighed as Léonie paced the floor of her sitting room radiating happiness.

"He wants me to go away with him, Caro, to this lovely little inn on the Côte d'Azur. He says it's beautiful, so quiet and peaceful. We shall be all alone and the sun will shine and the sea is warm and even bluer than the sky."

"Léonie, it's *December*," said Caro realistically.

Léonie was lost for a moment in her dreams, her thoughts turned inward on a vision of Rupert alone with her, in a simple whitewashed room that overlooked the blue sea, and a big white bed. "Oh, Caro, what do you think? Should I do it?"

"Of course you shouldn't do it! Léonie, think about it, and think about it carefully. It's the biggest step a girl can take, and it's one there's no going back from." She didn't want to hurt her, but she must tell her the facts, make it clear that Rupert would not be able to marry her. Love was quite another matter. "I'm sure he loves you, just as much as you love him. But Rupert's engaged to a girl in Germany. He'll marry her, Léonie."

"I know about her, he told me, of course. He didn't want us to have any secrets," Léonie said confidently. "But he'll tell her that he can't marry her. Not now that he loves me."

"His father arranged this marriage for Rupert. It's more than a marriage, Léonie, it's an alliance between two powerful families—you have more than just Rupert to contend with ... you've almost got the whole German empire!"

Léonie laughed. "Oh, Caro, you're so funny. You mustn't worry about me. Rupert will take care of everything."

Damn, thought Caro, this is all my fault and it can only end in disaster. Even if Rupert does go against his family and marry her, he will have no money, he can't afford a wife. A lover is a different matter. Every man can afford a lover.

Léonie glanced at the clock. She would be late for the theater. Thank goodness it would only be for a few more weeks; she had promised Monsieur Briac that she wouldn't leave until she'd done the circus role. She wished she could tell Caro now that she worked in the cabaret. She looked at Caro longingly, resisting the urge to confess. The fewer people who knew, the better. She never, never wanted Rupert to find out, and Caro might just, even if sworn to secrecy, she might just tell Alphonse, and Alphonse might tell a friend—no, it was better this way.

"Where do you disappear to all the time?" complained Caro. "You're so busy. You must come and see me more often. Come with us to dinner at Gilles de Courmont's next Tuesday. I'm sure he wouldn't mind if I brought you along." She'd get her away from Rupert, take her out a little, let her meet more people.

Tuesday was the opening night of the new show. "I'm sorry, Caro, I can't. But thank you anyway. I'll come to see you again next week." Léonie kissed her impulsively on the cheek. "I can never thank you enough for introducing me to Rupert."

"Oh, dear, Léonie," sighed Caro. "I do wish I hadn't."

Monsieur le Duc de Courmont had two lives: one formal life at home with his wife, the social events they were expected to appear at together, when she would grace his table for business and political purposes, or when he would be at her side at family events; and another, quite separate, one, where he would go his own way, always alone, meeting the people he chose to meet, playing host at a smart restaurant, returning the hospitality of people whose parties or dinners he might have attended. And the extraordinary thing was, thought Verronet, waiting outside Voisins, pacing the chill December street trying to keep warm, that no one ever refused his invitations. Like him or not, they came. He wouldn't like to bet on how many *friends* were sitting at that big table right now—and there were two dozen people there. That's power for you. He smiled smugly, secure in his little niche in that power. Nobody can ever say "no" when you're *that* powerful.

Caro had always like Voisins, she loved the restaurant's overblown intimacy, its deep coral walls and swagged velvet drapes, the heavy tassels and gilded mirrors that reflected the smartest diners in Paris. And, for those who preferred privacy, there were the special booths, each one a tiny secluded rendezvous—candlelight, sòfa, and table for two—hidden from curious eyes by velvet curtains heavy enough to muffle whispered words of love and the soft sounds of kisses. She had fond memories of those booths.

Gilles had taken a private dining room, and, as usual, everything was perfect. The staff at Voisins were used to Monsieur le Duc. He was civil, prompt, and undemanding; he simply expected the best and they were happy to supply it. "And God help us if we don't," said the manager feelingly.

De Courmont greeted his guests, savoring the evening ahead. Anticipation was an enormous pleasure, it always heightened his excitement, whether it was pulling off a coup in business or making love to a woman—the waiting, knowing what was to come, knowing he would win, was at least fifty percent of the game.

He liked giving these dinner parties; they gave him another opportunity to manipulate people, placing young men next to sophisticated older women, and foreign businessmen next to the most alluring girls, juggling the beautiful people of Paris, sparking off rivalries and love affairs. The results could be fascinating to watch. Tonight he had put Rupert von Hollensmark next to Marla, and he could see it was a good move.

Marla was flamboyant, arrogant, rich, titled, and forty, notorious for her liking for younger men. As Gilles watched she leaned closer to Rupert, affording him an even better view of her spectacular bosom. Even a man as in love as Rupert couldn't remain unaware of that body, or of her reputation for never wearing underwear. Marla fired any man's fantasies. She leaned closer, fingers resting lightly on Rupert's thigh, asking him some question. Gilles smiled. No young man was safe with Marla. He'd chosen her well.

Caro was flirting with the American millionaire. Why was it that Americans always wanted you to know how many millions they had? he wondered. This one had made his in oil and railroads—a useful combination. He'd left his yacht at Monte Carlo and was dividing his time between losing his dollars in the casino there and spending them on more earthly delights in Paris. Caro already had him so charmed that he thought he must surely be the most attractive man in the world—she was an expert flirt. She glanced up and caught his eye and he smiled at her.

There was a buzz of conversation and laughter as the wine flowed; he could almost sense the women relaxing, like flowers in the sun, while the men basked in a glow of well-being and good food. Two dozen people. Could he call any of them friends? The men were mostly business acquaintances, the women, well, some of them he knew more intimately than others. Gilles smiled, enjoying himself. His party was a success. But the best was yet to come.

"Ladies and gentlemen." He commanded their attention. "Friends," he added smoothly, "I have a surprise for you. We are going to a cabaret."

"A cabaret? What fun. Where?" they clamored, eager for excitement.

"There's a new show opening tonight. I've heard it's quite spectacular—amazing costumes, extraordinary girls, wonderful dancers—I thought it might amuse us." He smiled at Rupert, enjoying himself.

* * *

Léonie paced the dressing room tearfully in her high white leather boots, raging against the manager. "How could he—how could he, Loulou? Just look at me—look at this *costume!*"

Loulou stared at her. The white tights fit her like a second skin and the stiff white satin corselette, pulled tight by silver laces, pinched her waist, pushing her bosom upward until it spilled out at the top in two emphatic half-moon curves. A white leather belt, studded in silver, was slung low on her hips and padlocked strategically with a large silver heart. She carried a silver whip with a thin white thong and her blond hair was tightly tied back into a long plume plaited with tinsel strands exactly like the tail of the white horse she was to ride. She looked spectacular, a white virginal rebel from some masochistic dream of de Sade.

"It's too late to do anything about it now, Léonie. I don't understand why you didn't complain at the fitting."

"But it didn't *look like this* at the fitting. The top came up to here and it wasn't pulled as tightly, and there was supposed to be a little tutu to cover the tights—not this—this padlock! Oh, Loulou!" She was near to tears.

"I think if we put a little flesh-colored gauze here"—Loulou tucked the soft fabric over Léonie's bosom—"it should be all right. That way the audience will think they're seeing more than is really there—it's an old trick. Now," she said, shrugging, "it doesn't seem to matter anymore."

"It does to me," cried Léonie.

"I know, I know it does, but look in the mirror. You see, now you're completely covered."

Léonie stared; it did look a little better. "What about *this?*" she demanded.

Loulou examined the belt. It was attached to the tights and there was no way to take it off. "I *can't* go on stage like this. Oh, I just want to hide." The tears streamed down Léonie's face, ruining the elaborate makeup.

Loulou thought for a moment. "That's exactly what you'll do. You'll hide. Wait a minute." She rummaged through the big drawer that held scarves, gloves, and odd bits and pieces of costumes and pulled out a silver domino mask. "I wore it in a Pierrot and Columbine number last year. Put it on, Léonie, it's as good as hiding; your own mother wouldn't recognize you."

My mother, thought Léonie desperately, never did anything like this —she never shamed herself appearing on stage looking the way I do. She put on the mask and faced herself in the mirror. It didn't hide much but it was better, at least she didn't feel so exposed.

They could hear the orchestra crashing into the first bars of the overture. "I've got to go," cried Loulou, "I'm on first." She dashed off down the dim passage that led to the stage and Léonie followed her slowly.

Only four more weeks, she told herself, just four weeks and then I can leave all this. I'll go with Rupert to the south, to the inn with that big bed in that moonlit room where we'll begin our lives together, and I'll *never ever again* in my whole life set foot in a cabaret.

Their party filled the center block of the first two rows of the theater, crowding in together, laughing and chattering as they discarded furs and capes and took their seats, staring in anticipation at the advertisements for hair restorer and cough linctus on the stiff safety curtain still lowered in front of the stage.

The audience up in the balcony was a raucous group, mostly young men who came to see the girls, already rowdy and excited, passing ribald comments on the dancers and showgirls they had seen before. In the stage boxes and the stalls, other men, their white ties and starched shirtfronts gleaming, waited quietly; they, too, were here to see the girls.

After all, thought Paul Bernard from his seat at the back of the theater, that's what cabaret is all about: girls. He studied his program, linking names to faces, and in some cases bodies, checking to see what his rivals were up to. Of course, his was a classier cabaret than the Internationale, and more subtly presented. He always had excellent singers and he had the best chorus line in Paris. He was here to see Léonie Bahri—he'd noticed her last week when he'd dropped in to catch the previous show and he'd recognized her as the girl from the train—and, of course, she'd looked as spectacular as he had known she could. He'd like to use her in his next show if he could lure her away from the Internationale.

The horse, powdered to perfect whiteness, was waiting in its box by the stage, fidgeting nervously as the orchestra pounded through the first tunes and the dancers dashed on and off the stage on cue. Léonie could hear the audience laughing at Loulou's song and the applause for her as she finished and began a second number.

The dancer who was to play ringmaster eyed the horse warily as it whinnied and kicked out its back legs, scattering the stagehands. "I'd be careful with him if I were you," she advised. "He's not used to the lights and the noise."

Léonie patted his neck, stroking his nose gently, and the horse rolled an eye at her. "He'll be all right," she said sympathetically; she knew how he felt. Loulou came off the stage and Léonie went across to congratulate her, leaving the horse stomping his hooves in the straw. "Here," said one of the stagehands bringing over a bucket of water, "drink this, you stupid animal, maybe then you'll feel better."

"They're a terrific audience tonight." Loulou smiled, pleased with her success. "You'll have no problems, Léonie."

The pretty ringmaster stalked the stage cracking her whip as the "beasts" of the circus cavorted around the ring—long-legged girls dressed as leopards and tigers, ponies and zebras. Real little dogs in neck ruffles somersaulted over their backs and clowns in baggy pants and red noses did handstands and backflips along the catwalks.

De Courmont watched Rupert as he applauded, joining in the fun, bending his head to listen to the whispered comments of Marla, whom Gilles had again seated next to Rupert.

The pretty white horse was next, trotting in neat circles, lifting his feet gracefully to the music, tossing his silvered mane and rolling his eyes like a pony in a fairy story as the audience applauded admiringly. To a fanfare of trumpets a masked girl strode into the ring, sensational in silk tights and satin breasts. There was a whistle of approval from the balcony as she cracked her whip, tossing her head so that her plumed hair flashed with silver to match her horse's tail. Such marvelous hair, thought Caro, and such legs; she stared closer. No, it couldn't be, could it? "That *must* be Léonie!" whispered Alphonse. It *was* Léonie! So *this* was what she had been doing, *this* was why she was always so busy in the evenings! But why hadn't she told her? And why hadn't Rupert told her? Rupert's eyes were fixed on Léonie. Had he known? She turned quickly to look at de Courmont. Had *he* known? Was this why he had brought them here? His eyes were not on the stage, not on Léonie. De Courmont was watching Rupert intently. Caro could tell by Rupert's tense expression that he hadn't known. Léonie had kept her secret well—from everyone but de Courmont; she'd be willing to bet on that.

"It's Léonie. . . . It's Léonie, Caro's friend from the party." The whispered name flashed around their group and de Courmont settled back into his chair, a smile on his lips. "You knew," whispered Caro.

He shrugged. "I thought it would be a nice surprise if you saw your little protégée doing so well. Look, she's going to begin." Caro turned to Alphonse and raised her eyebrows inquiringly. What was he up to? Alphonse shrugged; he didn't know. She stole another look at Gilles—his eyes were on Rupert, who was sitting bolt upright staring at the stage, obviously shocked at seeing his Léonie, half-naked in the cabaret.

Léonie ran across the stage and vaulted lightly onto the back of the cantering horse, jumping off again neatly as it circled the ring. "Bravo," cried the American millionaire, applauding enthusiastically. "Bravo, Léonie"—the others joined in, calling her name and cheering her on as she performed her small feats of bareback horsemanship. She was really quite good, once you got used to her appearance. Rupert joined the applause and Caro saw that he was smiling again, enjoying Léonie's small success.

De Courmont leaned forward; he hadn't expected this, he'd wanted Rupert to be stunned, to be outraged by her appearance, shocked that she was not the virginal seventeen-year-old girl he was enamored with. This was meant to expose the "real" Léonie, to shatter Rupert's dream.

Could it be, Caro wondered, that Gilles doesn't want Rupert to have Léonie? Surely not, he barely knows Léonie—or does he? He'd been at that party, too. She frowned. Something was wrong and she couldn't put her finger on it.

The horse is too nervous, thought Léonie, gripping the trace tighter as she swung herself on its back, it's scared of the applause. It's those people in front, they're waving and shouting. What *are* they doing, don't they see they're upsetting the animal? She balanced herself warily on one leg and raised the other, toe pointed in bareback rider pose, as she circled the stage, peering across the footlights. Could that be Caro? and Alphonse? She wobbled dangerously. And all those other people she'd seen at Caro's, a whole group of them? And, oh, God, oh, no, don't let it be true! There was Rupert! He was smiling and cheering. The smart woman next to him leaned over and took his arm, whispering in his ear, making him laugh. They were laughing at her!

She wanted to jump off the horse, to run away, to escape, but there was no way out. She had to finish her act. It was almost over, thank God. Oh, what would she say to him? He was with that woman. Would he ever want to see her again now that he knew? Now that he'd seen her in this costume, this awful, humiliating costume! The music slowed and the white horse trembled as the trumpet began a fanfare, kicking its heels suddenly as Léonie attempted her final pose. She lunged forward, just righting herself in time to save herself from falling.

It was as she raised her arms aloft in a final flamboyant pose that she realized that the gauze so well placed by Loulou had slipped and so had her tight bodice. Her naked breasts were displayed to the entire theater. And to Rupert. Oh, God, Rupert!

The audience went wild, they stomped and whistled and applauded, jolting her from her first frozen immobility, and she clutched her arms frantically over her bosom. Over the racket she could hear a new noise, a strange hissing; the footlights spluttered and steamed as the foaming liquid hit them. The nervous horse, filled with water earlier, had chosen this moment to relieve itself, flooding center stage and sending the dancers leaping and giggling out of its path.

The audience howled as Léonie stared with horror at the group in the center stalls. Their heads were thrown back as they roared with helpless laughter, applauding and cheering. Rupert, too, was laughing; he was laughing at *her*—they were all laughing at her—she wanted to die. She just wanted to die. She leapt off the horse and ran from the stage, tearing through the dancers standing in the wings, pushing Loulou away. She had to escape, to get away.

Only Caro wasn't laughing. She was watching de Courmont. He was smiling quietly. "I didn't realize it would be quite this amusing," he said.

❧ 6 ❦

MAROC HURRIED DOWN the alley at the back of the rue Montalivet and into the connecting one at the corner, threading his way through a network of narrow streets that became increasingly dirty and mean as he made his way home. The shabby lodging house stood back from a busy intersection near the railway station, and he had chosen it because it was the cleanest he could find. The landlord was a meticulous old man who insisted on his lodgers being the same; he would have no garbage left in the halls, no cooking smells from the tiny communal kitchen, and each tenant had to wash his own window once a week and pay his rent on Friday. Those were the rules and you either lived with them or you left. But the old man asked no questions and took no interest in the personal lives of his lodgers, and it had been the cheapest place he could find for Léonie. When she had come to him that night, he had understood at once how desperate she was and had taken her in without even asking what had happened, or why.

He couldn't forget how she had cried; the tears had seemed an unending torrent, blotching her skin, puffing her lovely face, until he became worried that she might never stop. But she had, eventually. Then she'd told him the story of her humiliation, of her nakedness and her shame and how they had all laughed at her, laughing together. She never wanted to see any of them again, even Caro. When Léonie said that, he knew the depth of her humiliation. She adored Caro, she was her idol, she was everything Léonie longed to be. It was Maroc who had sneaked back to Madame Artois's and collected Léonie's things, slipping in after dinner when he knew Madame Artois would be alone in her sitting room, enjoying her brandy. There had been no one around. And it was he who had found her the job—it was only as a waitress at the café opposite the station, but at least it was work and she had welcomed it. She would never, never, she told him passionately, go back to the cabaret again. And she had sworn him to secrecy. He knew nothing about her, he had no idea where she was, he was to tell no one.

Verronet sat at a table by the door in the Café du Gare, lingering over a cup of what must surely have been the worst coffee in Paris. He was getting tired of spending so much time in this dreary place, the windows were perpetually steamed from the bubbling pots in a kitchen that smelled of too many layers of grease, and the woman who presided over the immense cash register near the door was beginning to look at him suspiciously as he sat for an hour at a time, ordering nothing but coffee. Weakly he summoned the waiter. "Brandy," he said, "and make it a large one." Catching her eye on him, he added hastily, "and a piece of that cake." He stared distastefully at the tired chocolate confection in its glass case under the zinc counter. Surely de Courmont must be satisfied by now that the girl did nothing other than come here to work and leave again when she had finished, heading straight back to the lodging house without speaking to anyone. Her routine had been the same for over a month now, and she was unlikely to vary the pattern. The young boy was her only friend and he was harmless. But de Courmont did not like it. He wanted her to have no one to turn to so that he could come along and save her. Verronet shrugged. What did de Courmont expect him to do about the boy? He was just a kid.

Caro was consumed by guilt and worry—it was her fault. If she had been less busy, less wrapped up in her social rounds, more caring, perhaps Léonie would have confided in her. She would have advised her against any association with a man like the manager of the Cabaret Internationale. Time and time again she told herself Léonie's public humiliation could have been avoided. But she blamed Rupert as well as herself for what had happened. "You've monopolized her time, and yet you say you didn't even know what she was doing! How could you Rupert, how could you let her do that?"

"I swear I didn't know, Caro." He was so miserable, so abjectly sorry, that she had relented. They had hurried backstage together that night, but Léonie had gone, thrown her coat over that astonishing costume and disappeared into the night. "I couldn't stop her," Loulou had told them. "She just pushed me aside and ran off. She must have gone home."

But she wasn't at home, Madame Artois hadn't seen her, and when she heard their story, she told them bluntly that she wasn't surprised the girl had run away. "Poor child, and her so modest," she had said, recalling her blushes as the girls had made her try on the dress that time. "To expose her in a costume like that in front of all those men!"

Caro had no idea where to search. At first they just hoped that she would return, but she didn't. Then the answer came to her in a flash. "There's only one person," Caro told Alphonse, after weeks of worrying, "only one person that she might trust. Maroc. It must be him. Why, oh, why," she wailed, "didn't I think of this sooner?"

At Serrat Maroc lurked in the background, avoiding her eyes, and she knew she was on to something. "I'll need the boy," she ordered, "to carry my parcels."

"Of course, Mademoiselle Montalva. . . . Maroc!"

He came forward reluctantly and followed her outside. "Tell me where she is," she demanded.

"I don't know what you mean . . . where who is?" he parried innocently.

"Léonie! And *of course* you know." He was silent. "Look, Maroc, I'm here because I want to help her. I feel responsible for what happened. I should have kept an eye on her. I should have known what was going on. . . . I must help her, and so must you."

"You should have left her alone in the first place." He flared up angrily. "She was all right before she met you."

"Oh, Maroc!" Could it be true? Caro wondered guiltily. Had she meddled in the girl's life? If she had, it was now up to her to do something about it.

Maroc stared at the ground miserably, torn between loyalty to Léonie and his worry about her. The double blow of lost love and hurt pride was taking its toll, diminishing her once-sparkling brightness to muted shadow. It had been five weeks now, and she was growing thinner and more lethargic. She was supposed to get her lunch and evening meal free at the café, but he suspected she didn't bother to eat, and she never went anywhere— just walked to the café at noon and back again at eight o'clock at night. What was he to do with her? The responsibility was enormous. He looked hesitantly at Caro. Maybe if she promised not to tell Rupert. After all, she was the only one who might be able to help Léonie.

Caro sensed his hesitation. "Please, Maroc, *please*. I'd do *anything* to help her. She needs another woman at a time like this."

She was right; Léonie did need another woman. He had done all he could, but women were a mystery, you never knew what they were thinking, what they might do. And he was becoming afraid of Léonie's black mood. "But you must promise to tell no one else," he said.

* * *

De Courmont was restless. He paced the decks of the liner *Ile de France,* avoiding the companionship of his fellow passengers as much as possible. The outward journey to America was boring enough, but the return seemed even longer. Shipboard life was too relaxed for him after the pace and action that always seemed so much a part of New York. Still, the trip had proved a profitable one, he would be one of the first men in France to get into the motor car industry. The vehicle of the future, just as railways had been not too long ago. He was well pleased with himself.

He thought about Paris, about getting home. He had promised his wife he would be back in time for their elder son's birthday; Gérard would be six years old—he must see to it that the boy had a good tutor, get him primed for school in the autumn. That fool governess was no good. Of course, Marie-France liked her, said she was kind. Kind! The boy needed knowledge, not kindness. Perhaps he'd try to spend more time with him, go down to the country, ride with him, that sort of thing. Now that they were no longer babies, he should take more interest in his sons—Marie-France had influenced them long enough.

"Morning, sir." The wireless officer saluted him. "There's a cablegram for you, sir."

Gilles tore open the cable and read it quickly. It ws another report from Verronet: the same thing, the girl was still at the café. No sign of Rupert. Yes, his plan had worked out very satisfactorily. Léonie would be just about ready for some comfort, a sympathetic listener, a little help; he'd ease her into a little luxury, a little pampering, gradually, until she couldn't do without it. She'd soon forget Rupert von Hollensmark. A few more weeks of hardship and loneliness wouldn't hurt; he'd let her wait a little longer . . . to make his own pleasure all the sweeter.

Caro dusted her hands fastidiously, removing what she felt sure were the imprints of a thousand greasy fingers from the banister of the rickety staircase, where she had thoughtlessly trailed her hand on the climb to the fourth floor. Nevertheless, it was cleaner than she had expected from the outside, and Léonie's room, though dark, was immaculate. And cold! Caro shivered; how cold it was, even though the sun was shining outside and the sky was blue—these old lodging houses had the chill of a dungeon. Maroc had said that Léonie would be home at eight o'clock and she wandered restlessly around the small room, her high-heels echoing on the naked floorboards, peering out the window at the thankless view of the railway station, lifting the cheap flowered curtain that hid Léonie's pitifully few belongings: two dresses hanging crookedly from a peg on the wall, a pair of gold boots—of course, she remembered she had worn them at the party—the start of it all. Caro turned expectantly as she heard footsteps on the stairs and the door was pushed open.

Léonie was lost in her thoughts, eyes downcast. It wasn't the sort of room you entered with any joy for its welcoming comfort.

"Léonie."

Looking up, she saw Caro waiting, framed by the window that never seemed to let in either light or fresh air—Caro, whose world was jewel-colored and bright, gleaming and sparkling. It was like finding an orchid in a prison. Léonie began to cry.

"Oh, Léonie, my poor Léonie." Caro wrapped her arms around her, cradling her head, kissing her hair, offering words of comfort. "It's all my fault," she cried guiltily, "I was your friend. If only you'd told me about the cabaret, I would have helped you, advised you, warned you. Oh, Léonie, it need never have happened." Her tears mingled with Léonie's and they sobbed together in relief. "The worst is over," she consoled her. "You'll come with me. We'll work it all out."

Léonie pushed her away, her eyes red-rimmed and wide with panic. She bore so little resemblance to the golden girl of the party, to the star of the cabaret, that Caro was shocked. She could see now how thin the girl had become, the bones of her face projected sharply and her thin shoulder blades protruded from under the cheap blouse. Her hands were red and chapped from washing dishes and her hair, dragged back into a coil on her neck and anchored by a dozen pins, lacked the luster and the wildness that had always sent it floating free with a life of its own.

"I can't ever see Rupert again."

Caro wondered what to say. She didn't want her to see Rupert again, it would be far better for all their sakes if she didn't, but he was so miserable, so terribly unhappy. He came daily to see if Caro had heard anything, and each time she sent him away with no news he seemed to become a little older, a little sadder. There was no doubt he was a young man very much in love. She hardened her heart. She'd seen young men in love before, and she wouldn't have Léonie hurt a second time.

"You need never see him," she promised. "We could work it out, Léonie, just come back with me. I promise I won't let him know you're there."

Léonie felt so *tired* suddenly. It was all too much. Too many decisions, too much emotion, too much despair. How nice life would be without it, a life where she need never feel love and despair and passion and hate and humiliation. Where everything just jogged along pleasantly. How easy, a life without love. She looked around her small room. It had never seemed a place of refuge, it had given her nothing, offered her no warmth, no comfort. One day she would find a place that did that, a place of her own.

"Leave everything," commanded Caro, "you need nothing of this. You'll start afresh, a new beginning."

Léonie hesitated. "Just these," she said, "I need them." She picked up the small bag, hugging it to her. It was just as Maroc had brought it to her—she hadn't bothered to unpack. She would never part with the two Egyptian dolls. They were all that truly belonged to her. As they slammed the door of that miserable room behind them and walked together down the stairs, Léonie wondered what the next tenant would think when she discovered those little gold boots.

❧ 7 ❦

THE BARONESS VON HOLLENSMARK loved to gamble. There was something about those green baize tables and the delicate flutter of cards in expert hands, the tension of the players and the impassive faces of the croupiers—and all those lovely colored counters and gold coins scattered across the cloth—that still gave her a thrill. "I'm eighty years old," she said gleefully to Rupert as he pushed her chair through the foyer of the Hotel Grand Park, "and I've an arthritic hip to thank for getting me back to Baden-Baden. Your grandfather used to bring me here often. Of course, he came for the races, but I always liked the casino best."

It had been fifteen years since she was last here and she still half-expected to meet some of her old friends, though, sadly, most of them were gone now, many killed more than twenty years ago in the Franco-Prussian War. Rupert adored his grandmother. Grandess, he called her, mixing her two titles. She'd always been the member of the family he'd been closest to; he had spent long, lazy summers at her castle overlooking the Rhine, and it had been she who had comforted him when he had been sent away to school, she who had promised to look after his pony and his dogs—and she hadn't forgotten. He'd been happy to escort her to Baden-Baden for treatment for her arthritis. Of course, she had her little entourage, her maid and her nurse, but she enjoyed the company of her favorite grandson.

Grandess sighed with satisfaction. Thank goodness the casino was still the same, things seemed to change so quickly these days. The Venetian chandeliers were as glitteringly beautiful and the tables as busy as in the past; the women were still pretty and the men, in white tie and tails, as solidly handsome. The ceilings still had the same floating cupids and clouds and the carpet was satisfyingly thick and red. "Now," she said happily, "I think we'll start with chemin de fer."

Rupert watched Grandess enjoying herself, allowing his mind to wander back to the previous weekend. It had not been a success. Puschi had wondered why he hadn't been writing to her and why he was so distant. It wasn't her fault. He hadn't meant to hurt her, he just couldn't forget Léonie. It had been three months and there was still no trace of her. He had wanted to hire an investigator but Alphonse had forbidden it, saying that if Léonie didn't want him to find her then he should accept that. She knows where you are, she could come to you, he'd said. Obviously, Léonie doesn't choose to do so. Alphonse's words had a ring of logic that Rupert had been forced to accept, but he still found himself searching through the faces in the crowds hoping to see her. He never did. He'd thrown himself into his work, burying his dreams in the complexities of expanding markets for Krummer—his future father-in-law's steelworks—working hard and late with a new dedication that had earned the surprised approval of the directors of the Paris offices. That was the reason her father had been so pleasant this weekend, despite Puschi's complaints.

"He's working hard, my dear," he'd told her. "He's a busy man," he added approvingly, as talk had shifted to the possibility of an autumn wedding. *An autumn wedding.* Oh, God! He loved Léonie. He would try to see Caro again when he got back to Paris, though she was so elusive these days, always away in the country.

"Excuse me, sir." Grandess's nurse was at his side. "It's time for the baroness to go to bed, sir. She has a treatment first thing in the morning at the spa and she needs her rest."

"It's only been a couple of hours," said Baroness von Hollensmark testily, "and don't treat me like an old lady. I don't like it, I'm not old yet. I can still win at the tables."

"I'll come back with you," volunteered Rupert. "Keep you company."

"No, no, there's no need to, Rupert. Unfortunately the woman is right. I do have to be up early and they tell me that the treatment is tiring. You stay here and enjoy yourself. Here, take these." She pushed the pile of chips toward him. "Try your luck. See if you can break the bank for us."

Rupert bent to kiss her cheek. She smelled of eau de cologne and pink powder, just as he remembered. He watched her disappear down the vast chandeliered corridor and turned away, feeling suddenly very lonely. The night was still young—and still empty. Gathering up the chips, he returned to the chemin de fer tables.

* * *

It had been Alphonse's suggestion that she take Léonie to the spa and Caro had leapt at the idea. Of course, it was the perfect place, a health resort that offered diversion, too. It was exactly what she needed, and besides, she didn't know how much longer she could tolerate hiding away in the country. No matter how beautiful Rambouillet might be, it was *quiet*. Baden-Baden was *fun*, she'd told Léonie, and what they both needed was a little fun.

While fun wasn't exactly what she felt like, Léonie enjoyed the lovely old town on the bank of the river Emz, and the hotel was so grand and so beautiful with its distant views of the Black Forest from the terrace. What she liked most of all was the swimming pool. She'd discovered it on her first morning, exploring the labyrinthine corridors under the Hotel Grand Park, wandering through echoing halls filled with faintly sulfurous steam and past swirling baths of mud, where white-coated attendants performed miracles on tired flesh. The lofty swimming hall with its twin marble colonnades had been empty, filled with the faint slap and rustle of the pool, transparently blue and inviting. She'd stared at it, imagining how it would feel to swim, a lovely cool world of soothing sensations where you might float suspended in soft mineral-filled water, just letting it take your weight, hold you, caress you. If only she could swim! She dipped a tentative toe in the pool, longing to be able to cast off her clothes and dive in, to cut cleanly through that blue water.

"Why don't you take lessons," Caro had said practically. "There's an instructor at the pool and the exercise would be good for you." So, early every morning, when it seemed the rest of the world was still sleeping, she walked alone through the vaporous halls for her lesson. The pool seemed so much bigger when you were *in* the water and not standing on the edge. By the end of the first week, she could swim a width, enjoying the sensation of her own strength as she made her way slowly through the water, excited by the feeling of power at conquering a new element. She was determined to become a really good swimmer, and after her lesson she stayed on to practice, only leaving when the pool began to fill up at midmorning.

"I'm surprised you're not permanently crinkled," commented Caro, "you spend so many hours in the water." Still, she was pleased—Léonie was looking better. She had gained back the lost weight and her hair, though it smelled faintly of the pool, had regained its luster. The next problem was what to do with her. Léonie was not just a problem to be resolved, she was a friend, a little sister—the odd attraction that she had felt that first snowy afternoon had become true friendship. "You are the first real woman friend I've ever had," she told Léonie. "I confided all my secrets the first time I met you. And now that I've found you, I'm not about to lose you so quickly."

"But I must get a job, Caro," Léonie answered. "I can't stay with you forever, and besides, it's not fair to Alphonse. You've both done enough for me."

But what sort of job? Léonie wondered, floating on her back in the pool. I'm different now from the girl who worked at Serrat. I've grown up a little. And, after all, I'm seventeen years old. Girls from her village were already married and producing their first babies by that age, or even their second! She hadn't thought about Normandy since she had left, and she locked the stray thought away now, just as she had locked away her memories of Rupert. She *never* allowed herself to think of him. But what was she to do in the future?

"Enjoy it," said Caro firmly, as they drove through the Black Forest that afternoon with a laughing group of her friends. But Léonie still felt the outsider, a temporary visitor who didn't belong. She had refused to allow Caro to buy her expensive clothes and accepted only the older ones in Caro's wardrobe, a couple of simple summer skirts. She didn't need anything elaborate because she never went out in the evening, eating her supper in her room and going to bed early. The truth was that she was afraid of all those people, the glittering casino and the glamorous dining room. Léonie wandered in the splendid solitude of the Black Forest, where the green silence was marred only by the sounds of their voices echoing along the grassy trails and where the tall trees filtered the sun into fractured sparkles and thin strands of clean light. Its beauty only made her feel sadder. The future stretched ahead, blank and endless, unpenetrable and lonely.

She couldn't sleep—the room was stuffy after the freshness of the day—and she tossed restlessly, waiting for dawn. As soon as it's light, she promised herself, I'll go to the pool. The very thought of the cool water was refreshing and she went out onto the balcony and stared out across the park. Lights still blazed in the casino, though the orchestra had long since stopped playing and gone home to bed. At this hour of the morning only the serious gamblers were left. Everyone else was either sleeping or at one of the dozen or more parties. A couple strolled on the terrace beneath her window and Léonie leaned over to watch, straining her ears to listen. His head was bent close to hers and his arm was around her waist. The woman seemed to melt into him as they kissed, lingeringly, reminding her of Rupert. She closed the window quickly, shutting off the memory.

Rupert stared blearily at the pile of chips in front of him. He hadn't broken the bank, but he'd had a phenomenal run of luck and Grandess would be furious to have missed it. He stretched his aching back; by God he was tired. Perhaps he should try the steam rooms, have a massage, clear his head a little.

The lofty marble halls were packed with men steaming away the excesses of the night, sweating silent and naked on benches amid clouds of vapor, preparing for a day at the races and another night at the casino or with a favored lady. The man manipulated Rupert's tense muscles, sluicing him finally with icy water. God, that felt good, he could almost feel his pores snapping shut! "You might try the pool, sir," suggested the masseur. "It's always empty at this time of the morning and it's very refreshing." Was it morning already? It was still gray and quiet, the sun hadn't yet pushed its way through the mist. A swim might be just the thing. Wrapping his towel around him, he padded through the steamy halls, losing himself in the twisting corridors, only locating the pool finally by the sound of water slapping against the tiles. Throwing off his towel, Rupert prepared to dive in. But someone was in the pool. A woman! Hastily he snatched up his towel.

"I do beg your pardon," he called. "I'm afraid I didn't realize that I wasn't alone. I didn't know that ladies were in here at this time."

Léonie floated on her back with her eyes closed. She must be dreaming, hearing Rupert's voice.

Was it possible? Could it be her? No, of course not. Rupert moved closer. The girl had the same color hair. It was her! "Léonie!"

It wasn't a dream. He was there. Rupert. Her breath came out in a great gasp, choking her as she swallowed water and sank like a stone. In a panic Rupert dived in, scooping her up from the bottom of the pool. "Léonie, oh, my darling Léonie." He held her close to him. "I can't believe it's you ... I thought I'd lost you, I thought I'd never see you again."

"Rupert, oh, Rupert, I thought you didn't care, that you were laughing at me. . . ."

"It wasn't you I was laughing at, Léonie, it was the horse—you were wonderful, so brave and so clever. And you looked so beautiful, I was jealous that all the other men were admiring you."

"But you were with that woman, whispering about me. . . ."

"No, no, no, my love, that's not so."

It took so few words to make the world all right again, she thought, so much pain erased by a few words. How stupid she'd been to run away! "I'm sorry, Rupert, I should have trusted you. It was all my fault."

"Oh, darling, it's my fault." He kissed her wet hair tenderly, stroking her cheek, gazing into her lovely long amber eyes. She was here, his little love, his darling, but what was she doing here?

"I'm with Caro and Alphonse. They've helped me, Rupert."

"But why didn't Caro tell me? God, she knew I was desperate to find you!"

"I asked her not to, I thought you'd just been playing a game with me."

He held her close. "It's just a series of misunderstandings," he murmured in her ear. "But now that I've found you, I'll never let you out of my sight again." He kissed her eyelids and her throat and remembered suddenly that he was naked. Leaping out of the pool, he wrapped the towel around his hips as Léonie averted her eyes modestly. Then he helped her from the water, snuggling her into the white robe and drying her tenderly. "Come and have breakfast with me," he whispered. "We must make plans."

"Plans?" Her eyes sparkled with new excitement.

He kissed her. "We have our future to think of." Their laughter echoed through the tiled halls of the spa as they ran hand in hand back to his room.

As he closed the door behind them, he took her in his arms. "I can't believe it's true," he murmured. "It's all I've dreamed of for months. Oh, Léonie, I love you so much."

Her mouth opened under his kiss and her body leaned into his. How could kissing feel this good, she wondered, how could her body feel this wonderful, as though it had turned to liquid, like mercury, molten yet heavy? Oh, this was what love was, this was what it felt like when you belonged!

"I love you, Rupert . . . it's different when you love someone, then it's all right. Isn't it?"

She looked so pretty and so young, she was irresistible. Rupert picked her up in his arms and carried her to the bed, kissing her, opening her robe, sliding the clinging wet fabric of her bathing suit from her shoulders, and gazing at her lovely body as she lay there proudly, pleased that he thought she was so pretty. She wanted to be beautiful for him, to please him; she loved him so much. Oh, it felt so good when he did that, it was so nice when he stroked her. She gasped with tenderness as he kissed her breasts and she closed her eyes unable to bear it when his hand parted her legs. It must be heaven, she knew it was heaven.

Léonie lay still with the weight of his body still on her and knew that this was what belonging meant, it was so simple, just two people making love, this wonderful, marvelous closeness.

He held her in his arms and told her how perfect she was, and they whispered their plans.

"You're mine now," he murmured in her ear. "We'll go away to the inn—remember, I told you about it?"

"The white one by the sea, with the big cool room with the bed?"

He kissed her again. "Our room . . . our bed. We'll leave this morning." He couldn't wait to have her all to himself. "I have enough money to keep us for a couple of months while I find some sort of work." He laughed, remembering the win at the tables last night; it was going to come in handy. He felt a pang of guilt as he thought about Puschi, but he pushed it away. He was too filled with happiness to think of that, he'd take care of it later. And Grandess? Of course he'd tell her, he'd leave her a note, swear her to secrecy until he had worked things out. She would understand, he felt confident about that. Caro was the one who might be a problem, she'd kept Léonie away from him and he wasn't going to risk that happening again. "You must leave Caro a note," he told Léonie.

"But Rupert, I can't do that. I want to tell her myself. I want her to see how happy I am . . . we are. She'll be happy for us, I know it."

"Caro blames me for hurting you and I know she's not going to let you go with me."

"But if I tell her, explain to her . . ."

"She won't understand."

Léonie was silent, thinking about Caro. She couldn't just leave. Caro was her friend. She loved her and she'd been the one to find her, to help her; she owed her the loyalty of telling her. Léonie pushed herself upright. "I must tell her, Rupert. Nothing she may say could stop me from going with you."

He stroked her thick soft hair, kissing the tendrils around her wide-boned face, loving her. "I'm afraid of losing you again." He knelt at her feet, pleading with her. He was so beautiful, his body so slender and so strong. "I can't risk that again, Léonie—write her a letter! Tell her what happened, beg her to understand. Say that we'll come to her later, in Paris . . . she can come to our wedding."

"Rupert! Oh, Rupert . . . do you mean it? Our *wedding?*"

She kissed him extravagantly. She would do *anything* for him. Even write the note to Caro, if that was what he wanted. Rupert came first. Caro would understand, she knew all about love and passion. And, of course, she would come to their wedding.

The inn was exactly as he had described it, sparkling white in the clear southern light against a gentle hilly backdrop of green-black cypresses and ancient olive trees. It perched above a strip of white sand with a flight of rickety wooden steps leading down the slope from the wide terra-cotta tiled terrace to the sea. The sea! Léonie couldn't believe any sea could be this blue. It seemed to reflect the sky and double it, deepening its color. Even under the moonlight, it was a deep inky blue. But at night she wasn't looking at the sea, she was in Rupert's arms in that wide white bed in the cool room with just the sound of the murmuring waves as a backdrop to their words of love.

It was everything Rupert had promised her it would be. Monsieur and Madame Frenard, who ran the little place, had few guests for their three rooms, an occasional traveler, perhaps, but the inn was off the beaten track, a little too far from Monte Carlo or Nice to be popular. They made their living mostly from the lunches they served to the locals, who ate in the dim little dining room at the back, leaving the terrace to Rupert and Léonie. The Frenards liked them, they were so young and so obviously in love and they were so beautiful—brown from days in the fresh sea air with their hair bleached whiter from the saltwater and the sun. Like a young god and goddess, they thought, turning away discreetly as the two dashed naked into the playful waves, cavorting and laughing as he made her practice her swimming.

Their life was so entirely physical that Léonie couldn't imagine how she had ever lived before without feeling like this. Her body was pampered with the sun and sea and tiny breezes and lavished with love. She was vibrating with energy and happiness from the moment she awoke in his arms until the time they fell asleep still entwined from making love. And they made love everywhere, on the beach, hidden behind rocks at the Point with the waves washing over them, or lost in the grasses behind the chalky paths that circled the Point Saint-Hospice, and she felt wild and ecstatic, a part of the earth and the sea and the sky. It was all exactly as it should be.

⅋ 8 ⅋

MARIE-FRANCE DE COURMONT was not happy to see her husband back from America, but her two small sons were. They rushed forward to greet him, knowing he would bring presents. He always did—at least she had to admit *that* in his favor. He might neglect her, but he never forgot the children. It was just that he didn't know how to behave with them, he was so stiff, so un-tender. She didn't know how to describe it, it was simply a lack of warmth. The fact was, the man was incapable of showing emotion, even if he felt it, and she suspected he didn't. If he'd had a daughter, she wondered fleetingly, would he have been any different? She knew he felt that the boys should be brought up to be little men. But it was hard for her to treat Gérard, a six-year-old, and Armand, who was only four, as little men. They were babies and she adored them. At least he'd given her that.

"Gérard, Armand . . . how are you?" Gilles rumpled their hair genially, smiling at them. Gérard looked tired, he thought, and a little pale, but he was dashing about just like Armand.

"Where are our presents, Papa?" demanded Armand, pulling at his father's trouser leg impatiently. Gérard hung back a little, keeping his distance.

"Here you are." He brought the parcels out from behind his back. "The blue box is Gérard's and the red is yours, Armand."

The little boy danced up and down with excitement, clutching his box, already tearing at the wrapping. "Come and see, Maman, see what I've got," he said, struggling with the box. Marie-France helped him, casting an anxious eye at Gérard. She knew the boy was worried about being sent away to school, she must try to convince Gilles that it was too soon. He was too young, too sensitive to leave home yet; another year or two wouldn't hurt.

Gérard knelt on the floor, opening his box carefully, peeling back the wrapping paper deliberately, delaying his pleasure in the gift.

He's like me, thought de Courmont, he enjoys the anticipation. He smiled at his elder son, and the boy stared back in surprise. "Well, do you like it, my boy?"

"It's beautiful, Papa. It's wonderful." He gazed at the little motor car, an impeccable copy of the prototype that his father was soon to produce. His was blue and Armand had the identical one in red. It was the best present he had ever had. He would like to play with it if his head didn't ache so; he wished he didn't have to go away to school. He was afraid. The boys at the park had told him such terrible stories about how cruel they were at school, especially to new boys. He hoped Maman would remember to ask Papa not to send him away.

Dinner alone with Marie-France was always hard work, but Gilles put himself out to be entertaining, telling her of his trip, describing New York and Chicago with a vividness that aroused her curiosity. "And the motor cars?" she asked.

He signaled the butler to fill their glasses, sniffing the dense bouquet of the Margaux appreciatively. "De Courmont cars will be on the roads of France next year," he said, raising his glass, "and in a few years' time we shall be exporting them to America."

"So I suppose that you will be devoting all your time to this new venture?"

"Not quite. I do have several other interests that I must look after."

"Like Gérard," she suggested, pinning him down with a smile. "He's very unhappy, Gilles, about being sent away to school. I think he's too young."

"Many boys his age go away to school, Marie-France. Why should he be an exception?"

"Why? Because he's your son . . . our son. He's not just any boy . . . he has feelings. He's a sensitive child, quiet and very intelligent. Right now he needs his home more than any school!"

"That's nonsense." He pushed back his plate and the butler signaled the footman to remove it. Gilles sipped the wine impatiently, his pleasure in it destroyed. How irritating Marie-France was, always so caught up in these small matters. He glanced at her over the top of his glass. She was still a pretty woman, in her own way, small and dark-haired, rather plump now— not his kind of woman at all. An image of Léonie flashed through his mind. Yes, he must take care of that tomorrow, it would be pleasant to see her at last, to make her his.

A nursery maid appeared in the doorway and whispered in Bennett's ear. The butler bent discreetly to pass on the message to his master. "You'd better go up, Marie-France," he said. "Apparently Gérard has a temperature. No doubt he's fretting too much about school."

Marie-France looked at him contemptuously and without a word rose and left the room. He sat staring at her empty place, finishing his glass of wine while Bennett waited patiently in the background.

There was no question that the boy was ill. The doctor, summoned in the middle of the night, came at once, wasting no time on the niceties of proper dress. He simply threw his overcoat over his pajamas and grabbed his bag. If Monsieur le Duc had said that it was urgent, then he meant it.

De Courmont paced the floor while Marie-France went in with the doctor. Gérard couldn't be ill, he was *his* child, *his* boy; he was strong, sturdy. Never had had anything really wrong in his life.

The doctor emerged and Gilles greeted him anxiously. "What is it? What's the matter with him, Doctor?"

"I'm afraid it's diphtheria. The boy is very ill. We must set up a breathing tent, and I shall have to put a tube in his throat."

"A tube in his throat!" Dear God, that was his boy, had the man gone crazy? "You can't do that . . . you can't cut open his throat . . . he might die."

"Monsieur le Duc," said the doctor gently, "if I don't, he *will* die."

Gilles stared at him in horror. How could this happen, and happen so quickly? He remembered Gérard opening his present with such anticipation. It had been the first time he had seen anything of himself in his children, until now they had been so much a part of Marie-France. He turned away. "Do what you must then, Doctor," he said humbly, "but please save my child."

He waited all that night outside the boy's door, while Marie-France sat at his bedside watching him. All they could do was wait, the doctor had said, the sickness would take its own time, but the boy was breathing easier with the help of the tube. When he could bear it no longer, he opened the door. In the gray light of dawn he saw his wife sleeping in the chair, still holding the boy's hand. Gérard's arm was clutched around his toy car, holding it tightly as his thin little chest heaved up and down, the liquid rattling grotesquely in his throat. Gilles turned and hurried through the silent house to his study. He watched the sun rise as he finished the bottle of whiskey.

It was two weeks before the boy was pronounced out of danger and another two before he could get out of bed, and even then he was so thin that he could barely walk. His dark blue eyes were enormous in his white face and Marie-France was almost as pale. She seemed to have aged years in the last four weeks and Gilles looked at her, for once, sympathetically. "Thank you," he said.

"For what, Gilles?"

"For taking care of him so well."

"I'm his mother . . . what else should I do?"

"He needn't go away to school, Marie-France."

"Oh? Why not? He'll be better soon . . . will you change your mind again, then?" she asked cynically. She knew him well.

He was serious. "You know best. Do what you think is right for both boys. I'll trust your judgment."

She stared at him in astonishment.

"I think we need a holiday," he announced suddenly. "Gérard needs some good sea air to bring back his appetite, and you do, too, my dear." He touched her shoulder lightly, almost tenderly. "We'll go to the south. The yacht is waiting. I've already told the captain to expect us. We shall all go to Monte Carlo."

❧ 9 ❧

LÉONIE sat at a table outside the Café de Paris in Monte Carlo waiting for
Rupert. It was still quiet, too early for the fashionable lunchtime patrons,
and she sipped her coffee in peace, enjoying the breeze, throwing crumbs to
the little birds waiting patiently for the rich pickings from this smart café.
Only one other table was occupied, by a man indulging his two sons with
ice creams. She could hear the children laughing, bickering happily over the
cherries on top, and she turned to watch with a smile. The man was half-
turned away from her and she could see only his profile, but there was something naggingly familiar about it. Hadn't she seen him somewhere before?

She hoped Rupert wouldn't be too long. He'd gone to the post office
to pick up his mail. She hoped there would be a letter from Caro. It had
been six weeks since they had left Baden-Baden so precipitously, six amazing, glorious, wonderful, happy weeks, but still she hadn't heard a single
word from Caro and she was worried. I knew it was wrong, she thought, I
should have talked to her before I left, but Rupert insisted. It all happened
so fast; when we're in Paris we'll go see her, she'll forgive me then, she'll
understand.

"Excuse me, but didn't we meet at Carolina Montalva's?" It was the
man from the party, the silent one. She recalled how he'd watched her as she
stood by the door, afraid and wondering whether or not to go in. But now
he was smiling at her, holding out his hand to her. She held out her hand,
feeling it gripped in firm cool fingers that sent little tremors of unexplained
excitement through her body.

"Gilles de Courmont, mademoiselle." The two little boys watched
curiously, spooning up their ice cream. His eyes were dark blue with heavy
brows, and his skin was smooth, faintly pink under the tan from a recent
shave. Her eyes dropped to his chest, where the dark hair curled in the open
"*V*" of his crisp shirt. He was an attractive man.

"Are you alone?" he asked.

"I'm waiting . . . for a friend."

"I see. And is Caro here, too?"

"No, she's in Paris, I believe."

"Well then"—Gilles gestured toward the bay—"I would be happy to have you and your friend dine with me one evening on my boat. As you can see, I'm here with my boys."

She smiled at them and they wriggled uncomfortably under her gaze. "I've promised to take them to the Oceanography Museum," he said, "and they're impatient to be off. The boat's name is *Bel Ami*. Leave a note with the captain if you can manage dinner one evening. I'd be happy to have some company."

He waved, smiling as he collected his boys, and they departed noisily, heading across the square. How different he is from the way I imagined him at the party, she thought idly. I thought him so sinister—but it's not that. He's interesting, mysterious—different.

There was Rupert! He was walking quickly, hurrying toward the café, a bundle of envelopes in his hand. "Darling," she called, waving to him, banishing thoughts of de Courmont from her mind. He kissed her hand and quickly took a seat. "Anything for me?" she asked anxiously.

"I'm afraid not." He glanced at her worried face. "It's all right, I'm sure Caro's just busy. When we get back, I'll explain that it was all my fault, that I'm a bad influence on you."

Léonie laughed, he always made everything seem all right. He ordered coffee and put the letters on the table. She could see that two of them had German stamps and she stole a look at his face, but he said nothing. She knew that they had to be from home, maybe from his fiancée. She dreaded the letters from Germany, he was always so quiet afterward, and he looked worried although he said nothing to her. His eyes met hers and he smiled. Taking her hand, he said, "Let's go to Nice. You must see it."

She was happy again, she knew the small trip would be fun, it always was when she was with Rupert. She touched the single strand of tiny pearls at her neck—she only took them off when they went swimming and then she hid them under a special rock. Rupert had put them on her himself. "A girl's first jewels should be pearls," he'd said as he clasped them and stood back to admire her pretty neck, adding a kiss or two. "I want to give *you* a present," she said now as they left the café hand in hand.

"*You* are my present ... you're all I want," he said, smiling again and tucking the letters away in his pocket.

I still find her fascinating, thought de Courmont, as the guide explained the complexities of marine equipment to his wide-eyed sons. Marie-France had returned to Paris and he hadn't really thought about Léonie in weeks—not since the night Gérard had become so ill. Verronet's reports from Baden-Baden and Léonie's letters he'd stolen from the letter box by the inn at Cap Ferrat had lain unread on his desk. Until now it had all been a game, anyway, tracking her, setting her up, stalking her like a wild animal, but she was beautiful. He remembered her golden face and amber eyes, and now her tawny hair was streaked lighter from the sun. It had been months since he'd thought of a woman. He'd busied himself with his sons, spending time with them—under Marie-France's cynical eye—that brush with death had frightened him, it was something he couldn't control, it was stronger than he. His thoughts returned to the girl. He wondered if von Hollensmark's family knew of his new liaison. He doubted it. Wasn't Rupert engaged to be married to Krummer's daughter? Gilles savored the thought of his old business enemy's embarrassment when he heard the news, and as for the von Hollensmarks, he could almost guarantee their reaction.

He called the museum guide over and tipped him lavishly. "Look after them for half an hour," he instructed. "I must go to the telegraph office." He strode across the square planning his moves; he could put the right pressure in the right place. The von Hollensmark family needed that alliance, they couldn't afford to see their only son wasted on a nobody.

The following morning the telegram lay next to Rupert's plate like an unexploded bombshell, drawing Léonie's eyes toward it no matter how hard she tried to pretend. Rupert sipped his coffee and stared at the sea. "Aren't you going to open it?" she asked finally, unable to bear it any longer.

"There's no need. I know what it says."

Léonie was quiet. She had a good idea of what it said, too. What she had really meant was, What was he going to do about it? She looked at him expectantly, waiting for him to come up with a solution. She trusted him, he was so clever; of course he'd know what to do.

Rupert paced the terrace impatiently, talking fast, thinking as he went. "I'll have to go back, Léonie, right away. It's the only honorable thing to do. I must tell Puschi myself. You do understand that, don't you, my darling?"

Her eyes were wide with panic; he couldn't leave her alone, what would she do without him? He took her in his arms. "Oh, my little love, it's all right. I shall come back to you. You mustn't worry. You know that it's you I love."

"But Puschi . . . ?" She was afraid.

"She *is* my fiancée, I have an obligation." He thought of the letter in his pocket from Grandess. She had been the only one to whom he'd told the whole truth, that he was in love with Léonie and wanted to marry her. He had thought that Grandess could be trusted; she was always honest with him, always sympathetic. But this time she had told him how wrong he was, that he was harming both Léonie and Puschi. His family had expected better of him; what had happened to his sense of honor, to his family duty?

He had thought that she, of all people, would have been on his side, and now it seemed that he had no ally. He hadn't written to Puschi yet, only sending a note to her father saying he was ill and needed rest. He had been putting off the moment to tell them and somehow the days had slipped into one another and it hadn't been done.

Léonie put the telegram into his hand. "Open it," she demanded.

He hesitated, reluctant to read what he feared it said, but her eyes insisted, and he ripped open the envelope. He read the message quickly and crumpled it into a ball and stuffed it into his pocket. It was signed by Herr Krummer and his father, and it commanded him to return at once, or they would see to it that he was without a penny. She watched him expectantly. "Just as I thought," he said. "My father wants to see me."

Léonie pushed back her chair and walked to their room. Lifting his bag from the top of the armoire, she began taking his shirts from the chest, folding things neatly, and packing them in the brown leather valise. He watched for a moment, feeling helpless and afraid. He loved her so much, he wanted to marry her, he hoped he would be able to come back, that he could work it all out.

"I'll wait here for you, Rupert," she said with a brave smile, picking up his brushes from the chest, searching the room for anything she might have forgotten. There were his bathing suit, his sandals. "I'll leave them here," he said, "for when I get back."

Her smile held relief. "Yes," she said confidently.

She watched while he dressed. He looked so unfamiliar in his suit and tie, almost a stranger. He was to go to Nice to catch the afternoon train, and he explained to Monsieur and Madame Frenard that he was leaving Léonie in their charge. He paid them a month's rent and gave Léonie the rest of his money, not that there was much left. "I'll be back, Léonie," he said, "you'll see. I'll be back within a week. I promise you."

"I'll try to be patient," she vowed.

He kissed her and walked away quickly, leaving her standing alone in the cool white room with the big bed. "I love you," she called, running up the path after him.

He turned at the top to wave to her. "And I love you," he answered.

❧ 10 ❧

THE FIRST FEW DAYS will be the hardest, she told herself, after that I'll be more used to being without him. But it wasn't like that, she missed him more every day. The first week she had counted the days, waiting until seven had passed before acknowledging that he wasn't coming back within a week as he had promised. The second week had been stormy, with black scudding clouds and angry rumbles of thunder over a faded, tossing sea and she'd huddled indoors, watching the rain fall on the terrace, counting the seconds between the lightning flashes and the thunder, until they were so close together that it crackled right overhead and she'd been afraid. When the skies cleared she took to going for long walks around the peninsula, wandering inland, finding little hamlets where she would buy fresh figs and goat's cheese and eat her own picnic in the hills while the butterflies and bees danced over the wild rosemary. At the end of the third week she had heard nothing from him and she began counting her money anxiously. It was disappearing quickly, but surely he'd be back soon.

On the Sunday of the fourth week she sat alone on the terrace, staring out to sea. A sleek white yacht slowly made its way across the bay, leaving a wake of glinting sun-tipped foam. It was the same one that was there every morning. She wondered about the lives of the people who had yachts like that. Rupert had told her of the millionaire whose yacht had a Turkish bath, and who kept a Jersey cow in a padded stall so that his guests would have fresh cream, and another whose yacht boasted a putting green and a theater. Quite suddenly she began to cry. What was she to do? Was he coming back? Why didn't he write to her? What had gone wrong? She wouldn't allow herself to think of Puschi; that would be too much to bear.

The following morning she sat down and wrote a letter to Caro, begging her to find Rupert, please to reply right away if she loved her. She wrote a note to Maroc telling him where she was, and then she walked along the lane and left her letters in the wooden box by the side of the road to be picked up by the mailman on his morning rounds.

* * *

The great yacht rode the blue swells of the Mediterranean while the crew of twenty, smart in white uniforms, stood at their positions, waiting for the commands of its master, whether they might make for Monte Carlo or Corsica, or steam further east to the Adriatic or the Aegean, or simply serve him a whiskey and soda. De Courmont paced the deck, staring across the water at the shoreline, at the white square shape of the inn, resisting the urge to use the telescope to peer closer. He was no voyeur. If he had not met Léonie in Monte Carlo he probably would have forgotten her, lost in the time before Gérard's illness. But now he could think of nothing else. She occupied his thoughts, waking and sleeping—it was disturbing. He must get her out of his system and then he'd be fine. Life would go back to normal.

In the main salon a bundle of letters lay on the table. Léonie's letters. He'd read them, of course, small pathetic missives from her begging for help. And the letter from Rupert—a plea, asking for more time, enclosing more money. Gilles almost felt sorry for her.

He pressed the buzzer on the speaker. "Sir?"

"Return to harbor at once."

"Yes, sir."

Léonie drew the shades and lay down on the bed. It was midafternoon and hot. She closed her eyes and listened to the faint, familiar sound of the sea. There had been no reply from Caro, none even from Maroc. She'd written to her again, even sent a note to Madame Artois asking for help, but no one answered her. Now she knew she was more than just lonely. She was alone. There were no more tears, she'd shed them all, and she lay quietly on top of the coarse white sheet, thinking about dying. It would be quite easy, she thought, you simply stopped breathing. She held her breath for a few moments to see how it felt and sat up gasping for air. How *did* people kill themselves? Poison, wasn't that how women did it? Women like her who had lost everything, whom no one wanted. It must taste so awful and be so painful. She held her hands over her stomach, hating the idea, but what else was she to do? Drowning! Of course, that was it. She'd drown. It would be easy. She'd just wade out into that lovely blue water as far as she could and then she'd just keep on swimming until she was too tired. It would be soft, gentle, caressingly easy. She pulled off her dress and stepped into her bathing suit so the Frenards would think it was an accident. She wished she didn't owe them any money, but she had nothing of value to leave them. She touched the pearls on her neck; of course, there were the pearls, but Rupert had given them to her. Oh, Rupert, Rupert. She stepped onto the terrace, staring out to sea. It looked friendly, inviting. The white yacht was there again. If she swam out far enough, maybe its owner would rescue her!

She heard a faint sound, a soft pattering, and then a low purr as a kitten rubbed itself against her feet. It was small and dainty, the most feline and feminine of kittens, chocolate brown with pink pads on its paws and a sweet pink-tipped nose. It rolled at her feet, making playful passes at her, and Léonie smiled. It looked familiar, the aristocratic arch of its back and the sleek little triangular head. Of course, it was exactly like the Egyptian cat, the "doll" of her childhood. She bent to stroke its fur. It was *so* soft, the softest fur she had ever touched. The kitten licked her hand with a rough pink tongue, purring loudly. Thinking of her father, Léonie began to cry, the tears falling onto the kitten's fur, spiking it as it licked them away, still purring. Her father had left her, too. This was the second time in her life she'd been abandoned.

She picked up the kitten gently. It lay on its back in her arms, staring at her with slanting golden eyes, waiting. It was her kitten. It had chosen her. She walked back into the room and lay down on the bed again, thinking.

❧ 11 ❧

THE WINDOW of the jeweler's shop on boulevard des Moulins was a sparkling treasure chest of emeralds, diamonds, and rubies and Léonie hesitated at the door, uncertain of her reception. The salesman hurried forward with a smile, wondering what she could want, but he was used to all sorts in here. This was Monte Carlo, where the most unlikely people won great sums of money and the first thing they wanted was to buy some expensive jewel as a symbol of their new wealth. On the other hand, he thought, as she produced the little pearl necklace, there were also those who lost.

"Would you please tell me what these are worth?" Léonie asked timidly.

"Of course, madame." He tested their weight in his hand, holding them to the light to examine their color. They were genuine but inexpensive. "A very pretty necklace, madame"—he smiled—"but not, I'm afraid, worth very much."

"How much?"

"Well, not more than a hundred francs, madame."

"Would you buy them from me?"

He hesitated, it would be a hard item to get rid of, not the sort of thing his customers would be looking for, but she was so young and looked so desperate. "Very well," he said, "if it'll be of any help."

Léonie breathed an enormous sigh of relief. "Oh, thank you. I don't know what I would have done if you'd said no."

"Do yourself a favor. Don't go back to the tables and gamble. You'll only lose again," he warned, as he handed her the money.

"Gamble? But I didn't gamble."

She bent down pulling something else from her bag on the floor and he peered curiously at the statue. Egyptian, obviously, and very old. Yes, he'd bet that it was genuine. Now where had she got that from? "Here's another." She set a second one on the counter beside the lion-woman. It was a cat, Bastet, the sacred cat of Egypt, he knew that much, but the first was a mystery to him, though his guess was that it, too, was a goddess. He handled them carefully. "Where did you find them?"

"They were my father's. He was Egyptian. My mother always said that they were very old. I wondered if you knew if they are valuable?"

"I'm afraid that I can't speculate as to their value, but I would be willing to bet that they're genuine and are indeed very old. You should take them to Paris, to the department specializing in Egyptian studies, they might be able to help you."

"Then you don't want to buy them?" She'd hoped so badly that they would be worth a lot of money, that they would save her.

"I'm afraid I have no idea what they're worth." He hesitated. "Look, I'll offer you a hundred francs for them both. I'm taking a gamble, but if it'll help . . ."

A hundred francs was a hundred francs more. Should she do it? She stared down at the floor—they were all she had, all that was really hers. The kitten poked its head out of the bag, sniffing inquiringly as it woke up, rubbing against her ankles and tangling the ribbon she had tied round its neck as a lead. "No," she said positively, "I'll keep them. But thank you anyway."

"Not at all. It was a pleasure, madame." He was as courteous and smiling as though she'd bought the crown jewels, escorting her to the door and opening it with a flourish as she said good-bye and walked off down the street, trailing the kitten on its pink velvet ribbon. He wished her luck.

The kitten had slept all the way home, curled in her arms like a baby, earning its new name, Bébé. It sat on the bed watching as she pulled the white dress over her head and inspected herself critically. It simply wasn't fancy enough for her purpose. Maybe the skirt would do, if she had something different on top, but what? She thought of the scarves Rupert had bought her in the market in Nice, long silky bands of color that he'd wound, laughing, around her hair. They had bought half a dozen in different golden shades—amber, bronze, terra-cotta, lemon, and gold. She pulled them from the drawer now, draping the amber one over her shoulders, crossing it over her bosom and tying it at the back. It looked quite pretty. She wound another around her waist and the golden one low around her hips, pulling it tight so the full skirt frothed from beneath. She stood back to examine the effect. It looked surprisingly good! Should she put one in her hair? No, perhaps she'd just pile it on top, it would make her look older. Bending her head, she brushed her hair forward and swirled it around in a tumble of curls, the way Loulou had shown her, and tucked in a sprig of jasmine. She flung a thin lemon scarf around her neck so that the ends floated behind her. Picking up her purse containing the precious hundred francs, she tucked Bébé under her arm and walked to the door. She hesitated a moment and then opened her purse and took out five francs, which she placed carefully under her pillow, tucking another five into the top of her stocking just in case—though of course she would win. Tonight she felt lucky.

Verronet stared after her in astonishment as the pony cart trotted off down the dusty road with Léonie sitting at Monsieur Frenard's side. Where could she be going—and in that outfit? She had certainly acquired a taste for the bizarre, this girl. He'd better see what she was up to.

She'd been walking up and down in front of the elaborate wedding cake of a casino for fifteen minutes and Verronet wondered if she would ever go in. He'd already sent a message to Monsieur le Duc, but now it looked as though she was not going to do it. He wished she'd hurry up, he wanted to get to the tables, he'd only been waiting to make sure that she wouldn't leave the inn before going there himself. He smoothed his starched white shirtfront impatiently; ah, at last. He followed her up the steps, tripping over the little cat on its lead. He could have sworn she was trembling, but she lifted her chin haughtily as she marched toward the door. "I'm sorry, madame; unescorted ladies are not allowed."

"Oh, I . . ." Léonie hesitated, thinking wildly of an excuse to get her in. "But—"

"The lady is with me." Verronet took her arm and led her into the crowded foyer, ignoring the doorman.

"Oh, thank you, it was kind of you. . . ."

"Not at all, mademoiselle. Good luck!"

He smiled politely and disappeared into the crowd as she stared after him in surprise, wishing he hadn't left her alone. She took shelter behind a life-size statue of a Greek god, peeking between its marble limbs at the immense chandeliers and curlicued mirrors, the gilt sofas and thick carpets, the bejeweled women in silk and sable and confident men who talked loudly and knew everyone. Catching a few speculative glances, she tilted her chin defiantly; she wasn't going to let them intimidate her this time. Tucking Bébé under her arm, she sauntered into the public gaming room, scanning the tables.

It was all much more complicated than she had imagined; there were so many different games and everyone seemed to know how to play them. How did you learn? The roulette wheel seemed easiest and the result was certainly quick and simple, either your number won or it lost. Easing her way to the table, Léonie set the curious Bébé on her knee and took a one franc piece from her purse, snapping it shut afterward. She placed the franc on red nineteen and waited for the wheel to spin. The croupier raked it back to her superciliously. "There is a five-franc minimum, madame, and please purchase your plaques."

"Oh, five francs!" She fumbled in her purse and took out fifty francs, counting them carefully, exchanging them for ten rectangular plaques. Only ten—they didn't look like very much! She stared hard at the numbers on the green baize table and finally placed her plaque on red nineteen, waiting while the others placed their bets and the wheel began to spin. The ball fell into black fifteen and Léonie watched the croupier rake away her plaque indifferently. She pushed forward her second plaque, placing it again on red nineteen. Again she lost. Third time lucky, she thought, parting with another five francs. But it wasn't and she glanced down at Bébé in dismay; she'd lost fifteen francs in five minutes, what should she do? She still had thirty-five francs in plaques and another forty in her purse. She waited, not placing a bet, watching others to see what they did. The man on her left seemed to have plenty of money, he had a whole stack of plaques—a wall of them! She watched him place a casual pile on black, sipping his drink unconcernedly as the ball fell obediently into place and the croupier pushed an enormous pile of plaques toward him. The man couldn't lose. He was betting on squares and areas marked around the table that she didn't understand—not just the colors and numbers in the center—she'd follow his bet. Léonie pushed forward two plaques onto his number and waited breathlessly. They'd won. She flashed him a grateful smile, but he didn't notice. This time she placed three plaques, feeling the excitement rise as she watched the spinning wheel. She won. Oh, she'd known she would win! Exhilarated, she leaned over the table, absorbed in the game, pushing her plaques back and forth less cautiously, sometimes losing, but mostly winning. She pushed twenty francs onto his numbers and sat back, enjoying herself. It was the most she'd placed yet and she felt sure it would win. But, no! She glared at the man as he pushed aside his winnings. "Keep this for me, Louis," he said. "I'm off for a bite of dinner."

"Certainly, sir." The croupier raked the plaques and gold coins into a box.

He was going, now what should she do? She counted her plaques—ninety francs. She still had forty in her purse, but she needed more, lots more. Wasn't this what they called a lucky streak? Like Rupert had had in Baden-Baden? Oh, God, she wished she hadn't thought of Rupert. The excitement drained from her and miserably she pushed forward her next plaque.

De Courmont sipped his whiskey, watching her as she leaned across the table. Her hair was tumbling from its pins, falling in thick springy waves down the elegant length of her back. He wanted to touch it, to smell its scent—it would smell of fresh clean air and sunshine, and so would her skin; no, that would be denser, more exotic, and it would feel smooth, so smooth. He signaled Henri, the manager, hovering nearby, anxious to please this distinguished client in a salon full of rich and prominent men. "A table for two, Henri, in the alcove and a magnum of Roederer Cristal"—he glanced at Léonie—"in about half an hour, I think."

She was tired and hungry, and she was losing. She must have been sitting there for hours. She stretched her back and glanced around the room. Where, oh, where was the man who'd disappeared for dinner, taking her luck with him? Why hadn't he come back? She stared at the green baize table—she was down to ten francs, even the forty francs she had kept in her purse were gone. She fingered the purse again to check if there were anything left, but it was empty. She looked around her. Chandeliers glittered on gold coins tossed easily across the green cloth by men who seemed not to care about the result, laughing when they lost and laughing when they won. It all appeared so lighthearted, was no one else playing for such high stakes as she? All or nothing was as high as you could go. She stared down at her two remaining plaques—ten francs. Money was meaningless, it only translated into other things—food, rent, shoes—it was so little. She thrust the plaques forward onto red nineteen, closing her eyes as the wheel spun.

De Courmont moved closer, watching over her shoulder as the ball dropped into red nineteen. He sipped his whiskey, smiling. He had time.

Léonie's eyes flew open in shock—her luck had changed! Boldly, she placed her plaques again on red nineteen, waiting breathlessly, not daring to look. She won again. Exhilaration swept over her; of course, this was how the game was meant to be played, you could never be cautious and afraid. Scooping her winnings into a pile, she divided them and placed half on red, oblivious to the woman pushing into the empty seat next to her, laughing loudly and tossing remarks over her shoulder to her companion as she thrust forward a handful of plaques. Her fringed shawl swept across the table. "I do beg your pardon," she smiled at the croupier.

"Not at all, Comtesse," he answered politely.

The comtesse's number won and Léonie watched her place another bet. Again the comtesse won. Léonie pushed forward ten francs following the woman's next bet. It lost. Fool, she should have trusted her own judgment. She chose a number and placed ten more francs on it. It lost. What should she do? She had ten francs left, she should leave now. She dithered nervously over the board, then taking a deep breath she pushed her two remaining plaques onto red nineteen—her lucky number, luck only favored the bold, she remembered. The comtesse leaned over her to place her bet at the last moment and Léonie sat back closing her eyes, waiting for the rattling sound of the wheel to stop. Red nineteen! Oh, thank God, she'd won. She'd quit now, leave right away before she lost any more. She reached forward to scoop up her winnings and the croupier looked at her in surprise.

"But your bet was *seventeen,* madame, nineteen was the winner." Léonie stared at him blankly as he pointed to her stake; it was on seventeen! The comtesse reached forward, and her fringed shawl drifted across the table, sending the plaques flying. Too late Léonie realized what had happened and she stared in horror at the woman, sipping her champagne and laughing carelessly with her friends. Panic seeped up Léonie's spine in a hot wave— she'd lost it all! No, not quite. She put her hand on her thigh, feeling the five francs she had tucked into her stocking. Yes, it was still there. She hesitated, caught in the gambler's dilemma. Should she? Wasn't it her last chance?

"Bad luck, mademoiselle." The voice was vaguely familiar. She turned and looked directly into the eyes of Gilles de Courmont.

They were blue, a darker, deeper, more serious blue than Rupert's, unreadable and masked even though he was smiling at her.

"Do you remember?" he asked. "We met at the Café de Paris."

She'd been waiting for Rupert; yes, of course she remembered. They'd gone to Nice later, it had been such a lovely day. Oh, God, what was she going to do, what was she going to do now? "Of course, I remember, Monsieur de Courmont." With an effort she pulled herself together.

Her eyes were almost tawny, a golden amber, the pupils dark and dilated with panic. He smiled, taking her hand. "I saw what happened," he said sympathetically. "It was very bad luck, especially as you had chosen the winning number, but I'm afraid the rules are the rules and your money was not on red nineteen."

She smiled at him shakily as he helped her from the chair. "Would you share a bottle of champagne with me," he suggested, "to soften the blow? . . . It's never pleasant losing one's money."

It was as though she had no will of her own; she felt lost, powerless, floating on his arm through the crowded casino with Bébé on her ribbon, as people moved to one side and stared. "Monsieur le Duc, your table is waiting, sir." Henri waved an imperious arm and flunkies hurried forward to the table in the alcove, dusting the already immaculate tablecloth and polishing fluted crystal glasses, as Henri placed her tenderly in a chair and waited for Monsieur's commands. "The champagne is ready, sir."

The room was intimate and relaxed, without the tension of the gaming tables, and Léonie breathed a sigh of relief, touching the delicate petals of the translucent greenish orchids in the center of the table. They felt surprisingly cold. Weren't they tropical flowers, didn't they need warmth and jungly places? Perhaps it was just she who was cold. A small orchestra played behind a screen of fronded palms, the banks of flowers creating small islands of privacy, veiling murmured conversations and the clink of glasses.

"I'm sorry," she said, "for calling you 'Monsieur,' I mean." She was suddenly surprised by the fact that she was sitting in this room with a duke—shouldn't she be more in awe, even overwhelmed? But he was so easy, so natural—perhaps dukes weren't any different from other men after all. "I didn't realize that you were 'Monsieur le Duc.' "

He laughed. "It's not important. You may call me whatever you wish."

She believed he meant that. It didn't matter to him if he was addressed by his title, he simply assumed everyone knew who he was, that doors would be opened for him and wine poured. How wonderful to be like that, to be so supremely confident.

"So, there was no beginner's luck tonight, Mademoiselle Léonie."

"No"—she lifted her chin haughtily—"but perhaps another time I shall win."

"I hope so. Meanwhile, if you are not playing the tables anymore tonight, would you have dinner with me?"

The Café de Paris opposite the casino was crowded and Maurice, the maître d'hôtel, was frantically turning away customers—it was breaking his heart but he'd already squeezed in five extra tables. He'd be relieved when Monsieur le Duc arrived, it wasn't easy convincing irate and distinguished customers that the empty table was reserved, and he was already over an hour late. But, of course, he wouldn't dream of giving it to someone else.

Like the Red Sea, thought Léonie in amazement as the crowd in the casino parted to let them pass, waved on by the deferential manager. The doorman, who just a few hours before had refused her admittance, held open the doors and wished them a polite goodnight.

Monsieur le Duc's arm felt reassuring and she glanced up at him as they walked across the cobbled square to the Café de Paris. His strong profile was severe, the nose slightly hooked and arrogant, and his dark hair waved crisply on his neck. There was a security about his presence, his confidence was absolute. Nothing could ever go wrong when you were with a man like this.

His eyes met hers. "You look sad, Léonie."

"No . . . well, perhaps." She had a sudden urge to confide in him, to tell him things—her secrets.

"Here we are." They were whisked immediately through the crowded room to their table, under the steely glares of those who had been left waiting, sipping drinks at the bar.

Swirling enormous pink linen napkins onto their knees, the head waiter presented the menus with a flourish, while the sommelier appeared with more champagne.

"We shall both have a dozen Belon oysters and your special salmon," said Gilles, without consulting the menu, "and a plate of fresh salmon for the cat."

Léonie stared at him in surprise. "I'm sure you'll enjoy it," he said. "I have the feeling it's exactly what you need."

Léonie relaxed, leaning back into her chair. It was comforting to be looked after, to have someone care for you, make decisions; she felt so tired. "You look troubled, Léonie. Won't you tell me what's the matter?"

His voice was low and sympathetic and she stared into his dark blue eyes, hypnotized. Champagne floated in her veins, bubbling in her head. "It's just that everything has gone wrong lately . . . everything." She was on the verge of tears and he leaned across the table and took her hand.

"It's always better to talk about these things, you know, and I'll bet you've had no one to talk to." It was true, she had had no one to talk to, no one at all, except Bébé. She glanced at the kitten crouched under her chair, hungrily licking salmon from a silver plate, totally absorbed in her own pleasure. At least Bébé was happy.

She began to talk, whispering so that he had to bend closer to hear her, the words and sentences confused and jumbled. "Begin at the beginning, Léonie," he said gently.

It took less time to tell than she had thought—it was surprising how hopes and dreams and fears and pain could be reduced to words that fitted into only thirty or so minutes. The plates of oysters sat untouched and Gilles signaled the waiter to remove them.

The relief was immense; she felt purged, clean of all secrets. Rupert had gone and she must face up to it. There was no more hope, she knew it now.

But there was no need to die, either. She would begin again, get another job, make a fresh start. Monsieur de Courmont had helped her just by listening. She smiled at him gratefully. "Thank you." She clutched his hand impulsively. "It must have seemed silly . . . a stupid little story that happens a thousand times every day."

"And now," he said, kissing her hand, "now that it's over . . . will you fall in love again?"

"Never!" Her voice was emphatic.

He smiled as the waiter placed fresh oysters in front of them. "Well then, perhaps we should begin our dinner."

Léonie lay in the big bed with Bébé curled up on her pillow, still purring softly, even though she was asleep. It was the hour just before dawn when the sky was still a gray haze and the air was chill as the night-cooled sea waited for the sun. She stared out the window, lost in her thoughts. She'd been surprised when he had put her in the cab. They had strolled along the waterfront together, looking at the stars and talking of her childhood, of the stories she'd heard about her elusive father, and of Normandy, and then he had suddenly signaled the cab and put her in it, lifting Bébé in beside her.

"But aren't you coming with me?" she'd asked foolishly, as he paid the driver, instructing him to take her home.

"I'm afraid not." He had waved good-bye as they drove off, and she'd turned to watch him through the back window as he strode away across the still-busy square. She'd been disappointed. Didn't he want to see her again? She was surprised that she should ask herself such a question—she was in love with Rupert. He hadn't kissed her, or even put his arm around her—he'd made no move at all—he'd just been kind and sympathetic.

She tossed restlessly as the first glow of the sun appeared and the sky began its rapid change from gray to flawless blue. Had she wanted him to kiss her? Was that why she was disappointed? No, of course not—she dismissed the thought angrily—but then why was she filled with this trembling excitement just thinking of his lips on hers? She was being foolish—he had just been kind to her, and she was grateful for someone to talk to, someone who understood. She would probably never see him again. Just as the birds awoke, she drifted into sleep, and for the first time she didn't dream about Rupert.

❧ 12 ❦

LÉONIE had awoken late and had been irritable all day. Madame Frenard, as kind as ever, had brought her coffee and fresh bread, but she hadn't felt like eating. Finding the five-franc piece under her pillow, she gave that, together with the five francs from her stocking, to Madame to pay something toward her rent. "I'm going to get a job," she assured her, "I'll be able to pay you soon."

With Bébé trotting eagerly at her heels, she rambled along the chalky path that rounded the peninsula of the Point Saint-Hospice, thinking of Monsieur de Courmont.

"Gilles," she said out loud, as Bébé paused in surprise. "Gilles." Somehow it felt uncomfortable, too familiar for such an important person. "Monsieur" was better. She climbed down the slope, dangling her dusty feet in the cool water of a rock pool, watching while Bébé fished with a cautious paw in a vain attempt to catch the myriad tiny sea creatures lurking beneath the green moss. She and Rupert had come here often. She remembered him, stretched out flat on his stomach poring over the pool, fascinated with the abundance of life it contained. And they'd made love there behind the sea grasses with just the blue sky overhead and never a soul to see them. Her flesh recalled how it had felt, naked in the sunshine, warm and sweating, loving and gentle, as though they were a part of the earth itself. She stood up briskly, she was not going to think about it.

"Come on, Bébé," she called. "It's time for your dinner, though I'm afraid it won't be fresh salmon tonight."

She helped Madame Frenard in the kitchen, preparing a huge *tian* of zucchini, eggplant, and tomatoes, all picked from the plot on the hillside behind the house, spicing the dish with garlic and sprigs of wild thyme, and anointing it with olive oil fresh from the old press in the courtyard. It was baking in the oven and, pleased with herself, Léonie sniffed the savory smell drifting over the terrace. At least she had done something positive, and Monsieur Frenard had promised to take her into Nice to see about a job next week.

She was sipping a glass of pastis with the Frenards, catching the last of the late evening sunlight, when a cab pulled up with a note for Léonie. She read it hurriedly. It was quite formal, absolutely unemotional. It was certainly no love note. Simply that Monsieur le Duc expected her for dinner at eight-thirty and the cab would take her to the Hôtel Métropole.

She rushed to get ready, wondering what to wear, sorting anxiously through her meager wardrobe and ending up with a white blouse flounced on the shoulders with *broderie anglaise.* It was simple but at least it left her neck and shoulders bare and hopefully looked suitable for evening. A white skirt wouldn't be smart enough, she'd have to wear the deep pink—with the amber scarf wound around her waist, it looked nice, the colors were unusual and pretty together. Cutting the end of Bébé's pink velvet ribbon, she pinned it around her neck. It matched the skirt perfectly and the choker made her neck look long and elegant so that her hair had to be swept up on top, more neatly this time, in smooth blond curves that she anchored as firmly as possible with long pins.

There, that would have to do. She peered at the result in the mirror. She hoped he would like it. Bébé watched from her perch on the window ledge, waiting. "Of course you're coming," Léonie called happily. "Don't worry, Bébé."

It was only later, as she sat in the cab joggling along the road to Monte Carlo, that Léonie began to wonder if she should have gone. Should she have been so quick to accept? He could have asked her last night. She frowned, suddenly angry with herself for being so easily available—and with him for assuming she would come.

A footman waited on the steps of the Hôtel Métropole. "Monsieur le Duc is expecting you, mademoiselle," he said courteously. "Would you come this way, please?"

The awninged terrace overlooked a sweep of smooth palm-fringed lawn and in the distance strings of lights curved around the bay like necklaces in the blue-black velvet of a jeweler's window. Gilles stood as she came toward him. She had forgotten that he was so tall. His grip was firm as he took her hand. "Léonie, I'm so glad you could come."

"But I'm not sure that I should have," she replied, putting Bébé on a chair beside her.

"Why on earth not?" His smile was lazy, faintly teasing.

"Well, isn't it more usual to *ask* a lady if she would like to go to dinner?"

"I'm a busy man, Léonie ... my time is not always my own." He shrugged. "Tonight I'm free. You wanted to come, didn't you?"

He was leaning over her as he spoke and she stared up into his dark blue eyes, aware of his nearness, of the width of his shoulders, of his hand against her arm. "Yes," she admitted.

"Well, then." He moved away and took a seat opposite her. "I'm very happy that you're here. Now, shall we start with champagne again?"

Dinner was more leisurely this time, more relaxed as he amused her, telling her stories of his travels in New York and Chicago and the strange ways of Americans. Again, he chose for them both, coaxing her to taste the caviar. "I might like it one day," she admitted doubtfully. But there was no doubt she liked the chicken he ordered, stuffed with rice and crayfish and truffles. She ate with such gusto that he offered, with a smile, to send for more.

"Oh, no, please don't." Léonie was embarrassed. She remembered the *tian* at the Frenards' and how good it had smelled and she laughed, telling him how she had cooked it herself. "Of course, it can't compare wth this," she said.

"Good food is like beauty," he replied, "it simply requires the right combination of good ingredients put together in an attractive way. Perhaps you'll cook it for me one day?"

"I'm not sure you'll enjoy it," she protested, "you're used to so much better."

"Do you know that every day in Paris I eat lunch at the Ritz Hotel and I eat exactly the same thing: an omelette."

Léonie stared at him, astounded. "But why, when you can have anything you want?"

"Maybe that's why."

"I think I understand," she replied, but she wasn't sure she did.

He sipped his wine, watching her. She was a lovely tawny animal in that blouse with her golden shoulders, so slender and yet round, and that great mane of blond hair. He stared at her mouth, wide and curving, showing strong perfect teeth when she smiled, and just the tip of a pink tongue when she licked her lips, as she did now. He imagined her with diamonds in those pretty ears, slinking round her lovely neck, decorating her fingers, and the texture of fur next to her skin. He wanted to rush out and get them now so that he could see her naked but for jewels and some rich tawny fur.

"Tell me, Léonie," he said, taking her hand, "what do you want most in life? What is it that would please you most?"

The answer flashed through her head immediately. To have Rupert back! But no, that was not anything she could have. No, she knew now what it was, she was sure of it. "I'd like a home," she said. "I've never had a proper home, a place that is truly mine. I think a home must be a place that welcomes you, a place of refuge. Like the old inn at the Cap. Somehow," she added thoughtfully, "I feel that is where I belong. It has a feeling of home about it."

Gilles was surprised. He'd thought she'd say jewels and money and yachts, wasn't that what most of them wanted? All she wanted was a home!

Léonie had been driven back alone again, waving good-bye to him as the cab drove away, and again he hadn't mentioned seeing her. But as the next day moved along toward six, and then six-thirty, she found herself waiting, listening for the sound of a cab on the lane above the inn. At seven she heard it, and read the same note, this time with a smile. She had a skirt waiting on the bed, freshly starched and pressed—how she longed for something silk, she thought, feverishly struggling with the buttons of the white skirt, instead of always wearing crisp cotton. She visualized herself in startling red silk, tight bodiced and revealing, and blushed as she realized that she wanted to look more daring, more tempting. What *was* she thinking about? Rupert would have hated her in red silk. Her only other blouse was black, high-necked and demure, and she felt hot and uncomfortable in it as she sat in the dining room of the Hôtel Hermitage. She'd endured the stares of the elegant ladies in lace in the foyer and the bejeweled matrons at the other tables and she felt shabby and ordinary. She wished she hadn't come. He was late and she sat alone at the table sipping a glass of water. She had refused the waiting champagne, not caring to drink it without him. Bébé was bored and had fallen asleep under the table.

The manager came toward her. "I'm afraid Monsieur le Duc is delayed, madame," he said deferentially. "He asks you to begin without him and he will be here as soon as possible. He has already ordered for you, madame."

"But . . ."

"Yes, madame?"

"Oh, nothing. . . ." She didn't want to sit there and eat by herself with everyone staring, but if he had said she should, it seemed she had no choice. She felt so foolish there alone.

A waiter arrived bearing an elaborate terrine in aspic, wobbling colorfully on its silver plate. He arranged a slice, placing it before her. Léonie stared at it miserably.

"Is the terrine all right, madame?"

"Oh, yes . . . yes, thank you." Picking up her fork hastily, she tasted it. It was delicious, but she felt too nervous to eat it.

The waiter removed her plate and a second waiter wheeled in a large trolley filled with elaborate hors d'oeuvre. "Would madame like to choose?" he suggested.

"I don't think so, thank you." The hors d'oeuvre terrified her, they were so fancy, she didn't know whether you picked them up and ate them with your fingers or used your knife and fork—and there were so many knives and forks. Oh, dear, it had all seemed so simple when he was there, she hadn't felt like this at all, she hadn't even thought about it. Oh, where was he?

"Allow me to choose for you." He piled her plate with tiny fish, and spears of asparagus, curls of meats and grapes stuffed with creamy cheese, pastes of eggplant and hearts of artichokes. And she ate nothing. She didn't know what to do with it.

After ten minutes they removed her plate and the sommelier offered to pour the wine. "It's a very good year, madame," he said, flourishing the label for her inspection. "Monsieur le Duc knows his wines well." Léonie sat stiffly while he opened the bottle and poured a little into her glass. She ignored it, she didn't want any wine. What she really wanted was to go home. She was conscious of eyes upon her, of whispered glances from other tables where people were dining in groups of four and more. Everyone was with someone else and she was alone, and obviously didn't belong there. They had to be wondering who she was, what she was doing.

"Would you care to taste the wine, madame?" suggested the sommelier, impatiently.

"What?" Her frightened eyes met his.

"Taste the wine, madame."

Léonie sipped obediently. "It's very nice." He filled her glass, placing the bottle in its impeccable white napkin on the side table.

She longed to escape, to hide in the ladies powder room, but she didn't know where it was and she was too nervous to ask; besides, it meant walking past all those tables full of people, all staring at her; yet if she did go it meant she could run away, not come back. Just get up and walk to the door, she told herself, that's all.

The maître d'hôtel arrived with two attendant flunkies and set up his little spirit flame. Other waiters appeared carrying silver-covered dishes of fresh vegetables, half a dozen different kinds, which they proceeded to serve, asking her bewildered permission, while the maître d'hôtel occupied himself with slivers of meat that he was heating quickly in butter in a copper pan, dousing it with cream and green peppercorns, splattering it liberally with warmed brandy that he then ignited with a flourish, scooping it onto a warm plate as the flames died out.

"Madame"—he placed it on the table before her—"enjoy your dinner, madame."

Léonie sat with her eyes lowered, trying not to look at the food. She felt sick. She wished she were anywhere else but here.

"Léonie?"

It was he. She grabbed his hand in relief.

"Aren't you enjoying your dinner?" He picked up the bottle from the

side table. "Yes, the Leoville . . . it's a good wine, don't you think?" He settled back in his chair without a word of apology for being so late and she
stared at him in astonishment.

"But I've been waiting for you. . . . I thought you weren't coming. . . ."

"I told you that my time isn't always my own, Léonie. However, I'm
here now." He smiled at her and took her hand. "You're so cold," he said.
"You should eat your dinner."

"What about you?"

He called the waiter. "Bring me some of the grapes stuffed with
cheese," he said, "and some Evian water."

"Yes, sir." The waiter sped off on his mission.

"But aren't you having dinner?" She gestured to the plate of meat in
its elaborate sauce, the vegetables glowing like jewels under a glisten of
butter.

"That was for you," he replied. "I wanted you to enjoy your dinner
even though I wasn't here. I'm not hungry." She stared at her plate, like an
enchanting upset little child who couldn't eat her meat. "Go ahead." He
smiled. "I'm sure it's delicious, this is one of the best restaurants on the
coast."

She tasted the meat cautiously. It was good, the sauce more delicate
than she expected. People at other tables were staring at them, but it didn't
seem to matter now. She relaxed. Everything was all right again. Now that
he was here.

Each morning she ran up to the mailbox on the lane still hoping there
might be a letter from Rupert. There never was, nor was there one from
Caro. How she must despise me, Léonie thought as she sat on the big white
rock at the top of the path that led to the inn, waiting for the mailman. She
must hate me for running off like that, without even talking to her. She was
my friend, she saved me before when I was desperate. If only she could
speak to Rupert for me, find out what is happening. But Léonie was afraid
that she already knew what was happening. An image of Puschi had formed
at the back of her mind, a laughing, blond, pink-cheeked girl, who loved
horseback riding and fun and lived in a castle, a beautiful fairy princess
waiting for her prince to marry her. She had accepted that Rupert wasn't
coming back, but not the hurt of it, and not without telling her. He would
write, he would explain—wouldn't he? She couldn't blame him for returning to Puschi. His family came first. That was always the way with families,
she supposed.

She found that she spent each afternoon in a state of anticipation, wondering whether the cab would come, and each night when it came she forgot about Rupert, excited by the mysterious quality of Monsieur le Duc and

their assignations, each time at a different place—a fisherman's café at Cap d'Ail, a famous restaurant in Nice, or the grand dining rooms of the grandest hotels. And she enjoyed it. Rupert disappeared for a while in the magic of being the girl on Gilles de Courmont's arm, the one for whom snobbish maîtres d'hôtel opened doors and flourished wines, for whom waiters hovered and flunkies arranged fresh flowers and for whom people stood aside to let pass. It was exciting and *he* was exciting. He was never the same man. Each night he seemed different. Sometimes sympathetic and understanding, sometimes distant and abstracted, sometimes amusing—and sometimes silent and watchful, the way he had been at the party. She liked the way he made her feel—more conscious of herself physically, aware of the contact of his hand on her bare arm as he escorted her into a restaurant, his breath on her cheek as he leaned closer to comment, the feeling of restrained power in his broad-shouldered body.

She thought about it as she lay on the warm sand early one morning. She had come back so late that she hadn't bothered to go to bed, but had sat by the window waiting for the dawn, and then she'd tiptoed down to the beach, thrown off her clothes, and waded naked into the sea, gasping as its early morning coldness touched her. It always excited her, swimming without her clothes, and Rupert had laughed at her for it. She cut through the water with a powerful crawl, covering the bay fast and gracefully, feeling the surge of the water beneath her, lifting her breasts, pushing between her legs. Yes, she was definitely attracted to Gilles de Courmont. All right, she asked herself, if you could choose now to have Rupert or "Monsieur," who would you choose? Whose hands would you like to caress you? Whose lips would you like to taste? Whose body would you like next to yours? Flinging herself into a dive, she plunged beneath the blue-green swell. She knew the answer.

She was ready early that night, sitting on the terrace watching the sea and the sky and the pretty white yacht anchored out in the bay. The cab usually came at seven and at seven-fifteen she went inside, tidied her hair, and returned to her seat on the terrace. By seven-thirty she was pacing its length restlessly, and at eight o'clock she began to worry. At nine-thirty she was still sitting there with Bébé sleeping on her knee, a glass of pastis in her chilled hand. By ten-thirty she realized that for the first time in ten nights the cab wasn't coming for her. She watched the twinkling lights of the yacht in the dark bay, wondering if it were his *Bel Ami*. She made excuses for him. Of course, he must be busy, he always says his time isn't his own. "I expect it'll be here tomorrow night, Bébé." Picking up the cat, she went to her room and undressed slowly, hanging up her dress with care, ready for tomorrow.

It took a long time to get to sleep, and it wasn't Rupert she was thinking of.

Verronet was tired of the train journey back and forth between Paris and Nice and then the drive along the coast to Monte Carlo. De Courmont was needed in Paris and he knew it—nothing was being accomplished by this long-distance traveling. He was needed on the scene. He had invested heavily in the railway link with Russia and their people would be in town this week and, more important, because of de Courmont's total commitment to the development of the automobile, key discussions were to take place the following week with automobile men from Chicago. Verronet had suspected that for once his employer had found a consuming interest in making cars instead of money. And now this girl was upsetting everything. Was de Courmont really expecting them to come all the way down to Monte Carlo just so he could hang around there, waiting for that girl; hadn't he had enough of her yet?

After boarding the yacht, he made straight for the main saloon. De Courmont was waiting. "Let's get down to business at once," he said impatiently. "I have an appointment at three."

He went over the papers, making rapid decisions, raising points that had seemed hidden under a mass of complicated contractual language. Verronet admired him; whatever it is, he's not losing his mind over her, he thought.

"I'll be back in Paris for a day at the end of this week to meet the Russians," de Courmont told him, "but I think perhaps we'll have the Americans come down here—we'll lay on a few diversions for them. They'll enjoy the atmosphere, and the casino." He knew it would work in his favor, thought Verronet admiringly. He always knew exactly what to give each one, how to sweeten the bait.

De Courmont left the offices of Grimaud and Gagnac, notaries of the city of Nice, and strolled down the narrow cobbled street feeling very pleased with himself. Things were going exactly as he had planned and that was always satisfying. He turned onto the main boulevard and stopped in front of the jeweler's window. There were rings and necklaces, bracelets and pins, ruby-studded cigarette cases and gold bags beaded with diamonds—everything to tempt a lady. He wondered, he just wondered what might tempt this one. He pushed open the door and went in, imagining her surprise when he gave her the jewels, the way she would look as she tried them on, her cries of joy and feminine greed for the pretty, glittering baubles—and maybe her softer cries as she allowed herself to be seduced by him. Anticipation was a marvelous pleasure, he thought, leaning lazily against the glass counter while the man brought out tray after tray of jewels for his inspection.

It had been six nights now and each night Léonie had dressed and waited for the cab that had never come, and Madame Frenard was worried about her. Not worried as she had been when Rupert went away, when they had been afraid she might try to do something bad to herself, but worried by her anger. She'd bristled with it, sparked with it; she'd stormed up and down the terrace, seething with anger. "Damn him," she'd cried to the cloudless heavens, "what is it that men want from me!"

"You mustn't say things like that," protested a shocked Madame Frenard. "He'll come back, you'll see."

"Oh, yes," sneered Léonie, "he'll come back, just like Rupert did." She'd dashed off along the path round the Point, still screaming her anger to the sky, and had come back an hour later, sullen and tearless. From her usual place on the window ledge Bébé stared at her. "And you . . . you traitor," Léonie muttered, "you liked him, you purred for him, you sat on his knee."

The cat yawned, stretching herself to full length along the ledge, rolling on her back, peering at Léonie mischievously, upside down. Léonie tickled her chin, smiling. "Oh, you," she sighed, "you know how to charm . . . you should teach *me*, little kitten."

She went humbly to the kitchen to apologize to Madame Frenard and to help her prepare supper. At least she was working for her keep now; she was becoming quite a popular waitress among the lunchtime locals. Back where I started, she thought cynically.

She didn't hear the cab when it came along the road because it was the first night she hadn't listened for it, and when the driver came to the door with the note she was taken by surprise. Wiping her hands on her apron, she looked at the familiar writing on the envelope in disbelief. He'd sent for her again, she supposed, just like that. She should drop everything and put on her best dress and go and pander to his perverse whim of being the duke out with the little servant girl. Well, not this time. She was damned if she'd go.

She handed back the note, unopened. "Tell Monsieur le Duc," she said in a voice that trembled, "that Mademoiselle Léonie refused his invitation. She is too busy to see him."

"But mademoiselle . . ."

She turned away, leaving him standing, open-mouthed, on the doorstep. "That's all," she said curtly, stalking back into the kitchen.

Madame Frenard watched Léonie's rigid back as she stirred the bubbling tomato sauce on the stove and sighed. Would things never go right for the poor girl?

The cab returned at breakfast and this time a young man accompanied the driver. "I'm to give these documents to you personally, mademoiselle," he said smoothly. He bowed and turned to walk back up the path.

"Wait," she called, "don't you need an answer?"

"No, mademoiselle. There is no answer," he called, turning into the lane.

She took it down to the beach to read. His writing was pointed and severe, the crisp letters unelaborated with loops and curls, and his words were equally direct.

"I'm sorry you were unable to have dinner with me, Léonie," she read, "especially as I was here for only the one night. I had hoped to give you this personally, but in the event, may this gift make you happier than love did."

She stared curiously at the small parcel that accompanied the letter, then ripped it open, hastily pulling off the ribbon and the pretty marbled paper. "Title Deeds and Documents Relating to the Property Known as LA VIEILLE AUBERGE with 10 Hectares of Land, fronting onto the bay of—" her glance traveled rapidly down the page "—in the name of Léonie Bahri." *Her* name! They were the title deeds to the inn—in *her* name. She remembered the night he'd asked her what she wanted most from life and she'd told him. "A home," she'd said, "like the old inn." He'd given her a home. He'd waved his magic wand and made her dreams come true. This from a man who chose only omelettes because there was nothing he wanted, nothing for him to dream for, nothing to long for.

Léonie stared at the inn. It stood square and solid, whitewashed and clean, against its background of olives. She had known that the Frenards ran the inn—as had Monsieur Frenard's father before him—for the owner, who lived in Nice. And now suddenly she was the owner.

She sat down in the sand staring at the deeds, running her finger over the page with her name. She was a woman of property. The inn was hers. And what about all the nights she had waited—when there had been no message, no explanation? You're always waiting, she told herself, waiting for Rupert to come back, waiting for the carriage to come—waiting for the man to beckon, added a sneaky little voice in the back of her mind. She looked again at the title deeds, at all they implied. Men are all the same: the moment you accepted, the moment you gave in, you were owned. She stood up briskly. "I'll give them back, of course," she announced to Bébé. "I'll get a job—in a café, in the music hall if I have to—but I won't be bought!"

❧ 13 ❧

HE KNEW EXACTLY how she would react. It was lunchtime and he sat on the terrace outside the Café Riche in Monte Carlo, imagining how she would have looked, the expressions that must have flitted across her lovely peach-fleshed face, amazement, bewilderment, speculation, excitement—certainly anger—and maybe a little fear. He knew she must have been prepared to hate him, he'd primed her anger, deliberately neglecting her for a whole week after seeing that she was pampered and comforted and looked after. Oh, yes, she'd be angry all right. He smiled to himself. She'd come tearing back to see him—right about now, if he'd calculated correctly. She wouldn't be able to wait, Léonie always acted on impulse. But what was she going to do now? Would she throw the deeds in his face and scream at him? Or would she throw her arms around his neck and kiss him? He sighed with satisfaction, either way was all right with him. He knew he finally had her.

As if on cue, Verronet hurried along the terrace toward him. "Mademoiselle Léonie is on board the yacht, sir."

He sat for a while, enjoying the sunshine, savoring the anticipation; his staff had their instructions, they knew what to do. "Waiter," he called.

"Yes, sir?" the man came running.

"I'll have an omelette, please . . . and a bottle of Evian water." There was plenty of time, Léonie would wait.

Léonie had been there for an hour, sitting nervously in the main saloon with its wide windows overlooking the busy little harbor. The saloon was immaculate—too much so. It was a room that could have belonged to any rich man of taste. There were no personal mementos, no telltale signs of the presence of two small boys, though they had left only recently to be with their mother in the country. No one had disturbed her, she had been quite alone, only the clock ticking on the large square desk had sounded the passing minutes. At one o'clock the steward had come to offer his apologies for Monsieur le Duc's absence, he was expected back at any moment, meanwhile would madame care for some lunch?

"Oh, no, no thank you," she had said, but he'd smiled and said that Monsieur le Duc would have insisted on it.

She'd drunk a glass of champagne to calm her nerves, and then a second because the first hadn't seemed to work, and then she'd wandered restlessly onto the deck of the big boat, curious to see what this "home" of his was like, what clue it gave to the true man. She had expected ostentatious luxury, but there was none, just the special gleam of everything that was the best—polished mahogany and shining brass. A big immaculate white boat.

The sun was hot and Léonie returned restlessly to the saloon; the clock on the desk said two-thirty. Perhaps she should leave. After all, wasn't she waiting—again? The thought annoyed her. Yet she had to stay, she had to give back the deeds before she changed her mind. She couldn't stand the ticking of the clock! There was another door leading off from the saloon and she peeked through. It was a small study—a desk covered in papers, books on tall shelves, polished boards with a small Persian silk rug in faded blue-green and a deep sofa under the window that looked out onto the sea. It was quiet, no clock ticking, just the sound of the waves, and she sat on the edge of the sofa to wait. The champagne and the sun made her feel sleepy and she arranged the cushions, making herself more comfortable. How long would he be? she wondered.

The boat was absolutely silent, swinging gently on the rippling water under the hot midafternoon sun. The crew had been dismissed for the rest of the day and even the seabirds were taking a siesta.

Gilles found her in the study, asleep with the packet of deeds on the sofa beside her. Walking across to the desk, he poured himself a glass of whiskey, sipping it thoughtfully. She was so very young and so very lovely. He wanted to kiss her eyelids, they were so transparently delicate, blued with tiny veins under the tender skin—but he waited.

He read her thoughts from the expressions that crossed her face as she awoke—confusion, surprise, and relief. She sat up quickly, smoothing her skirt. "I must have fallen asleep."

"I expect it was the champagne—and the heat." He smiled at her. "I'm sorry you weren't able to have dinner with me the other night."

"But I waited for you—*all week,* I expected to see you!"

He shrugged his shoulders, staring indifferently through the window at the sea. "I told you that I'm a busy man, my time is not always my own."

He was right. It was silly to expect that he had time only for her. He had to attend to meetings and business matters—and a wife and family. She remembered the two little boys eating ice cream. "I came to return these"—she held out the packet—"it was very kind of you, but I can't accept."

His eyes met hers and he smiled lazily. "But why ever not, Léonie?"

"It's too much . . . it's . . . well, it's not the kind of gift a girl should accept from a man."

"It was my indulgence to give it to you, it's of little value, just an old inn."

"But you knew it was more than that to me."

"Yes. Your name is on the title deeds. It belongs to you. It was your dream."

She moved closer to him, holding out the deeds. "Please," she said, offering them.

"There are no strings attached, Léonie," he said, breathing in the scent of her hair. It smelled as he knew it would, of fresh air and sunshine and the sea.

"There aren't?" she asked uncertainly. Did a man give a woman a gift like that without expecting anything in return? "I insist," she said firmly, pushing the papers into his hands.

"You mean that you expected me to make love to you in return for the inn?" He put his hands on her shoulders, gazing into her eyes. "I didn't have to give you the inn to do that, Léonie. I could have made love to you any time."

His touch on her shoulders was light, she could have turned her head, moved away, run off the boat—but she didn't. She waited for him to kiss her and when his mouth was on hers she accepted it willingly, as if this were the true reason she had come here. She wanted him to make love to her.

He pulled her closer, holding her body tightly against his as he explored her mouth, tasting its sweetness, touching her little pink tongue, running his hands down the elegant length of her back, feeling the gentle hollow at the base of her spine and the cushioned swell of her buttocks. He tilted back her head, kissing her neck; he wanted to bite her ears, to grip her hair and force her head back, he wanted to take her violently, passionately—and right now. He thrust himself against her, holding her tighter so that he could feel the curve of her belly through the thin summer skirt and he knew she could feel him, his hardness, his excitement. He lifted her, carrying her to the sofa. Léonie gasped, clutching her arms around his neck, moaning in his ear with soft sighs of passion. He knew what she wanted, he'd known she was wild—all she needed was to be shown how. Oh, God, but she was lovely. He unfastened the blouse, watching as she slid the chemise over her head, stopping her, holding up her arms to gaze at the twin curves, so round, so golden, the nipples large and erect, waiting for him. She stroked his hair as his mouth closed on her breast, holding him tighter, wanting him to do it, to do anything to her . . . marvelous things. He knelt between her legs, lost in the ecstasy of tasting her breasts, stroking her smooth back, gripping a soft curve as she trembled and moaned. He stood up quickly and unfastened her skirt, sliding it over her slender rounded hips, running his hand down the slope of her thigh as he undressed her, until she sat naked before him, waiting. Her eyes fastened on him as he stripped, and leaning forward, she took him in a trembling hand as he moved toward her, caressing him. Gilles pushed her away, thrusting her back violently against the pillows and she stared at him, her eyes dark gold with excitement as his hands found her, opened up her secret places, stroked her and cajoled her, tantalized her until the juices flowed and he licked them up and made her scream with ecstasy. And then he made love to her. Not gently, but powerfully; not tenderly, but with a driving force; and not quietly, but with shouts of triumph as they rolled in shuddering union on the sofa.

She lay back in the big black onyx tub in his bathroom examining the marks of love on her body, the faint bruises, the small bite on her breast, the skin still pink from the pressure of his body and the tender swollen area between her legs. Her body felt wonderful, relaxed, confident in its ability to please and take pleasure. But she was thinking of Rupert. How could she have done this when she loved Rupert? How could she betray her love? But it had never been like this with Rupert, it had been different—warm and loving and gentle, though she'd imagined it was passion. Was it *she* who had changed? Or was it Monsieur who had changed her? She had liked it when Rupert made love to her, she had lain in his arms loving him, holding him, enjoying his body and their closeness, but she had never wanted to do what she had done with Monsieur—she'd never felt that wildness. It was a need, an urgency, that she hadn't known she possessed. She sat up guiltily in a swirl of water as Monsieur came through the door. She shouldn't have done it. Not only had she betrayed Rupert's memory, but she'd put herself in a bad position. She must make him take back the deeds.

He held out the soft robe for her. "Come into my bedroom, I've got something to show you."

The shades were drawn against the heat and the narrow bed was covered by a throw of plain blue cotton. There was no luxury in here and Léonie was surprised—she thought that such a sensual man would have had deep carpets and glowing colors, silver lamps and velvet hangings. If it were not that everything were of the very best quality this room would have been spartan.

"I have a gift for you." He held out the box.

"A gift?" Had he expected to see her then? She stared suspiciously at the box in her hands.

"Open it," he said, enjoying his power, "it's for you."

The smooth suede box clicked open easily, revealing its velvet blue interior. A thin rope of diamonds sparkled prettily, throwing off rainbow lights, the enormous pear-shaped pendant gleaming with a stab of metallic blue. The stone was enormous—smooth and cold under her fingers, as big and as round as the stopper on a crystal decanter. It was a jewel fit for a kept woman, the kind of bauble that proclaimed that you had been bought, that a man had paid for you. Léonie felt the rage rising in her. "Damn you, Monsieur," she yelled, throwing back her head, stalking the floor like a wild animal. "You can keep your jewels—give them to your other women." She tossed the pendant onto the wooden boards. "You don't have to pay for the services rendered; you got them for nothing! And here"—she threw the title deeds after the pendant—"take these, too. You haven't bought me, Monsieur. You don't own me and you never will."

Gilles laughed. "But I haven't paid for you, my dear, that was merely an advance on my account. Come and live with me, Léonie, you'll have a house in Paris, you can have whatever you want . . . name it and you shall have it. You'll be my Léonie, my creation. We'll dress you in silk and jewels, you'll have only the best. You will always be beautiful."

She stared at him in horror. What was he saying? He wanted her to live with him, to be his woman—for as long as he wanted her, and then he'd discard her. She thought of the nights waiting for the cab to come, just like a mistress even then. She would have none of it; she would not be owned by any man, be at his beck and call, be there when he wanted her and deserted when he didn't.

He caught her in his arms. "Come on, Léonie"—he smiled confidently—"you know you want me, remember, you told me so, just a short while ago. Of course, I have my private life in Paris, but you'll be well taken care of."

She tore herself away from him and began throwing on her clothes rapidly. "Never," she stormed, "I'll never be your kept woman."

He watched her with lazy, confident eyes. "Think it over," he suggested, amused by her anger, "but take these with you." He picked up the deeds and handed them to her with a smile. "Remember, these were given without strings attached . . . they weren't for services rendered."

Léonie took a deep breath, then snatched them from his hand. "Damn you, I will keep them," she shouted. "You got what you wanted."

He laughed as she ran from the room and across the deck, hearing her footsteps on the gangway as she hurried from the boat. "You'll be back," he murmured.

* * *

Léonie had no money—she had spent the last of it getting to Monte Carlo that morning—and she began the long walk back to Cap Ferrat. The sun was already low in the sky and thank God it wasn't as hot, but her knees felt weak and she was still burning with anger. After a mile or two she hitched a ride in a farm cart on its way back from the market and sat in sullen silence, thinking over the afternoon and her dilemma.

There was no doubt that she had adored his lovemaking, even now her body reminded her of the excitement. She wriggled uncomfortably. But he hadn't said he loved her; he said she was beautiful, wonderful, the smoothest, the most glorious woman, and lots of other things, too; words she repeated as he thrust himself into her. She blushed with shame. Oh, Rupert, why did you ever leave me? This would never have happened! But now it had—and she was different. The cart bumped uncomfortably over the rutted lane and she remembered riding along the road from Masarde to the cottage she had called home. Face it, Léonie, she said to herself, you're right back where you started—riding home in a farm cart, with no money and no job—and no one who cares about you. Wait, though—one thing was different. She stared at the title deeds in her hand, in the name of Léonie Bahri. She did have a home! She began to laugh, laughing until the farmer joined in, wondering what the joke might be.

The anger and the elation left her as soon as she was back in the security of the inn. It was going into *their* room that did it, seeing the bed, its white sheet spread smooth across its width and the pillows plump and unruffled, waiting for the imprint of their blond heads. But she was no longer Rupert's girl, the blond head that had lain there next to him was an innocent one and loving, not this wanton creature who had begged for more, who had sold herself for this place. For wasn't that what she had done? When he'd said there were no strings, had she really believed him? It was all so bewildering. Was she in love with him? Was she in love with Rupert? She felt defeated by her own body, thinking about Gilles in spite of herself—no, she still couldn't call him Gilles, even now. He was Monsieur le Duc de Courmont. Monsieur.

She cuddled the little cat in her arms, rubbing her cheek against the fur. "What are we to do now, Bébé?" she wondered.

❧ 14 ❦

GILLES HAD LEFT for Paris the next day, confident that she wouldn't be back for a day or two. There had been urgent business to take care of, but he would return within two days. He estimated that that was about the length of time it would take her to arrive at the right conclusion: that she did want to be with him, that she couldn't live without him and what he offered. He'd led her into it subtly, not overwhelming her with flowers and presents, just allowing her to sink gently into the luxurious ease of life when she was with him, entertaining her, sympathizing with her so that she no longer felt lonely and unwanted, allowing her to feel that she was pretty after all, despite Rupert's rejection. He had watched her blossom with new confidence, and then he'd taken it away from her, left her for a week racked with insecurity and rejection, only to lift her up again, to take her back into his world, to offer it all. How could she resist? But now he'd been back for more than a week and it seemed Léonie *was* resisting!

He paced the deck of the yacht while the bored crew waited for a command to head out to sea that never came. He was afraid to leave the harbor in case Léonie arrived, worried that she'd think he'd stopped waiting for her and had left Monte Carlo. He stared gloomily over the side of the boat, watching without seeing the bustle of activity on the little harbor front. Had he misjudged her? He thought not. No woman who had responded as she had could feel indifferent now. Even thinking about her excited him, he could sense the texture of her skin, smell the light scent of her body, taste her. The thought of the gleam of her flesh as she leaned over him was driving him crazy, he wanted her and nothing was going to stop him now.

He paced the little study where they had made love, trying to decide what to do. For the first time in his life he was incapable of making an immediate and decisive decision.

Monsieur and Madame Frenard were delighted to find that Léonie was the new owner of the inn. When they'd heard the inn had been sold, they'd been afraid that the new owners might want to run the place themselves and they would have to leave. "But now, we must pay our rent to you instead of you paying us." He laughed appreciatively at the twist in fortunes.

"There is no rent," said Léonie. "You've both given me so much already. As long as I have my room I shall be happy, and I'll still help in the kitchen, Madame Frenard, in return for my food."

Madame Frenard bustled about the room preparing lunch. "You should do something better than work in my kitchen. There's more to life than this for a girl like you."

"What? What is there, Madame Frenard?"

"I'm not sure." She wiped the floury pastry from her hands. "But you're different, Léonie, different from the girls of families like ours. There will be a lot more to your life than just being a waitress—I'm certain of it."

"Do you think there'll be happiness, Madame Frenard?" Léonie's voice was wistful.

"I expect so, my dear, there usually is, somewhere around the corner. Of course, you have to grasp your opportunities. It takes a lot to climb from this level. But you've already started. You're a woman of property already, and only seventeen."

Léonie thought over what Madame Frenard had said. Yes, she was a woman of property now—a landowner. Those olive trees and that patch of hillside were hers. The land was solid, secure, the only security she had ever known. She'd like to expand it, to own all the hillside, to put fences round it, to plant and grow things. And no one would ever take it away from her. She wasn't destined to find some nice young husband who'd love her and give her children. She was already cast in the role of mistress, the other woman. Women like Puschi and Marie-France were so secure in their charmed lives, they would never be abandoned. The Ruperts and de Courmonts of this world never left their wives, and if they dallied a little, well, how could anyone as insignificant as she dent the smooth surface of their lives, even just a little? But she wanted security, too, absolute security so that no one could play games with her. Security enough so that if the man she loved abandoned her, she wouldn't be defenseless. A home—her own property—land. They would be her security.

Her plan had grown from that. She would play Monsieur at his own game—it was, after all, a successful one. If he really wanted her, then he would come after her, just as she had gone to him. If he didn't, well then, she had lost the gamble. She would wait and see, and meanwhile she would decide what it was that she wanted. He had asked her once before, and this time she intended to have the answer ready.

One thing she knew she did want was his lovemaking. She thought of it every night alone in bed, she fantasized it lying in the sea grasses on the Point, she imagined him with other girls, doing things to them, finding the idea exciting, and she stared at herself in the mirror, imagining how she had looked to him, how she had felt.

Bébé was becoming used to the long daily walks around the Point, though often she had to be carried back on Léonie's shoulder, sniffing contentedly at the sea air as she joggled along. Léonie's feet were still damp and sandy as they made their way up from the beach to the terrace, and it was Bébé who saw him first, running to him and purring against his legs. Gilles picked her up, watching as Léonie climbed the hill. He could feel the nervous dampness on the palms of his hands and he rubbed them fastidiously on his handkerchief.

She looked up and saw him. "Oh, it's you."

"Weren't you expecting me, then?"

She tilted her head to one side, considering. "You're such a busy man. . . ."

He sighed with exasperation. "Is this the tone our conversation is to take then, Léonie?"

"What other tone should it have?"

"I came to tell you that I haven't changed my mind. I want you."

"Really." Her tone was calm, indifferent. She sat down on the steps of the terrace, brushing the sand from her feet. "How could you want a woman with feet as big as this?" she said, waving a toe in the air, laughing.

"I'm serious, Léonie!"

"What do you want me to say? That I can't live without you? Aren't you supposed to say that?"

"I can't live without you."

She looked at him surprised, searching for the truth. "Are you saying you love me?" she asked slowly.

He sighed, choosing his words carefully. "I'm not sure you know what love is, Léonie. Oh, I know you thought you were in love with Rupert, but you've forgotten him quickly enough." He sat beside her on the steps of the terrace. "I want you," he said, "because I can't erase the memory of you from my body. I want to give you things, to make you even more beautiful. I'm known in business as a ruthless man, one who will stop at nothing to gain his ends. But I won't tell you I love you, Léonie. I want you with passion. Isn't that better than love? You've found out already, as we all do in time, that love is a fool's emotion."

Léonie wrapped her arms around her knees and gazed out to sea. What had she expected? That he would come on bended knee declaring his undying love? And was she in love with him? She certainly didn't feel for him what she had felt for Rupert, but she did *want* him. Despite everything, there was something about him that pulled her toward him, something that she couldn't resist—that she didn't want to resist. He was right though. Love was a fool's emotion. She had fallen into that trap once and seen where it had gotten her. Much better to live without love in the future. They understood each other. "Then it's a business contract, Monsieur, your terms and mine."

"Just tell me what you want."

"I want to become a rich woman. Oh, I don't mean just your giving me money; what I want is for you to show me how to use money to make more money. I'd like to buy land and property ... will you help me, will you show me how?"

She was full of surprises. He had thought she might demand an apartment in Paris, servants, money, jewels, clothes from the best couturier, that she might want to return to the theater, to become a star. But no, she wanted to become a businesswoman! Very well. It would be amusing to teach her—though he doubted the lessons would be successful. The disciplines of business were contrary to her nature—she was too emotional, too volatile, to pay serious attention to the intricacies of finance. He certainly preferred it that way. He wanted a mistress, not a business partner.

"I'll help you," he said, taking her hand, turning it palm upward, kissing the soft part in between her fingers.

She curled them around his. "Then it's a deal? We have a contract, Monsieur?"

"We do," he said with a triumphant smile.

The cat leapt onto Léonie's knee, claiming her position, staring at him haughtily. "I can see I have a rival." He laughed, bringing out a box from his pocket. "I didn't dare give you this before, in case you thought I was trying to bribe you."

In the box was a tiny necklace, a thin strip of pavé diamonds. From its center hung a thin gold disc, and inscribed in tiny rubies was the name Bébé. It was as dainty and charming a collar as any cat had ever had and Léonie loved it. "How clever you are, Monsieur," she said, laughing, "it's exactly what Bébé would like."

He refused to let her stay at the inn another night. "Leave everything," he commanded, "you don't need anything. Now you can buy whatever you like."

Léonie returned to the white room just long enough to pick up the Egyptian statues.

"To remind me of my past," she explained quietly, putting them safely in her bag.

She said good–bye to the Frenards, thanking them for everything. "Take care of the inn," she said. "I'll be back. It will always be my home."

They dined alone on the yacht, sitting out under the stars on the top deck, sipping Roederer Cristal champagne while Léonie picked tentatively at salmon and asparagus, ignoring the tempting mound of *fraises des bois*.

This is the first time in my life that I have been nervous with a woman, Gilles thought. I have exactly what I set out to get and now I'm unsure of myself.

What is he thinking? wondered Léonie. He's so quiet. My God, can he have changed his mind? Now that he's got me, maybe he doesn't want me!

Tension crackled between them. He stood up suddenly and went to the speaker. "Cast off, Captain, we'll make our way along the coast to Cannes."

There was a sudden flurry of activity as sailors appeared on the lower deck, and from below came the quiet smooth chug of powerful engines. Gilles watched restlessly. Why didn't they move quicker? He needed the bustle and activity of the boat to cover the growing silence between them. There, that was better.

The yacht slid from the harbor, past a dozen others already twinkling with lights as the deep blue dusk began to fall, and then they were out to sea, dipping with the slight swell, picking up the cool evening breeze. Léonie felt herself relax. She lay back on the divan under the awning gazing up at the emerging stars.

Monsieur stood over her, watching.

She held out her hand to him. "I want you," she said softly. She had grown up.

≫ 15 ≪

LÉONIE swept into the shop on Monsieur's arm as though she owned the place. "Bring whatever madame wants," he commanded, and they leapt to do just that. The smart shops of Cannes were only too honored to serve Monsieur le Duc and Madame.

She sat on a tiny stiff sofa while models paraded every kind of garment. There were dresses for morning and for afternoon, dresses just for taking tea, robes for the time between tea and supper, and evening gowns of such breathtaking brilliance that she gasped. "Oh, they're all so beautiful," she whispered to him, "I don't know how to choose."

He called over the vendeuse. "Kindly advise madame on what to choose."

"Of course, sir."

Léonie waited eagerly to see what she would show her. "Of course, when we return to Paris you'll go to Worth," Monsieur said.

Worth! He was the best couturier in Paris. Caro went there. What would Caro think of her now, she wondered, running off with one man and coming back with another? If she was even speaking to her—she had never written. She felt sad thinking of Caro. But now Monsieur would help her, he would explain everything. She glanced at his thigh, next to hers on the sofa, his firm, hard thigh. She touched it with tentative fingers; he glanced sideways at her and their eyes met. She removed her hand with a smile as the vendeuse returned.

"I think these colors would suit madame." The models paraded again, showing simple skirts in white banded with brilliant colors for mornings and fluttery afternoon dresses in cool silk in sea colors—blue, aquamarine, and jade—with pretty belts twisted and tasseled with beads. For evening there was a dress of cream-colored lace, woven with a gold thread, tightly waisted and full in the skirt with a ruffle of lace on the deep neckline, and a barbaric-looking dress that hung from the shoulders in a soft fall of fine pleats of the supplest amethyst silk, held loosely at the waist by a belt of thin golden discs.

"You must have that," said Monsieur suddenly, "it'll be wonderful on you." She looked at him in surprise as he called over the vendeuse. "Madame will have all of them," he instructed, "and kindly make up the last one in other colors, anything that will suit her. Oh, and take that belt to Cartier—I want it copied in gold."

"Yes, sir. Naturally it will be more beautiful in gold. And now perhaps madame would like to choose the accessories, and be fitted for the models?"

"Take care of madame, then," he said firmly, walking toward the door, "give her whatever she wants. I'll be at the Café Cézar, Léonie, when you're finished. Enjoy yourself."

Léonie's spirits soared. "Very well," she decided, "we must begin with lingerie." It was a field in which she was expert, and she knew just what to choose. Then there were shoes and bags and gloves, and she just adored the hats—big straw ones with streamers, and bunches of flowers, and lacy ones for grand occasions. She chose a hat to go with each outfit. And shoes in the softest kid, that matched exactly the tiny bags that went perfectly with the dresses.

With a sigh of complete satisfaction she marched out onto the promenade clad from head to toe in new things: her underwear was sea green crêpe de Chine, her stockings were a thin cream silk, her dress was cool fine lawn in aquamarine, and her bag and shoes were a pale cream leather, matching the wide straw hat that perched uncertainly on her boisterous hair. She felt *wonderful*.

Gilles smiled as he saw her walking haughtily behind the head waiter escorting her personally to his table, casting regal glances from side to side as heads turned to watch her. She was magnificent!

"Well?" she asked, unable to resist a small twirl in front of him.

He threw back his head and laughed out loud. "Dazzling," he announced, "you are *dazzling!*"

They cruised up and down the coast, lingering at Menton and Nice and Monte Carlo, so that she might wear her new finery and be suitably admired on his arm, or anchoring off the little fishing village of Saint-Tropez, so that they could dine barefoot at the tin-roofed café on the beach that cooked the best lobster on the Côte d'Azur, with lashings of fresh garlicky mayonnaise. Or merely lazing on the yacht, when she would wake late to find he had been up since dawn, working in his study, and she'd persuade him to go for a swim with her, climbing down the rope ladder over the side to a special little platform where she dived and cavorted, swimming under the clear sea, eyeball to eyeball with tiny fish. He swam as he did everything else, excellently, with clean smooth strokes that drove him through the water in a straight line and back again to the boat. "You just don't know how to play," she called, frolicking around him, splashing him with water as he sat on the diving platform. "You're simply taking the required amount of exercise . . . come back in and we'll play!"

She raced him, losing hopelessly, laughing with the effort, and then they stretched naked on the privacy of the top deck, while the sun dried them off and rewarmed their sea-cooled skin.

Lunch was simple, though she refused to let him eat omelettes. "Never again," she commanded, enjoying her new authority. "You will eat something different every day." And they did, though it might be just fruit and cheese, or a mound of shrimp fresh from the bay.

And, of course, they made love, if that was what you could call their trembling driving union. It was moody, intense, adventurous, and always it was wild and overwhelming. It was never, never tender.

❧ 16 ❦

CARO HAD HEARD the rumors. It was impossible not to. Paris was abuzz with the story. "Do you really think it can be *our* Léonie?" she asked Alphonse over breakfast.

"I'd be willing to bet on it." He buttered his toast neatly and took a bite. "I was there the first time they met, at your birthday party."

"I didn't even know that they *had* met."

"It was strange, now that I think of it. Gilles seemed to make a point of coming over to be introduced and then he said he had to leave. . . . Just said hello, and went. Knowing de Courmont, he probably fancied her then and saved her up for when he had the time."

"Really?" Caro was thinking. "Alphonse, do you remember that night at the Cabaret Internationale when there was the disaster with the horse? I always had the strangest feeling that it wasn't just an accident . . . that Gilles had set it up. Could that be true?"

"But why would he go to such lengths—Gilles can get almost any woman he wants."

"But what if," said Caro thoughtfully, "what if he wanted Léonie and she already belonged to Rupert?"

"Then it seems all he had to do was wait."

"I wonder . . ." said Caro, pouring his coffee. "I wish she'd written to me. I feel responsible for all this. I hope she's happy with de Courmont, but I can't imagine how . . . she's such a child, Alphonse. Don't you think we ought to do something about it?"

"Caro, she ran off with Rupert. That wasn't the act of a child, she was a young woman in love. And now that Rupert is married, she's moved on to de Courmont." He shrugged. "It happens a thousand times."

"Yes," sighed Caro. She knew that was true.

"Anyway, they're back in Paris," said Alphonse. "They arrived yesterday and he's installed her in a suite at the Crillon. Apparently they're living there pretty openly, despite Marie-France."

"I didn't know that!"

"I just heard it last night. I meant to tell you, but I forgot."

Caro pushed back her chair and hurried to the door. "I'd better see if she's all right, Alphonse. After all, she is my friend."

Léonie fluffed up the pillows and lounged back against them, arranging her lace gown so that it sat demurely high against her collarbone, tying the virginal white satin ribbons in a large bow at her neck. Julie, her maid, had already arranged her hair, and for the first time in her life it remained in place, caught back simply with a matching white ribbon. It knew when it was beaten. What, she wondered, should she do today? It was her first day without Monsieur. He'd left early, while she was still asleep. She looked around the room, *her* room—that is, until they found a house. He'd suggested buying an apartment, but Léonie had insisted on a house—anything could happen to mere buildings, they could burn down, but the land would always be there. Meanwhile, this room would do very nicely, although she really preferred her room at the inn. Bébé in her diamond collar had already ripped her pretty lace pillow to shreds and adopted the blanket, although she didn't look nearly as decorative on it.

The suite was all blue; the immense deep blue Chinese silk carpet was bordered with flowers, and the Louis XIV bed had gilded finials and blue damask upholstery with a painted oval of elegant courtiers taking a stroll by a blue lake. The windows were draped with the same blue damask fabric and the sofas, of the same period, were in blue velvet with tasseled edges—even the lamps were blue, though, thank heavens, they'd had the sense to use peach-colored shades.

It was more than just a suite; it took up half a floor of the Hôtel Crillon on the place de la Concorde, and it was very, *very* smart. There was a large salon for entertaining, and a small salon just for her, a large *and* a small dining room, a study, kitchens, dressing rooms, and a separate bedroom for Monsieur, bathrooms, and even rooms for the servants. "What can I do with all these rooms?" she wondered aloud.

"Madame." Julie offered a card on a silver salver.

"Carolina Montalva," she read. "Caro . . . it's Caro! Oh, how wonderful, send her in, Julie, no, wait a minute." Pushing aside the tray, she rearranged herself. "Does my hair look all right?"

"Perfect, madame."

"Then send her in."

The door swung open and there she was, in a sapphire dress, her black hair shining and glossy, and her eyes sparkling with pleasure. "Oh, Caro." Léonie leapt from the bed and hurtled across the room. "Oh, Caro, I'm *so* happy to see you."

They hugged each other so tightly they couldn't breathe. "I knew everything would be all right once I saw you," gasped Léonie.

"Of course it's all right, but are you?"

Caro took stock of her. "You've grown up," she said accusingly. "You're sophisticated and glamorous. What happened to the little girl in Baden-Baden?"

"That was such a long time ago—really another lifetime. Caro, tell me, have you heard from Rupert?"

Caro hesitated. Should she tell her? If she didn't, someone else would. "He's married, Léonie. It was inevitable, his family needed it."

Léonie's shoulders drooped under the lace gown. "If only he'd written to me, Caro," she whispered, "he should have written."

Caro said nothing. Of course he should have written. And why hadn't he? Rupert wasn't cruel; it was very odd.

"This is all very grand," she said, shrugging off her coat, "although it's a bit *blue,* isn't it?"

Léonie burst out laughing. "Caro, tell me, what do beautiful mistresses of rich men do all day?"

"What do they do? I'll tell you what," replied Caro. "They have *fun.*"

"Will you help me to have fun?"

"We'll start today! First we'll visit Worth, then we'll have lunch, then we'll go to Cartier, and then, let me see, do you need a house or an apartment?"

In the south the air had been soft as though summer longed to linger. The sun had warmed the sea for them to swim and the breezes had been welcome, fluttering leaves and skirts gently, but in Paris the autumn trees were already bare, feeling the icy grip of an east wind that made Caro and Léonie quicken their step as they paced arm in arm along the Bois de Boulogne.

Léonie had needed to talk and Caro had wanted to listen, and the Bois, with only the wind to catch their words, had seemed the most private place for such confidences.

Caro listened in silence, not wanting to interrupt the flow of words, the torrent of truths that poured from Léonie, flinching as she described Rupert's desertion, wondering about the letters that never arrived, and shedding tears alongside a dry-eyed Léonie as she described how she had wanted to die, until Bébé had adopted her and become her only friend. And then she had met Gilles de Courmont. Caro heard in amazement of his sympathy, his nightly dinners with her, his gift of the inn—without strings—and their incredible lovemaking.

"If you find me different," said Léonie, "it's not simply that I'm beautifully dressed and have learned how to behave in smart restaurants, although Monsieur taught me that, too. It's his lovemaking, Caro. He's changed me. Sometimes when I'm in his arms, I don't recognize myself and then afterward I'll look in the mirror, searching for traces of what I had felt only an hour before, and thank God there are none."

Caro was stunned. It wasn't the confession of a woman in love, they were the words of a woman enthralled. "But you loved Rupert. . . ."

"Yes. I loved Rupert—but Rupert left me. He never wrote, Caro. He said he would come back—all those weeks waiting, just *waiting!*—and all the time he was planning to marry Puschi. He lied to me!" She turned to face Caro, her lovely face as bleak as the sunless light filtering through the naked trees. "I swore that I would never be put in that position again. Caro, I want to be so secure that *no one* can destroy me. I made a bargain with Monsieur—a contract. He will make me a rich woman, but not just by giving me money, paying for me. He will teach me how to *make* money. I'm going to increase my capital so that I can buy property. Giving me the inn started something that I can't explain. Land is the ultimate security and I want acres of it, parcels of it—fields and streams and corner plots." She sighed with satisfaction. "Gilles de Courmont is the key to my independence. You'll see, one day I'll be my own woman."

They huddled next to each other on a cold bench staring at the dry copper leaves scudding before the wind in a desperate final rustling of life before they were changed to anonymous brown mud by the winter rains. "Then you don't love him, Léonie?"

Léonie's eyes met hers. "It's a sort of love. It's not what I felt for Rupert, but it's *our* sort of love, Caro, mine and his. And it's what I want."

They began to walk again, hurrying before the wind, trying to get warm. "Aren't we supposed to be having fun?" demanded Caro. "Come on, let's go to the Brasserie Lipp for lunch."

"Wait." Léonie paused, staring at a ragged poster, torn by the wind and faded by rain, the last remnant of a summer circus long since departed for warm winter quarters in Spain. She ran her fingers down the names, wondering if she would *ever* be able to pass a circus poster without checking. "I always think that perhaps my father's name might be there," she said, in reply to Caro's questioning face, "but of course it never is."

Maroc hunched his shoulders against the wind, staring at the whirlpools of dust eddying down the alley, thinking about the homeland he had left long ago, where it must surely always be warm.

"Do you have a sandwich to spare for an old friend?" The voice was familiar.

It was Léonie! It really was Léonie! Different—glamorous and sparkling—but the same. She threw her arms around him, laughing as he swung her off the ground with a shout of joy. "Why didn't you write to me?" she demanded. "I thought we were friends?"

"How could I write when I didn't know where you were?"

"But *I* wrote to *you*—with my address, explaining everything!"

Maroc shrugged, grinning happily. "I never got any letters, but it doesn't matter because now you're here. What's happened to you? You look wonderful."

"It's a long story, Maroc, but for now this will be enough. *I*, my *dear* Maroc, am a rich woman. I am buying a house in Paris, and I want you to be my butler."

"Your butler!"

"Just what I said, my *butler*. *More* than my butler, you will be what's known as a majordomo: *you* will run my household."

"But I don't even know what a butler does," he protested.

"Then you'll learn very quickly. After all, look at me, haven't I learned?" She twirled in front of him, laughing at the amazed expression on his face.

"I have a lover," she announced, "who adores me and I can have anything I want. And I want you, Maroc, as more than just a butler, as a friend. *Please* say yes."

"Won't I be the youngest butler in Paris?"

"So, we'll set the style. You'll see, everyone will want a *young* butler. And you'll be the most fashionable butler in Paris, your tailcoats will come from London and your shirts will be specially made. Other women will try to tempt you away from me to work for them, there'll be offers that'll be hard to refuse!"

He laughed at her vivid flights of imagination. "You're crazy, Léonie."

"I'm on top of the world, Maroc, and I like it there very much. Throw away the turban and the feather and come with me." She held out her hand, smiling at him.

"I can't wait to see Marianne's face when I tell her." Maroc laughed.

❧ 17 ❧

GILLES DE COURMONT pushed back his chair, propped his feet up on the desk, clasped his hands behind his head, and thought about Léonie. The blueprints of the design of the proposed de Courmont cars lay neglected in front of him.

Léonie was there, he thought, in the suite at the Crillon, probably just having her breakfast by now. She'd be wearing that lace robe that he liked so much; her hair would be freshly brushed and her cheeks pink with the morning bloom of youth. He felt almost content, imagining her there like that, waiting for him. He remembered Marie-France; even in the beginning he'd never thought of her once he was away from her—except, of course, on the days his children were born. His boys. It was time they went away to a decent school, despite what Marie-France thought. He had been sent to school at their age and it had been good for him, but then he didn't have a mother like Marie-France. There wasn't really much to choose between being at home and being at school—except that at home there was more food—it certainly wasn't the presence of his mother, or his father. For all he saw of them, they could have lived in another country.

How he had hated that dark, silent house in the country. It only came to life when *they* arrived on one of their rare visits, and then the servants would run around getting everything ready for Madame la Duchesse. The whole house would be in a turmoil. He remembered the gardener arriving with plants from the hothouses and great armfuls of cut flowers; the maids lighting fires in the enormous grates and fueling them constantly with great buckets of coal so that the vast frozen rooms glowed into warmth; the butler polishing the silver to a final sheen; and the chefs busying themselves in the smokerooms, selecting pink-fleshed hams. Sometimes he'd creep after them into the vast cold rooms where the hooks hung waiting for the new season's grouse and woodcock and where wild geese and ducks from the home farm sat plucked and trussed, ready for the oven. He'd hang around watching the pastry chef weave strands of spun sugar into little baskets, ready to be filled with some mouth-watering dessert that he would never taste. The preparations seemed endless, building his excitement. It was like waiting for Christmas Eve, only better.

And then at last came the day of the arrival and he'd be up at dawn, climbing from his narrow bed in the old nursery to peer from the window to check the weather. It was always misty when they were coming for the shooting, but later it would burn off and be bright and clear, so that the targets of the massacre stood little chance of escape. He'd been often with Monsieur Talbert, helping to scatter the grain that fed the little birds, and he felt sorry for them.

He could remember, even now, the feeling of the cold water he splashed on his face in a sketchy attempt at a wash, and throwing on his clothes, making sure to brush his hair properly. His hair was like hers, thick and dark and crisply curling, and he had her eyes, they said.

The carriages would bowl briskly up the drive—he'd see them in the far distance from his vantage point at an attic window, they'd come past the woods and through the parklands, a dozen of them with liveried attendants and the coachmen in top hats—and they'd curve to a halt in front of the west portico, and *she'd* be there. His mother. The most beautiful woman on earth, and he adored her. They'd pile out of the carriages laughing and chattering, the women all so beautifully dressed, and the men checking on their guns with their handlers. The guns were wonderful; he'd sneak into the gunroom in the evening and the bearers would let him hold them, stroking the beautiful stocks inlaid with silver and the sleek lethal barrels. "It's time your dad let you out with the shoot," they'd tell him with jolly laughter, "you're old enough to hold a gun at six."

He remembered the last of these occasions so well. She had swept into her great house calling to her friends, throwing commands to the servants as she went, complaining about the chill despite the enormous fires that had been burning in every room in the house for a week, day and night. "How I hate this place," she had cried, hurrying up the marble staircase to change, "I so much prefer Moulins"—their other house in the Loire Valley—and then halfway up, she remembered. "Where's the boy?" she'd called, and he had come forward from his hiding place behind Nanny and run up the stairs toward her and she had bent down to inspect him, smoothing back his hair with a soft hand. She'd been so close he could smell her perfume— he could recall it now with perfect clarity—a base of jasmine with some other more earthy tone.

"And are you being a good boy?" she had asked in her high clear voice.

"Yes, Maman."

"Good, then have Nanny dress you properly this evening and you may come into the drawing room before supper. Off you go now, surely you have lessons to do." And she had sent him off with a careless pat on his rump.

Of course, he had no lessons to do; the governess she'd hired had left after a month, unable to bear the big lonely house any longer, and Maman had not remembered to hire a new one, even though Nanny had said it was scandalous. So he still couldn't read, even though he was six. Nanny was English and not a very good reader herself, so she was no help, and he had desperately wanted to read. He'd pored over the books he'd found in the big, gloomy library, not even ones with pictures in them, running his fingers along the words, threading together the letters of the alphabet, teaching himself until he could sort of half-read, but the words had been so big and didn't sound the way the letters did.

He'd waited all that day for evening to come. Upstairs in the nursery wing he couldn't hear the sounds of music and jollity from the other side of the house and he'd lurked behind the baize door, peeking out when Nanny wasn't around, just to catch their laughter. He had even sneaked down to her room on the first floor, hiding behind the door while she dressed, smelling her drifting perfume. He wanted to stay near her forever, to hear what she said when she spoke to those strange people, to know what it was that she did when she wasn't with him that was so important and glamorous and wonderful—and that took her away from him. Afraid of her anger if he were caught, he'd crept back through the big house to the nursery and Nanny, to wait.

And then it was time—and this last time was burned in his memory forever. He'd walked in holding Nanny's hand and they had turned to watch him, all the smart ladies and the tall gentlemen, smiling at him as he basked in their warmth, like a foolish puppy displaying its charms. "And what are you learning in the schoolroom, young man?" his father had boomed, awaiting the opportunity to display his son to his friends.

"Nothing, sir."

"Nothing? What does he mean, nothing?" He turned to his wife.

She shrugged. "I don't know. Come here, Gilles." He'd walked over to her obediently, smiling up into those dark deep blue eyes with the thick curling lashes. He'd put his hand on her arm, touching her soft peachy flesh, longing for her to put her arms around him. "Why are you not learning, Gilles?" she'd asked.

"The governess left, Maman, and you never got me another."

She had flushed with embarrassment. "Nonsense," she'd said, "you're old enough to be at school anyway . . . surely he should be at school now?" She'd turned to his father angrily.

"Well, he's old enough, Régine. . . ."

"Then that's it: next week you'll go to school, my boy. I shall arrange it myself," and she'd turned her attention to the young man by her side, taking his hand and seating him next to her, charming him easily. He had stood there forgotten. She had just carelessly condemned him to twelve years of loneliness and misery and he had hated her for the rest of her life.

When she had died, ironically in a shooting accident at the same house, he had felt nothing, not even a lessening of the hate. But he always remembered how beautiful she was, her perfume and her skin.

Gilles stood up abruptly as Verronet came into the room. "Excuse me, sir, but I have the new figures you requested on the rubber for the automobile tires, and the various comparisons on the durability of the paints."

"Thank you, yes, put them on my desk. I'll look at them later." He glanced at his watch, it was almost twelve. "I'll be back around three, Verronet."

"Of course, sir." Verronet followed his employer down the hall, hurrying to hold open the door, watching as Gilles strode out into the icy wind without even seeming to notice it. I'll bet he's going back to see her, he thought with a lewd smile. This is the first time *that* has ever happened.

The big room was silent and empty, the bed smooth and untouched. He had hurried into the suite expecting to find her still pottering about the way she had on the yacht, but she was gone.

Where had she gone? He paced the floor angrily, calling for Julie.

"I believe she's lunching with Mademoiselle Montalva, sir, they were to look at houses together."

Of course. He'd been so lost in his need to see her, to watch her smile, to have her tease him; fool, he should have known she wasn't going to just sit around here all day. He closed the door to the blue suite and made his way down to the restaurant.

The head waiter seated him at a quiet table by the window and another took his order.

"An omelette *fines herbes,* please, and bring me the wine list."

"Well, what do you think?" Léonie spun around in the center of the main salon, throwing out her arms expansively to take in the row of eight french windows with ornamental iron balconies, the high ceilings with their molded cornices, the vast expanse of polished boards, and the twin marble fireplaces, one at each end.

"It's a perfect room for entertaining," replied Caro, "and look, here's a smaller sitting room with a very pretty Adam mantel."

They wandered through the empty rooms, followed by the echoes of their own voices, exclaiming over each new discovery—a master bedroom with his dressing room and her dressing room and two bathrooms and her boudoir, small enough to be cozy, with a fireplace for chilly weather and two long windows that overlooked the leafy square and opened out onto a tiny balcony for warmer days.

"I think it's perfect," said Léonie, surveying her future domain, for she had already decided. This was to be her house.

"It's suitable," agreed Caro. "There's plenty of space for entertaining."

Léonie stopped in her tracks as a thought struck her. "Caro, *who* am I to entertain?"

"My dear Léonie, that will not be a problem. Monsieur knows everyone there is to know, and besides, every woman in Paris is dying to see who has finally melted the ice in Gilles de Courmont's veins!" She laughed at Léonie's surprised face. "You'll be amazed at how quickly you get used to it," she warned.

"But I don't know what to do, Caro. I don't know how to give a party."

"The first thing you do is hire a good chef. And, if you insist on having Maroc as your butler, then you must have an experienced housekeeper—she'll teach you how to run a household. An efficient staff will know exactly what to do. As for clothes, take my advice, Léonie, *always* wear exactly what you feel like wearing. Forget all the rules and regulations. I've never forgotten the way you looked at my party—even then you had a style of your own."

"And what about the house, Caro? It's so big. Where do I start?"

"Come with me." Caro led her to the middle of the vast salon. "Now, close your eyes and just think about it. It's your house. This is your room, and it's going to reflect your personality. What do you want from it? Imagine yourself in it."

Léonie closed her eyes and saw the blank walls, the tall row of windows with their balconies; it was like an empty stage. Of course! The place was exactly like a theater, and this room was the stage where everything would happen. It couldn't possibly be conventional and ordinary—it demanded flamboyance, textures, wonderful gleaming light, as though lit by stage lamps. "I know exactly what I want," she announced, opening her eyes. "This room will be silver."

Verronet's eyes tracked his employer as he strode past him into his office, slamming the door behind him. Back so soon? De Courmont emerged again an hour later. "Verronet."

"Sir."

"I want you to get someone to keep an eye on Mademoiselle Léonie. I want to know where she is and what she's doing—the same as before."

"Yes, sir." Verronet was surprised. Surely he couldn't suspect her of being unfaithful already! "You'll have a daily report, sir."

"Oh, and Verronet"—de Courmont paused by the door—"I'll have the answers on these figures you gave me sometime tomorrow."

"Yes, sir." Verronet's face was blank. Normally he would have had them back within an hour.

❦ 18 ❦

IT SEEMED TO LÉONIE that the house consumed all her time. It didn't matter anymore that Monsieur was up and out by dawn, she herself was up by seven, dressed and ready by eight, waiting impatiently for Caro and the first task of the day. Monsieur's team of surveyors and experts had found evidence of dry rot on the upper floors of the house and damp on the lower ones, and advised that an enormous amount of work was needed. "If this is the house you want, then it will be done," he told her.

Of course she wanted it, she could already see it finished; it was going to be wonderful. It was a house built from a poor girl's dreams. She who had bathed in cold metal tubs had ordered a bath of rose quartz with taps fashioned from leaping gold dolphins and studded with turquoise—she even had her monogram in gold on the bottom—though Monsieur had refused the gold taps and initials on his plain cream marble tub. With a vision of the entire house in her mind, she'd ordered translucent silk brocades specially woven in Lyons, while factories at Aubusson were weaving delicate pastel-colored rugs and carpets. She was determined that the house should have a unique style that she had created. There would be no other house in Paris like it. "Do exactly what you want," Monsieur had told her, "it's your house."

"Our house," she'd corrected him.

She walked through the courtyard of their house and up the short flight of stone steps, pushing open the big double doors with a possessive hand. The hall was quiet this morning, the heavy work had been completed, just the painters were in now, putting on the final touches. She wandered through the rooms that had already taken on a new life, imagining herself with Monsieur. They had been together for almost six months now, and she still didn't really know him. He allowed her just so close, and then no closer. It was disconcerting. She was so wildly in love with him, not the wonderful gentle love she'd felt for Rupert—this was different, crazy. She thought about him all the time, planned how she would look for him, how she would be for him, fantasized him covering her with kisses and telling her he loved her, loved her forever.

She peered into the room that was to be his study. It was already completed and it was the only room in the house, apart from his dressing room, that felt masculine. She'd found a wonderful carpet from Scotland in a dark green tartan and had chosen plum-colored walls—making the painters fade it slightly with cream so that they were just warmly rouged—and the curtains were heavy ribbed green linen with a border of plaid braid. She'd sought out a marvelous old ebony desk in Drouet's salesroom and an immense dark green padded leather chair. Walking to the desk, she unwrapped the writing set. A simple silver tray held round crystal bottles for inks, a silver pen and pencil, and a little curved blotter with a handle. She had bought it yesterday in Cartier and had been meaning to give it to him when she showed him the finished house, but she decided now to arrange it on the desk to surprise him. Just by the groove where the pen rested was a tiny inscription. "To Monsieur," it read, "with love from Léonie." She ran a finger over it thoughtfully. She hoped he would like it.

Voisins was busy, as always, and Léonie happily surveyed the crowded room from their corner table. They were alone tonight, just the two of them having dinner together. She couldn't remember the last time they'd been alone for an evening, there always seemed to be something arranged— a theater or a party, or dinner at some restaurant with a dozen friends. "Remember," she asked, taking his hand and squeezing it, "remember all those dinners at all those grand restaurants along the coast?"

"Of course I remember, you ate such enormous quantities of food."

She laughed, studying the menu. "I don't know what to choose," she said, closing it finally. "I think I'll just have some fish."

"I also remember at one of those dinners you asking me why I always ordered the same thing when there was so much to choose from."

Léonie looked at him, wide-eyed, surprised that she had become so blasé in so short a time. "Are you bored already?" he asked her.

"Of course not; it's just that I'm excited at being alone with you," she flirted with him. "And you must choose for both of us, just as you did on that first night."

"Then we'll have the very same things," he said, ordering oysters and salmon.

It was a sort of anniversary, she'd explained to him that morning, because it was exactly six months since they had been together. This evening he had said they would go to Voisins to celebrate. He checked his watch and she frowned; surely he couldn't be going home to Marie-France tonight? She felt a flicker of jealousy for her unknown rival—not even a true rival, really, because there was no contest. He belonged to his wife. They were sitting together on the red velvet banquette and she moved closer to him and placed her hand lightly on his thigh. Their eyes locked and she caught her breath. He took her hand, kissing her fingers as she leaned back against the seat, feeling weak, wanting him. She always wanted him; he had a magic hold over her body that she had no wish to release—she just wanted to feel him next to her right now.

"I'm afraid I have to go away tomorrow," he said as the waiter poured their favorite champagne.

"Go away? Where?"

"To Vienna first, but there's a possibility that I may have to go on to St. Petersburg."

"But that's in Russia!"

The waiter placed the oysters in front of them. They glistened juicily in their own brine.

"But what shall I do all day, without you?"

He shrugged. "Whatever it is that you do all day now, I suppose." She stared at him. "Take me with you."

"I can't do that."

"Why not?"

He shrugged impatiently. "This is a business trip."

"But surely—"

He cut her off abruptly. "I told you in the beginning that my time is not always my own. I'm not sure how long I'll be gone. Surely you can amuse yourself until I get back."

Léonie stared down at the oysters. Why wouldn't he take her with him? She could wait in a hotel suite in Vienna, just as easily as a hotel suite in Paris. She felt the old fear creep around her heart. Maybe he wouldn't come back to her. She turned, the words on her lips, but caught herself just in time. She wasn't going to think about it; of course he would come back. And if he didn't? She steeled her heart against the thought. Wasn't she protected this time? She had the new house, it was almost finished, and she had money in the bank, though somehow she hadn't yet gotten around to learning about stocks and shares and how to increase her capital. Monsieur was always so busy and she'd been caught up in decorating the house. She thought longingly of the inn, so white and simple it hadn't needed anything to make it beautiful. There, she would simply have planted a garden, perhaps added a little pool and some shade trees.

"I have a present for you." It was another of those long boxes, like the one he'd given her on the yacht. He hadn't given her any jewelry since then, just Bébé's collar, and she had felt no need for any, though she'd bought lots of clothes. She enjoyed wearing them because she loved the way they felt, the touch of the fabrics and the way good clothes used her body and made it their own. Breathless with admiration, she stared at the double row of perfect pearls, the large cabachon sapphire clasp surrounded by diamonds and the matching drop earrings. "I was wrong before when I gave you the diamonds," he said, clasping them around her neck. "A girl's first jewels should be pearls."

An image of Rupert flew into her mind, of how he had put that other string of pearls around her neck, lifting her hair, kissing where the pearls fit—he had used exactly the same words. They had been so much in love, and she had been so *young.*

"Don't you like them? You can take them back if you wish, change them for something else."

"No, oh, no." She picked up the earrings and clipped them onto her ears, swinging her head for him to see. "They're beautiful, Monsieur. Thank you. I shall treasure them."

What a strange girl she was. He remembered giving jewelry to other women in his life, how they'd grabbed greedily, rushing to the mirror to try it on. He wondered what she would do when he was away. It would be a test—for him, as well as her.

He ate little, preferring to watch her, as she picked up the *fraises des bois,* one by one in her fingers, biting into them carefully, round-eyed with pleasure; oh, she was such a creature of pleasure. Sometimes he'd watch her through the mirror when he was tying his tie and she'd be lying in bed, curled lazily with the cat, or he'd stare at her from behind the door when she didn't know she was observed, watching as she fixed her hair, just the way he had watched his mother.

The night had turned to heavy rain as they drove back through the gleaming streets of Paris and the street lamps flickered from the gloom in a halo of rainbow drops as they sat together in the intimate warmth of the cab, not touching each other but aware of the other's nearness. He took her arm as they walked across the foyer of the hotel, waiting silently for the elevator. As the iron grill clanged shut, locking them into its cage, he took her into his arms, crushing her against him, pushing back her fur cape so that he could get at her breasts, sliding her dress straps from her shoulders until she was naked to the waist, devouring her hungrily as she leaned against the padded wall and cried out her passion. The elevator jolted them to some sort of sense as it stopped on their floor and he folded the cape across her naked breasts as they walked sedately, hand in trembling hand, along the corridor under the curious gaze of the night chambermaid.

As the big doors slammed shut behind them he was pulling off her cape, unclasping the heavy gold belt around her waist, sliding the dress down over her hips, leaving her clad only in thin silk knickers, as golden as the hair on her body—it was all she ever wore underneath. It was the way he liked it. He guided her into the salon. The lamps were lit and the big windows stared uncurtained onto the rain-slick streets. The room was quiet except for the sounds of their breathing and the rain on the windows. He took off his jacket and laid it carefully across the chair as she waited, her hands on her breasts, anticipating his touch. He came over to her, naked and ready, wanting her, *needing* her. She sank beneath his weight into the blueness of the carpet, opening to him unresistingly, accepting his passion as he plunged into her, thrusting hard against her until she fought, scratching his back with demanding nails, begging for more as they rolled together on the rug sweating and crying like animals engaged in combat, striving toward an ultimate goal as if they were never sure that it had been reached.

❧ 19 ❧

CARO COULD SEE that Léonie was upset by Monsieur's absence. She never actually said so, but she was quieter than usual and seemed at a loss as to how to fill her time. "We'll go to Drouet's salesroom," she told her one afternoon, "and see if we can find the sort of bed you want—although I'm not too sure what it is you're looking for."

"Nor am I," said Léonie, cheering up at the thought of the bed, "but I'll know it when I see it." Monsieur had been gone now for three weeks and she hadn't heard a word from him, and despite herself she was worried. Oh, she knew he wasn't in Paris, she was sure of that, so he must have gone on to St. Petersburg. It seemed so far away. God, how she hated *waiting!* I'll never do it again, she promised herself for the hundredth time.

"At least the house is almost finished," said Caro as they strolled toward Drouet's in the early spring sunshine. "When Monsieur gets back, you'll be able to move in."

Léonie was suddenly inspired. "I want to move in right away," she said, tugging Bébé as she paused to sniff the new buds on the bushes. "I want to be there when he gets back. It will all be finished, Caro, and I'll show him his new home . . . our home," she added triumphantly. "I *must* find that bed today, Caro, it's important."

Caro looked at her anxiously, she was talking like a new bride, like a girl in love. Did she really know the man she was dealing with?

"Tell me," she asked casually as they pushed open Drouet's big glass doors, "have you been having your lessons?"

"What lessons?"

"You remember, you were going to learn how to invest your capital. Monsieur was going to show you how to buy stocks and shares, and land."

"I shall start as soon as he gets back," she announced confidently. "Now that the house is finished, I shall have more time."

"I warned you once," said Caro, "that it's too late at the end of an affair to wonder why you didn't make sure things were in order."

"But they are in order, Caro, I have my account at the Agence de Credit de Paris, and the house is in my name. I can have anything I want," she fingered the pearls at her neck, "but somehow now that I can have it there isn't much that I do want . . . except a bed." Grasping Caro's hand and tucking Bébé under her arm, she ran laughing down the corridors of the august salesroom, turning heads as she went.

The house was absolutely silent. Léonie walked slowly through the rooms with Bébé pattering uncertainly at her heels, drawing the curtains carefully over each window and turning on lamps. She rearranged cushions on newly upholstered sofas and straightened stacks of books piled on convenient tables, waiting for readers. She had hung the walls of the great salon with a transparent film of silver tissue, so fine that the silk weavers in Lyons had warned her against it. "It's meant to be the train of some wonderful bridal gown, madame," the man had said, shocked into disbelief when she told him she wanted hundreds of yards for her walls. "But, madame, it will disintegrate in a few years," he'd protested.

"Then you shall weave me more," she had said, dismissing his cries of dismay at the expense. And she had been right, she thought, pulling the silver cord that released the matching curtains, watching as they drifted in soft folds with the subtle glimmer of stars under a veil of fog. She had achieved her aim. The room was theatrical, a backdrop for a glittering cast of people that she would invite. The enormous carpet was a pale dove gray garlanded with flowers in such muted pastels that they looked submerged beneath some translucent rippling lake. The sofas and chairs were covered in heavy slubbed silks in cream and fawn, moonlit gray and charcoal, and the lamps and sconces were silver with pleated peach-colored shades designed to cast warm pools of light. She had arranged bouquets of pale flowers, choosing only those with a heavy scent so that one was aware of their texture and perfume rather than their individual beauty. Cabinets and tables in rare woods displayed exquisite objects of porcelain and silver. Léonie sighed. Yes, the room was ready. All it needed was people.

She picked up Bébé and walked through the house to her bedroom, touching the immaculate cream-colored bedspread, running a hand across the champagne moiré walls, turning on the taps in her vast rose-colored bathroom, remembering the first time she'd taken a bath in a tub like this, at Caro's.

It was no use pretending, she thought miserably as she curled up on the big bed. He wasn't coming. She knew he was in Paris, she'd heard yesterday that he was in town, and she'd had the servants scurrying around making sure everything was in place, preparing a special dinner just for two, to be held in their own new small dining room, with candlelight and flowers. She had waited, eager to see him, waiting to hear his words of approval for their house, anxious to show him his study and the present she'd placed there, with its inscription. She had worn his favorite dress, the barbaric amethyst one that he'd chosen in Cannes with the belt that he had had copied in gold at Cartier. She'd brushed her long hair, flinging it back to float loosely so that he might run his hands through it and grip it, pulling back her head to kiss her. And she had had the Roederer Cristal champagne iced and ready.

He hadn't come. She had waited all night. And then all morning and afternoon. And then she'd sent the servants away, telling them to take the next few days off, that she would pay them anyway. She was only glad that Maroc was not yet there to witness her humiliation.

She was alone in the great house. Just she and Bébé, who watched her with eyes of love, comforting Léonie with her warmth. She ran the bathwater, throwing in a handful of fragrant salts, steaming the air with jasmine and green-growing scents, and then she lay back in the water with her hair floating around her and wondered again, what should she do?

He smelled the jasmine as he came up the stairs, stopping with a shock of recognition as he remembered the boy hiding behind his mother's dressing room door. Putting the parcels he was carrying carefully on the bed, he walked to the bathroom door. Bébé stared at him from the chair but didn't move. Léonie was stretched out in the tub, her eyes closed. She hadn't heard his step on the soft carpets. He closed the door and went back into the other room, glancing at the silken hangings with a smile. He opened the large box and pulled out the fur, tossing it casually across the end of the bed. And on top of it he put the papers, scattering them equally casually over the bedspread. He went into his dressing room, inspecting the narrow iron campaign bed, the sort that had been used by generals on the march to battlefields—this one had the twin bees of Napoleon emblazoned at the head. He had stipulated that she must find him a bed like this, like the one he had at the house on the Ile Saint-Louis that had come from his father's room. The walls were gray linen and the rug a caramel color. He liked its simplicity. She had understood what he needed.

Léonie wrapped a towel loosely around her and trailed, still wet, into her bedroom. Bébé trotted after her, leaping onto the bed sniffing cautiously at the fur, then curled up on it comfortably. Léonie stared at the bed, the fur, the papers. She picked one up. Securities, the envelope said. Putting it down, she lifted Bébé off the fur and touched it hesitantly. It was tawny and rich and infinitely soft. She ran, still holding it, into his room, trailing the towel and the fur, her wet hair shedding drops of water as she threw open the door. He was leaning against the window, arms folded, looking out into the night. He turned his head as he heard her.

"You're back," she said accusingly.

"So it seems," he answered dryly.

"What's this?" She lifted the envelopes.

"Those are the stocks and shares I promised you."

She dropped the towel and tore them open, examining their contents. The European Iron and Steel Company, she read, a thousand shares, her name across each one. And the de Courmont Automobile Company—the same. Her hand trembled. Why did he do it? Why did he torture her and then give her exactly what she wanted? Why did he make her so insecure and then make her dreams of security come true?

He walked over to her and picked up the fur. "Are you glad to see me?" he asked.

"I don't know." She turned her head angrily, avoiding his eyes. "I heard you were in Paris yesterday."

"I was here the day before that, but there were things to be taken care of, and naturally I had to see my family."

"Naturally."

"You're all wet." He touched her damp arm, brushing off the drops with his fingers, and then he turned the rich tawny fur inside out, wrapping her in it, closing the fur onto her still-wet flesh, rubbing it against her, drying her with it. He carried her over to the narrow bed and tossed the sable coat across it, lying with her, crushed together in the intimacy of the small bed. She smelled of jasmine and wet fur and he began to kiss her.

She awoke hours later, still crushed beneath him on the narrow iron bed, his head nuzzled against her breast. "Tell me," she whispered in his sleeping ear, "tell me that you love me."

He'd rolled over, instantly awake. "Don't be ridiculous, Léonie," he said, walking toward the bathroom. "We had this discussion once before. I explained my feelings for you then. They haven't changed." She heard him turn on the taps and the tub beginning to fill and then she threw on a robe and ran down the stairs. She opened the door to his study and crept in the darkness to the desk, feeling for the little silver desk set, her present to him with its futile, childish inscription. She ran back upstairs clutching it to her breast and then she hid it at the very back of her armoire, where it would never be found.

Caro looked at Alphonse with exasperation. He was such an ordinary man with his round cheeks and brown hair, already thinning into a neat little circle on top. His glasses were as round as his brown eyes—in fact, he was made up of circles, she thought affectionately. He must have been the sweetest little boy. "You haven't asked me to marry you this week, Alphonse."

"Marry me, please, Caro?"

"Well, perhaps not this week." She stretched out next to him on the big four-poster, drawing the rioting cornflower and poppy-strewn drapes around them cozily. "It's like being in a summer meadow," she said with a sigh of satisfaction.

"I'm a patient man," he said, kissing her tenderly. He knew there were those among their friends and acquaintances who questioned just why a woman as beautiful and fun-loving as Carolina Montalva chose to live with a man as ordinary as he, but he didn't care about mere gossip. It was enough that she stayed with him. And he knew she loved him, even though she steadfastly refused to marry him.

"I do love you," she said as if reading his thoughts. "You're the only one who'll put up with me. You're the only one I can complain to that my feet hurt, who doesn't mind when I eat enormous chunks of bread and cheese at four in the morning, or will allow me to fill that great barn of a country house of yours with my frivolous friends. I've given some of my best parties there," she added reflectively.

Alphonse laughed. "But you know I hate parties—I'm really the pipe and slippers type."

She grinned at him. "I know, I know, but you're learning to love them, aren't you?"

He kissed her eagerly. She brought adventure into a life of banking and tradition and had changed his entire world. "Never leave me, Caro, even if you never agree to marry me." He wrapped his arms around her, capturing her warmth, her vitality, the many colors of her life.

"If only I could find someone like you for Léonie," Caro murmured in his ear. "I just feel in my bones that Gilles de Courmont is a dangerous man. There'll be trouble, I know it."

The Office of Egyptian Studies was an ancient building hidden away in a tiny back street behind the Louvre. Léonie had been there once before and had no difficulty in finding it this time. Today she was excited. Monsieur Lamartine had told her that he was sending photographs of the hieroglyphs on her Egyptian statues to Monsieur Mariette at the new museum in Cairo and he expected to have an answer by now.

Lamartine had been able to identify the statues, of course. He had held the little cat statue tenderly. "The ancient Egyptians loved cats, to them they were sacred animals. This one is known as Bastet."

But it was the other statue that he had found exciting, handling it reverently. "This is from the eighteenth dynasty, the reign of Thutmose," he told her. "She is the goddess Sekhmet, mistress of the great god Ptah, who was the ruler of the ancient city of Thebes."

"A goddess," she'd breathed, touching the smooth stone with new respect, "but what was she a goddess of, Monsieur Lamartine?"

"Sekhmet had many roles, but she was known to be the protector of the sun god Ra on his nightly journey through the underworld. The Egyptians believed that when the sun sank below the horizon it went beneath the earth to the underworld through a gate guarded by a fierce dog, Cerberus, and then floated down the river Styx—facing many evils—until it reemerged with the dawn. Sekhmet's power protected the sun god from harm and therefore she was important—without the sun there was no life, and without Sekhmet it was believed there would be no sun god. This disc behind her head symbolizes the sun, the lion head denotes her power, the woman's body, her fertility.

"Sekhmet had a dual character: mistress of the powerful, and the lover who was strong and would protect her lands and the lives of those she loved. But Sekhmet was also ruthless against her enemies, she was said to kill with such ferocity that soldiers talking of a terrible battle would say that the enemy had 'killed like Sekhmet.' This goddess has always been a controversial figure, loved by some and hated by others, right down through Egyptian history." Lamartine looked at her keenly. "Might I ask you where you got this from, madame?"

"It belonged to my father—he was Egyptian. How it came into his possession I don't know, but I've had them both all my life." Léonie had clutched the statue to her as if afraid he might take it away.

"There was a great deal of tomb robbing in the past," he had explained gently. "No doubt your father came across one of these in his village if he lived near Luxor?"

"I don't know; I don't know where he came from."

"Most of the statues found of Sekhmet came from the Temple of Ptah at Memphis, once known as Thebes. It's just outside Luxor on the Nile River. But this one is rare in that the stone is most unusual. Even the great statue in the temple itself is of black granite. Ah, there are many strange stories about that statue, many strange stories. . . ."

"Stories?" Léonie had been eager for information, but Lamartine had been lost in his thoughts.

"I must know what the message is on the statue." She had pressed him. And today, hopefully, she would know.

Monsieur Lamartine's office was covered in the dust if not of dynasties, at least of several years. He swept off a chair for her and sat her down with a pleased smile on his face. "At last we have it, madame. Now we know what it says!"

"Oh, Monsieur Lamartine, quickly, tell me." She leaned forward, waiting breathlessly for his words as he began to read.

"It is a fragment of a poem," he said, "that was found inscribed on the gates of the Temple of Mut at Karnak—alas, now only a crumpled ruin. Sekhmet, in her loving and protective role, was associated with Mut."

"And the poem," she urged anxiously.

"I shall read it to you, madame.

> Praise to Sekhmet
> She is the mistress of all the gods
> It is she who gives the breath of life
> to the nose of her beloved
> She is the one who is great of strength
> Who protects the lands.
> Protector of those she loves.
>
> Sekhmet with fearful eyes
> The mistress of carnage
> The messenger who brings pestilence and death
> Sekhmet the great mistress of power
> Who sends her flame against her enemies
> Her enemies have been destroyed. . . .

Léonie shivered as the words, written thousands of years ago in ancient Egypt, echoed into the dusty silence of the room. Sekhmet, she thought, the name ringing in her head. Sekhmet. Yet the words, now she knew them, were ambivalent.

"I think, madame," Lamartine said, smiling, "that like all the gods, Sekhmet is only what you seek in her. The perfect mistress of the powerful man, the mother figure who will fight to protect her children, or a ruthless woman who will stop at nothing to gain her own ends, even murder."

Léonie took a deep breath. "Well," she said with a shaky laugh, "I've had the statue all my life—I even slept with it in my bed when I was a child, I loved her, she was my friend—I don't believe Sekhmet is evil."

"Then that is what you see in Sekhmet, madame, and that is the way it should be." Lamartine handed her the transcription of the hieroglyphs. "I'm happy to have been able to help you, madame, at least we've solved the mystery."

"Yes," Léonie answered doubtfully. "I suppose we have."

❧20❧

MAROC, immaculate in his black frock coat and starched shirt, walked down the sweeping staircase from the first-floor drawing room and sent the footman to fetch a parlormaid. "Yes, sir?" The girl came hurrying toward him. "Louise, the flowers in the main salon are already drooping. I shall complain to the florist tomorrow, but meanwhile put them in fresh water and remove the pollen dust from the tables."

"Yes, sir, of course." She bustled off, anxious to please him. This was the best household to work for in Paris; they paid the best wages, gave more time off, and madame always had a nice word when she saw you around the house. She knew all of the servants by name—*and* where they came from *and* about their families—and often asked about her little sister, she did. She was a nice lady, no matter what people thought of her. And Maroc was the best butler in Paris, she should know, she'd worked under some tartars who fancied themselves as good if not better than their bosses, but he was all right. He ran a good, tight household and that was what counted and nobody took the role more seriously than he, young though he was, you had to admit that. *And* he adored madame. Gossip in the kitchen said she used to work with him in a lingerie shop years ago, but it was probably only gossip. Madame was such a lady.

Maroc watched as she carried the big flower arrangements carefully down to the garden room. He could trust her to take care of them, but he'd give that florist hell in the morning. He'd have sent them back now—he glanced at the walnut and gilt grandfather clock ticking mutedly in a corner by the big double doors—but it was already too late. Guests were expected in an hour and everything must be perfect.

The dining table was set for sixteen, the most Léonie would allow at the big table. If there were to be more, they used the small round tables for six, arranging them in groups, which she enjoyed—said it was more intimate and made for better conversation—but Monsieur always liked to have everyone at the same table. Privately, Maroc thought it was because he could keep an eye on her that way. If she were off at a table without him he didn't know what was going on. Not, of course, that anything was. But Maroc had no doubt that Monsieur de Courmont was a very jealous man.

He inspected the table critically, smoothing the skirt of the exquisitely embroidered peach linen cloth. Again, Monsieur preferred plain white damask, but this was Léonie's choice. The silver candelabra were heavy and the crystal glasses, which he picked up to check quickly their unmarked clarity, were so thin he wondered they didn't crumble in the mouth of some too-hearty drinker. Putting down the glass carefully, he thanked God he wasn't the one who had to wash them. A single gardenia floated in a crystal bowl next to each lady's place, their heady fragrance pervading the room, and a ribbon of tiny lilies twisted with ferns and greenery lay along the center length of the cloth.

At the sideboard Maroc checked the wines he had decanted earlier. Monsieur was very particular about his wines and in the two years he'd been working for them, he'd become something of a connoisseur himself. Léonie had explained his ignorance of his new job to Monsieur and he'd accepted it because that was what she wanted, even going out of his way to show him things, like how to decant the wine properly, though that was more because he cared about the wine than from kindness of the heart. Yet he was civil and he appreciated good work.

Maroc made his way through to the kitchen to check with the chef. To the chef's chagrin, Léonie preferred simple food—though, of course, by simple she didn't mean cheap. Maroc grinned, remembering the shared sandwiches in the alley behind Serrat. Now Léonie served fresh salmon and simple roast pheasant in season, and the best vegetables that the markets could provide, and Monsieur had baskets of fresh out-of-season fruits sent from the hothouses at his château twice a week. Léonie had taught the chef herself to make the Provençal *tian* that she liked so much. But mostly, when she was alone, she ate an omelette.

Bébé whisked through the kitchen door at his heels, snatching in her tail in the nick of time before it snapped shut. "That cat'll lose its tail one of these days," said the chef, setting down Bébé's dish of chopped chicken livers, receiving a purring rub of the head from her. He loved that cat, he had never allowed one in his kitchen before, but Bébé was different. Special.

"Everything in order, Chef Mougins?" Maroc scanned the immaculate kitchen, quietly busy with everything under control, as always.

"Can we expect to start serving on time then, Maroc?"

"Yes, Monsieur le Duc is already here." The cat sped through the door after him, scampering up the stairs to find Léonie. Bébé rarely let her out of her sight.

The vast bed with its headboard that looked as though it might once have graced the carved splendor of some Renaissance Italian palace was set on a raised dais in the middle of the room and Léonie lay alone in the very center of it, looking, without seeing, at the pale moiré silk walls. Champagne color, it was called, and it almost matched the color of her hair, unless she'd been swimming or out in the sun, when it became paler. The statue of Sekhmet, polished to a translucent luster, faced the bed on a tall plinth of solid marble, with that of Bastet standing next to her. Bébé, attracted by the warmth of the lamp that illuminated the statues day and night, often curled at the foot of Bastet's plinth, making Léonie smile as she looked at her twin cats, but not tonight. She could hear Monsieur in the next room, he'd already bathed and was, she supposed, dressing with his usual speed, already preoccupied with other thoughts.

She ran a tentative hand down her body, still damp from their lovemaking. This was his first night back after a long trip to Russia and, as he always did, he'd made love to her, claiming her again as his own. And she wanted him, wanted the dominance of his body. And when it was over, he had moved from the bed and gone to take his bath without even saying he'd missed her or that he loved her. But then, she smiled wryly, he had never said that—nor had she. But I would, if he would, she thought.

"Monsieur," she called. He appeared in the doorway fastening his studs, clasping the onyx cuff links. He was remote, preoccupied, already thinking of the next matter on the agenda, she thought bitterly. And she knew what that was. He was going home tonight after the dinner party, to Marie-France and the children. He spent a meticulous amount of time with his family, despite the fact that he now went his own way so publicly. Once Léonie had envied Marie-France her security as Monsieur's wife, but now she understood that she, too, was vulnerable.

She remembered with a shiver the time Marie-France had come to see her. It had been a lazy morning and she hadn't been prepared for visitors. She'd dressed hurriedly, having Julie pull her hair back as severely as possible, so that she wouldn't look as if she'd just emerged from some warm, tumbled bed. Marie-France had been pale and composed, with a calm smile playing about her mouth. "I know this is difficult for both of us," she'd begun, as they sat opposite each other drinking tea from exquisite china cups, paid for by her husband. "But I had to meet you. It wasn't just vulgar curiosity. I wanted to know what he needed that I couldn't give him."

Léonie had gasped with shock at her next words. "Do you love him, my dear?" Léonie had been unable to answer. She'd stared at the pale carpet, wishing she could hide in it. There was no way this gentle woman could know what it was between her and Monsieur.

"It was all right before I met you," she had told Marie-France quietly, "but now you have a face, one that I'll remember. And feelings—just like I do. Madame"—she had taken a deep breath—"I understood it was otherwise, but if I am ruining your life, causing you a deep misery, then I shall leave him."

"Gilles and I have been living separate lives for a long time. There were others, you know, before you. It's just my children I care about. I won't have them harmed and I won't have any scandal." She had shrugged. "Many men, as we both know, have mistresses. I feel he is lucky to have found someone as young and lovely as you. I have never understood what it was that Gilles needed, but hopefully he's found the answer." She had put down her untouched cup of tea and walked to the door, turning to smile at her. "Just remember, though, my children will come first if there should be any conflict." And with a gentle smile she was gone.

"Yes?" Monsieur's voice was impatient, interrupting her reverie.

Léonie leaned forward, gripping his hand. "Do you care about me, Monsieur? Tell me the truth, what do you feel for me? Do you care at all?"

"Of course I do, Léonie," he said as he shrugged on his jacket. "You belong to me."

She sighed and lay back against the pillows, watching as he adjusted his tie in her mirror. "I'm lonely, Gilles."

"How can you possibly be lonely? This house is never empty! And you have sixteen people coming for dinner in less than an hour's time—so perhaps you'd better get out of bed and get ready."

She had organized a dinner party as a welcome home for him, inviting a mixture of old friends and new acquaintances, but now she regretted it. She needed him, she wanted to be alone with him—to *talk* to him. "Let's send them all away; let's not have a dinner party. You and I could have supper together right here in my room."

"Don't be ridiculous, Léonie. Anyway, the party was your idea." He checked his watch. "Don't forget that I want to leave by twelve."

"I won't forget." She pulled the sheet over her head and buried her face in the pillow as Bébé leapt onto the bed, curling up in the curve behind her bent knees. "I don't know, Bébé," she whispered, "it's not that I'm bored, it's just that there must be something more than this."

* * *

She looks wonderful, he thought, watching her at the foot of the table. Léonie was wearing a black organza dress, sleeveless and high-necked, with a deep ruffle at the throat, and the black emphasized the velvet texture of her bare arms. Her skin had the smooth warm bloom of summer apricots and it still excited him. She was talking intently to some new young man she'd acquired, an artist, she had said when she introduced them, and he watched their heads bent together as they talked. She seemed absorbed in what the young man was saying. He felt a pang of jealousy, though he knew he had no reason—she was faithful. Verronet had a man on her all the time, he had daily reports on her every movement from the time she left the house to the time she came home. What had started out as a game was now a need—he had to know what she was doing, whom she met, and where she went. So consumed was he with the minute details of her life that he wished he could have the man eavesdrop on her conversations.

Why, he wondered, had she said she was lonely? She was never alone. But at least she was mostly with people he knew, like Caro and Alphonse. When he was away she went to parties or to the theater, he didn't keep her in prison—though he'd like to. The thought lurked in the back of his mind. He'd like to lock her away and keep her just for himself, then he'd be sure he'd never lose her. She belonged to him—hadn't he just proven that upstairs in her bed? He could still excite her, make her want him. She was wanton, his Léonie—the Léonie that only he knew.

She wore her hair loose, floating around her shoulders like a mantle of light, and she tossed it back impatiently. Her long amber eyes watched him watching her, and she smiled. Bending down she picked up Bébé and placed her on a corner of the table next to her. She knew he hated the cat to be on the table. Pouring some cream, she allowed the cat to lick it from her plate, glancing at him from under her lashes. His expression didn't change, he sipped his wine and continued to watch her with dark unreadable eyes.

Damn, she thought, why doesn't he at least *react?* I want him to be angry! To shout at me, yell, throw things—strike me! I can't bear this indifference, isn't he human? Doesn't he know we are allowed to show our feelings? Sometimes I think he feels nothing. The only time he's out of control is when he makes love and then I'm not sure it's pleasure he's experiencing—it's certainly not happiness.

The young artist was sketching on the stiffly starched linen napkin, a quick pencil study of Bébé, sitting on the corner of the table licking her whiskers. "But it's charming." Léonie laughed, pleased with the result. "I shall save it and have it framed." She had deliberately seated him on her left in an attempt to provoke Monsieur, hoping it would make him jealous—

someone new, a stranger in her life. She leaned closer to him, smiling. "Tell me," she said, "what's it like to be an artist? Is inspiration very hard to find?"

Monsieur signaled Maroc to fill the wineglasses as the hum of conversation flowed around the table. The bosomy opera singer on his right and the pretty young actress on his left began in desperation to talk to each other across the table, unnerved by his silence.

He had been away for a month and he missed her. Life was empty without her. Before it had seemed full to overflowing, with everything neatly in its place, everything under control. There had been Marie-France and the children, and then there had been his real life—his business world. The part allotted to women had had its place, but it had never taken over, business had always come first. But Léonie had crept into the corners of his mind and lingered there the way her fragrance—the sweet, earthy scent of jasmine—lingered in his nostrils. She had invaded his world, his public life and his private fantasies. He wouldn't allow it! He must keep her in her place. She was vulnerable, he knew what she needed to keep her happy. He'd show her the new property in the Loire. She had fancied a vineyard and this one was for sale—that would excite her—and he would give her the new share certificates tonight. He glanced down the table—and he'd have Verronet put someone on to that young man.

≫ 21 ≪

CARO FELT SURE that Léonie would wear a track on her beautiful sapphire blue Aubusson rug if she paced its length one more time—she'd been there for an hour already and so far she hadn't sat down once.

"Please stop," she begged her, "you're wasting your time fretting about Monsieur. You have to accept that this is the way he is."

"But, Caro, I never know if he even cares about me! Oh, I know"—she sat down abruptly on the couch next to Caro—"I shouldn't grumble, I made my bargain and I have everything any woman should want." She threw the envelope of securities onto the couch between them. "Even these! I have a beautiful house filled with beautiful things. Look at me: I'm one of the best-dressed women in Paris, the envy of other women because I live with Monsieur le Duc. I have everything I want . . . or so it seems. Do you know, Caro"—she leaned forward, whispering the words—"no other man has even made the slightest advance toward me . . . I don't even know if I'm desirable anymore."

Caro was shocked. "Doesn't Monsieur desire you?"

"Yes. Yes, he does, but sometimes I wonder . . . I'm not sure why he wants me, whether I'm even really there for him or whether he's just lost in his own needs and desires. And why should he want me, Caro, if he doesn't love me?"

Caro put her arms around Léonie as she began to cry. "Please don't, Léonie," she said, stroking her hair. "He's a strange man. I don't know if he's ever felt love for any woman. But I do know that he's obsessed by you—I'm willing to swear that he thinks of you all the time, that he *needs* you."

"Then let him tell me so . . . oh, why doesn't he tell me so?" Léonie sat up and dried her eyes. "Damn it, I'm never going to cry over another man. I swore that when Rupert left me."

Caro held up the envelope. "What's this?"

"His welcome home present to me."

Caro opened the envelopes and scanned the contents rapidly. They were share certificates—all in companies owned by de Courmont. She placed them carefully back in the envelopes.

"Well, at least he takes good care of you."

"But it's not enough, Caro. I dress the way he likes to see me dressed, I wear the jewels he gives me, I throw the right parties, invite the people he chooses, I go with him when and where he wants, and I'm always there—waiting—when he needs me. I'm the perfect mistress," she said bitterly. "I am everything he wants me to be. I feel as though he's created me!"

"Léonie, that's not true. You are *you.*"

"I envy those young people I invite to my parties, the opera singer who studies every day, and the pretty young ballet dancers who are struggling to make a name for themselves. At least their lives are real. I'm part of a fantasy, Caro. It's one long game—a tug of war. Sometimes I think I should take a lover." She resumed her pacing of the rug. "There was a young man at dinner the other night. . . ."

"You must be crazy," Caro said quietly. "No one cheats on Gilles de Courmont."

"I've never even kissed another man since I met him." Léonie was lost in her own thoughts, carried away by the torrent of her own words. "I think about Rupert sometimes, about how young and innocent we were, and how lovely it was."

"Rupert left you, Léonie, have you forgotten that?"

She had shocked her into silence. "I'm warning you now, Léonie, that deceiving Gilles de Courmont would be a dangerous game. Why do you think no one makes a pass at you—it's not that you're not attractive or desirable. It's because they're *afraid* . . . afraid of Monsieur! He's known as a ruthless man in business and I've seen how he is with women, he can turn to ice in a moment and leave you wondering why, what it was you did that upset him. But a lover . . . my God, Léonie, you must be crazy! He'll never let you leave him!"

Léonie stared silently at the floor, and Caro took her hand, feeling sorry for her. "Anyway," she added, "remember you made a bargain. A contract, you told me. Isn't Monsieur keeping to that?" She held up the stocks and shares.

Léonie sat down with a sigh, her anger exhausted. "I suppose you're right, Caro."

The crowd of smartly dressed people swarmed out from the theater onto the rue Royale laughing and talking about the show they had just seen as they drifted slowly down the street. Monsieur signaled the waiting driver. "No, please, let's walk," suggested Léonie, "it's a lovely night."

"Very well, if you'd like. I've booked a table at Voisins."

"Why don't we go to La Coupole, it's full of interesting people, artists and writers."

"I like Voisins and I thought you did."

"But we always do the same thing, go to the same places—see the same people. You never take me anywhere different."

"Nonsense." He took her firmly by the arm, hurrying her across the street.

"Anyway, you're here so rarely."

He laughed at her grumbling. He knew she was angry because he was leaving for New York.

"I think I'll leave you," she said, testing him.

He kept on walking. "Of course you won't," he said.

"Why won't I?"

"Why should you? Don't you have everything you want?"

"Do I? Do I, Monsieur?" She willed him to say he loved her. Say it, say it, her mind throbbed with the words.

She stopped, forcing him to turn and face her. The tree-lined street was cheerful, the brightly lit cafés filled with people enjoying themselves. There was a snatch of music in the air, a feeling of gaiety. "Take me with you to New York," she begged, "let me come with you just this once . . . please, Monsieur."

"I can't do that, Léonie."

She didn't bother to ask why not. The answer was always the same.

"We'll go to the south for a few days when I get back."

"But that's not what I want," she said bleakly.

"What do you *really* want?" His eyes bored into hers, dark and unreadable.

She wanted to force him into revealing himself, provoke him into a reaction that was more than passion. She wanted to be loved by him. "I want to be with you. I love you, Gilles."

He turned his face away. "I told you in the beginning, Léonie, there was to be no talk of love."

"I'd like to have a child."

For the first time his face showed real anger as he stared at her, his eyes blazing. "That is the most stupid thing you have ever said, Léonie. You are my mistress, not my wife." He walked to the curb and hailed a cab. She climbed in sullenly. The words had just come into her head out of the blue, and they had reached him. At least he was angry.

"I didn't mean it," she said in the silence.

"I won't discuss it," he replied stiffly. "Except to say this: my children are with their mother, my wife . . . and those are the only children I intend to have. What is between you and me is another matter."

They drove the rest of the way in silence, dinner forgotten, climbing the steps of their house together, each heading for their own room. Bébé ran toward her anxiously; Léonie picked her up and held her comfortingly close, but there were no tears. She was not going to cry any more tears for Gilles de Courmont. She recalled her own brave words as she had waited for him to come to her at the inn: she was going to be her own woman. She had played him at his own game and won then. Well, she was tired of being the docile, waiting Léonie.

≈22≈

MAROC sat at a table outside La Coupole waiting for Léonie. The café was crowded and noisy and the white-aproned waiters hurried at a reckless pace between tables, balancing metal trays of beer and *citron pressé*, brandy and coffee, somehow keeping track in their heads of everyone's tab as money clinked busily into the little saucers left for their tips. The iron-curlicued awning kept out the shower of rain that had suddenly darkened the midday sky as Léonie ran toward him, clutching Bébé, who refused to get her feet wet in the rain.

Panting, she brushed the raindrops from her hair. "Oh, Maroc," she said, kissing him on the cheek, "I'm so glad to see you."

They met regularly, once a week for lunch at some brasserie or inexpensive café. She had told him in the beginning that even though he was to be her butler, he was also her friend and they must never forget that. And he knew she valued their friendship as much as he did. She told him everything, pouring out her heart to him, and he watched over her in the house, observing Monsieur, wondering how she could stand his coldness. In Maroc's view she was imprisoned in that wonderful house, trapped in a luxurious life-style—and not only by Monsieur, but also by her own needs.

"Let's have cheese," she said, "and lots of crusty bread, and a bottle of white wine ... I'm starving, Maroc."

She was exceptionally cheerful, he thought, calling the waiter. "You look happy today," he said, watching the man who had just taken a seat at the next table. Hadn't he seen him before? He couldn't place the face, but the thought nagged at him.

"I'm thinking of going to the inn for a while," she said. "I'd like to see how the garden is looking and I want to put in a new kitchen. It'll make Madame Frenard's life easier. I've got lots of plans for it, Maroc; it's going to be even more beautiful. I'd like to extend the terrace and make the steps wider so there's easier access to the beach, you know how difficult that slope can be just before you get to the house. . . . Oh, I forgot, you've never seen it. Well, soon you will ... and you'll be my guest, not my butler."

He was glad to see her looking happier. She'd been so quiet the week Monsieur had left, never leaving the house, barely even leaving her room. And now here she was, bouncing with energy again. "Is it making new plans for the house that's cheered you up?" he asked.

"That and my new approach to life." She broke off a chunk of bread from the baguette, buttering it lavishly. "I'm leading my own life from now on, Maroc. I'm no longer just a 'lady in waiting' for Monsieur."

He'd observed all their battles, knew her secrets. He knew Monsieur. "I hope you're not going to do anything foolish, Léonie."

"Like take a lover?" She grinned at him mischievously. "I'm not looking for one, but ..." She shrugged her shoulders.

"Léonie, you can't do that! Don't you wonder what he might do if he found out?" Maroc leaned across the table and grabbed her hand. "Listen to me, Léonie, he's dangerous."

"What can he do? He's made me an independent woman, he can't throw me out because the house is mine, I have enough money, and," she added confidently, "men like Gilles de Courmont don't kill their mistresses.

But don't worry, Maroc, I'm not looking for a lover. I'm simply going to use my time the way I please. I'm not sure what that means, but I'm tired of this fantasy world." She reflected bitterly on her lack of education. She was improving, thanks to Monsieur and to her own addiction to books and newspapers. Now she could converse on current events and discuss the latest novels or criticize the newest opera or play, but she feared she would never catch up on those lost childhood years when she might have learned so much more. Yet there was time, and her instincts were good. She knew what she liked, and if her conversation wasn't that of a scholar, at least it was bright and amusing. "I wish I could paint or write books or sing . . . that's real. But as I don't do any of those things, maybe I can help some of those who do. There are lots of struggling artists who need someone to buy their work and Monsieur has enough money to become a patron. Perhaps I'll even start my own gallery. . . ."

Léonie was carried away on a wave of enthusiasm and it seemed harmless enough. She fancied herself a patron of the arts now, and why not? She had good taste, and plenty of money.

"I must dash." She kisssed him good-bye. "I'm going to see the new exhibition at the Gallerie Marechaux."

She set off at a brisk pace down the street, her blond hair flying like a flag behind her, a smartly dressed, beautiful woman who turned heads as she hurried by. He frowned as the man at the next table tossed some money into the waiting saucer and pushed his way through the crowd, disappearing in the same direction as Léonie. *Where* had he seen him before? He remembered suddenly. He was usually to be seen sitting at the café at the corner of place Saint-Georges, opposite the house.

Léonie wandered slowly through the Gallerie Marechaux, staring at the paintings on the wall, occasionally consulting the small catalogue she held in her hand. Impatient with such slow progress, Bébé tugged the lead from her hand and, claws skittering on the polished boards, trotted toward a patch of sunlight in the window. Sniffing the solitary painting displayed there, she dismissed it as uninteresting and, nose tucked under tail, curled herself up for a quiet snooze.

Alain Valmont watched in amusement as the cat arranged herself in front of his painting, noting the long velvet ribbon that dangled from a thin collar of what looked to be diamonds around its neck. Well, the creature didn't detract from the painting, in fact it added an extra touch of sensuality, it had the same quality of relaxed abandon as his women. He'd been talking to Marechaux, but the man's attention had been quickly diverted by the woman at the end of the long gallery.

She must be rich, Alain supposed, studying her. That dress was expensive and she wore it with the sort of unconscious ease that breathed money. No jewelry, her hair just tucked into a band and pulled back severely from a surprising profile, not classically beautiful, it was too dominant for that. He analyzed her face with a painter's critical eye: the chin was a little too firm, the cheekbones flared so widely that the eye sockets were deepened. There were wonderful hollows and angles to that face, and a slumbering eagerness to her expression as she became aware of his gaze and her eyes met his. Oh, yes, she was lovely, there was no doubt about that. Léonie turned to speak to Marechaux. So she was a buyer, well, he just hoped she would buy one of his. He needed the money.

He lounged in a chair by the window waiting for Marechaux to finish; perhaps he could coax another small advance out of him, he needed paint and the tab at the Café Alsace was getting bigger. Monsieur Lucien was tolerant with his artist customers but every now and then he had to be given something on account—he already had more paintings on his walls than most galleries possessed, all given in lieu of payment.

Léonie couldn't stand Marechaux hovering at her elbow like that, she'd rather be alone. She wanted to take her time, to look at the paintings that caught her eye, not the ones he pointed out as being of special merit. She wanted to find out what it was *she* liked. And besides, she thought sneakily, I want to take another look at that young man.

He was sprawled in a chair and his feet in their shabby shoes were propped on a second chair as he lay back enjoying the patch of sunlight by the window. He looked relaxed and perfectly at ease. Léonie circled nearer, pretending great interest in a small and muddy landscape. I hope I don't have to buy this in order to get to know him—she smiled to herself, peering more closely at its tortured trees—I'm not sure it's worth it.

"You should take a look at the painting in the window," said Alain, without moving his position. "It's much better than that."

She hadn't expected him to speak to her and she was flustered. He could tell by the way she spoke, hesitating at first and then in a sort of a rush. "Oh, I'm just looking around, I wanted to see everything."

"The one in the window is mine and it's by far the best painting in this bastion of commercialism."

"If that's the way you feel about the gallery why do you exhibit here?"

"Money." He opened his eyes and stared at her. "Money, my dear . . . so that some rich lady such as yourself can come along and buy them, so that I can buy more paint and a little wine and a crust of bread, so that I can paint more pictures to put into commercial galleries like this one. I'm your typical starving artist." He got slowly to his feet and bowed deeply. "Alain Valmont, madame, at your service."

Léonie eyed him cautiously. There was a fascination about this tall emaciated young man with the penetrating greenish eyes that made her unsure of herself. He wasn't handsome and he certainly wasn't smart—in fact, staring at his paint-stained fingers and unshaven face, she wasn't even sure that he was clean! But he was attractive. "Show me your painting, Monsieur Valmont," she suggested.

"It's in the window, though I think your cat is attracting more attention from the passersby than my painting."

Bébé rolled onto her back and stretched, displaying her perfect slender furry belly and elegant limbs, turning her head to one side with coquettish charm, making them laugh.

"She's like every woman I've ever known," he commented. "No matter how angry you might be, when they flirt like that, you can forgive them anything."

Léonie avoided his gaze and looked instead at the painting. The woman lay in bed amid a tangle of sheets, a delicate back and a swirl of hair—nothing much to it, just a few brush strokes, a veil of color, pale yet passionate. It held a feeling of intrigue, she didn't know why, it was quite innocent really. "It's very interesting," she said, slightly at a loss to know what to say to an artist who stands waiting for your judgment. "I'd like to see more."

He hunched his shoulders and turned away. "I only give Marechaux one at a time, that way he can claim it's unique and ask more money."

He was attractive, this young man. He was dark and thin and vital, with a tense expression and eyes that seemed to notice everything, every detail of her face, her body. "I'd like to paint you," Alain said suddenly.

"Paint *me?*"

"You're different. I like the bones of your face and the length of your spine, the way your body arranges itself—like the cat. Of course," he added, "you realize that I paint only nudes." He watched her face for the reaction, smiling as she blushed. So this rich girl could still blush, could she? "Think it over," he said with a casual wave of his hand as he made for the door, "Marechaux has my address."

Léonie looked again at the delicate painting in the window. It was disturbing, but she couldn't think why.

She went to the desk and told Monsieur Marechaux that she would buy it without even asking the price. "Oh, and by the way," she added casually as she made out the check, "you'd better give me that young man's address. I may have a commission for him."

Place Mirabeaux was not squalid, as she had expected, nor was it seedy. It was just worn down to the gray poverty of the respectable people who made up half its tenants and the negligent life-style of the artists who were the other half. Léonie wished suddenly that she hadn't worn the white kid shoes, they looked so clean, so unscuffed and out of place. She pulled off her white gloves hastily and hid them in her purse before knocking on the door. There was no answer and she shifted nervously from foot to foot. Of course she shouldn't have come and of course she wasn't going to let him paint her, but she wanted to help him and she liked the painting. She had propped it up on the table next to her bed, examining it carefully under the light. It was more complex than she had first thought, it had taken layer after layer of brush strokes to achieve the veiled texture, and the girl was so eloquently alive, even though she was relaxed. She wanted to see more, perhaps buy another.

She knocked again. "Oh, for God's sake, come in if you must, the door's open."

"Hello," she called, peering inside, "it's me, Léonie Bahri. We met the other day at Marechaux's."

He didn't turn from the canvas he was priming. "Have a look around if you want. I'll be with you when I've finished this."

She looked around the big bare room. Its whitewashed walls were splashed with color where he had tested his palette and adorned with dozens of canvases. The big window on the far wall filtered a cold gray light through its grime-encrusted panes and she wondered with a smile if that was the reason his paintings had that particular quality of veiled color. She gave a pleased sigh, it fitted exactly her romantic idea of how the studio of a struggling young artist should look. She liked it, she liked the smell of paint and thinner, the piles of canvases, the sketches made quickly and tossed aside. Feeling bolder, she prowled the room examining the canvases, some completed, others started and abandoned. It was exciting, seeing these living paintings, quite different from staring at them on gallery walls. And *she* felt different in this room, it had an energy that was lacking in her rooms, in her life. She stared again at the paintings. They were all of women, sullen half-beauties in cluttered feminine disarray—displayed on tumbled beds in cramped, darkened rooms. There was a quality to their nakedness, she could feel it, they emitted vibrations of sexual energy, either of love just consummated or just about to begin. Do I look like that for Monsieur? she wondered fleetingly.

She could feel Alain's eyes on her and she met his gaze, raising an eyebrow as he took her in from head to toe. "Do I take it that your work is autobiographical?" she asked.

Alain threw back his head with a shout of laughter. "They're all girls from around here, some are professional models—others just came along."

Léonie turned back to the paintings. They were of girls like she had been—poor, yet attractive, working girls. She didn't blame them for accepting what Alain Valmont had to offer. Life with him, she thought with a pang of envy, though it might have been for a short while—maybe only for as long as it had taken to paint them—would have been interesting, and real. There was a down-to-earth quality about him that was very appealing. "I would like you to paint me, Monsieur Valmont," she said. "Of course, I shall pay your fee. But I want a portrait exactly like those."

He wiped his hands on an oily rag. "You bought my painting from Marechaux?"

"Yes."

"It's a good one. It'll be worth some money one day. Meanwhile, of course, he overcharged you. This one will be cheaper."

"I want it to be a large painting," she protested.

"The size has nothing to do with the quality, you know," he said scathingly. "I don't paint the kind of nudes you find over the bar in a cheap gaming club."

"I'm sorry, I didn't mean that, of course. It's up to you what you paint."

"Léonie Bahri, I shall paint exactly what I see."

At first it was difficult because Léonie was surprisingly shy about taking off her clothes. She had lingered behind the screen. Only after Alain had called her impatiently had she emerged, clad in a robe of soft gray cashmere that covered her from neck to ankle like a monk's habit, except where it clung to her curves. It was probably the sexiest garment he could ever have imagined, though she had obviously worn it for precisely the opposite reason.

He sat her on a chair and sketched her face while she held the robe closed around her neck, staring out of the window expressionlessly until he threw the charcoal to the floor in a rage. "For God's sake, where have you gone?" he asked her.

She looked at him with concern. "Did I do something wrong?" There was a length to those amber eyes, a slumberous upper lid, and he sketched quickly.

"Keep quiet and keep looking at me like that."

Finally he'd gotten something on paper—just a glance, but it was a start. "Right, just loosen the robe a little, ease it off one shoulder."

Léonie arranged the robe neatly around her shoulders and Alain tugged at it, until it slid sensuously down one arm, revealing just the upper curve of her breast. He tilted her head so that she looked over her shoulder at him, warily, chin slightly down. Perfect—he caught the expression in rapid strokes, smudging the curves with his finger to soften the line.

"Now take off the robe," he said, walking to the littered table and choosing a brush. He'd prefer to sketch her body in watercolor.

She couldn't do it. With a shock she realized that she had only undressed for two men in her life and they were men she had made love with. This man was asking her coldly and dispassionately to stand naked in front of him and she couldn't do it. She'd thought it would all be so easy, she'd just lie on a bed while he painted. She hadn't thought beyond that.

"Well?" Alain had the paper already dampened and was impatient to start.

She stood frozen in front of him, clasping the robe around her. "I'm sorry, Monsieur Valmont," she said in a small voice, "but I don't think I can."

He threw the sketchbook on the floor. "Goddamn it," he yelled at her, "you're wasting my time! Why? Why can't you take your clothes off? You must have done it for a dozen other men!"

Léonie drew back, stung by his remark. "What do you mean?" she glared at him angrily.

"You *know* what I mean! There's a body under that robe and I wouldn't be the first to have seen it."

She turned on her heel and stalked across the room to the screen, kicking at it angrily and remembering too late that she was barefoot. "Oh, oh, *damn* it!"

"That'll teach you to keep your robe on in my studio, you stupid woman. All I wanted to do was paint you!"

Léonie pulled on her clothes hastily, before he could reach her, fumbling with the buttons on her blouse, and tugging the skirt over her hips. He leaned companionably over the screen, resting his arms on top, watching as she thrust her feet into her shoes. "You've got big feet," he said with an amiable grin, "but then I suppose every goddess has to have one flaw." His anger seemed to have disappeared as quickly as it had come, but still she eyed him warily. He was unshaven and the blue workshirt he wore was splattered with paint. He had rolled up the sleeves and she noticed the fine dark hair growing smoothly on his forearms.

"Léonie Bahri," he said, "I think what you and I need is a nice relaxing lunch. A glass of wine, a little pigeon pie . . . I know just the place." He headed for the door, turning as he opened it. "Aren't you coming?" he asked with a grin. Léonie picked up her purse and hurried after him. "Oh, by the way," he said as he followed her down the stairs, "you're paying!"

He supposed it was the café and the wine that had relaxed her more than anything else. Monsieur Lucien's carafe red was potent and fruity and she had blossomed as he knew she could in the steamy little café with its mirrored walls and tiled tables. They had paused by the door to watch the chess and domino players, and they scanned the blackboard, choosing the dish of the day which, as he had known it would be, was pigeon pie. Alain had grabbed the carafe of red that Monsieur Lucien pushed across the zinc counter and swept her to a table by the window. It was early and still quiet and Léonie sniffed the atmosphere like Bébé, smelling the sawdust on the floor and the garlic from the kitchen, the cheeses on the counter and the coffee constantly on the brew. She settled back against the faded leather banquette and smiled at him. "I used to work in a place like this," she said.

Nothing she said could have surprised him more. She was, then, a girl with a past! "I assume it wasn't by choice," he said, examining her face intently—had he got those eyelids quite right, weren't they hollowed a little more right there, by the nose?

Léonie laughed. "No, it wasn't by choice."

"Tell me why you wouldn't take off the robe." He was leaning toward her, elbows on the table, resting his head on his hands; his young face looked almost haggard, he was so thin. His greenish eyes grew darker when he was angry.

"I don't know. Yes, I do. I've only taken my clothes off for the men I loved."

"Then you had to love them . . . to make love I mean?"

He was too inquisitive. "You know what I mean," she said lamely.

"We could have done that," he said with a grin. "I'd do anything to sell a painting."

She laughed and drank her wine. "Here's our pigeon pie," she said, as Monsieur Lucien appeared bearing steaming casseroles.

"So fresh they're almost flying, madame," he said, presenting her plate with a flourish and placing a second carafe of wine on the table. "Here come your friends, Monsieur Valmont."

The table was suddenly crowded and extra chairs were dragged forward as a group of young people shouted hello, calling their orders to Monsieur Lucien and darting back and forth as they greeted other friends.

Léonie sat quietly, watching the activity with eager eyes. They all seemed to know each other intimately and were immediately friendly, treating her as part of their group. "I'm Laura," said the dark-haired girl, squeezing in next to her on the banquette, and Léonie recognized her immediately as the girl in at least four paintings in Alain's studio.

"And I'm Jacques." A blond boy, no more than nineteen and thin as a reed, pushed in on her other side. "Sorry, but there's not much room. I made a sale this morning. What's everybody drinking?"

There was a camaraderie and an intimacy about them—and the café—that felt warm and comfortable, in the same way the inn did. It was a place that put people at ease and made them welcome and where they knew they would always find a friend just to talk with, or to listen to their complaints and problems and offer consolation. This wasn't fantasy, they were real people with real lives, struggling to succeed in a perilous vocation, gambling on their talents. How she envied them!

"We must go," said Alain finally, "I've got work to do."

Her feet felt lighter, and smaller, she thought, still stung by Alain's remark about them. "What are we going to do now?" she asked, as he took
her hand and walked across the street.

"We're going to take your clothes off," he said with a grin.

And he had. Discreetly at first, dropping the robe low over her back, so
that he could sketch the spine and the twin hollows at its base and the lean
curve of her hip. "Further," he had commanded, "just drop it a little further, Léonie." And she had, holding it behind her in her hands so that she
stood naked, her head tilted so that her hair flowed back, almost touching
her waist. "Wonderful, wonderful . . . you're lovely, Léonie, now move
around just a little, let me see your breast, raise one arm. Perfect, my darling, you have perfect breasts . . . rest your foot on the chair . . . ah, you're a
wonderful model . . . throw your head back, my beauty, feel how lovely you
are, don't you feel it?"

She felt it and it was marvelous. She was loving it—posing for him,
flaunting herself as he directed her, adding a little extra, a provocative gleam
in her eye, an arch to her back so that her breasts pushed forward, lifting her
rib cage until her belly was one taut lovely line. She trembled with the excitement of it, and he sketched her, capturing her flagrant arousal. And
then, inevitably, he made love to her.

She spent all her time with him, arriving at eight every morning and
tumbling into his bed with hugs and kisses and laughter, bringing with her
fruits and cheese for their breakfast. They'd hide naked under the covers,
nibbling on the peaches and licking the juice from their chins, gossiping
cheerfully about their friends from the café, and then he might make love to
her, or he might be too anxious to get on with his painting, and either way
she was happy. Although she didn't know if she was too happy with the
pose. He had arranged her, finally: stretched out on the bed, covering it first
with a ratty piece of bronze fur borrowed from a friend. "You're an animal," he said, "and I intend to paint you that way." Léonie was afraid to
imagine the result and he wouldn't allow her to look. She'd thrown her
heavy hair forward and then tossed it back, so that it tumbled and flowed
around her shoulders, partly covering her breasts, and she'd rolled onto her
side, like a contented cat after some enormous meal, stretching her long
legs. It wasn't difficult to be naked in front of him now, laughing as she
posed, until their excitement was too much and she pulled him onto her.

Sometimes, she thought, as they sat in the café at night, I think this is
what I like most. I like the bustle and clatter and the plat du jour and the
rough red wine and Alain's friends. They had accepted her as Alain's new
girl and that was all that was needed to belong. And she'd always wanted to
belong. Sometimes she would slip in there alone and share a glass of Pernod

with Monsieur Lucien, who was always glad to see her, for she would discreetly pay off their outstanding tabs and for once the slate behind the bar would be clean.

Caro had been waiting for Léonie all afternoon, pacing the lovely salon and staring anxiously out of the windows. At last she heard her footsteps and ran to meet her. In a simple blue dress with her hair tangled and windblown, Léonie had the aura of a woman who was enjoying herself. There was a secretive gleam in her eye as she greeted Caro.

"That look can mean only one thing," Caro groaned. "You've got a lover."

"It's not the way you think," began Léonie defensively.

"Léonie, don't you realize that Monsieur will *kill* you if he finds out."

Léonie shrugged. "He won't find out, Caro," she said confidently. "I have a perfect alibi. I'm having my portrait painted."

"That's funny. I always thought painters needed good light for their work, unless of course your artist works by moonlight."

"Well, naturally, we have a little dinner and some drinks afterward— but always with his friends. We're never alone."

"And you're never alone in the studio?"

"Oh, yes . . . yes, Caro. We are." She laughed at Caro's startled face. "I can't help it," she said triumphantly. "Monsieur always said I was a wanton woman. And Alain is . . . oh, Caro. It's different from me and Monsieur. It's . . . it's sort of friendly. It's just . . . fun," she added lamely. "That's all."

"Monsieur gets back next week," said Caro, "and I suggest you have your portrait finished by then. Otherwise, I'm afraid there'll be trouble. Please take care, Léonie." She put her arms around her friend and hugged her. "I love you, you know, I don't want anything bad to happen to you."

"Like what, Caro? Nothing bad will happen to me, I promise you. This has been good for me. I feel better. I'm even looking forward to Monsieur coming back . . . although I'll miss my evenings in the café," she added wistfully.

"I'll need a few more days to complete it," said Alain, standing back from the canvas and eyeing it critically.

She swung her legs off the bed and came toward him. "Let me look, please?" she begged him. "After all, I'm the one who posed—it's my picture."

He wiped his brush on a rag and shrugged his shoulders. "Take a look then."

She stared in surprise at her painted image. It was her all right, stretched full length with her arms in front of her and her chin resting by her shoulder, staring slumberously out of the canvas from a tangle of hair that partially covered her breasts and matched the soft triangle just revealed by the curve of her leg. But it was the light that was so extraordinary, the painting had a sort of golden glow, a special illumination, as though the sun had crept into some shady spot and left wisps of golden light, veiling the body with mystery, layered with tender minute brush strokes of fading color until it was more than a picture of a lovely woman, it was a transparent fairy creature from another world. "It's beautiful, Alain . . . it's more than me. More than I deserve."

"It's you all right. One part of you, Léonie Bahri." He kissed her lightly on the forehead. "When will I see you?"

She hesitated. "I don't know. Not for a week or two perhaps."

"It'll be finished by then. I'll miss you."

"And I you. But I'll be back."

They parted lightheartedly and she ran across the road to pay Monsieur Lucien before she made her way back to her wonderful house on the leafy square.

❧23❦

WAS SHE DIFFERENT? She looked the same, sounded the same. She had welcomed him cautiously but warmly, and considering the way they had parted, he couldn't have expected more.

The yacht was berthed at Antibes and each morning at dawn he stood at the wheel and personally guided her through the tangle of craft in the busy little harbor and out to sea, watching as the sun emerged from the haze.

He hadn't made love to her yet. He slept alone in a cabin at the end of the deck, not trusting himself to touch her. He brooded silently at the wheel.

Léonie wondered what was wrong. Was he still angry because she had said that she wanted a child? Or was it that she had said she loved him? He hadn't mentioned it, but there was a distance between them that wasn't of her making. They were alone, except for the crew. He had invited no guests and after a week of silent dinners and long empty days when she had thought she might go crazy, she had begun to wonder if perhaps *he* was crazy.

She swam before lunch, cutting a solitary path through the swell, glancing up at the storm clouds scudding toward them.

He helped her from the ladder and put a towel around her shoulders. "I shall be leaving for Paris this afternoon," he said curtly. "I have some business to take care of."

"Am I going with you?"

"No need, amuse yourself here." He put a hand on her shoulder and she bent her head suddenly and kissed it. She lunged for him, wanted his arms around her, wanted desperately to create the old magic between them. Monsieur said nothing, just removed his hand and walked away. "I'll get changed then," she said. It sounded like an offer, but he turned his back and leaned on the rail, staring at the villa-dotted coastline.

Was this his way of dismissing her, of saying he was tired of her? Would he come back? She smiled wryly. That's the story of my life, she thought, always waiting, always wondering if some man will come back to me.

When he had finally gone, she and Bébé went to the inn. She'd been there one or twice in the past couple of years, but Monsieur hadn't liked to let her out of his sight and she rarely had the time alone. Now she realized what she had been missing. It had the old magical quality of peace. The sun-warmed tiles of the terrace felt comfortably familiar to her bare feet, the hills still smelled of thyme, and her room was cool and simple and held memories of the girl she had once been, making her feel guilty as she thought of Monsieur and of Alain. She had told Caro the truth, that the affair had just been fun. She had liked being with Alain, but it was casual. They were friends.

Her relationship with Monsieur was complex and troublesome, and she lay on the bed wondering what she should do. He couldn't possibly know about Alain, there was no way. She was sure of that. So, therefore, he had to be angry with her for saying she loved him. But *why?* Even though he may not love *her*. She felt sure now that he didn't. He didn't even touch her anymore. He hadn't touched her once—oh, yes, just that one time on deck when he'd put his hand on her shoulder and she'd kissed it.

She refused to wait and worry, and instead put her energy into planning out the gardens, ordering shade trees and plants, and dashing between Nice and Monte Carlo in search of rare species, even managing to persuade Monsieur Blanc to let her have some of the wonderful tropical plants from his casino gardens.

Monsieur had been gone for ten days and she had given up expecting him, or rather she had not been waiting for him—she didn't wait for anyone anymore. Those were her rules. When he was not there her time was her own and she'd fill it as she pleased.

She was sitting on the terrace, barefoot as usual, with her hair tied back in a scarf and her skirt hitched above her knees, shelling peas into a bowl in her lap. "The very picture of domesticity," he said with a smile.

She looked up at the sound of his voice. He was smiling. What was it that Alphonse had once said to her? "He only smiles when he's winning." "Hello." She went on shelling the peas.

"Are those for our dinner?"

"If you're staying for dinner."

"You once promised me you'd bake that Provençal dish with the eggplants ... how about keeping that promise tonight?"

She looked at him in surprise. "Would you like that?"

He slipped off the canvas espadrilles he was wearing and sat next to her on the steps. Picking up a pod he shelled it, putting the tiny yellow-green peas into his mouth.

"You're supposed to put them in the basin," she told him.

He caught hold of her hand. "I know. Léonie?"

"Yes."

"Let's be friends. I missed you. That's why I was so miserable ... don't ask me why, but I couldn't say it—I wanted to. I'm saying it now. I missed you on that trip."

She looked at him, suspicious of this sudden change. What could have happened in Paris? Had he made some fabulous business coup? Bought out a rival or taken over another company? It could be the only reason for such elation. Or was he trying to bribe her with words now, instead of diamonds? She felt a flutter of anticipation, wanting to believe that he meant it. He'd said it, hadn't he? Said *he'd* missed *her!* Wasn't that almost as good as saying he loved her? She put the basin on the step beside her and moved closer. "Why didn't you say that before?"

"It's not easy for me, Léonie."

She stood up, shaking out her skirt, and he bent and kissed her ankle, holding it tightly in one hand, gripping it with his fingers until it hurt. "Ow," she cried out, laughing as she limped away.

"That's just to let you know you belong to me," he called, "and, Léonie ..."

"Yes."

"I've brought the champagne."

She smiled as she went into the house and her spirits rose. Maybe this time everything would be all right.

* * *

They ate on her terrace with just the light of the moon and a single candle that burned steadily in the breezeless night and he talked of his cars, passionate about the details of their engines and design, and of his travels, amusing her, entertaining her with all his old charm. So that she knew why she cared—she loved this side of him—and he was so attractive. They walked on the beach, wading in the water that was colder than either of them had expected, and hidden by the curve of the Point, he finally made love to her, slowly and deliberately claiming her as his own, until at last she cried out that she loved him.

❧24❧

THE MAN WAS almost invisible, he was so ordinary—one of a million who looked just like him—brown hair, small brown ragged mustache, brown clothes. It had taken weeks for Maroc to realize the fact that he saw this man almost every day, and although obviously not wealthy, he seemed to have no work. He idled away his days in the Café Saint-Georges at the corner of the square, or he sat on a bench in the gardens reading a newspaper, always just within view. And then next time Maroc looked, he'd be gone. And it was always when Léonie had left the house. Today he would find out why.

Dressed as inconspicuously as his prey, he sat four tables away and sipped his coffee, watching the man. He was reading his newspaper and yawning, apparently in no hurry to go anywhere. Maroc knew that Léonie would leave the house at ten o'clock and it was now five minutes before the hour. He folded his arms and waited. The waiter appeared with a plate of hot croissants and coffee, and putting his paper aside, the man began to butter his croissant just as Léonie emerged from the house. Cursing, he broke off a chunk of croissant, stuffing it in his mouth; throwing some money on the table he set off down the street after her. He signaled to a cab and climbed in as Léonie drove off around the corner of the square.

So that was it. Monsieur was having Léonie followed. With a pang of fear, Maroc remembered her visits to the artist. But no, Monsieur had been back several weeks now and everything seemed quite normal. He stared worriedly at his coffee. Naturally he must tell her, but what would they do?

* * *

Léonie ran light-footed up the familiar dusty stairs to the studio and tapped on the door. "Open up," she called impatiently, "it's me." There was no reply. "Alain." She turned the handle, but the door was locked. She stared at it in surprise, it was never locked. She hurried back down the stairs and across the cobbled street to the Café Alsace.

It was exactly the same, the big glass windows were still steamed over and the old men in the corner still played dominoes, nodding a polite bonjour as they recognized her. She glanced around quickly. Alain was not there, nor were any of his friends. It was early yet and they probably wouldn't be there until after twelve. Monsieur Lucien hailed her from his usual place behind the zinc counter.

"Monsieur Lucien . . . have you seen Alain? I've been to his studio, but it's locked."

He looked at her in surprise. Could Alain have gone without telling her? That was very unfair, it was certainly no way to treat a girl as nice and as generous as this one. "I thought you would have known," he said. "Alain left for London a few weeks ago."

"London!"

"Alain had a stroke of luck . . . some visiting gallery owner from England saw a painting of his at Marechaux and came to the studio to buy. He was so impressed with his talent that he offered to take all Alain's paintings and mount an exhibition in London. In fact, mademoiselle, he offered to become Alain's patron: he will make sure that he has a studio, everything he needs, and his paintings will be sold through his gallery. But he insisted that Alain move to London for a year—it was the only way to have continuity of work, he said. Alain was thrilled by his good fortune and we had such a party in here that night, mademoiselle. I'm sorry you missed it."

"But wasn't it all rather sudden, Monsieur Lucien?" asked Léonie uncertainly.

He shrugged, throwing out his hands expressively. "But, mademoiselle—that's the way fortunes can change in his business. One painting can alter the course of a man's life."

Léonie pushed aside the selfish feeling of regret at losing Alain and the happy times they'd shared. "I'm glad he had such a marvelous opportunity," she said. "Maybe my portrait will be worth a lot of money one day. Did he leave it with you, Monsieur Lucien?"

"As far as I know, mademoiselle, he took everything with him—they just packed it all up the next day and he was gone. It was fast—before he could change his mind." Monseur Lucien shrugged at the thought of such foolishness. "As if Alain would turn down an offer like that."

Léonie slid from her stool at the counter. "Then I suppose he must have kept it." Perhaps it's as well he did, she thought, remembering Monsieur.

She walked slowly down the drab street that had ceased to be drab for her when she was part of it with Alain and his friends. Somehow they'd warmed it into color and life. Now it was gray again . . . a drab little street in a poor *quartier*. The inconspicuous little man in the brown suit blended so exactly into the drab background that she wasn't even aware of his presence.

"Of course he's capable of it, Léonie," stormed Caro. "Didn't I tell you that a long time ago? Monsieur is capable of *anything!* And he's clever, he'll never do the obvious thing, so you won't know what to expect."

"But to have me *followed*, Caro! How could he do that? Oh, I wish Maroc were wrong." She didn't want to believe it.

"He's not wrong, Léonie. Of course, if you hadn't had this stupid affair there would be nothing to worry about. The man would have found out nothing. The thing we don't know is *when* he started following you—and *why*. Don't you think there is something *odd* about Alain's disappearance, Léonie? That he should have such a sudden stroke of good fortune, be discovered just by chance—a chance that was only offered if he went to London . . . out of the way. . . ."

Léonie stared at Caro in amazement. Could it be true? "I don't believe it," she protested.

"You don't believe it because you don't *want* to believe it. If Monsieur even *suspected* you were having an affair, don't you think he would find a way to get rid of the man? He does it in business all the time. He finds out what they want and provides it and then he takes over. Alphonse told me his method. And it never fails."

Léonie began to laugh. "Then I'm glad that at least Alain will benefit from my folly," she said. "I always wanted to be a patron of the arts!"

"Léonie," said Caro, exasperated, "you don't seem to realize the position you're in. I believe that if Monsieur had known for sure that you were having an affair with Alain, he might have *killed* you, or *him*, or *both* of you."

"He'd never do that." Léonie was quite sure about it. "Do you know why? Not because of me, but because of his children. He has two sons, Caro, and they come first. Nothing will be allowed to sully *their* name, there'll be no breath of scandal. Marie-France de Courmont will make sure of that. Anyway, if it amuses him to spy on me, then let him. My life is blameless from now on."

"I hope so," sighed Caro.

* * *

It was an odd sensation, knowing that she was being followed. Now that she was aware of it, she seemed always to be noticing the man, he was always there—just at the corner of her eye, hiding behind a newspaper, sitting in a cab, or loitering aimlessly along the street. Léonie felt sometimes that she ought to stop and tell him where she was going—it would make it all so much easier—but at other times, she became bitterly angry. She wanted to confront Monsieur with his spy, tell him how despicable it was, how underhanded and mean. But how could she? She was guilty. It might force a confrontation about Alain and she didn't want that, not now when things were going so well.

Monsieur was spending more time with her, teaching her at last the things she had wanted to learn. He took her to inspect properties, not only in Paris but in industrial cities where he bought up land on speculation, knowing where industry would need to expand and where factories would be built. She invested her money alongside his, buying more shares in the de Courmont Automobile Company. His cars were his passion—he talked of little else, neglecting other business matters to devote more time to them, and already the first models were on the road. He drove a bright red one himself and to her it looked a clumsy vehicle, long-bodied, strapped with leather, glinting with brass handles and lamps and gadgets. It had padded brown leather seats and even a small Lalique crystal vase to hold flowers. She had rushed to Worth and bought a dress of scarlet silk, as bright and brassy as the car itself, and he'd driven her to the theater, enjoying the sensation they had caused in their wonderful automobile. "It's the best advertisement I could have," he had said, as he helped her from the running board. "You'll see, Léonie, soon Paris will be full of cars—and most of them will be de Courmonts." For the first time, he had allowed her to share his excitement in his new business and she had been pleased to be even such a small part of it.

Best of all, he had promised to take her to New York with him. He was to leave the following week and Léonie was busy shopping, buying suitable clothes for the occasion—the first time he had so publicly acknowledged that she was more than just his mistress. She would be on his arm as his woman, the one he had chosen to share his life with, the woman he loved. And she felt sure he loved her—hadn't he said that he'd missed her? Missed her so much that he was taking her with him this time? She wanted so much for him to love her. She wanted to be secure in his love.

She hurried into the Fortuny salon, hoping they would have her evening gowns ready. She'd chosen them with Monsieur in mind and they were all the same style: long fluid sheaths of pleated silk open to a *V* almost to her waist, curving to her body when she moved, clasped low on the hips with a barbaric belt of semiprecious stones of the same color and silken tassels. She had bought the same model in amber and jade, aquamarine and amethyst, topaz and crystal. They were superb.

"Madame looks marvelous in this dress," the vendeuse murmured admiringly as Léonie inspected herself in the mirror, twisting around to examine the back. The delicate fabric swung in a loop from her shoulders, bare to the waist. It was sensational. Monsieur would be proud of her in New York.

She smiled at the vendeuse. "They are perfect. Please have them delivered to my house—no, wait, I'll take this one with me." She picked out the crystal dress. She would wear it tonight, just for him.

He could forgive her anything, he thought, when she looked like that. She was waiting for him in the big salon and she'd chosen her setting well. The dress had the same opaque quality as the fabric on her walls, a veil of mist that skimmed her body, sparkling where the belt of crystal beads clasped her narrow hips. In the lamplight even her hair seemed paler. She'd braided it into a thick elaborate plait entwined with beads so that it hung, glistening, down her smooth back.

The windows were open to catch the breeze and he recalled suddenly and vividly the night at the hotel when he'd made love to her in the blue salon. He accepted the whiskey from Maroc and took a seat by the window. It was very hot tonight.

"Do you like it?" Her face was eager for his approval.

"It's wonderful."

"I've arranged a special dinner for tonight, come and see." She held out her hands to him.

"Are we having guests?"

"No guests. Just you and me." She showed him the table. "We are having omelettes," she said, "and a salad, and a simple glass of wine." She laughed. "Like an old married couple."

"I'm quite happy with an omelette," he said indifferently.

"Ah, but you see, you can have any sort of omelette you like—an omelette with caviar or smoked salmon or truffles. Or *fines herbes?*"

"I must leave right after dinner"—he checked his watch—"in fact, in half an hour."

She wondered what was wrong, surely not the children? "Monsieur, the children, they're not ill?"

"No, they're not ill. I've decided to send them to school in America for a while. They'll be leaving with me next week. As will their mother."

"Their mother? Then . . ." She couldn't finish the sentence.

"Exactly, my dear. I'm afraid you won't be able to go on this trip. Perhaps next time."

Léonie could actually feel the tremor inside her body, as though the blood were shivering in her veins.

"Please don't bother to stay for dinner," she said, her voice very quiet. "I'm sure you have more important things to do."

"I'm sorry to disappoint you, Léonie, but as you can see, I have no choice."

"I don't want to discuss it any further. Your life obviously goes on without me." She trailed from the room, a gray wisp of shadow, her blond braid swinging as she went.

His eyes were cold as he watched her go. I could forgive you *almost* anything, Léonie Bahri, he thought, remembering Alain Valmont, but not *quite* all. We must all accept our punishment.

Léonie heard him leave. She wandered aimlessly down the stairs and peered into the dining room. The table for two looked so inviting, set with the thin crystal glasses that were his favorites and the simple fine porcelain she'd chosen because she knew he preferred it plain. Her anger boiled suddenly, tearing at her, consuming her. With one blow of her arm she swept the table clear amid a splintering of glass and a crashing of china. "Léonie Bahri," she screamed into the empty echoing silence that followed it, "you're not meant to be any man's mistress!"

She fled the next day to the south, taking only Bébé and one valise, hastily packed with the simplest clothes.

Maroc accompanied her anxiously, pacing the platform with her as the train steamed and puffed, preparing for its journey.

"But Léonie, what shall I say to him? Are you coming back?" This time it was serious; he felt it from her attitude. She had contained her anger, but it flowed inside her like a volcano ready to explode, a layer of heat to cover the hurt that she felt at the core.

"I never want to see Monsieur again. Caro warned me about his methods: he promises exactly what people want and then he takes them over. That's what he does to me, Maroc: he finds out what *I* want most and then he takes it away. He tortures me . . . how can I live with a man like that!"

"Léonie." He patted her hand gently. "You've always come back before. This has happened many times, it's a game the two of you play."

"Is it, Maroc? Am I as guilty as he?" Maybe she was. But weren't her faults the ordinary, human ones? She didn't wield godlike power over people the way he did.

She could see the despised man, like a shadow at the end of the platform. "Anyway, he's sure to know where I've gone," she said bitterly. "His spy will hurry off to telegraph his report as soon as the train pulls out. Oh,

Maroc." She held him tightly as her tears began to flow. "The trouble is that *I love him.*"

Bébé began to howl, a thin eerie wail, and Léonie picked her up, hugging her comfortingly. "It must be the steam," she said. "The train has frightened her."

She leaned from the carriage, holding Maroc's hand. "Who would have thought, Maroc, when you and I first became friends, that our lives would turn out like this?"

"Life isn't over yet, Léonie," he said, as the train began to move.

❧25❧

BÉBÉ ROLLED in the sunshine on the terra-cotta tiled window ledge, abandoning herself to its warmth, waving a lazy paw at a bee as it droned across her line of vision. Léonie was out on the hillside planting things in her garden. They had been there for almost two months and she was up with the sun every day, digging, raking, hoeing, and planting. In the evening, when the sun was low, she watered her plot, treating each of her precious plants tenderly, as though she could urge it to grow strong just by kindness. "One day you'll see," she'd said to Bébé, "this will be a beautiful garden and I will have created it."

Monsieur Frenard had terraced the hillside down to the beach and the two of them pored over her plans and sketches, for she knew exactly what she wanted: a line of shade trees here on the west and an ornamental pool on the bit of headland that curved around the beach with a bench beside it so that at sunset she could sit beneath the jacarandas and look out across her pool and the sea. She'd planted palms and jasmine and yucca and oleander, and she loved them all.

"It's the most satisfying thing I've done in my whole life," she told Monsieur Frenard as she cleaned off her hands. "Look at me"—she held them out for inspection—"there's dirt under my nails and calluses from digging. I'm a woman of the fields, Monsieur Frenard. Back to my peasant beginnings."

At night she was so exhausted that she slept like a log, not dreaming or worrying. She did that in the daytime. All day. She had gone over the scene with Monsieur endlessly, wondering why? *Why* had he done it? *Why* did he *always* do it? One thing was certain, she never wanted to see him again. Or maybe she did so she could tell him that she hated him, that he was a monster and she wanted to tear his eyes out, to kick and bite and hurt him! How could she love him? But sometimes she would want him desperately, long for the power of his presence, feeling waves of passion for him that she fought against, telling herself that she didn't want him.

After a few weeks, the first pain had passed and she had thrown herself into her work, which was at least disciplined and satisfying—at the end of each day there were results that she could see and each week her plants grew and the garden developed.

She had heard nothing from Monsieur and had no idea whether he had returned or if he was still with his wife and children in New York. It was none of her business anymore. That part of her life was over.

She had become a country girl again, not even venturing into Monte Carlo or Nice. The inn was truly her home. The peace that she had always felt in its welcoming warmth comforted her. One thing she knew for certain: the little man in the brown suit was nowhere to be seen. Monsieur Frenard checked every day and confirmed that there were no strangers in the village. "Anyone hanging around here would stick out like a sore thumb," he reassured her. "I know everybody around these parts. This is no place for a spy, Mademoiselle Léonie."

Straightening her aching back, Léonie examined the path that she had made leading across the garden and down to the rocks where she liked to bathe. She had dug it and smoothed it herself and then paved it with broken slabs of rock and old terra-cotta tiles in a patchwork of shapes and colors, filled in with smooth pebbles from the beach. The sky was darkening rapidly and even as she looked there was a flicker of lightning on the horizon. She gathered up her tools quickly, cleaning off the trowel with a tuft of grass and wiping her hands on the cotton skirt she had bought in the village of Saint-Jean. Bébé trotted eagerly toward her, hoping it was time for a walk.

Thunder rumbled across the water as the lightning flickered again, illuminating the sail of a small boat tacking toward the shore. There wasn't a breath of wind and its sails hung limply under the menacing purple sky as it tried to outrun the coming storm. Léonie watched anxiously from the headland above the rocks, wondering whether he would make it. A zigzag of lightning cleaved the sea suddenly as the wind and rain began, thrusting the boat toward the rocky Point. She ran down the slope to the beach, barely able to see through the driving rain, slithering over the rocks, trying to keep her sodden hair out of her eyes as she struggled toward the spot the boat had been heading for. She was upon it almost before she saw it, beached neatly into a sliver of sand in between the rocks. There was no sign of anyone on board and Léonie stared at it in concern. Could he have been swept overboard? The sea boiled and foamed, soaking her feet, spitting back at the lightning and rain, roused angrily from its usual blue tranquillity. "Is anybody there?"

A head appeared from behind the sail. "I'll be with you in a minute. I'm just trying to get this damned sail down before the wind rips it to pieces."

Léonie sank onto a rock, her knees weak with relief. "I thought you were dead."

There was a laugh from behind the sail. "What, me? Never. I've been in worse storms than this one—and in smaller boats. There, that's that." He jumped from the deck and surveyed his work with satisfaction. "Did a good job, didn't I? I spotted this bit of sand from out there and realized it was the only place to head for, just made it before the storm really caught me." He turned to her with a smile. "But thank you for your concern."

He was young—probably her own age—and as wet as she was. His hair was plastered to his head and water was dripping down into his eyes. Léonie began to laugh. "What a sight we must both be," she said, struggling to her feet.

He put out a hand to help her. "Well, if *you're* here, there must be food and shelter to be found—or is this a desert island? I don't know how good I am at building huts from palm leaves and hunting for wild berries to feed you."

She laughed. "There's no need for that, there's an inn at the top of the slope."

"Wonderful. The boat should be safe here until the storm blows over." He rechecked his vessel, making sure she was secure. "There's more weather in that sky yet."

Léonie watched him curiously; he was efficient, capable. He knew what he was doing. She needn't have worried about him.

"Let's go." He took her hand as they bounded up the hill together, arriving laughing and panting at the top, slithering together through the mud of her sodden garden until they reached the terrace, where they sat down for a moment to take off their wet shoes.

He looked appreciatively at the inn. "I couldn't have been shipwrecked at a better place. Do you think they'll have a room for me?"

"Oh, I dare say," she replied. "I'll speak to Madame Frenard for you."

"You work here then? Fantastic—I was rescued by the fair maid from the inn. I should write a song about you."

"Wait here," she said, leaving him dripping in the hallway. "I'll get you some towels and some dry things and then I'll show you your room." In the kitchen she explained their visitor to the Frenards, returning minutes later with an armful of towels, a pair of workman's pants, and an old shirt. "I don't suppose they'll fit." She smiled ruefully. "Monsieur Frenard is wider than you, and shorter."

"They'll do," he said cheerfully. "Now lead the way, fair maiden."

Léonie showed him to a room and hurried off to change. She wondered what he looked like when he was dry and, catching a glimpse of herself in the mirror, mud-spattered and rain-soaked, her hair an unkempt tangle of sodden strands, she laughed. No wonder he had thought she worked here. Well, there was no reason to disillusion him. She did work here.

She bathed quickly and changed into a fresh cotton skirt and a soft white shirt, rolling up the sleeves in a workmanlike fashion. She toweled her hair, braiding it loosely out of her way, and went off to help Madame Frenard in the kitchen. It was almost suppertime and the inn had a guest. Her first guest. It was exciting.

Charles d'Aureville buckled the old blue pants around his lean waist, smiling as he rolled up the ankles—at least if they were too short it was better to make them shorter than having them flap around his calves. His canvas boat shoes were still wet so he had to go barefoot. He hoped they wouldn't mind. His glance took in the small room overlooking the rain-swept sea and he counted himself lucky to have found such a snug haven. He'd better find the girl, buy her a glass of pastis, and thank her for her help. He could smell food cooking.

Following the delicious aromas, he made his way along the corridor to the small dining room. The girl, neat now in a skirt and shirt, was setting a table with blue-glazed dishes. She looked up as he came in, swinging the blond braid from over her shoulder, smiling at him with the most amazing eyes. Was this the same girl? "Hello, it is you, isn't it?" he asked with a grin.

Léonie stared at him. He was tall with the wiry, muscular leanness of an athlete. His dark hair curled crisply and his curiously light eyes—were they gray or hazel?—regarded her quizzically.

"And it is you," she answered. "I can tell by Monsieur Frenard's pants!"

"You certainly look better than I do." He laughed. "I must thank you for coming to rescue me. There's just one thing ... what would you have done if I'd been swept overboard?"

"I'd have gone in after you, of course, I'd have fished you out."

He believed she would! "Well then, my brave rescuer, will you share a bottle of wine with me?"

Léonie plunked the bottle on the table. "This is on the house," she said, "we never charge shipwrecked mariners. We usually find they have no money in their pockets."

He slapped his hands to his pockets—of course, he didn't have any money! "I'll pay you back," he promised. "My mother taught me always to be honest and never to take money from a woman."

Léonie laughed, filling their glasses. "The sky is clearing. Shall we go out onto the terrace?"

"Look," he said, "if you've got work to do I'm quite happy to hang around the kitchen. I used to do quite a lot of that at home when I was a kid . . . I'm a terrible scrounger, no one was safe from my charm. I could get anything I wanted from the cook, even her best chocolate cake before it was really cool enough to slice."

"I bet you were thoroughly spoiled."

"You're right, though I always thought Edouard more spoiled—he was older, so he'd had more opportunity."

"Edouard?"

"My brother."

"I see. Well, we needn't go into the kitchen, I'm allowed a little time to myself."

"I don't even know your name," he said, surprised.

"Nor I yours."

"I'm Charles d'Aureville."

"And I'm Léonie Bahri."

They wandered onto the terrace, laughing. Madame Frenard, peeking through the kitchen door, watched them go. "That's better," she said. "She needs some company."

He lived at the family château, near Tours, where he managed their estates. "What I really like most are horses—the racing sort—and boats, not necessarily in that order," he told her. "I was in Monte Carlo for the yacht race last week—no, I didn't win. I came in third, but I gave it a good try. Next time I'll do better." He glanced at her work-roughened hand holding the glass of wine. "And what do you do?"

"Oh, a little of everything. I cook, I work in the garden, do the dishes . . . the usual things."

"Isn't that boring? I mean, a girl like you . . . well, you are very pretty." She was looking at him with those lovely long eyes, an enigmatic look that he couldn't read. "I'm sorry, I didn't mean to offend you . . . I mean I wasn't making a pass or anything."

She frowned. "That's all right. Every girl likes to be told she's pretty. Tell me more about yourself." She leaned against the wall at the edge of the terrace. "What's it like to be nineteen and be in charge of vast estates and to have a big family and horses and boats?"

"Hey, wait a minute. First of all, I'm twenty-two, and the estates are not that large. Just a decent size. The house was built three hundred years ago by a d'Aureville and we've managed to live there ever since. My mother seemed to run it like a hotel—it was always crowded with friends and grandparents, uncles and aunts and cousins. It brimmed over with people and pets—dogs, hamsters, guinea pigs, cats, rabbits, horses—you name it. The river ran through our parkland and Edouard taught me to swim."

"Your older brother," she prompted.

"Yes. Edouard was the perfect older brother; he taught me all the things older brothers should—how to swim, how to sail a boat, to ride— and helped me with my schoolwork."

Madame Frenard poked her head through the window. "Dinner is ready," she called.

Charles was disappointed, he liked being with her. "Will you have to go and help?"

"We don't seem to have any other customers tonight—no one goes out around here when it's wet!"

"Then would you have dinner with me? I'd be awfully lonely all by myself." He smiled at her winningly.

"I'd like that," she said, eager to hear more about his family.

For her, his life was more fantastic than any tale from the Arabian Nights, he was a Scheherazade telling her the stories she longed to hear, tales of a mythical childhood in a château on the Loire, where summers were full of long, sun-dappled days with favorite ponies and faithful old dogs, of swimming with great troupes of friends in a chilly pool dammed from the river, of stealing apples and plums from their own orchards. And there were always strawberries in June and a lovely mother who made sure they washed their hands before supper, refusing to banish them to a nursery, claiming that she needed her family around her constantly, that they were the joy of her life. Winters were crisp and there were hunts in the forest when they were older and Christmas Eve was a festival, always with the same traditional food and Midnight Mass and trooping back again afterward, not sleepy at all, to have mulled wine—more lemonade than wine really—and hot sticky buns in front of the roaring fire in the hall, while the grown-ups laughed and kissed each other and wished "Happy Christmas" and everyone opened presents.

"And your brother?" she asked. "Tell me about him."

"Edouard is the adventurer of the family," he said, in between mouthfuls of her *tian*.

"Go on," she prompted.

"There's a story about Edouard my mother always loves to tell," he continued. "One morning when he was only six, he packed a bag with the necessities of life—an apple, two slices of chocolate cake, and a teddy bear—and set off for the village, en route for Paris. When he arrived in the village he sat on a bench outside the inn to eat his cake—walking, he'd decided, was a hungry business. The patron spotted him and, recognizing him as the young one from the château, sent someone to tell my mother, meanwhile giving Edouard a big glass of milk to go with the cake. When she arrived, she threw her arms around him in relief and asked where he was going. 'Adventuring,' he said, 'I'm going to the jungles and the lakes and the mountains, in Africa and China.' 'Can't you go later?' she asked him. 'When you're a little bit older? After all, I need you now.' He looked at her very seriously, thinking it over. She always swears it was touch and go—her or the jungle—and then he agreed to stay. 'But only for a while,' he said, 'and because you really need me.' " Charles laughed. "He managed to keep his promise until he was sixteen, and then he was off: first to Africa, the land of his dreams, and then all the other places. And now he's twenty-five years old and he's in Brazil . . . miles away, up the Amazon, bringing rubber from the jungles."

"You must miss him," she said enviously, "such a perfect elder brother."

"Edouard is my best friend. There's nothing I couldn't tell him. It's hard to explain but . . . well, Edouard has a quality of tenderness that's rare in a man. That probably sounds strange, but if you ever met him you'd know what I mean. As an elder brother he loved me almost like a father; he always allowed me to join in his games without being pressured by my mother. He used to stand in front of a semicircle of his friends and say, 'This is Charles, he's my brother and he stays with me,' daring them to refuse. And they never did . . . and so I stayed." He laughed reminiscently.

"And you, Charles, did you ever want to run away to far off lands like your brother?"

He looked into her eyes—those strange wonderful eyes, like a sleepy animal's. "No, I like it here. I like my horses and my dogs, and the farms. I like everything the way it has always been." Bébé leapt onto the table next to him. She began to purr, rubbing her head against his arm. "Why, you flirt," he said, laughing, sleeking back the fur on top of her small head. He looked up in astonishment. "My God," he said, "this cat is wearing diamonds—and rubies!"

Léonie shrugged. "Perhaps she had a rich father," she said with a smile.

"But can they be real?"

"I doubt it, but she looks equally pretty wearing fakes, don't you think?" She pushed back her chair. "Let's go out onto the terrace and see if the stars are out. Maybe you'll be able to rescue your boat tomorrow."

The sky was cloudless and the air balmy and warm, as if Odin and Thor had never heard of the Côte d'Azur. "Tell me about yourself," he urged as they paced the terrace together. "There's a mystery about you. You're too exotic to belong here." He watched her face, waiting for a reply. Her lower lip was round, cushiony, tempting.

"Exotic? I'm afraid not. I'm just an ordinary kitchen maid. The only exotic thing about me is that my father was Egyptian."

"Then," he said, taking her hand and kissing the harsh, worn fingers, "perhaps you're a goddess . . . a maker of destinies, a weaver of spells. . . ." He put up his hand and unfastened her braid, fanning the hair about her shoulders. She smelled fresh and cool, of jasmine and peaches.

Léonie walked away, leaving him foolish and stranded at the end of the terrace.

"Léonie. I'm so sorry. I didn't mean that. Well . . . yes, I did mean it, but not the way you think."

Dear God, she thought, he's so very sweet. He thinks that I think he's taking advantage of the poor servant girl! When really I didn't want him to kiss me because I didn't know where it might end.

Charles was abject in his apologies. "Forget it, forgive me. I lay myself at your feet." And he did, spread-eagling himself on the terrace and kissing her toes until she laughed, wanting him to kiss her mouth this time. He did, tasting deliciously of sun and wind and wholesome goodness and all the things she craved.

It was very late, they had talked their way far into the night. Taking his hand, she led him to her room and they lay there together side by side in the big bed, holding hands and talking in whispers about how he must be up at dawn to check the boat, and how lucky he had been to find her, and how lucky she had been to find him. And then he kissed her and held her and she relaxed in his young loving arms, letting him make love to her and dreaming that she was part of his big happy family, that she, too, was one of the d'Aurevilles of the sun-filled summers and the happy Noëls. As long as she was in the arms of this purveyor of her dearest dreams, she, too, belonged.

She woke him at dawn and they went down to the boat together, climbing the rocks and wading across little tidal pools to its secret harbor. "I hate to leave you," he said, holding her hands and gazing into those beautiful eyes. "It's a night I shall never forget as long as I live. You are a goddess, Léonie Bahri. You have magic about you." He put his arms around her and kissed her tenderly and she smiled as he waved to her. The boat rode easily in the water, waiting for its master, and with the brisk morning breeze he hoisted sail and set his course. "Good-bye, Léonie," he called, standing at the helm.

"Good-bye Charles . . . take care." I'll never forget you either, she added in a whisper.

A week later there was a letter from him. She took it down to the beach to read, sitting on the rocks where she had met him.

"Dear and lovely Léonie Bahri," it read.

"I told you that my mother said that I should always be honest and I should never take money from a woman . . . therefore as an honest man I'm enclosing a sum in payment for my room and board at the Frenards. Please thank them for me.

"And, magical Léonie—sorceress, goddess, weaver of spells—thank you for being with me, for giving me a night from your charmed life, for being as beautiful as you are, and as loving and gentle . . . need I say you have a place in my memories. . . . Charles."

She folded the letter carefully and walked slowly back to the inn, thinking of him. She would keep his letter forever—he was her memory, too.

⫸26⫷

MARIE-FRANCE DE COURMONT had never seen Gilles quite like this. He'd been many things—charming, bitter, amusing, cold, remote—but never indecisive. He had insisted quite suddenly on taking the boys to America to look at schools, overriding her protests that she couldn't bear to leave her children so far away; then stay there with them, he had replied, indifferently. And once they had gotten there he looked at a dozen schools, narrowed his choice down to two, and then the whole subject had been dropped as though it never existed. When she had asked him about it, he had said he'd think about it later. She'd heard Verronet questioning him about the new cars and again he would put off making an important decision, and she knew from Verronet it wasn't the first time. It was as though

Gilles, who had never left his desk with a paper on it, who'd stay there until he had everything under control, couldn't concentrate. And work was his passion.

Now that they were back in Paris, it was no better. He was up most of the night—she knew because she'd see the light on in his bedroom—and he wasn't working, so what *was* he doing?

"You look tired," she said to him over dinner one night.

"Really?"

"Are you not feeling well, Gilles?"

"I'm perfectly all right."

"Perhaps you've been working too hard. You should take a rest. Why don't you go down to the south, you know being on the yacht always does you good."

Gilles stared at her in surprise. She was offering him the excuse he had been looking for. "I'll think about it," he replied.

She pushed back her chair and Bennett hurried to help her. "I'll go and say goodnight to the children and then I think I'll have an early night myself. Goodnight, Gilles . . . and Gilles . . ."

"Yes."

"Maybe you should see a doctor, have things checked out?"

"You're exaggerating again, Marie-France. I'm perfectly all right."

She shrugged. "As you wish."

Gilles lit a cigar and sipped his brandy, alone in the dining room. The long table, polished to perfection, reflected the silver candelabra, pointing up his loneliness—candlelight was meant for two, for romance and attraction. Oh, God, how he missed Léonie. He was desperate for news of her. There had been no letter from her, no message. She had gone for good. The man in Saint-Jean had a rough time trying to keep a watch on the inn and had found it impossible to infiltrate the locals. The cigar went out and he relit it: he walked through the hall to his study, pulled the big chair close to the window, and gazed out across the Seine.

He'd intended never to see her again, she demanded too much. Oh, not like other women—not money and jewels and furs—Léonie wanted love. And love was the one commodity he didn't have to give. What did he feel for her then, he wondered. For feel something he most certainly did. It was painful, his need for her. And why had she said that she wanted a child? A child! She must have been crazy. Didn't she know the demands children made—no, not made, expected? They expected love—and he wasn't prepared to give it to anyone. Except that was the one thing she wanted, the only thing she needed. Léonie wanted to be loved.

He leaned back in the chair thinking about what to do.

If he wanted her back, he must tell her he loved her. It was so simple he wondered why he hadn't thought of it before.

* * *

The stormy weather had lingered, lurking on the horizon and darkening the evening sky with purple clouds, just as it had when Charles had been washed up on her doorstep two weeks before.

Léonie eyed the clouds warily as she hurried back from Saint-Jean, running the last few yards as the heavens opened and the rain came down in torrents. "My poor trees," she gasped to Madame Frenard, shaking the drops from her hair. "If this goes on much longer they'll be washed away." She peered out of the window at the young cypresses she'd planted on the western boundary of her land, but it was impossible to see anything through the sheets of rain.

Madame Frenard had lit a fire in the sitting room, and Léonie sat before it drying her hair and watching Bébé enjoying its unaccustomed luxury.

"There's a visitor for you, Léonie," Monsieur Frenard spoke in a conspiratorial whisper from the doorway.

"A visitor? But who is it?" she whispered back.

He closed the door carefully behind him. "It's him, Léonie; it's Monsieur le Duc."

The shock sent a tremor up her spine again. Her throat felt dry and her heart was pounding. Was it nervousness? Or excitement? So he'd come at last! But had he come to claim her as his property or to say his final farewells?

Monsieur was standing in the little hallway, dwarfing it with his presence. Water dripped from his hair and his clothes, forming a pool on the tiled floor.

"My car broke down," he said. "I walked the last couple of miles."

"You'd better come in." Léonie held open the door to the sitting room. "I'll get some towels." She left him standing by the fire gazing after her and ran to the safety of the linen cupboard, giving herself time to get used to the idea that he was actually there. Damn it, she hadn't expected to feel this way, but he looked so vulnerable, all wet like that. And he was thin, he didn't look well. My God, was there something wrong with him? Léonie, Léonie, she said to herself, you're not supposed to care, you hate him, he's out of your life forever.

He was waiting where she had left him, and she handed him the towels. "Better take off your jacket," she suggested. "I'll put it here to dry."

She turned her head, unwilling to watch even such a small intimate gesture, remembering how she used to unbutton his shirt and put her arms around him, loving the way his naked chest felt next to her, feeling his heart beating.

"Léonie?" His hair was rumpled from the toweling and his shirt was soaked, too, as wet as his jacket had been. "I had to see you. I came to say that I'm sorry for what happened."

"I seem to remember you were sorry last time you came here. . . . Isn't it the same story?"

He shrugged. "It's difficult for me, Léonie," he pleaded. "You know that. I see now that what I did was cruel. But somehow when I did it it didn't seem that way—it just seemed the most convenient thing to do, to take the children to New York with me. I hadn't realized quite how much it meant to you."

"Oh, I think you did, Monsieur . . . you always know exactly what you're doing."

"You give me credit for more than I'm capable of. Surely if I'd known what I was doing, I wouldn't have behaved so stupidly, I'd have taken you with me."

"Oh, I can't bear it," she cried suddenly. "I can't bear to go through it all again. You'll say you're sorry and then I'll come back to you, and then you'll find some other way to torture me. Well, no. No, no. Never again!"

"Léonie, I need you." He held out his hands toward her. "Please Léonie, come back to me." She walked to the far end of the room as if she were afraid he might try to touch her, and he slumped weakly into the chair by the fire.

"What is it?" she cried in panic. He looked dreadful, he was white and shaking.

"I'm sorry, I'm really sorry, Léonie. I must have caught a chill."

"Madame Frenard, Madame Frenard. . . ." Léonie dashed from the room in search of brandy and he watched her through eyes that seemed to be rapidly dimming. He felt a numbing pain in his shoulder and began to cough; he hadn't planned on feeling like this, he'd wanted to sweep her into his arms, overpower her, make her feel that she needed him—and now he needed her.

He heard her come back into the room, but somehow it was too much effort to open his eyes. He smelled the brandy as she held it to his lips and forced some down him, making him cough. "Monsieur," she cried, "oh, Monsieur . . . open your eyes, tell me you're all right."

"I'll be all right—just give me a moment. I felt as though I couldn't breathe." He gasped as the pain hit him again, and she fled back to the Frenards. "We must get help," she cried. "Monsieur Frenard, please go into Saint-Jean for the doctor."

She knelt beside him on the rug, holding his hands. He could feel the warmth of her fingers on his frozen ones. The pain was lessening, not gripping him quite so agonizingly, and the sensation was coming back into his numb hands, tingling in his fingers. He pushed himself upright in the chair. "I'll be all right now," he murmured.

He was breathing more easily and she watched as the tension left his face. Gilles opened his eyes and gazed at her. "Léonie, this is ridiculous . . . I came to tell you that I couldn't live without you." He laughed and began to cough, his face contorting with pain.

"Don't, please don't," she urged.

"I came to tell you that I love you," he gasped. "I love you, Léonie."

She remembered Caro's warning voice. He finds out exactly what they need most and then he uses it to undermine them, everyone has their price. It's not true, she thought, he's telling me the words I've wanted to hear for so long only because he thinks he might die.

"It's all right, Monsieur," she said gently, stroking his fingers as they tried to grip hers, "don't hurt yourself by trying to talk now."

He moved restlessly in the chair. "I have to tell you. I must. Come back to me, Léonie. I need you. I love you. Please say you will." His eyes closed and he lay back against the cushions.

"Just lie still," she murmured. "The doctor will be here soon."

With the doctor's help they moved him into her bed and Gilles sank into its softness with relief. "I really should insist on sending you to the hospital in Nice," said Dr. Marbeuf, "even though you seem better at the moment."

"It's happened before, Doctor," Gilles replied, already impatient with his weakness, "and no doubt it will happen again. I'll stay here."

"The heart is an unpredictable organ, Monsieur le Duc," the doctor said warningly. "My advice would be to return to Paris as soon as possible and consult with your own specialist. However, if you choose to ignore my advice then at least take a rest. Go back to your yacht and do nothing for a few weeks. If you've been under too much stress, then you must try to remove as much pressure as possible."

Léonie listened from her seat in the corner. It was his heart then; she hadn't known there was anything wrong.

"It's all right, Léonie," he said after the doctor had gone. "I'll live. But I'm sorry I frightened you . . . except . . ."

"Except what?"

"Except it showed you still cared."

It was dark outside and the rain pattered on the windows, drumming on the terrace. Bébé stared out into the night, hating the rain. The silence hung heavily in the air.

Léonie walked over to the bed and looked down at his tired face, gazing into his eyes. "Did you mean what you said?"

He reached up his hand, touching her hair with gentle fingers. "I meant it. I love you, Léonie."

He lay back on the pillows watching as she unbuttoned her shirt and pulled it off slowly, and then the skirt, sliding it over her hips—her body so familiar, so beautiful. She slid beneath the covers, putting her arms around him, holding him close to her, comforting him with her nearness, sharing her strength. He felt like a child in her arms, protected and loved, soothed into sleep. Oh, thank God, he thought as his eyes closed, thank God she's still mine.

❧27❧

HE'S LIKE a young man in the throes of first love, thought Caro, as Léonie and Monsieur strolled arm in arm up the path from the inn to the waiting car. Monsieur was returning to Paris and she had never seen a man more reluctant to go. It was Léonie she was worried about; one minute she seemed like a woman in love, happy and carefree, and the next she would be remote and distant, preoccupied with her own thoughts. Caro waved as he climbed into the car and, with a last kiss from Léonie, drove off down the road to Nice.

Well, she thought to herself, maybe now I'll hear the truth. Has she found out she doesn't love him after all? Caro had been at the inn for only two days, hurrying down at Léonie's urgent request that she had something she must tell her, but Monsieur had lingered and there had been no opportunity to talk.

"Well, he's gone," Léonie announced with a sigh.

She sat on the steps leading to the shore, her knees hunched under her chin and her arms clasped around them. Was it just that she was going to miss him? wondered Caro. They'd been together on the yacht for over a month. Léonie always hated waiting.

"Caro, I'm pregnant."

She let the words sink in. "Oh, Léonie, oh, my God, are you sure?"

"Yes, I'm sure. I must have an abortion."

"Léonie!" She was shocked. "You can't do that . . . it's so dangerous." She shuddered at the thought. "But why not just tell him? I know what he's like, but surely we can work something out."

"Caro, it's not Monsieur's child."

175

Caro's stunned gaze met Léonie's.

"Then . . . who?"

"It's the one I told you about . . . the shipwrecked mariner."

"But it was just one night."

Léonie smiled. "Oh, Caro, that's all it takes."

Caro was silent, wondering what to do.

"You've seen the way Monsieur is now," said Léonie. "He's different, he loves me. This last month has been so happy, so calm, for the first time in years we weren't tearing at each other, trying to provoke each other. The games were over."

"Léonie, is there no way that Monsieur might think it was his child?"

"He told me once that his children were his and his wife's and those were the only children he intended to have . . . Monsieur is a very thorough man, Caro. He doesn't make mistakes."

They stared at each other, searching for a way out of the dilemma. "I must have an abortion," said Léonie flatly. "There's no other way."

She began to cry and Caro put her arms around her. "Don't, please don't cry. Of course, you can't have an abortion. I won't let you do such a terrible thing, Léonie. Think of the risk, you could die."

"Oh, Caro, don't you understand? Finally I have everything. Monsieur loves me. It's all I really wanted. And now, because of one night—just one sweet night with a young man who came along at a moment when I needed someone—I'll lose everything. Oh, how could I have been such a fool!"

Caro put her arms around her, letting her cry. "Don't worry, Léonie," she said soothingly. "Everything will work out. I won't let you kill yourself with an abortion . . . we must think of a plan. There *must* be some other way."

Verronet knocked on Monsieur's door. "Mademoiselle Montalva to see you, sir."

He looked up in surprise. "Caro?" What on earth was she doing here?

Caro swept into his office, kissing him on the cheek and taking a seat without her usual confident smile. "I've come to see you about Léonie."

He stared at her in surprise.

"I don't know whether you've noticed, Gilles, but she's not been looking well for the past few weeks. She's been complaining of fatigue and listlessness—and you know that's not like her."

It was true. Léonie had always brimmed with energy, even sitting still she seemed just to be holding back, waiting for action, and now all that had gone. She was quiet, too quiet; and since they'd been back in Paris, she hadn't wanted to go anywhere. He thought she was content just to be with him. Fool! Why hadn't he realized that something was wrong?

"She says she's not interested in food anymore," said Caro, breaking into his thoughts, "nothing tempts her. . . ." Well, that was true enough, she thought with a sigh. Léonie wasn't eating in a desperate attempt to stay thin so the pregnancy wouldn't show.

"She must see a doctor," he said anxiously. "I know just the man."

"I took her to a doctor this morning." She hesitated. "I'm afraid what he said was not good."

Oh, God, what was she saying? He pushed back his chair standing over her, gripping her shoulder. "Caro . . . what's the matter with her, what is it? Tell me, for God's sake."

"It's her lungs, Gilles, the doctor says that it's tuberculosis."

Léonie. His lovely Léonie was ill, maybe even . . .

Caro turned her head away, not wanting to meet his eyes. "There is a good chance that she can be completely cured, Gilles, but she needs expert care. She must go away at once to a sanatorium in the mountains. The doctor says it's essential for her to have complete rest and quiet, that she may have no visitors until he gives his permission. It could take months."

"Then I must speak with this doctor. She must have the best man, Caro, the most expert treatment." He tried to quell the panic rising in him—he had to save her.

"This doctor is the best. He has his own clinic in Switzerland and his work is the most advanced of any in the field. He'll take care of her, Gilles, you can trust him. If you wish, you can speak with him yourself." She knew she could trust the doctor to confirm their story—he had already been well paid.

It was exactly as she had said. Dr. Lepont merely confirmed her story, adding that the presence of Gilles and Caro, distressed as they were, would be harmful to Léonie's delicate state of health. She must have no visitors at all until he gave permission. But they mustn't worry, he had his own private sanatorium in the mountains, he would take her there himself, and his team of doctors would supervise her treatment. He would keep them informed of her progress, naturally, but she must leave right away.

"Do whatever is necessary," Monsieur replied quietly. "But Dr. Lepont, I want her back *cured!*"

He walked the streets of Paris for hours, cursing himself for not knowing she was ill, for not noticing sooner. He remembered the night when his son had almost died. It was only then that he'd known how much he cared for him. And he remembered Léonie at the inn, when she had held him in her arms all night. No, oh, no—Léonie couldn't die!

* * *

He took her to the station himself, making sure she was comfortably installed in the special compartment he had reserved for her. Léonie watched him anxiously as he paced the platform waiting for Dr. Lepont.

He lavished departing gifts on her, soft ruffled nightdresses and robes, a fur rug for her bed, the latest books for her entertainment in the long hours she was to spend alone. The train puffed clouds of steam along the platform and Bébé on her knee growled softly and settled closer.

He came back with Dr. Lepont. "I shall be in the next compartment, madame," said the doctor with a smile. "I'll keep my eye on you, don't worry."

He left them alone discreetly as the conductor began slamming the doors.

"I expect you to return as my old Léonie," Gilles said, gripping her thin shoulders, his deep blue eyes commanding her.

"I shall, Monsieur," she replied obediently as he kissed her, "I promise you I shall."

She watched him from the window, one arm raised in farewell as the train pulled away. As he disappeared from view, she sank back into the cushions with a sigh of relief. Maybe it would work out after all.

❧28❧

THERE'S NO DENYING it now, thought Léonie, running satisfied hands across the low bulge of her belly. And I love it, I love it. I want to have a dozen babies. I'd like to spend the rest of my life being a mother. "Imagine, Bébé, that I can grow a child. You should try it, my kitten. We must find you a husband." A husband. Her spirits crashed from elation to dejection as they had so often since she had come to the little chalet on the grounds of the sanatorium. There had been times when she had felt so isolated and sad she wanted to die, and peaks so high that she had felt invincible, promising herself she would keep the child, that Monsieur would accept it as his and everything would be wonderful. But, of course, it was all just a dream. The reality was that she was almost eight months pregnant and the child had no father. Worse, she was to give it up as soon as it was born.

All the arrangements had been made. The nurse would take the baby from her at birth and then it would go to friends of Madame Frenard's sister, who lived in Menton, and who had promised to look after it as though it were one of their own. They were good people, simple and kind and already with three children—one more would just add to their happy little family. And, of course, she had made sure that there was a generous amount of money in the bank at Menton, enough to take care of the whole family. Léonie's child would not be deprived, she had seen to that.

She had tramped the eucalyptus and pine-studded hillside behind the chalet endlessly, thinking about life, about the baby, coming helpless into the world, as unwanted as she herself had been, and she had shed bitter tears for yet another child born without love. But at least you'll be taken care of, you *will* be loved, she promised, even though I shall never see you again, after the beginning.

Time had passed slowly in the tiny Swiss village nestled in the clutch of jagged peaks that pierced the sky with white-tipped fingers. The early autumn air was clear and touched with frost, and she would sit on the veranda warmly wrapped against the chill, watching the squirrels running through the branches and feeding the bright-breasted robins her breakfast crumbs. And with the approach of winter the sound of bells rang through the valley as the cows were brought down from the high pasture before the snows began.

The color returned to her face and she ate everything the doctors said she should, going for long walks with Bébé in the hills behind the chalet until her body became too clumsy for such an effort, and then she strolled the grounds of the sanatorium, avoiding the village just in case there might be any strangers, though she felt confident there weren't.

Monsieur was allowed to write to her once a month and she opened his letters eagerly. They were always the same, brief notes saying that he hoped she was stronger and feeling better and that he looked forward to seeing her when she was well enough. They were always signed simply, "Monsieur." What does he do when I'm not there? she fretted, stalking the isolated hills. She wanted it all to be over so that she could be back with him, secure now in the fact that he loved her, that everything would be all right as soon as they were together again.

Quite suddenly late in the eighth month, the pains began. At first it was just a low ache in her back, which she ignored, but then the cramp hit her and she gasped, surprised by its intensity—this child was determined to be born now. Like her, it had waited long enough.

Now that the time was here she felt afraid, and taking Bébé she sat on the veranda for a while, gazing at the familiar mountains. Their immensity calmed her, putting what was to come into its proper perspective: mortals gave birth and mortals died, but the mountains watched over them forever. The act of creation was something that happened every day; she was a woman about to do the thing she was meant for, to give birth to a child.

The night seemed so long, spaced between periods of calm and peace and a frenzied battle with pain. She hadn't expected *this* pain. Did the child have to fight its way out of her body, wasn't there some easier way? She lost track of time, drifting between the contractions, hoarding her strength for the next onslaught—she would beat it, she wasn't going to give in and cry that she could take no more. She pushed and panted her way through the pain-filled night, and with the dawn the baby was there. She heard its cry as the nurse took it and she laughed in triumph, lying exhausted in the tangle of her long, sweat-soaked hair.

Then she saw her daughter for the first time—and she loved her instantly.

"Just leave her with me for a little while," she pleaded, holding the tiny, blanket-wrapped, day-old bundle that was Amélie. "Just let me have her for a week."

The nurse looked at her helplessly. "But you said, madame . . ."

"I know, I know, but now I can't. Don't you see, she's the most beautiful baby in the world? I just need to hold her, to look at her for a while longer."

She touched the baby's hand, smiling as the slender, starlike fingers gripped hers with surprising strength. Tenderly, she kissed the wisp of blond fluff on her head. Oh, yes, she thought, this is my baby and no one is going to take her from me.

The doctor came to plead with her and she lifted the child from the crib at the side of her bed, clutching the infant protectively like a wary animal, in case he should try to take her away by force.

"Of course I won't do that, Léonie," he said gently, "but it's up to you to weigh the circumstances. I know that it's difficult for you right now, you've just given birth, but you must keep in mind what's best for the child. Remember the reasons you came here. The decision is yours. No one will take her from you—you must do that yourself."

It was clever of him, she thought moodily, as the days passed. Of course no one would take the baby from her. Only she could make the decision. But what if she left Monsieur? She could keep the baby. A thrill of fear chilled her. And what sort of life would a child have, anyway, as the illegitimate daughter of a woman like her—a kept woman? No, Amélie was better off with a normal family, with brothers and sisters to play with and a mother and father who would love her. Léonie knew she had no choice.

But she would keep her just for a little while longer, a month perhaps. Surely a month wasn't too much to ask. She could take the baby south to the inn, to the sun. It would be spring there, the mimosa would be in bloom. A baby would grow plump and healthy with all that fresh air. Just one month, she promised herself, and then Madame Frenard can take Amélie to Menton.

❧29❧

MONSIEUR PACED restlessly through the big house on the place Saint-Georges. Everything was immaculate, the polished tables gleamed, the gauzy silvered curtains hung in neat folds, shading the spring sun from the unused rooms, and empty grates waited for a warming fire.

He didn't come here often, it reminded him too much of the gloomy house in the country when his mother had gathered up her friends and departed, taking with her all the sparkle and glow that had for a short while brought his world to life.

He felt the same now as he wandered into Léonie's room, touching the smooth, cream-colored bedspread and the pillows, imagining the imprint of her head and all her lovely hair, that wonderful hair. The scent of jasmine lingered in the closet and he stared at the dresses hanging there, at the crystal Fortuny dress she'd bought to wear in America, remembering how she had looked in it when she had worn it for him that evening of their parting, how he had wanted to punish her.

He lay on the bed, staring at the ceiling. He had no contact with her. There were no more daily reports, no secret details of her life. There had been a time when he couldn't live without them, when he'd needed to know everything, when he'd been obsessed with knowing what she did every minute of the time she wasn't with him, but now all he wanted was that she might get better, that she would live. He couldn't bear it if she didn't.

It was difficult to sleep in his old room at the house on Ile Saint-Louis. He stayed up most of the time, working until he was so exhausted that sometimes he fell asleep at his desk. He closed his eyes. At least here he felt closer to her. He felt at peace.

It was dark when he awoke, but he didn't feel rested. He leaned over and turned on the lamp, swinging his legs over the side of the bed. There were a couple of books on the bedside table that she must have been reading before she left—should he send them to her? he wondered, flicking idly through the pages. A note slipped to the floor and he picked it up, looking at the writing curiously. It was addressed to her at the inn, dated last September. He opened it and read it quickly, and then again more slowly. It was from a man: Charles. He enclosed money for his room and board at the Frenards; he called her magical, beautiful and thanked her for a night from her charmed life. It was dated just two weeks before he'd gone to her at the inn, when he'd told her that he loved her.

It wasn't anger that he felt, it was different. It was as though ice were filling his veins, as though he was cutting off all emotion. He had allowed a chink, a single tiny gap in the armor of defense that had grown over him since his mother had so easily, so carelessly condemned him to a life without her, without love—sending him away to that school, where she hadn't even come to visit him, never even written. He had never again allowed any woman that kind of power over him—never. Until Léonie.

He folded the note carefully and put it in his pocket. There were few clues. Just the name: Charles. And the fact that he had been a "shipwrecked mariner"—that meant a boat, and not a large one. If he'd been washed up near the Frenards', it would be a small boat. A racing yacht, for example. Weren't there races at Monte Carlo at that time of year? Verronet would find out.

And Léonie? What would he do about Léonie? He walked down the stairs thinking about her. First he needed to know the whole story, and then he'd make his move. But he wasn't going to let her go, he knew that.

"I was right to bring her here, Madame Frenard," said Léonie, watching Amélie sleeping in her crib out on the terrace, shaded from the sun and wind by her canopy. "Just look how she's growing."

The two of them hung over the side of the crib, examining the little blond face, her mouth pursed tightly in sleep as though she were concentrating very hard on it. "Ah, she is beautiful, Léonie, and so like you."

It was true, even now at three weeks she looked like her. Léonie searched her daughter's face for a trace of her father, but could see none. Amélie's hair was blond and when she opened her eyes and gazed at the world it was with that same long, golden, slumberous look.

Bébé had quite taken to this new, small-sized human being and had become its guardian, placing herself next to the crib and purring loudly and contentedly at her new responsibilities, making Léonie laugh at her self-importance. "I'm not sure if I'm the mother, or you Bébé," she teased, picking up the small cat and hugging her, receiving a rasping lick on the nose in return.

This month was heaven. May had blown in across the Mediterranean bringing clear skies and a warming sun, and the blessed blue days were ones of gentle happiness, of looking after the baby and feeding her, watching her with the fascination of a new mother as she slept, and waking with a new instinctive alertness to her tiny cries in the night. And Amélie thrived, blossoming from her first battered difficult journey into life into a plump-cheeked, blond infant content in her mother's arms.

Léonie enjoyed each day for what it brought, each small gain in weight, the wave of a tiny arm, her gripping perfect fingers. It was the happiest month of her life and she refused to count the days until the last one.

There was no going back, and she knew it, even though she paced the terrace through the night, plotting ways to keep her, agonizing over the thought of giving her away. There must be some way, but it all came back to the same thing. She was no good for the child. With her Amélie would never have a normal life—she would be the illegitimate child of a notorious woman, and Monsieur's vengeance would be terrible. She shivered with fear for Amélie as she thought about him. She remembered the property she owned, the house in Paris, the factories in Lille, the railway shares and the stocks and bonds—she would have traded them all in in an instant to be able to keep Amélie. If only it were that simple. Once she had thought that was all it took—security. Then life offered no more problems, no one could hurt you. It wasn't true, it just wasn't true.

The sea barely moved under the morning sunlight as she sat on the terrace holding Amélie in her arms. She had packed all her little things—the tiny jackets and minute nightdresses, the little pink hairbrush for her blond fluff of hair. There was no way out. Amélie deserved a better mother than she, and a real father. And then she would be safe from Monsieur.

Madame Frenard hesitated in the doorway, afraid of what was to happen. "We're ready to leave now, Léonie," she said gently.

Léonie looked down at her daughter, at the small, lovely, innocent face. "It's the last time," she whispered. "I'll never see you again, Amélie, but I'll always love you. Oh, yes, you'll always be loved."

"Madame Frenard," she whispered, as she handed her the baby, "this is the most terrible thing I've ever had to do in my life."

She turned away, stony-faced and dry-eyed, unable to watch as they drove down the lane, and the little cat sat quietly at her feet, knowing as she always did that she needed comfort.

❧30❦

CARO HELD LÉONIE'S HAND as they drove from the station toward the place Saint-Georges. "Come and stay with me for a while," she urged. "Tell him you're not strong enough yet to return to town, we can go to the country." She was terribly worried about Léonie. It wasn't so much the way she looked—she was thin but she seemed healthier than when she had left and there was color in her face from a month in the sun. It was the dead look in her eyes that was frightening.

"No," said Léonie determinedly, "I've done it now, Caro. I'll regret it for the rest of my life, but it was best for Amélie, and now I have to live with it. Monsieur has been patient and kind—and I've deceived him. I want so much to tell him, Caro . . . it's a terrible secret."

"You mustn't even think of it. He'd kill you, Léonie! Think of Amélie. My God, if he knew there was a baby. . . ."

Léonie hadn't told Monsieur that she was coming home. Only Caro knew—and Maroc. He was waiting for her on the steps, and he took her cold hands, scanning her face anxiously. "Is a butler permitted to kiss madame?" he asked with a faint smile.

"Oh, Maroc, of course you are." She flung her arms around him. "I'm just so glad to see you, both of you, my friends." They followed her into the hall, eyes meeting behind her back.

"Is she all right?" whispered Maroc.

"I'm not sure . . . she looks well, but she should never have kept the child, she'll never get over it now."

The house looked just the same. Even in the afternoon sunlight the salon was theatrical—a stage for a play that no longer held her interest, she thought wistfully. And her room was as beautiful, filled with flowers by Maroc, pillows temptingly arranged on the wide bed, her little sitting room waiting—with the chaise placed by the open window and its leafy view, ready to catch the first breeze. But all she really wanted was to be back at the inn. She began to cry.

"Oh, Léonie," begged Caro, "please don't cry. I'm here, I'll help you—and Maroc . . . we love you, darling, please don't cry."

"Caro, how could I do it? How could I make such a mess of my life? All I really want is to be with Amélie."

"All right, Léonie, that's what you want. But you can't have it! Yes, you have made a mess of your life, but you're not going to ruin that child's. Pull yourself together . . . this is the way things are. We planned the deception and we carried it through. Monsieur suspects nothing. Only you could give away the secret—and if you do, God knows what will happen. It's time, Léonie Bahri, to start thinking with your head and not with your heart."

They'd left her alone to rest and to think things over. Of course, Caro was right. It was all her own fault and she had no right to be self-pitying. It was time to pick up the threads of her own life and go on. Her heart lifted as she thought of Monsieur—he'd been so kind, so understanding. He really loved her. Hadn't he said so? And, once, that had been all she wanted.

Verronet's report was on his desk waiting to be read. He had pushed it away, hidden it under a pile of papers, busying himself with blueprints and layouts, financial reports and share dealings. But now he had to read it. He had to know. It hadn't been easy, Verronet had said, there were a number of little boats in the harbors along the coast in September, and the only clues he had had were the name Charles and the fact that they thought it must be a sailboat there for the races. But he had done it; he'd gone personally, as de Courmont had instructed, trusting no one else, and spoken to harbor masters, sailboat owners, and to the promoters of the various races—and then he had had a stroke of luck. He'd met someone who had remembered that Charles d'Aureville had been out in the storm, and he remembered it particularly because it brought a spell of bad weather, several weeks of rain and thunder and high winds. Charles had been lucky to find shelter, let alone to have escaped with his life.

So that was it. The shipwrecked mariner: Charles d'Aureville. He threw the papers back on the desk. The name meant nothing to him. He looked at the address. Château d'Aureville in the Loire.

He paced the floor of his office, thinking of his next move. There was a tap on the door. Léonie stood framed in the doorway, smiling at him. "I was just thinking about you," he said calmly.

"And I was thinking of you . . . so here I am. Quite better, as you see."

She looked thin and tired. There was something, he wasn't quite sure what it was, she was different. But in his arms her sleek-skinned bones felt the same under his hands, she smelled the same, of fresh air and jasmine—he could drown in that scent. He wanted to kill her!

"Did you miss me, darling?" she asked with a smile.

"You know I did." His eyes searched her face. He knew he couldn't live without her. "And are you better?"

"Oh, yes, Doctor Lepont said that I'm cured and there should be no recurrence if I'm careful."

"I should take you for a holiday—to the sea, maybe even to your precious inn, so that we can build up your strength again, but I'm busy."

"No, not the inn . . . I want to stay here with you. I've been isolated for too long, Monsieur. I'm quite happy now that I'm back here—with you."

Her smile wrapped itself around him.

She was still his Léonie, his old Léonie come back to him. He thrust the papers into a drawer and took her by the hand. "I'm finished for the day, Verronet," he said as they walked down the hall together. "We are going home."

He drove to the house himself in the new model of the de Courmont car—a deep blue tourer with creamy leather seats—concentrating on the machine. When they arrived at their house he took her hand and walked silently with her up the stairs to her room.

If she'd expected him to be tender and considerate, she was mistaken. He didn't so much make love to her as reclaim her, branding her body as his with a dark thrusting passion that left her gasping. And he didn't say he loved her. But then, she hadn't said she loved him.

Verronet always enjoyed the Côte d'Azur. It wasn't so much the sunshine and sea breezes as the gambling. The casino was a terrible lure, but so far he'd always managed to stop before disaster struck. There was one great advantage to working for de Courmont: he was a very generous employer. He demanded every minute of your time and your life was never yours to call your own, but he paid well and the expenses were unlimited, so if a little of it got lost in the casino, who was to worry? And that was another thing: over the last couple of years his job had become more that of a "right-hand man," a personal confidant. He was closer to de Courmont than anyone else; he took care of all his *personal* business. Only he knew de Courmont's secrets, his weaknesses—the private desires of a man whose public image was so distinguished, so powerful, and so ruthless. In fact, what he knew might surprise a lot of people. Yes, he was sitting pretty and for the moment he was content to leave it that way. But there'd come a day when he'd have had enough of being de Courmont's spy—he didn't intend to be a high-paid lackey all his life. When the moment was right he'd use what he knew to move up in the world. He would go to all those parties as an equal, not as some sort of servant—people would invite *him*. And there'd be plenty of money; de Courmont wouldn't like the world to know he had an under-belly as vulnerable as any shark's.

He'd a feeling that there was more to this Charles d'Aureville affair than just one night. It had seemed implausible that a woman like Léonie and an attractive young man like d'Aureville would be satisfied with only that. De Courmont had sent him back to see if there was any foundation to his suspicions, and at first it seemed that that was the way it had been. Except now there was something new, and Monsieur was not going to like it.

Léonie had spent a month here when she was supposed to be still up in the Swiss mountains getting cured from whatever it was she was supposed to have. He'd found out quite by chance when he'd gone to the village of Saint-Jean near the inn—sometimes you could pick up gossip from the locals in the bar there, or in the store. Small things, like at the pharmacy. He had dropped a glass onto the floor in the bar, spilling his beer, and had cut his finger quite badly. They had directed him to the pharmacy and the owner had supplied plaster and ointment—and a little gratuitous information. The Frenards did the best lunches around, he'd told them, thinking he was a casual visitor, and now that the lady from Paris had gone he thought they would be serving again. It had taken only a little probing to find out that there had been a small child staying, a baby in fact. Madame Frenard had come herself to collect the gripe water and powder and things that small babies need; she had seemed quite pleased about it, though she had been very close-mouthed. He didn't quite know why.

A baby. And Léonie away in the mountains for six or seven months; things were beginning to add up, and Verronet knew Monsieur wasn't going to like it. It gave him a good deal of pleasure to write that telegram. He could just imagine him reading it.

Well, there was no hurry. He might as well enjoy himself at the casino for a few days before he began to look for the child. After all, he was enti-tled to a little pleasure, too.

"Caro, isn't that Verronet—you know, de Courmont's lackey?" Al-phonse pointed out the man at the chemin de fer table, a pile of plaques stacked beside him.

Caro stared in surprise. "You're right, but what on earth is he doing here? I thought he only left Monsieur's side when he went to bed."

"I wonder," said Alphonse thoughtfully. "De Courmont is up to his eyes in these American negotiations for his cars. I would have thought he needed Verronet—he can put his hand on facts and figures in a moment and that's just what de Courmont needs right now. It's very strange that he should be gambling in the casino in Monte Carlo instead."

"Do you suppose he's run off with de Courmont's money?" Caro laughed at the idea. "That would be something!"

"I don't think it's that. You know, Caro, Monsieur uses Verronet as a sort of a business spy—he has him find out all the secrets of the men whose companies he wants to take over—and he's very good at it. Now, what secrets are there here in Monte Carlo that Verronet might be looking into?"

Caro's eyes widened as she realized what he was saying. "But it's not possible, Alphonse. Why would Monsieur suspect?"

"I don't know, but for Léonie's sake, I think we must find out."

"Oh, Alphonse, what shall we do?"

"We'll follow Verronet."

"But he's sure to recognize us. We must get a spy of our own, Alphonse."

"We'll do better. The chief of police here is an old friend of mine. I once did him a favor. He'll be only too pleased to return it now."

Amélie will be five months old next week, thought Léonie, as she dressed for dinner in the suite overlooking the ocean in the Grand Hotel at Deauville. Her legs will be brown and strong from lying in the sun and she'll be lifting up her pretty head to look around. Her own face stared back at her from the mirror. "It's no good, Léonie Bahri," she told herself firmly. "You have to stop thinking like this."

"Like what?"

Monsieur was behind her. Léonie hadn't heard him come into the room and she realized she must have spoken the words aloud. "Oh, nothing. . . ."

"It didn't sound like 'nothing' to me. What could it be that you have to force yourself to stop thinking about it?"

"I was thinking about you—going off to New York again. You promised you would take me, remember?"

"Indeed, I do remember. And I shall take you . . . one day."

She didn't know what was the matter with him—or maybe it was she who had changed. Perhaps he sensed that she was different, that she hadn't come back the same girl who had left. They rarely went out together, Monsieur worked late almost every night, and he'd been spending time with his sons. It was odd, though; she had thought he would be overjoyed to see her back. It wasn't like the time at the inn when he'd come to find her, to tell her that he loved her. It's probably just that we're more used to each other by now . . . an old married couple, she thought grimly. His suggestion that they go to Deauville for a few days had come out of the blue; it'll do you good, he'd said, to get some fresh sea air.

But Deauville was so different from the Côte d'Azur. Even though the sky was blue this was no gentle little sea, it was an ocean, pulled by tides that sent it surging and crashing onto the miles of lonely windswept beaches.

"I thought you might like to see the yacht races tomorrow," he said casually, bending to fix his tie in the mirror.

A memory of Charles d'Aureville racing his little boat to safety came vividly to mind. "Oh, I don't know," she replied carefully. "I'm quite happy just sitting on the terrace and doing nothing. I'm not interested in sailing."

"It might be amusing. We'll take a look."

She felt him standing behind her and turned with a smile, kissing him on the cheek. He smelled of shaving lotion and crisp linen and she liked it; he was as attractive as ever. She took his fingers and kissed each one and held them to her breast.

"You'll spoil your gown," he said, disengaging himself and walking to the door. "We're late for dinner. I promised the Massenets we'd meet them at eight."

It was another brisk blue day of scudding fluffy clouds and swirling little winds that tossed up a fine dust from the sandy paths in the hotel gardens. Léonie heard the sailors among the guests congratulating themselves on having such perfect weather. What's good for sailors obviously doesn't suit me. She frowned, rubbing the grit from her eyes and making for the shelter of the terrace. She'd refused to go with Monsieur down to the harbor to watch the races. "I'll see them go by from the hotel," she had said, escaping thankfully from the drafty launch.

She settled herself at the table on the glass-enclosed terrace that overlooked the bay and ordered a *citron pressé,* glancing casually at the program of events that Monsieur had thrust into her hand as she left. There were six different classes of vessel, graded from large to small. In the third class was the *Isabelle,* crewed by Charles d'Aureville.

The name sprang from the printed page as though illuminated in scarlet. Charles d'Aureville was *here—Charles,* oh, my God, what should she do? What if they were to meet? It was quite possible that he was staying at the same hotel. Or she might see him strolling along the promenade, or in a restaurant, and, of course, he would come over to her, he'd wonder what she was doing there, his little kitchen maid from the inn at Cap Ferrat. She must leave, plead that the air was no good for her, the winds were too strong and took her breath away. She *had* to get away from here.

Could Monsieur possibly know? The idea struck her like a blow. Wasn't it an odd coincidence that they should be here at the same time as the races, and as Charles? But they could just as easily have gone to Monte

Carlo and Charles would probably have been there for the races, too—all the resorts had them this time of year. Of course, it must be just a coincidence. There was no way that Monsieur could know. It was impossible. But still the idea nagged her.

The races were well under way; she could see the boats skimming over the choppy gray water, their sales ballooning in the wind, and she watched for a while, wondering if one of them was the *Isabelle,* remembering the night he had sailed into her life on the edge of a storm.

De Courmont adjusted the binoculars, focusing them on the *Isabelle.* He stared at his rival circled in the lenses. He was young and attractive, smiling cheerfully as he adjusted the rigging, throwing a casual comment to the crewman he'd picked up in Deauville when his own man suddenly became sick. He was certainly a competent sailor, he thought, lowering the glasses as the little boat tacked its way through the turbulence outside the harbor to join others in its class.

He'd seen enough. He made his way back to the bar and ordered a large whiskey, drinking it neat in quick gulps. He ordered another immediately. He took the glass, sipping the spirit this time, drawn despite himself to the window and its view of the bay. The little boats were still there, scudding gaily before the wind. He watched for a while and then went to find Léonie.

❧ 31 ❦

GRAY CLOUDS BANKED threateningly over the wide silent stretch of the Tapajoz River in Brazil and Edouard d'Aureville, standing on the wooden jetty of the Oro Velho rubber trail, glanced at them with concern. "Just another few days," he said, "that's all we need to get this loaded and off to Santarém." Even as he spoke, there was a low rumble of thunder in the distance—it looked as though the rains would come early this season and that meant no more work. An early rainy season cost money. He sighed with frustration, you couldn't win with this forest, it always had an answer. You hacked the trails through it every morning, and every night it grew again, hiding its rubber trees in underbrush and lianas that the sweating laborers, out before dawn, hacked back once again in the flickering light of kerosene lamps strapped to their heads.

The laborers hauled the great two-hundred-pound balls of rubber in slings, stacking them in the hold of the launch ready to take them to Santarém at the junction of the Tapajoz and the Amazon, where they would be transferred to the steamer and taken to Manaus for onward shipment to Europe or America. It had meant six months spent in the Amazon, enduring its unnerving tall spongy green silence, its humidity, its vicious biting insects, downing quinine to ward off malaria and yellow fever, fending off the river pirates who would kill to take over a good trail, and supervising the work force of laborers drawn mostly from the drought-ridden savannahs of Ceará, who worked from dawn till dusk and then drank themselves into frenzied fights with machetes.

It was a rough, tough life and Edouard, after six months, felt the way the laborers did—exhausted. He needed civilization: some good food, wine, women, and fun. "I need Manaus," he said to his partner, Wil Harcourt.

"Damn right," said Wil. "The only good thing about six months in the jungle is that the price of rubber will have gone up twenty times since our last shipment. It's the black gold of the Amazon. We'll be millionaires yet, Edouard."

"If the rain holds off we'll have another half a ton ready, the men'll work right up to the last minute."

"Okay, but let's not leave it too late; I don't want to get caught in the storms."

Edouard strode across the compound to the curing sheds, wrinkling his nose against the acrid stench of the latex bubbling in caldrons over the smudge fires. Wielding fifteen-foot-long paddles, the laborers stirred the congealing mass, lifting and turning, wrapping it around each paddle until it formed a solid black ball of rubber. The sweat poured from their backs as they heaved its weight, peering through smoke-blackened eyes to see how much longer it would take.

The compound sweltered in the sunless heat and Edouard strode past the tumble of workers' huts and outbuildings to the main house. It perched on stilts with a rickety veranda fronting the river and was what he and Wil laughingly called home. The wooden boards were bare, there were thin little snakes in the palm-thatched roof that they picked off with rifles when they spotted them, and termites were eating the stilts, causing the whole flimsy structure to lean dangerously. All it contained was a couple of iron beds, a few extra hammocks for visitors, and, out on the veranda that acted as their dining room and sitting room combined, a wooden table and a couple of chairs. Opening a bottle, he poured himself a beer, grimacing at the taste. It was warm. God, he could use a cold beer and a hot bath! And a woman. It was time to get back to Manaus and catch up with the world.

* * *

The looming nearness of the equator bisected Manaus with a knife blade of heat that left them breathless and sweltering as they walked along Marashal Deodoro Street toward the Chamber of Commerce, eager to check the price of rubber on the world market before they sought the comforts of the Hotel Centrale. The blue-tiled building was packed with trail owners and rubber barons, the élite of Manaus, newly and staggeringly enriched by the black gold.

"I told you"—Wil slapped Edouard's back in triumph—"up thirty percent since last time . . . we've made a killing on this lot, Edouard."

Edouard beamed. "Let's celebrate: a bath, a shave—send to Atelier Simmons for some new shirts—and then dinner and a bottle of champagne, maybe even a few bottles, who knows?"

Theirs were familiar faces at the Centrale. "I'll have your trunks taken out of the storage room, sirs," the manager promised, "and the man from Atelier Simmons will be here shortly."

The bath was porcelain, wide and long enough to wallow in, and the water was steaming hot. The barber from the hotel shop wrapped their weatherbeaten faces in hot towels, shaving them luxuriously with long clean sweeps of his blade and patting on a crisp cologne. The clerk from Atelier Simmons brought fresh shirts and the valet pressed their white linen suits. White suede shoes and jaunty panama hats finished their ensembles and they inspected themselves in the mirror. Wil, burly and bearded, and Edouard, slender and tanned, grinned with pleasure as they closed the door and headed for the delights of Manaus.

The well-paved streets were busy: fountains sparkled in the light of the street lamps: the tiled dome of the opera house gleamed under the moonlight; bars, cafés, and restaurants were crowded with smart women in the latest fashions from Paris with jewels from Cartier, and immaculately dressed men with great rolls of money in their pockets. Green electric streetcars carried passengers through the new city to its very edges, where paved streets met the jungle.

"I've made a reservation for dinner at the Montmartre," said Edouard, "and after that . . . the night will still be young."

Their spirits were high, they were free of the forest, they had made a killing on the rubber market—the world was theirs.

"Oh, by the way," said Wil. "I forgot to give you this. I picked it up at the telegraph office today. It's been waiting for you for days apparently, so I guess it can't be too urgent."

"A telegram?" Edouard turned it over in his hand. "From France." He read it quickly, and then again in disbelief: "Regret to inform you that your brother Charles has died in a boating accident . . . please return at once." The signature was that of the family lawyer.

He stared white-faced at the telegram, oblivious to the noise of the crowds and the snatches of laughter and music from the cafés. The night was sweltering, the humidity so dense it was almost tangible—and he was shivering with cold, the terrible cold chill of Charles's death. Charles, his baby brother, the energetic young man, the expert sailor, dead in a boating accident? He didn't want to believe it. It couldn't be true.

Wil took the paper from Edouard's nerveless hand. "God," he whispered. "I'm so sorry, Edouard."

"I must go home," he said, his face tense with shock. "My mother is alone. She'll need me."

❧ 32 ❧

"MAROC," CALLED CARO, "I'm going to need you." She hurried up the stairs to Léonie's room as he stared after her in surprise, wondering what was going on. Monsieur was away again in New York and Léonie had been very subdued, staying home alone, seeing no one.

He followed her into Léonie's sitting room and closed the door behind him. In the square the sharp autumn wind was blowing the leaves from the trees, and he could see the man sitting on a bench reading a newspaper. He was always there, waiting.

"Léonie, I've got something very important to say, and I wanted Maroc to hear it because we are going to need all the help we can get."

"Caro, what is it?" asked Léonie, alarmed.

"First I must tell you that Monsieur knows about Charles d'Aureville. When Alphonse and I were in Monte Carlo, we saw Verronet there, gambling in the casino. Alphonse thought it odd that he wasn't here with Monsieur at a time when he needed him for business—therefore he was obviously in Monte Carlo on more urgent affairs. As a spy, Léonie. Something had triggered Monsieur's suspicions and somehow he got on the trail and Verronet found out the rest."

How had he known? Léonie wondered frantically. What had aroused his suspicions? Of course it must be the letter—when it was missing she had thought she had left it behind at the inn. Oh, my God, the baby.

"Caro . . . then . . . does he know about Amélie?"

Caro took her arm sympathetically. "It's not easy to hide new babies in a small community, Léonie. Everyone knew about the lady from Paris staying at the Frenards', and that there was a baby. The only thing he doesn't know yet is where she is."

Maroc leaned against the door, his arms folded, watching the two women, wondering what they were going to do.

"I'm afraid, Caro—if Monsieur finds her he'll take her away, he'll hide her from me."

"Léonie, there's one more thing."

They both stared at her, waiting.

"Charles d'Aureville is dead."

Maroc drew in his breath sharply. The color had drained from Léonie's face, and her eyes were blank with shock. "Dead?" she whispered incredulously. "But how did he die?"

"He drowned at Deauville a month ago."

"But I was there . . . I was in Deauville, Caro. I saw his name in the list of competitors for the races, he was to sail the *Isabelle*—the same boat he had the night of the storm."

Caro gripped her arm. "You were there? With Monsieur?"

"Yes, I told you. . . . He wanted to take me away for a few days. Caro, Charles couldn't just drown . . . I saw him handle that boat in a storm—he was an expert sailor."

"Alphonse found out what happened. The story is that Charles's crewman got sick just before the race and he picked up a new man at the harbor. He wasn't a local man and no one seemed to know him. The *Isabelle* went out with the other boats and at one point almost capsized. The crewman came back alone. He said that Charles had been caught by a sudden shift of wind and had fallen overboard. He'd thrown him a line, but he seemed stunned and was going under. He went in after him and tried to get him back, but the sea was too rough, he slipped from his hands. The body was washed up the next day on a beach five miles away. The skull was fractured as if from a strong blow on the back of the head. The coroner said that Charles probably struck it as he fell and therefore was unable to save himself."

Léonie and Maroc stared at her, horror-struck.

"Alphonse found out more, Léonie. The inquest took place the same day—normally these matters take a week or more—and afterward the body was sent back to his family in a sealed coffin. Charles was popular, he had many friends, and there were rumors among the yachtsmen, murmurs of suspicion against the stranger, the crewman who had disappeared as quickly as he came."

Their eyes met. "You don't think Monsieur . . ." Léonie couldn't say it.

"Do *you* think Monsieur had anything to do with it, Léonie?"

She thought of Charles, beautiful young Charles, alive and loving, giving her his warm body and his magical world, just one simple loving night—and now he was dead. The enormity of Monsieur's obsession struck her like a blow. It had gone beyond game-playing; he was capable of anything—even killing. And if he killed Charles, then he would kill Amélie, too; he wouldn't be able to bear the thought of there being another man's child around. "Yes," she answered. "Monsieur killed him. I'm sure of it."

Caro felt faint; she knew it was true—she'd known it as soon as Alphonse had told her. Dear God, what now? Was he going to kill Léonie, too?

Tears of sorrow and anger ran down Léonie's face and the bitterness caught in her throat.

"We must get Amélie, Caro, for you can be sure that once he finds her he'll kill her, too."

"I'll go," said Maroc. "I'll get your baby. You can't do it yourself; Monsieur's spy is right outside waiting for you."

"And then what?" asked Caro. "Where shall we take her? Remember, Léonie, she's been with this family for five months—the woman is her mother. Must we take her away?"

Léonie was bewildered. What should she do? Where could she hide the child? Where would Amélie be safe from Monsieur? Oh, Charles, dear sweet Charles, what should we do? She remembered the stories of his childhood, the lovely uninhibited sunny days at the château and his wonderful elder brother. What was it he'd said about him? Edouard has this quality of tenderness—unusual in a man—you can tell him anything. Edouard, the brother who had loved him; surely he would love his child, too? Of course, that was the answer. She would send Amélie to Edouard d'Aureville in Brazil—there was no way Monsieur would be able to find her there. She would be with her father's family, where she belonged.

Caro and Maroc stared at her in amazement. She must be crazy. "But how, Léonie? They don't even know she exists."

"I'll tell them. I'll go there now, to the Château d'Aureville, and I shall speak with Charles's mother, Amélie's grandmother. I'll tell her the truth and I'll beg her to take the baby to Edouard in Brazil." Her brain was working fast, spurred on by the adrenaline of fear and the need to protect her child. "Maroc, I want you to go the the inn and explain the situation to Monsieur Frenard. He will take you to Menton where you will collect Amélie. I will leave right away for Tours and wait for you there. Caro, you will have to divert the spy somehow, so I can escape without being followed. But we must act fast . . . who knows what plans Monsieur has made, Verronet may be there before us. Oh, Caro, we must *hurry!*"

"Alphonse will go with you, you'll need some support with the d'Aureville family. But Léonie, have you considered the fact that they might not believe you, that they might not believe it's Charles's child, and might not want to take her?"

"Edouard d'Aureville will believe," she said simply. "He will believe it when I tell him that Charles said that he would understand anything, even your darkest secrets . . . he's a man of compassion."

The nondescript man caught a flash of blond hair as the woman ran across the courtyard and jumped into the waiting cab. He lumbered to his feet, cursing as he raced across the square to follow her. He hadn't expected her to rush out like that, almost as if she were making a dash for it; she must be up to something.

Maroc watched him go and then hurried back into the house. He grabbed the hastily packed bags waiting in the hall and carried them to the tradesman's entrance at the back, looking impatiently for the cab. Léonie, discreetly dressed in a dark coat with her blond hair swathed in a scarf, stepped in and he closed the door behind her. "Don't worry," he murmured as she bent to kiss him. "I'll get her, all right. You'll have your baby back, Léonie."

"Oh, Maroc, why was I fool enough not to realize that he would go this far? It's all my fault. Charles is dead because of me . . . and Amélie is in danger."

"It's *his* madness, Léonie, not yours. He's tried to control your life for years now, and I've watched him do it, maneuvering and playing games with you, spying on you . . . his infatuation became an obsession—and now madness and murder."

She leaned back against the seat, shaking. "I'll never let him get Amélie," she whispered. "Never! I'll kill him first." Bébé leapt in beside her with a piercing yowl, shocking Léonie. "Oh, Bébé, this is the first time I ever forgot you," she said as her tears fell on the soft fur.

Maroc watched anxiously as the cab drove off through the mews at the back of the house on a roundabout route to the small hotel south of the river where Alphonse would meet her, then he climbed into the second cab that was to take him to the station to catch the train to Nice. He prayed that he would get there before Verronet—if he didn't, he would never be able to face Léonie again.

* * *

The man stomped the pavement outside Caro's house impatiently. His feet were cold, he'd been waiting for more than four hours and she was still inside waiting for that friend of hers. She hadn't left yet, he was sure of it, just the man had left, and he hadn't looked as though he were going anywhere important; he had just sort of strolled away down the street. He blew on his hands, he wanted some supper, but he supposed he'd better wait and see what happened. Still, it wouldn't harm to go to the café across the street. It looked cozy in there, and a brandy would warm him up.

Caro peered out of the window. Thank God, it had worked, now they had at least three hours' start. The man was going into the café—good, that meant he thought Léonie was still here; no doubt he'd have some supper and then hang around a bit longer and assume that he'd missed her. He'll probably go back to the place Saint-Georges and wait there. It might be a day before he realizes that she's given him the slip.

Léonie waited restlessly for eleven o'clock to come. She'd sent the note round to the Comtesse d'Aureville as soon as they had arrived last night, asking if she would see her, saying that she had something important that she must discuss with her personally, and she had received a note back asking her to come to the château at eleven the next morning.

She didn't know what she would have done without Alphonse. He was like a rock, thinking logically and sensibly where she inevitably was acting only on her emotions. Surprisingly, he hadn't discouraged her from going to see the countess. "If that's what you feel is right for Amélie, then you must do it," he'd said. "But remember, she might not believe that this is her grandchild. She's just lost her son, Léonie, she may think it all a fraud."

"But why? Why should she? I'm not asking for money. I'll give her as much money as she needs. I just want her to take her grandchild to Brazil for me . . . to save her from a man's madness."

They had agreed that there should be no mention of Monsieur, or his part in Charles's death—"We have no proof," Alphonse had said, "and it would only cause her more grief. For now, things must stay as they are."

Léonie glanced at the clock. Only seven. It had been a long and sleepless night, one of the blackest of her life. She had lain on the bed with Bébé beside her wondering where Maroc was, whether he was already on his way to Menton, praying that Verronet was not yet on the trail. And she had lived and relived the day in Deauville, remembering herself on the terrace watching the boats skimming gaily across the bay, wondering which one was Charles's. And then later, Monsieur had stormed into the suite, carrying her off to bed and making love to her with the same ferocious passion of their early days together. Oh, God, she'd wailed into the night. The monster, the monster. Oh, Charles d'Aureville, it's my life he should have taken, not yours!

❧ 33 ❧

THE COMTESSE ISABELLE D'AUREVILLE walked along the terrace on the southern front of the château, enjoying the unexpected warmth of the October sunshine, stopping here and there to inspect a plant or to snip off the last of the withered roses. She was still a lovely woman, although the events of the past few years—the death of her husband and now her son—had combined to leave their mark on her. Her thick russet hair was clouded with strands of gray and there were lines around the fine eyes. And she smiled less often.

The mellow stone walls of the château behind her had been standing for over three hundred years and the ancient building had the kind of weathered charm that had lent itself to expansion, over many years of d'Aureville family life, to become the lovely, rambling home that it now was. She had loved it since she had first come there as a bride of eighteen.

Putting her garden basket on the terrace beside her, she sat on the carved wooden bench looking out across the lawns to the parkland beyond. The sun glinted off the waters of the moat and she could see the swans and the mallard ducks drifting effortlessly; it was all so peaceful. Charles had always liked the autumn, the smell of woodsmoke and the crisp mornings, but she must stop thinking like that. It did no good. It was just too painful to remember. He had been so alive, so vital, and now, quite suddenly, there was nothing.

Edouard strode along the terrace toward her, waving. Thank God, there was still Edouard. Yes, she still had him, although not for very long. He'd go back to Brazil soon, now that he'd seen where Charles was buried. He had his own life to lead. And then she'd be here in this big house, all alone. She remembered with a pang how it had always been filled with Charles's friends.

"Good morning, Maman." Isabelle looked at her elder son affectionately as he kissed her. His tanned skin made his gray eyes look even lighter, almost transparent in the sun, and his hair was like hers, russet color, waving thickly from a broad brow. She recalled the attractive sixteen-year-old boy who had left on his first "adventure" and smiled now at the handsome man. Only she knew how much he had loved Charles, and how shattered he was by his death, only she had seen his tears.

"What are you thinking about now?" he asked, putting his arm around her.

"I was wondering what I'll do here all alone. Perhaps I should buy a little villa somewhere, in the south maybe, or an apartment in Paris. I don't think I can bear to be here without either of you."

He looked at her worriedly. "Why not come back to Brazil with me ... not to Manaus, but to Rio? Luiza and Francisco would be happy to have you. Francisco do Santos has never forgotten you—though I suppose he still thinks of you as the beautiful seventeen-year-old girl he met all those years ago."

She laughed. "I don't know, Edouard. I don't know what I want to do."

"There's no hurry, I intend to stay here just as long as you need me. Now, who is this mysterious woman who wants to see you so urgently?"

"I've no idea. Her name is Léonie Bahri and she is with a Monsieur Alphonse de Bergerac."

Edouard frowned. "I wonder what they want?"

"We shall soon see," she said, picking up her basket and walking back along the terrace. "They'll be here at any moment."

"Alphonse"—Léonie gripped his hand nervously—"this isn't going to be easy."

"Do you want to leave?"

"Oh, no ... I must see her."

"Then let's go in. Don't worry, I'll help you. I'm here to corroborate your story. She'll believe you."

Isabelle d'Aureville came toward them with a smile. "Do sit down," she said pleasantly, as they introduced themselves, "I'm most intrigued to hear what it is that you have to tell me."

"It's about your son, Comtesse, about Charles. ... I'm so sorry, I can't tell you how very sorry I am."

"Of course, my dear." What could she want, this lovely girl? She was obviously upset. She glanced questioningly at the man beside her, but he said nothing.

Edouard closed the door quietly behind him as he came into the room. The woman was sitting near his mother, with her back to him. She had the most marvelous hair and he glimpsed the velvet skin of her neck, and her long slender back.

"You see, I knew Charles," she was saying, "not for very long but . . . well . . . we were lovers, madame." The words came out in a rush.

Edouard leaned against the door, listening. His mother looked surprised but not shocked. Why should she be; Charles was an attractive young man, of course he had lovers, but what did she want? She didn't look as though she had come here to ask for money, and the man with her looked the pillar of respectability. Was he her lover now? Somehow Edouard didn't think so.

"Madame, I don't want to shock you and in other circumstances I might never have come to you, but . . . there is a child."

A child—could she mean Charles's child? Was what she was saying true? Edouard looked at his mother. She was gripping the arms of her chair tightly and he could see she was shocked now. He walked across the room and stood beside her. "I am Edouard d'Aureville," he said, meeting Léonie's eyes. "Before you go on, I want you to remember that my brother is only recently dead. My mother is very upset; she cannot bear any more shocks."

"Edouard . . . it's you!"

He stopped in surprise.

"But you see, Edouard, I'm here because of you. Charles told me about you. He said he could tell you anything, all his secrets . . . that you always understood. That's why I knew I could trust you with Amélie."

"My dear," said Isabelle, "where is this baby?"

"She'll be here soon. Don't you see . . . I want you to have her. I'm giving her to you . . she's *your* grandchild." She turned to Edouard, her eyes desperate. "She's your niece . . . she's a part of Charles. And she needs you."

"I think perhaps I had better explain," interrupted Alphonse. "It's a bizarre story and I see no sense in complicating it with detail. Léonie and Charles were lovers, briefly. A daughter, Amélie, was born from this relationship, though Charles knew nothing about it. Their relationship had been a . . . casual one; Léonie was involved with another man at the time. He's a very jealous man, capable of anything. She decided to conceal the birth of the child from him, and Amélie was taken to be brought up by a family on the southern coast. He has since found out about the child, and we feel now that he is a threat to her, that his jealousy could drive him beyond the bounds of sanity. Quite simply, Amélie is in danger. In an effort to remove her daughter from this danger, Léonie has come to you to ask you to take her and, more specifically, to take the child out of the country, back to Brazil with you. Obviously she asks nothing in return: in fact, she will give you any sum you stipulate to provide for her daughter. And once the child is handed over to you, she will never ask to see her again. It is the only way to ensure her safety."

His words rang with truth and Léonie thanked God he had come with her. Without him she would have seemed just some hysterical woman, distraught over her lover's death. But Alphonse was so cool, so precise; they must believe him.

"But I must see her." Isabelle's eyes had filled with tears, and Léonie knelt at her side.

"Madame, I had to give away my baby when she was only one month old. I have not seen her since. She will be here soon and I'll see her one more time, and then I'll trust her to you . . . you must take her, madame. If you don't, I don't know what I will do."

"Are you saying that your lover will kill the child?" asked Edouard in amazement.

Léonie's eyes met his. "He is no longer my lover. Yes, he will kill her. Believe me, he will."

The evening mist was rolling in as Edouard walked silently with Léonie by the river. The torrent of words had stopped and there were no more tears. He could sense that she was feeling calmer, just from the relief of telling him her story, about Charles, her shipwrecked mariner, and "Monsieur," her lover, and their strange relationship. They had walked alone by the river for hours. She had left nothing out, or almost nothing. The mystery of Charles's death. It wasn't simply that he'd been caught in a squall and washed overboard in a rough sea—conditions were perfect for sailing. Edouard had spoken with some of his yachting friends and they had complained of the quickness of the autopsy, the disappearance of the crewman whom nobody knew, and the fractured skull—as if from some heavy blow. Charles had probably been dead before he went into the water, they had said. Some thought the man had murdered him—but why? What was the motive? Well, now he had one. He had been Léonie's lover, and Léonie was associated with a jealous man, a man who was angry enough to kill her child.

"And now you'd better tell me exactly what happened to Charles," he said quietly.

"What do you mean?" Léonie stopped in surprise.

"Did Monsieur kill him?"

His eyes asked only for the truth. "We have no proof," she said.

"But?"

"Yes, I believe he did kill Charles. That's why I'm convinced he'll try to kill Amélie."

He hadn't been prepared for it, even though he'd asked her. His dear little brother—the boy he'd taught to sail and to swim—killed by this woman's monstrous lover. "Where is he? I'll confront him. I'll get evidence . . . damn him!"

"No, no, no. Please, Edouard. Don't you understand? You can't—

there's no way we can accuse him publicly. Don't you see, it was all arranged, the autopsy and the coroner—even the police, for all we know. He's too powerful, Edouard. . . . No one can go against him. He controls it all."

"Then I shall kill him."

She took his hand and held it to her burning cheek. "Please, no . . . no more killing. Think of your mother, think of Charles. Oh, I should never have told you! All that matters now is Amélie. She's Charles's daughter. Only *you* can save her, only *you* can look after her. You will be her father. You can't become a murderer because of Monsieur . . . and because of me."

A murderer. He felt helpless. What was he to do? How could he let Charles's death go unavenged?

Léonie read his thoughts. "I will take care of Monsieur. One day I will have my revenge."

Madame Frenard had accompanied Maroc to Tours with the child, refusing to let him take charge. "You'll never manage without a woman," she'd insisted, "a baby needs a woman around."

Alphonse met them in the hotel lobby and the baby smiled at him delightedly. She loved company, and why not? Wasn't everyone always so pleased to talk to her, to tell her she was pretty and tickle her cheek? Oh, dear, thought Alphonse, now what? How will Léonie ever be able to give her up? She's a charmer.

"Léonie's at the château," he said. "It's all arranged. Was there any trouble, Maroc?"

"None so far. It seems Verronet has been spending more time at the casino than looking for the baby; we were lucky."

"I hope he lost," said Alphonse calmly.

Maroc smiled. He liked Alphonse. "I'll wait here then," he suggested. "You should take the baby to her."

Alphonse picked up her basket gently, carrying it like an awkward parcel. He was not used to babies and Amélie crowed with laughter, enjoying being joggled so inexpertly. Oh, yes, he thought, this is going to be hard.

Edouard sat opposite Léonie as Alphonse put the baby in her arms. He had never seen anything so beautiful as her face when she saw her child. She was lit with such radiance that he wanted to hold her, to save her from what was to come. Such joy was fragile.

"Amélie," she whispered, smiling into the eyes of her little girl. "Here I am . . . remember me? We were together in the beginning, maybe somewhere in the recesses of your little mind you remember. . . ."

Amélie reached up and grabbed the pretty beads swinging above her, tugging them in an attempt to get them into her mouth, wasn't that where everything good went?

Léonie laughed, holding her closer. She was so beautiful, this child of hers.

"Léonie," said Alphonse, "I'm afraid we must remember why we're here."

"Of course, but just a few minutes, please?"

They left her alone with Amélie: just ten minutes, though, warned Alphonse. Just ten minutes for the rest of her life!

Amélie was exactly as she had known she would be, a plump-faced, blond, smiling infant—already with two tiny white teeth and a dazzling smile. She stroked the soft hair with her finger, feeling its silkiness, studying her child's face intently, catching up on the missing months and storing memories for the coming, lonely years. Amélie waved her arms, smiling at her mother, and Léonie smiled back at her, whispering little words of love as the child grabbed again for her pearl necklace. "Here," she said, "take it, my darling, I brought no toy for you, take this instead." She laughed as Amélie took the necklace in her tiny fist and swung it, dangling, backward and forward. Oh, she was enchanting, this daughter of hers, and they had only ten minutes together, ten last private minutes.

"I know I shouldn't ask you this," said Edouard as he and Alphonse paced the terrace together, "but who is he . . . her lover?"

"It's better that you don't know."

"You realize it would be easy for me to find out if I wanted to."

Alphonse looked him in the eye. "Yes. It would. But I'm trusting you not to. Believe me, Edouard, when I say that it's better you don't know. Once you did, you might be tempted to do something about it. I don't want to put that burden on you—and neither does Léonie. Remember, the child comes first."

Edouard sighed. "There's only one good thing to come out of this, and that's that baby. My mother has a grandchild, a memory of Charles."

Isabelle came toward them, hurrying along the terrace. "Is she here? Has she arrived yet?" she called.

Alphonse glanced at his watch. The ten minutes were almost up. "We left her alone with the baby," he explained, "but now it's time."

The tension was unbearable, thought Isabelle. She wanted to see the baby and yet she didn't—what if she looked exactly as Charles did when he was that age? Oh, dear, she couldn't bear it.

But this baby was blond, golden eyed, and peachy skinned, smiling at her with a merry grin. "Amélie," said Léonie softly to her child, "this is your grandmother and she will look after you. And this is Edouard, your new father . . . he will love you as your real father would have." She placed the baby in Isabelle's arms and in a voice she struggled to control said, "We must leave now, Alphonse." Turning her back on her child, she ran from the room. Isabelle started after her, holding the baby.

"Léonie," she called, but Léonie kept going.

It was Edouard who caught up with her as she ran through the hall and out across the lawn. "Léonie!" He grabbed her arm. "Please stop, Léonie, don't run away."

He folded her in his arms, holding her trembling body close to him until she had calmed, and then when she turned her face up to him, he kissed her. It was gentle and without passion, but it was full of love.

34

THE VAST SILVERY ROOM was cold. No fires burned in the grates of its twin fireplaces and there were no flowers to cast lingering sensuous scents into the air. Monsieur didn't notice. He'd been there for hours, waiting. She had to return eventually. And when she did? What then? He sank wearily into a chair, remembering how he'd felt when he heard she was ill, that she had to go away for months. He'd been in agony, telling himself she *had* to get better, she couldn't die and *leave* him! And all the time she'd been plotting, she'd been planning to go away and have another man's child. God, how she had fooled him—worse. How she had let him make a fool of himself! Well, all that remained now was to find the child. Verronet would know in a few days, the man was efficient. If it hadn't been for his intuition, he never would have known about the child. And now Verronet knew how he'd been made a fool of, that his mistress had had a child by another man! But he didn't know what had happened to Charles—it was never good business to keep all your secrets in one safe so he had gone to other agents for that.

The door clicked. Her hair was wild, blown by the wind, and her stare was as icy as the room. "I should kill you," she said, standing by the door, "but it's probably just what you expect me to do. I'm never sure whether my actions are my own or just the result of your planning. I don't want you to die. You can live with the disaster you've made of your life . . . a great man, son of a noble family," she mocked him, "a rich man, a powerful man. A murderer, Gilles de Courmont."

"Nonsense," he said crisply. "You don't know what you're talking about."

"Don't I? I'm not the only one who believes Charles d'Aureville was murdered."

"Murdered? You're being ridiculous, Léonie. I heard that he died in a boating accident."

"An accident that you planned just as you plan everything."

"I don't know on what evidence you're basing these statements, but of course they are not true. I suppose it's only to be expected, though, from a woman as treacherous as you. I give you everything you want and you use it to cheat on me, to flaunt yourself with other men . . . d'Aureville wasn't the first."

It clicked suddenly. "Of course, Alain—the important gallery owner in London, the offer too good to refuse—why didn't you kill him, too? Or didn't you 'love' me then, Monsieur? Oh, that's right, 'love' only came later—when you decided you needed me and to love me was the only way to get me back. But that was after Charles."

His rage was ice-tipped as he towered over her. "You made a fool of me. No woman does that."

"You made a fool of yourself, Monsieur. You should have told me you loved me long before. I begged you to, I wanted you to. All I wanted was to be loved by you. There would have been no Alain, no Charles—"

"And no child."

She looked at him warily.

"Where is she, Léonie?"

She turned her back on him, staring out of the window. "I don't know."

"You don't know?"

"I gave her away when she was born; she has her own life, without me."

"Don't you want her back?" He moved closer to her. He could smell jasmine. "Léonie. Find the child, get her back. Bring her here, we'll live here together. I'll bring her up as my daughter, take care of her, provide for her. . . ."

She turned and stared at him in astonishment.

"Stay with me, Léonie."

Their eyes locked. "Do you imagine for one moment that I would give you my child? You're crazier than I thought, Gilles de Courmont. Charles d'Aureville is dead because of me—I have to live with that for the rest of my life . . . and so do you! I wasn't the one who struck him on the head, but we're both guilty."

"Léonie, I swear I had nothing to do with it. You can't leave me, Léonie, I need you. Stay with me!" He gripped her arm, pulling her toward him.

"There is no power on earth that would make me stay with you. You're a monster."

He pulled her closer, thrusting his face next to hers. "If you leave," he said quietly, "I'll ruin you. I gave you everything, and I can take it all away. You'll be left with nothing . . . *nothing!*"

"You forget, you made me an independent woman. You put money in my bank account, bought the stocks and shares, invested in property—"

"All in companies that I own and all with a clause that they revert to me at any time I should say. You never learned to read the small print, Léonie—every business contract's first rule."

She began to laugh. "Of course. How typical, Monsieur, how very typical. You only lent them to me for as long as I behaved! Well, you can keep them all. I shall be back where I started. I'll leave the jewels in the safe, the money in the bank—it'll be all you have to console yourself with. You'll ruin me, but you'll ruin yourself . . . you're just a shell, a façade of a civilized man. You're a cold, arrogant, ruthless killer."

"I'll find your child, Léonie. And when I have her, you'll have to come back to me, or . . ."

The unspoken threat dangled in the air between them. "If it takes me years," he whispered, "I'll find her."

"And if it takes me years, Monsieur, I'll find the evidence that you had Charles d'Aureville killed. It will all catch up to you, Monsieur, one day, I promise."

"Think of your child, Léonie. . . . Wouldn't it be nice to know that she was safe?"

Her heart was beating so wildly she felt sure he must be able to see it, that he must surely feel the fear that was sweeping through her, and then she remembered him with his sons in Monte Carlo, remembered him telling her that it wasn't until his son almost died that he knew how much he meant to him. If Amélie were his child, would he be able to kill her? She took a deep breath. "But what if Amélie were yours, Monsieur? What if Amélie was really your daughter?"

The door shut behind her and he stared after her in disbelief. What was she saying? He wanted to run after her, to beg her for the truth. Was the child *his?* Could it be possible? Had he killed Charles d'Aureville for nothing? He walked to the window, gazing unseeing at the gardens in the middle of the square. She had gone. Left him. The only key was the child. Once he had her, Léonie would come back to him. He would offer her her daughter—alive—there would be no danger, so long as Léonie stayed with him.

But how was he ever to know if Amélie was his child? Was Léonie fooling him again? He *must* find her. If it took him a lifetime, he would do it. And then he would have Léonie again.

He walked along the line of curtains, releasing their tasseled ropes until they swung in a silvery mist, closing out the light from the room.

BOOK
2

1902-1909

❧ 35 ❦

AMÉLIE D'AUREVILLE swung back her thick blond braid impatiently and peered from the loft at Roberto and Diego waiting in the stable ten feet below. It looked a very long way down and she glanced longingly at the ladder. "I told you she wouldn't do it," said Diego contemptuously. "What do you expect? She's a girl, and anyway, she's only eight."

"She'll do it," replied Roberto do Santos stubbornly. "She's no coward."

Damn, thought Amélie, now there's no way out—I'll have to jump, Roberto believes I can do it and I'm not going to let Diego Benavente beat me. Dangling her skinny legs over the side, she wriggled to the very edge, balancing uncertainly. Diego had closed the door so that no one would see them and it was quite dark. She could just make him out, leaning against the wall with his arms folded, waiting. Roberto's hair, as blond as her own, gleamed in the dimness as he looked up at her. "It's all right, Amélie," he called, pushing a bale of straw into place beneath her, "this'll cushion your fall . . . it won't hurt, I promise you." She had to do it, he told himself, quashing the pity he felt for her. She couldn't let Diego win or he'd never let her play with them again, and he couldn't bear for her to be left out. "Come on," Roberto encouraged her, "I'll catch you."

Gripping the beam, Amélie shut her eyes tightly and slithered over the edge, dangling uncertainly in space, seconds passed, her arms hurt, she could hold out no longer. The ground came up to meet her in a rush and she sprawled on the hay with Roberto, who had broken her fall by grabbing her just before she hit the ground.

"Are you all right?" he asked, peering at her to see if she were crying.

Amélie sat up. "'Course I am, why shouldn't I be?"

"You cheated," complained Diego, "you had the hay there and that makes at least a couple of feet difference. Anyway, Roberto helped you."

"I did not cheat," yelled Amélie angrily. She could never win with Diego—he always had an answer. He put her down for being a girl and for being only eight years old, always boasting that he was already eleven, and a year older than Roberto. He provoked her into deeds of daring that were almost too much for her. But he hadn't beat her yet! Still, her ankle hurt, it was beginning to throb painfully, and she felt she might cry.

"Of course she didn't cheat, Diego," said Roberto reasonably, trying as usual to keep the peace between them. "She did really well."

Diego pushed open the stable door. "Oh, come on," he muttered, "let's gallop the horses up to the coffee fields."

"Why do we always have to do what *you* want to do, Diego Benavente?" yelled Amélie, pulling her throbbing foot under her and curling up on her bale of straw.

"Come on, Amélie, please," begged Roberto. "I'll let you ride Bicho." She adored his pony Bicho and to ride him was a treat he accorded her when he was being extra nice.

Amélie hung her head. "I don't want to," she muttered. "I'd rather stay here."

"Leave her, Roberto," said Diego impatiently. "Let's have a race; I'll bet Vinicius can beat Bicho any day."

Roberto hesitated. "Are you sure, Amélie?"

" 'Course I am!"

"Come *on,* Roberto!"

"Well . . . all right. I'll see you later, Amélie."

Amélie waited as they crossed the yard to the paddock, holding back her tears until they were out of sight. Ow! Her ankle really hurt. "I hate you, Diego Benavente," she sobbed, as she scrambled to her feet and hobbled after them.

From the veranda Sebastião do Santos watched Amélie limp across the courtyard, no doubt in search of Roberto. He fought an impulse to dash after her and find out what was wrong, but if she wanted to be with the boys and play boys' games, then she must work things out for herself. Still, she looked so small and vulnerable in the baggy shorts she insisted on wearing so that she could be like Roberto—she even wore his shirts and pulled back her thick mane of hair as tightly as she could so it would look short like his because, of course, Isabelle wouldn't allow her to cut it. More often than not, when the d'Aurevilles were staying on the Fazenda Castelo do Santos during the holidays, they'd find Amélie curled up asleep in Roberto's bed, their two blond heads side by side on the pillow, her two little cats dozing at their feet. Anyway, whatever had happened to her, he'd bet that Diego Benavente had something to do with it. Diego made him uneasy, despite his dark good looks and his charming grin—he could talk his way out of any trouble with his glib tongue. It was a pity that Roberto was so close to him, but then, as their parents were lifelong friends and the Benaventes had the neighboring *fazenda,* it was only natural that Diego would be Roberto's best friend. And poor Amélie wanted that role very badly.

He had loved Amélie from the very first day he saw her, a blond beaming baby girl who'd come to stay with his family and their houseful of boys. He, as the eldest do Santos son, had been seven years old, and his brothers Flavio six, Marcus four, and Roberto just three. She had moved into their house and into their hearts as easily as if she were a do Santos daughter, and her soft curls, her amber eyes, and her very feminine charm had made him her particular slave. The first thing he had always done when he got home from school was find Amélie, and he'd spent hours riding her around on the back of Zeze, Roberto's dehorned pet ram, her little fingers clutching its woolly coat and her low merry chuckle delighting him as her tiny heels drummed on the gentle beast's sides in an attempt to make him go faster. As she grew up, it was Roberto, of course, so close to her own age, who had become her playmate, but it was still Sebastião who was her confidant, the one to whom she told everything—all her secrets and her fears and her worries. It was he who had taught Amélie to swim when she had confided to him that she was afraid of drowning like her mother and father, and with his help she'd overcome those fears.

Sebastião counted it as his lucky day when Isabelle d'Aureville had decided to come to stay with her old friend and distant cousin, Francisco do Santos. The family ties went back to 1567 when François de St. Chapelle had sailed from Honfleur to Brazil, becoming one of the vast new country's first settlers. The family had never lost touch with their native country and, though their name had become Brazilianized, each generation had sent its sons back to France to be educated. Francisco Castelo do Santos, his father, had never forgotten the warmth of the welcome of his French family for the painfully shy young man who had arrived in Paris to take his place at university, and in particular the kindness of their youngest daughter, Isabelle. She had taken him to parties, sharing her friends, and initiating him into the manners and customs of French life, giving him a new confidence and making him feel at home.

In fact, Francisco had fancied himself a little in love with Isabelle—that is, until he had returned home and met dark-eyed Luiza with the long black hair. How they had managed to have a family of Nordic-looking blond sons confounded them.

Tia Agostinha emerged from the wide doors that led from the dining room onto the veranda, her heavy tread sending small tremors through the springy cedar boards. Her eyes followed Sebastião's gaze as Amélie's distant figure paused, then bent to rub her ankle, and slowly turned around and retraced her steps.

"That child's in the wars again," she sighed.

Sebastião grinned at her. Agostinha was their old nurse, she'd brought up all the do Santos boys and their father and his brothers and sisters before them, and she loved them all equally. But he suspected that for her, too, Amélie was special.

"What happened this time?" called Agostinha, bustling to help Amélie up the steps to the veranda.

"It's my ankle," said Amélie, avoiding the question. "I think it's broken." She gazed in relief at Agostinha. Everything would be all right now; Agostinha knew how to take care of everything. She'd find some herbs and leaves and soak them in water for a poultice, muttering incantations in Yoruba, her native language, that probably worked some magic spell. Tia Agostinha looked magical, she was so *big*—over six feet tall and almost as wide—and she was a lovely smooth soft mahogany color and her hair was a frizzled reddish halo around her smiling face. And she had the biggest, most comfortable lap for cuddling children.

Agostinha laughed, a loud rumbling sound that always made Amélie laugh, too. "It's not broken, *mia filha,* just a sprain, that's all. We'll soon fix that."

"Exactly what did happen, Amélie?" asked Sebastião, not letting her off the hook.

Amélie avoided his eyes. "I was just jumping, that's all."

"And where was Roberto? And Diego?"

Amélie hid her face in Agostinha's vast bosom as she swept her into her arms and carried her off toward the kitchen, making her reply too muffled for Sebastião to catch. It didn't make any difference; he knew she would never tell on Roberto anyway.

Isabelle had thought that life in Rio was sixty years behind that of France, but on the *fazenda* it was like going back centuries. That was exactly its charm, it never changed. Isolated in its thousands of acres of rolling coffee fields, the big house was as all-embracing and comfortable as Tia Agostinha's arms, and Isabelle could never decide when she liked it more: in the daytime, when the sunlight filtered through slatted shutters in the lofty salons and the happy family house rang with the voices of children; or in the evening hours, when the sun cast long calm shadows across the lawn, as they gathered for drinks on the veranda, to enjoy the cooler air and each other's company; or at night, when the only illumination came from antique oil lamps and tall wax candles that lent a tender flickering dimness to the family scene around the vast dining table that could, and often did, seat two dozen with ease.

If anyone had asked her eight years ago where she would most like to live in the world, she would have stated unhesitatingly the Château d'Aureville. Now, she would have to pause, to give herself time to consider the question—and even then she might not have been able to answer. This house was a favorite, but then her new home, the Villa d'Aureville, was just as special in its own more modern way, built as it was on the long empty stretch of beach behind the last hilly spur of the Sierra Nevada mountains that isolated Copacabana from the rest of Rio.

It was Edouard who had chosen the site, buying it for a song, knowing that one day its value, set as it was facing Copacabana Beach—where long curling emerald waves plumed with white unfurled themselves slowly to crash in a smooth line, bubbling into the soft sand—would skyrocket. Edouard had thrown himself into the plans for the house, busying himself with the minutest details, planning and replanning, seeking perfection in the d'Aurevilles' new home, as though not allowing himself time to think of anything—or anyone—else. He gave the same energy to his toil in the rubber plantation, buried in the Amazon forests for months on end, sending telegrams from Manaus when he could to let Isabelle know he was all right, and long, loving messages for Amélie. Even now, Isabelle suspected he still carried a lonely torch for a woman he barely knew and to whose child he was now father. Léonie. What a miracle she had worked on their lives. She had brought them a bounty of blessings by giving them Amélie. It wasn't only that Amélie brought back tender memories of Charles as a boy—in the way she tilted her head when she smiled, or clenched her fists in determination when she walked, or in her low, bubbling, joyful laughter—but because of her own loving nature and intelligence. And there was no mistaking whose child she was. Amélie was the image of her mother.

Amélie had finally won her battle and was to go to school. Of course, she had wanted to attend the Collegio Pedro II with all the do Santos boys, but she had been forced to settle for a girls' convent school. And that, thought Isabelle, was the problem. Not for Amélie, but for herself. With Amélie as its center, her daily routine of nannies and governesses had dominated Isabelle's life. And now, with Amélie away all day, time would hang heavy on her hands. Unless, of course, she went ahead with her plan. The idea had evolved from the compliments of friends. Compliments earned by the faithful Celestine, her old cook from the château, who, with her husband, Georges, had refused to be pensioned off when Isabelle left France. The couple had resisted all of Isabelle's arguments against their coming to Brazil. Celestine had learned new ways in the kitchens of the do Santos villa, where she had been initiated into the mysteries of Brazilian cooking, with its African origins and its special oils and spices, black beans and chili peppers. There had been other mysteries perpetuated by the do Santos servants that they hadn't cared to penetrate: the rams' horns tied to the trees, the strange plants brewed into mysterious potions, the fires lit some nights on the kitchen doorstep—all meant to keep out the devils. "Whatever next," Celestine had said in amazement as she'd discovered the tiny labels affixed to the jars of preserves and jams. "They're prayers to keep out the ants!" It never failed to surprise her that such nice people could have such heathen ways. But her cooking, always superb in France, had taken on a new dimension, and the Villa d'Aureville—with its name written in an arch of delicately wrought iron across the immense gates and its guardian griffins from the old pillars at the château—had soon become known as the house that served the best food in Rio, and in the loveliest, most civilized surroundings. An invitation to dinner at Isabelle's was prized indeed. And, after all, thought Isabelle, I ran a château with thirty bedrooms for most of my life; what could be so difficult about this idea?

The question was, how would Edouard and Francisco react to it? There was, she decided as she descended the stairs for lunch, no time like the present for finding out!

"I have been thinking," she said some minutes later as Francisco poured her a glass of pale pink wine, "that with Amélie away so much, my life may become a little boring."

Francisco's and Luiza's dark eyes met hers and Edouard's quizzical gray ones lit with a smile. What was she up to now?

"I am considering," said Isabelle clearly, "opening a restaurant. It will be called the Pavillon d'Aureville."

The office was stifling. Gilles ripped off his jacket and flung it across a chair, and loosened his tie as he paced to the window and gazed out across the leafy abundance of chestnut trees. It was a perfect day in May, perfect for being on the Côte d'Azur—on the yacht, maybe, with a woman, enjoying the sun and the breezes and the freshness of early summer. But with what woman? Oh, he had tried it. There had been women since Léonie, all they did was satisfy the urge of the moment. There was never anyone who fulfilled the *need*.

From his desk piled high with papers he picked up the latest report—she was still at the old place, living there quietly, eking out a small living running it as an inn. Why—when she could have everything? She hadn't even cared when he had taken it all back, she'd sent him the keys to the safe deposit in the bank—his own bank, where he had the master keys anyway—and told him to take back his jewelry. She had left her clothes hanging in the closets—the sable coat and the floor-length blue fox, the gowns from Worth and the negligées from Serrat. She'd ripped the worthless share certificates to pieces and scattered them across the bed, and he had had her name eliminated from the title deeds to all the properties—except one: the inn. Its title belonged to her free and clear and he cursed the day he had given it to her; it was the one thing he couldn't get back and it had saved her. She had her rufage, her place to run to for safety.

It was proving impossible to spy on her in such an isolated spot and reports were sparse. She'd been into Saint-Jean to the market, or had been swimming in the morning—the usual things. Sometimes she went into Nice or Monte Carlo and had lunch in a café and mailed some letters at the post office. She never left them in the mailbox at the top of the lane anymore, so he couldn't discover whom she was writing to.

He threw the paper back on the desk and paced the floor restlessly. He needed that day-to-day information! He needed to know what she did now that he wasn't there, now that she had condemned him to loneliness—again. Throwing himself into the big leather chair, he buried his head in his hands. If he knew it would be better, then he could visualize her doing what she did, almost as if he were there, just as he used to at school when he would think of his mother. With her he'd had to imagine it all, invent the scenes and the dialogue, but with Léonie it was real. Oh, God, Léonie, Léonie . . . come back to me.

Amélie was her one vulnerability, but there was no trace of her. He had combed Europe for the child, following the minutest leads, using top men, but all to no avail. He had started on the coast with the foster parents, but they had known nothing; he had had Caro and Alphonse followed for two years, and Maroc . . . everyone she knew. He'd even—farfetched though it was—had someone make inquiries at the Château d'Aureville. He had had just a glimmer of an idea that she might take the girl there—ridiculous, of course, to think that a family like the d'Aurevilles might accept a bastard child some woman claimed was their son's, but then that woman was Léonie. His man had reported that the château was closed and shuttered and that the Comtesse Isabelle d'Aureville—a broken woman since the death of her son—had gone abroad. He was upset by the news of Isabelle d'Aureville; he hadn't considered Charles's mother when he'd made the arrangements. He had called off his man at once and tried to forget her.

It always came back to the same thing: Amélie was the key to Léonie. Without Amélie he had nothing, with her he could offer Léonie everything, a home with her child, security—and himself. If she didn't agree, then the child became his weapon: Léonie would have to come back to him to make sure her daughter came to no harm. And, of course, once she came back, everything would be all right, it would be like it was in the beginning. He could remember that summer when she had swum from the yacht, and afterward fed him plates of shrimp and cheese . . . no more omelettes, she had said . . . they had laughed together and afterward he had made love to her. He had possessed her . . . owned her.

He *had* to find Amélie. The idea came to him suddenly. If he couldn't trace her, then there was only one way left to get her. Pulling on his jacket, he strode to the door. "I shan't be back this afternoon, Verronet," he called over his shoulder. "Something important has come up."

Verronet watched him go with a raised eyebrow. Monsieur le Duc de Courmont was not the dedicated man he used to be.

❧ 36 ❧

THE ENVELOPE looked very official and Léonie balanced it in her hands. There was something ominous about the brown thickness and the pink sealing wax over the flap; it was from a firm of notaries in Paris.

"Bébé," she called, hurrying through the garden toward the beach. The little cat scrambled down the wooden steps after her as she slipped off her shoes and walked barefoot across the warm sand to a sunny rock and sat there for a while, gazing at the calm sea, getting up enough courage to open it. She shrugged; maybe it was good news. She ripped the envelope open and unfolded the document.

It couldn't be true! Monsieur must be *crazy*. He was claiming her child as his own; he was going to force her to give him *his* daughter. The court would be told that she was an unfit mother who had given her child away, that she was unwilling to look after Amélie herself and that he, the father, had a legal right to his daughter, that he wished to provide for her and to ensure her welfare.

"Oh, Bébé," she whispered, "I thought we were safe, after eight years I thought maybe he had forgotten ... how could I have been so foolish?" She glanced back at the papers in her hands. What was she to do? There was no way that the court could make her tell where Amélie was, and anyway, she didn't know. She'd never heard a single word from the d'Aurevilles; a precaution she had insisted on, fearing that Monsieur would intercept her letters and trace Amélie through them. Now she knew she had been right, for at least she couldn't perjure herself when she said she didn't know where Amélie was, and she would say no more than that. Except, of course, that the child wasn't his.

She picked up Bébé and sat the cat on her knee while she thought. Monsieur must have realized that she would say the child was someone else's; could he really be prepared to go through with it? Was he—Gilles, Duc de Courmont—really going to give Paris the gossip it would love, let the world know that his mistress had cheated on him, that he wasn't enough to satisfy a woman! Oh, she would humiliate him all right, she would make him look a fool. She had learned how to play him at his own game.

"If only I'd found the evidence, Bébé," she murmured. "I could accuse him of Charles's murder, but there is no evidence. He was too clever for that." She and Caro and Alphonse had tried their best to break the barrier of silence that surrounded the case in Deauville, but it had proved impossible. It had all been done too quickly, no one knew anything. There was just a physical description of the man on the boat given to them by the other yachtsmen: a burly man with sparse reddish hair, an oddly small head on a large body, running to fat, and he knew about boats. The description of Charles's assassin was engraved on her mind. Alphonse had hired detectives to search for the man, but without any luck.

She brushed off her skirt and, picking up Bébé, wandered barefoot by the edge of the water. The inn, gleaming white under the cloudless May sky, was truly her home, her refuge. She would have been content bringing up Amélie here, watching her grow. It would have been a simple life. "But we're not meant for a simple life, Bébé," she said, kissing the cat's little pink nose. "We must go back to Paris and fight. The only trouble is that the fight will take money, and we have none."

Paul Bernard studied the two women at the table by the window. Pale sun filtered through the long net curtains, throwing into relief Léonie's dominant profile and her mane of hair. She looked from this angle like an image from some ancient coin. But the dress was quite wrong. Oh, it was expensive and fashionable, discreetly navy blue with a white collar and tiny pearl buttons, but Léonie needed something flamboyant, extravagant—she had a natural ostentation that would turn heads whatever she wore, and in the right outfit she would be more than just beautiful, she would be stunning.

She had come a long way from the little girl he had met on the train, running away from Masarde. She was even more beautiful now at twenty-eight than she had been at sixteen. She was the talk of Paris. He could see heads turning in her direction even here, in the smartest restaurant, whose clientele were almost immune to gossip and scandal, it being such a part of their daily lives.

He lit a cigarette and sat back, watching her. He had seen her twice on stage, the first time as the showgirl La Belle France in feathers and leotard—he remembered those long legs. Then the second time, when the horse had created such confusion and she'd almost lost her balance—and her top! He had tried to find her afterward but it had been impossible. He could have taken her then and made her a success, he'd known from the first moment on the train that she had what it took—all she needed to learn was the craft—and now her prospects were even better. Everyone in Paris already knew her—she was both a celebrity and a notorious woman. The man in the street read about the proud sexy mistress of a duke, and the woman read about the desolate young mother who had been forced to hide her child from a cruel lover—each one seeing exactly what he wanted to see in her. Either way they would flock to a theater just to get a look at her. He wondered if she would do it—it was worth a try. He'd send a note across with the waiter.

Paul Bernard—the name was familiar. Léonie read the note quickly. Of course, the man from the train! Had she ever repaid him the money he'd lent her for the extra train fare? He had played a small but important part in her life—if she hadn't met him, she would never have gone to Madame Artois, would never have worked at Serrat, never have met Maroc or Caro and Alphonse—and Rupert. And Monsieur. She might never have had the joy of Amélie.

"I must see him," she said to Caro, "though I don't know what he wants; probably just to say hello to the scandalous woman of the year!"

Caro laughed. "Don't forget you're also a beautiful woman," she said, "and from what I can see, he looks like a very attractive man."

Léonie examined him as he threaded his way through the tables toward them. She had thought him so old when she had met him on the train, but now she realized that he could have been no more than thirty. She smiled, at sixteen, thirty *is* old. He was short and wiry, with dark hair, prematurely graying at the sides, and amused brown eyes that met hers admiringly as he took her hand.

"I wasn't sure you'd remember," he said.

"You played a more important role in my life than you know, Monsieur Bernard, and, besides, I couldn't remember whether I ever paid you back the train fare—am I guilty?"

"I had a note from you with the money a few weeks later. I think you sent me your first wages."

She laughed. "I probably did. I was an honest woman then. Caro, this is Paul Bernard, a theatrical entrepreneur—I think that was what it said on your card?"

"That's exactly what I wanted to talk to you about. . . ."

"We were just about to have some coffee," said Caro quickly. "Won't you join us?"

Léonie stared at her in surprise. Why the sudden enthusiasm for Paul Bernard? Of course, Caro wanted her to meet some attractive men.

"Now, what was it you were saying, Monsieur Bernard?" asked Caro with a smile, as he accepted the chair pulled forward by the waiter.

"Do you remember when we met on the train, I told you that you had what was needed to become a success in cabaret? Even as a simple country girl, you had the looks—no, more than that, there was an arrogance, a flamboyance lurking under those layers of woolens. I saw you again, twice. At the Internationale."

Léonie groaned. "Oh, God, I'll never forget it."

"You shouldn't forget it, it was probably the best introduction you could have had to show business—nothing could ever be worse. It was humiliating, especially for the young girl you were then."

She raised an eyebrow. "You mean 'innocent'?"

He thought about it. "Yes, possibly. But that's in the past. What I want to talk about is the present. Where you are now. You are a public figure—known to everyone in Paris, probably in the whole of France. People would flock to a theater just to see the beautiful mistress of the Duc de Courmont. . . ."

She was shocked. "Like a freak in a circus!"

"I didn't mean that, and it's certainly not true. They'd come to see *you:* a beautiful woman, tragically forced to hide away her child so that a rich, powerful man can't take the child away from her. The public would adore it, they would pay just to see you."

"To see me? But what would I do?" she asked, remembering that she had posed exactly the same question all those years ago on the train.

"You'd make a fortune," he replied quietly.

Money. Once again she needed money, this time to pay for the lawyers—or at least to be able to pay back Alphonse and Caro, since it was they who were spending a small fortune hiring lawyers on her behalf. She had worked in the cabaret before when she needed money and she flinched at the memory. No, it was too much, too humiliating. No money was worth it.

So that was it, he thought, he'd said the right thing, she needed money. "I promise you that it would be nothing like before. You'll be prepared this time, you'll learn what to do, how to move, how to use your voice. It will take a little time, but we'll make you the most famous—*not* the most notorious—woman in Europe, Léonie Bahri. And a rich one."

She shivered at the thought of the cabaret—a fortune, he had said. She could pay back Alphonse, pay for her sins, pay for Amélie. "I'll think about it," she agreed finally.

Caro sighed as they shook hands. All I thought was that he was an attractive man, and it's time she met someone—and now look what's happened. Oh, dear, I've done it again!

*   *   *

"Léonie, you can't," protested Caro as they drove toward the law courts. The preliminary hearing was that afternoon, and the purpose of the lunch had been to boost Léonie's morale, but now, instead, she was disturbed.

Léonie sighed. "I wish I were brave enough to do it—he said I could make a fortune, Caro. I'd be able to pay back you and Alphonse; after all, Amélie is my responsibility, not yours."

"We've already discussed that. Alphonse is doing this for himself now, as well as you." He'd been there when Léonie had had to part with Amélie, he'd gone through the search for Charles's killer, he hated de Courmont now almost as much as Léonie did. "It doesn't matter, Léonie, he can well afford it. Of course, he's not as rich as Monsieur, but he's still very rich."

Léonie was silent. They had both been so good to her, it was only because of them that she had survived. Caro had helped her to pay for the expansions to the inn, adding extra rooms so she would be able to take more guests. And now this court case. There must be some other way to make money, but what could she do? She knew only how to be a kept woman—and she wasn't very successful at that. The cab drew up in front of the law courts and she stared at the solid, intimidating stone building with a pang of fear.

Caro took her arm and squeezed it. "It's all right, it's only a preliminary hearing. It'll just be between the lawyers today—no one is going to ask you any questions." They walked down the gloomy, echoing corridors together and the usher held open the door to let them pass. The small courtroom was crowded, spectators lined the benches and journalists waited avidly, pens poised over notebooks. Her lawyer came forward to greet her, and taking a deep breath she entered the courtroom.

She could feel the curious eyes on her, crawling all over her, searching for signs of emotion in her face, taking in the details of her dress as she walked with him to his desk, sitting with her eyes lowered, waiting. She remembered Loulou's words from so long ago: chin up, spine straight, look them in the eye. She lifted her head, tilting her chin at an arrogant angle, and looked directly into the eyes of Monsieur sitting opposite. She hadn't expected it; wasn't it just going to be the lawyers? *No one had told her that he would be there!* Panic flowed through her body. She couldn't move: she gazed into his eyes as though mesmerized—those familiar dark, deep blue eyes, those eyes that knew her as no other man's ever had. There had been so much between them, so much passion, so many storms—and now so much hate. But she would have loved him if he'd only let her; how different life would have been then. He was thinner and there were lines around his eyes and deep grooves by the sides of his mouth. He looked different, but he was still an attractive man. She wondered, with a flicker of jealousy, if there were other women; did he have new lovers?

When Léonie lowered her eyes he felt as though she had shut him out of her world. For a moment she had been his again. What was she thinking as she sat there? Did she hate him? He remembered those first days on the Côte d'Azur, when her thoughts had been so transparent he'd been able to read them in her face. No longer. I'm only doing it for your own good, Léonie, he wanted to say to her, to bring you to your senses, so you'll come back to me.

The judge took his seat and the lawyers conferred and the reporters scribbled busily. Léonie felt isolated, quite separate from the whole scene, as though it were happening to someone else, like a dream. How odd, she thought, that this is all happening to me and because of me, and yet I feel like a spectator. I sit here and people all around me discuss Amélie and make decisions about her future and I'm helpless to do anything about it. It was the same feeling she'd had when Rupert left her and she had been alone and penniless at the inn—Monsieur had won then, but he wouldn't win now. She had resolved then that she would never again be poor and at any-one's mercy. Today Paul Bernard had offered her a way out and she had been too proud to accept it, but not anymore. Monsieur wouldn't stop at this court case, she knew it now. He'd meant it when he said he would get Amélie if it took him forever. This was a lifelong struggle, and if she were to win she would need money. If Paul Bernard were right and people would pay to see her, then she would do it. Then she'd be able to protect Amélie always—even if it cost every sou she ever made.

It was over. The case had been stated and an adjournment declared for preparing fresh documents. Léonie could feel Monsieur's gaze, forcing her to look at him.

Her lawyer took her arm and escorted her from the court, followed by murmurs of admiration from the crowd. Caro had been right about the navy blue dress, she thought grimly; it was the perfect image. But it would be a different one on stage: there she would have to be the mistress, not the mother.

Monsieur walked from the court flanked by his lawyers and watched by the now-silent crowd. Léonie was in front of him, her blond hair coiled tightly on her neck, tied with a girlish blue velvet ribbon. He longed to touch it, to feel its silken texture . . . if only she'd turn around and speak to him. But she didn't. Caro rushed forward and took her arm, hurrying her from the building. He watched until they had disappeared in the crowd, and then he walked alone down the steps, back to his splendid house on the Ile Saint-Louis.

* * *

Marie-France stared at the newspaper in disbelief. The words of the article jumped out at her—it was a full account of the previous day's court hearing in the custody battle for a daughter between Léonie Bahri and Gilles! There were even descriptions of the protagonists—the slender, beautiful, young blond mother and the arrogant, rich aristocrat. Oh, the papers loved it, it was the kind of story they would follow for weeks—months—in all its juicy details. And she had known nothing about it. Nothing! She had been away for more than a month at the château and had returned only yesterday—and Gilles had said *nothing*. All Paris had known before she did! She was so angry she was shaking; she hadn't even known about the child. She picked up the paper again to check—a daughter, it said, Amélie, now eight years old. *Eight years!* He hadn't seen Léonie in years; why was he suing her now for the child—and one she claimed was another man's? She reread the words, letting the details sink in this time. Dear God, how could Gilles do this, didn't he realize what a fool he was making of himself—and of her! Had he even considered her feelings when he took this action? He was humiliating himself and her; their name was being dragged through the courts and daily newspapers for everyone to read and speculate over. It was the scandal of the decade! She thought of Gérard and Armand—what was he thinking of, to do this to his sons. It couldn't go on.

She walked to the sideboard and poured herself a glass of brandy. It was the first time in her life she had ever done such a thing, but the spirits calmed her and she began to think more logically about what she must do. First she must speak with Gilles and then there must be a family meeting. Her own family as well as his would be against him, they would use all their efforts to stop him. Nothing would harm the good name of her children, she would make sure of that.

≥ 37 ≤

LÉONIE'S DAYS were divided between lengthy meetings at the stuffy wood-paneled offices of her lawyers and the bare cold room where she was learning her craft, being put through her paces by Paul Bernard's team of choreographers, voice teachers, writers, and costume designers. They exercised her, danced with her, and sang with her until she was on the point of exhaustion and knew that she would never be any good, crying her anger at Paul, accusing him of trying to humiliate her.

"It's not so, Léonie," he reassured her as she sat on the bare wooden boards, sweating and limp, tears running down her cheeks. "I promised you that it wouldn't be like last time, and it won't, even more so, because now we know you have a voice."

"But it's so small, they'll never hear me."

It was true, her voice was small, but it had a roughness, a core of emotion, that was appealing, and it was a bonus he hadn't counted on. Of course he had known they could get her into shape so she would know how to hold herself and be able to pace through some simple dance movements—it would have been enough for the audience, who only wanted a glimpse of the notorious Léonie—but the voice was *good*. "Dry your tears," he commanded, "there's someone I want you to meet."

"I don't want to see anyone. I'm too tired." Wearily she pushed the damp hair from her brow.

"He's a songwriter; he'll be writing special songs for you."

"For me? But why . . . I've just learned all these others." She was too tired, she didn't want to be bothered. All she wanted was to go home and forget the whole thing, but she couldn't, she had to go on. It was for Amélie.

Jacques Miel was probably her age and was neither attractive nor unattractive. He was just sort of ordinary, except that he wrote the most incredibly romantic songs, songs of love and loss—and sex. An inner life burned behind those rimless spectacles and within that thin body. It seemed as if all his energy and emotion was poured into his music and his lyrics. God may have made his features ordinary, but his was one of the most inspired talents she had ever known. He was fascinating. From the moment she met him, the stage act that had loomed in her mind as a near disaster took on a different aspect, and for the first time she felt that it might possibly succeed. And all because of Jacques's songs.

She began to spend her evenings at his apartment, going over the lyrics with him. He knew exactly the phrasing she should use; he was better than the voice teacher.

"You don't have a trained voice," he told her, "but what you do have is a special quality. It's rough on those lower notes, a bit raw and sexy . . . that's what we need to use. We don't want you singing sweet little songs, that's not you, Léonie."

"Isn't it?" she asked wistfully. It would have been nice to be sweet and simple.

"It's not you on stage." He amended his statement.

"That's the problem. I wish it weren't me on stage. I'm afraid of all those eyes crawling over me, looking at Léonie Bahri. What do I have to offer them? It just makes me want to hide."

"Look," he said. "I've worked with actors and actresses since I was fourteen and I learned early that no one is himself on stage. The funny co-median is a quiet, unassuming man of few words offstage, the arrogant ac-tress becomes the sweet young girl in front of an audience, the beautiful ethereal ballerina is sweating backstage in pain from strained muscles. They take on another image, become someone other than themselves. You must never give the audience yourself, Léonie, give them what they would like to see. That's the image you should hide behind."

He was right, of course. She wanted to be someone else on that stage, not Léonie. She wanted to be a new person. And, after all, didn't the audi-ence expect that, weren't they expecting to see someone out of the ordinary, someone different from themselves—the Léonie of the newspapers, more ex-otic, more glamorous, and more exciting. But who was she?

"There is nothing else but me, Jacques. I'm just like they are."

"That's not true . . . you don't even look like anyone else I know. Apart from being beautiful, you're different—foreign-looking."

"That's my Egyptian father's influence."

"There you are! It's perfect."

"What is?"

The Egyptian image. Hide behind it if that's what you want. Give them something exotic to look at, take their minds off the Duc de Cour-mont's mistress. You've got more to offer than just the fact that you were his woman, Léonie."

She thought of Sekhmet and the clinging robes like the Fortuny gowns she used to love—maybe even then, subconsciously, she'd been adopting an Egyptian look.

Jacques pulled books from the shelves and they pored over the illustra-tions of ancient Egyptians. He pointed out the hair ornaments, the strange blue painted lines emphasizing the eyes, and the supple clinging robes. Oh, yes, it was perfect; she could hide behind her ancestors.

"Jacques"—she threw her arms around him—"you're wonderful. I thought I'd never be able to go through with it, but if I'm someone else, then maybe it will be easier."

"Will you do something for me?" he asked, still holding her.

She gazed at him expectantly.

"Save 'Léonie' for *me*."

She hesitated, looking into his eyes; they were dark and long-lashed be-hind those thick glasses. She took the spectacles off his nose gently. "A part of me, Jacques," she breathed, "only a part of me."

It felt so good to be in a man's arms again—so good—and he was such a sweet and tender lover, gentle with her at first, kissing her, stroking her hair, whispering how lovely she was. And then she undressed for him, turn-ing to look at him, naked as she. He was thin but muscular with slender hips and small firm buttocks and surprisingly strong legs; he was ready to love her, and she was ready for him. He kissed her and coaxed her and stroked her until she demanded more and then he entered her, filled with passion, and she was as passionate as he. It had been a long time; there had been no other man since she had left Monsieur, but it was in that final moment that she thought of him—and remembered the feel of his body in hers that first time.

And she had forgotten how nice it felt to wake curled up with a man and to make love early in the morning and then sip coffee, tucked in together under the crumpled sheets. "This deserves a toast," she said with a smile, "to a whole new era in my life."

He lifted his coffee cup. "To Léonie's new life," he said solemnly, "and to her happiness."

"Ah, Jacques, I'm happy here with you . . . I'm content."

He put down his coffee and gave her a kiss. "Content or not, darling, you're a working woman—it's time to get up."

"Slave driver." She laughed, remembering that she did indeed have to be at the rehearsal hall at ten, and then a meeting with the lawyers at two, and then back for more rehearsals. And now, of course, there would be a lot more for them to talk about with Paul—new ideas for costumes and stage design—a whole new approach. For the first time she was interested, excited by the idea. It even made her forget Monsieur for a while.

Gilles watched warily as Marie-France stormed around the room. He had never seen her so angry. It was more than anger, it was rage. She was incensed. He had promised her weeks ago that he would take the case no further, though of course he had. He didn't know how she had found out that his lawyers were still going ahead with the suit; he had counted on her not knowing until it was too late. She had threatened him with the entire family—and with the family behind her, he would have no choice. There were certain things over which even he had no final control, and the family set-up, with its trusts and foundations, was one of them. If they decided that what he was doing was against their interests, then they would take action. Marie-France was still pacing the floor, talking about mental instability, that she would remove the children from his care. *His sons!* He would have to find some way to appease her, but he would never give up his chance to get Léonie back!

"What I don't understand," she fumed, "is *why* you want this child. Léonie even claims it's not yours. Why? Why do you want to take another man's bastard? Are you prepared to sacrifice your own family—the children you *know* are your own—just to torture that woman? You are crazy, Gilles. You are completely *mad!*"

"You don't understand, Marie-France." He kept his voice deliberately calm. "It's *because* she is my child that I must have her. I can't bear to think of her lost in some peasant household simply because Léonie doesn't want her."

"That's not what she claims. She says she had to hide Amélie from you—that she's afraid."

"Marie-France, you are a mother . . . the child is a de Courmont. She is my daughter!"

"And if you get her—then what? What do you intend to do with her? Bring her here?"

"I need her, Marie-France. She is my child, too."

She stared at him, the anger leaving her. He looked ill, worn out. Desperate. Could he be sincere? Had he been foolish enough to give Léonie a child? Only one person could know the truth. She sank into a chair wearily. Humiliating as it might be, she must ask Léonie.

Léonie stretched luxuriously. There had been no rehearsal this morning, and after the fiasco of the dress rehearsal the day before that had run half into the night, she was thankful for the reprieve. Paul hadn't seemed too perturbed, even when the lights didn't work properly and the costumes didn't fit. The final straw had been when the beautiful panther, black and silent for most of the night on the end of her chain, had snapped at him, lunging forward, claws and teeth bared. "It's all right," he said philosophically, "it missed me," and they had all laughed uproariously in relief. Paul was wonderful, calm and unflappable in the face of every new disaster. "I've seen it all before, love," he had said, opening a bottle of champagne. "Here, you need reviving."

"What I need are some new nerves," she told him, sipping the drink gratefully.

"Léonie, you're wonderful. You're exactly the way you should be. Trust me, I know. All these other things—the lights, the costumes, the sets—are just technical, they can be worked out. But you and the music are exactly right. I don't want you to worry anymore . . . go home and get a good night's sleep."

He knew she was sleeping with Jacques—they all knew now—and he was glad of it. She was a different woman since she had met the songwriter; he only prayed it would last as long as the show.

Jacques brought her breakfast in bed, appearing in the doorway with a loaded tray. "Mmm," she said hungrily, inspecting the brioches and croissants as he sat beside her on the bed, shifting Bébé with a gentle push of the foot.

"At least you haven't lost your appetite," he commented as she dunked her brioche in her coffee.

She grinned. "Try me later ... just now I'm not thinking about anything except breakfast—and you." Reaching behind her, she pulled a small parcel from under the pillow. "This is an opening night present—for you."

"For me?" His brown myopic eyes lit with pleasure as he searched for his glasses before ripping open the paper.

She had bought him cuff links—gold set with turquoise, the Egyptian stone—and she could see his pleasure reflected on his face. "It's to say thank-you, Jacques"—she kissed him—"for helping me. I might still be a disaster, but at least it won't be because of the music, and I can hide my fear behind the new Léonie."

"And I have a present for you," he said, "but it's at the theater—to be opened later."

She laughed. "Ah ha—a surprise. Perhaps it'll take my mind off stage fright."

"Nothing does that except going on."

"I'll remember that tonight," she promised, snuggling up to him.

By two o'clock she was restless. Jacques had left for the theater and a final run-through with the orchestra, and she prowled his apartment with Bébé for company, unable to settle. She went to the mirror and inspected her face. It looked as it always did, smooth and unlined—apart from the worried frown between her eyebrows! She sighed and turned away, at least the makeup was wonderful. Paul had been right not to allow it to be too dramatic and masklike; it was mostly the eyes that were painted with the deep teal blue lines that the ancient Egyptian women had used, and her hair would be braided into a hundred small plaits, each with feathers and turquoise beads. Oh, God, it took hours. She checked the time—half past two—the hairdresser would be at the theater at four. She'd go now. At least if she were there, she might feel better—and she wouldn't be able to run away!

Marie-France had had trouble finding Léonie; she didn't have her husband's ways of knowing things. She had known so little about Gilles's mistress that she had no idea where to look for her. She hadn't asked Gilles's lawyers, for obvious reasons, and although she knew the name of Léonie's lawyer, she hadn't wanted to approach him. She had no idea who Léonie's friends were, or where she now lived; she had had no reason to think about her since her visit to Léonie's house years earlier. It wasn't until she had read in the newspaper that Léonie was opening at the Théâtre Royal that night that she had even known Léonie was involved with the theater. Well, she thought, opening night may not be a good moment to see her, but I have no choice. My need is more urgent than hers.

The concierge at the stage door recognized quality when he saw it and he jumped from his usual fixed position on his chair to do her bidding.

"Please take this note to Mademoiselle Léonie," she commanded.

"Yes, madame, shall I say who it's from?"

She glanced at the man, who was waiting eagerly to find out who she was—there had been enough gossip. This was between her and Léonie. "No," she replied coldly, "you may not."

He shuffled off down the corridor and she peered after him impatiently. She'd never been backstage in a theater before and looking at the shabby peeling walls and the dusty floors, she had no wish to see more.

The concierge returned after a few minutes. "Come this way please, madame," he beckoned.

The corridor outside Léonie's dressing room was a bit cleaner and more brightly lit, but not much. The paint on the door was new though, a bright shiny gold, and when she knocked it swung open to reveal a different world. The walls and ceiling were hung with a bronze-red fabric patterned in gold, so that the room resembled a tent. Low, cushioned divans lined the walls and a sweet, musky scent came from candles burning in bronze sconces. Léonie waited on a gilded thronelike chair in front of a vast mirror lined with lights.

Her eyes were enormous, glittering like canary diamonds between their liner of deep teal blue. Her cheekbones gleamed beneath a coral blush dusted with gold powder and her mouth was rouged a wet glossy red. She walked towards Marie-France flicking back the feathered braids, and held out her hand. She wore a loose silk kimono and her feet were bare, their nails enameled red to match her fingers and her lips.

"I don't know why you're here," said Léonie, as Marie-France ignored her outstretched hand. "It's your husband I'm fighting, I have no quarrel with you."

"I'll get right to the point," said Marie-France. "I'm not here to argue with you. I'm here to find out the truth. You may remember the only other time we met I warned you that if ever there should be any conflict, my children—and their good name—would come first. Well, now there is a conflict. Gilles is destroying our name. It's an old and honorable family and my sons have a right to inherit that name unsullied by any scandal. Gérard is at a vulnerable age—he's almost seventeen—the boys at his school are aware of what's happening with his father. It's unfair, mademoiselle."

"Then why don't you ask him to stop; surely *you* can do that? Don't you think *I* would have stopped him before now if I could. I'm helpless, madame."

"There is a way, but I must know the truth. Gilles swears the child is his—and if she is, then he has a legal right to her. Give her to him, please, I beg you. We can end this court case, resolve it in a civilized, private fashion. I promise you—as a mother—that I would look after Amélie; surely it would be better than hiding her away. You would be able to see her, I would make sure of that."

"And if she's not his child?"

Marie-France looked at her levelly. "Then I will use all my power—and that of our family—to stop him from taking this action any further."

Léonie brushed back the feathered braids from her throbbing head. It was tempting to believe that Marie-France could take the child and protect her, but it wasn't true. Monsieur would still have power over her.

"Amélie is not your husband's child," she said clearly. "Her father was Charles d'Aureville. He is dead . . . drowned in a boating accident."

Marie-France breathed a sigh of relief. She didn't know what to say. Beneath the makeup the girl's face looked so bleak.

"My daughter is Amélie d'Aureville, and you can tell Gilles that. It's the truth."

"Thank you, Léonie," she said quietly. "You can trust me to do all I can now to stop the case. You will have no more trouble from the de Courmonts."

Léonie stared after her as she swept from the room. No more trouble from the de Courmonts! With a shaky laugh she sank back onto her gilded throne. Monsieur would haunt her for the rest of her days—and Amélie.

Jacques hurried into the room, clutching a small packet in his hands, his face cheerful behind the rimless glasses. "What's wrong?" he asked. She looked odd, and she was very pale under the bright makeup.

Léonie stared at him. There was still opening night to face. She began to shake, she didn't know if she could make it. "Oh Jacques," she whispered, as tears sprang to her eyes.

"For God's sake, don't cry," he gasped, "you'll ruin the makeup."

She began to laugh. "Oh, Jacques, but I want to cry." Her laughter and tears mingled and he dabbed at her eyes feverishly with scraps of cotton.

"Kiss me instead," he commanded. "It's easier to redo the lips than the eyes."

She kissed him obediently and he pushed the present into her hands. "Here," he said eagerly, "it's for you."

Bébé basked under the hot lights around the mirror, peering curiously over Léonie's shoulder as she unwrapped his gift. The Egyptian gold coin, ancient and worn thin with use, dated from the eighteenth dynasty. He had had it set in a delicate gold band and it swung from a slender gold chain so that she might wear it around her neck.

Léonie traced the delicate worn pattern with her finger, the papyrus scroll and the strange hieroglyphs. It was a reminder that the role she was playing was based on reality. Only Jacques would have thought of it—and only he would have gone to the trouble to find it. It was a gift from a sensitive, caring man and it meant far more to her than mere diamonds.

"Thank you, Jacques," she breathed, kissing him and leaving red marks on his face, "you've made me feel better. You always know the right thing to say and do."

≥ 38 ≤

CARO DIDN'T KNOW who was more nervous, she or Alphonse. He was fidgeting, rubbing his hands together, fiddling with his program, and staring round at the auditorium, though there was no need to worry, it was obviously going to be a full house. They had invited everyone they knew, so that at least Léonie would be sure to get *some* applause. But she didn't know about *them*—she glanced apprehensively at the rapidly filling balconies. There were groups of girls who had come, she supposed, out of curiosity to see how you looked when you were the mistress of the Duc de Courmont, and there were solitary men, whom she knew must be there to fantasize how it must be to have a mistress like the beautiful Léonie, how her skin felt under your hands, what her breasts were like when you touched them. There were middle-aged women and young mothers, and crowds of young fellows eager for the glamour and sex that was Léonie. And in the circle and the boxes were the others, those who had come to gloat over Gilles de Courmont's downfall, as his mistress showed herself on stage for all to speculate over. She knew now what Léonie had meant when she had said that their eyes crawled all over her—they wouldn't, any of them, miss a single detail. With the memory of Léonie's last stage appearance still clear in her mind, Caro prayed that it would be all right this time. But she had an awful feeling inside that it was all going to be a terrible disaster.

Maroc waited at the back of the stalls, watching the crowds pouring in. Léonie had asked him specially to come, she couldn't do it unless she knew he were there, she said. Hadn't he seen her through all the important events of her life? And she needed him desperately for this one. He didn't know how much help he was going to be, he was as nervous as she had to be. His palms were damp with sweat and he rubbed them fastidiously with his handkerchief. Since he'd taken the job at the Hôtel Lancaster, he hadn't seen Léonie as often as he would have liked, though they always wrote. He managed to get down to the Côte d'Azur once or twice a year, but his time was not his own—the job was all-consuming. He had worked his way up to assistant manager and one day he wanted to open his own place. On the stage the safety-curtain slid up slowly as the orchestra began to file into the pit. Not much longer. Oh, God, he hoped she would be all right. She had seemed calm enough half an hour ago when he'd been backstage, but anything could have happened since then.

The orchestra began to tune their instruments, grating on his already taut nerves, and he paced the aisle at the back of the stalls restlessly—could he bear to watch this? He remembered the last time—when she had come to him, broken and humiliated. The house lights dimmed and he took up his position against the wall, arms folded. He wished now he had had a drink.

Caro gripped Alphonse's hand tightly as the lights went down, casting a final glance at their friends—at least they knew what to do: they were to applaud whatever happened. The piano picked out the first notes of the overture, the violins joined in, and the buzz of excited conversation faded into expectant silence. It was time to begin.

Léonie had been all right until Jacques had left. He was to conduct the orchestra for her and he needed to check that the musicians had their parts and that all was in order. He was meticulous about his music and he wanted to leave nothing to chance.

Now there was just Paul Bernard left, and her dresser, still fiddling with the tissue-thin silk of the gown. She glanced at the clock—the orchestra was playing the overture, that meant there was a half hour before her entrance. The first part of the show was filled, music hall style, with other acts—dancers, a comedian, showgirls, a big splashy stage set, all spangles and glitter. "But why," she had asked Paul, "why can't it just be me? Shouldn't I go on myself and do what I'm supposed to do? After all, that's what they're here for."

"You have to make them wait," he'd explained, "build their anticipation and their excitement . . . make them want you a little bit more. We'll give them all the brash, flashy dance routines and then we'll present them with the contrast: a solitary woman alone on stage. You'll be magnificent, Léonie."

She stared in the mirror. Yes, she looked magnificent. The trouble was that inside she didn't feel magnificent. Oh, Jacques, she thought desperately, could you have been wrong? How do I become "another person"? I don't think I can do it.

Paul dropped a light kiss on top of her braided head. "Keep calm." He smiled. "You're going to be fine."

"Am I, Paul?" Her eyes betrayed her panic.

"Everyone feels like this on first night," he said gently. "We'll all be here to help you through it, Léonie. You're not alone. Jacques will be there in the orchestra pit—you'll be able to see him—your friends are in the audience. Courage, my girl." He waved as he made for the door to check on the progress of the show. Courage, he thought apprehensively to himself. He hoped she'd make it.

The dressing room was filled with flowers—masses of yellow roses from Caro and Alphonse, enormous bouquets of summery-smelling flowers from Paul, and delicate camellias from Jacques—even her lawyer had sent roses. Their perfume filled the room; if she closed her eyes she might imagine she were in a garden. There was one scent dominating all the others, even stronger than the camellias; it came from a spray of jasmine that had arrived just a few minutes ago. It lay in front of her on the dressing table along with a note. The familiar writing, severe and unelaborate, loomed from the paper. She read it once again. "I haven't forgotten you, Léonie." It was signed, simply, "Monsieur."

Paul appeared at the door again. "It's time, Léonie," he said.

She took a deep breath and with a final glance in the mirror at the woman who was not her, she turned and faced him. "I'm ready," she said, lifting her chin arrogantly.

Paul had been right. The audience were primed for her, eager for their first glimpse of the mistress of France's richest man. She waited at the side of the stage as Jacques picked up the signal, the stage lights dimmed, and the music began. Remember Loulou, she murmured to herself as she lifted herself taller, shoulders back and down. Flaunt it, she had said. She gripped the animal's chain tightly, wrapping it around her wrist, and with the panther padding at her side strode arrogantly on stage.

The audience gasped as she faced them, challenging them to look at her—at this exotic creature—different from them, grander, more powerful. The big cat lay docilely at her feet and the amber spotlight encircled them intimately as she raised her arms, allowing the tiny crystal pleats that formed the sleeves of her tunic to spread like a fine golden fan. There was a murmur of comment, a ripple of applause from the stalls, and the silence of stunned admiration from the balconies. They didn't know what they had expected, but not this: this wasn't just a pretty girl who'd made it the hard way, or the poor distraught young mother, or the humiliated, discarded mistress of a ruthless man. This was a being from another world.

She began to sing, a small soft song of a woman in love, of how she loved her man, how she loved to touch his skin, how she felt when he lay next to her holding her.

Alphonse glanced quickly at the audience. They were riveted, leaning forward, eager to catch her words—listening for nuances and underlying meanings—captured by her low, rough, flagrantly sexual voice.

The spotlight faded as her song ended, illuminating only her bowed head. And the applause began, a ripple at first, gathering momentum as people recovered their breath and joined in, dying into stunned silence as Jacques swung into the next number and the stage lights revealed six enormous Nubians guarding a bronze couch. They stood, all of them, well over six feet tall, naked but for golden cloths tied Egyptian style around their loins, their massive chests gleaming a glossy black under the lights and the tight muscles of their abdomens rippling as they moved. Léonie stalked the arena, long-legged and lithe as the panther, as she sang her second song, its barbaric Latin rhythm underscoring the words of the temptation of forbidden fruits, the lure of the forbidden. . . .

Of course, Maroc knew it was her, but it was a part of her he had never known existed. The audience were loving it; they couldn't keep their eyes off her, watching her every movement as if to capture it in their minds forever. The door to the foyer swung open behind him and a figure slipped quickly inside; a latecomer, he doubted he'd find a seat now. The man leaned against the wall, watching. In the dimness there was something familiar about the figure, those broad shoulders. The stage brightened and he caught a glimpse of the strong profile: it was Monsieur! He was staring fixedly at the stage, unaware of anything but her. Why was he here? Would he try to see her afterward? Maroc hoped not. It would only mean trouble.

Here, in the dark, it was almost like being alone with her. She was close to him, just a few yards away on stage. Her gauzy golden tunic gleamed under the lights, the crystal pleats flickering around the curves of her body, skimming her flesh like a warm tongue. She was beautiful, flamboyantly, sybaritically sexual. She was no stranger to *him*. This was the Léonie only he knew. He became annoyingly aware of the audience as the applause and cheers rang through the theater, intruding on his dream. It wasn't right, these people shouldn't be here; this was meant for him alone. Didn't they know she was his? Angrily he turned to leave, he would not endure this exposure of the woman he loved. But he couldn't do it, he couldn't leave her—he had to stay to the end. And then what? He remembered the scene with Marie-France just before he left. She had won this round, but he wasn't finished yet. He'd find Amélie. And then Léonie would come back to him. He fixed his attention on the stage again, drinking in her presence like a thirsty traveler at an oasis. At least now he would always know where she was, for the price of a ticket he could see her whenever he wished—it was a start.

Maroc watched Monsieur watching Léonie, remembering him as he used to be—a tall, arrogant, civil man, always icily polite, always in control.

When had the destruction begun? Was it with Léonie? Or was it before then—earlier in his life? Had he been damaged so badly by women that he needed to treat them with contempt, or was it Léonie who had driven him to terrible deeds? He had murdered because of her, he had humiliated himself because of her; look at him now, here in this theater, braving the recognition of the crowds to catch a glimpse of her. He couldn't let go of her! He was truly a man obsessed.

The last bars of music faded into silence and Léonie and the panther faced the auditorium with identical topaz stares. She stood unsmiling as the audience rose to its feet and the theater echoed to the cheers and bravos. Sweat trickled coldly down her back, whether from exhaustion or fear she didn't know. She felt numb. The panther stirred restlessly on its chain and she bent and stroked its sleek black head, feeling it throb in a gigantic purr. She knew she had no need to fear this creature, it was a cat and she loved it. Ushers were bringing bouquets to the stage and looking down she caught Jacques's eye. He smiled encouragingly, and suddenly she felt normal again. It was over. She smiled around in surprise as the audience demanded an encore. Could it be true? Was it really all right? The ice had melted in her veins, she couldn't sing anymore. She was Léonie. She tossed her feathered head, laughing out loud as the cheers rang out, and floated off the stage on sandaled feet and a wave of exhilaration, the big cat loping at her side.

Paul clasped her in his arms and kissed her as the dancers and stagehands burst into a spontaneous round of applause. "Wonderful . . . you were wonderful, Léonie. I always knew it."

Chilled champagne waited in her dressing room as she pulled the gold band from her head wearily and sank onto her golden throne. Jacques burst through the door, his thin young face lit with excitement, brimming with happiness for her success. He knelt dramatically and kissed her bare feet. "Léonie Bahri, you were amazing . . . far, far better than at any rehearsal. What happened? Where did it all come from?"

She laughed. "I don't know—I don't even know what I did that was different. I suppose I became the other person, the one the audience wanted."

"Whatever it was it worked," said Paul, lifting his glass to her. "You are a success."

She smiled and sipped the wonderful champagne, the tiredness leaving her. "Only because of you, Paul. And you." She kissed Jacques lingeringly as Paul watched, smiling. "What would I have done without you?"

The dressing room was suddenly crowded with friends. Caro flew toward her, laughing and crying and hugging her. Alphonse held her close, patting her hair as though she were a small child to be comforted, and Maroc hugged her and hugged her, laughing with her at her triumph. Reporters tried to gain admittance to the charmed circle inside the room, but were kept firmly away by guards. Léonie slipped behind the big Coromandel screen—a present from Paul—to change.

The party was to be at Voisins, the scene of many of her triumphs and battles and a restaurant she hadn't been to in years—when Alphonse had asked her it had seemed the only one to choose. If the show had been a disaster, Voisins would cushion her in its velvet comfort, and if it were good, nowhere else was better.

The laughter and chatter flowed with the champagne as she stared into the mirror while Julie removed the feathers from her hair. She was wearing a favorite dress, one of the few she'd kept from the old days because it happened to be at the inn. It was amethyst silk, pleated, like her stage costume. There was a memory attached to it. Monsieur had chosen it himself that sunny morning in Cannes when the world had suddenly become wonderful again for her. It was a perverse idea to wear it now, and she hadn't meant to—there was a special new one waiting in the closet. But she felt drawn to this one. She snapped the golden Cartier belt around her waist and began to remove her makeup, creaming away her exotic stage-being until she was herself again. She hesitated as she came to the eyes, she liked hiding behind that new person, it allowed her to be two people at once—like Sekhmet. And after all, wasn't she like Sekhmet: protecting those she loved, terrible against her enemies? Léonie shivered remembering Monsieur, remembering why she was doing this, remembering Marie-France, and Amélie—oh, Amélie—maybe one day I'll have you back with me, but each year that goes by puts you further away from me and closer to your own family. Soon, it'll be too late. She gazed silently into the mirror.

Caro touched her shoulder. "You should be smiling, not sitting here looking sad." She had caught the look in her eyes. "After all," she said gaily, "tonight everything is all right. It's more than that, it's wonderful."

Léonie laughed as Jacques came over and took her by the arm. "Come on, then. Let's go and celebrate."

Crowds thronged the stage door, making it almost impossible to pass, surging forward to catch another glimpse of her, trying to touch her. Léonie drew back in alarm as Jacques and Paul stood protectively in front of her until a path could be cleared. "Léonie, Léonie," they called, and she stared back at them in amazement; what more did they want, what more could she give them?

"Smile at them," whispered Paul in her ear, "wave, call hello—anything. . . . That's all they want."

She waved and smiled obediently, catching the eyes of a young girl—young like she had been. She understood suddenly what it was that they wanted, remembering those lonely walks around Paris on Sunday afternoons when she had been sixteen and felt that she didn't belong, that everything was happening somewhere else, if only she could find it. These girls thought that she had found it. It's all an illusion, she wanted to tell them, it's not real.

The news had already penetrated Paris and Voisins was eager to welcome an old customer—and a new star. The Roederer Cristal was waiting, and caviar and quail eggs and the grapes stuffed with cheese and salmon and asparagus—all the things she'd always liked here. It was Alphonse and Caro, of course. They had wanted it to be perfect. Exhilaration swept over her again as she began to enjoy her party, accepting the congratulations of total strangers who came to shake her hand, hovered over by waiters eager to do her bidding—and with Jacques by her side she felt wonderful.

They waited for the early editions of the newspapers, eager to see what the men of the press would have to say. Jacques read them for her, but she had already seen the smile on Paul's face. "They say you have a triumph," he said, watching her anxious face for a reaction.

Léonie threw back her head with a laugh. "Isn't there an old saying, Jacques, that 'out of adversity comes triumph'?"

She was tired but content as they left the restaurant together, eager for some fresh air. The night was changing to the dusky grayness of dawn as they strolled down the street, arms around each other, neither of them noticing the big de Courmont automobile parked across the way, its darkened windows shielding its occupant from view. As they disappeared around the corner, its engine roared into life and the big car swung around, making its solitary way back to the Ile Saint-Louis.

❧ 39 ❧

ISABELLE WALKED through the gardens to her restaurant, the Pavillon d'Aureville, built on a plot of land adjacent to her villa so that it faced the sea. Amélie skipped along in front of her, sniffing the ocean breeze enthusiastically, her two cats, Fido and Minou, trotting behind like a pair of faithful hounds. Bustling into the kitchens ahead of her grandmother, Amélie cast a quick glance around to see what goodies were to be had, snatching up a tiny fruit tart with a giggle as she caught the indulgent scowl of Celestine. Amélie could do no wrong in Celestine's eyes, there was always a spare

pastry for her and for Roberto. It was Diego she didn't like: he was an un-
pleasant boy, always smiling to your face and smirking behind your back.

Amélie enjoyed being in the restaurant. It looked like a pretty octago-
nal summerhouse, with a roof that came to a point in the middle and french
windows leading onto blue-awninged terraces, for alfresco lunches or candlelit dinners on still summer nights. The tablecloths were a pretty aquamarine overlaid with a second cloth in crisp white, and the silver, bought from
Cristofle in France, was heavy and simple. It was a very satisfying room,
Amélie thought, straightening a knife as she passed, running a finger over
the immense displays of fruits, and breathing in the scent from the enormous baskets of fresh flowers; no wonder people enjoyed coming here.

Though her cats were banned from the restaurant, they were welcomed
in the kitchen, where there were always scraps, and she rushed back to collect them. Roberto would be home soon. His new house was next to
theirs—just along the sandy Avenida Atlantica.

Sebastião saw her coming, hair flying in all directions, jumping every
fourth step, her long thin legs covering the ground rapidly. "Amélie." He
waved. "How about a swim?"

"Not now," she called, shading her eyes against the sun, "I've got to
find Roberto."

Didn't she always? he thought, making his way across the garden to
the beach. He was going to miss her when he left for France, he couldn't
imagine life without Amélie. He really loved her, but France held the promise of a new life for him with access to the best teachers in his chosen field of
architecture. Where better to study than in Europe? He would see at last
those wonderful Renaissance palaces in Italy, the castles and churches of
England, and the great cathedrals of France. And, of course, Paris!

Diego Benavente pretended not to listen as Roberto conferred with
Amélie in a corner—she had said she had a secret to tell him. Diego's lip
curled as he watched her, didn't she know yet she couldn't win? Roberto
was *his* friend, his *special* friend; they were inseparable at school—and at
home. It was only when *she* was around that there was any trouble—when
they were alone Roberto was different, more easygoing, always willing to go
along with what he suggested. Well, today he had a surprise for little
Amélie. He sauntered away casually, a dark-haired attractive boy of thirteen,
with a stocky muscular body and intense greenish eyes under heavy black
brows.

Amélie watched him out of the corner of her eye. What was he up to?
He didn't usually leave her alone with Roberto. "Here," she said, taking the
squashed pastry from the pocket of her shorts, "I saved this for you—it's
one of Celestine's, the sort you like."

Roberto wiped off the sand and fluff and offered her a bite. "No
thanks," she said, skipping away. "It's all for you." She peered around the

fountain, dunking her head quickly into its splurging arc of cool water, shaking the drops from her hair like a puppy. "Roberto?"

"Mmm?" He finished the pastry quickly.

"Roberto, where do you suppose Diego has gone?"

"I don't know; he was here a minute ago."

Amélie was uneasy. Diego was up to something, she sensed it.

Glancing about to make sure no one was around, Diego took out the little sack he'd hidden behind the stable door. Its top was fastened tightly with a string and he held it away from his body carefully. Fido and Minou lazed by the stable wall enjoying the sun, watching him with sleepy eyes. "Here Fido," he called, tapping the ground with a stick. "Here girl . . . come and see what I've got." It was typical of Amélie, he thought contemptuously, to call the cat by a dog's name and a masculine one at that. "Here girl," he coaxed.

Intrigued by the tapping stick the cat moved cautiously toward him. Diego grabbed her quickly by the scruff of her neck, sliding a piece of string through her collar to hold her. Then he gingerly unfastened the sack and threw it to the floor. A thin black snake slithered from the opening, tongue flickering, head moving balefully, seeking its captor. Diego threw the struggling cat down in front of the snake and backed away quickly as the snake lunged forward. Fido leaped backward and the snake spat its venom into the air. Crouching low, Fido stared fixedly as the reptile, tail lashing slowly from side to side. "Go on," murmured Diego, prodding her with his stick. The cat backed away again. Diego thrust his long stick toward the snake, goading it exasperatedly toward the cat, just as Amélie and Roberto rounded the corner. As Amélie screamed the snake reared once more, striking at the cat, who leapt high, biting it sharply in the back of its neck, almost severing its head. Sitting back on her haunches, Fido watched bemusedly as the snake writhed on the ground.

Sebastião tore around the corner, frightened by Amélie's terrified screams. Taking in the scene at a glance, he grabbed Diego by the arm, twisting it up behind him.

"Tell me right now, what's going on," Sebastião said menacingly. "The *truth* Diego!"

"I saw the snake," yelled Diego, as Sebastião inched his arm higher. "I tried to get it away from the cat, I could see it was going after her."

"And where did the snake come from, Diego?"

"*I* don't know!"

"Not from this sack then?"

"*I don't know!*"

Sebastião gave his arm a final twist. "That'll teach you to try to kill Amélie's cat," he said. "It's time you had a little of your own medicine. You're a bully and a coward, Diego Benavente. If Amélie were a boy you wouldn't dare do the things you do to her—I saw you whipping her pony the other day. If there's any more trouble from you, I shall tell your father—he'll probably make you go back to the *fazenda*." Diego was a true city boy and the threat of banishment to the *fazenda* was a terrible one.

"You'll apologize to Amélie," commanded Sebastião, his gaze contemptuous, "and tell her that you'll never try to harm her cats again."

"But I'm sure he didn't mean it, Sebastião." Roberto rushed to the defense of his friend. "It's just as he said—the snake was there and he was trying to save Fido."

Amélie sat hunched on the steps, clutching Fido protectively as Diego approached. "I'm sorry, Amélie," he said, staring down at his feet. "I'll never try to harm your cats, I promise."

Amélie made no reply, watching warily as he walked away from them, a lonely figure heading toward the long empty stretch of beach. Roberto stared after him, agonized. He turned back to Amélie. "I'm sure he really didn't mean to harm Fido, Amélie . . . and, anyway, now he's apologized." He looked anxiously across the yard as Diego disappeared around the corner, he could bear it no longer. "I'm going after him," he said, breaking into a run.

Amélie stared down at the ground, fighting back the tears. Sebastião glanced at her worriedly. This episode was more than meanness. Diego was getting vicious, there was no knowing what he might try next, and whatever it was it would be directed at Amélie. "Look," he said, sitting next to her and taking her small rough hand in his, "you'll have to watch out for Diego when I'm not here. You can't trust him."

"I know," she whispered, hugging Fido close to her face, so that he wouldn't see her tears. "Oh, Sebastião, I do wish you weren't going away. Paris is so far. Will you write to me?"

"I'll write every week," he said. "I promise."

And I'll write every day," she vowed. "I'll tell you everything. Oh, I do love you, Sebastião!"

Edouard d'Aureville was adrift in the middle of the blackest of seas. He watched the lights of the ferry disappear across the Gulf of Mexico with a feeling of panic, wondering how he had managed to get himself in this position. They had omitted to mention, when he took the ferry from Tampa, Florida, that St. Petersburg was only a hamlet and had no pier. They had simply put him over the side in this rotten little boat and pointed to an invisible shore.

"It's a ten-minute row," the captain had said. "Don't worry about the boat, the next passenger from St. Petersburg will bring it back."

This is ridiculous, he thought, hefting the oars. If I survived in the Amazon, I'm damned if I'm going to die here!

He pulled in his oars and listened. He must have been rowing for at least twenty minutes and the captain had said ten. But then he was a Mexican. A few minutes either way would still be accurate.

The tide seemed to be changing, he could feel its surge and an increased pull and then, at last, the sound of waves breaking on the shore. Almost at the same time he saw the lights, twinkling and bobbing across the waves, and he headed toward them helped by the incoming tide, wiping the sweat of relief, and fear, from his brow as he tied up at the little wooden jetty and his trembling legs found dry land again.

He was here because he'd heard that Henry Flagler, oilman and railroad entrepreneur, was opening up this young state, parts of which were still a wilderness. Because of his wife's ill health, Flagler had been forced to spend his winters in St. Augustine and had discovered the delights of both the ideal climate and the long windswept Atlantic beaches. Realizing their potential as winter playgrounds for chilled northerners, he had bought the railroad, extended it south as far as Miami, and intended to take it even farther, right to the furthermost point—Key West.

Edouard zigzagged restlessly across Florida, sometimes on horseback and sometimes catching up with the railroads, wending his way east through the little coastal towns of Daytona and Rockledge, down to the sleepy village of Miami, whose white arches dripped purple bougainvillaea in tropical disarray against the clearest blue sky. Flagler's grand new hotel was rising from the ground and would soon be completed. Edouard knew there'd be room for more than one good hotel in a place like this and land was cheap—he could take his pick of plots. He bought along a wide stretch of beach reaching back through sea grasses and dunes into windswept rubble. One day, he thought, pacing it with the satisfaction that only his own land can give a man, I'll build a hotel here that will be better than Flagler's—better than anyone's.

It wasn't easy to get to Key West. The ferry called at dozens of tiny islands that formed the tail of Florida, but the journey was worth it. The town's ancient Spanish name was Cayo Huesco—Bone Key—so named for its white coral reefs that were pounded by the waves to a fine powder, the color of men's bones. The powder mingled with the sea, turning it an astonishing opaque turquoise, and the pretty little port sent forth its fishing fleet on these milky waters, bringing back a daily bounty of shrimp and soft-shell crabs and fish of every sort. Key West's sandy streets were bordered by wooden sidewalks and lined with shade trees and white-fronted houses, and in the hills beyond, hidden in the privacy of thick groves of magnolias, laurels, and orange trees, were breezy pastel villas, whose only disturbances were the dry rattle of palm fronds and the shrill call of the ci-cadas.

Calling for a chilled beer, Edouard watched the passing parade from the veranda of the St. James Hotel on Main Street.

What better haven of peace and quiet would he ever find than this? He'd buy one of those houses in the hills and bring Amélie here—she'd love it. Oh, how he missed her. He missed her curling up on his knee, asking for the old stories of when he and her father were just boys at the château in France. Sometimes she'd speak wistfully of her mother, Léonie. "Why did she have to die, Edouard?" She'd asked the same questions, so sadly, so many times. "If my father were such a good swimmer, why couldn't he save her and himself?" He'd answered her with small protective lies. Léonie had become a myth: the lovely young mother who had died so tragically with her husband. She was just a dream figure in Amélie's mind—and in his also, almost. Every time he looked at Amélie, he remembered. She was so like her—the same peachy skin, the beautiful amber eyes, and, of course, the same champagne-colored hair.

Edouard stared unseeingly across the blue seas toward the exotic island of Cuba, just a ferry ride away. He felt suddenly very lonely. What I need, he thought with a wry smile, is the love of a good woman. Maybe then I'll be content!

⊱40⊰

VERRONET SIGHED with exasperation as he searched through the mass of papers on Monsieur's desk. Something would have to be done, he thought resignedly; it was impossible to find anything these days. There were still papers about the long-dead court case for the child—he had kept them all. He picked up a document and stared at it in amazement—it was a report on a proposed merger of the two steel companies. He thought it had been taken care of weeks ago. Hadn't de Courmont told him that? The man must be going crazy. Just look at this desk! He pushed at the pile impatiently, who knew what was lost in here. All de Courmont cared about these days were the reports on Léonie and the futile search for that child. He was ob-sessed with that damned child! *She* was the reason he neglected his business matters. Why didn't he give up on her—and Léonie? It wasn't as though he had no other women. God, there was a succession of them—and they cost him a fortune. But he was like a child who'd lost a favorite toy—he only wanted *that* one!

The only things he cared about with any passion, besides Léonie and her daughter, were his automobiles—and thank heaven for that, at least he still kept those under his personal control—almost everything else was delegated these days so that he could follow *her* around Europe. Whenever Léonie went off on one of her tours, he'd disappear for a few days here and a few days there. He simply couldn't keep away.

Ah! Here was what he was looking for—the breakdown of the component prices for the new limousine they had scheduled for production next autumn. As usual, rubber cost more than steel, more than almost any of the other items on the list. Those tires were becoming prohibitively priced. He thought about the rubber for a while, something must be done about it— he'd speak to de Courmont when he came in. He had a couple of ideas.

Monsieur stood at the back of the darkened theater not watching the stage, lost in his thoughts. He was there every night, as he always was when Léonie was in Paris. This was the last night of her third season and she grew more accomplished each time. He brooded on her success—it was more than success, she had become a cult, a celebrity. She was treated like a queen wherever she went, not just in France but all over Europe, and he'd heard a rumor today that she was to go to America. America! How often had she begged him to take her there. And now she was her own woman; she set fashions for others to follow, they copied her style, her hair, her look. Even the one who was waiting for him now in the blue suite of the Hôtel Crillon had blond hair, swinging smooth around her shoulders in the same long Egyptian bob that Léonie had.

The usher glanced at him disinterestedly—the man was always there, never took a seat, said he preferred to stand. Maroc noticed him, too. He checked every night to see if he was there—Léonie always asked him. And the spray of jasmine was delivered every night, too; the dressing room was choked with their scent. But, oddly, she refused to throw them away. He glanced at his watch as Léonie paced onto the stage, facing the audience with her usual challenging stare. They were running five minutes late tonight, he must find out why. He'd been Léonie's manager for three years now, organizing her tours, coordinating the production with Paul Bernard, helping her find new music and new designers, making the deals for ever-increasing sums of money, amounts now so large that even he was astounded that theater managements agreed to pay them. But they did—and they begged for more. They had traveled Europe together, and soon they'd be off to America where, even though she was still an unknown quantity, the management had guaranteed the substantial amount of dollars he had demanded. It was exciting: she had conquered Europe and now she would conquer the New World!

Léonie's private life, when she had time for it, was very much her own, as simple in contrast to her public person as she could manage. Any free time she had she spent at the inn, her refuge from the people and the publicity that followed her everywhere.

He glanced at Monsieur. He was watching her intently. She hadn't spoken to him for well over ten years and yet he still came every night to see her. Shaking his head in amazement at the power of the man's obsession, Maroc slipped through the door and made his way backstage.

"Sir." Verronet gave a tentative cough.

De Courmont looked up from his desk wearily. "What is it now, Verronet?"

"It's about the tires, sir . . . for the new cars. You remember I spoke with you about it before. The price is now truly prohibitive."

De Courmont sat back in the green leather chair and considered the matter. It was true. The cost of rubber seemed to increase every time he checked it, and the manufacturers hiked up their prices accordingly—and then some. Their profit must be enormous.

"I know you'll agree with me, sir, when I say that the amount spent on tires for our cars is completely out of proportion, but I have an idea. There is at present no way to cut our costs, but with the expansion of the automobile industry, perhaps we should think seriously of becoming manufacturers ourselves—we could supply Europe with tires and associated products, undercutting the present prices and at the same time reducing our own costs. There's a large margin of profit to be had. Here are some figures, sir. It'll take a bit of work, of course, but I've been doing some research and I think if you considered buying your rubber direct from Brazil—perhaps even taking over a plantation—it would be more than viable."

De Courmont listened. Verronet was a good man, he was loyal and he had the schemer's instinct for a loophole in a contract or an advantageous deal. Picking up the little scarlet model of the new de Courmont limousine from his desk, he balanced it in his hands, liking its crisp clean lines, the lack of gadgets and clutter that had spoiled the first cars. This was sleeker, longer, and with a lot more power. He remembered when he had given Gérard and Armand little models of the first car—wasn't it that time when Gérard had been so ill? He had hoped Gérard would follow him into the business, but he was set on becoming an architect. Armand would take over the business, he loved the cars.

"Sir?"

He glanced up. "What is it now?"

Verronet held his temper in check. "The rubber, sir, for the tires. If you're interested I've found a couple of contacts in Brazil, there are several estates producing the high grade 'Pará' rubber we need. It must be the hardest quality and I understand that it only comes from the southern banks of the Amazon—the northern reaches grow only 'weak' rubber. There are several trails, the Agencia Hevea Belem, the Puntamayo Company, and the Oro Velho Trail are the best possibilities. It would necessitate going to Manaus and arranging to purchase an entire season's production of one or more of these companies at a favorable price."

It was a good idea. They could put up a factory on the site next to the components' depot—de Courmont glanced at his watch. The train for Nice left in fifteen minutes; he pushed back his chair hurriedly, reaching for his jacket. "We'll discuss it later, Verronet."

"But . . ."

"Not now, Verronet, I don't have the time."

Verronet heaved an angry sigh. It might mean a delay of another month, maybe two. De Courmont never said when he would be back.

❧ 41 ❧

MONTE CARLO welcomed Léonie on her own terms these days—as the star, the celebrity, the glamorous young woman in Fortuny silks and barbaric emerald-studded bracelets and swirling tawny gold hair. Léonie carried off the role with aplomb, smiling at the crowds as she strode through the casino, remembering her amazement that first night she had met Monsieur, when people had moved aside to let the Duc de Courmont pass with her on his arm. Now the crowds parted for her, managers bowed and doormen saluted. And the Café de Paris always held her table.

But fame had its price. She had worked hard to achieve it—and worked even harder to maintain it—and her public life left little time for private pleasures. Jacques, unhappy with the scattered moments spared from her busy life, had reluctantly departed. And here, in her favorite place, she went back to the inn, alone, to that white room still virtually untouched from the day she first went there—just a lamp and a small rug—and maybe, now and then, a man.

Occasionally she would catch a glimpse of Monsieur in the distance, at some smart restaurant or in the casino—and always with some young blonde on his arm. But she ignored him.

It was always easy to avoid Monsieur's spies when she was at the inn. It was impossible for them to hang around too much and there were limits to how many times they could drive past; anyway, they were becoming lazy. He changed them every now and again, but he knew that she knew about them—they had become almost a token threat, a last hope that she would lead him to Amélie. She knew how to avoid them when she had to.

She was up and dressed before dawn, ready and waiting on the terrace when Monsieur Frenard appeared to drive her to Nice. The roads were empty and the little white town was just beginning to awaken as they arrived. He dropped her at the railway station and she hurried along the platform to catch her train, praying no one would recognize her. There was no trace of her Egyptian image, no eyes elongated with kohl, no braided mane, no jewels and silken tunics. She was discreet in a plain cotton dress and jacket, her hair pulled back severely and tied with a ribbon at her neck. She was just another woman, a lovely woman with haunted eyes.

The train journey was a long one and Léonie fidgeted for the last hour, unable to read her book, eager to reach her destination. The car was waiting at the station and they drove through the lovely countryside of the Loire, crisscrossed with rivers and dotted with moated medieval houses, toward the Château d'Aureville. The twin stone pillars flanking the big iron gates were empty of their griffins, flown with the d'Aurevilles to grace their new home. But the château looked exactly as it had when the family had left it, only its occupants were different.

A round-faced smiling nun stood on the portico to greet her, embracing her cheerfully as she ushered her into the hall. "The children will be so happy to see you, Madame Léonie," she said. "They always look forward to your visits."

They stood up with a great scraping of chairs as she came into the room, two dozen small faces beaming at her, chanting *"Bonjour,* madame," and waiting, like leashed puppies, for the signal of freedom.

"Come," she called joyfully, holding out her arms as they rushed toward her with whoops of excitement, clamoring to be the first for her kisses, pushing and shoving to be the preferred one whose hand she would take as she walked to the tables. "All right, all right, now *everyone* has been kissed—and it's time for lunch. And then . . ." She smiled at their expectant faces. "And then," they chorused.

"And then there will be presents!"

Sister Agnes laughed. "They'll never eat their lunch now," she said. "There'll be no holding them until they see the presents."

"Now let me see," said Léonie, walking around the table. "Whose turn is it to sit next to me this time?"

"Me, me—it's me."

"And me . . . Cécile . . ."

"Come along then, Cécile, and you, Véronique . . . let's see how much lunch you can eat."

She cut their meat and encouraged them to eat the vegetables, listening contentedly to the chatter of the small events of their daily lives. It was only here that there was any reality to her memories of Amélie.

The idea had come to her out of the blue. Money had begun to flow in—more money than she had thought possible. She had been shocked to see that the Château d'Aureville was for sale—it had always been there, d'Aurevilles had always lived there. Charles had said so. And as long as it still belonged to them it had meant that one day they would come back, but now she knew they wouldn't, and neither would Amélie. Léonie had never forgotten the stories Charles had told her of his idyllic childhood; it was a house that needed children. If Amélie were never to live at the Château d'Aureville, then other children should have the chance.

The rest had been simple. She had bought the château—discreetly, using the name of one of her companies—and she had endowed it as an orphanage. Twenty-four children who by some unfortunate trick of fate had been left alone and without parents, had found a home here, lovingly cared for by a team of young nuns, chosen for their youth and understanding of childish problems, under the gentle and capable supervision of Sister Agnes. The youngest child was now two years old and had been found on their doorstep, a tiny newborn infant whom they had named Léonie, after their patronne. And the eldest was almost twelve—Amélie's age. Léonie loved them all.

The day passed too quickly, the presents distributed—cuddly toys and bouncing rubber balls and dolls and toy horses and engines and puzzles and lots of books. There were kites to fly in the wind and colored paper bags of sweets—the latter given furtively and with much giggling behind the indulgently turned backs of the sisters.

The journey home seemed even longer than had the one there. It wasn't exactly a restful day, and Lord knew she needed rest, but it had been the happiest day she had spent in months.

She had been at the inn for two weeks—two blissfully lazy weeks—gathering strength for the American tour. First there would be the rehearsals and the costume fittings and the new songs and—oh, the million details that she didn't want to think about now. Now was for idling, loafing, lazing, hanging around, busily doing nothing important, like drying her hair in the sun and choosing fish and vegetables for Madame Frenard in Saint-Jean, and lying on the terrace after supper with Bébé on her lap.

The sunset was wonderful tonight, she thought sleepily, stroking Bébé's fur, staring across the darkening sea to the crimson horizon, flecked with fluffy lilac clouds. Her eyes were closing already and she yawned, wondering how she managed to get so tired here at the inn. In Paris she was never tired, perhaps she just saved it all up until she came here. "Early to bed tonight, my darling," she said, tucking Bébé under her arm and making her way sleepily along the terrace to her room.

Bébé watched from the bed as Léonie braided her hair, waiting for the moment when her mistress would climb in and she could make her way up the quilt to snuggle safe in Léonie's arms. That was the way it always had been.

Léonie couldn't remember what it was that woke her. She thought maybe it was because the purring had stopped, or was it Bébé's strange coldness? The fur was still as soft, the tiny head was still tucked next to hers on the pillow, but Bébé had gone.

She lifted her and held her close, praying that her own warmth would revive Bébé's already lifeless body, but Bébé was dead and Léonie had lost her dearest, most beloved friend, the keeper of her secrets, sharer of her sorrows, bestower of laughter and comfort. It was as though the tears would never end.

Taking the scissors, she cut up her cashmere robe, Bébé's favorite soft resting place, and wrapped Bébé gently in its folds. She emptied her carved rosewood chest of the jewels and placed Bébé's tiny limp body in the casket. Then she took the chest into the garden and buried it in the place where they had always sat together to watch the ocean and the birds and the sky. She planted a tree over the place, a flowering pear that would bloom every spring and always be part of Bébé.

The tour was postponed. She couldn't work. She was distraught, distracted, limp, without energy.

"She's mourning for Bébé," said Maroc to Caro as they stared at her helplessly.

"We must find her another cat. A kitten . . . the same sort."

"But I've never seen one like Bébé anywhere else . . . she was so small, so brown. I don't know what breed she was, Maroc."

"I'll find out," he promised. "I'll get her another kitten. I can't bear to see her like this."

It took him a month of intensive searching—no one on the Côte d'Azur knew of any cats like that; where Bébé had come from was a mystery. He went further inland, thinking perhaps she had come from some sort of farm, or the hills, but no one knew. He had to find an expert. Madame Hermione was an expert. She had fifteen cats of her own and she knew immediately what he was looking for.

"They're Swiss Mountain cats," she told him as if surprised that he should even ask. "You'll find them up in the Alps, right on the border. I'd try up near Annecy if I were you."

He would make the weary journey willingly, if only at the end of it there would be another Bébé.

At Annecy he found another clue: there was a small lake just over the border, nothing much there—a few farms, a few chalets—but it was possible they had that sort of little brown cat there.

He walked around the track by the lake, wishing he had time to enjoy the crisp clean air that smelled of eucalyptus and pine, making his way to the farm at the bottom of a meadow scattered with blue and yellow flowers, hearing the sound of cowbells. As he came to the dairy where the farmer's wife was busy churning butter, he almost fell over a little brown kitten. She lay on her back waving her pink-padded paws in the air. He had found Léonie's cat.

She was only a shade darker brown than Bébé and a little lighter on the belly and under the chin, but she had the same triangular head and oblique yellow eyes, and she was just as soft. She snuggled in Léonie's arms as though she belonged there, purring trustingly. Léonie hadn't thought it possible that she could love any cat after Bébé, but this one was irresistible.

"Oh, Maroc," she said, "how can I ever thank you?"

"There's no need," he said with a smile. "As long as you're happy."

"I'll never forget Bébé," she vowed.

He sat down beside her and took her hand. "Nor should you," he said, "but this is a different one . . . a chocolate color kitten. And look, she loves you already."

The tiny paws were kneading her arm affectionately and Léonie smiled through her tears. "Chocolat," she said, "that's her name." The loneliness without Bébé had been unbearable, the rooms at the inn empty of her mischievous presence, the terrace silent without the skittering paws, and the bed sad without her small comforting weight. She hugged the new kitten to her tenderly; they would be friends.

❧42❧

SEBASTIÃO DO SANTOS was enjoying Paris. He liked everything about it: the street life of terraced cafés and bistros, the *bal musettes* where you could meet girls and dance and drink a little, and the open spaces of the Bois and the Luxembourg Gardens and the bridges and the *bouquinistes* in the *quais,* where you could find wonderful old books for a few sous. He was happy, immersed for weeks on end in draftsmanship and blueprints and the buildings ancient and contemporary that made his architectural studies come alive at last. He enjoyed his freedom away from the confines of home and family, living in the world's most fascinating city in the company of his new friends.

His rooms were in a crumbling old stone building that opened onto a cobbled courtyard guarded by a fierce concierge, who watched with an eagle's eye to see that the young men were not bringing back girls—though the fact that she was almost stone deaf and disappeared every evening at eight, shutting herself away in her apartment with a bottle, meant that his rooms were the venue for many a rowdy party. Like the one they'd had the night before.

Sitting up in bed, he ran his hands through his thick straight blond hair and walked yawning across to the window, throwing it open to let in the fresh morning breeze.

He inhaled deeply. Gérard was still asleep on the couch. "Come on, wake up," he called. "I'm hungry."

"Ugh" was the only reply.

Sebastião laughed. "I'm off to the Dôme for breakfast, are you coming?"

"Oh, all right ... I suppose so." Gérard emerged grumbling from beneath the blanket, blinking his dark blue eyes at the bright morning sun. "How can you eat after last night?" he said, surveying with distaste the row of empty wine bottles on the stained table. "Where is everybody?"

Sebastião shrugged. "If you mean the girls, they left before the dragon was up ... they're terrified of her."

"You really must change your rooms, Sebastião," Gérard said, laughing. "How can you put up with that interfering old girl?"

"I like it here. I like this old building . . . it suits me. Anyway, let's get going. I'm starving."

Gérard de Courmont was as dark as Sebastião was fair: dark brown, almost black hair, dark deep blue eyes that always seemed to see more than you meant him to, and a slim, strong-boned face with a touch of arrogance in the profile. He had met Sebastião at college and though he was a year older, the two had soon become friends. He practically lived at Sebastião's apartment, preferring its freedom to his family's home.

"You'd better go home this week," said Sebastião, reading his thoughts, "your mother will be getting worried."

"She's in the country most of the time these days, it doesn't really matter whether I'm there or not."

"And your father?" Sebastião was curious.

Gérard shrugged. "Who knows. I think he spends most of his time at the factories with the designers—they're bringing out a new sports car this year." He didn't want to think about his father, he rarely saw him these days, and when he did it only made him feel guilty for not going into the business. His father had always lived his life on his own terms—and so would he.

They ran down the stairs together, calling a cheerful *bonjour* to the old woman in her black dress and boots sitting in the courtyard, knitting yet another black garment. "Here," she called after Sebastião, "here's a letter for you."

He looked at the envelope. "It'll be from Amélie again," he said with a grin. He loved to get her letters.

"And what will she have been up to this time?" Gérard smiled. Amélie's letters were a great source of amusement. She wrote constantly to Sebastião, long scrawls filled with details of her daily doings, the rides with Roberto and Edouard along the beach, getting caught in the thunderstorm all the way out at Barra de Tijuca, the direness of exams at school, the exploits of Fido and Minou, and her continuing feud with Diego Benavente. She illustrated these sagas with funny little drawings of herself, a round-faced, fuzzy-haired, skinny-legged girl in boy's shorts, smiling or scowling or standing on her head—just so you'll remember what I look like, she wrote.

The Dôme was quiet and they took a seat outside. Gérard ordered coffee while Sebastião opened her letter. He smiled as he read it, passing it across page by page to Gérard: this time she was in trouble. On one particularly hot day she had cut off her hair, shearing it raggedly above her ears, and a distraught Isabelle had rushed her down to Hellot's beauty parlor, where they had trimmed it into short fluffy curls that lay close to her head. She was pleased with it, she said, because now she looked more like Roberto, but poor Grandmère had wept for the loss of all her beautiful hair and had gathered up the thick glossy hanks and tied them into braids to keep forever. She'll soon get over it, she added, because she's so busy with her plans to expand the Pavillon into a small hotel—sometimes I can't believe Grandmère, and neither can she. She swears she was meant to be part of the bourgeoisie—being the lady on the high stool behind the cash register in a bistro would have suited her. She complained that Roberto thought she was too bossy and drew a little picture of herself with downturned smile next to it, and another of her face with a huge grin where she told him of her birthday lunch at the Pavillon and the enormous sugar-frosted cake with twelve candles. And now she was looking forward to going to Key West again with Edouard, she loved it there, especially going fishing on the boat and then cooking the catch over a smoky grill on the terrace in the evening—and Roberto was going this time, too. Diego was furious!

Gérard took a deep breath and laughed—Amélie's sentences and thoughts flowed in one continuous line, leaving the reader breathless but amused.

"I can't wait for her to grow up," said Sebastião.

"Oh? Why?"

"So I can fall in love with her," he replied with a smile.

Gérard looked at him curiously. "I believe you really mean it."

"If you ever met her, you'd know why. Amélie is a charmer, you can't help but love her."

Gérard felt a pang of envy. How nice to have a family like Sebastião's—united and happy—instead of torn and bitter like his. He sighed; he'd like to meet someone like Amélie one day.

"Why don't you come back with me for the holidays?" offered Sebastião suddenly. Gérard gave off such waves of loneliness that at times he felt sorry for him. "You'd love Rio. We'll go down to the *fazenda* with all the family—we can work outdoors in the fields instead of poring over technical drawings and perspectives all day! And you can meet Amélie."

Gérard's spirits rose. "I'd love it. Of course, I'll have to get permission from my father."

Sebastião laughed. "You may never come back," he warned. "Rio is as seductive as a beautiful woman."

❧ 43 ❧

VERRONET HATED MANAUS. He hated the humidity that made him sweat uncomfortably in his white Paris suit, he hated the insects and mosquitoes that bit him insistently, he hated the moist jungle smells of rot and decay and the hot town smells of perfume and sweat and sugar-cane rum. And he loathed the all-pervading acrid stench of rubber.

Averting his eyes from the flashy brothels and bawdy painted women with teeth studded with diamonds and filed to feline points, he stared nervously at the Winchester carbines slung carelessly across the shoulders of fierce swarthy men, in town from remote upriver rubber trails. He was waiting to meet the last of the trail owners on his list. He'd already spoken to half a dozen—some of whom, with their flinty eyes and casually toted pistols, had put the fear of God in him, and some of whom, flaunting their new wealth in linen suits from London, Charvet ties from Paris, and women on their arms decked in emeralds from Cartier, had quoted prices as high as their life-style. There had been one or two possibles, but their plantations had turned out to be too small. De Courmont was going to need a lot of rubber and Verronet hoped that Wil Harcourt would be the one to provide it. If not, it could mean at least another month in Manaus, searching. He doubted he'd be able to bear it.

The Churrascaria Onça was named for the beautiful tame jaguar lounging lazily on its chain at the far end of the long, mirrored mahogany bar, and Verronet kept as far from it as possible as he ordered an American beer from the vast refrigerated cabinet.

"You must be Verronet."

He wheeled around in surprise. "You look so damned uncomfortable, I guessed you were a newcomer to Manaus."

Verronet assessed him quickly: a strong face, the straightforward manner of a man with nothing to hide, and he toted no pistols and wore no diamond rings! Just let him have enough rubber, he prayed, and of the right quality.

Wil led the way to a table, past the guardian Onça. Her eyes followed Verronet as he skirted her nervously. "She's tame enough." Wil grinned. "Playful as a kitten—with her owner!"

Verronet got straight to business, listing the European Iron and Steel Company's requirements: details of quantities, the five-year contract at a fixed, initially high price that they estimated would amortize itself over a period and which, in any case, would be substantially less than they would have paid buying from brokers. To his relief, Wil was able to confirm what he hoped to hear: the Oro Velho Trail had only the best *hevea brasiliensis* trees, supplying "Pará fine hard" rubber, and they had sufficient quantity for his needs. Wil promised to discuss Verronet's terms with his partner and let him know in a day or two. It seemed probable they could make a deal.

Verronet glanced again at Wil Harcourt, who was digging enthusiastically into his plate of grilled meats. Harcourt was demanding payment for two years in advance. That was a very great deal of money, though his reasoning—that it must offset any great price rises for the next season's rubber—was valid. Still, it made him nervous. Could he trust him? What if the rubber was of inferior quality when it arrived in France? De Courmont would hold him responsible. Verronet shuddered as he thought of the consequences. It was no use checking the rubber in the warehouses, they could show him anything they wanted. There was nothing for it but to go upriver and inspect their trail. De Courmont, I hope you appreciate this, he thought bitterly, because it's going to cost you! He thought greedily of the rise in salary, the possible bonuses in de Courmont stocks that he stood to gain from such a deal, and sighed. It would be worth it.

Verronet felt a fool in his brand-new jungle outfit; the long-sleeved shirt was hot and the high boots uncomfortably tight on his already swollen feet—and besides, Wil Harcourt was wearing his normal clothes. He fumed silently, wishing Harcourt's partner would hurry, the *Liverpool Lady* was already preparing to leave.

"There he is," said Wil, leaning over the rail. "Come on," he yelled, "Captain Beckwith will be furious if you make him miss his sailing!"

Edouard threw his bag onto the deck of the steamboat and hurried up the gangway. "Had to stop by the telegraph office to send a message home," he said, grinning. He held out his hand to Verronet. "It's a pleasure to meet a fellow Frenchman. I'm Edouard d'Aureville."

Verronet blinked. Had he heard right? He offered his moist hand. "Monsieur . . . d'Aureville?"

"Didn't I mention," said Wil, "that my partner is French?"

"A lapsed Frenchman," said Edouard. "I haven't been home in twelve years."

A fixed smile hid Verronet's interest—of course, there had been a brother who lived abroad, and wasn't it twelve years since Charles d'Aureville had died and Léonie's baby had disappeared? "And where was your home, Monsieur?" he asked.

Edouard caught the faint tremor in Verronet's voice. Why was the man so nervous? "The Loire, close to Tours. Would you excuse me?" he added. "I must check with the captain about an extra load we're bringing back from Santarém."

Verronet turned to Wil. "An odd coincidence," he said casually, "a Frenchman supplying France with rubber from Brazil. Tell me, why has he never returned to France? There are ships from Belem every week."

"Edouard's family moved with him to Rio—his mother and his little girl. They're happy there."

"His little girl?" Verronet's voice rose to a squeak. "He's married then?"

"No, he's not married. Amélie is Edouard's brother's child. He died when she was very young and Edouard has brought her up as his own."

Verronet drew a trembling breath. Oh, the mysterious ways of fate! Here he was, on a steamboat, a thousand miles along the Amazon River, and he had found Amélie! He shook with excitement. He had to be alone; he had to think. He needed to consider his next moves.

He sat on the narrow bunk in his tiny cabin and stared at the blank wall opposite. He—Verronet—held the key to Gilles de Courmont's obsession. Amélie was the one thing in life de Courmont *needed*—and it was going to cost him dearly!

Verronet laughed out loud. He needn't be so careful now about this rubber deal. He'd go to Rio instead, track down the girl; he peered through the porthole, but Manaus was only a faint silhouette on the darkening horizon. *Merde.* Now he'd have to go through with it. He sighed and threw himself on the bunk. Well, Amélie had waited all these years, a few more days wouldn't matter.

Gray clouds misted the roofs of Santarém, and Edouard, watching the last of the rubber being loaded onto the *Liverpool Lady,* cast an anxious glance skyward. If it hadn't been for Verronet, they wouldn't have made this journey so late in the season; he hoped they would make it back to Manaus before the heavy rains began.

It had been a tough couple of days. Verronet made him uneasy, but he couldn't think why. There was just something odd about him. It had been amusing, though, watching Verronet treading warily through the tall green silence of the jungle, shooting glances right and left as though expecting to be eaten alive at any moment, swooning with fear as the howler monkeys screamed their dawn chorus, shattering the still forest like a pane of breaking glass. Verronet had scurried thankfully back on board the *Liverpool Lady* and was now soothing his frayed nerves with a bottle of Captain Beckwith's Scotch.

Verronet composed the telegram to de Courmont carefully. "Rubber situation successful," he wrote, "delaying return for a further few weeks to follow up information of an important personal nature. Will report as soon as possible."

Did it say enough? He wanted to feed de Courmont the information slowly, allow him to think that this would be extremely difficult, even dangerous, work. Then he'd tell him he had found her. Léonie's long-lost daughter! And he'd make him pay every step of the way!

With a great blast on her siren, the *Liverpool Lady* pulled away from the dock and out into the sluggish silt-brown river—at last returning to Manaus. Verronet sipped his Scotch contentedly, he had finally won the game.

The sound of rain drumming on the decks woke Edouard. He glanced at his watch—after three o'clock—and turned over again, closing his eyes, but the noise of the rain beat incessantly through the darkness and the boat wallowed uncomfortably on the churning river. He was now completely awake; cursing the rain, he pulled on trousers and shirt and went in search of a drink.

He found Captain Beckwith in the wheelhouse, peering out into the rain-washed night. "Good weather, isn't it," commented the captain, filling their glasses, "for ducks!"

Edouard grinned and sipped his Scotch. The rain was a solid sheet, isolating the little steamboat as she plowed her way upriver. The wheelhouse seemed a tiny haven of security in a wild alien world. Flickering lights threw back their reflections from the useless windows as Edouard listened to Beckwith's tales of ships and storms that spanned his fifty years at sea. A stocky Yorkshireman, who unbuttoned his tight-lipped silence only after his third whiskey, Beckwith alternated his drinks with mugs of steaming dark brown tea, brewed by the mate who stood in charge of the wheel.

The rain stopped suddenly, as though God had turned off the tap, and the captain looked up in surprise. On deck he sniffed the air like a pointer, scanning the gloomy predawn sky and the dark mass of river, searching through the spiraling mist to where he could just make out the bank on the port side. "Mmm," he muttered. "I don't know . . . something doesn't feel right."

"Perhaps we're in for a thunderstorm," suggested Edouard, stretching wearily.

The captain held up a gnarled hand as they strained their ears into the silence. Distantly, beyond the movement of the river, they could hear a low rumbling, like a far-off train surging through the night.

"By God," roared Beckwith, "we're in trouble! First Mate, ring that bloody bell . . . all hands on deck . . . it's the riverbanks, the bastards are being ripped apart by the floodwaters. They're tearing off in great chunks—mile after bloody mile of them. The force of the fall will create a freak wave maybe twenty feet high. Better wake up your friends, Edouard, and get below. We'll run for the shelter of the islands in midstream."

Wil was already awake and throwing on his clothes as Edouard pounded on Verronet's door.

"What is it?" called Verronet irritably. He'd only just fallen asleep after spending restless hours tossing and turning, despite the bottle of whiskey he'd consumed.

"Get dressed," yelled Edouard, "we're in for trouble: the riverbanks are caving in."

Verronet appeared at the door, white-faced. "You mean we're *in danger?*"

He was obviously going to be of no help. "Better stay below," advised Edouard, heading for the companionway. "You'll be safe enough down here."

Verronet stared after him, his face pinched with panic. He glanced up and down the corridor—no one was in sight. He was all alone down here! He heard the sudden running of feet overhead as the ship pulled hard to starboard, gathering speed as she moved into the current, flinging him to his knees. Terrified, he scrambled to his feet and lumbered up the companionway, peering out at the wild, swirling, muddy river, the great roar ringing in his ears. A wave slapped viciously across the deck, pouring down the steps and slamming him backward. With a whimper, he picked himself up again, coughing river water, and clambered back up the stairs. He scurried toward the wheelhouse, passing Wil, who was working with the sailors on deck, frantically battening down hatches and portholes.

In the engine room stokers fueled coal into the roaring furnaces as Beckwith swung the ship into the shelter of the islands. Edouard focused the binoculars on the misty horizon, waiting.

Verronet stood in the doorway, dripping water. "What's happening?" he demanded hoarsely. "You left me down there alone. . . ."

"Shut that blasted door!" roared Beckwith, as the boat wallowed and water slopped through the cabin.

Verronet slammed the door, cowering against the security of its solid wood, following their gaze as they scanned the river, his breath escaping from terrified lips in a long hiss as he looked out. Less than a quarter of a

mile away, a solid wall of water spanned the width of the river, curving toward them, gathering momentum as it came. With a shriek like the twisting of steel girders, the Amazon riverbanks crashed, rending up giant
centuries-old trees by their roots and hurling them into the torrent as
though they were twigs. There was another sound above the roar of the
falling lands and Verronet realized suddenly that it was his own terrified
scream. He was going to die, here in this wilderness. They'd brought him
here to drown him. He spun around as Edouard pushed past him and
hurled himself on the bucking wheel with Beckwith, lending his weight to
the captain's, striving to keep the ship steady. Then the wave engulfed
them.

The *Liverpool Lady* shivered under the impact like a dying animal, timbers splintered with a sound like pistol shots; metals ripped and screamed as
the torrent poured in. Verronet fought the weight of the water, choking on
the silt-thick mass that pressed on his eyes, invaded his nose, crushed his
lungs. It was bottomless, endless; he was drowning beneath the formless
heaviness.

"Bastard river," roared Beckwith, surfacing, still clinging to the useless
wheel, which bucked wildly, flinging him backward with Edouard into the
water. There was a sharp pain as a shard of broken glass crashed into
Edouard's forehead. Beckwith surfaced again, grabbing Verronet, shaking
him like a rat, slapping the water from him with great thuds on his back,
until Verronet choked and gasped air. Edouard staggered to his feet, shaking his head, spattering blood across them both. Where was Wil? he wondered fuzzily. Oh, God, where was Wil? Water still flooded through the
wheelhouse. Staggering upright, he pushed his way across to the door, tripping over Verronet, who clung, paralyzed with fear, to the stair rail. The
boat shuddered again, wallowing deep in the water as Verronet grabbed
him. "Where are you going?" he screamed. "Don't leave me here alone . . .
you want me to die, you want me to die. . . ."

The poor fellow's crazed, thought Edouard, heading single-mindedly
for the door to find Wil.

He's leaving me here to drown, thought Verronet, frantic with fear.
That's it! He's found out that I'm working for Monsieur, he knows that I
know where Amélie is and that I'll tell Monsieur that she's in Rio, waiting
for him. *Waiting for whatever he might do!* He wants to get rid of me. *To kill
me! He'll shut me in here to drown—and nobody will ever know!* Verronet lunged
toward Edouard as he disappeared up the steps, grabbing him by the legs.
Edouard floundered on the treacherous wooden steps, sliding backward,
pushing Verronet beneath the water that flowed, two feet deep, through the
wheelhouse. Verronet scrambled for a hold; the river was claiming him
again, its mud was choking him, sealing his eyes, his lungs. Struggling to

his feet, he shook the water from him. "Murderer," he shrieked, his voice a thin knifeblade of fear. "*You want to murder me because I know* . . . you planned this, you and your partner. . . ."

Blood streamed down Edouard's face from the gash over his eye—were there two Verronets in front of him?

"The bastard's gone mad!" yelled Beckwith.

Edouard tried to focus, to concentrate; what had Verronet said about him and his partner? *His partner! He had to find Wil!* He staggered again up the steps.

"You're not leaving me here," screamed Verronet as Edouard disappeared and the boat wallowed suddenly, sending another crushing wave of brown water to engulf him.

Edouard clung to the doorway as the river tossed the *Liverpool Lady* like a cork. Water flowed from every aperture. Tattered awnings flapped wetly over the slippery boards and steel deck rails, twisted like ladies' hairpins, sagged uselessly from their fittings. Wiping the blood from his eyes with his sleeve, Edouard moved cautiously forward.

Verronet slithered after him. "Wait!" he yelled. "Wait for me, you're not leaving me down here to die!"

An ominous rumbling came from beneath the decks and the *Liverpool Lady* shuddered and then slowly and gracefully tilted her bows from the water, lifting them to the top of a treacherous slope.

"Help me . . . help me . . ." screamed Verronet, scrabbling for a foothold on the smooth slippery boards.

That man is screaming again, thought Edouard, shaking his head to try to clear his vision. Why doesn't he shut up, can't he see the ship is listing?

Verronet rolled past him, sliding fast across the deck, and instinctively Edouard reached out a hand to grab him. Verronet's fingers latched onto his like a claw, dragging Edouard with him across the deck. Edouard's left hand searched frantically for a hold; he could see the river sucking at the ship. I'm just a foot away from death, he thought, his brain clearing. They were going over together, the river was waiting for them just a foot away. "I can't die . . . I can't," he roared.

The metal bollard thudded into his belly, knocking the breath out of him as he curved his body around it. Edouard sucked desperately for air, searching the smooth metal with his free hand. His fingers locked around the metal ring as Verronet, still clinging desperately to his right hand, slid over the side.

White hot pain shot through Edouard's shoulders as the muscles ripped. I must hold on, he thought, closing his eyes against the agony, I must hold on. Verronet dangled from his right arm, his legs and lower torso in the water. The thick brown river sucked at him eagerly.

"Murderer, murderer," screamed Verronet.

Edouard's puzzled eyes met his. "Murderer," screamed Verronet again as the boat swung around, forcing him beneath the water. The clawlike hand gripped Edouard's with fearsome strength, dragging at him, refusing to let go, the nails biting into his flesh to the bone. The *Liverpool Lady* swung with the current and the hand slacked its grip and was gone.

Wil pulled himself to his feet, wading through the debris in the salon, kicking aside floating pieces of wood and lethal shards of broken glass, bobbing whiskey bottles, and the sodden newspapers that wrapped themselves around his legs. Hefting aside the splintered slab of oak that had once been the door, he emerged, trembling, onto the deck. He didn't know by what miracle, but he was *alive!*

Beckwith appeared from the wheelhouse, running and sliding toward him across the slippery deck. "It's Edouard," he yelled. "Get Edouard. . . ."

Edouard lay, half over the side, one hand clinging to the metal ring. They eased him back onto the deck and Wil examined him anxiously. "He's unconscious," he exclaimed, "and my God, look at his hands!" Edouard's right hand was black and swollen, every finger broken.

His left was frozen around the metal ring, and as they pried his numb fingers free, blood ran where the metal had cut deep into the flesh of the palm. Wil looked helplessly at his partner. Edouard was very cold, and there wasn't even a dry blanket to wrap him in. Wil lifted him gently and carried him into the saloon.

Men were emerging from below decks, staring with stunned, frightened eyes at the scene. The boat trembled fitfully and there was another ominous rumble.

"My God," yelled the captain, "we're not holed, it's the blasted rubber that's shifting ballast—it's rolling. A few degrees more and we're under!"

Wil had never realized how terrible the stench of rubber was until now. He'd thought he was used to it, but here in the waterlogged, stinking hold it overwhelmed him. Head down, shoulders straining, he sweated with the others, heaving and rolling the great two-hundred-pound balls of rubber from the flooded stern to the bow, dodging the rolling balls as they broke wild and careened past, snapping men's bones in their path, like some nightmare billiard game. Endless hours passed, lost in the rancid, stinking, sweating hold, as Beckwith snarled commands and one by one the rubber balls were captured and tethered securely with steel cables. Gradually, the *Liverpool Lady* settled back into the water to lick her wounds.

It was two weeks before Captain Beckwith guided his ship into the great floating dock at Manaus. Like many other riverboats caught in the *terras caidas*, the falling lands of the Amazon, she had been given up for lost.

Manaus's finest doctor, fresh from Harley Street, London, tended Edouard's wounds. He refused to stay in the hospital and sat with Wil at a café on Avenida Edouardo Ribiero, his shoulders strapped, his hands in plaster, and a jagged row of stitches across his forehead. Passersby turned to stare and whisper, but Edouard didn't notice. He couldn't get the image of Verronet out of his mind, the crazed eyes, the hand clawing his, sliding away. *Why,* he wondered for the hundredth time, *why did he call me a murderer?*

Wil sighed. "You know," he said as last, "you and I are lucky to be alive. I don't believe in pushing my luck. Let's sell the Oro Velho to the highest bidder and get the hell out of here."

❧ 44 ❧

GILLES TOOK OFF his jacket and loosened his tie, glancing wearily at the two telegrams that lay side by side on his desk. He had come to the office directly from the station, after a much delayed train journey from Milan, and had almost forgotten that Verronet was in Brazil.

A puzzled frown crossed his face as he read the first message. What on earth did Verronet mean by "information of an important personal nature?" Had he got some new angle on the rubber deal? An idea for extracting more money for himself? He flung the piece of paper on the desk irritably. Or had he simply found a good gambling club in Manaus? He knew Verronet's little weakness. He always knew a person's weaknesses.

With a sigh of exasperation, he ripped open the second telegram, addressed to the European Iron and Steel Company. It was signed "Wil Harcourt of the Oro Velho Trail." He drew in his breath sharply as he read it, placing the telegram next to the other on his desk and staring angrily at them both.

The fool! How could he get himself killed in some storm on the Amazon? Verronet had been with him for fifteen years, he knew everything—just where to lay his hands on the right information, who was involved with whom, where the secrets of their rivals were buried. Damn it, how would he manage without him? And what had he meant by this odd message? God, the man was a *fool!* If he weren't a fool, he wouldn't be dead!

Gilles paced the floor angrily. What about the Brazilian rubber deal? Who was there that he could trust to take Verronet's place? Who was as devious and as clever—and as loyal? He knew the answer. There was no one.

Gérard hesitated at the heavy oak door to the office. You never knew whether Father was going to be furious at an interruption or so lost in his own thoughts that he scarcely even knew you were there—or whether he might be pleased. It had always been the same, even when they were small: one moment he'd be smiling and giving you all his attention and the next it was as if he had never seen you before. Gérard had learned to live with it, but he still couldn't fathom his father's moods.

Gilles looked up irritably. Ah, it was Gérard, he was a good-looking boy—no, *young man!* How old was he now? Nineteen, twenty? He couldn't remember.

"Did you have a good trip, Father?" Gérard was still cautious. He didn't want to get to the point until he knew what sort of a mood Gilles was in.

"A lot of problems, but everything went well in the end. I wish you'd been with me," said Gilles suddenly, "you would have enjoyed the negotiations—it's like a game, a complex fascinating game."

"And you always win."

Gilles shrugged. "So far. Won't you reconsider, Gérard? The business is all here waiting for you—waiting for both my sons."

They'd played this scene before, many times. His father knew he was set on becoming an architect—it was what he had always wanted. "You have *two* sons, Father, and Armand is crazy about cars. When he's old enough, he'll join the business." Gérard seized his opportunity. "Father, I've been invited to spend the holidays with a friend. I wanted to ask your permission."

"I don't see why not," replied Gilles abstractedly, his thoughts still on Armand and his future.

"Then may I go to Brazil?" Gérard pushed home his point eagerly.

"Brazil?" The two telegrams lay on the desk in front of him. Verronet was dead. *Dead in Brazil!* "You can't go, Gérard," said Gilles abruptly. "Look at this." Gilles thrust the telegram into Gérard's hand. "Verronet's been killed in the Amazon. Do you think I'm going to let you go there?"

"But, Father, I'm going to stay with the do Santos family in Rio. . . ."

"I forbid it, Gérard. You'll stay here in France."

And that was that, thought Gérard bitterly. If his father hadn't received that telegram about his assistant, everything would have been all right. He thought about Verronet, his father's shadow, always in the background. No one had really known him, except his father. "I'm sorry, Father—about Verronet, I mean."

"The man was a fool." Gilles's face was expressionless. "It was his own idea to go to the Amazon for the rubber . . . he had only himself to blame. And he's left me in a hell of a mess!"

Gérard watched his father as he busied himself with the papers on his desk. He didn't even seem to care about Verronet. What about the man's family, if he had one? No use asking his father about that, he'd take care of things in his own way. And there was no use asking him again about the holiday, he knew it.

Gilles was already reaching for the telephone, his mind on other matters, as Gérard made for the door. He didn't even notice his son leave.

⅍ 45 ⅍

LÉONIE placed the spray of jasmine in a glass of water on her dressing table and looked at it thoughtfully. He still sent it, wherever she was in the world, he always knew the country, the city, the theater; even in the depths of winter she had jasmine. It was a romantic gesture—or it would have been if the man were anyone but Monsieur—still, she could never bring herself to throw it away. It sat there on her table, scenting the room with memories.

But tonight was different. There was a letter with the flowers. She eyed the envelope warily; what could he want now? Shaking back her hair impatiently, she fixed the gold circlet around her forehead, scowling at her image. It was time to go on stage—the last night of the season, thank heaven. And tonight she'd go south, like a migratory bird, back to her refuge. She stretched wearily. She was more tired this time than ever before, and there was the new American tour ahead. Sometimes she thought she was getting too old for all this. It was true, she thought suddenly. She was thirty-one years old. It's thirteen years since I left Monsieur and still the battle between us continues. She glanced at the jasmine again, and then at the envelope lying untouched next to it. What had he said, she wondered. The envelope gleamed whitely, tempting her the way he knew it would. Turning abruptly, she walked to the door, slamming it shut behind her.

There was something exciting about traveling on the wagons-lits, she thought. Perhaps it was the idea of hurtling through the night across plains and mountains toward your destination, tucked up in crisp white sheets, and then waking to find yourself in another city. There was a magic about it.

She relaxed in the luxury of the private compartment, whose dark paneled walls were inlaid with designs of garlands and flowers in lighter woods and lit by discreet, pink-shaded lamps. The ruby velvet banquettes were deeply padded and soft and a crystal vase held a matching ruby rose.

Chocolat explored the new territory, sniffing it with interest, and then settled down on the velvet cushions, watching Léonie.

"Will you be taking supper, madame?" asked the steward. "The dining car will be serving soon after we leave."

"I don't think so, thank you." She felt too tired to bother with food. "But will you bring me some tea, please, with lemon, when you have a moment?" She smiled at the steward.

"Of course, madame."

The carriage door closed smoothly behind him and Léonie closed her eyes. Tomorrow she'd be home.

Gilles strode across to the waiting train, already billowing steam and groaning as though with eagerness to be off. He still enjoyed traveling in the wagons-lits, it made him feel like a child enjoying an adventure—going off to mysterious places in the middle of the night.

The steward escorted him to his compartment, making sure he was comfortable. "Will you be having supper, sir?" he inquired.

"Supper?" Now that he thought about it, he was rather hungry, but he couldn't face a crowded dining car. "Is the train full?"

"Oh, no, sir, we're very quiet tonight."

"Then yes, I will be taking supper."

Gilles settled back against the cushions and poured a shot of whiskey from his silver flask. Why in God's name hadn't Léonie answered his note? He had *humbled* himself. He'd *begged* her to see him. Every time he saw her on stage, it was torture. He had gotten through these past years in the belief that one day she would come back to him. Now he must go to her at the inn, and speak with her. He would beg her to come back—it was the only way.

The hot tea arrived and Léonie sipped it, enjoying the lemony fragrance as the warmth soothed her tired body. She wished she'd asked for a sandwich to go with the tea, she really felt quite hungry now. Perhaps she'd ask the steward to bring her something, but no, it was probably quicker just to get it herself.

The dining car was empty—just a solitary person at the other end of the softly lit carriage—she could just see the top of his head over the high banquette. "A table for how many, madame?" the attendant asked, smiling graciously.

"I'm alone," replied Léonie.

Gilles de Courmont froze. His hand still holding the wineglass trembled as he watched the attendant go through the door toward the kitchen. He was alone with Léonie.

The length of the carriage seemed infinite as he walked toward her. "Léonie."

Her startled golden eyes collided with his penetrating look. The adrenaline of shock rushed up her spine, forcing the blood through her veins, burning her cheeks with heat. Her eyes widened with panic: what was he doing here, was he chasing her?

"I didn't mean to startle you; I didn't know you were here." His voice was gentle. "It's as much of a surprise to me as it is to you."

It must be true, she thought. How could he have known that she would be in the dining car—she hadn't known herself until a few minutes ago. But what was he doing on the train? She stared at him. There were lines around his eyes, spiraling from the corners, and his thick hair was graying, brushed back from the temples in smooth silver streaks. She shivered, unable to take her eyes from his face.

"May I sit down, Léonie?" He asked the question but she knew he wouldn't take no for an answer. She had no choice. Except, of course, to get up and leave. But she didn't. She couldn't.

Monsieur leaned across the small table toward her, taking her hand in his. It lay small and unresisting between his palms, and he closed his eyes, so that she wouldn't see the emotion in them—even now he must hide what he truly felt. It was just the way it had always been; holding her hand in his, he could smell her perfume, hear her breathing—feel her hand trembling. He turned it palm up and kissed it, smoothing the skin of the wrist with his finger.

Léonie let her hand lie in his, feeling the shock of his flesh on hers, watching in fascination the long square-tipped fingers, the immaculate, slightly ridged nails, and the tiny dark hairs on the back of his hands, as though she were looking at them under a microscope.

She lifted her eyes with an effort. It seemed as though time was passing very slowly, unfolding second by lethargic second, and she was without strength to move. His eyes were still so dark, such a deep blue. She was a different woman before those eyes, a shocking, daring, demanding woman who wanted him as much as he wanted her—whenever and wherever he wanted her—and now she felt as powerless against him as she had in Monte Carlo when she was seventeen. He was still such a sexual lure for her that his touch burned the memory of response. With an effort she forced herself to her feet.

"Please speak to me, Léonie. I beg you."

The train gathered speed, thundering through the night, hooting its presence into the silence, isolating them in its rose-shaded luxury. "Please let go of my hand." Her voice sounded small and weak.

He gripped her hand tighter. "Stay with me for a few moments, Léonie . . . let's be civilized . . . you must speak to me, I beg you."

The waiter appeared in the doorway, staring at them curiously. "Shall I serve your meal now, sir?"

"Léonie, will you at least have a drink with me . . . just let me talk for a few moments." His gaze held her transfixed. She sank back into her seat and he called an order to the waiter, taking the seat opposite and at last releasing her hand. She rubbed it surreptitiously under the cloth, grasping Chocolat for comfort. What was she doing here, what was happening to her?

"Léonie, I was on my way to Cap Ferrat to ask you to see me . . . you know why, don't you? Why do I think of you every day, dream of you at night? Why can't I forget you and live in peace without you? Why do I send you jasmine, remembering the scent of your skin when I kissed you? And why do you never throw the jasmine away? Is it because you remember, too? It is, isn't it, Léonie." His voice was a low, soothing murmur, insinuating itself into the corners of her mind. "You haven't forgotten those nights, those long wonderful naked nights . . . how warm your body was under mine, how smooth and honeyed with juice and how much you cared. . . ."

The waiter coughed discreetly, placing the wine cooler by the table, and Léonie leaned back against the seat, her cheeks flaming.

Gilles poured the champagne himself. "You see," he murmured, watching as she sipped the familiar wine obediently, "I forget nothing."

Léonie held the glass tightly, staring at the night flying by in the darkness beyond the window and at their reflection—a handsome couple sipping champagne in a rosy, comfortable world. She wanted to touch him again. Oh, she knew she shouldn't, but she wanted to. . . .

He leaned closer, still talking in that hypnotic soft voice, telling her things: how he'd missed her, what he had missed—exciting her.

Chocolat jumped on her knee suddenly, tipping the glass of champagne over her skirt, startling her back to reality. The cat sat proudly on her knee and tentatively licked the drops of champagne.

Léonie pulled the cat to her and struggled to her feet. Monsieur stood in front of her, tall and commanding. "Don't go."

Léonie hesitated. She was torn with a longing she knew she shouldn't feel: she was vulnerable, shorn of all her defenses, here alone with him on a speeding train. This wasn't reality, it was a dream. She pushed past him, running down the car, wrenching at the door. He held it closed as the waiter turned his back and pretended to busy himself at the table. "Léonie," he said urgently, "let me speak to you—at least hear me out."

"Open the door," she whispered, "or do I have to call the waiter?"

Their eyes locked as he hesitated and then he moved slowly from the door, holding it open for her. She passed through it quickly, breaking into a run as it slammed shut behind him. He trapped her at the next door, holding her with his body against the paneled walls of the corridor, an arm on either side of her head. She turned her head away as his mouth approached hers, holding the startled cat in front of her as a barrier. Chocolat struck out with frightened claws at his face, raking them down his cheek, and he drew back with a cry, dabbing at the bloody wounds.

"I know what you want to say," she said, brought back to reality by the violence, "and the answer will never change. It is impossible, Monsieur—you have made it impossible."

"But I know you want me. You do, don't you . . . you feel the same as you always did. I saw it in your eyes."

"You were wrong," she replied coldly. "It's all in your imagination, Monsieur. And surely it's time you faced reality."

"Let's leave what happened in the past where it belongs, let's begin again." His voice was harsher now, it had lost that commanding murmur, that insinuating, soothing lure. His dark eyes glittered so that she could see her face reflected minutely in the enlarged pupils. "You can have Amélie, we'll all live together—the three of us. I'll make you happy, Léonie, you can have anything you want, anything, I promise you."

Amélie—how dare he even mention her name, how dare he! She'd missed Amélie's childhood because of him. Her hate flowed back, twisting in her like a blunt knife. "We said good-bye years ago, Gilles de Courmont. Your life is your own, and it will never include me—or my child." She pushed past him, walking quickly along the corridor and through the door and then, as panic hit her, running down the train until she reached her compartment. She slammed the door behind her, thrusting the bolts closed with trembling hands. Chocolat meowed nervously by her side as she waited for the trembling to stop.

He was insane. She must have been crazy even to listen to him, to let him even try to seduce her with his words—he'd always been able to do it. He knew what she was like. Oh, God, and she had wanted him: for a few moments she had actually wanted him more than anything else in the world. She stared at herself in the mirror, twisting the lamp so that she might see herself better. She wanted to see what kind of woman she was that she could forget murder and danger, betrayed by memories and longings of her own body.

In the morning she was the first off the train, striding alongside the burly steward in charge of her bags, running through the barrier. She caught a glimpse of him hurrying toward her as she stepped into the taxi and the steward slammed the door. He was too late. She was safe.

The inn had never looked more welcoming, nor its square whitewashed walls more solid and secure, and the simple sanity of the Frenards brought her back to comforting reality, making the events on the train seem like a nightmare.

❧ 46 ❦

EDOUARD HAD JUST SEEN Wil off on the train to Miami en route for New York. The Oro Velho was sold and he was a richer man than he had ever dreamed possible.

Thank goodness, his days as a rubber baron were over. He rubbed his hand over the aching scar on his forehead—even though a year had passed, it still gave him trouble. Remembering the look in Verronet's eyes as his hand had slipped from Edouard's broken grasp, he counted himself a very lucky man.

The ferry from Key West to Havana jostled its way fussily out into the bay as he strolled its decks. Life was in a lull, decisions had been made, changes accepted, and the future lay ahead with a big question mark.

Xara Rosalia O'Neill de Esteban rode her horse slowly across to the ridge that divided the two estates, the westerly one belonging to her brother, Tomas, and the one to the east that of her dead husband, Don José. From this height she could see the road that curved like a dusty white ribbon around the perimeter and the royal palms that stood as seventy-foot-high markers to the Flor de Sevilla estate. Its tobacco fields lay neatly furrowed in front of her, dotted here and there with patches of white, where the tender young plants were covered by cloths to protect them from the burning rays of the sun. Immediately below, in the lee of the hill, the evening sun glinted off the red tiles of the spreading roofs of the hacienda and the magnificent avenue of mango trees bordering the drive that led, straight as an arrow, to the boundary road—one of the few straight roads in Cuba, where all the original old estates had been circular.

José de Esteban's *vega* lay exactly as it had been left by the bandits two years before: endless naked fields that were only now beginning to show a sparse covering of rough grass, and the ruin of a great house, a vivid black scar amid the burgeoning purple-pink and scarlet bougainvillaea that sought to hide its wounds.

Tethering Florita beneath a tree to crop the lush grass, Xara wandered along the top of the pleasant little hill, looking contemplatively at her old home, the scene of her married life. "José," she said guiltily, "it's not that I don't love you, I always will, but there must be something more for me than this." Her eyes embraced the scene, the secluded narrow world of the *vega*. "Maybe if I had children, it would all be different, but twenty-six is still young." She turned back from the dead shell of her old home regretfully; she wanted so much to find life again—and romance and love.

The pearly dawn exploded into morning as the Port Authority cannon boomed across the harbor, signaling that ships could now enter, waking Havana into bustling, chattering, vigorous life. The city's narrow streets, strung with awnings for precious shade, teemed with people. Storekeepers arranged their wares in open-fronted shops: colored pastel pink, lilac, and lemon with stacked bolts of organdies and lawn, black and scarlet from spreading lace fans, or eggplant and orange, green and yellow from the shiny heaps of fruits and vegetables. Housewives and servants filled their baskets with bananas and mangoes, papaws, pineapples, and passion fruit, bargaining busily over cages of small game birds and scrawny chickens. Chinese and Creole beggars loitered in the shade of the terraced cafés in the Paseo Tacon, where the white-suited businessmen drank thick black coffee and talked over games of checkers and dominoes. Guitars throbbed an accompaniment to the clattering wheels of the country carriages on the cobblestones, and an aroma of spices and coffee and flowering mignonette mingled with the heavy scent of the powdered women, gossiping outside the Café Dominica.

Edouard breathed it all in, letting it flow like wine through his blood; gay and extrovert or smoldering and secretive, whatever you wanted it to be, Havana beckoned with promise.

The Boutique Oberon on Calle Fundador specialized in the very latest fashions from Paris and Xara headed toward it purposefully. It's now or never, she told herself firmly as she pushed open the door, I'm going to change my life and I'm starting right here.

"Doña Xara," greeted the saleslady, "we haven't seen you for a long time."

"No, Marcella, you haven't, but today I'm making up for it. Take a good look at me . . . look at these drab colors, these out-of-style garments. I've become a cross between a country cousin and a weary widow. I need *change,* Marcella. Change me, *please.* I need *color,* pink and yellow and turquoise, and white silk stockings and pretty shoes with flirty little bows on their toes! I want lacy blouses and ruffled swirling skirts. Marcella, you don't have to *sell* me anything, just bring it all out and I'll buy it!"

Marcella laughed. "Very well, but remember, it'll be very expensive."

Xara sighed. "I'm a rich, childless widow and I'm twenty-six years old. What else is there to spend it on?" She sank into a deep velvet chair with a frown. You're not to think of the past, she reminded herself. This is the day of change, remember?

Young assistants were pressed into action and garments paraded in front of her: day dresses in the finest linens, cool and crisp, in banana and strawberry and pistachio, with the very latest long, lean lines; blouses in handkerchief linen, in peach and vanilla, with matching skirts that swung in layers of tiny points above creamy silken legs. She bought them all, and the little white and blue jackets and skirts for traveling, and the matching shoes and strappy little sandals with a glitter of colored beads across the front for evening, and the long straight white silk sheath that fit as though it were poured over her, banded with a delicate glimmer of crystal at the hem, its wispy fling of silk shawl ready for needless protection against the tropical night air. But her favorite was the scarlet taffeta, tight bodiced and ruffled skirted, sexy as a Spanish gypsy dancer's dress.

It was an orgy of buying, she thought, looking happily at her purchases as they were packed carefully in boxes by the dazzled young assistants; it had purged her of widowhood at last. And the nicest part was that José would have wanted her to do it; he wouldn't have wanted her to be buried, like him, at the Vega Flor de Sevilla.

"Send it all round to the Santa Isabella, Marcella," she called. "I've got several more stops to make before siesta."

The lingerie store sold the slitheriest, silkiest, most heavenly undergarments imaginable, and her hands ran riot in the pastel softness of chemises and slips, of lace-hemmed knickers buttoned at the waist in pearl, of nightdresses in virginal white and less virginal rose and taupe, and even scarlet to match the taffeta dress. Silk stockings and satin slippers with puffs of swansdown and pearl buckles. She sighed with satisfaction. What an absolutely perfect morning this had been. There was only one question, she thought, as she sank thankfully into a chair in the fountained marble coolness of the Café Dominica. Where am I going to wear it all and—even more important—for whom?

Staring into the swirl of dark coffee, she stirred it pensively. It wasn't going to be an easy question to answer. Why, oh, why, couldn't some tall dark stranger come into her life and sweep her off her feet?

* * *

Those ankles, thought Edouard, peering beneath the palm fronds that stood between him and her, were very nice ankles. They were trim and wore silk and ended in slender feet in pretty Paris shoes with flirty little bows on the toes. If he edged his chair slightly to the right, he could probably see more, but then it might spoil his fantasy. She'd probably be some plump Spanish matron waiting for her husband to take her to lunch after a hard morning's shopping. Wasn't it better just to sit here and enjoy the sight of the pretty feet beneath the palm fronds—and they *were* pretty, especially when she crossed her legs like that, giving a man a glimpse of nice silken calves. Ah, well, he thought, signaling the waiter for his bill, I'll keep my dreams.

Now that, thought Xara, sipping her coffee, was a very nice back. Pity he was leaving, now she'd never know what the front was like, but she liked the back. He was tall and lean and he wore his brown hair a little long, so that it curved into his collar. It looked thick and strong; it would feel soft under your hands. He walked with a touch of arrogance, striding through the crowded tables with his white jacket tossed casually across his shoulders. Xara sighed as she called for her bill. Now why couldn't she meet someone like that? Don't be ridiculous, she told herself firmly, he's probably a married man with a plump provincial wife and four children waiting at home while he goes off to visit his little lady friend at some too-hot apartment. As she thought about the lady friend she felt a little pang of regret—or was it envy? She wished she hadn't invented her.

The baroque, rose-colored building that was once the palace of the counts of Santavenia was now the Hotel Santa Isabella, run by an American from New Orleans, and its marble-tiled hall was deserted. Edouard rang the bell on the desk with a sharp ping and waited. The only sounds were the gently splashing water in the pretty blue-tiled fountain and the lethargic whirr of two long-bladed fans strung from the soaring, beamed ceiling. A cage of songbirds, doubled by the reflection in an ornate gilt mirror, remained silent as if they, too, were taking their siesta. He pinged the bell again, impatiently.

A boy appeared, buttoning his white jacket hastily, obviously not expecting guests to arrive at siesta time, but he cheerfully showed Edouard up the galleried staircase and across a hall to a wide airy room whose shuttered windows overlooked the now-silent square. Well, if all Havana were sleeping, who was he to be different? Edouard lay back in the big brass bed and closed his eyes. I wonder, he thought as he drifted into sleep, I wonder if the rest of her was as pretty as her ankles?

* * *

Xara took stock of herself in the long mirror on the door of the vast armoire in her room. The face wasn't *too* bad, she decided, but then she was used to looking at it, so how was she to know? She ran a finger along the slope of her cheekbone; did it slope too sharply? And were her eyes just a little too slanted—wouldn't they be nicer as a bright sparkly blue rather than this glossy brown? Why hadn't she inherited some of her grand-mother's Irish coloring instead of this cream-colored skin with its olive un-dertones? And her hair? She lifted the shining blue-black mass that fell smoothly almost to her waist; perhaps she should have it all cut off and try some new, more interesting style? Her teeth were pretty, though, she ad-mitted that; they were white and even and if she ever had someone to smile at, he would surely be dazzled by her teeth!

She flung off her robe with a sigh and looked at the rest: a tall slender body. Was she too tall, too slender? High pointed breasts, long legs—at least her legs were nice—trim ankles and pretty feet. How did she look to a man? It had been so long, she had no way of knowing. She'd married José when she was seventeen and he had been more than twenty-five years older. Might not a stranger—some other man—find flaws? Things about her that she hadn't realized? She put a tentative hand on her breast. How would she feel to a man, under a man's hands? She put her robe back on with a frown. That was the problem. How did a young Cuban widow meet a handsome, eligible man—and not someone she'd known all her life?

The boxes from the Boutique Oberon with their ransom of Paris-labeled clothes were piled unopened on the bed and she looked at them longingly. They were so pretty, they were meant to adorn some wickedly witty woman traveling alone on a long sea voyage who would be a constant lure to all the men on board and the cause of endless speculation and com-ment. They were clothes for a daring woman.

She began to unpack them, tossing them onto the bed in a flurry of pleats and flounces and splashes of color. Yes, the red taffeta was definitely her favorite. She longed to wear it. She took it to the mirror and held it in front of her. If she wore her hair pulled back, Spanish style, and the ruby earrings— "Damn it, Xara," she said to herself, "you'll wear it tonight. You'll dine at Velasquez and you'll dine alone."

Edouard opened his eyes and took in the strange room. Padding across to the window, he flung back the shutters onto a rose-tinted world. The sky was a dazzling red curtain suspended like gauze over the bustling square, where café terraces were already filling up with people ready to enjoy what the evening might offer. And what, he wondered, would it offer him? Well, first a bath, and when had he last eaten? He had had nothing on the ship last night, a cup of coffee, a beer; he was starving! That was it. He'd find the best restaurant in town and he'd dine in style—alone.

The scarlet taffeta rustled pleasingly as Xara walked along the gallery toward the stairs, and she smiled. She felt the way she had when she was a small child and her mother had dressed her in pretty flounced lawn. Tying the pink satin sash tightly and turning her around to look at her, she'd said with a smile, "How pretty you are, Xara"—and to this day she could remember *feeling* pretty. Well, tonight she felt pretty again and it added an extra lift to her chin, a provocative languorousness to her walk.

She looked, thought Edouard d'Aureville, waiting in the hall, like an aristocratic gypsy girl on her way to an assignation. Lucky man, he thought enviously as she walked toward the door. Oh, yes, whomever she was meeting, he was a very lucky man.

The night air was warm and Xara breathed it in eagerly. This is an adventure, she told herself as she waited for a cab, well-brought-up Cuban girls don't go to restaurants alone, they go with their fathers or brothers or cousins or husbands; there's still time to go back, a small voice inside her added doubtfully. You could have a quiet dinner in the hotel dining room. After all, the Velasquez is a very smart restaurant, you never know whom you might see there, think of the talk. "No," she said firmly, "I'm going to do it."

"I beg your pardon?" said Edouard, standing next to her.

"Oh, I'm sorry, it was nothing, I was just talking to myself." Xara climbed into the cab. "The Velasquez," she said, turning to look at him out of the window. Their eyes met for a moment—were his gray, she wondered, leaning back against the seat, or were they silver? Or maybe they were transparent like glass, so you could see into his soul—if you were close enough? Who was *he* going to meet tonight? Probably some lovely foreign woman, cool and blond and British, or maybe some elegant American—whoever she was, she was a very lucky woman.

Edouard speculated on those brown oblique eyes. Had she smiled at him, a sort of half-smile? The fragrance of the gardenias she wore in her hair lingered tantalizingly. The Velasquez, she'd said. He had meant to go to the Habanera. He hesitated for only a second. "The Velasquez," he instructed the driver.

The restaurant was quieter than Xara had expected and if the maître d'hôtel was surprised that she was alone, he didn't show it. He escorted her to her table in an alcove by the ornately tiled Spanish fireplace, banked tonight with flowers instead of flames. "Señora," he said, casting the huge crisp white linen napkin across her knee and presenting the menu. "Would you care to order something to drink?"

"Manzanilla," she said with a smile—a dry sherry was appropriate as she was so very Spanish tonight. She looked around disappointedly, the alcove held just two tables directly opposite each other, and only by pushing her chair around slightly could she see the main part of the restaurant and the other diners. Damn, she thought, I wanted to be the observer, to see people together, the married couples and the lovers. I wanted to watch their happiness, to catch up on life, if only vicariously. She sipped the thin, dry Manzanilla sadly.

Edouard glanced around the restaurant. She wasn't there; could he have made a mistake? Was this the wrong restaurant?

"Señor," the maître d'hôtel ushered him into the alcove by the fireplace. There were just two tables and the girl in the red dress sat alone at the other one. Edouard nodded politely to her as he took a seat. Her lover must be late; obviously she was waiting for him. He could smell the fragrance of gardenias again.

Xara peered at him from beneath her lashes—it was him! Oh, this was awful; she'd have to sit opposite while he dined with his lover. The tables were so close she'd be able to overhear their most intimate conversation, see their faces as they gazed at each other, glimpse their clasped hands beneath the table. She sipped the Manzanilla nervously.

Edouard studied the menu, glancing over its top at the scarlet lady. Who could she be? And what sort of man would keep her waiting? Only a fool, he answered regretfully, the man must be a fool to waste a single minute without her. Her shoulders are like cream next to the berry-red dress, and her blue-black hair shines like a blackbird's wing.

"Sir?" prompted the waiter.

"The swordfish—and a bottle of Roederer Cristal." This might prove to be a long night. He hadn't intended to have such a firsthand view of his scarlet lady and her lover. Why do I think she's meeting a lover, he wondered suddenly. It could be her husband, her brother. No, he knew it wasn't. This woman had dressed for a lover, her scarlet taffeta rustled with promise. She looked like a flower amid the petals of her skirt, a gardenia flower.

Xara studied the tablecloth nervously. He'd ordered. He wouldn't do that if he was meeting someone; he would wait. Could he be alone? Why don't you invite him to join you? After all, you came out looking for romance. How can I do that? she asked herself in panic. I can't do that—can I?

"Señora?" She looked up at the waiter. "Will you be having any wine?"

"Wine?" She glanced at the cooler with the bottle of champagne on his table. "Champagne, please." Perhaps it would give her courage; she wanted those silver-gray eyes to look into hers.

She must be alone, thought Edouard in surprise. A woman like her—dining alone? But why? Don't ask why, you idiot, he told himself, she's here alone, and so are you; ask her to join you. There was probably an irate Cuban husband around the corner ready to shoot him, but the hell with it, it was worth it.

"Excuse me," he said.

"Pardon me," she said.

Their eyes met—hers glossy brown and tilted at the corners, swept by a fringe of curling lashes, his as transparently clear as a mountain pool.

"Oh," she breathed, "how did you get that terrible scar?" She didn't know why she said that, she hadn't meant to say it at all, it had just slipped out. Oh, God, now what would he think of her?

"It's a long story," he said with a smile, "but one I'd be delighted to tell you. I meant to ask—as you seem to be alone tonight, and I, too, am alone—whether you might join me? I know we haven't met, but we seem to be at the same hotel. It's a sort of introduction, isn't it?"

"But we've both ordered champagne," she said foolishly. "Now we'll have two bottles."

Edouard walked the three paces to her table, smiling down at her. "Then I suggest that we drink them together," he said, taking her hand. "My name is Edouard d'Aureville."

"'I'm Xara . . . Xara O'Neill de Esteban," she said breathlessly. Is this how it happens—just like this? The man of your dreams walks up to you in a restaurant and tells you his name is Edouard—such a lovely name—and you drink champagne together and you flirt with him until the end of the evening when you know he wants to make love to you.

"Yes." She remembered looking into the mirror earlier and thinking that at least her teeth were pretty and she laughed.

Edouard looked at her with delight; he could almost sense how that coral mouth would feel under his—it was a mouth to be dwelt on, lingered over, touched with a tongue, bitten tenderly. It was definitely a mouth he very much wanted to kiss.

"Tell me," he said, sitting next to her, "how you can be called both O'Neill and Esteban."

"The O'Neill is because of my father's Irish ancestry—the family set-tled in Cuba two hundred years ago. De Esteban was my husband's name."

"Your husband?"

His eyes looked surprised. "My late husband," she said quietly. "He was killed two years ago by bandits. They burned our estate . . . José had the finest tobacco *vega* on the island, the Flor de Sevilla." She shrugged slightly and the taffeta flounces on her shoulders rustled prettily.

"I'm so sorry," Edouard said to her.

"It's been two years." She looked into his eyes. "It's a long time." She sipped her champagne. "I shouldn't tell you this," she said, "but today I decided to change my life. I had stayed on in the country at my brother's estate and suddenly I couldn't bear it any longer. I wanted to be free of it all. I came to Havana, bought myself some new dresses"—her hand rested lightly on the ruffles across her bosom—"and I came here to dine alone. I wanted to force myself out into the real world again."

"How lucky for me that you did," said Edouard. "I, too, have a confession to make. I followed you here from the hotel. I thought you must be meeting your lover."

"My lover?" She was startled. "Why should you think I had a lover?"

"You looked," he said with a smile, "like a woman en route to an adventure, dressed in scarlet silk, flowers in your hair . . . a ravishing gypsy."

"And you," she whispered, "I thought you were meeting some cool British blonde . . . she would be icily aristocratic and as tempting as chilled wine on a hot summer night."

He gazed into her glossy tilted eyes and she moistened her lips nervously. She felt breathless. She took a sip of champagne. His eyes held hers.

"Xara O'Neill de Esteban," murmured Edouard, "I'm afraid I'm falling in love with you."

She was oblivious to the restaurant, the waiters, the guitars, and the busy hum of conversation—he was falling in love with her; was she looking at him as longingly as he was at her?

Edouard bent his head and kissed her softly on the lips; she tasted of champagne and softness. "We've come too far already, Xara," he murmured, "there's no turning back."

She wanted to kiss him some more, she was *committed* to kissing him. Oh, yes, they had come too far to go back now, but she shouldn't be doing this. Well-brought-up girls didn't behave like this, kissing perfect strangers in restaurants. But she was in love with this *perfect* stranger.

The waiter interrupted them with a discreet cough, carefully avoiding looking at them as he served the food. In Cuba, he thought, anything could happen.

"I don't know you," Xara said. "I don't know anything about you." It was suddenly terribly important that she know all about him, where he was born, where he lived, but she didn't want to hear that he was married— please don't let him tell me that, she prayed, even if it's true, not tonight.

She listened as he told her, sipping her champagne, fascinated by his mouth. She reached up and placed a finger on it, running it lightly along his bottom lip. He pressed the finger to him, kissing it tenderly. She turned away as tension crackled between them, it was as though they were suspended in time and space, just the two of them.

Neither of them wanted to eat. "Let's go." He took her hand firmly in his. "We'll walk."

All of Havana was out on the streets, seeking a breath of air on the hot windless night, crowding the brightly lit café terraces where beggars slipped from shadow to shadow, making their rounds. Pretty girls flirted behind lace fans with dashing young men in immaculate evening dress, lounging at tables next to jolly families, whose children in their best beruffled finery ran laughing and indulged among the throng, and lissome young girls with heavily painted faces and flashing dark eyes paraded the cafés looking for customers. The mingled scents of flowers and cigar smoke, spicy foods and heady perfume lingered in the night air, heavy with promise and intrigue.

Edouard took her arm, feeling the smooth coolness of her skin under his hand. I've never felt like this before, he thought, never. She's a dream, a fantasy image in scarlet silk and high heels—and I'm in love with her.

In the shadows at the edge of the square, they turned instinctively, folding their arms around each other, pressing their bodies close as they kissed, an endless, deep, searching kiss. There was no going back.

Hand in trembling hand they walked through the shadowy streets to their hotel, stepping softly up the curving marble stairway to the galleried hall above. Xara leaned against him weakly as he turned the key in the lock. The door closed behind them and she was in his arms, lost again in his kiss. She never wanted him to stop kissing her. He tasted like wine. She pressed closer as his hands slid down her naked back. She wanted to touch every part of him with her body, to be so close to this man that she would see his soul through his transparent eyes.

The windows of the room were open to the hot night, and the sound of guitars strumming in the cafés reached them faintly in the darkness. The big bed with its tall Spanish headboard could have come from some cloistered convent, its carved cherubs and winged angels muted and mysterious under the protective white mesh of mosquito netting. Unpinning the gardenias, she placed them carefully on the table by the bed and shook her hair into a loose slide of shining black silk. He reached out to touch its soft luxury; he wanted to bury his head in the fragrant mass. Her shoulders under his hands were fragile as he slid the scarlet dress from her body, letting it fall in a rustling petaled heap at her feet. "You're beautiful, Xara," he whispered, picking her up and carrying her to the bed. "You are perfect."

The pile of Paris dresses were swept impatiently from the bed and she lay inside the gauzy tent looking—he thought as he stripped off his clothes—like a painting by Goya.

He lay beside her, trembling from his need for her. Her skin was cream satin stretched taut on a framework of delicate bones. They were drowning in each other's eyes, lost in the first ecstatic passionate touch as their hands explored each other, pressing kisses onto eyes and mouths and throats, onto curves and softness, promising pleasure to each other, loving the way the other felt, longing for more, and more. He knelt over her, slender and strong, postponing that final moment from which there is no going back. "You are perfect, too, Edouard, my perfect stranger," she whispered, reaching out to him. He engulfed her with passion, clasping her body to him, winging her to new heights of fulfillment, as his sweat mingled with hers in the hot Cuban night and the guitars in the square throbbed an accompaniment to their thrusting tangled bodies, masking their moaned desires, her pleas, their final cries.

Still entwined with her, he pushed the silken hair from her damp neck to kiss it, burying his face in the curve of her throat, breathing her scent, soothing her still trembling body beneath his hands. "I love you, Xara O'Neill de Esteban," he said. "We're strangers because we only met today, but we've been looking for each other all our lives. I love you, oh, yes, I love you."

Xara smiled, lying there in the semidarkness with a man who loved her. Life was wonderful. Sometimes all it needed was a little push and then things happened, wonderful things, like Edouard d'Aureville.

Edouard lay on his back staring at the ceiling. Xara's silken leg was still flung across him and her head lay on his shoulder. She slept on, breathing deeply and with a look of such contentment on her vulnerable, sleeping face that he closed his arm around her protectively. How could he let this woman go? She was his as completely as if they had known each other forever. It didn't matter that they had only just met, he knew the way she looked, the way she thought, what she felt—the way she responded. Xara O'Neill de Esteban was his woman and he wanted her to be his wife as soon as possible. He wouldn't leave Cuba without her.

She stirred slightly in her sleep and he brushed her blue-black hair tenderly from her warm face. He would wait until she woke and then he would ask her to marry him. Or maybe he should *tell* her she was going to marry him so that there could be no room for any doubt. In any event, he wasn't going to take no for an answer.

The pale, early morning sunlight filtered through the green slats of the shutters as she awoke and he kissed her before her eyes were open. "Marry me," he murmured to her closed lids, "marry me today. Now. I want you this very minute."

Her eyes flew open, the curling lashes tickling his smiling mouth. She kissed him back, winding her arms around his neck. "Are you sure it wasn't just the scarlet taffeta," she whispered, "and the romantic Cuban night?"

"This is the morning, and I'm very romantic, and I love you. Please be my wife, Xara O'Neill."

"We hardly know each other," she said hesitatingly.

"We have the rest of our lives to find out what we've been missing. Marry me, Xara, please."

"When?" Her mouth fluttered across his lips in tiny sighing butterfly kisses.

"Today." His hands caressed the nape of her neck. "I can't today. I must speak to my brother first, and you must meet my family." She wriggled closer to him, her long leg still wrapped around him, anchoring him to her body.

"Tomorrow, then . . . this week. . . ." He kissed her throat, moving his lips down further across her breast.

"Yes," she murmured breathlessly, "oh, yes, Edouard. I'll marry you."

☙ 47 ❧

NEW YORK! Amélie jumped out of bed and ran to the window to check that it was still there outside the Waldorf Hotel.

Fluffy flakes swirled from an invisible sky, settling silently on the ground in a plump white blanket. Her eyes grew round with astonishment. *Snow!* It was really snowing! With a whoop of joy she sped across the salon and into a darkened bedroom, shaking the form buried under a mound of blankets.

"Roberto, Roberto, get up! It's snowing!"

"Oh . . . go away, Amélie." He burrowed deeper under the covers.

"Roberto! You must get up! It's snowing out there."

"Amélie"—his sleepy blond head emerged from beneath the covers—"it's seven o'clock in the morning. This is meant to be a holiday . . . go away will you."

"But Roberto, don't you understand," she cried in exasperation, "I've never seen snow before."

He sat up slowly, pushing back his hair and yawning, his clear blue eyes taking in her excited face.

"Oh, all right." He smiled. "I'll get up."

"Hurry then," she said, bouncing on the bed, "you must get dressed right away." She grabbed the covers to pull them off him and he gripped them in alarm.

"Don't do that, Amélie," he protested

"But why ever not?" She looked at him in surprise. His naked chest was tan against the white sheets. "Aren't you wearing pajamas?" she asked suspiciously.

"I don't wear pajamas anymore. I don't like them."

"How silly," said Amélie, tugging at the covers. "Anyway, I've seen you often enough without your clothes on."

"It was different when we were just kids," Roberto announced firmly, "but I'm sixteen and you are fourteen—it's time you started to behave like a young lady."

Amélie was crushed. "Oh, Roberto, I never thought you would say that to me. Everyone else, but not you."

"Well, it's true." She looked so downcast that he had to smile. "We're all growing up, Amélie. What about your friends at school, aren't they becoming different now, too?"

"Oh, them," she said contemptuously, "all they can think about is clothes and boys."

"Well, thinking about clothes isn't a bad idea," he said, swinging his legs over the side of the bed, modestly wrapping the sheet around himself. "You would look a lot better in some pretty clothes."

Amélie stared down at the complicated pattern on the hotel's green carpet. She hadn't even realized that he didn't think she looked nice; looking pretty hadn't been something she had even considered. She was the way she was. Looks hadn't seemed important, not nearly as important as being cool in the heat, or cutting off her hair because it was so much easier to manage—though it had grown again since the disastrous occasion when she had shorn it close to her head. As for being a young lady! Amélie heaved a sigh. Everything was so complicated lately. She and Roberto had always been together—she'd crept into his bed to snuggle up to him and whisper secrets when they were little, she'd worn his baggy white linen shorts clasped round her waist with one of his belts, she'd borrowed his sweaters, swum naked with him in the river at the *fazenda*—and now he wanted her to be a young lady! She supposed that he must now be a young man, whatever that meant. She glared at him, swathed in his sheet, what was he hiding under there that she hadn't seen before? And what difference did it make anyway? She flounced off the bed and made for the door. "I'm going to get dressed and then I'm off to see the snow," she announced. "You can come if you like."

He caught the faint tremor in her voice. "Of course I'll come," he said. "I want to be the first to throw a snowball at you."

"A snowball?" Amélie paused with her hand on the doorknob. "A snowball, Roberto do Santos! I bet I get you first!"

It took her exactly two minutes to throw on her clothes and stuff her hair under the new woolen hat she'd bought yesterday when her ears were so cold. She had never felt such cold; it gripped you, chilling even your bones until they felt tight and cramped, and the freezing wind scratched at your face. It was never like that in Rio, but then, they never had this wonderful snow either. She peeked through Isabelle's door. She was still asleep, her lacy robe folded neatly on the chair by the bed. The room smelled sweetly of perfume—like flowers, thought Amélie. Grandmère always smells like summer flowers, was that what Roberto meant by "growing up"? Should she smell of flowers now instead of soap and water, should she have lacy peignoirs and fluffy feminine little slippers? She stared down at her feet looming large from beneath her warm new winter coat. How could her feet ever look small and pretty? She dismissed the idea impatiently. *Where* was Roberto?

"Come on, then," he said, emerging from his room and making for the door. "You're keeping me waiting."

"Oh, Roberto!" She shot after him furiously, running down the corridor to the elevator, waiting impatiently for it to clank its way up to the sixth floor, pushing him aside so that she could be the one to press the buttons. The metal grill slid across, closing them in as it began to descend. "We're animals in a cage trapped by the wicked circus owner." She laughed.

Roberto smiled at her fondly. She was really such a little girl. He felt so much older than she, much, much older.

Amélie dashed across the lobby of the smart hotel, empty but for a surprised desk clerk and a couple of lounging porters, pausing at the big revolving glass doors to stare at the vision outside. The street in its coat of white had a new brightness, and the gray buildings opposite were hidden by a veil of swirling flakes. "Wait," said Roberto, turning her around to face him. "Let me fix your scarf before you go out there in the cold." She tilted her chin, watching his face as he tied the blue woolen scarf. Roberto was really very good-looking, such nice thick straight blond hair and the clearest blue eyes, you could trust him with anything. He patted the scarf into place under her chin and with a quick tug pulled her woolen cap down over her eyes, then he dashed through the revolving door to be first out in the snow.

"Beast," cried Amélie, hurling herself into the door after him and erupting onto the sidewalk with a laugh as she skidded in the unexpectedly soft snow. "Isn't this supposed to be crisp?" she asked, picking up a handful and rubbing it against her cheek. It was wonderful—cold and sparkly clean.

In the new blanketed stillness, even her voice sounded oddly muffled.

Fifth Avenue was empty, the unseasonable October snowstorm had brought New York to a standstill, and there was only the crunch of her own footsteps as she trod carefully across the sidewalk.

The snowball smacked into her shoulder and she turned to protest, ducking as another sailed toward her. "I'll get you," she yelled, her voice bouncing off the walls as she scooped up the snow and hurled it at Roberto.

"Wait, wait," he called, "*pax,* Amélie." He held up two crossed fingers. "*Pax,* come with me!" He took her hand and led her out into the middle of the street. "Look at that," he said in an awed voice. The length of Fifth Avenue stretched before them, immaculate and white, unmarked by human feet or traffic. "It's like being the first men on the moon," cried Roberto. Shrieking and laughing they ran hand in hand down the center of the avenue, a zigzag of slippery tracks marking their erratic progress.

"Stop, stop," protested Amélie as they reached Thirty-fourth Street. "I'm quitting, are you?"

"Not yet . . . come on." He tugged her down a pristine Thirty-fourth Street, dragging her by the hand, too breathless to protest. She skidded weakly to a halt near Macy's. "I can't run anymore." She leaned against the plate-glass window, gasping.

He grinned at her. "Had enough, huh? Girls can never run properly, they always wave their arms around too much."

"Oh, Roberto, if I had the strength left, I'd rub your face in the snow."

"Never threaten when you're at a disadvantage," he leered, holding a dripping handful of snow over her head.

"All right, all right," Amélie said with a laugh. "I'll give in if you'll buy me a cup of hot chocolate and a donut. I'm starving."

Roberto peered into Macy's glossy window. "Look, Amélie, why don't you wear something like that?" He pointed at the dress, a pink silky confection with a wide white collar. "You would look really pretty in that—if you fixed your hair properly, of course."

Amélie inspected it critically; it was everything she hated: silk, so you had to be careful with it, and pink—ugh! And that silly collar! Why did she have to be pretty all of a sudden just because she was fourteen? With a doubtful backward glance at the pink dress, she crossed the street hand in hand with Roberto to the steamy storefront café. Would she look pretty in it? And why had he said that?

"Hello," called Isabelle as the door to the suite slammed shut. "Where have you been so early?"

"Grandmère!" Amélie pulled off her wet hat and coat, dropping them in a heap on the floor. "How are you feeling today?"

"Much better, darling, thank you." Isabelle flexed her fingers in satisfaction. Two weeks of treatment had straightened out what she had feared was the onset of arthritis. It had been worth the trip to New York just to have her fears put to rest.

"Grandmère, it's snowing! It's *wonderful*. Roberto and I have been snowballing, we ran all the way down the middle of Fifth Avenue"—she peered from the window—"you can still see our tracks."

Amélie's cheeks were still pink from the cold and her clear eyes sparkled with enjoyment. Isabelle smiled at her. "Your first snow, Amélie . . . that's an unexpected treat in October."

"Grandmère, will you go shopping with me?" she asked suddenly. "I want to buy some new clothes, a few dresses and things, you know—more grown-up stuff."

Isabelle put down her tea and took her granddaughter's hand. So the little tomboy wanted girls' clothes, did she? Was she finally admitting that she must grow up? "Of course we'll go, darling," she promised, "there's nothing I'd like better."

De Courmont checked his watch wearily. The train from Chicago was already an hour late, and at this rate it looked as though by the time they got to Grand Central Station it would be closer to two hours. Who would have expected a snowstorm this early in the year? He leaned back against the cushioned seat trying to concentrate on his papers, but the figures danced in front of his eyes and he pushed them away with a sigh, thinking about the meetings that had just taken place with the automobile manufacturers in Chicago. They had not been good meetings. De Courmont cars were slipping in the sales race as more and more companies invaded the marketplace. His cars were too "special," they had told him, too exclusive and up-market, if he wanted big sales he had to do what Ford had done. Ford! He was like Citroën in France, making cheap little cars for cheap little buyers! They put the working man on the road in their little black boxes and called them automobiles! The new de Courmont was a thing of beauty, long lean lines, the deep luster of a dozen coats of special enamel paint glittering in scarlet, or rich royal blue, or a deep opulent green. Everything about his car was perfectly crafted and carefully thought out. The leather was ordered specially from a single tannery that used only flawless hides, softening them to exactly the right buttery degree of suppleness and then tinting them buff or cream or bronze to blend perfectly with the lacquered bodywork. The brass fittings were made at a small factory in England that had specialized in quality brassware for more than a century, the woodwork was a rare burled walnut and the engines were masterpieces of French and Italian design, a combination that had produced the smoothest precision instrument to provide speed and power.

Then why weren't the damn things selling? The question nagged him. He knew they were the best on the market, and people were buying expensive cars, he saw them everywhere—Rolls-Royce, Bugatti, Hispano-Suiza, Mercedes-Benz, Lagonda.

He heaved a sigh of frustration and glanced again at his watch. Oh, God, it was going to take hours yet, he knew it. Did it really matter? There was no one waiting for him, no one he wanted to see. He had no reason to linger in New York. He'd try to get a sailing as soon as possible, maybe even tomorrow or the day after, though no doubt everyone had decided to leave now that the weather had turned bad, no one wanted to hang around and face a crossing in the winter storms. It was terribly cold on this train. Gilles rubbed his chilled hands together. He'd go and see if he could get a whiskey to warm him up. He'd be glad when he arrived: at least the Waldorf would be comfortable.

Roberto waited in the sitting room for Amélie and Grandmère; they were certainly taking their time tonight, he'd been ready for ages. "Come on, you two," he called through Amélie's closed door. "Remember, it's our last night in New York you're wasting."

They were to go to Delmonico's for dinner and he was looking forward to it. It would be something to boast about to Diego for a change, instead of Diego always bragging of where *he'd* been. Madame Susana's and all that. He wondered what Madame Susana's was like. Diego said the girls were wonderful, big Nordic blondes from Germany and Sweden; smooth-skinned, almond-eyed girls from Asia; dark, fiery, blue-eyed girls from Romania and Ireland; as well as the beautiful sensuous local mulatto girls. Roberto shivered as he thought about them, wondering again where Diego got the money. He never told him. Diego *never* told him *everything*, he always held something back, kept some secrets.

The silk felt nice, thought Amélie, sliding it over her shoulders and smoothing it down. She hadn't realized it would feel like this, sort of cool and soft. The pleats in the skirt swirled quite prettily as she clasped the belt with its neat small buckle around her waist and inspected herself in the mirror. There was no doubt it made her look like a girl, it showed off the small breasts that she had tried to pretend weren't there but, somehow, now looked nice. Tightening the belt a couple of notches, she swirled around to see the back. Roberto had been right. It did suit her.

"I'm ready," announced Amélie, sweeping haughtily into the room, stopping in front of Roberto to allow him the full benefit of her new appearance.

Roberto dragged his thoughts guiltily from Madame Susana's and white thighs. He stared at Amélie in surprise. She looked so pretty, lovely in fact. The bright pink silk fell in soft pleats, concealing her still girlish slenderness, making her look rounder and more grown-up. Long sleeves bloused into tight cuffs, white to match the wide collar banding the *V* neckline, and she wore pink stockings on her too-thin legs and silver sandals with tiny heels. Her beautiful mane of hair had been brushed and brushed until the fizz had calmed into a subdued wave and she had tied it back on her neck with a big velvet bow.

Amélie waited anxiously for his verdict, ready no doubt, thought Isabelle, to rush back into her room and tear off all her new finery if he said one critical word.

Roberto gave a low appreciative whistle. "Isn't that the dress I pointed out in Macy's window?"

Amélie smoothed the skirt nervously. "Yes," she admitted.

"You can always trust my good taste, Amélie," said Roberto with a grin. "You look *terrific!* I shall have the two loveliest women in New York on my arm tonight—Delmonico's, here we come!"

It was seven-thirty when Gilles de Courmont finally walked into the Waldorf and he went directly to the main desk to learn that week's sailings to France. Thank God, the first bit of luck since he'd arrived: there was a British liner sailing at eleven the next morning. It couldn't come soon enough. He glanced down the list of names as he signed the register—there was no one he knew. He was alone in New York. The manager, hurriedly summoned by the desk clerk, took care personally of his distinguished guest and Gilles cut short his effusive greetings wearily. He waited irritably for the elevator, it seemed to be stopping on every floor. The manager glanced at him apologetically as the first elevator stopped in front of them and a well-dressed woman with a handsome blond young man emerged smiling broadly. Gilles stepped into the cage and the ornate iron gates meshed neatly together behind him, imprisoning him in a sudden overwhelming loneliness. He thought of the opulent suite awaiting him, empty.

Isabelle waited in the lobby with Roberto for the other elevator to descend bearing Amélie, who was playing tricks on Roberto again. Who was that man? His face was familiar, it was someone quite well known, she was sure of it, and he was French. It had been so long since she was in France she couldn't even recall the faces of her own friends anymore—at least not in detail, they were just a pleasant blur of memory.

The second elevator gates opened and Amélie emerged, grinning happily. Roberto helped her on with her cape, arranging it carefully around her shoulders while Amélie smoothed back her already unnaturally smooth hair. She was such a golden girl, thought Isabelle, overly tall for her age but with a coltish grace that she was completely unaware of. She would be a lovely woman, like her mother, and yet there were traces of Charles in her spontaneous nature, her devil-may-care attitude. Poor Charles, he had never even known he had this lovely daughter. And poor Léonie, who was still alive but who would never see her.

"Come along, Grandmère," cried Amélie, sliding her arm through Isabelle's, "you're dreaming again."

The liner *Normandie* had had a rough crossing. October wasn't renowned for good weather in the Atlantic, but this trip had been exceptionally stormy and the dispirited passengers had spent much of it in their cabins. Maroc tapped on the door to Léonie's stateroom. "It's snowing out there," he said, brushing the melted flakes from his jacket as he entered, "but the news is that we'll be arriving in New York early in the morning."

Léonie sighed with relief, they were already a day late and she would feel a lot better with her feet firmly on dry land. She pushed aside her unwanted supper tray and peered out into the stormy night. "How early in the morning?"

"Around six."

"Six! Oh, Maroc!" She flung herself into a chair, pouting. "Why did I agree to do this concert?"

They both knew why. It was for her favorite charity. He'd been astonished when she had accepted, though he knew she would do anything for children. But to travel all the way to New York for one concert and one charity ball was asking a lot, especially as it meant taking time away from her hard-earned rest period.

The request had come at the last minute and Léonie hadn't hesitated. "Do you have any idea how much money those society women can raise in one night?" she asked him when he'd argued against it. "They can make enough to take care of hundreds of children, the newborn babies left on the doorsteps like unwanted kittens, the poor young children, starving and homeless." She had flung her arms wide, gazing around at her lovely home: the old inn, ever-expanding, always beautiful. "How can I stay here in all this comfort when I know I could be doing something to help?"

The big liner lurched with the waves. "Here we go again." She laughed as the sound of crashing glass filtered from above and Chocolat scurried terrified across the room and into her lap. "You'd better get out the whiskey, Maroc, and the cards . . . and find any of our fellow passengers who are still standing. It's going to be another of those long nights!"

* * *

James Homer Alexander Jamieson III relaxed in the red leather chair, enjoying his brandy and watching the group at the card table. He had seen one or two of them before—they'd been among the few who had shown up for dinner on this crossing—but this was the first time he had seen the woman and he liked what he saw. She had rolled up the sleeves of her simple linen blouse in a workmanlike fashion and her marvelous blond hair was brushed back firmly from her smooth arrogant face without any concession to feminine vanity, or perhaps just one: the childish blue velvet ribbon that she had tied carelessly at her neck. He liked her hair, it spiraled in rebellious tendrils that every now and then she swept impatiently aside with a slender unringed hand; he had noticed that particularly, no rings. She was unattached!

She was taking this poker game very seriously, playing with panache and no fear of losing, sipping neat whiskey from a constantly refilled glass, keeping them guessing with her lively play and making them laugh occasionally with some sharp comment.

The ship still lurched beneath them as if searching for a grip on some slippery surface, and most of the passengers had not ventured from their cabins. The card room was quiet and soothingly dim, there was just the lamp illuminating the green-topped table and its players, and there was one solitary steward on duty clearing ashtrays and supplying fresh drinks. He glanced at his watch—three o'clock—they would be in New York in a few hours' time, and a few hours ago he would have been glad, but now? How, he wondered, can I get to meet her before we disembark?

Léonie flung her cards onto the table and stretched, lifting her arms above her head and tilting her chair backward as she pushed her long legs out in front of her. "That's it for me, gentlemen," she said. "I'm tired and I've drunk too much whiskey . . . and I've taken too much of your money." She grinned at them wickedly. "I should have warned you I'm an expert." It was true, poker was a passion with her, she'd taken it up first to pass the interminable hours traveling on trains, learning from the musicians who toured with her, and now she could out-bluff almost anyone.

She picked up her purse and glanced around the room. Maroc had retired hours ago. There was just that one man sitting in the corner. He'd been there most of the night, watching them—she had felt his eyes on her and had glanced up once or twice, but it was impossible to see him properly in the dim light. She supposed he was just another passenger who couldn't sleep in this tossing ship and preferred to pass the night awake instead of fruitlessly searching for rest. Léonie nodded goodnight to him as she went by. He stood up with a smile. "Please don't leave," he said.

He was tall and rugged with dark hair, nice hair, soft and wavy, and he wore it rather long. A full mustache curved over his wide mouth. She definitely like his mouth, the lips were firm with an upward tilt that made him seem ready to smile. She liked the rest of him, the way his well-tailored jacket fit smoothly over his broad shoulders and the way his body looked muscular and tight—and very fit. He was decidedly handsome. Positively American. And probably ten years younger than she.

"It's very late, Mr. . . . ?"

"Jamieson—James Homer Alexander Jamieson the third—Jim."

Léonie laughed. "Your mother obviously expected a lot from you . . . Homer *and* Alexander! I hope you didn't disappoint her."

"I tried not to, but you know how it is with mothers."

Do I? she wondered, do I know how it is with mothers? She was suddenly very tired. Too tired for conversations like this. "I'm sorry, Mr. Jamieson, but it's late, I'd like to get some rest before we get to New York. Goodnight."

She strode toward the door but he matched her stride, talking fast as they threaded their way through lurching empty corridors. "Why haven't I seen you before? We've been on this boat for over a week and yet we didn't meet. I don't even know your name."

Léonie stopped at the door of her cabin. He didn't know who she was? Could that be true? She remembered her shirt with its rolled-up sleeves, her hair tied back with a ribbon, and her unadorned face. Of course, she didn't look like "Léonie"—she was just herself. "It's mademoiselle," she replied, "Mademoiselle Bahri. Goodnight, Mr. Jamieson."

With a final smile she closed the door, sliding her feet out of her shoes, unbuttoning her shirt, and flinging it onto the still lurching floor along with her skirt, peeling off her stockings and letting them drop in a trail toward the bed; she crawled naked under the sheets. Fatigue claimed her; nothing, not even the sliding lurch of the boat, could keep her awake another moment. Jim Jamieson's face with his nice mouth was the last thing she thought of before she drifted into sleep. That nice mouth that curved up at the corners as though he were just about to smile.

Maroc shrugged off his coat, thankful to be in the warmth of the Waldorf Hotel at last. It had been freezing on the pier, even though they'd been ushered through immigration and customs with a minimum of delay. He'd had a hard time waking Léonie, but she had finally dragged herself out of bed and into a hot bath, hiding the fatigue beneath a wide-brimmed hat and a brush of artificial color on her pale cheeks. She huddled miserably into her furs, managing to smile charmingly when necessary, though all she really wanted to do was climb back into bed. She must get some sleep, she had the show to do tonight. She cursed the weather for delaying the ship, it left her so little time.

"I'll have them send up some hot tea with lemon for your throat," said Maroc, "and then you rest until this evening. I'll take care of everything."

The manager of the Waldorf considered Léonie one of the few guests worth getting up to meet this early in the morning. He showed her the suite with a flourish, opening doors and switching on lamps. Fires glowed in the marble hearths and flowers bloomed on every table. Léonie thanked him and collapsed on the sofa, kicking off her shoes, as the door closed behind him. "Julie," she called to her maid, "I'm going straight to bed, and I don't want to be disturbed until five o'clock."

Maroc took the pile of envelopes and messages from the desk clerk and glanced through them quickly. There was the usual stuff, a note about rehearsal time—five o'clock—earlier than he'd expected. They wanted to know about the lights. The pianist would be there at two o'clock to check that the Steinway was to their liking. What would Madame like in her dressing room—champagne, wine, whiskey, food? Would she need the services of an extra dresser? There was a charming note from Mrs. Van Wyk, president of the Charitable Homes Trust, welcoming Léonie to New York and offering any assistance she might need. One from Mrs. Austin, who had organized the ball, selling tickets for two hundred dollars each, saying she could easily have sold twice as many. The fund raising was already a success, and that was without the donations yet to be demanded from the wealthy guests later that evening.

He picked up the pen to sign the register. The harsh, uncompromising, black script jumped out from the page. "Duc de Courmont!" Monsieur was here? He pushed the book away angrily. How the hell had he known Léonie would be here? Wait a minute, though, did he know? Monsieur was often in America on business.

"The Duc de Courmont," he said casually to the desk clerk, "I see he checked in yesterday. Is he staying long?"

The clerk checked his list. "No, sir. He's just here for the one night. He's sailing for France this morning."

Maroc heaved a sigh of relief. Thank God, that meant he didn't know. And he wouldn't tell Léonie that Monsieur was here in the same hotel. There was no point in upsetting her unnecessarily.

"Excuse me, sir." The desk clerk broke into his thoughts. "But you forgot to sign the register." He pushed the book toward him again, apologizing as the pages flipped forward.

It was the wrong page and Maroc paused, pen in hand, as his eye caught the looped continental swirl of the French name. "D'Aureville . . . the Comtesse Isabelle d'Aureville, Mademoiselle A. d'Aureville, and Senhor R. Castelo do Santos."

The names exploded in his head like rockets, reverberating in sound waves of shock. Could it be? It *must* be the same one—there couldn't possibly be two Isabelle d'Aurevilles! But then A. d'Aureville. He stared again at the neat script. That must be Amélie!

The full implications of the situation hit him suddenly. Somehow he had always known it would happen like this. They would go on for years, being cautious, never communicating with the d'Aurevilles, not even attempting to find out where Amélie was, parrying Monsieur's every spying move. And then one day there would be the coincidence that would trigger the sequence of events that they had all been dreading.

What must he do? He turned urgently to the desk clerk. "When are the d'Aurevilles leaving?"

The desk clerk glanced at him in surprise. Maybe it was the rough sea voyage, but this guest was behaving a little oddly. "The Comtesse d'Aureville leaves this morning, sir." He looked at the clock on the wall. "In fact, in about fifteen minutes. They're catching an early train to Florida."

Maroc hesitated. The decision was a terrible one. "Oh Léonie," he murmured, "will you ever forgive me for this?"

The desk clerk looked at him in alarm. "Is something wrong, sir? Is there anything I can do?"

"No. Thank you."

Maroc glanced uneasily around the lobby. It was empty but for a couple of cleaners and porters. Of course, it was still very early, only seven o'clock. Amélie would be safely away from the hotel before Monsieur was down. And, with luck, Monsieur would also leave without knowing that Léonie was there. God, he needed a cup of coffee, he felt chilled to the bone, but he had to wait. He had to see Amélie. It was the least he could do for Léonie. He took a seat in the lobby, half-hidden by a pillar but with a good view of the doors.

He didn't have long to wait and he recognized them immediately. The grandmother, the young boy, and the girl. They were both blond and almost the same height—the girl was tall for her age. Isabelle hurried them through the lobby to the big doors and Amélie revolved twice around, laughing, before darting out into the street.

Maroc let out the breath he hadn't realized he was holding. This was the baby he'd carried to safety from Menton, the infant who had slept in his arms. Amélie looked *exactly* as Léonie had when he had first met her, a young bright-faced innocent girl, still too slender, but with the promise of beauty. And her mother's special magical quality.

He wandered slowly across the lobby to the elevator. He knew he should feel relieved that the danger was past, but all he felt was sad.

Léonie's smart Vuitton steamer trunks waited under the awning at the front of the hotel to be carried inside and the porter hurried forward with a trolley. Amélie and Roberto stared at them curiously. "Look, Roberto," said Amélie. "Imagine having all that luggage—there's enough for six people and yet they all have the same monogram." She ran a curious finger across the gold initials emblazoned on the top of each trunk.

"LB," she said, "I wonder what it stands for. She must be very grand to need so much luggage."

"How do you know they belong to a woman?" asked Roberto.

Amélie looked at him scornfully. "What man would have sixteen matched pieces of luggage, silly?"

They watched the porter maneuvering the mound of baggage onto the trolley.

"It's Léonie's," said the burly Irish porter with a smile. "She always stops here—and she always has enough luggage for six. More than this, usually."

"Who's Léonie?" asked Roberto curiously.

"You don't know who Léonie is? Where do you live? On the moon?" asked the porter incredulously. "She's the singing star, that's who! The most beautiful woman in the world."

"Imagine," said Amélie in an awed voice. "Imagine, Roberto, she's the most beautiful woman in the world!"

"Huh, I don't believe it, there are lots of beautiful women."

"Yes, but still . . . how nice to be called that," sighed Amélie. "Léonie, the singing star, the most beautiful woman in the world. My mother's name was Léonie," she said to the porter.

"Well, I'm sure she was lovely, too. Come to think of it, you look a lot like her." He stared at her in sudden surprise. She was only a little girl, but there was something about her.

"Did you hear that?" she said triumphantly to Roberto. "He says I look a lot like the world's most beautiful woman!"

"He should see you in a pair of baggy old shorts with your skinny legs and big feet," teased Roberto, dodging as she aimed a kick at him.

"Come on, you two," called Isabelle. "The baggage is loaded. Let's go or we'll be late."

Maroc spent the morning restlessly pacing his suite, consuming vast quantities of black coffee and worrying about de Courmont. The minutes ticked by and at ten-thirty he went back down to the lobby, where he bought a newspaper and wandered casually across to the concierge's desk. "Better weather for the crossing today." He smiled, pointing to the headlines on yesterday's storms. "We were unlucky enough to get caught in this."

"That was bad luck, sir," the clerk smiled politely.

"I think a friend of mine sails today. The Duc de Courmont?"

"Yes, sir. He booked at the last minute, he was lucky to get a cabin, but some people were canceling—afraid of the bad weather, you see. He's on the *Empress* sailing at eleven."

Maroc folded his paper neatly and placed it under his arm. The relief was so intense that he felt weak. It was all right, Monsieur didn't know.

He walked across to the porter's station at the left of the lobby, tipping the waiting man casually as he asked him, "Did the Duc de Courmont leave yet?"

"Oh, yes, sir," the porter said appreciatively. "Well over an hour ago."

"Do you know where he went?"

"He took a cab, sir, to the West Street Pier."

That was it then. He had gone. And Amélie had gone. Léonie would see neither of them. Shrugging on his overcoat, he strode out into the icy street, turning up his collar against the wind. He made up his mind not to tell Léonie before the concert tonight.

Jim Jamieson was not a man to be put off by a difficult task. He'd panned for gold in the Rockies, mined for silver in California, and made a fortune in oil in Texas. He'd lived the rough, tough life of frontier towns and now, at twenty-six, he was head of his own building and land company with headquarters in San Francisco.

Miss Bahri was difficult to contact, but he would do it. She was at the Waldorf, but she wasn't taking any calls and she wasn't seeing anyone. He had picketed the hotel lobby all afternoon, and had finally spotted her, swathed in a vast fox-fur coat and half-hidden beneath an enormous hat, as she had sped across the foyer into a waiting car. She was accompanied by a short, dark man—he'd seen him on the ship—but he'd never seen them together. And, he remembered, there were no rings on her fingers.

He took a cab to his apartment on Gramercy Park, where he hastily packed a few things, drove back to the Waldorf, and checked in. Then he went downstairs to wait. Hours passed. He had dinner. He waited some more. He stared at the large gilt clock on the wall, it was almost two in the morning, he must have missed her. He sighed. He'd try again tomorrow. He was surely not going to give up.

* * *

Maroc glanced at Léonie's face as she sat beside him in the limousine. It was just after two o'clock and she was obviously exhausted. Quite apart from her superb stage performance, she had been wonderful at the ball afterward. She had smiled, chatted, danced; she had kissed the men who had given the biggest checks; she had given out prizes and congratulations and she had made a speech—all without a single sign that she was bored or tired. She had worked hard for those children. He wondered when he should tell her. How much longer could he put it off?

"Was it really all right, Maroc?" she asked from behind closed eyes. She always asked him the same question, she still needed his reassurance, though the applause must have told her the answer.

"More than all right," he replied, holding her hand. "You will have made a lot of children happy because of tonight."

"I hope so," she said wearily, as the car pulled up at the hotel. The big lobby with its sweeping staircase and marble columns was very quiet and they waited in tired silence for the elevator.

"Léonie," he said finally, "I need to talk to you."

"Can't it wait until tomorrow?" A vision of the nice soft white bed, with Chocolat curled up on her pillow, purring, was all that was on her mind.

He hesitated. She was so very tired. "It can wait," he said simply.

❧48❧

THE LOBBY of the Waldorf was not where he wanted to spend the rest of his life, decided Jim Jamieson, as he tried one more time to get Miss Bahri on the telephone and once again was informed that she was not taking any calls. He banged down the telephone in frustration. What the hell was going on? It had been three days now and she hadn't left the suite. Flowers were delivered to her, but she had received no visitors. Who, he wondered, were the flowers from? Could she be ill? No doctor had been summoned, he knew that. But why would she come to New York and spend all her time in a hotel suite?

He strode into the main salon and took a seat at a desk, writing rapidly on a sheet of hotel paper. He signed it firmly and walked back across the lobby and down the corridor to the florist, where he chose a single perfect peach-colored rose, short-stemmed and plump, just opening into full-blown softness—he wanted none of those tall sharp-pointed scarlet roses for Miss Bahri. She was a woman of summer roses that grew in gardens and smelled of sunshine and wind-blown scented petals.

Too impatient to wait for an elevator, he leapt up the curving stairway to the fourth floor and sought out the room service waiter in his little kitchen at the end of the corridor. With a few words and a lavish tip he achieved his aim. "I'm just about to take in her breakfast, sir," said the man with a smile. "I'll put it right here next to her plate."

Jim glanced at the tray—there was just a pot of coffee, some juice, and toast—not a very lavish breakfast.

"Is Miss Bahri ill?"

"No, she's not ill, sir. She always stays here when she's in New York and usually she's very lively, but not this time."

Jim turned away thoughtfully. What could be wrong? She had been fine on the ship; she was probably the only woman on board who hadn't been ill. Well, there was nothing to do but wait. It didn't come easy to a man of action, but if that was the only way, he would wait.

The rose was beautiful, thought Léonie, picking it up and holding it to her face. It smelled wonderful, too, a sweet heavy scent that reminded her of the garden at the inn in early summer, green and fresh and moist. Oh, she wanted to go home, she wanted so badly to go home. She had done her job. Saturday couldn't come soon enough.

There was a note with the rose and she glanced at it disinterestedly. It was from Jim Jamieson, the man from the ship—the one with the nice smiling mouth. "James Homer Alexander," he'd signed it. Such a ridiculous name! "I've picketed the lobby of the Waldorf for three days now, dear Miss Bahri," she read, "and I am in grave danger of being arrested for loitering. Could you please take pity and have lunch with me? Or tea! Or supper or dinner? My floral offering may not be as lavish as some I've seen being delivered, but it describes you better. Please say yes? I shall telephone at noon for your answer."

She looked at the rose with a smile. He thought it described her. Well, it was a perfect choice, it was her favorite sort, but did she want to see him? She put the rose aside with a sigh.

Chocolat purred contentedly in the crook of Léonie's arm, almost hidden by the long fur of her big coat. There was only one other person in the elevator and Léonie nodded politely to his good morning, turning up her collar and hiding beneath the brim of her hat. As the elevator bounced gently to a stop, she hurried left down the corridor, and out the side door. The first blast of icy air took her breath away and, bending her head into the wind, she cuddled Chocolat closer to her. This was a mistake, she decided, struggling forward, it was much too cold and Chocolat would never walk in this gale. Besides, she didn't like city pavements, she liked grass and gardens and beaches, and so did she. "What are we doing in this cold city, Choc?" she whispered, cutting down a side street out of the wind, running the last block back to the hotel.

The revolving doors swung behind her as she strode across the lobby, pulling off her hat and running her hands through her hair.

"I knew if I waited long enough I'd get lucky. Good morning, Miss Bahri."

The American voice was cheerful and unmistakable. Léonie turned and looked directly into the bright blue, dark-lashed eyes of Jim Jamieson. They were as smiling and cheerful as his voice and she felt her own mouth curve upward in response. There was something quite irresistible about such confident charm.

"Good morning, Mr. Jamieson. And thank you for your rose."

"The question is, would you have thanked me if I hadn't waylaid you like this? There was a letter with the rose. Remember?"

Even his persistence was confident. "I remember." She pressed the bell for the elevator.

He moved around so that he stood between her and the cage. "You don't strike me as the kind of woman to stay silent for very long," he said, "so I'll say what I have to say while I have the chance. I've wanted to meet you ever since I saw you playing poker on the ship. I've picketed this lobby for days now. I'm a very determined man, Miss Bahri. And you haven't answered my request. Lunch? Tea? Dinner? I'll even walk your cat."

Léonie threw back her head and laughed. "Very well, Mr. Jamieson. Why don't you come to my suite for tea? At five o'clock."

Jim consulted his watch. "But it's only twelve-thirty. We could have lunch—and then tea. You can't ask a man to wait all those hours." The gates closed behind her and the elevator began to ascend.

"Five o'clock, Mr. Jamieson."

Her voice floated down to him and he gazed after the disappearing cage, smiling. Five o'clock it was.

"Make yourself comfortable," Léonie called from her bedroom, "I'll be with you in a minute." She surveyed her face in the mirror. She didn't know if Jim Jamieson was here to see "Léonie," but if he was then that's what he would get. She applied the eye crayon expertly, smudging the line into a softer shadow, creaming on a blush of rouge and fluffing on powder, while Julie brushed her hair into a smooth golden mane. She slid a gold circlet around her forehead and examined herself critically in the mirror. Yes, that would do. She was ready for Mr. Jamieson. It had taken her exactly ten minutes to become "Léonie" again.

Jim prowled the sitting room. Despite its too-opulent decor, crowded with too many fragile gilt chairs, the room had become very much Léonie's. Photographs in silver frames were scattered on tables and moiré silk cushions in a springtime softness of mint green, almond blossom pink, and lilac overflowed from sofas and chairs. A velvety moleskin rug was draped across the big couch in front of the fire and Léonie had banished the usual enormous floral trophies to the hallway, filling her sitting room with growing green plants—gentle spreading ferns and small graceful trees. Jim's rose in a thin silver flute spilled its petals onto the rug. Piles of books were strewn on tables, on chairs, on the floor, and there was music on the stand of the grand piano. A pair of Léonie's gold sandals lay where she had cast them off and Jim smiled as he picked them up and placed them neatly side by side.

He peered closely at the photographs: a dark-haired beauty, very Spanish-looking with a smaller, bespectacled man beside her: another of an older couple standing in a garden in front of a white square villa on a hill surrounded by cypresses and olive trees. There was no picture of a man, surely if there were a man in her life she would carry his picture with her?

A painting was propped on a small gilt easel near the window and he stepped back to look at it more carefully: a naked girl on a tumbled bed, a wonderful wash of light and color, it was sensual, beautiful.

"Well? Do you like it?"

Jim hadn't heard her come in and he swung around with a smile.

Oh, God, what a fool he'd been! Why hadn't he realized who she was? Mademoiselle Bahri, the shirt-sleeved, midnight-hour poker-player of the tumbled hair and luminous eyes, was the famous "Léonie." He was such a *fool* not to have recognized her!

Léonie watched the bemused expressions flitting across his face. His astonishment was so patent that she laughed. She had been wrong. Jim Jamieson had wanted to see Mademoiselle Bahri. There was an innocence about him. It wasn't naivete, just a good wholesome innocence.

"I'm sorry," said Jim, smiling ruefully, "I must be the only man in America who wouldn't recognize you. Will you forgive me?"

Léonie settled herself on the couch in front of the fire with Chocolat curled into the corner beside her. "I'm flattered," she told him, "and glad that you recognized that there are two Léonies. Only my closest friends know that secret."

"Then I hope that puts me in the same category?" Jim's bright blue eyes smiled into hers.

His gaze was intimate. Or was it just that she felt that way about it? Léonie decided to ignore his question. "Do you like the painting?"

"It's wonderful."

"I knew the artist—a long time ago."

"Not now?"

"No. Not now." He was clever, too, she thought, he caught all the nuances.

The waiter arrived with tea—a trolley filled with tiny cucumber and salmon sandwiches, crustless and thin, and toasted muffins oozing butter, still-warm scones with strawberry jam and thick smooth cream to be spooned on top, and a dark moist chocolate cake. Léonie and Jim gazed at each other in delight over the top of the feast. The fire crackled in the grate and the chilly sky was already darkening outside the long windows. Somehow the laden trolley and its silver pots of tea gave the hotel room an air of domestic intimacy, as though they were a comfortable married couple sitting down for tea on a cold winter's afternoon. Except they weren't married, thought Léonie, and she barely knew this man.

"I feel," said Jim, pulling up a spindly gilt chair with an expression of distaste, "as though we've known each other for years."

He took charge, picking up the pot and pouring tea. His firm square hands looked capable even performing such a small task, she thought, looking at them. They were long-fingered and a scatter of smooth dark hairs silkened his skin.

"But I don't know you, Jim Jamieson. I don't know which part of your name is really you. Are you Homer, the scholar? Or Alexander, the warrior? And if not, then who is Jim? I don't know what you do, or even where you live."

"Right now I live in San Francisco, but I'm thinking of moving."

"Oh? Where to?"

He handed her the cup of tea. "Paris."

Léonie laughed. "I thought only prospectors lived in California—wild men, covered in gold dust!"

Their eyes met over their cups. "It all depends what you're looking for ma'am," Jim said with a grin.

She felt that familiar warm flutter of response. She liked him. She liked his nice smiling mouth, his blue eyes with their long lashes, his bigness, his broad shoulders that looked strong enough to cope with any disaster, and the way his body looked so firm and tight. There was an endless list of things to like about him. She wondered what that silky mustache would feel like when he kissed you.

Chocolat jumped from the sofa, stretching each leg slowly, before walking across to Jim, her tail waving like a banner. Leaping onto his knee, she rested her paws on his chest and peered into his surprised face, sniffing curiously. Satisfied, she curled up on his lap, tucking her tail neatly around her paws and resting her head on his knee. She purred gently.

"Well," said Jim smugly, "it looks as though I've been accepted by the family. Now all I have to do is persuade you."

"Persuade me to do what?"

"I have plans," he said mysteriously.

Léonie stirred her tea, a smile edging its way across her mouth despite his brashness. She watched him piling a scone with scarlet jam and a mound of cream. "Eat this," he commanded. "You need more flesh on your bones, Léonie Bahri. What you need is a man to look after you."

"Do I?" she murmured, enjoying herself. There was a take charge quality about Jim that was very appealing, he made her feel looked after. He made her laugh. And he sent big peach-colored roses. She bit happily into the scone, licking the cream from her lips.

Jim leaned forward in his chair, watching her. Every move she made was a delight. Even eating the scone, the pinkness of her tongue flickering across her lips, the curve of her long eyelashes on her cheeks as she half-closed her eyes to savor the creamy delight, the flutter of her hair as it rebelled against its firm brushing. It was odd, he thought, that such a successful woman should seem quite so alone, and quite so vulnerable.

"You didn't ask what my plans were." he said suddenly.

"Tell me." She laughed. "I can't wait."

Those luminous tawny eyes gazed directly into his. "I'm going to ask you to marry me," he said, holding her gaze.

Léonie felt her heart pounding. This stranger was planning to marry her? Or at least he was planning on asking her. Had anyone else ever asked her to marry him? Rupert had promised to marry her, and Jacques had cared about her enough to do so, but circumstances had driven them apart before they had reached that stage. The others, well, they'd been just lovers. And Monsieur? No, Monsieur had never said those words, he had never really loved her. Edouard d'Aureville had loved her, she'd felt it that night by the river when he had kissed her. There had been a future in that kiss, but it couldn't be. She must be careful with Jim Jamieson, he was going too fast for her.

"Don't worry," he said, touching her wrinkled brow. "I don't mean to confuse you. I just thought I'd let you know that my intentions are honorable."

Despite herself, Léonie laughed. He was very attractive. "Why don't we just begin at the beginning?" she suggested, relaxing again.

"An excellent idea." He beamed. "Just leave everything to me, Léonie."

* * *

Maroc was astonished when Léonie canceled the Saturday sailing. "But why?" he asked. "I thought you couldn't wait to get back to France."

"But I feel better now . . . and I've got good company."

"Jamieson?"

Léonie grinned at him. "Jamieson."

"There's the meeting of the Château d'Aureville trustees on the twenty-ninth," he reminded her.

It was the first time she had ever forgotten. The Château d'Aureville trust was the most important thing in her life. Still, that gave her two weeks, two more weeks with Mr. Jamieson.

Jim courted her with a very American single-minded thoroughness, sending her flowers each morning, always the same generous-scented peach roses, and showing up each afternoon to take her to lunch at some special restaurant in town, or off on some expedition to the coast to eat lobster and scallops and small delicious oysters. In the evenings they went to shows and drank late-night glasses of champagne in fashionable cafés while he showered her with installments from his life story.

Jim came from Savannah, Georgia. A "true American" was how he described himself to her as he looked around the crowded restaurant. "Not like these Yankees."

"But all Americans are Yankees to the French," said Léonie, laughing at his pretend-shocked expression.

He told her that he was thirty-five, but she knew he was lying: he could be no more than twenty-six or twenty-seven, but it touched her that he had been sensitive enough to think the age difference might bother her.

Each night he asked her to marry him. And each night she refused. Each night he asked her to let him come in for a last drink, and each night she refused.

Lying alone in bed she wondered why. Was it because she was older than he? She flung back the covers and climbed out of bed, stripping off her nightgown and assessing herself in the long mirror. At thirty-three her body was still firm and rounded and she eyed it with satisfaction, remembering those hard mornings in the cold studio when she had forced herself through the dance routines and exercises. Most women her age were all downward slopes of flesh by now, supported by corsets, she thought, running her hands across her body. It was good to have breasts that still pointed upward and a bottom that was still round and trim.

No, it wasn't her age that worried her, or that her body would betray her. Then why not? There had been other lovers. But this was different. Jim wasn't the sort of man to play a secondary role in her life. He was very much in charge, which was rather nice, she thought wistfully. She liked being taken care of, relaxing in his arms might be just as pleasurable. She pushed aside the thought. There would be no compromising with a man like Jim. He might want more than she was prepared to give. And, anyway, it couldn't work. He was American, he lived and worked in America. She lived in Europe. And she *must* work. Her children were dependent on her.

She climbed back into bed. The Château d'Aureville seemed to eat up money and the investments she had made hadn't been too successful. She tossed and turned worriedly. Life was always so full of problems. Jim's strong honest face followed her in her disturbed dreams. He was a man to lean on, a man a woman could depend on, but she didn't have the right. Her destiny was different.

Jim's approach was direct and uncompromising, but still touched with that southern charm and an irrepressible humor that kept her constantly laughing.

"Léonie, will you come out to California with me?" he asked her one night as they returned from dinner. "You'll enjoy San Francisco, it's much more your sort of town than New York."

Léonie felt a pang of dismay. "But when do you have to go?"

"Next week." He put a finger under her chin, smiling into her eyes. "Don't tell me you might miss me?"

Next week, thought Léonie in panic. Next week he was going to San Francisco. And she was returning to France.

"Perhaps I will miss you," she admitted. She knew she would.

"Then come with me."

His voice was persuasive, and he was looking at her eagerly, waiting for her answer. He really thought she could go with him. Jim's life was so simple, so uncomplicated. "I can't go with you, Jim. What would people say?" She noticed how his eyes crinkled when he laughed, and he laughed a lot. Life with Jim Jamieson would have been such fun.

"Certainly no more than they are saying already. Most of New York thinks we're lovers by now, you know. After all, we spend so much time together—I might almost have thought we were, too!"

Léonie sighed. "You Americans, you're always in such a rush."

He put an arm around her pleadingly. "Léonie, at least invite me in for a drink before you send me off for the night."

"Very well," she said, handing him her keys as they walked down the corridor, "but only one."

The brandy waited on a table near the fire and there was a warm red glow still left in the coals. Jim poured himself a drink, prowling the room, shifting spindly gilt chairs out of his way irritably.

"All this French clutter," he grumbled, "and there's nowhere to sit."

"Sit here by me," she suggested, snuggling into the moleskin-covered couch.

He sank down carefully next to her. "Are you sure it won't break?" he asked with pretend concern.

Léonie sighed with exasperation. "Jim, stop pretending. You know perfectly well you're not the wild man from California. You're a proper, well-brought-up southern gentleman."

"I think I'm about to forget my southern manners," he said, sliding his arm around her shoulders.

Their eyes met and Léonie leaned toward him. She kissed him lightly on the mouth. A timeless few seconds passed as she moved her head away and their eyes met. Then he wrapped his arms around her until she felt like a part of him and he explored her mouth, savoring its sweetness, like strawberries in June. Her hair smelled as good as fresh-cut grass, he wanted to grab handfuls of it, to wrap its long silken strands around him, to bind her to him forever with her own beautiful hair.

It was meant to be just one kiss, thought Léonie, running her hands down the length of his back, feeling his taut muscles as he held her to him. Just one kiss.

Jim smiled into her surprised tawny eyes as he flung the soft fur rug onto the floor in front of the fire and then began to undress her, removing each garment as though he were unveiling a precious statue in some rare peach-colored marble. Except her skin didn't feel like marble, it felt warm and infinitely soft and he wanted just to hold her, naked, next to him forever.

She felt safe held against his hard body. He was firm and muscular, his skin was bronzed from the California sun, smooth and silky under her trembling hands. His lovemaking was joyful and uninhibited. He lavished her body with kisses and caresses, licking her, tasting her, stroking her. Open your eyes, look at me, *look at me,* he demanded, and their eyes locked as deeply as their bodies, until his face contorted with passion and she cried out in triumph.

Jim lay back laughing and Léonie smiled at him, baffled. "But *what* are you laughing at?" she asked. "Did I do something funny?"

"I'm laughing," he said, "because I'm *happy.* People do sometimes, you know."

Léonie laughed, too. "I only meant to kiss you, but this is the best thing that's happened to me in New York. I must say," she added smugly, "you southern gentlemen certainly know what you are doing!"

He rolled over. "Now that's a romantic statement, and here I am, madly in love with you."

She had a sudden terrible memory of lying like this with Monsieur, longing for him to say he loved her, just to tell her—even if he didn't truly mean it. Other people had said they loved her since then—other lovers— but it hadn't been as important. And Jim *was* important. He had made love to her as passionately as Monsieur, but there was an edge of tenderness in his caresses, a warmth to his kisses that made her long for more. "Are you really in love with me, Jim?"

"Of course I am. Didn't I just tell you that?"

"Well, yes, but . . . you know, I thought you were just being gallant."

He smiled. "I didn't hear you say you loved me. You were using other words, but I don't think any of them meant that."

Léonie sat up, hugging her knees. "I'm not sure I can say it. Oh, I don't know, I just can't commit myself to love, it involves too much. I'm my own woman, and believe me, it took a long hard fight to become that. I want to keep my independence. And, besides, I have other commitments."

"We've all been through other loves, other lives, Léonie. None of us grow up without bruises and scars. Anyway, it's too late, you're already committed to me. You're going to marry me, make no mistake about it."

"I'm tempted," she added reluctantly.

"Good." He clasped her triumphantly in his arms. "Then come to California with me, we'll get married there. I know the perfect place in Mill Valley, a simple little redwood church, you'll love it."

"Jim, Jim," she protested as he scrunched her in his arms, "don't go so fast, I can't keep up with you. We only met two weeks ago."

"But think about it," he whispered, kissing her ear, "that lovely little redwood church . . . like a log cabin."

She did think about it—with regret—as she kissed him.

Maroc had been trying to get up his courage for days. Now he knew he must tell her, courage or not. It would be better now, while Jim Jamieson was still around and before they left for France. She would need all the help she could get.

"You're not easy to get ahold of these days," he said, leaning against the mantel and pushing the log with his foot. It sparked, shooting out thin orange flames, and he stared at it in fascination.

"What's the matter, Maroc?" asked Léonie, concerned. "You look . . ." She hesitated, searching for the word. It wasn't "ill," he didn't look ill— "upset" was the best she could manage. And nervous.

"I have something to tell you," he said gravely, "and when I do, I hope you will remember that what I did was for your own good. It was what we had agreed on years ago, all of us who were involved, that there would be no contact with Amélie."

She tensed at the mention of her daughter's name. "What are you saying, Maroc?" she cried. "What about Amélie?"

"Amélie was here in this hotel."

Léonie stared at him numbly.

"She was with the Comtesse d'Aureville. They were leaving just as we were arriving. By chance I saw the name in the register. I waited. And I saw them."

"You saw Amélie?" Léonie's voice was as thin as glass, as though it came from a distance.

"I saw her, Léonie. I saw your daughter." The words Maroc had been holding back for so long tumbled out in a haste of confession. "Remember how you looked when you first came for the job at Serrat, all thin arms and legs and a mass of hair . . . she looks exactly the way you did then, Léonie. *Exactly* like you."

"Why didn't you tell me? Why didn't you let me see her?" Léonie's heart was breaking all over again. She rolled in agony on the sofa, banging her head against the cushions, hiding her screams in their softness.

"Léonie, I couldn't . . . I couldn't. There's more. Monsieur was here, too, in this hotel."

Frozen into silence, she stared into the silk cushion, its zigzag pattern echoing her disjointed thoughts. Had Monsieur found Amélie at last? She turned her face slowly from the cushion, afraid of the answer to her unspoken question.

"No!" said Maroc. "He doesn't know! It was a coincidence, it just happened. No one knew, except me."

Léonie's face was so full of despair that he wanted to cradle her in his hands, to brush away the tears, the smudged rouge, and the eye pencil. She was so utterly defenseless, like a kitten in the current of a fast-flowing river. He couldn't let her go under, she couldn't be defeated now.

"It was sheer chance, Léonie, I swear it. Amélie is safe."

"Are you sure, Maroc? Are you absolutely sure?"

"I'm sure, Léonie."

She began to cry again, quietly this time, the tears falling unheeded down her cheeks. "Tell me again, Maroc, how did she look?"

"She's lovely, Léonie . . . a lovely girl. Tall and too slender, with your hair and your eyes exactly."

"Oh, I should have seen her, I should have seen her . . . just this once," she wailed, hurling herself again into the pillows.

"You don't have the right, Léonie," murmured Maroc. "Amélie has her own life now, her own family . . . it's over, Léonie."

She stared at him, aghast. But she knew he was right. It was over.

* * *

"What the hell have I done?" said Jim out loud as he paced the lobby of the Waldorf once more. It had been three days now that Léonie had stayed in her room. She wasn't taking any calls and she didn't answer any messages. He was supposed to leave for San Francisco tomorrow—he *had* to leave for San Francisco tomorrow. But how could he go and leave things up in the air like this? What the hell was going on? He headed for the telephone, he would try again—he had tried every half hour for the past two days!

Léonie hurried in through the side door of the hotel, clutching Chocolat in her arms. Pulling the brim of her hat further down over her pale face, she strode toward the elevators. She had had to take poor Chocolat out, the poor darling had been in for days now, but neither of them had enjoyed the walk. She just wished Saturday would come quickly so they might leave. Why did the elevator take so long! It was odd, but her legs felt suddenly weak and her head was spinning; she leaned against a pillar wearily, clutching the cat.

"Léonie?"

She looked up guiltily. She stared at Jim, unable to speak.

"Are you all right?"

She heard the concern in his voice and turned her head away.

"What's the matter, are you feeling ill?"

To her horror she felt the tears slide down her cheeks and she turned away. She couldn't cry here in the lobby of the Waldorf.

He took hold of her arm. "Lean on me, Léonie," he said firmly. "I'm looking after you."

She did lean on him, hiding her face against his jacket, unable to stop the tears.

He helped her into the elevator. "It's all right, you know," he murmured into her ear. "I'm here now, I'll take care of you. I'll take care of everything. Don't worry, it's all going to be just fine."

She leaned against him again in the corridor, grateful for his sustaining arm around her shoulders. In her suite, he commanded Julie to help her undress and to wrap her in a warm robe while he summoned the doctor to come see her and room service to send up a light lunch.

Léonie lay back on the moiré silk cushions in front of the fire and watched him prowling the room silently, waiting for the doctor to arrive. He looked so big, so rugged—and so determined. He looked like a man a woman could rely on. It was a long time since a man had looked after her like this; in fact, had any man looked after her? Jim was a lot like Edouard d'Aureville. Edouard was a tough adventurer but a tender man. And under that rugged façade Jim, too, was a tender man.

He left them alone discreetly while the doctor examined her, confirming that the only medicine she needed was rest and food, and then he watched over her while she sipped a little of the consommé. He then wrapped a blanket around her, tucking her up on the sofa to rest. "I'll be back later," Jim said, dropping a light kiss on the top of her head, "and you are to go to sleep." For the first time in days she slept a light effortless sleep, untroubled by a single dream.

Jim was back at four with tea, standing over her while she ate a cucumber sandwich. It was so different from their first tea that she felt even sadder. "I've waited for three days down in that lobby and when I finally catch up with you, you're not the same woman. You're pale and worn and tired—even a rough Atlantic crossing hadn't done that to you—what happened? What have I done? I'm willing to bet those tears are not just from fatigue, but whatever the reason, Léonie Bahri, there's no need for despair. There is nothing in this world that can't be worked out."

Somehow when he said it she could almost believe that it were true. She pushed the plate aside with a sigh and he peered at it, checking. "It's all right," she said. "I ate three. Now can I talk?"

"Please talk, tell me what's the matter, Léonie. I want to help you."

"There's nothing anyone can do, and I can't tell you what it is. It's something that's been going on for years now, and there's no solution. But you have helped." She leaned across and took his hand. "Just by being here."

His blue eyes were worried. "I can't make you tell me, Léonie, but just remember, in case you change your mind, I'm a very sympathetic listener." Jim hesitated. How could he leave her like this? "Come with me tomorrow," he urged, "please, Léonie. You'll see, things will look quite different in a different place. Please come."

"I can't, Jim." His blue eyes were so pleading and for once his face was serious. If only it were possible. But now, more than ever, she must go back to France. Her responsibility was clear.

"Then promise me you'll wait here until I return next week. Promise me." His voice was commanding. He was allowing her no leeway.

"I'll see," she said evasively.

He put his arms around her, holding her close. He felt so good. His chest felt strong, his arms so secure. "It's not good enough, Léonie, promise me."

"I promise," she said, listening to his heart beat next to her face.

* * *

Léonie reread the letter before she folded it and placed it in the envelope and sealed it firmly. There, it was done. If she didn't mail it right away, she might change her mind. She glanced around the room. It looked naked without her things. There were just the steamer trunks with Chocolat perched nervously on top of the pile as she always did when they were traveling, making sure she wasn't overlooked and left behind, she supposed. But all she was leaving behind was Jim—and a way of life that couldn't be hers.

She ran a finger across his name on the envelope. Jim Jamieson. She could have been Mrs. Jim Jamieson. But she was "Léonie" and she had her role to play. Work awaited her. There was the meeting of the trustees of the Château d'Aureville home—she must go through the lists of figures, study the financial report and the investments—and then she must go on tour again and make some more money. She had pledged her life to it, for Amélie.

Jim had left the day before yesterday, still begging her to come with him, and then reminding her of her promise to wait.

Léonie went downstairs to mail the letter to San Francisco, watching it drop down the narrow glass chute, sealing her fate. There was no going back now. The ship was to sail at noon and at the end of the journey were France and reality.

ঌ49ঌ

AMÉLIE WANDERED BAREFOOT along the terrace of the Villa Encantada, comfortable again in her old shorts and shirt. She leaned happily against the rail, gazing down at the green tree-tangled hillside and the view of the tranquil bay below, enjoying the warmth of the sun on her bare arms and legs. Snow was all right, she thought, remembering Fifth Avenue, but this was better. They were to go to the St. James for dinner that night and she planned to wear the new pink dress. Edouard hadn't seen her in that yet. She stretched lazily, wondering why he was being so mysterious. They were to have a grand celebration, he had told them before he disappeared into Key West an hour ago, leaving them all mystified and curious. Amélie kicked a pebble off the terrace and watched it bounce down the hillside. Life was good, she thought, especially when Diego wasn't around. Roberto was so different when it was just the two of them, he was happy just being with her, she *knew* he was.

A donkey cart appeared around the bend in the lane piled with melting blocks of ice, leaving a watery trail as the animal sauntered slowly through the lemon trees, pausing to nibble a bit of grass here, a leaf there, until he was prodded back into action by the boy in charge.

"Your champagne"—the boy grinned, waving to her—"well chilled."

Edouard's tiny car chugged up the hill behind the donkey, leaving a swirl of dust in the flawless air. His laughter and that of the dark-haired woman sitting beside him floated toward her. Amélie stiffened. Who could that be? She leaned over the rail to get a better look as the car jolted in low gear the last few yards and shuddered to a stop behind the drooping donkey.

Edouard waved. "That's Amélie," he told Xara. "I just know she's going to love you."

Xara smiled doubtfully as she waved to the tall slender figure on the terrace. Amélie turned and darted into the house. "I'm not so sure, Edouard," said Xara. "Stepmothers are not usually very popular."

"This one is different." Edouard helped her from the car. "Because it's you, and because Amélie has never had a mother. You're her first."

Amélie was surely going to consider her, a stranger now in Edouard's life, her rival. After all, she was fourteen—almost fifteen—now. She would be beginning to know how it felt to be a woman—all the pain, the uncertainties, the jealousies. Poor girl, she thought suddenly, walking up the steps to the house. Poor little girl.

"Maman," called Edouard, "Amélie . . . Roberto. I'm back—with the surprise and the champagne!"

Roberto ambled into the hall behind them. "Hi," he said, "what's the surprise? Oh, hello." He held out his hand to Xara. "I'm Roberto do Santos."

"This is Xara O'Neill de Esteban," said Edouard.

"Edouard." Isabelle hurried from her room, tidying her hair as she went. "I didn't know we were to have a visitor."

"Maman, I want you to meet Xara." The two women regarded each other, liking what they saw. There was no doubt that this was someone special, thought Isabelle, taking the girl's cool soft hand in hers. "Welcome, my dear, to the Villa Encantada." She smiled.

"Where's Amélie?" Edouard looked around. "She's usually first out."

"She's helping the boy unload the champagne," said Roberto. "I'd better go and help her."

"Hurry then," called Edouard. "We'll have it out on the terrace."

Xara picked up the long box Edouard had been carrying and took it out onto the terrace with her. At least Edouard's mother was nice, though how she would react to the sudden announcement of her son's engagement to a widow he'd known only a few weeks would be the true test!

Amélie lifted the icy bottles from their nest and carried them indoors, while Roberto helped the boy unload a block of ice, hauling it with his big tongs into the kitchen.

"What's the surprise?" Amélie asked, licking her cold fingers to warm them.

Roberto grinned at her. "Old Edouard is in love," he said. "I can see it in his eyes when he looks at Xara O'Neill de Esteban."

"Xara," breathed Amélie, recognizing it instinctively as the name of a rival.

"My bet is that he's going to announce their engagement," continued Roberto, "and I don't blame him. She's gorgeous—dark and exotic and very elegant."

He placed the glasses on a tray, taking the silver wine cooler and filling it with ice crushed with a few efficient hammer blows.

"Their engagement," echoed Amélie numbly. Edouard was going to *marry* this woman? If Edouard got married, he would leave her. Maybe he would even have children—his own *proper* children. She felt desolate suddenly and her high spirits of an hour ago plummeted to new depths.

"Come on," called Roberto, carrying out the tray, "let's get on with the celebration."

Amélie hesitated by the kitchen table. She didn't want to meet Xara. She didn't want to know that this woman even existed.

"Amélie." It was Edouard's voice calling her. She must go. It's only an engagement, she told herself, it takes ages before people get married; maybe it won't even happen.

Xara stood by the rail admiring the view that had entranced Amélie just a short while ago. It was perfect, she decided, turning with a smile as Edouard announced Amélie at last.

That the girl was too thin didn't matter. She would be a beauty—a tall rangy golden girl. The look in Amélie's eyes as she shook hands politely made Xara recall her own parentless insecurities at the age of fourteen. The girl was afraid and Xara's heart went out to her.

Xara's smile was so warm, so sisterly, thought Amélie, as though they had known each other a long time and shared the same secrets. She shifted uncomfortably from one foot to the other, wishing she had thought to wear the pink dress instead of these awful old shorts. Xara was so smart in her cool blue-and-white linen dress and perfect white shoes. And she was beautiful. *Very* beautiful. Amélie hadn't known jealousy could feel like this, it was suffocating her. She felt hot and her heart was pounding.

"Well," said Edouard, pleased with his family, "now for the surprise." He took Xara's hand in his and turned to the three waiting faces.

"Xara is to be my wife. We shall be married the day after tomorrow, here in Key West."

"Edouard . . . Xara!" Isabelle throw her arms around them both, tears brimming in her eyes. "It's silly to cry," she sniffed, "but it's really only because I'm so very happy for you both."

"We hoped you wouldn't mind it being so sudden," explained Xara, "but we love each other and there seems no reason to wait."

"I've no intention of waiting." Edouard's eyes met Xara's and the look that passed between them seemed to Amélie to shut out everyone else from their world. Their own private world.

"May I kiss the bride?" asked Roberto, shaking Edouard's hand and planting a firm kiss on Xara's cool cheek.

"Amélie," cried Edouard cheerfully, "what do you have to say?"

"Congratulations," she murmured, stepping forward dutifully, barely touching her lips to Xara's cheek.

Edouard flung his arms around Amélie and swung her into the air. "It's not every new wife who gets a ready-made daughter like you," he said, ruffling her hair.

"Don't do that!" cried Amélie sharply, brushing her hair back into place with her hands and retreating again behind the table.

Roberto stared at her in surprise, but Edouard was too busy to notice her tight little face. He poured the champagne lavishly, handing a chilly glass to each of them, raising his own in a toast. "To Xara," he said, his face brimming with love, "my future wife."

Amélie thought the champagne would choke her. She swallowed a mouthful and stared miserably at the terra-cotta tiles. How could he do it? It had always been just Grandmère and Edouard and her. Now what would happen? Edouard was talking to Isabelle, talking about Xara, she could tell by the expression on his face; she'd never seen him look like that before, all sort of thrilled. Damn her, she thought suddenly, as the tears pricked at her eyelids. Damn Xara. I hate her.

"Amélie"—Edouard put his arm around her—"we have a present for you." He handed her the long box emblazoned with the elaborate Boutique Oberon script.

"A present." Amélie looked at the box doubtfully.

"Come on, open it."

Amélie ripped off the ribbons, pulling at the lid impatiently. Beneath a layer of tissue was the prettiest dress she had ever seen. It was the blue-pink of wild lilac, its fine cotton-lawn ruffles edged with satin ribbon in lavender and rose. "It's beautiful," she said, touching its softness.

"Xara chose it for you. We want you to be her bridesmaid." Edouard beamed.

Amélie's eyes met Xara's. The tears were going to come, she knew it.

Dropping the dress back into its box, she ran along the terrace and through the hall.

Edouard stared after her in astonishment. "What's the matter?" he asked. "What did I do?"

"Poor Amélie," said Xara gently. "She's shocked, Edouard. It is too much for her to accept so quickly that her father is to be married. I understand how she feels."

"I'll go to her," said Roberto, heading indoors.

Amélie slammed the door shut behind her, hurling herself onto the bed as the sobs shook her. She didn't want Edouard to marry that woman. He was her father, he had no right to marry and leave her. She didn't want to lose him.

Roberto could hear her sobs even before he opened the door. He sat on the window ledge watching as she lay on the bed, her head hidden beneath a pillow. Poor silly kid, he thought compassionately. He went over and pulled back the pillow. Amélie's face was blotchy and swollen and her eyes still brimmed with tears.

"You look a mess," he said, bringing over a wet cloth and wiping her face gently. "There's really no need for all this fuss, you know. He's only getting married."

"You don't understand," she whispered despairingly.

"*What* don't I understand?" He knelt by the bed and took her hand. "Tell me, Amélie."

"You'll *never* understand, Roberto, because you have your own big family. Grandmère and Edouard are all I've got and I'm so afraid of losing them. Don't you see?" she cried. "He'll probably go away to live and then he'll have other children—his *own* children. Oh, Roberto, this woman won't want an almost grown-up girl around and she won't want to be my mother. Why should she? She'll want Edouard all to herself."

"That's not true, Amélie. Edouard would never let that happen. You *know* he loves you. You are his daughter, just as if he were your real father."

Amélie red-rimmed eyes were anxious. "If only I'd known my mother, just known what she was like, then I'd know about myself."

Roberto looked puzzled. "What do you mean—about yourself?"

"No one ever talks about my mother. Her name was Léonie, she was lovely and good and sweet. And I look exactly like her. But what was she *like*, Roberto? Did she ride horses and did she like cats? Did she laugh at silly things the way I do and did she like to dance and wear pretty clothes . . . or maybe she liked mucking about barefoot in the sand. I don't know if she ever felt jealous. Or did mean things. Don't you see, Roberto? I'm like a jigsaw puzzle with a piece missing, it's lost under a rug somewhere and the picture is spoiled. It's almost there, but you can never be quite sure what it was really like!"

"Amélie, there's no use worrying about a mother you've never known. You're one of us—part of *my* family as well as Edouard's. You know my father thinks of you as one of us. Doesn't he always call you 'his other son' when he's teasing you?" He dabbed at her eyes with the damp cloth. "You are what you are, Amélie d'Aureville, and it's very nice. And I love you."

Amélie sat up, pushing away the cloth. "Really, Roberto? Do you really love me?"

"Of course I do." His clear blue eyes emphasized his sincerity and Amélie heaved a sigh of relief.

"Well, at least I have you," she said, taking his hand.

"Come on, dry your eyes and wash you face, and let's tell Edouard and Xara that you are pleased for them." They walked hand in hand to the door. "Let them be happy, too," he said.

Edouard smiled compassionately as Amélie came toward him, brushed and neat and very subdued, with Roberto beside her. She looked so vulnerable with her skinny arms and legs and tear-blotched face.

"I'm sorry," she said shyly. "I didn't mean to be rude. I was just surprised and a bit afraid of losing you, Edouard. I really want you to be happy—and Xara, too."

Edouard wrapped his arms around her. "Thank you, my little daughter, thank you."

The wedding day dawned as blue, clear, and perfect as all Florida days, and Amélie and Isabelle waited in Xara's tiny sitting room at the St. James while she dressed for her wedding. This is it, thought Amélie miserably, nothing will ever be the same after today.

"You're going to be a beautiful bridesmaid," said Isabelle encouragingly. "You look so pretty in your lovely dress, and so like your mother."

Amélie looked up hopefully. "Do I *really* look like her, Grandmère?"

Isabelle stroked her pretty hair; it hung loose and tawny, streaked with paler gold from the sun, tiny ends curling around her face despite the vigorous brushing she had given it to make it lay smooth. The circlet of pink flowers she wore was already turning faintly brown at the edges from the heat and its sweet scent filled the room. There's no mistaking that you are Léonie's daughter, it's all there—your hair, your eyes."

At least I know that I look like her, thought Amélie, that's something. Now if I only knew what she was *like*.

* * *

Xara sat in front of the dressing table brushing her long black hair. Her wedding dress of white organdy, banded on its full skirt and flounced neckline with satin ribbons, waited on its hanger and she could see its reflection in the mirror. Marcella and the Boutique Oberon hadn't let her down, it was beautiful. She wondered what Edouard was doing now. He'd left her discreetly in the lobby of the St. James last night, after pulling her into the shadow of a doorway and covering her face with kisses. She closed her eyes, remembering the sensation of his warm lips on her skin. Tomorrow, he had whispered, you'll be the Comtesse d'Aureville. Tomorrow, she had whispered back, you'll be mine at last. No, he'd said, you'll be mine. Either way, she had murmured from beneath the kisses. I'll be happy.

There was just Amélie to worry about. And she *was* worried about her. There was no way to be a mother to the girl. Isabelle was already doing a good job of that. If Amélie could think of her as a sister, it would be easier for them to become friends.

Xara put down her hairbrush and went to the door. "I don't know what to do with my hair," she called, lifting it up on top of her head. "What do you think, Amélie, should I pin it up like this?"

"Oh, no," responded Amélie instinctively, "please leave it loose."

"Could you help me? I feel so nervous somehow, I just can't seem to do anything right."

Their eyes met. She looks like a little girl, thought Amélie, puzzled. Is she really nervous? It's only Edouard, after all. Still, it's her wedding day, all brides are nervous.

She followed Xara to the dressing table and began to brush the heavy blue-black hair. It was so smooth and silky, not like her own unruly mop. "There," she said, brushing the ends over her fingers, "now all you need is a flower or something." She picked up the gardenias and held them to Xara's hair. "These are perfect."

"You're right, Amélie." Xara clipped the flowers into place. "Thank you for helping me."

"You're welcome," said Amélie uncomfortably. "Do I look all right— for a bridesmaid, I mean?"

Xara had been afraid to comment on the dress, or on how she looked. Amélie was so prickly, looking for hidden hurts in every word. But she looked adorable, the flounced neckline and ruffled skirt disguised her coltish thinness, and the color suited her tawny blondness. "You look like a Renaissance princess," she said, touching the mass of blond hair lightly. "You are a perfect bridesmaid."

They smiled at each other. It was turning out better than she had expected, thought Amélie, withdrawing from the room. If Xara wasn't marrying Edouard, she might even think she was very nice.

Xara's brother, Tomas, and his wife, Lola, had arrived on the ferry from

Havana. Lola was a vision in yellow silk, beaming with such excitement and happiness that even Amélie was won over by her charm. "Ah, you look so pretty, little one," she cried, "the dress was a perfect choice . . . and such hair. Look at her wonderful hair, Tomas." She hugged Amélie to her. "How nice to have you for a new sister-in-law . . . or is it daughter-in-law?" she asked, wrinkling her nose in puzzlement as Amélie laughed. "One of those 'in-laws,' anyway. Here, let me straighten your ribbons." She pulled the sash tighter, adjusted a ribbon here and there, and fixed the circlet of flowers firmly on her hair. "There, you're ready. All we need now is the bride."

Xara emerged from her room, pale and perfect, nervously holding a spray of creamy gardenias. They stood for a moment admiring her in her demure white gown that set off her dark exotic beauty to perfection.

"Xara," said Lola softly, "you look beautiful. Oh, Tomas, look at her."

Tomas took his sister's arm. "It's the beginning of a new life for you, Xara. I know you'll be happy."

Passersby smiled admiringly as the bridal party walked the short distance to the tiny white frame church where Edouard waited with Roberto. Edouard turned as the organist began to play and he and Xara smiled at each other as she walked down the aisle and put her hand in his.

Amélie stood behind them, listening to the quiet words of the service, watching Roberto as he handed Edouard the ring. She caught the expression of love between Edouard and Xara as he slipped it on her finger. They looked so, so *nice,* she thought helplessly, at a loss for the right word. Is that how marriage made you feel? Sort of loved, as though you belonged to someone? She looked at Roberto again. His back was toward her, his shaggy blond hair was combed neatly, and his white jacket looked very smart. He looked very grown up. We'll get married one day, she thought, and then we'll feel just the way Xara and Edouard do.

❧ 50 ❦

LA VIEILLE AUBERGE. The name flowed in stylish script across the little wooden gate at the top of a rocky path and Jim checked it against the scrap of paper in his hand. Yes, this was it all right. He slammed the door of the yellow Mercedes-Benz and put on his jacket. Might as well look smart even if it's hot. You can't ask a woman to marry you in your shirt-sleeves, even if she did know you a lot better without your clothes on. He grinned as he opened the gate and strode down the path.

The house stood white, four-square and green-shuttered, amid a riot of flowers on an olive-strewn slope leading to the sea. He smiled in satisfaction. He liked that blue sea. He liked this place. All of it. Naturally she would live here. He started for the front door that stood open to the sun, flanked by great earthenware pots of geraniums, but stopped suddenly. He followed the path around the side of the house, emerging onto a broad terrace over-looking the sea. Another little path led from the steps down the slope past a silent pool that reflected the blue of the sky and a vine-covered arbor. It was the perfect garden in which to sit and dream in the shade, idling away the hours, recuperating from life's mortal blows. It was Léonie's garden, and he knew that was where she would be.

He followed the path until he found her. She was tending a bed of flowers beneath a blossoming tree, while Chocolat chased her feet. The sound of Léonie's laughter floated toward him.

"At least it's good to hear you laugh again," he said.

Léonie wore a simple blue cotton skirt and blouse and her face was golden from the sun and lit with surprise. She had never looked more beautiful to him.

"Jim Jamieson," she said, "what are you doing here?"

"You know us Americans, we never know when to quit." He walked toward her down the path and took her in his arms beneath the tree. "You mustn't leave me like that again," he whispered, as he held her close to his heart. "I'll always find you. Don't fight it, Léonie Bahri," he said, kissing her. "We belong together. You're going to marry me."

They argued for a week in between making love, drinking wine, and eating huge meals, for he discovered a passion for the food of Provence.

"This is the real thing," he pronounced, digging into a dish of lamb braised with rosemary and olives. "I'm used to New York French food in fancy sauces, it's like the hotel chairs: phony."

"You'll get fat," she cautioned. "All those sausages and soups."

"No chance," he replied smugly. "You'll see, I'll have the same waist-line when I'm seventy."

She sighed. "That's another thing, I'm older than you."

"So?"

"My waistline will be the first to go."

He laughed at her. "Léonie, you will always be beautiful."

He was wearing her down and she knew it. "I can't leave France," she argued. "I couldn't live in a place where I would always be a 'foreigner.'"

"Then I'll commute, or I'll sell my business and start again here . . . whatever you want."

"How can you commute across continents?" She was amazed by his energy.

"One month here, one month there—and one month traveling—as long as you promise to travel with me."

That was it. They were down to reality. She couldn't travel with him. She couldn't marry him. She had to keep on working as long as audiences wanted her; the money just got eaten up by the château, and whatever the children needed she would give them.

"I couldn't do that, Jim," she said quietly. "I have my work."

He looked at her shrewdly. "I had the feeling that you had had enough of being 'Léonie,' that you didn't need her anymore. Am I right, Miss Bahri?"

She avoided his eyes. "Of course not. That's what I do. I told you I was an independent woman. I like it that way."

He took her hand. "All right, tell me the truth. You're hiding something from me and I want to know what it is."

His clear blue eyes were serious, waiting for her answer. "I need to make money," she said simply. "No, don't say anything, it's not just a *little* money. I have to make a *lot*. I have forty children who depend on me . . . that's where 'Léonie's' money goes."

He stared at her, trying to understand what she meant.

"Forty children . . . whose children?"

"They're orphans. I provide a home for them. They are my children."

In his wildest dreams he could never have expected this. Forty children stood between him and marriage! What next? "I've never considered it," he said slowly, "but I imagine that your fees must be substantial and you told me yourself that you work nine months out of every year. Surely there must be plenty of money by now?"

She shrugged helplessly. "There were some bad investments. I followed the advice of my trustees . . . a lot of money seems to have been lost along the way." She sighed. "I don't know, Jim, no matter how much I earn, it never seems to be enough."

He leaned toward her across the table. "Do you remember when we met I told you that there was nothing that couldn't be resolved? Leave it to me, Léonie . . . your children will be taken care of—all of them. I'll straighten out those investments—and I'll add to them. My God, Léonie, is money the only thing standing between you and me? That's the easiest of problems to solve."

Could he really do it? Hope flickered in her eyes.

"Put me in charge," he told her with a smile, "and there'll be no more problem." When he said it she knew it would be true. She lay back in her chair and relaxed, everything would be all right now.

"I love you, Jim Jamieson." She sighed. "What would I do without you?"

"Isn't that what I've been saying all along?" he cried triumphantly.

It was because of Sekhmet that she finally said she would marry him. The statue gazed at them nightly from its marble plinth opposite her bed and he glared back at it. "Let's turn her face to the wall," he said. "She's always watching!"

"No. No, you can't do that."

He looked at her, surprised by the vehemence of her reaction. "It was just a joke, Léonie."

"I know. I'm sorry, but it's important to me."

"Because they were your father's?"

"That . . . and other reasons," she replied evasively, lying back against the pillows.

He propped himself on one elbow and looked at her. "Well?"

"Well what?"

"Are you going to tell me? Or is there some terrible secret that no one can ever know . . . the curse of Sekhmet!" he said with a laugh.

"Oh, Jim! Don't say that!" She turned her face away so that he couldn't see the fear in her eyes.

"Hey, now, wait a minute. What's going on here?" He pulled her gently around to face him. "You don't mean to tell me that you believe that there is a curse of Sekhmet?"

"It's not a curse exactly, it's more. . . . Oh, I can't tell you. You'd only laugh and say I was being silly."

Jim put his arms around her comfortingly. If she was this upset, something was really wrong. "Try me, Léonie. Just tell me what it is."

She sat up, pushing back her hair. "Very well, I'll tell you. But first you must read this." She walked to the desk and pulled out a piece of paper. "It's a transcription of the hieroglyphs on the statue."

He read it and looked up at her inquiringly.

"I've no idea where my father got them from, but I've had the statues since I was a child. They were my dolls, they slept in my bed at night and I loved them. It wasn't until I was eighteen that I found out the secret of Sekhmet, who she is and what she is. And when I did everything changed. It was as though Sekhmet took over my life. Oh, damn it," she said, bursting into tears. "I told you it would sound ridiculous. That's why I never told anyone before, not even Caro."

"Tell me," he urged. "Go on, I'm listening."

"You think you know me, but you don't," she whispered. "You'd better know what sort of a woman you are asking to be your wife. I can't marry anyone, Jim. I'm haunted by my past and I'll never be free unless . . . unless I am like Sekhmet. Unless I kill my enemies."

He picked up her robe, wrapping her in it, folding it around her lovingly. "Come on," he said, taking her arm and leading her outside onto the terrace. "Let's just sit here together in the dark and you can tell me about it. Don't leave out a single detail. I want to know it all."

She glanced at his profile, silhouetted against the warm blue-black night sky. It would be such a relief to tell him, to unburden herself of the fear. The story spilled out of her, about Monsieur, about Amélie, her fears for her daughter's safety. "And I know," she said finally, "that one day some small coincidence will lead Monsieur to Amélie . . . and when he finds her, then I shall have to kill him. Sekhmet's destiny is mine."

Her words drifted into the velvet night. She waited nervously for his reactions, but he said nothing, staring out to the dark horizon across the faintly rippling sea. I knew it, she thought despairingly, I knew he would think I'm crazy—I've lost him. I'd better leave, just go away. I'll go down to the beach and walk and when I come back he'll be gone. And I'll be alone again—except for Monsieur. And Sekhmet. She stood up quickly and turned away. He caught her hand. "Where are you going?" he demanded.

"I'm going down to the beach. I need to walk . . . you can leave if you want to."

"Leave? Of course I'm not leaving. I'm just trying to figure out how your life got so complicated and what we can do to straighten it out." He put his arm around her and they walked together down the steps to the beach. The sand felt cool and damp under their bare feet as they paced by the edge of the silent water. "All right," he said, "now it's my turn to speak. First of all, this man . . . Monsieur. He still spies on you, still has someone following you?"

"Yes. Wherever I am . . . and *he* follows me, too. He is always there, in the theater, or I'll see him in a restaurant, or outside a shop, and when I'm here, he'll be on his yacht waiting."

"Waiting for what?"

"For me to say I'll come back to him. Or for me to lead him to Amélie."

"And this 'murder' . . . are you sure of it? Was it murder?"

"Yes, I'm sure. When I found out that Charles was dead, I knew what had happened. Monsieur had even taken me to Deauville . . . he wanted me to *see* it happen! I confronted him about it and that's when he threatened Amélie, because he knew I would believe him."

"But you have no evidence?"

"None. Only a description of the man who did it. He was on the boat with Charles, a casual crewman picked up in Deauville. He came back alone and said that Charles had been swept overboard. His skull had been fractured. The autopsy was hurried, it was all over in a day. Monsieur had arranged everything," she added bitterly. "Caro, Alphonse, and I searched everywhere for the man, but without any luck."

"And Amélie? Does she know about you?"

"No," said Léonie wearily, "I doubt she even knows I exist. It was the safest way."

"Right, now I have the facts. Monsieur still doesn't know where the girl is—despite his constant vigilance. So at the moment she is safe . . . and has been for almost fifteen years. Yet he's crazy enough to keep after you, to keep on spying and following you, he still believes he can force you to go back to him. There's only one way to stop a man like that and that's a counterthreat. We must discover the identity of Charles's assassin. Monsieur must have paid—and paid well—for him to remain quiet all these years."

"But we tried," she said despairingly. "And it was all so long ago, who would remember?"

"Will you let me try?" he asked gently. "I promise you, if he's still alive, I'll find him. And then I'll take care of Monsieur."

"You don't know Monsieur . . . you can have no idea what he's like. Don't forget he's a public figure, Jim, he has so much power, he can do anything."

"Léonie, no one—not even a powerful man—can escape a charge of murder. He would have to face it . . . or he would have to give in. He sounds like a proud man to me. Those two sons you mentioned must be growing up, how can he let them think their father is a murderer! No, we'd have him, Léonie. I'm going to trace that man. Leave it to me."

She sagged against him as relief flowed through her. How had she ever lived without this man, but could he really make it all right?

"And now there's the other problem," he said, putting his arms around her and holding her. Her hair floated around them in the sea breeze and he tilted up her face, lit by the stars and a scudding moon. "Is this the face of a goddess? Or is it a woman? A mortal like the rest of us. Léonie, you can't seriously think you are the reincarnation of some Egyptian goddess . . . don't you see, it's something you've brought on yourself. Sekhmet's destiny isn't yours. It's you who are allowing the poem to influence your life. You told me yourself there are two 'Léonies.' Isn't that Sekhmet on stage, not you?"

"But it's true, don't you see. . . ."

"No!" he replied firmly. "It's not true and I'm not going to let you believe that. Don't you realize what you're doing . . . you're preparing yourself to kill Monsieur!"

He was right. She was preparing herself. She had always known that one day she would kill him.

"You are Léonie Bahri," he said firmly. "You are not Sekhmet and your destiny is not ruled by some mysterious force from Egypt. Because of what happened, you've allowed yourself to believe that her fate is yours. You've dwelt on it for years until it seems like reality. But it's over now. Do you understand, Léonie: it's over!"

She wanted so much to believe him—he was always right, he always knew how to solve problems. Had she just in her isolation lost her identity to Sekhmet?

"There'll be no more Sekhmet, no more Léonie—not even Léonie Bahri. You'll start a new life as Mrs. Léonie Jamieson."

"Oh, Jim, can you really make everything all right? Can you free me at last of Monsieur?"

"I promise you. And without Monsieur, there's no need for Sekhmet."

She leaned against his hard chest while he held her close, crushing her against him so that she would never run away again.

"And I promise you something else, Léonie. One day you'll meet your daughter . . . we'll find her."

"Amélie—but how? She doesn't know I'm alive."

"Sshh," he said soothingly, "leave it all to me."

The burden she had carried alone for so long seemed suddenly, miraculously lighter, shared by Jim with his strong shoulders and his calm logical thinking. "Jim Jamieson," she said holding him tightly, "your mother was right to call you Homer and Alexander . . . you're a thinker and a fighter, and I don't know how I ever lived this long without you."

"Then marry me, Léonie," he whispered.

"Yes," she said, "I want to be Léonie Jamieson."

The first thing he did was turn Sekhmet's face to the wall. "We ought to get rid of her," he had said firmly, but Léonie had been so upset by the idea that he gave in.

"It's because she was my father's," she pleaded. "I must keep her."

"Not because of Sekhmet?" he demanded. "Are you sure?"

She was almost sure.

"And what about this one . . . the cat?"

"That's Bastet, the sacred cat."

He smiled. "Do I detect a strange resemblance to Chocolat? Is that why you got her?"

"Oh, no . . . no," she said, remembering how it was Bébé who had found *her*.

So the statues stayed and he turned his attention to other matters.

True to form, he charmed the mayor of Nice into giving them a special license. He arrived home waving it triumphantly in his hand. "We can be married tomorrow," he announced happily.

"Oh, but I can't . . . not tomorrow."

"Why ever not?" he groaned. "What's wrong now?"

"It's just that I've never been married before . . . and I want to be your bride. I want to look beautiful and special. Besides, I couldn't possibly get married without my dearest friends here with me."

He smiled. "Now you're going to tell me that they all live in Vienna or St. Petersburg and it'll take weeks for them to get here!"

"No. Just Paris. It'll be Caro and Alphonse—and Maroc, of course."

"And I expect you have to go and buy yourself a new dress or something."

"Well, of course I do."

"All right. We'll send telegrams to everyone telling them to be here on Thursday if they want to see you get married. But I warn you, I can't wait any longer than that. I want to take you on a honeymoon . . . anywhere you want: a houseboat on a lake in Kashmir, a chalet in the woods in Vermont, an island in the southern seas—what shall it be?"

"A honeymoon? But Jim, I can't. I have to be in Paris next week for rehearsals. The tour begins in a few weeks . . . there are costumes and fittings and music—everything."

"Léonie Bahri," he roared, "are our problems never to be over? Cancel the damned tour."

"Certainly not," she said, facing him angrily, "and you've no right to ask me. I'm committed to those concerts. The theaters are sold out and I shall be there. It's not just me, Jim, there are a lot of other people involved, it's their livelihood, too. If I don't work, then neither do they."

"You're right, of course." He sighed, grabbing her and hugging her. "But I wish you didn't have to do it."

"There's one other thing," she said in a small voice.

He looked at her with a faint smile. "All right," he said, "let me have it."

"Would you mind very much if we kept our marriage a secret at first—not from our close friends, of course, but from the public. It's because of the concerts. Léonie's image is not that of a married woman. She's just, well, a woman."

"Does it matter to you very much?"

"Yes," she replied, "it matters, at least for a while. Afterward, when there are no more concerts, I shall just be Mrs. Jamieson."

"I don't like it," he told her, "but if that's what you feel is necessary . . ."

Her smile covered the relief she felt. She hadn't wanted to tell him her other reason for keeping it a secret. She was afraid of Monsieur's revenge, afraid for Jim.

Caro sat with Monsieur and Madame Frenard at the front of the little English Church in Nice. It was pleasant, she thought, dark and cool, with a glimmer of silver candlesticks and a touch of color from the stained glass. Yes, it was a nice place to get married. She smoothed her dress and smiled at Madame Frenard, smart in navy blue silk—bought by Léonie, she suspected. And Monsieur Frenard, his red-bronzed outdoorsman face solemn as befitted the occasion, buttoned into a neat gray suit. The organ music was soft and sweet—Handel—and the two men stood at the top of the aisle chatting softly with the minister. Maroc, who was Jim's best man, was smiling at something he had said. It had all been so sudden, but very satisfactory. She had good feelings about Jim. He turned and caught her eye and smiled. And he was very handsome—those blue eyes and black eyelashes were quite something—and he looked rugged and somehow dependable. He was exactly what Léonie needed. It had been a long road to happiness, but at last it seemed as though it were within her grasp. Remembering Monsieur, she hoped so.

A shaft of sunlight filtered down the short aisle as the church door opened and Léonie entered on Alphonse's arm. She looked wonderful: her cream silk suit was soft, a flutter of pleats in the skirt, the simple jacket tied with a velvet ribbon at the waist. Her blond hair was pulled back into a gleaming chignon and she wore a wide-brimmed flowery hat and carried a small posy of peach-colored roses. Caro dabbed at the tears of happiness in her eyes.

She's beautiful, thought Jim, as she came toward him. My lovely bride. Her amber eyes met his, loving him. He took her hand and held it, and they smiled at each other. It was just them now, together for always.

Madame Frenard wiped her eyes. She had told Léonie that one day she'd find her happiness and now look at her. She'd never seen anyone look so happy. When Jim put the ring on her finger, her face was just like the shaft of sunlight when the door opened—she lit up inside. She reached for her husband's hand, holding it in hers. The best thing in life was to be with the man you loved.

Caro followed the bridal party into the vestry to sign the register, kissing Léonie through her tears. "But you shouldn't be crying," said Léonie, tenderly dabbing her face with a lace handkerchief.

"It's just because I'm so happy for you," sniffed Caro, "that's all. They're happy tears."

Alphonse took her hand. "We could always make it a double ceremony," he suggested.

"Oh, Alphonse, I'm happy as I am. You know I love you."

"I know," he said, kissing her, "forgive me, it's just a habit."

Jim burst out laughing. "Are they always like this?" he asked Léonie.

"Always—and they're the most 'married' couple possible."

"Well, Mrs. Jamieson, talking about married, how does it feel?"

She tilted her chin arrogantly, her eyes smiling at him from under the brim of her hat. "Mr. Jamieson," she murmured, "it feels wonderful."

⊰ 51 ⊱

ARMAND DE COURMONT lay in bed contemplating with satisfaction the day ahead of him. It was his twenty-first birthday, the sun was shining, and there was a beautiful dark-haired girl waiting in Paris to help him celebrate. He glanced at the clock on the mantel—seven-thirty—still early. He padded to the window and looked out across the pillared portico of the Château de Courmont. Hoskins, his father's English chauffeur, was already out there, his shirt-sleeves rolled up, adding a final loving polish to the already spotless scarlet lacquer of the new sports car. The radiator with its eagle mascot glittered in the early morning sun and the car's lovely low raking lines held a promise of power and speed. It was his birthday present from his father—the first of the new de Courmont sports cars and the one on which his father was placing his hopes for reviving his ailing automobile business. Armand knew that engine backward. He'd worked on the prototypes, he'd tested them, and he'd labored over them up to his elbows in grease along with the mechanics. It was a good car.

There was a clatter of hooves on the gravel as Gérard rode into view on his big bay hunter with Sebastião behind.

Armand threw open the window. "Hey, wait for me. I'll be down in a minute."

Throwing on his clothes, he ran along the corridor and down the stairs to the hall.

"Armand?"

His father emerged from the breakfast room, a cup of coffee in his hand.

He looks tired, thought Armand, as though he hasn't slept—not just last night, but in weeks. He felt a pang of pity, his father was such a desperately lonely man.

"Happy birthday, my boy," said Gilles with a smile. "Have you seen your present?"

"I saw it from my window, sir, I'm just going out there now to show it off to Sebastião and Gérard."

They walked together through the soaring malachite columns of the vast hall. "Well," said Gilles, "what do you think, Armand? Have we done it this time?"

"I'm sure of it, sir. It can't miss, it's a great machine. I'll bet in six months the sales figures will have skyrocketed."

"And what do *you* think, Gérard?" called Gilles.

"It's wonderful, Father, a beautiful car. Sebastião was just saying he'd love to take one back to Brazil with him."

"Trouble is I can't afford it yet," Sebastião added, laughing.

"Do what I did," said Armand, climbing into the driver's seat, "get your father to give you one as a birthday present."

He switched on the ignition, touching his foot gently on the accelerator. The horses backed away nervously as he spun the car around amid a splutter of gravel and sped off down the drive. "Yes," murmured Gilles with satisfaction, "it's a good car."

"See you later then, Father," called Gérard, heading for the river with Sebastião.

Gilles watched them go, two nice-looking young men on a nice sunny summer morning. It was a pity Gérard hadn't wanted to join him in the business, but he had Armand—and he couldn't have wished for anyone better. The concept for that new sports car was his and he had followed every stage of its production meticulously.

He wandered back into the hall, glancing at the big grandfather clock with its gilt pendulum ticking away the hours as it had done for two hundred years now. But it didn't make the time go by any faster. It was still only eight o'clock in the morning and he'd been up since five.

He could never sleep at the château, it oppressed him with its memories, though Marie-France, to her credit, had brought it to life; it wasn't the gloomy house of his childhood. She had spent a fortune refurbishing it and had done it beautifully. Marie-France spent most of her time here now and it felt more like her house than his. The house on the Ile Saint-Louis saw her rarely, and even his sons seemed to prefer living elsewhere when they were in Paris. Gérard had rooms with Sebastião do Santos, and Armand had taken an apartment closer to the factory, though he suspected he lived most of the time with some girl. And why not, he thought indulgently, the boy should enjoy himself.

De Courmont strode across the hall into his study. He'd reread the financial report from the man who had taken Verronet's place. God, he missed Verronet. How *could* the man have been stupid enough to get himself killed? Satère had been working for him for three years now and he still didn't seem able to get the details he needed the way Verronet had. His reports never showed anything more specific than where Léonie was and when—what city, what country, what theater. And sometimes whom she was with. One name had been cropping up often recently: James Jamieson, an American. The latest of her lovers, he supposed. It was the question that had run through his head in the sleepless hours of the night: What was he going to do about Jamieson? He knew the answer. Nothing. There was nothing he could do, unless he found Amélie—and that was a lost cause. There was no trace of the child, every possible lead had been followed. Verronet had been thorough. He would never find Amélie and without her he would never have Léonie. He put his head in his hands and stared sightlessly at the polished surface of the desk. Léonie! he thought helplessly. Oh, Léonie, you must come back to me soon, I can't stand this loneliness much longer.

Marie-France surveyed the table happily. It wasn't often that she had both her boys here, and even Gilles was putting himself out to be amusing. The thing that always surprised her was that he was such a charming man when he wanted to be. Why couldn't he be that way all the time? But Gilles was two people, even to his sons. He'd be the indulgent father one moment and the cold disinterested businessman the next—they had never known where they stood with him. They had come to terms with it years ago. Gilles was the only one to suffer now. He suffered, she knew it—and she knew why: he had never forgotten Léonie and that child.

"When Sebastião goes back to Brazil, Mother, I'd like go with him," said Gérard. "I feel I know his family as well as my own, I've heard so much about them."

"It's true," said Sebastião. "He reads my young cousin's letters, so he knows all the family squabbles."

"What do you say, Father?" asked Gérard.

"Yes, why not?" Gilles said absently, looking at his watch. Two-thirty. If he went back up to town now, he could catch the night train to Monte Carlo. He knew Léonie was there. "I must get back to Paris this afternoon," he said to Marie-France.

Can't he even wait till Armand's birthday lunch is over? she thought irritably. She lifted her glass. "Here's to you, Armand," she said with a smile for her son. "Happy birthday, my darling."

"And many more happy birthdays, my boy," said Gilles, smiling at his favorite son.

* * *

Armand lifted the long hood of the de Courmont, folding it back on its side to inspect the immaculate engine. He took out a wrench and tested a bolt, thrusting his hands beneath the gleaming pipes and fiddling with the wires. He thought he'd felt a faint wobble when he'd driven it to the garage, but everything seemed fine. Good. He'd leave in about half an hour, he could give his father a lift to Paris if he liked, it'd save him taking Hoskins. Wiping his hands on a rag, he pulled the hood back into place. It closed with a satisfying click and he smiled. It was a good, solid, well-crafted car.

Back in the house, he poked his head around the study door. "I'll be leaving in about half an hour, Father. I'll give you a lift if you like. We can see how she drives."

Gilles packed his papers away in his case and went to the drawing room to say good-bye to Marie-France. She was sitting by the open window, a swirl of colored wools beside her, working on a piece of tapestry. Her dark hair curled neatly around her face and she looked at him with those big skeptical brown eyes as he came in.

"I shall be leaving for Paris with Armand," he told her, "and then I expect to be out of town for a week or two."

"Where is it this time?" she asked with a faint smile. "Chicago or Cap Ferrat?"

"Does it matter?" he asked coldly.

"I don't know why you bother telling me, Gilles, it hasn't 'mattered' for years." She bent over her needlework and he watched her for a moment. They had been married for twenty-six years and they were strangers. He turned and walked quickly from the room.

Armand was waiting in the car. "Right," he said. "Let's give her a workout, Father. We'll see what she can do."

The long red car rushed along the country roads, controlled perfectly by Armand's capable hands, taking the corners steadily as he put her through her paces. He knew exactly how this engine should sound and it was like a symphony, every part in tune.

Armand glanced at the clock on the dashboard; it was almost six, which meant he'd be in Paris just before eight. He'd drop his father at Ile Saint-Louis and go straight on to Claudine's. She'd be waiting for him, wearing, he hoped, that pretty lilac robe, and then later he'd take her to dinner at Café Cézar, she'd enjoy it there.

The steering wheel trembled slightly under his hands, had they gone over a stone in the road? It felt all right now. Still, perhaps he should stop and check it out, wasn't that the same tremor he'd felt this morning? He glanced at the clock again, he was already late. He swung the big car around the bend into the hill. It had been a good birthday, he thought happily. Father had been civil, and he and Mother had seemed to get on all right. It was always a strain when they were together. Jesus, what was that? The tremor from the wheel ran up his arms and he took his foot off the accelerator. He felt rather than heard the crack of the steering column as it broke loose from its bearings and the next bend loomed before him. He slammed his foot on the brake and felt the car go into a skid, somersaulting twice before it landed upside down in the ditch, its wheels still spinning futilely in the air.

Gilles knew something must have happened but he couldn't think what, his mind didn't seem to be working properly. He forced his eyes open and looked around: everything was black. Panic rushed along his spine, he could feel himself trembling. He pushed desperately. His face was pressed into the black leather seat. Where was Hoskins? Or had he been driving? Oh, God, Armand. He pushed ineffectually at the weight above him, he had to get to Armand. Wait, he could hear voices, there were people, they would help him reach Armand. "Here," he called, his voice sounding thin and cracked, "here, help me. We must get my son."

The weight was lifted from his chest and a florid, anxious face looked down at him. "Don't move," said the man. "We've sent for the ambulance, you'd better just stay still until the doctor gets here and the police."

"But my son," he cried weakly, "you must help my son."

The man looked away from him. "All right," he said, "they'll be here in a minute." Poor devil, he thought sympathetically, looking across the road to where the young man lay. He'd already checked him and there was no doubt he was dead.

Sebastião watched Gérard pacing slowly up and down the corridor of the hospital. He wished desperately there were something he could do, something he could say that would help. He felt ill remembering Marie-France's stricken face, remembering what she had said. "Why wasn't it Gilles?" she'd screamed. "Why couldn't it have been him instead!" Gérard had put his arms around her and held her, his own agony visible on his stark face. "Maman," he whispered. "Maman, please. . . ." Her normally sweet face had set in a stony resolve. "I must go with you to the hospital," she said. "My husband is there. It is my duty."

Her duty! thought Sebastião in amazement. What could these people's lives be like? She was at her husband's bedside now. They had operated on his legs and he was still unconscious, but she refused to leave until she had spoken to him. And he knew that was what Gérard was worried about. What was she going to say to him?

"Gérard," he said, taking his arm, "let's go for a drink, there's no point in waiting here. The doctor said he won't come around for hours yet."

"I can't leave her here alone, Sebastião. I must stay with her."

Sebastião returned to his seat. "Very well," he said, "we'll wait."

Was it dawn, or had all the world suddenly lost its color? wondered Gilles, peering through half-closed eyes into a veiled gray twilight. He could make out a ceiling and a light in the middle. He turned his head slightly to the left and a pain shot through it, red pain like heat. Someone was there just by the bed. Damn, he wished he could see who it was. He tried to speak but his mouth felt odd; he couldn't move his tongue, it felt thick and heavy. He needed a drink of water, wouldn't someone give him a drink of water? He must speak! "Léonie?" he forced his tongue around the syllables. "Léonie?"

She leaned over him and he waited for the familiar scent. He couldn't see her properly, but he would know it was her by the jasmine.

"Gilles." It was Marie-France's voice, high-pitched and icy. "Gilles," she said, "I've been waiting here for you to wake up, because I wanted to be the one to tell you. Armand is dead. Dead because of *your* faulty car . . . *your* negligence. You killed our son, Gilles." Her face was implacable and her voice relentless. "You called for Léonie just now, Gilles, but she left you years ago. And I'm leaving you now. I never, in my whole life, want to see you again."

He heard the click as the door closed quietly behind her and he was alone again with the terrible truth. Armand was dead. His son was dead! He wanted to scream, to blast his agony from him in a spear of sound. This was how it felt when your son died, this tearing agony. An image of Charles d'Aureville's young smiling face framed in his binoculars flashed through his mind, he must have been about Armand's age when he had died. And his family had felt what he was feeling now. Except Charles's death was no accident, he had killed him . . . and now she said he had killed Armand. "Oh, God," he cried. But God was not merciful.

❧ 52 ❧

A CHILL WIND blew from the ocean, crackling the tarpaulins lashed across the small boats in the marina at Deauville, gusting viciously along the pier. Jim turned up his coat collar, lengthening his stride as he turned the corner into a side street just off the seafront. The street was narrow, lined with two-story gray buildings, mostly small shops—a chandler's, a sail maker's, a garage, a small warehouse that smelled strongly of fish, and a couple of bars, both with nautical names, the Pêcheurs and the Trident. The Bar des Pêcheurs on the left at the end of the street was the one he was looking for.

The bead curtain rattled in the wind and a faded green shutter flapped against the window, swinging back and forth on a single hinge. Jim pushed through the curtain and found himself in a small lobby facing a shabby wooden door. The wind swept in after him as he pushed it open and went inside. The bar was brightly lit and cleaner than he had expected. Behind the familiar French zinc-topped counter a small mustached man was drying glasses and smoking a Gauloise, coughing. A couple of old fishermen playing dominoes in the corner looked up as he came in.

Jim took a seat at the counter. "Beer, please," he said, placing his wallet on the counter.

The man eyed it warily. "Alsace or Normandy?"

"I'll take Alsace."

He opened the bottle and poured the beer carefully, placing it on the counter in front of him. The foam was cream color and the beer tasted cold and good. "Have one yourself," suggested Jim with an amiable smile in the barman's direction.

"Merci, monsieur." The barman thanked him laconically, pouring himself a shot of Pernod.

"Not too busy today," said Jim.

"We're never too busy at this time of the year."

"I don't suppose there's much fishing from Deauville anymore," said Jim. "It's become too smart for that. Too many yachts now, there's no room for fishing boats."

"That's true, monsieur."

"I hear you're a pretty good sailor yourself."

"Who told you that, monsieur?"

"The barman at the Grand, Jean-Luc Grenier, he said to mention his name."

"My wife's cousin," said the barman, permitting himself a faint smile.

"Yeah. He told me you sometimes crewed for the races—when they need someone to fill in."

His face lit up suddenly. "Yes, monsieur, and I'm very good. But you can't be looking for a crew now, the races are over until next season."

"No. No, I'm not. I'm looking for someone else. Someone who also picks up a casual job crewing. A big guy, sort of reddish hair, running to fat a bit." He picked up the wallet and opened it suggestively. "He must have been around for years now, probably disappeared for a while and then came back. And he's not a local man."

The barman leaned on the counter eyeing the wallet. "Why do you want to find this man?" he asked, sipping his Pernod.

Jim sat back, closing the wallet with a snap. "I think that's my business."

The man jumped. "Yes, yes of course. I was just curious. Well, I suppose I could tell you what I know. . . ." His eyes were on the wallet and Jim took out a note and laid it on the counter. He took out a second note and laid it next to the first. "Well?"

The man swept the notes into his pocket and took another sip of Pernod. "There is only one man who looks like that, and he's here only in the summer . . . and not every summer. He picks up a casual job for the season, ferrying pleasure trips or working in the marina, a bit of painting, a bit of carpentering, things like that. He was here last season, but he's not popular—there have been fights, drinking. . . ." He shrugged. "He is not a good man to know, monsieur."

Jim took out another note, placing it on the counter. "After the season," he said quietly, "where does he go then?"

"I think he goes south, monsieur, that's all I know. I'd guess that he goes to Cannes or Monte Carlo—their season goes on much later, right into the winter. There's always work to be had in the marinas there."

"And his name?"

The barman refilled his glass with Pernod. "That I can't tell you, monsieur, but if you ask at the marina someone there might know—he worked quite a bit for Lesage this summer."

Jim finished his beer in a gulp and made for the door. "Thank you," he called over his shoulder.

The barman sipped his Pernod, shivering in the draft that whipped in through the door as Jim closed it behind him.

Was this it? thought Jim excitedly. Had his hunch paid off? He had guessed the man must be an itinerant laborer, moving from resort to resort as the mood and the season took him. Deauville was a smart resort, there was plenty of money to be made there, plenty of jobs. Why wouldn't he have returned after a few years, when everything had blown over? After all, he had been accused of nothing—there was nothing to be accused of. And people's memories where short. Now all he needed was a name.

Lesage was the biggest proprietor on the marina. Their premises took up half the pier and their boats—pleasure steamers for day trips, small boats for hire for fishing, and the smart yachts of their customers keeled for the winter—ranged along the waterfront.

The gray-haired man behind the desk put on his jacket hastily as Jim entered the office.

"Good morning, sir." He smiled. "What can I do for you?"

"Good morning. You've got some nice boats out there."

The man beamed. "We have several for sale, if you're interested. Unless, of course, you prefer one specially made to your specifications. We have our own yard, sir, just down the coast."

"I might be interested in a boat," Jim replied casually, "a smallish one—my wife fancies herself a sailor. Although with her on board I expect I'll have to pick up someone extra to crew for me."

"No problem, sir, there are always extra hands looking for work in the season—they'll crew, sir, and keep the boat clean and in trim. We can arrange that for you."

"A friend of mine said he had a good fellow last season, a reddish-haired chap. I forget his name."

"Red hair, sir? You must mean Marigny. Oh, but I wouldn't recommend him, sir—he's a good worker all right, but he's an odd fellow. No, we weren't happy with him at all." He sucked in his cheeks and rubbed his hands together agitatedly. "A little too fond of the brandy, sir, to be honest. I think we can do better than that for you. Now, can I show you our craft, sir? We have several that would be suitable for your needs."

"If you don't mind," said Jim, heading for the door, "I'll come back later. I'm late for an appointment."

He just made the three o'clock train to Paris and settled back against the cushions studying the name he had written in his notebook. Marigny. Possibly the man who assassinated Charles d'Aureville. And hopefully the key to Léonie's freedom from her past. All he had to do now was find this Marigny. He glanced at his watch, if he were lucky he might make the night train to Nice. It would take time, but he'd comb every marina, every harbor and pier between Menton and Marseilles until he found him.

*　*　*

Maroc picked up the copy of the French newspaper *Le Monde* from the shop in the arcade near Brown's Hotel in London, meaning to read it later, after the show. He glanced at the headlines and ran his eye quickly over the page. The report of the serious injuries to the Duc de Courmont and the death of his younger son in an accident involving the latest de Courmont sports car blazed from the page in graphic captions and heavy type.

Folding the paper carefully so that the wind couldn't blow it, he read the report quickly. Although Monsieur had suffered crushing injuries to the chest and legs, he was expected to live. My God, he thought bitterly, why couldn't it have been him!

He strode back along Dover Street and into the hotel. They had two more nights left in London, should he tell Léonie now, or after she'd completed the shows? He remembered the last time he'd held back information from her. But this was different—he'd tell her now. She'd want to know.

Léonie was up and dressed and planning on doing some shopping. She wanted to buy things for Jim—nice English things, soft cashmere pullovers and striped silk pajamas—there were such wonderful places in Burlington Arcade and Jermyn Street. She smiled as she brushed her hair, it was so much nicer when you loved someone. And when you were loved. "It took you a long time, Léonie Jamieson," she told herself, "but you finally found out what it was that makes you 'belong.' "

Maroc called to her from the sitting room and she put down the brush and walked through to see him. "Hello," she said, kissing him lightly on the cheek, "would you like to come shopping with me?"

"There's some news in the paper, Léonie. It's about Monsieur. There's been an accident."

She stared at him, eyes wide with apprehension.

"He's not dead, Léonie, but he is badly injured. It was in one of his own cars; his younger son was killed."

"Killed!" She remembered the two little boys solemnly eating ice cream in the Café de Paris in Monte Carlo all those years ago—poor, poor little boy. And Monsieur was still alive. God, it was ironic—an innocent boy dies and he lives! She held the paper in trembling hands, serious injuries to the chest and legs—an image of his strong hard body pressed close to hers flashed through her mind. No. He couldn't be injured, nothing could ever hurt him. He was invincible. Hadn't he proved that over the years? She didn't want to think of his body broken like that, he was better dead; he should have died.

Maroc took the paper from her hand and she gazed at him despairingly. "Oh, Maroc, why? Why wasn't it he who died? Is there no justice?"

"I don't know about justice," he replied, "but you could call it retribution—a young life for a young life. He'll suffer now, Léonie, make no mistake about it."

❧ 53 ❧

THE HOTEL VILLA D'AUREVILLE on Copacabana was exactly like a small and exquisite country house. Its walls were plain and white and its ceilings dark-beamed. The polished wooden floors were dotted with wonderful rugs brought by Isabelle from the Château d'Aureville—the opulent blue of Kermans, the glorious golds and lilac of a Kashan prayer rug, a creamy golden Senne, and the multitude of reds of Ferahan and Bokhara. The most delicate and rare examples decorated the walls, glowing silkily from dim corners, alongside portraits of past d'Aurevilles and vast canvases of glorious flowers, so exquisitely painted by a long-dead Dutch artist that you could almost smell the perfume of the roses and peonies, whose living cousins crowded from vases and bowls on tables and cabinets and were massed in baskets along the corridors.

Comfort, thought Isabelle, walking through her hotel, and *luxury.* The luxury of only having the best. Not ostentation—that was never what she would seek. The wide sofas were *comfortable,* covered in muted floral chintz in faded corals and greens, or soft brocades in pale watery blues and buttery gold, piled invitingly with cushions. Small tables with peach-shaded lamps, carefully placed to give pools of light, held magazines and books and on one circular table in the salon was an enormous jigsaw puzzle, half-completed and which no guest could resist trying. The whole effect was of a home that had been there for a couple of centuries, but without its inconveniences.

The bathrooms had the most up-to-date equipment and the biggest, softest towels, the beds were the most temptingly comfortable, and the embroidered linens the finest Europe could provide. There were fresh flowers in every room and bedside books for insomniacs and little bottles of water imported from France with a silver tray on which were brandy and soda and biscuits. Every guest was known by name and their preferences as to rooms, food, and wine, their likes and dislikes and special requests, were kept on file so that when they returned they were greeted as though they had never been away and everything was exactly the way they would have liked it, but without the effort of having to ask.

It was an oasis in a desert—a corner of France blended into Brazil—and it was perfect. At least Isabelle thought it was, and as their ten rooms and eight suites were always full, she assumed her guests thought so, too. And Amélie certainly did. She spent more time here than at home these days. It had been hard for her at first when Edouard had married, but thank heaven Xara had been sensitive enough to understand how Amélie had felt. Now that the baby was on its way, Amélie was as excited as Edouard.

She could see her now at the reception desk talking with Senhor Vasconcellos. I hope he's not being difficult, she thought, hurrying toward them. Senhor Vasconcellos was one of those men who are born complainers, nothing was ever right while he was here, and yet he always left thanking them for a wonderful stay and promising to be back again soon—and he always was!

"I expect you've had a tiring journey, Senhor Vasconcellos," Amélie was saying. "Paulinho will take you up to your suite—yes, it's the same one, the Auvergne, and I'll see that a bath is run for you and send up a tray of tea ... camomile, wasn't it? You'll find the menu for dinner in your room—we have some marvelous grouse in from Yorkshire that I'm sure you would enjoy."

Isabelle watched her with a smile. Well, well. Who would have thought it! Vasconcellos was smiling and satisfied, he obviously felt welcome and cared for and that was what it was all about. The fact that it cost the earth was not important, there were always people who would pay for the best.

"Madame la Comtesse"—he bowed over her hand, smiling—"your granddaughter has inherited your charm. She has taken care of everything for me."

"I'm very happy to hear it, Senhor Vasconcellos. I understand you're to be with us for a week this time. I hope you'll be able to lunch with me one day at the Pavillon?"

"But of course, madame, I would be delighted."

He hurried after Paulinho, and Amélie grinned at her grandmother. "I'm getting quite good at it," she said triumphantly. "I think I could almost run this place myself."

"Not quite," said Isabelle dryly, "but you're doing very well. You're learning."

"Grandmère, when I finish school next term, I don't want to go to college. I want to work here, with you."

Isabelle stared at her in surprise. "But Amélie, you could go to America, there are wonderful colleges there for you."

"I know, I know, but this is what I *like* to do, Grandmère. Please say yes. You *know* how much help I am to you already."

Her lovely face shone with enthusiasm. She was almost sixteen years old and beautiful. Flesh had finally rounded out her limbs and she was tall, not elegant yet, but with the grace of a young animal, and she approached everything with the same eager energy she always had. Whatever she was doing was the most absorbing thing in the world at that moment and whoever she was with was the most interesting—her attention was total. Whether it was Roberto telling her of his latest exploit on the polo field, or Vasconcellos voicing a complaint, she would fix him with those marvelous tawny eyes and listen with slightly parted lips and such breathless attention that he felt he was the most interesting and important person in the world. Amélie had a devastating charm that at present was totally innocent but, thought Isabelle, once she learns how to use it, we're in for trouble. Or would be if she weren't so devoted to Roberto.

"Well, Grandmère?" pleaded Amélie. "I really don't want to go away to college. I want to stay here with you and . . ."

Her voice trailed off. Had she been going to say Edouard, wondered Isabelle, or Roberto? "I'll speak to Edouard," she promised, "though I'm not sure he's going to like it, Amélie, you know he thinks you should go to college."

Amélie beamed. "If you just tell him how much help I could be to you, he's sure to give in."

"We shall see. Oh, by the way, there's a letter for you from Sebastião. It came this morning. It's on the shelf over there."

"Fantastic!" Amélie grabbed the letter and tucked it into her pocket. "See you later, Grandmère," she called, heading for the beach.

She always took his letters to the beach to read. She would open them facing the green immensity of the Atlantic, feeling that surely she must be facing France and that made her closer to him somehow. Of course it was silly, but she'd always done it, and now that she was older she felt superstitious about it. She cast off her sandals, leaving them beneath a palm tree, and ran barefoot across the wide stretch of still-warm sand to the water's edge, facing it symbolically and ripping open the envelope. Three pages— oh, good, it was a long one, and about time, too; it had been ages since she'd heard from him. He was in Italy! Gosh, he was *so* lucky, Paris and now Italy. He was traveling with his friend, they were in Venice, he was making sketches for her—the bridges, the gondolas, the palazzos, and piazzas, all were glorious. He thought of her and missed her, she could write to him Poste Restante, Roma, where he was going next. He hoped things were better between her and Roberto.

She stuffed the letter back in its envelope and sank down onto the sand, knees crossed, chin in her hand, staring at the horizon. Roberto. She hadn't seen him in over a week. Of course, he was studying for his exams, and she knew that they were very important. Getting into a good university depended on it. "Oxford," he'd said grandly, "or Heidelberg"—he always chose the romantic-sounding places, but never seemed too sure what he wanted to study. He would think about it later, he said, after the exams.

Oxford, she remembered bleakly, was lost in the middle of England some-where. She'd lose him if he went there, just as she had lost Sebastião, except that she couldn't trust Roberto to write as dutifully as he did. The only ad-vantage was that it would get him away from Diego. It's not a contest with Roberto as the prize, she thought, it's just that I love him. What will I do when he leaves? She stood up, brushing the sand from her skirt. Well, he hadn't gone yet, she'd go see him this evening and wish him luck on the exam tomorrow.

Diego and Roberto walked along Rua Ouvidor deep in conversation, oblivious to the passersby. They were an attractive pair, Diego dark and swaggering and Roberto blond and athletic, both deeply tanned from a summer spent on the *fazenda* and their year-round outdoor life. They stopped at the Café Miltinho and took a seat at one of the tables outside.

"Two *cafezinhos* and two Cachaça," commanded Diego to a passing waiter.

"I'm not having Cachaça," said Roberto, "and neither should you."

Diego shrugged indifferently. "What's the matter? Think you might get drunk on one Cachaça?"

Roberto sighed. "I know I won't," he said, "but I also know it won't stop at one and we're supposed to be studying for the exam tomorrow."

"Oh, come on, Roberto, you're taking it all too seriously. You know you'll breeze through the exams."

"That's the trouble, I don't know, and if I keep wasting my time with you I know I *won't!* Listen, Diego. How much time have we put in this week? My father thinks I'm at your place studying with you—and yours thinks you're with me!"

Diego laughed. "Come on, stop worrying. You'll get a C, you always do."

"But I need at least a B to go to Europe . . . and it would really please my father."

"Why bother, Roberto, he'll be happy with a C. If you get more, he'll expect it every time. Just do enough to keep them happy, that's what I say."

"Damn it, Diego, I *want* to go to Europe next year!"

Diego hunched his shoulders angrily, drinking the Cachaça in one gulp. "Terrific," he scowled, "you'll be off enjoying yourself in Europe and I'll be stuck out in the wilds on the *fazenda.*"

"Maybe if you worked a bit harder you'd be able to go, too."

"There's no chance! The estate's in a mess. My father says he needs all the help he can get. Why did this country ever get rid of its slaves?" he added nastily. "The Chinese immigrants are no good and the Italians are even worse—none of them can work—and now he expects me to go home and help out. Goddamn it, it's not fair!"

Roberto knew that the Benavente *fazenda* was in trouble and it wasn't the only one, serious labor problems and a couple of poor seasons were wreaking havoc on many of the old coffee estates. "If my father were in trouble I'd help him," he said.

Diego looked at him calculatingly. Did he really mean that? Yeah, he probably did. He'd give up going to Europe to work on the *fazenda* if his father needed him. There was a side to Roberto that was unquestionably stupid—or maybe "soft" was a better word, the exploitable side. "It's my father's fault the *fazenda* is in trouble, why the hell should I have to suffer because of it?"

"Working on the *fazenda* is hardly suffering."

"It is when you hate it as much as I do. My brothers both got lucky, they were old enough to escape before this happened. Now there's only me left—and my sister, but she's no help. God, I can't stand her, she's not even pretty."

"That's not fair, she's all right, and Amélie says she's very sweet."

"Sweet! Amélie *would* say that! Damn it, why did we have to get stuck with such useless girls? Listen, Roberto, do you remember what I said before, about Madame Susana's? Let's go where they've got real girls!"

Roberto stared at him. The vision of scarlet garters on soft white thighs and long black-stockinged legs flashed through his mind; he dreamed of them every night, thighs and soft breasts and how they would feel, and what she would smell like.

"Susana knows me," bragged Diego, catching the hesitation in Roberto's eyes, "she'll fix us up with some real beauties. I tell you, Roberto, this Swedish one I had before was fantastic ... she was insatiable ... I had to screw her all night."

Roberto gulped the Cachaça. "I don't have time, you know I've got to work tonight. Besides, we don't have any money."

Diego pulled out a wad of greasy notes from his shirt pocket. "What do you call that?" he said, waving it in front of Roberto's nose.

"Where did you get that?"

"I saved it up for a rainy day! Jesus, what does it matter where I got it? It's here, I have it. Let's go!"

"I'll bet it's not enough for Madame Susana's anyway."

Diego frowned, counting it quickly. He was right. "Well then, I know another place, a little cheaper, a little rougher, a little more ... exciting? They let you do whatever you want there." He smiled. "Come on, Roberto," he whispered. "They'll look after us ... lovely girls, two, maybe three at a time." He leaned closer. "You can't imagine what they may get up to . . . you're going to love it, Roberto."

Roberto felt himself tremble at the thought, but he couldn't go, he shouldn't go. Oh, my God, two girls or even three—what must they do to you?

Diego pushed back his chair and tossed a couple of coins into the saucer on the table. "Well," he said, "*I'm* going. . . ."

"Wait," said Roberto, pushing back his chair hurriedly, "wait for me."

The dingy marble stairs leading to the Hotel Orfeo were protected from the eyes of curious passersby by a rattling bead curtain and an enormous doorman. He leaned aganst the wall, burly arms folded, his peaked cap with Hotel Orfeo inscribed across the front in faded letters tilted over his eyes, seemingly unaware of anyone or anything. Sweat beaded his massive chest, staining his white shirt, and he scratched the day-old growth of beard on his chin contemplatively, gazing at the dusty sidewalk.

Diego walked confidently to the door and stopped suddenly, staring down at the large foot that had appeared between him and the stairway. "You kids got money?" The doorman's eye flickered over them.

Roberto stared at him nervously; his flat tone held a threat. "Sure." Diego produced the wad of notes. "We've got plenty. You know me, I've been here before."

The foot was removed indifferently and the doorman went back to contemplating the sidewalk.

"Are you sure about this place?" whispered Roberto, following Diego up the stairs. "It looks a bit rough to me."

"Wait," said Diego over his shoulder, "you'll see, it's the best place in Rio."

A dusty velvet curtain covered the entrance and he pushed it aside, swaggering confidently into the room. Roberto hovered wide-eyed behind him. The place was festooned from floor to ceiling in deep dusty red velvet looped with tarnished gold cords and fringes and lit by dim glass chandeliers. Their thin glimmer illuminated the bored, painted faces and naked breasts of the dozen or so girls sitting around on the sofas lining the walls. It was intolerably hot. A couple of lethargic ceiling fans whirred monotonously, doing little more than moving the dust. Beads of sweat trickled between the pointed breasts of the girl as she came toward them.

Roberto felt a shock of disappointment. There were no black stockings and scarlet garters, no gay laughing blond women in satin knickers drinking champagne. These girls were not here to flirt and tempt and seduce; they were ready for action. Am I? he wondered in panic. What do we do now?

"Senhores." The girl's lips were red and wet-looking as she smiled at them. She had pretty teeth, he thought abstractedly, white and even, and her breasts were wonderful. He'd never seen a girl's breasts before—he lowered his eyes quickly. She wore a peacock-colored scarf wrapped around her waist and a pair of high-heeled shoes. And that was all. Her thighs were heavy and the triangle of hair was dark and crisp-looking. He felt hypnotized by the triangle, that secret place. "Welcome to the Orfeo," she said. "What can I get you to drink?"

"Cachaça," commanded Diego, putting his arm around her and caressing her breasts familiarly. She giggled and pressed closer to him as Roberto averted his eyes. The curtain was flung back suddenly and a caricature of a woman appeared in the doorway. Her mouth was a shapeless scarlet gash in a white-powdered face that was folded and creased with fat and age. Small pale eyes as hard and as dead as discarded nutshells peered from spiked black lashes and her thin reddish hair was brushed in elaborate curls around the mask of her face. A shiny, low-cut black dress, bejeweled with the glittering rewards of her profession, slithered over her shapeless body and rings flashed from every finger of her plump hands. Her face contorted into a replica of a smile. "Good afternoon, senhores," she said, "and what can we offer you this afternoon? You see our girls . . . and we have, of course, a selection of 'specialties.' Just tell me what you like and I'll make sure you have it; payment in advance, of course."

"Of course," said Diego coolly, tossing back his glass of Cachaça at a gulp, watching her disparagingly as she tottered toward the bar in shoes that were too tight for her plump feet. "She calls herself Madame Victoria," he murmured mockingly to Roberto, "because she thinks she looks like the old English queen." He laughed. "But that's one of the advantages of a place like this: they'll be anyone you ask . . . anything your fancy takes." A dark girl sauntered across the floor and stopped in front of him. She flicked back her hair and licked her wide pink lips invitingly. "I'm Marisa," she said, moving closer. Roberto gasped as Diego touched her heavy breasts, feeling them, lifting their weight, crushing them without tenderness under his groping hands. His fingers closed over her erect nipples, twisting them cruelly. The girl screamed in protest. "She's a cow," Diego said. "Let's see what else there is."

"Jesus, Diego, you didn't have to hurt her like that!" cried Roberto.

"You don't know these girls, they're used to anything. I told you, you can do what you want here."

Roberto drank his Cachaça rapidly, aware of the waiting eyes of the girls on the sofa. He felt the sweat trickle down his back and reached for another drink, watching as Diego settled himself between two of the girls, who giggled as they wrapped pale naked arms around him. "Come on, Roberto, bring the bottle over here and join us," he called.

Roberto walked cautiously across the room, stumbling slightly as the strong Cachaça hit him, hearing the girls laugh as though from a distance. He paused, shaking his head to clear it. That was better. He sat down carefully on the edge of the red plush sofa, staring into those waiting eyes—brown eyes smiling at him mockingly, blue eyes sullen and impatient, eager to get it over with, green eyes that had seen it all before—welcoming scarlet smiles on blank faces, naked breasts with rouged nipples, predatory hands that fluttered over him, caressing his hair, his face, his thighs. A girl settled herself on his lap, putting her arms around his neck, and desire surged through him so uncontrollably he was afraid he'd make a fool of himself. He tood a deep breath and she wriggled appreciatively, laughing. "I'm Romana," she murmured. "Here, I have another drink for you." She held the glass to his lips. "Let me do it for you, there, drink it up. My, but you're pretty. I'm lucky today. I don't usually have boys as pretty as you."

She had wild red hair and pale blue eyes and skin the color of fresh milk. He put his hand on her breast, blue-veined and soft. "That's better," she whispered. "Don't be shy." She leaned back, pulling his head down, and his mouth found her hard pink nipples. "Isn't that better . . . isn't it nice? Ah, yes, you like that, don't you?" He was lost in the sensation of her breasts, her soft flesh, her nakedness.

Diego pushed the dark-haired girl from his lap and stood for a moment watching them. Romana smiled at him secretively as he walked across the room to speak to Madame Victoria. Diego wanted to laugh. It had been so much easier than he had thought, Roberto hadn't been able to resist.

With all that Cachaça in him and the services of a couple of the girls, he'd never get through those exams tomorrow. He'd have to stay in Brazil. With me, he thought triumphantly. He couldn't have borne it if Roberto had left. He'd have been stuck out there alone on the *fazenda* with no money, no girls—nothing! Now he had him. His hand trembled as he whispered in Madame Victoria's ear, counting out the notes. Romana nodded as the madame gestured to the corridor.

"This way, my blond boy," she said, pulling Roberto to his feet and putting an arm around his waist to support him along the corridor.

His knees felt odd and this room looked odd—weren't the walls too close, or was it that the bed was so big? He fell backward onto it, turning his head away—the light hurt his eyes. Romana untied the scarf from her waist and flung it across the lamp, dimming it to a red glow. She looked warm now, he thought dazedly, warm and soft. She unbuttoned his shirt, sliding it from his shoulders, and he put his hands on her breasts as she unbuttoned his pants. She laughed as she eased them over the bulge of his erection. "Oh, yes," she murmured, "oh, yes, my boy, you're ready all right."

She straddled his body, leaning over him so that her breasts tickled his chest, the crisp red triangle of hair rubbed against him, she was warm, moist, soft. He was going to die from excitement, to burst, to explode; she was doing something to him, touching him, rubbing him. . . . Oh, my God, he was inside her, sliding, rubbing; she was squeezing him inside her, crushing his testicles with her hands. Oh, God, he was coming.

Diego and the dark-haired girl rolled next to them, on the bed, naked, laughing. He felt wetness as Romana moved away. His head reeled. He felt exhausted, drained.

Roberto awoke with a start. He was still lying on the bed, naked, and he could hear the murmur of voices and soft cries from somewhere close beside him. Opening his eyes he saw Diego crouched next to him. He was watching the two girls. They lay together in a tangle of arms and parted legs, caressing each other, kissing, tongues flickering, nipple pressed against nipple, hands searching. Roberto's body throbbed in response, his throat was dry and the Cachaça flowed in his veins. He shut his eyes. The image of the two bodies still burned behind them, scarlet in the lamplight. He felt a hand snake across his belly, a tongue flicked across his thigh, closer, closer. A second soft mouth fastened on his, and Romana's red hair brushed across his face as the dark girl bent over and took him in her mouth. Oh, he couldn't bear it, she was wonderful. He moaned and bit at Romana's flickering tongue. He could see Diego behind Romana and heard her gasp as he thrust himself into her. Oh, my God, he was fucking her. He kissed her again, sucking on her tongue, watching as Diego ground himself into her. He couldn't stand it, his body trembled; he closed his eyes, lost in an ecstasy of flesh and sensation—writhing, touching, trembling. The dark girl moved away from him; there was a new mouth, new hands, harder, more forceful hands, a familiar, more brutal mouth. He screamed with lust; his body was rocketing into new heights, new explosions of light, color, fantasy. It was Diego and he knew it. And he wanted it. It was the ultimate pleasure.

❧ 54 ❦

IT WAS FIVE-THIRTY on an August afternoon in Key West and the day was following a familiar pattern. First the warm pleasant early morning, then a gradual building of heat and rising humidity, until by evening it was stifling. Amélie sat by the open window of her room at the Villa Encantada, watching the purple clouds banking over the bay while the earth waited in breathless silence. No bird called, no insect buzzed, and even the rattling palm fronds were stilled. Then promptly at six o'clock, the jagged fluorescent fork of lightning split the lowering sky, its brilliant zigzagging blue plunging into the bay as thunder rolled across the heavens, rattling the timbers of Villa Encantada. Simultaneously the first heavy drops of rain began to fall, blocking out the angry sea, drumming on the roof and bouncing off the terrace, streaming from gutters and steps and flooding down the hill.

The ritual evening storm lasted for an hour and then quite suddenly the rain would stop and the sky would begin to brighten, the evening sun would reemerge and the sodden ground begin to steam as it dried in the heat. Birds trilled happily, insects continued where they had left off, and the palms rustled once more in the small fresh breeze. In a little while the terrace would be dry and they would sit out again, enjoying the cooler air and the smells of the garden refreshed by the rain, contemplating whether to go down the hill to the St. James for dinner or whether to barbecue the fish she and Edouard had caught that day. They were getting quite good at it—once Edouard had even caught a shark, a small one that the boatman had superstitiously cast back into the water.

Tonight Xara seemed especially tired and Amélie glanced at her anxiously. She was sitting in the big rattan chair with her feet up on the stool; the bulk of her full-term pregnancy made her look uncomfortable. Xara was enormous and even her own amazed eyes wondered how her body could cope with the expanding needs of the twin babies that kicked and wriggled contentedly inside her.

"I'm really not hungry tonight, Amélie," she said with a smile. "You go with Edouard to the hotel for dinner and bring me back some mango ice cream." The local ice-cream parlor had come to know them well. Xara's sudden passion for mango and Amélie's for chocolate with marshmallow had become, like the storm, a nightly ritual.

"Are you sure you're all right?" asked Edouard with concern.

She looked so tired and he knew that she was having trouble sleeping. "Why don't we stay here with you?" he said, taking her hand and kissing it. "I don't want to leave you alone."

"I'm all right, Edouard . . . I'm just pregnant. I'm certainly not ill. Besides, I'll sleep better if you're not here."

"Very well, then, if you're sure. Come on, Amélie. I'll buy you the biggest steak at the St. James."

They walked with their arms around each other down the sandy path, turning to wave at the corner as Xara waved back, thanking heaven that finally things had turned out so well between her and Amélie. It had been difficult until Amélie had realized that there was no threat to her relationship with Edouard, and though Amélie would never think of her as a mother, they were friends. She closed her eyes happily. She needed a couple of hours to herself. She knew these babies meant to be born that night, she had known all day.

Edouard sipped his wine and watched Amélie munching her steak appreciatively. She still veered between uncertain adolescent and young lady, though nowadays, he thought regretfully, she was more often the young lady. Roberto's unexplained banishment to the *fazenda* had left Amélie bewildered and lonely and it had been Xara's suggestion to take her to Florida with them. "Amélie will be company for me," she had said, "when you're busy poring over plans with the architects, or have to dash off to Miami."

"Edouard," Amélie interrupted his thoughts. "Why do you think Roberto hasn't written to me?"

Her face was worried and he felt that pang of regret and helplessness that a man feels for his daughter when, because she is no longer a child, it becomes impossible to shield her from life's bruises. He wished for a moment that she was still a carefree six-year-old tomboy; it had all been so easy then. "I'm not sure, Amélie, but it's probably because he's working so hard."

She put down her knife and fork and contemplated the tablecloth. She didn't know what Roberto had done, only that he hadn't come home for two nights—he hadn't even shown up for his important exams—and when he had finally come home she'd heard that he looked terrible. No one would tell her, but she'd pieced the story together from the maids' gossip and from snatches of conversation between Isabelle and Edouard and Edouard and Xara. He'd been disheveled and ill and he'd been confined to the house for a week. She hadn't been allowed to see him—no one had—and it was the only time in her life she could remember seeing Francisco do Santos in a rage. Luiza had tried to calm him, to tell him that it had been just a boyish prank, but he had been adamant. There would be no European university for Roberto—he automatically failed the exam by his absence. He was banished to the *fazenda* for three months while his father contemplated what to do with him. "He can work out in the fields with the men," he had said. "The hard work'll do him good, give him time to clear his head." But Diego was at the *fazenda,* too.

"It's all Diego Benavente's fault, you know," she said seriously, "whatever happened, it was because of him. He's a bad influence on Roberto. But because Teo Benavente is a good friend of Francisco's, no one seems to notice. Diego is bad, Edouard . . . I know it."

"Are you sure it's not just that you're a little bit jealous of him, Amélie? You've always thought of Roberto as *your* friend, just the two of you together. That was all right when you were kids, but now you're growing up. You'll be sixteen soon—and Roberto is eighteen. He's a young man, he'll have to make his own way in the world."

She pushed back her hair impatiently. Why would no one except Sebastião see how bad Diego was? "I think he's evil," she said passionately, her amber eyes glinting with tears. "I know Roberto will have his own life, but all this has happened because of Diego, and I'm sure it's *because* of Diego that he hasn't written. Don't you see, I'd rather he was away at a university in Europe, at least he'd write, he'd tell me things ... he'd share things with me."

Edouard sighed. "Perhaps you are right, Amélie, but Roberto is down on the *fazenda* as a punishment. I hardly think he's having fun with Diego. We must wait until he gets back and then see what happens. Come on," he said, taking her hand, "let's go and watch the sunset over the bay and then we'll get the ice cream for Xara. I bet I know what flavor you're going to have."

"Bet you don't," she said, cheering up.

"Chocolate with marshmallow?"

"No!" she said, slipping her arm through his. "Tonight it's peach. I feel like peaches."

The ice cream lay forgotten in a melting puddle on the kitchen table. They had returned to find that Xara was already in labor. "My girls are on their way," said Edouard, grinning.

"Our boys," Xara had corrected him gently.

"Boys or girls, I'm happy," he promised.

Amélie waited on the terrace with Edouard, watching the twinkling lights of the town below them. She had wondered how she would feel when the time came and now she knew. She heard Xara cry out, it was terrible, frightening, she didn't care about anything else, not the babies—nothing. Oh, God, she prayed, just let Xara be all right.

Edouard put his arm around her and she turned to hug him, hiding her face against his chest.

"It's all right, Amélie," he said, stroking her soft hair. "She said to tell you it's all right."

Vicente d'Aureville was born at three in the morning. Edouard stood beside Xara, smiling down at their small scrap of a son. "Isn't he the most beautiful baby you've ever seen?" she murmured proudly.

"The most beautiful." He smiled. "And you're the loveliest mother. I love you, Xara—and I love him."

"Wait," she cautioned him with a smile. "Save some love for Jean-Paul—he's next."

Jean-Paul was born exactly two hours after Vicente and weighed one pound less. But he was just as beautiful and just as perfect, thought Amélie, gazing at them in awe.

They lay in twin cradles, their crumpled pink faces looking like flowers still in bud, eyes tightly shut against the alien new light, as exhausted as their mother from their long journey into life.

"Xara, they're wonderful," she breathed, touching a tiny hand, marveling at the perfect fingernails, fearful for its very smallness. "I love them already. I can't wait to hold them."

"You shall, darling, as soon as they're awake. They're yours, too, you know—your brothers."

Amélie looked at them regretfully. She's being nice, she thought, they're cousins really, not brothers. She glanced at Xara, lying back against the pillows. She looked exhausted but lovely in a fresh blue nightdress with a lacy shawl around her shoulders. My own mother must have felt like that when she had me, she thought, and Charles, my father, must have stood by my crib and admired me, just like that. "Xara," she said, sitting on the bed and taking her hand, "what does it feel like to be a mother?"

"Oh, Amélie"—she smiled at her gently—"you can't imagine what it's like, it's the most wonderful feeling in the world."

⊱ 55 ⊰

LEÓNIE was quiet as she sat beside Jim in the silver Bentley on their way to Paris. Too quiet, he thought, maneuvering the car through the sudden spurt of traffic on the outskirts of Tours, and I know why.

They had spent a marvelous, satisfying, happy day at the Château d'Aureville, supervising the combination of sports day, prize-giving, and birthday celebration—Amélie's birthday. The children had crowded around them as they left, pressing kisses on them and demanding huge hugs, exclaiming with renewed delight as Jim handed over the box of presents to be distributed after they had gone. Yes, for them it had been a perfect day.

He glanced at her again. She was gazing straight ahead, a frown creasing her smooth forehead.

"All right," he said, putting his foot down on the accelerator as they came to a good straight bit of road, "let's have it . . . what's the problem?"

Léonie unwrinkled her brow and looked at him. His profile was strong and handsome as he gazed ahead, confident hands firmly on the wheel. Of course he knew what was wrong, he just wanted to make her talk about it. It's better to talk, he always said, don't keep things locked up inside anymore, talk to me!

"Amélie's sixteen today," she said. "Up until now I've always hoped that some day, by some miracle, I would see her again, but as each year goes by the possibility becomes more remote."

Jim frowned, thinking about it. He still hadn't discovered the whereabouts of the red-haired assassin, Marigny, but he hadn't given up hope. He'd covered the south of France from border to border, but the man simply hadn't been there. Maybe he'd gone to Spain, they said, or Italy. Each marina and each boat yard was alerted to contact him if Marigny should ever return. There was nothing more to be done.

Léonie was still convinced that Monsieur was a threat. He had overcome an accident, which might have killed a normal man or at least left him crippled for life, and within a year was back at the helm of his vast empire.

De Courmont strode around on legs whose shattered bones were pinned together with steel, covering Europe with an energy that a younger, fitter man might have envied. One thing *had* stopped, though, and that was the spying on Léonie. After the accident he had been too ill, but for some reason it hadn't picked up again. Yet he still sent her flowers—always jasmine—at the theaters. Was he giving up on her? Jim doubted it. The white yacht was there every now and again, anchored in the bay. Could he know that she was married? Was that it? Few people did. It was one of the best-kept secrets in France, and Léonie still insisted on it—just until she stopped performing. Well, this was her final year. Afterward she would be simply Mrs. Jamieson, his wife and lover. But he couldn't let her give up hope of seeing her daughter.

"I promised you when we married that you would see Amélie again," he reassured her, "and one day you will, Léonie. Just give me time."

She lay her head back against the cushions with a sigh. "I'll wait," she said simply.

"I had fun today with all your other kids," he said with a smile. "You're like the old woman who lived in the shoe, you have children coming out every door and window. But they surely love you."

She smiled reminiscently. "Did you see the look on little André's face when he heard he'd won the prize? And the amount of food that Genevieve ate?" Jim was right, she had forty children, not just one. And she had Jim. Even though he was busy, traveling often to New York to take care of his many business interests, he was always there when she needed him. When he was gone, she never felt abandoned and desolate, the way she had when

Monsieur left her. Her days were busy and filled with happy anticipation of his return, secure in his love. She was a lucky woman.

"We'll just make the theater in time," he said glancing at the clock. "We've cut it a bit fine, but we'll be there."

She didn't doubt it. Jim always took care of her.

Voisins was crowded, as usual, but Gérard de Courmont had no trouble getting a table for three. "How do you do it?" marveled Sebastião, following the maître d'hôtel through the busy room.

"It's not me," whispered Gérard, "it's my father, he's been coming here for years."

Agneta Lofgren took the chair he offered and stared around in surprise. This was much grander than she had expected when they'd invited her to their farewell dinner. In all the years they had been students together, she had never been taken anywhere other than the bistros and cafés of Paris. "I hope you two can afford this," she said suspiciously. The enormous menu showed no prices, as though money were too vulgar to be discussed.

Sebastião glanced around the room appreciatively. This had definitely been a good choice. Trust Gérard, he always knew where to find the best, though with a father like his he supposed he'd had a good apprenticeship. This was such an intimate room despite its size—it was a place meant for lovers, like those two at the next table. The man couldn't take his eyes off the woman. They held hands under the table and every now and then he would stroke her naked arm. It was a lovely arm, he conceded, and she had beautiful hair, a tawny blond mane. He liked it, pity he couldn't see her face—her back was to him—but he bet she was beautiful.

"I see you're staring at Léonie," murmured Gérard. "I don't blame you."

"Léonie? Is that who she is? I've only seen her on stage—she probably looks quite different in person."

"She does," said Gérard quietly. "I have good reason to know."

Sebastião and Agneta looked at him curiously. "Do you know her then?"

"Not really, but she dominated my childhood—from a distance, of course. You might say she changed de Courmont history."

"But how, Gérard?" persisted Agneta.

"Léonie was my father's mistress. He was obsessed by her. For all I know, he still is."

Sebastião stared at Léonie in surprise. Then she was a femme fatale as well as a great singer. This man she was with must be her latest lover. What, he wondered, does a femme fatale look like?

"Is she still your father's mistress?" whispered Agneta.

"Of course not, but she's still very beautiful."

Sebastião stared at her again. She was tall and very slender and she was wearing some sort of misty, silvery dress, high-necked and yet not at all demure—at least not from the back.

Jim glanced around the restaurant. The young people next to them were obviously having a good time, two young men and a pretty girl. One of the young men was obviously smitten with Léonie. "I think you have an ardent fan at the next table," he said with a faint smile as he caught the young fellow's eye.

"Oh? Really?" She turned to look, nice young people having fun. How lovely to have such an uncomplicated youth, not to always have to struggle. Her eyes met the shocked-looking ones of the nice blond boy and she smiled in surprise. Good heavens, did she have that much effect on them? He looked amazed that she had even smiled at him. She turned back to Jim apologetically. "You'll see, darling," she said, "this time next year no one will even recognize me. They may not even remember me. Only a few more appearances and then I'm all yours."

Sebastião put his hand on Gérard's arm. "Gérard," he said urgently, "it's extraordinary!"

"What is? God, you look weird! Whatever's the matter?"

"Léonie," he whispered, "it's Léonie ... she looks exactly like my cousin Amélie."

"Then you're a lucky fellow."

"No, you don't understand," he repeated urgently, "she looks *exactly* like her—they could be sisters!"

Agneta and Gérard stared at him in surprise.

"I'm telling you," repeated Sebastião, "that Amélie is the image of her. It's uncanny."

"Things do happen," whispered Agneta. "I've heard of strange coincidences like that."

Sebastião took a gulp of his champagne, staring at Léonie. They were leaving; Victor rushed forward personally to take her chair and she thanked him—she had a charming voice, low and musical. He waited; he must see her again. Léonie tucked her purse under her arm and turned round, smiling directly at him—amber eyes with that special mischievous gleam he knew so well, and that same wide coral smile. She nodded politely to them and swept off, bestowing smiles on the charmed diners, who turned eagerly to see her go by. "It's Amélie," he said to Gérard, his voice incredulous. "I'm telling you, Gérard, that's Amélie!"

≥56≤

ROBERTO DO SANTOS brushed his straight blond hair carefully and examined his reflection. He didn't like what he saw. The mirrored image seemed all right—the blond, blue-eyed, suntanned athlete, a sober and enthusiastic young businessman who worked with Edouard on the endless details of the construction of the Florida hotel—but he could see beyond that. Could others? he wondered nervously. Especially Sebastião. His brother knew him too well, he could sense when things were wrong. Sebastião had wanted to know why he hadn't shown up for the exam. He'd been tempted to tell him what really happened. But, of course, he couldn't, not now. Months had passed, things had gone too far. He wanted that other nighttime world of Diego's—prowling around the cafés and brothels where women with tired eyes and flamboyant flesh promised them anything they wished, the bars where nervous men bargained furtively for the favors of knowing young boys, and the rough cafés where you met the drug peddlers and the misfits and the other night-world drifters, like themselves. He couldn't be without Diego, he needed him. He felt the heat again as he remembered the night in the bordello. Diego had laughed it off casually; it happens, he had said, when there's a group of you making it like that. It's just sex. Was it? Roberto wondered uneasily. It hadn't happened again, and he had no desire for sex with the men they met in the homosexual clubs, although he'd been asked often enough. No, it was just Diego. He stared despairingly at his clean-cut untroubled reflection in the mirror. It was a perverse and twisted love, but he knew he loved Diego Benavente.

The receding tide had left the sand firm and cool and the horses were enjoying their gallop along the flat length of Ipanema beach in the cool of the early morning. Sebastião slowed his horse to a canter and looked back at Amélie. She was a hundred yards behind him wading her horse in the surf and he waited for her to catch up. She rode bareback, her long legs in her baggy old shorts gripping her horse with casual authority as she guided it through the edge of the waves. Her hair streamed behind her in the wind and she looked, he thought, like the valiant figurehead of some old ship.

One thing was certain, the little girl he'd known last time he was in Rio had grown up. She was still naive and innocent, still impetuous and out-spoken, but she had gained a new maturity, and she was now, at sixteen, a beautiful young woman. And he loved her. He'd always loved her, but now it was different. Now he wanted to press kisses on that curving coral mouth, he wanted to hold her in his arms and feel her heart beating next to his, he wanted to stroke and soothe her into loving; now he was *in love* with her. When she was eighteen, he would ask her to marry him, even though right now she treated him as her best friend, the recipient of her confidences, the keeper of her secrets, soother of her fears, audience to her daily life—he knew her soul as intimately as he wanted to know her body. She thought she was in love with Roberto. It would pass, though, he was sure of it. The two had been thrown together since they were babies, it was just familiarity and proximity. She hadn't been out in the world, hadn't yet met any other men.

"Sebastião," she called, trotting her horse up to his along the firm sand, "I'm starving, aren't you? Let's have breakfast at the *churrascaria* at Barra de Tijuca."

He glanced apprehensively at the gray sky. "I think we're in for a storm."

"We'll beat it," she said, ever the optimist. She was enjoying herself, it was fun to have someone to ride with. Roberto never did these days, he was always too busy, or too tired. She didn't want to think about Roberto, it was too nice being with Sebastião again, she didn't want anything to spoil that. She leaned across and took his hand with a smile. "Tell me about Paris," she asked. "I keep trying to persuade Grandmère to take me, but so far without any luck. I can't think what she imagines would happen to me there. Is it really a wicked city, Sebastião? Is it all whiskey and champagne and tense games of chance played for high stakes by suave men of the world with fancy women dressed in satin and bedecked with jewels?"

"Of course it is," he replied teasingly. "Why do you think I stayed so long?"

She giggled. "Then I better get there quickly, it sounds like fun. Can't you just see me as one of those women—draped in ermine, flirting with kings and princes? Oh, why won't she take me, Sebastião? It's really not fair, after all, I was born there—it's my homeland. There are still relatives there, more d'Aurevilles and Grandmère's old friends . . . she should go back to see them."

Her words took him back to the warm red intimacy of Voisins, to the vision in misty chiffon with Amélie's eyes, Amélie's hair—she *must* be a d'Aureville. "It's odd you should say that," he said, "but I saw someone in Paris who must be related to you—you look exactly like her. I was tempted to speak to her, to ask her, because the resemblance was so uncanny, she had to be a d'Aureville. But she's so famous, I didn't want to intrude on her privacy."

"Famous? You mean we have *famous* relatives in France? Sebastião, how *exciting*. Why is she famous, what does she do?"

"She's a singer. She has her own style, her own way with popular songs. She has a very different look, very exotic."

Amélie threw back her head and laughed. "Not quite like me, Sebastião, there's nothing exotic about me."

"I'm telling you, Amélie, she could have been you—except she's older, of course. She's still very beautiful, even though she's old enough to be your mother."

"Sebastião, you're so romantic, I hope someone will say that about me when I'm older—that 'she's still very beautiful.' " She tossed back her hair, tilting her chin at him in an arrogant flirtatious pose. "I'll look sort of like this, but a bit more 'experienced'!"

He laughed. "Well, that's just the way Léonie looks."

Her eyes opened wide in surprise. "Who did you say?"

"Léonie, the beautiful singer. . . ."

"Her name is Léonie?"

"Yes. She doesn't seem to have another name, she's just known as 'Léonie.' Perhaps the d'Aureville family cast her out when she went on the wicked stage."

Amélie reined her horse and stared at him. Léonie? There was a Léonie who looked like her—*exactly* like her, he'd said—and she was old enough to be her mother? It was surely more than a coincidence. She didn't know if she really wanted to hear the answer, but she had to ask him. "Did she really look like me . . . I mean *really?* It wasn't that you'd drunk a little wine and she was blond like me and she was beautiful—and you were feeling romantic?"

She was so serious all of a sudden that Sebastião was surprised. "No," he said, "it wasn't like that at all. She looked so like you, Amélie, that I was shocked."

"Sebastião, almost the only things I've ever known about my mother—the only *positive* things anyone has ever told me about her—are that I look exactly like her and that her name was Léonie. I don't look like the d'Aurevilles, I'm not like my father or Edouard . . . I look like my *mother!"*

What did she mean? That Léonie was her mother? "Your mother is dead, she died in a boating accident when you were a baby. You *know* that."

"I don't *know* that, Sebastião. I only know what they've told me. Oh, you can't understand, you just can't imagine what it's like not knowing about her. She's always been a mystery, like a secret that no one wants to talk about. Sebastião, could that be because she is still alive and they don't want me to know?"

Oh, my God, thought Sebastião, what have I put into her head? I should never have said anything. Of course it can't be true, she's just always had this yearning for her mother. What were the words I used? She could have been your mother? Fool, what a stupid fool!

"Amélie, it can't be true."

"My mother's name is Léonie. I look like her. That's the truth, Sebastião. Maybe you were right, maybe the d'Aurevilles hated her for being on the stage, perhaps they thought she wasn't good enough for them. Charles might have run away with her. Oh, I don't know, but I mean to find out." She turned her horse and set off down the beach at a gallop.

He matched his horse to hers, racing along the beach toward home. "What are you going to do?" he yelled over the wind.

Amélie looked at him exultantly. "I'm going to ask Edouard," she cried. "I want to know if my mother is still alive."

Edouard folded his newspaper neatly and poured himself a second cup of coffee. Amélie's two cats lurked beneath the breakfast table, hoping for the small treats that they knew Xara would give them, though Edouard had forbidden it. "They have such a sweet tooth," she said indulgently. "Look, they adore melon, see how they lick the juice?"

They glanced up in surprise as the door was flung open and Amélie burst in, barefoot and windblown and straight from the stables, where she had left Sebastião taking care of the horses.

"I must speak to you, Edouard," she demanded.

"Is something the matter?" he asked, surprised by her tone.

"I must speak to you, in *private.*"

He smiled at her. "This is private, it's just the three of us—and the cats, of course."

Xara caught the glint of tears in her eyes. "Go with her, Edouard," she urged. "She needs to be alone with you."

Amélie led the way out of the house and through the garden, heading instinctively for the wide space of beach where there was nothing but the ocean to overhear.

Clouds banked and scudded in the pull of the wind and the sky was rapidly losing its light, changing the sea from green to blue-gray flecked with white. Edouard picked up a pebble and skimmed it across the waves, watching until it sank with a plop into their depths, waiting for her to speak. What could Roberto have done this time? he wondered. She cares too much about him, she should go to more parties, meet other young men.

She was old enough now. "What is it, Amélie?" he asked gently. "Are you in trouble?"

"Edouard—who is Léonie?"

He looked at her in surprise. "Why, Léonie was your mother, of course."

Amélie moved closer to him, pushing the hair from her eyes impatiently, her heart beating faster. Should she ask him? If she did and he had been lying to her all these years, she'd never be able to trust him again—not him, or Grandmère—and yet if it were true, and surely it must be, the coincidence was too great, if it were true, then she had a mother who was alive. *She had to know.* "And is she the same Léonie, the famous one? The singer in Paris who looks exactly like me?"

Edouard's heart sank like the pebbles into the sea. My God, he thought, I expected some small story of how mean Roberto has been to her and she asks me this. How had she found out? It could only have been Sebastião. What was he to do? What could he say? She was staring at him, waiting, her tawny eyes already accusing.

"Edouard, I must *know,*" she cried.

"Yes," he said with a sigh, "she is your mother."

She couldn't stop the trembling, it seemed to sweep across her in uncontrollable waves. "Why did you *lie* to me?" she screamed. "Why did you do it? Why did you tell me she was dead?" The wind tugged at her words and carried them echoing across the crash of the waves until they faded, sighing, into the surf.

He threw his arms around her. "Amélie, it's all so difficult, we had to tell you that. We had to do it for your own safety. Léonie asked us to, Amélie, when she gave you to us to look after."

She pushed him away shouting at him over the wind. "She gave me away . . . to you? Why? Didn't she want me?"

"Yes, yes, of course she wanted you. But she couldn't keep you. It's a long story, Amélie."

"And my father . . . is he alive somewhere, hidden from me, too?"

"No! Your father was killed in the accident. That was true." He looked at her worriedly. Her face was ashen and she was shaking. "Let's go back to the house, Amélie, come on, darling, come home with me."

"No. I couldn't bear to be shut in . . . I need to be out here." She threw her arms wide, staring out at the wild tossing sea as the tears came. She remembered Xara's tenderness with her newborn babies, but *her* mother had abandoned her, given her away. "How could she, Edouard?" she cried, crumpling in his arms. "How could she leave me? Didn't she know what it would do to me? Other people have mothers who love them, who want them . . . what was wrong with me?"

He brushed the tears from her eyes with a gentle finger. What should he tell her? How much of the story should he edit to save her the pain? He couldn't tell her that her father had been murdered—he could *never* tell her that. "Come on, little one," he said gently, "let's walk and I'll explain everything. But when I do, Amélie, you must remember two things. First, that your mother loved you. I saw her holding you in her arms and she loved you. Never doubt that. And it was because she loved you that she gave you to us—your grandmother and your father's brother. Second, though you are very young, you are going to have to try to understand some very complex adult relationships. It may be difficult for you, but you must try."

They walked slowly along the beach hand in hand in the gathering gloom. "Where to begin," he wondered out loud. "Yes, I suppose it all begins with Léonie."

It was the story she had told him that evening by the river, the story of her poor childhood, of her tangled relationship with the mysterious Monsieur, and finally of her surrendering her baby to their care, convinced that it was the only way to save her life. "And she knew," Edouard concluded, "that you would have a good life, a better one than she could give you. It broke her heart, Amélie d'Aureville, when she put you, her baby, in Grandmère's arms and kissed you for the last time. It's a scar she'll bear forever."

Amélie clutched at his hand, struggling to comprehend the emotions that were filling in the missing pieces of her life.

After he finished the story, there was silence between them, broken only by the crash of the surf. The rain began, heavy drops that pounded into the sea, eroding the smooth surface of the waves, and soaking them as they stood oblivious to the storm, locked by memories of the past.

"You do look like her," he said finally, "more and more as each year goes by." He stroked her wet hair back from her face. "Your hair is exactly the same," he said, his voice faltering. Amélie flung herself into his arms and they clung together, their tears mingling with the rain on their faces.

"I must see her, Edouard. You do understand that, don't you?" Her voice was muffled against his chest. "She is my mother."

"But, Amélie, after all these years . . . she didn't want you to know. Would it be right?"

"Don't you see, now that I know I have a mother, I must know her to know who I am!" Looking at the determination in her face he knew that, by whatever means it took, Amélie meant to find her mother. Could he let her go to France? Surely it must be safe now, after all these years, and she did have the *right*.

"Very well," he said, kissing her gently, "we'll go as soon as possible."

"Oh, Edouard, thank you, thank you," she sighed, hugging him.

"Come on, we're soaked," he said. "Let's go back to the villa . . . we have arrangements to make."

They ran the length of the beach with the glowering sky pressing close, back to the warmth and security of the Villa d'Aureville.

Diego sauntered through the gate of the Villa d'Aureville. He wasn't welcome here and he knew it, but he was looking for Roberto. He hadn't seen him all week and he knew he wasn't at home because he'd called there first. The garden was empty, as were the stables, and he wandered around to the shady terrace. A table held an empty glass and on a chair was an open book, but there was no one around. The door stood open invitingly and he walked in. His glance swept the hall, assessing the trinkets displayed on the polished chests. Edouard's gold cigarette case lay next to a bowl of flowers on the circular rosewood table in the middle of the hall. He slid it silently into his pocket and then walked back outside. That should be worth a bit, he thought with satisfaction. Just so his trip wasn't wasted if Roberto wasn't here!

Avoiding the paths that ran near the windows of the villa, he slipped through the gardens to the Pavillon and in through the kitchen door. The atmosphere was frantic as pots steamed on the big stoves and meats were lifted spitting from the oven. It smelled wonderful and he sniffed appreciatively. He wouldn't mind having lunch here. Why did Roberto never take him?

It was an easy matter to slip unnoticed through the kitchen to the corridor where the small office was; he'd bet that was where they kept the money—and knowing them, they probably trusted everybody and left some lying around. More fool them. He grinned, treading soft-footed down the corridor. The door to the office stood slightly ajar and he could hear voices inside. Edouard was speaking.

"You see, Maman, it seems the best thing to do. If we don't let Amélie go to Paris to see her mother now, she'll find a way to do it later—alone. It would be safer this way."

Diego sucked in his breath in a gasp of astonishment.

"Surely Monsieur can no longer be a threat to her? It's been so long, Edouard," said Isabelle.

Edouard recalled the fear in Léonie's eyes as she'd spoken of Monsieur as a threat to Amélie. He would kill the child out of jealous rage, she'd said. But that had been sixteen years ago. Maman was right, surely the threat must have lessened. What man could sustain such a passion for so long? Léonie had thought he was capable of anything, but she had been so young and so helpless then—and she had to protect her baby. "You're right,

Maman, so much time has passed. Now Amélie has a mother who's a famous woman, a celebrity ... I told her *almost* everything ... about Charles and Monsieur's threat to her. I didn't want her to feel that Léonie had abandoned her. She *has* the right to see her mother. We can't keep them apart any longer. I want you to take her, Maman ... it's a woman's help she'll need in Paris, not mine."

Hurried footsteps sounded along the corridor and Diego slid silently back through the kitchen and out into the garden. He turned out of the gates into Avenida Atlantica and strolled, hands in pockets, along the sandy road smiling to himself. So there was a mother, was there? And a mysterious one, a celebrity with a past! And "Monsieur," who was a threat—well, well. He'd bet not too many people were aware of Amélie's sudden acquisition of a mother. You never knew when information like that could be valuable.

Sebastião glared at his brother. "What do you mean, you don't want to go?" he demanded. "How could you refuse, Roberto? You know how much your support means to Amélie."

Roberto avoided his eyes. "It's not that I don't want to go," he said miserably, "it's just that, well ... I should stay here. There's work to be done." Even to his own ears the words sounded hollow, and he really wanted to go to France, he wanted to be with Amélie. She was afraid and he should be there to help her. But Diego had threatened to tell her about him if he went. It was blackmail and Roberto knew it. Suddenly Amélie and the normal orderly life she represented seemed infinitely desirable. Roberto wished he'd never been with Diego, had never known the Hotel Orfeo and the lure of that other life. He hated it, he hated Diego for introducing him to it. But it's part of you now, an inner voice warned him, it's your life now. "I'll go with you," he said suddenly, "I really want to go, Sebastião. I know she needs us there for support."

"Then why didn't you say so in the first place?" Sebastião demanded in exasperation. "You would have saved us all a hell of a lot of trouble." He looked at his younger brother wearily. "Come on, Roberto, tell me what's wrong. Why are you so difficult these days, so elusive?"

Roberto shrugged, turning away so that Sebastião wouldn't see the fear in his eyes. He'd done it, he would go. He'd call Diego's bluff. And if Diego told, well then, he'd face up to it. But he couldn't tell Sebastião, he couldn't.

❧ 57 ❧

GILLES DE COURMONT'S assistant sprang to his feet and held open the door for his employer. "I shan't be back tonight, Satère," he called, as he strode through the vast offices of the de Courmont Automobile Company. Satère looked after him in surprise; he usually worked until ten or eleven at night, and he was always there before any of the staff in the morning. He spent so much time in the office that sometimes Satère wondered if he had a private life at all. Maybe he's got a woman waiting tonight, Satère thought with a grin.

"Damn," muttered Gilles as pain shot through his knee, "why does that still happen?" He thought of those long months in the hospital after they told him that he wouldn't be able to walk and the despair he had felt. How he struggled to master the painful exercises with weights strapped to his feet, forcing himself from his bed to stand on his own two feet, proving to the doctors that he *could* do it, that he *would* do it. But he would have traded both legs for Armand's life, and without legs he was better dead. He had contemplated it. There had been only one thing left to live for: he had wanted to see Léonie again. He couldn't bear the thought of dying and leaving her.

The big blue limousine drew up at the curb and Hoskins leapt out, opening the door apologetically. "Sorry, sir. I hadn't heard that you were leaving early."

"I should have warned you." Gilles looked at his watch. "The Ile Saint-Louis first, then I'll be leaving for the theater at seven o'clock. I'll be driving myself."

"Yes, sir."

It was Léonie's farewell performance. He couldn't miss that.

Léonie's dressing room was filled with flowers; they spilled out into the corridors, lining the drab walls with splashes of color like a village flower show. "It's nice, folks, that you appreciate her, love her, adore her . . . call it what you will," announced Jim, bowing to the floral offerings as he made his way toward her room, "but this is it . . . no more flowers are needed by

Mrs. Jamieson. *I* shall be the only one allowed to buy her flowers. Thank you, thank you."

"You're cheerful, darling," she said, as he swung into the room laughing.

"Just my own silly joke," he said, kissing her soundly. "How does it feel to be *almost* plain 'Mrs. Jamieson'?"

"I'm not even going to think about it until after the show," she said firmly. "If I do, I'll never get through it. I'd just want to go home with you and curl up next to you in bed."

"And that, my love, is exactly what you're going to do *after* the show . . . curl up with me and a magnum of Roederer Cristal—nothing but the best for the famous *ex*-star!"

"Oh, Jim, you are crazy." She laughed, tilting back her head to apply the eye pencil. "What is it like outside?"

"People are arriving in droves, the place will be packed and scalpers are selling tickets on the street asking five times the box-office price and getting it."

"See what a gold mine you're turning down," she teased. "People are getting rich out there and you scoff at it."

"You're rich enough, you don't need any more money, besides, there are easier ways of making it than this. You'll see," he promised, "I'm going to turn you into a tycoon."

"I thought I was going to be just plain Mrs. Jamieson," she said, standing up and taking off her kimono.

"Oh, Mrs. Jamieson," he said softly as she smiled at him temptingly, standing there in nothing but her high-heeled slippers, "you'll never be plain anything."

She walked into his open arms and hugged herself to him, loving the way his hard body felt next to hers. He kissed her hungrily. "You've smudged my makeup," she murmured with her eyes closed.

"Oh, Léonie," he murmured, "thank God this is your last night!"

Paris, decided Amélie, was the most romantic city in the world. It wasn't a place you had to take time to like, it was instant, and for her it wasn't just liking, it was love at first sight. The chestnut trees were in blossom under a blue early May sky, the café terraces were crowded, the women were chic, and the young girls far more stylish than in Rio—she was definitely going to have to buy some new clothes, maybe try her hair a different way. "Paris," she said to Roberto, sitting opposite her at the café table sipping Pernod, "is an inspiration for a girl. Everyone looks attractive here, even if they're not really pretty."

"Then there's hope for you yet," he teased.

"Do I look awful?" she asked anxiously. She'd bought this suit especially for the trip and the pale peach-color linen skirt and jacket had seemed very smart then. But no one else was wearing pleats like that and weren't their jackets a bit shorter?

"You look lovely," he assured her. "You always do."

She smiled at him, pleased. "Why are you being so nice to me?" she asked, suddenly suspicious.

"Because I love you," he said simply. He didn't know why he said it quite like that, the words just came out—and he did love her. He felt free with her, alive again, part of the *real* world. The weeks on the ship with Isabelle, Sebastião, and Amélie had felt like a convalescence from a serious illness. He had become himself again, and it was all because of her, her innocence had redeemed him. She was looking at him rather shyly and he took her hand. "I'll always love you, Amélie," he said.

Amélie breathed a sigh of contentment. She'd never doubted that he loved her, but she needed to hear him say so. She rubbed his hand against her cheek, feeling dazzled with happiness. Roberto loved her and now she could face anything. "I'll always love you, too," she murmured.

Sebastião wound his way between the tables and took a seat. "Isabelle is too tired after the journey to face dinner tonight," he said, "so we're on our own." He tossed the newspaper on the table, signaling the waiter to bring him a beer.

Amélie sighed. "All I really want to do is see Léonie," she said, "but Grandmère thinks it will take a few days to contact her and make arrangements. I'd just like to get it over with. Oh, Sebastião, I'm so nervous."

He looked at her sympathetically; of course she was nervous, who wouldn't be under these circumstances? He'd been stunned when she told him that Léonie was her mother. She'd said little else, and he had asked no questions, but he had to come with her. He couldn't let her face it alone, she might need a strong shoulder to cry on. He picked up the newspaper with a frown. Should he tell her? How could he not? He opened the paper to the page where the announcement spelled out Léonie's name in bold black letters and passed it to Amélie.

"Here," he said quietly. "You could see her tonight if you wanted to."

"Farewell performance," she read. "Léonie at the Théâtre de l'Opéra. Tonight at eight." The words danced in front of her eyes: this was her mother, she would be there tonight! She was suddenly becoming a reality, not just someone her imagination endowed with a voice and a smile and words of her own creation. Léonie was real. "I have to see her, Sebastião— can we go there? If I see her on the stage first maybe it won't be as strange later when I meet her," if, she added silently, I still have the courage.

359

Roberto looked at his watch. "It's already seven," he said. "We'd better go . . . if it's her farewell show, it's going to be crowded."

Sebastião elbowed his way through the throng outside the theater. The box office had a sign saying "No more tickets available," but he knew there'd be scalpers in the crowd. There was one! He grabbed the man by the arm and spoke to him, bargaining angrily in rapid French. The tickets were ridiculously expensive, but they were good ones—center-front in the dress circle. He pushed his way back to the steps where Amélie and Roberto waited anxiously. "I've got them," he called, waving the tickets in the air as he pushed his way toward them.

"Oh, I knew you would," cried Amélie. "Sebastião, you're so clever, you always know how to work things out."

Roberto felt a pang of jealousy toward his brother. He wanted Amélie to say things like that to *him*. "Come on then," he said, taking her hand, "we'd better go in."

This is it, thought Amélie, staring around the big rococo theater. All these smart people in evening dress and all those crowding into the balconies are here to see my mother; they all know her better than I do, they know what to expect—and what she's like. She smoothed her skirt nervously, tucking her hair back behind her ears, leaning forward to watch the constant stream of people as they took their seats in the stalls, wishing she had had time to dress properly for the occasion. But if there had been time, she might have changed her mind. The orchestra filed into the pit and there was a sudden ripple of applause as the conductor took his place, bowing to the audience before he took up his baton and began the overture. The house lights began to dim. Amélie took a deep, shaky breath. She felt Roberto's hand on hers. "It's all right, Amélie," he whispered, "I'm here with you."

Caro, rustling in silk taffeta, hurried down the aisle with Alphonse, murmuring apologies as they took their seats in the fifth row, center stalls. "Thank God," she said, "we're just in time. I would have hated to miss any of her final show."

"Did you see the car outside?" whispered Alphonse.

She had seen it. The familiar dark blue car had been parked directly across from the theater. "You didn't think he'd miss this one, did you?" she whispered back. "I'm sure he's still not given up hope of getting her back . . . wait till he reads the announcement in the papers. Then he'll know he's beaten." She felt almost sorry for Monsieur. He'd destroyed his life in a futile quest for Léonie and yet he had never really loved her—or if he had then it was a strange kind of love. To them it all seemed so far away—lost in the past—but he still lived it, day and night. He was an extraordinary man. Under other circumstances, he might have been a wonderful man.

Jim stood in the wings with Léonie, waiting for her entrance. She stared silently ahead, concentrating on the music, already remote from him. He'd seen her do it a thousand times, change from the Léonie he knew to the exotic stranger on stage, and the metamorphosis happened right here. She'd wait, quietly, head drooping as she listened to the music, and then when the moment came, she'd stretch herself tall, throw back her head, and stride onto the stage, pacing it arrogantly as she conjured with the lyric of her first song. It was a moment of pure magic and as the orchestra played the first bars he almost regretted that this was the last time he would see it.

The applause was rapturous as she strode onto the stage, cheers rang through the theater and Léonie paused for a moment, surprised. And then she raised her arms in acceptance and bowed to them, smiling.

Amélie bit her lip, trying to stop the tears from coming. She stared at the stage, at the golden, magical being smiling at the welcoming crowd. They were cheering her, calling bravo, and she hadn't even sung yet. They wanted to show her that they loved her. The hand that gripped Roberto's felt damp with sweat, she could hardly bear to look.

Sebastião watched her face—was she all right? She was just staring at Léonie, absorbing her. There was no mistaking their profiles: they were the same.

Léonie began to sing and Amélie leaned forward eagerly. It was a gentle song of a springtime love when she was very young and the world was all butterflies and blossom, but there was an undercurrent of sadness, a hint of loss. Amélie listened intently, wishing she were closer, wishing she could see her better. She was very tall and slender, and her hair was like hers, only it was brushed out like a golden cloud, with tiny braids meshed over the top, glinting with jeweled beads. Her dress was beautiful but very daring, she'd never seen a dress like that before—two thin gold straps held the wisp of fine silk cut low on her bosom, falling straight and simple to her sandaled feet. The sides were slit so that she might prowl the stage unhampered, like some tawny lion, enrapturing her audience.

Could this beautiful, extravagant, flamboyant woman really be her mother? She gripped Roberto's hand tighter. Did she really look like *her?* It all seemed so remote and so unreal, and she glanced anxiously at Roberto. He caught her eye and smiled at her encouragingly.

"Roberto . . . I don't feel anything for her," she murmured sadly. "I can't feel that she's my mother. She's just a beautiful stranger."

Maroc was in his usual place at the back of the stalls and he gazed around the crowded theater with satisfaction. It was a wonderful gala fare-well, everything was going splendidly, the audience loved her—for them she could do no wrong. He remembered the first concert with a smile, how scared she had been, and how nervous he had been for her. Every moment she was on stage had been an agony for him, and now look at her. It was almost a pity that she had decided to retire, except it was time Léonie had her happiness. She had worked hard and so had he. He wouldn't be sorry to say good-bye to this way of life—always traveling, another city, another hotel room—maybe he'd even settle down and get married now, get back into the hotel business.

The door opened behind him and he turned to look, knowing who it would be. Gilles de Courmont nodded to him as he walked past—they al-ways acknowledged each other's presence now, they'd long since given up pretending. The bastard was still handsome, thought Maroc, watching him, you'd never know the accident almost crippled him. There was no trace of the past in his face, none of the scheming and plotting, none of the crazy passion—none of the violence. He was unmarked by it all. He was invincible. This was his final night to see her; what would he do now? He would read the announcement in the papers and then he'd know that he had finally lost her. And then what? You never knew with Monsieur, just when you thought he'd given up he was likely to be at his most dangerous.

Look at them, thought Gilles, staring at the audience, they're eating her up, devouring her—fools! Don't they know that they could never know the real Léonie? Only I know the real one. He leaned against the wall, wishing his leg didn't ache so. What would she do now that she was retiring? Was she going to hide herself at the inn, work on her beloved garden? He wished to God he'd never given her the deeds to that inn. The scent of jasmine from the spray in his buttonhole drifted in the warm air and he closed his eyes, imagining her as she used to be. He had sent her jasmine tonight, of course, he'd taken this spray from it. She always kept the jasmine in her dressing room, he knew. She never cast it away, she kept it—to remind her. Look at her, stalking the stage just the way she had stalked into Caro's party the night he first saw her. Ah, Léonie, Léonie, if only we could turn back the clock. But I'll never give you up, never.

* * *

It's like a love affair, thought Léonie, between me and the audience. Whatever I do tonight, they are prepared to love me. She bowed one more time as they called for an encore; she turned to smile at Jim, waiting in the wings, and then at the conductor, waiting for her signal. She nodded to him and moved to center stage as the lights dimmed. She was alone in the small amber circle of the spotlight, head bowed, body taut, legs slightly apart. The audience waited in a breathless hush for what was to come as the music threaded its way softly around the melody. She lifted her head slowly and stared out at them, strong, unsmiling, beautiful. Her low passionate voice caressed the opening words of the song that Jacques had written for her, the one that had made her famous, the song of how it felt to love a man, how it was when he lay next to her holding her. She was lost in it, her whole being felt it. The music died away and the spotlight faded into darkness and silence. Suddenly the audience was on its feet, applauding and cheering as the stage lights went up, bouquets lined the footlights, the crowd pleaded for more, Léonie was gone. She had sung her final song.

The crowd of stagehands applauded her as she walked with Jim, arms around each other, down the bleak backstage corridor. They stopped at the door of her dressing room and she turned to look back. "That's it, darling," she said with a happy sigh. "I left Léonie there on that stage. Now it's just you and me."

He kissed her gently. "And that's just the way it should be, Mrs. Jamieson," he said opening the door.

Chocolat yawned and stretched under the lights on the dressing table and they laughed as they watched her. "You're a theater cat no longer, Choc," called Léonie triumphantly. "We're free!"

Jim took the bottle of champagne from the cooler and opened it with a flourish as Maroc came through the door, followed by Caro and Alphonse.

"Just in time," he called, pouring. "We're just about to drink to freedom."

Léonie flung her arms around Maroc. "Are you sad, Maroc?" she asked.

"No, I'm not sad, it was a fantastic farewell. They always say it's better to quit while you're on top—and you would never be able to top tonight's concert."

"That's true, Léonie," said Caro, settling herself on the sofa with a rustle of sapphire silk. "I almost cried, and I'm quite sure Alphonse did . . . he had to wipe his glasses, anyway."

"You know I'm sentimental about Léonie," said Alphonse. "Here's to the two of you . . . and to true love."

"I'll drink to that." Jim smiled. "And to the future."

"Excuse me, madame," the concierge poked his head around the door, "but there are these young people who insist on seeing you."

"There are probably hordes of people who'd like to see you tonight," Caro said, laughing.

"Really, I can't see anyone just now," said Léonie. "Tell them I'm sorry, will you, but I'm too tired."

"They said you knew them, they sent you a note, madame, they told me you should read it right away, it's important."

Maroc took the note and handed it to her. It was just a scrap of paper torn from a notebook; the handwriting was unfamiliar, round and girlish. She glanced at the signature at the bottom. "Amélie." Amélie? She read it slowly. "I hope you won't be too shocked," it said, "that I am here, but I only recently found out that I am your daughter. Edouard and Grandmère said that it was all right for me to come to you. Would you please see me, just for a few minutes?"

The numbness of total shock left the smile still on her face. She stared at the words, reading them again; Amélie was here.

"What is it, Léonie, what's the matter?" Caro's voice seemed to come from so far away, she forced her eyes from the note.

"It's Amélie," she said, her voice sounding small and controlled, "it's my daughter. She's here."

Caro took the note from Léonie's nerveless hand, reading it quickly. "My God," she cried, "it *is* Amélie. Jim, what shall we do?"

Léonie was sitting pale and frozen at her dressing table. "Of course I'll see her," she said. She was trembling and Jim took her arm, steadying her.

"Are you sure you're all right?" he asked quietly. "It could wait, you know, until you're over the shock. You could see her later. I'll tell her to come around to the hotel."

"Oh, but I want her . . . I must see her now, right away. I've waited so long and now she comes to me from nowhere . . . just suddenly appears."

Maroc looked worriedly at Alphonse. The same thought was in both their minds. The circumstances they had all struggled so hard all these years to avoid had finally come about. Léonie and Monsieur and Amélie were all here, under the same roof.

"I'll go get her." Jim strode to the door and Léonie sank back onto her chair, watching him. Chocolat crept from the dressing table and curled up on her knee, purring, and she rested her cold hand against the soft fur. There was silence in the room, the others looked at each other apprehensively.

"Shall we leave you alone, Léonie?" asked Caro gently.

"No. No, don't go. You were all involved from the beginning . . . you're like her family. Please stay with me."

Amélie waited with Sebastião and Roberto outside the stage door. "What if she won't see me?" she whispered nervously. She could hear the tremor of panic in her own voice and struggled to control it.

"She will," replied Roberto confidently, "but I expect she'll be a bit shocked at first. Amélie, do you think you'd better see her alone? I mean, we have to think of her, too. She might not like a couple of strangers being there at a time like this."

Sebastião agreed. "We could wait for you outside . . . it's a very private moment and we don't even know her."

Amélie took a deep breath as a man appeared in the corridor, walking toward them quickly. "All right," she said, "I'll go in alone."

Jim looked at the three blond young faces turned toward him expectantly, two young men—bronzed, good-looking—and a girl. He drew in his breath sharply, she might have been Léonie. Just that she was so young. But there was no mistaking her. The concierge was peering at her curiously from behind his spectacles—he hadn't missed the resemblance even with his poor eyesight.

"Hello." Jim held out his hand to her. "Of course, you're Amélie—I would have recognized you anywhere. I'm Jim Jamieson. Léonie asked me to bring you to her dressing room."

"How do you do?" said Amélie politely. "These are my cousins, Roberto and Sebastião do Santos."

"We'll wait outside now, Amélie," said Sebastião, backing toward the door. "Remember we're right here."

"Don't be afraid," whispered Roberto, turning away reluctantly as she walked with Jim down the long green-painted corridor.

Jim look at her walking silently beside him, her shoulders squared, chin up, ready to confront any adversity. Oh, she was Léonie's daughter, all right. "Your mother is a bit shocked," he said as they came to the door, "but that's understandable, isn't it? After all, she had no warning, but she wants to see you very much."

Amélie looked at him with Léonie's amber eyes. "Does she really?" her voice was small, uncertain.

He put his arm around her slender shoulders. "There hasn't been a day when she hasn't thought of you," he told her quietly. "You are the most important person in her life."

He opened the door and stood back to let her go through. Four pairs of eyes stared at her and she hung back nervously.

A little brown cat ran toward her, rubbing itself against her legs, purring. Amélie looked at the golden woman sitting on the stool by the dressing table. Even with the makeup and the wild hair she looked like her. If she had had any doubt, now she knew for sure: this was her mother.

Léonie walked toward Amélie, taking her hands. "Amélie," she said softly, smiling into the face that was so nearly her own. "I've wondered so often what I would say if ever I saw you again, and now I can't think of the words . . . except to say that you've made me very happy. I always thought that it would be I who would have to find you, but now you've found me." She kissed her on the cheek.

Amélie blinked back her tears. "I'm happy to be here, madame," she said shyly. Then she added impetuously, "Oh, you see, madame, when I found out about you, I *had* to see you . . . I had to know you, and then . . ."

"Yes?" prompted Léonie gently, still holding her hands.

"And then I would know who I am."

"Well. . . . and now you know. What do you think?"

"I think you're very beautiful," replied Amélie cautiously.

Léonie gestured to the people standing watching them. "These friends all knew you when you were a baby," she said gently, "they held you in their arms, they protected you, they loved you. They are part of your life, too."

Caro let out her breath with a sigh. She hadn't realized she'd been holding it, or that her hands were shaking. She must do something to break the tension. She put down the glass of champagne she'd been clutching and went to Amélie. "I'm Caro Montalva." She smiled. "And your mother is right. I held you when you were a baby and even then you were lovely. I can't tell you how happy I am to see you now." She put her arms around Amélie and hugged her. "Jim, how about some champagne for everyone . . . surely this is a celebration?"

Maroc kept an eye on Léonie. She was nervous, unsure of what to do. Obviously she was afraid of frightening the girl by showing too much emotion. He smiled as Amélie shook his hand politely, remembering how he'd taken her on the long journey from Menton to Tours.

"And this is Alphonse," said Caro. Alphonse took her hand and kissed it. "I'm happy to meet you again, Amélie. I can see your grandmother has taken good care of you for us."

"Do you know Grandmère then?" Amélie was surprised, but everything was surprising tonight.

"Indeed I do, please give her my regards."

"But she's here with me. At the hotel I mean, madame. . . ." Léonie flinched at the word, but what had she expected? That Amélie would call her Mother? How could she, they were strangers. She wanted to enfold Amélie in her arms, hug her tightly, cover her sweet young face with kisses, brush her hair, chat with her about clothes and boyfriends. Oh, God, I want to be her mother.

"Madame . . . I'm sure Grandmère would like to see you all."

"Of course." Léonie smiled. "We must see her. And Edouard? Is he with you?"

"Edouard wanted very much to be here, but he had to go to Florida. He asked me particularly to send you his love. It was Edouard who told me all about you." She sat down beside Léonie on the stool. "He told me how wonderful you were, and how beautiful . . . and that you hadn't wanted to leave me."

Léonie reached out a hand to stroke her hair. "You'll never know how much I hated it," she murmured, "and how I've missed you."

Amélie smiled at her, a smile of such beaming radiance that those watching felt warmed by its glow. "Oh, and I've missed you, too," she said, throwing her arms around Léonie. "Oh, Mother, I've missed you so."

Sebastião and Roberto stood at the top of the wide steps leading from the theater, watching the crowds as they dispersed in taxis and limousines or on foot, making for the busy restaurants, smiling and chatting, still elated from the performance. "I wonder what's happening," said Roberto nervously.

Sebastião paced along the top step and back again. "I hope she's all right." He glanced at his watch, she'd been gone fifteen minutes; it couldn't be an easy situation for her or her mother.

There was something familiar about the car across the road, a long dark blue de Courmont. Of course, it was Gérard's father's car! Could Gérard be here? No. It was the duke—there he was, walking toward the car. Sebastião dashed down the steps. "Sir?" he called. "Sir. . . ."

De Courmont looked up in surprise. "Why, Sebastião. . . . I didn't know you were back in France. How are you?" He shook his hand. "Did Gérard know you were coming?"

"No, sir," replied Sebastião, smiling. "It was an unexpected trip, in fact we just arrived this afternoon. This is my brother, Roberto. Roberto, this is the Duc de Courmont."

"I'm happy to meet you, sir," Roberto said politely. "Sebastião has often mentioned how kind you and your family were to him when he was in Paris."

"Well," said Gilles, "are you on your way somewhere? Can I give you a lift? Or maybe you're free for dinner? I'd be happy to have you join me."

"Thank you, sir, but I'm afraid we can't. We're just waiting for our cousin and then we have to get back to the hotel. But would you tell Gérard I'm at the Ritz and that I'll call him tomorrow."

"Tomorrow? But Gérard's out of town. He went to London on business, he'll be back in a few days. He still has your old apartment, you know, he seems to like living there. Well," he added briskly, "I'd better be going. Come around and see me, Sebastião—and you, too, of course, Roberto." He waved as he stepped into the big car.

They watched as he drove away, the engine purring meticulously in the now almost silent street. "He always seemed to me to be such a desperate man," Sebastião said compassionately.

Léonie was watching Amélie like a hawk, thought Caro. She was observing her every move, listening to every word with such total attention. She's storing it up because she knows she's going to lose her again. What else can she do?

She knows Monsieur is out there waiting. Damn it, why doesn't she just tell him to go to hell, that Amélie's hers and no one can hurt her, why doesn't she just flout him, call his bluff, be daring? Caro looked at Alphonse despairingly. She knew why. Because Léonie would be risking Amélie's life, that's why, and Monsieur had killed once. Even now, seventeen years later, she was afraid.

"But you must all come and have dinner with us tomorrow," said Amélie, cresting on newfound confidence. "Now that I know you all"—she laughed and sipped her champagne—"my new family. Oh, I forgot. Roberto and Sebastião."

"Your friends," said Jim.

"My cousins. They're waiting for me outside. We have to get back to Grandmère. You see, she doesn't even know we've come here. We were supposed to wait, to write to you or telephone first, but when we knew you were here I'm afraid we took the chance. I just couldn't wait, you see." She looked apologetically at Léonie. "I've always been impatient," she sighed.

Léonie laughed. "But must I lose you so soon? We've only just found each other."

Amélie stood up shyly, needing to escape—it was as if this room, all these people, all this emotion were crowding in on her. She looked at them uncertainly. She had herself under control, but she didn't know how much more she could take. Half of her recognized Léonie as her mother and the other half cried that she was still a stranger. She wanted to throw her arms around her, and yet she wanted to run away. "I must go," she said carefully, "but we'll meet again tomorrow."

Léonie took her hand. "I'll walk with you to the door."

The corridor loomed empty in front of them as they walked hand in hand toward the heavy iron doors. "I know how you feel," said Léonie quietly. "You are part of me and I am part of you, but we're strangers. It will take a lot of meetings, maybe even a lot of years, Amélie, but you are my daughter and one day we shall really know each other." She kissed Amélie gently on both cheeks, holding her face tenderly in her two hands. "The last time I did this," she whispered, "you were a baby, and now you're almost a woman. But I never forgot you."

Amélie hugged her, tears spilling from her eyes. "I'm here now," she said comfortingly. "Everything is going to be all right."

Léonie watched her go, running up the alley to the street, turning at the corner to wave. She had always imagined how happy she would feel if she saw Amélie again, but she had never realized she would feel the same joy as when she first held Amélie in her arms.

"Amélie!" Sebastião swept her into his arms, hugging her tightly. "Are you all right?"

"I don't know. I just don't know, Sebastião. It was all too much. She's so beautiful and lovely and gentle . . . and I loved her . . . but she's a stranger. Sebastião, I don't know what to say to her, what she expects from me. Oh, I don't know how to explain it."

"All right, all right, don't try," he said soothingly, "let's go back to the hotel and think things out."

Roberto took her hand. "Was it very hard?" he murmured sympathetically.

"It was only difficult because of me, Roberto—*she* was wonderful. Maybe it was easier for her, she's always known about me, always remembered. I didn't know her. Oh, I'm so confused."

"Don't worry," he said, taking her hand firmly, "we'll take care of everything. It will all work out, Amélie."

The conversation stopped as Léonie opened the door, and she knew they had been talking about her. "Well?" she asked with a shaky smile.

"I think we'll leave you and Jim alone," said Caro. Her brown eyes met Léonie's sympathetically. "I'm glad she found you," she said gently, "that at least you saw her."

Léonie stared after them as they drifted silently from the room.

"Come on, darling," said Jim, "let's go home." He wrapped the cape around her and tucked Chocolat under her arm, and they walked together along the corridor for the last time. She turned once to look back, she could still smell the jasmine over all the other flowers.

Léonie sat beside Jim in the car, holding Chocolat on her knee, and waited for what he was going to say.

"You know that Monsieur was in the theater," he said calmly. "He was at the back as usual."

Monsieur! For the first time in her life she had forgotten him! The shudder startled the little cat, who meowed at her complainingly. Léonie felt the sweat of fear break out along her spine. Amélie had been in the theater with Monsieur; he might have seen her—could he possibly know?

"I'm sure he doesn't know," said Jim, sensing what she was thinking. "But if she stays here and if you see her again, he *will* know."

"What should I do?" she asked in a small voice.

He glanced at her, huddled next to him. "Only you can make that decision," he said finally. "Only you know just what he's capable of. If you think he's no longer a threat. . . ."

"No. He's still a threat." The jasmine was still in her dressing room, he had still been at the back of the theater—and when she went home to the inn his yacht would still be there. "Dear God," she cried, "will I never be free of him!"

Jim took her hand and held it tightly. "One day you will. I promise you, Léonie. I'll get him one day."

❧ 58 ❧

ISABELLE GAZED at the empty pillars flanking the gates of the Château d'Aureville—the griffins that had once surmounted them now adorned the entrance to the Villa d'Aureville in Rio. "They were transplanted, like we were," she said, pointing out to Amélie the place where they had stood for three hundred years.

"Oh, Grandmère," breathed Amélie, "how could you bear to leave this place?"

The park unfolded before them, first the woodlands, the copses of beech and silver birch and ash, and then the glint of the river through the trees as it wound its way around the edge of the estate, touching the long sloping south lawn in a little tributary that was a sanctuary for ducks and swans and for wild geese and herons, river otters and a hundred small creatures. The lawns lay like smooth velvet covers dotted with shade trees, oak and chestnut, banked by flowered terraces in the blues and lilacs, pinks and yellows of late spring.

"You'll see the house now," she told Amélie, gripping her hand tighter and leaning forward eagerly, "just around this bend." There it was, the familiar yellow-gray stone, the solid lines, the tall windows that always seemed to catch the sun. She felt the tears prick at her eyes. It was good to be back.

"It's wonderful," cried Amélie, "beautiful."

Roberto stared through the car window at the rambling old house as the drive curved around it. She was right, it was wonderful. There was such a sense of solid security about a place like this, you felt nothing could ever go wrong here, that lives were orderly and planned and other, darker worlds didn't exist. The air was fresh and clean, there was no steaming tropical heat to inflame you, to taunt your body into wilder cravings. What must it be like, he wondered longingly, to be the sort of person who lives in this house, following tradition, upholding the family honor—with someone like Amélie by your side, straightforward and honest and strong?

They followed Isabelle up the broad steps of her old home, reluctant to disturb her memories as she stopped for a moment to look at the familiar view. "I came here as a bride," she said with a faint smile, "when I was eighteen. I lived many happy years here . . . many loving years, but I don't want you to think that this return is a sad one. Since I took Amélie to Brazil my life has changed, and developed, and I have changed, too. I'm not the same woman who lived here. I wouldn't alter anything, my home is with you all, in Rio."

"Grandmère," cried Amélie, hugging her, "I don't know what I'd do without you."

The big front door stood open to the warm spring day but Isabelle rang the bell, hearing again the familiar sound echo through her old house. It had been wonderful of Léonie to suggest that they come here. It was just the same, she had said in her letter, but filled with children. Still, it hadn't been easy to accept that Léonie couldn't see Amélie again. If it hadn't been for her nice husband, Isabelle might not have believed it true after all these years, but he had convinced her. Strangely enough, Amélie had taken it calmly. "I've met her now, Grandmère, and I'm happy," she had said. "She's my mother and I'll always think of her that way, but we're strangers. I didn't know what to say to her. She doesn't know anything about me or about my life . . . and where do you begin? How do you catch up? Grandmère, I'm almost glad, because I don't know how to do it." Isabelle had felt sad for her, she had gained only to lose.

"You'll see her again, Amélie," she'd told her. "Later . . . when you're older. One day you'll need your mother and that's when you'll go to her."

They had left Paris the same afternoon reluctantly, telling the surprised

Sebastião and Roberto that they had decided to visit the château and then drive on through the south into Italy. We'll go to Florence and Venice, she promised.

The sound of hurrying feet came from the back of the hall and suddenly it was full of children. They lined up on either side as a smiling young nun came to greet them. "I'm so sorry," she apologized, "we wanted to be ready for you. The children have their greeting planned, but we expected you a little later."

Forty eager young faces smiled at them curiously as they entered the hall, chorusing a beaming "Bonjour." The youngest girl, hastily pulling up her socks, presented Isabelle with the posy of wildflowers picked early that morning in the woods and meadows around the château and tied with a twist of thin fluttering ribbons.

"How lovely," Isabelle said, bestowing a kiss on the expectant four-year-old's face. "They're the nicest flowers I've ever seen." Their familiar sunny fragrance brought back decades of spring meadows and bluebell-carpeted woods.

"We thought it would be nicer if the children showed you around themselves," said Sister Agnes, "although, of course, there's no need. If you prefer, you can just wander where you wish . . . I don't want to disturb your privacy."

Isabelle took the four-year-old by the hand. "I can't think of a better way to see my old home than in the company of children," she replied with a smile as they walked down the hall. "And then afterward, I'd like to visit the chapel alone."

Amélie slipped through the door of the small chapel and walked back along the path that led to the château, pausing for a moment to look again at the d'Aureville tomb. Its pale marble surface was graced with winged angels trumpeting the glory of God, while plump comforting cherubs played around its borders. Isabelle's posy of wildflowers lay at the foot, beneath the inscription to the memory of her husband, Jean-Paul, and her son, Charles. Impulsively Amélie ran across the grass to the tomb, leaning her body against it and placing her warm cheek against the cool marble. "I would have loved you," she whispered. "I'm sure I would have loved you, Father, if I had known you."

She stepped back, gazing at the angels as if waiting for some sign that they had heard, and then she turned and walked, light-footed, across the grass to the avenue that led to the château.

Isabelle had wanted to be alone for a while in the chapel, and Amélie had left her in peace with her memories. Peace, she thought as she wandered slowly beneath the avenue of yellow and green trees, that's what I feel here.

I'm close to my father, this is where he grew up, I know all these places—the avenues, the riverbank, the flowered terraces—from the stories I've been told. It's as if it were *my* home. And now I have a real mother, not some shadowy dream. We'll know each other one day, but for now, I'm content. I know who I am.

"Amélie," Roberto waved to her from the other end of the leafy tunnel and she broke into a run, dashing into his arms as he caught her, swinging her around in the air.

"Roberto, I'm so happy," she cried. "This place is wonderful, it seems to sort out all your problems."

Arm in arm they walked down to the river. "I'd like to stay here forever," he said as they watched the mallards skimming the water with rushing wings. And, he added to himself, I never, ever want to see Diego again. Amélie's wild hair was blowing in the breeze and she looked poised for flight, bursting with eager energy, ready for whatever was to happen next.

"Amélie d'Aureville," he said softly, "I love you. Will you marry me?"

Her amber eyes sprang wide in surprise, followed by a look of such contentment and happiness that he had to kiss her smiling mouth. She laughed under his kiss, and, wriggling herself free, she ran to the top of the bank and stood there for a moment looking at him, laughing with pure joy.

"Of course I'll marry you," she yelled triumphantly, throwing her arms wide to the heavens. "I *always* meant to marry you, Roberto do Santos." She leapt into the air exuberantly, cavorting like a young animal in spring. "On my seventeenth birthday!"

He leapt up the bank toward her and she fled laughing along the path, turning teasingly to look at him. "I could always run faster than you," she shouted over her shoulder.

"No you can't," he cried, gaining on her. "You see!" He grabbed her by the arm and swung her, laughing, toward him, folding her in his arms as she covered his face in kisses. And then he kissed her, taking her sweet fresh mouth in his, loving her as she moved closer in the circle of his arms. This was true happiness and now it was his. He would never see Diego again.

❧ 59 ❧

JIM SAT ON THE TERRACE with the newspaper in his lap, looking down across the garden where Léonie was busy installing a border of pansies around Bébé's tree. Chocolat was stretched out on the grass nearby, lazing in the sunshine. He could faintly hear Léonie's voice as she talked to the cat. He smiled; she was probably telling her about Amélie. She had talked of Amélie constantly since they had met last week, telling herself that she had no right to be sad because at least now she knew her, she knew what her daughter looked like, sounded like, how it felt when she hugged her, how it was to kiss her, and she felt sure that one day she would see her again. One day, when she was free and Amélie needed her, they would be together. He didn't know how such conviction had emerged from the despair of her decision to send Amélie away—again—but it had, and she was happy.

He looked back at the newspaper. The announcement was there, the bold caption said it all. "Léonie secretly married . . . Mrs. James Jamieson, wife of the American property tycoon." He smiled as he read it; why were all American businessmen automatically "tycoons" to Europeans? he wondered. Anyway, there it was at last.

"Jim." She waved to him. "I'm just going up the road to get the mail. Ask Madame Frenard for some fresh coffee, will you—and some brioches, I'm starving."

He put down the paper and wandered inside. He loved this house as much as she did, he liked its cool thick white walls and terra-cotta tiled floors, its arched doorways and long, green shuttered windows, and he liked what she'd done with it, bestowing soft rugs on the gleaming floors, interesting paintings on the walls, and comfortable cushioned chairs for relaxing. It was truly a home. He passed their room. Its windows stood open to the sun and the rays picked out the statue of Sekhmet—still with her face to the wall. "I've almost got you beat," he promised, as he continued down the corridor.

The big cool kitchen smelled of herbs and flowers and fresh bread. A scrubbed pine table held a comfortable clutter of jugs and baskets and a rack of lamb lay in a flat dish, marinating in wine and bay leaves. Supper, he thought appreciatively, cutting a sliver of meat from the smoked ham in the larder. "Madame Frenard," he called, "could we have some coffee?"

She bustled in smiling. "I'll bring it out on the terrace for you."

"Thank you ... and some brioches, please, for Léonie."

He wandered back to the terrace, enjoying the lazy tempo of the day. Léonie was already sitting by the table, reading a letter. "Nothing much," she said, "just a note from Caro. Oh, and there's one there for you from Marseilles."

He opened it quickly, it was from Legrand Boat Yard—the man he was looking for had applied for a job there last week, but had not returned to start work. He looked up jubilantly. It was the first real contact. If this was his man, he was alive and he was here in the south. At last he was on the trail. He glanced at Léonie reading her letter and put the note carefully in his pocket. He wouldn't tell her yet, he'd wait until he was sure.

Gérard de Courmont had enjoyed the walk to the Ile Saint-Louis. The sky was a bright cloudless blue, the sun was shining and every bright little city sparrow and pigeon was flaunting itself as though it were in some leafy country lane. Paris was alive and spilling out onto the pavement, concierges sat black-stockinged and scarved in sunny doorways knitting fragile lacy white jackets for babies, builders labored shirtless in the new heat, and pink-cheeked girls in pretty swirling dresses flirted with shirt-sleeved young men at terraced café tables beneath blossoming chestnut trees. Summer was almost here, except at the big house on the Ile Saint-Louis.

The butler closed the door behind him, shutting out the sunlight, and his exhilaration with the perfect blue day faded. There was no early summer joy here, just the immaculate polished grandeur of long, dead years.

"Is my father home?" he asked, striding through the hall, his footsteps ringing in the silence.

"You'll find him in his study, sir," replied Bennett.

The study door was shut and he tapped on it and went in. His father looked up from his desk, unsmiling. "Gérard," he said, "I didn't expect you back until tomorrow."

His voice was tired and he looked dispirited, as though all the joy in the beautiful summery world outside had left him forever. He looks now, thought Gérard, the way he did when Armand died.

"I caught the night ferry," he said, keeping his voice cheerful, "and I'm glad I did. It's such a wonderful day ... you can't beat Paris in the spring-time. I thought of having lunch at the restaurant in the Bois. Why don't you come with me, Father, we could sit out on the terrace and share a bottle of wine, it'll do you good." I never, he thought, expected to be telling my father that something would do him good.

"I don't know, Gérard." Gilles picked up some documents on his desk, aligning them into a precise pile in front of him. "I've got work to do."

"Oh, come on, Father, leave it for once. I'd like your company."

"Would you?" The question was laced with bitterness and Gérard stiffened angrily. What did he expect from him? He moved the newspaper from the chair next to the desk and sat down. "I'd like to take you to lunch, Father," he repeated. "It's a beautiful day and I'd like your company."

"I'm sorry," said Gilles wearily, leaning back and closing his eyes. "Yes, I'd like that. Just give me a moment to finish writing this note."

Gérard picked up the newspaper. It was folded carefully to the report of the disclosure of Léonie's secret marriage to a Mr. James Homer Alexander Jamieson III. So that was it! How could he still care about a woman he had barely seen in sixteen years? What sort of woman must she be? How deep was that kind of emotion, he marveled, and why had he let it wreck his life?

"By the way," said Gilles, looking up from his letter. "I met your friend Sebastião the other night, he asked me to tell you that he's at the Ritz."

"Sebastião? But what on earth is he doing here? He hasn't been back in Brazil for more than a couple of months."

"He was with his younger brother Roberto at the Théâtre de l'Opéra. They were just waiting for their cousin. They had been to Léonie's farewell concert."

Gérard looked at him in surprise. He'd never heard his father speak her name before. Maybe now that he'd finally lost Léonie, he was going to accept it and begin to live his own life again.

"That's odd," he said, determinedly cheerful. "Last time I was with Sebastião we saw Léonie in Voisins and he swore then that she was the image of his young cousin ... or else Amélie looked exactly like her. He said it was uncanny, she could almost have been her mother."

Monsieur stared at him. What was he saying? There was a cousin Amélie who looked like Léonie? His throat was dry, and his voice rasped as he framed the question. "Sebastião's cousin ... what did you say her name was?"

"Amélie. She's only sixteen, but he's crazy about her. Her name is Amélie d'Aureville."

The cramping pain ran the length of his arm and along his shoulder the way it had that night he had gone to find Léonie at the inn. Gilles gasped, leaning back against the green leather chair. All these years he could have had her, she was there in Rio with Sebastião. Oh, my God, he'd been such a fool, so stupid not to have realized. All these wasted years! And now she was here in Paris. If he could get the girl now, he'd finally have Léonie.

The cramp moved through his shoulder and into his chest and he cried out as it clenched around his heart, the same gripping burning pain.

Gérard leapt to his feet. "Father, what is it?"

Monsieur's eyes met his, agonized and unbelieving. "Bennett," yelled Gérard, running out into the hall, "get the doctor at once. My father is seriously ill." The butler hurried to the telephone.

"Father," Gérard spoke gently now, but Monsieur couldn't hear him. He breathed in short labored gasps. His eyes were closed and his face looked white and bleak beneath the vigorous silver hair. "Oh, Father," said Gérard, taking his cold hand, "don't you understand that you cared *too much?"*

❧60❧

THE LITTLE BOAT YARD on the outskirts of Nice was just a jumble of sheds set back a pace from the water's edge. The sound of a saw buzzed across the sandy yard and a couple of men working on the keel of a neat twenty-foot sailboat looked up from their task as Jim paused beside them.

"Sorry to interrupt," he said with a smile. His French was heavily American-accented and completely colloquial, and always raised enough curiosity to gain him the attention he wanted from the indifferent boat yard workers. As did the bank note he held forward with the name written on it. "I'm looking for a man," he said. "This is his name: Marigny. He's a reddish-haired fellow, big, running to fat you might say."

The note disappeared into the pocket of the blue overalls. "Red hair," said the workman, "yes, that's Marigny. He used to work here."

"Used to?"

"Yeah. He got fired about an hour ago . . . for drinking. He was never really drunk on the job, but he'd always had a few. It made him aggressive, see; he picked one too many fights this morning—and with the boss. That's no way to keep a job, now is it?"

"Apparently not," said Jim, producing another note and passing it over. "Do you know where he lives?"

"You're too late. He already left. He never lived long in one place anyway. He must have had three different rooms in the few weeks he's been here. He's gone to Paris; said there was a lot of money there for him, money he wouldn't have to work his ass off for, like us fools. He's crazy," he said, spitting contemptuously into the sand. "If you're looking for him," he suggested suddenly, "he's probably gone to the railway station to catch the Paris train."

"Thanks a lot," called Jim, striding through the yard. The next train to Paris was at noon. He might just be in time.

Jim spotted his prey as he went through the barrier, a burly figure in a blue workshirt carrying a small bag, shambling along the platform. Jim watched as he disappeared into a second-class carriage of the Paris train, and then he followed him down the platform, sauntering past the carriage, casually glancing inside. Marigny had taken the last seat. People were already standing in the corridor and the conductor was checking tickets. "Paris," he said, clipping Marigny's ticket and moving on to the next.

He was bound for Paris to get the money that was waiting there, the money that "he didn't have to work for." It seemed that Marigny was finally coming out of hiding. He was going to Paris to find Gilles de Courmont.

Jim walked down the platform, took a seat in a first-class carriage, and considered what his next move should be. Suddenly it seemed so simple and so clear. There was no need to confront Monsieur with the evidence of his crime, the assassin would do it for him. And he'd bet Monsieur would pay up. He smiled. That would be the time to let Monsieur know he knew. The threat of exposure of his crime was a terrible one. He took out his big gold pocket watch and looked at it. Noon. The train was leaving right on time, as usual. He might as well relax and enjoy some lunch. This would be a very satisfying day.

Marie-France de Courmont sipped her tea from a rose-patterned cup of infinite fragility, without enjoying it one little bit. Gérard was reading the newspaper to his father and she watched them coldly. She should never have come here, Gilles meant nothing to her—nor, she supposed, did she to him. I shall only see him because of family duty, she had warned Gérard when he had pleaded with her. Gérard had remained silent and she had wondered if he could possibly understand what it had been like living with his father for all those loveless years. She had been young when she married him—only eighteen—she could have had a happy family life. She sighed and put down the cup, she hadn't been the sort of woman who would take a lover; instead she had bestowed all the caring and loving on her children.

Gilles was gazing out of the window, listening, she supposed, to the detailed report of some merger between two steel companies that Gérard was reading to him. She had meant it when she had told him she wished it were he who had died in the crash and not Armand, and now he had cheated death a second time. Nothing could beat him.

His profile against the pale wash of the sky was still arrogant, still strong, but then he had always been a handsome man. He leaned back in the wheelchair he hated, dressed as immaculately as ever, the same striped shirt, the silk tie neatly tied by his valet, for his own trembling hands were powerless even for such a simple task—he couldn't even hold the newspaper still enough to read it. His feet in beautifully polished handmade shoes had been placed on the footrest by the valet and his perfectly pressed trousers concealed his useless legs. What the crash hadn't succeeded in accomplishing the heart attack and the stroke that followed it had. Gilles was paralyzed from the waist down. And there was one other, even more terrible thing: Gilles had no voice. No one knew why, the doctors and nerve-specialists had puzzled over the question for three months now and were none the wiser. Maybe it will return when the shock is over, they had told Gérard, it's possible.

Gilles turned his head to look at her and their eyes met. His dark blue ones were cold, empty. What was he thinking? she wondered. There was no way to know. He couldn't write because his hands shook too much, and he couldn't speak.

She stood up hurriedly. "Gérard, I must leave," she said, avoiding Gilles's eyes.

"I'll take you home, Mother." Gérard put down the paper. "I'll be back later this evening," he promised, taking his father's hand for a moment. "I'll read some more to you then. Or maybe I could get tickets for the theater or a concert?" Gilles shook his head and resumed his gaze out of the window.

Gérard watched his father sadly. He never went out. He refused even to be taken to the park—he was so desperately ashamed of being crippled.

Marie-France paused by the door. "Good-bye Gilles," she called. She knew he could hear, but he didn't acknowledge her. She *knew* she should never have come.

I was right, thought Jim, following Marigny at a discreet distance across the Pont Sully. He had been uncertain about the man for a while when he had turned into a building across from the station, but it had been a cheap rooming house. He'd obviously taken a room and left his bag there and then he emerged ready for action—or almost. First there'd been a visit to the Bar Augustine, and then to the Bar Michel, and then a couple more bars. His man drank a *lot,* there was no doubt about that, and the guy at the boat yard had said it made him aggressive. Maybe he was just getting up his courage for the task ahead. He had to be Charles's killer.

He stopped as Marigny paused at the gates of the great private mansion. Marigny hesitated for a moment and then shambled across the courtyard and up the broad steps. He thrust out a stubby hand and pulled the bell, stomping his feet impatiently as he waited.

The butler opened the heavy doors and Marigny said something to him. The butler shook his head and began to close the door. Jim crossed the road, slowing down and loitering past the gates, taking in the scene. A footman had come to the aid of the butler and they were trying to force Marigny outside, but his foot was in the door. Someone else was in the hall. It was Gilles de Courmont, in a wheelchair. Then it was true, he was crippled. The door closed suddenly on the scene and he stared at it for a moment or two. Marigny was inside.

Gilles faced Marigny across his desk. They were alone in his study. The man was talking, threatening him. Of course, he thought wearily, it's blackmail. Oh, God, Verronet, why did you have to die on the Amazon River? I need you now! Only Verronet would have known how to deal with this—Verronet would have been his voice, his hands; there was no one else he could trust. No one who cared.

Marigny prowled the study confidently. Who'd have thought the old boy would be in this state? Well, it only made it easier, didn't it? He could do all the talking and the old bastard couldn't even answer back. This might be the easiest day's work of his life. "I'll go to her," he threatened, "I'll tell her everything. I'll tell her what you did—you wouldn't like that, would you? She's famous now . . . and rich. Of course," he added, wiping the sweat from the pasty flesh of his hairless face with the sleeve of his shirt, "then I may have to go elsewhere . . . to your son—or your wife."

He walked to the side table and picked up the decanter of whiskey, pouring himself a healthy slug. "Like some?" he asked, waving the delicate Venetian crystal decanter in the air. He grinned at Gilles' expressionless face as the decanter hit the ground, splintering into a hundred fragments with a delicate tinkling sound, splashing whiskey across the cream and gold of the old Chinese rug.

Gilles felt the sweat break out on his back and he pushed himself away from the desk, maneuvering his wheelchair awkwardly as he fumbled with the key to the bottom left-hand drawer of the desk. Oh, God, he thought, why is it so difficult, why won't my hands do what I want them to do? The key went into the lock at last and with a scrabbling pull, the drawer opened. He leaned sideways and put his hand inside. He always kept cash in there, you never knew when you might need instant money for business—or for blackmail, he added ruefully. He watched his trembling hand with fascination as it attempted to curl itself around the bundle of notes; it was as though it were not his hand at all. With a final jerking leap the hand managed it; exhausted, he pulled back his arm, resting it in his lap.

Gilles recoiled from the sour odor of sweat and drink as Marigny leaned over him. "Thanks," he said, picking up the notes and tucking them into his pocket. "Thanks very much, Monsieur le Duc." Marigny began to laugh as he made his way to the door, kicking the broken glass as he went. "They say, Monsieur le Duc," he said, pausing by the door, "that God smites the wicked. Well, he certainly took care of you." He patted his shirt pocket with a grin. "I'll be back," he promised, "when this runs out."

Oh, my God, thought Gilles. Oh, my God, he'll come back and I'm powerless. I can't move, I can't speak. There's no way I can get rid of him. I'll have to sit here waiting, wondering when he'll be back—and who he might tell. Gilles stared mutely at the closed door.

Marigny had already visited three bars by the time he reached Le Six Zero Un on the busy corner of the rue Ponsard. Jim followed him inside. He took a seat at the opposite end of the room and ordered Scotch, sipping it slowly, keeping an eye on his man. Marigny sat alone at the bar, drinking whiskey and talking to no one. Had he accomplished what he went for? How was he to know? Wait, he ordered another drink. Marigny's hand went to his shirt pocket and pulled out a wad of notes. He gave one to the bartender, who looked at it in surprise before he went to the till and came back with a handful of notes in change. Marigny had given the bartender a big bill, so he must have succeeded in blackmailing Monsieur.

Marigny stood up suddenly, knocking back his whiskey like a man in a hurry, and making for the door. His normally rolling gait was becoming even more uneven, and he stumbled over the step, turning back to look accusingly at it, before lurching onto the pavement. Jim followed him, waiting to see what he would do next—he was obviously too drunk to talk now. Would he go back to the rooming house to sleep it off?

Marigny lurched forward again, striding into the road purposefully, making for the bar opposite just as the car turned the corner of the rue Ponsard. Jim had time to glimpse the horror on the driver's face before the car hit Marigny, knocking him clear across the street. The big flabby body seemed to be suspended in the air for minutes before it crashed with a sickening thud to the ground.

The car hit the curb and stopped, its driver crouched in shock over the wheel. Jim ran across the road to where Marigny lay, face up on the edge of the pavement. His eyes were open and he was dead. One hand still clutched a thick wad of Monsieur's notes and they drifted gently one by one down the grimy street, blown by the wind.

So Marigny had done it! Monsieur had paid the blackmail money. Every day, he'd wait for Marigny to return, every day he'd wonder if he would be coming back. He would sit there, in his wheelchair, crippled, mute, and afraid—afraid that his secret would be out at last. Jim gazed at Marigny's body, grotesque in death. Monsieur would never know that his blackmailer was dead. He would live with fear. Marigny had succeeded where everyone else had failed: Monsieur was powerless.

Jim looked at the face of Charles d'Aureville's assassin. "Well, Léonie Jamieson," he murmured, "there's your revenge."

BOOK
3

1910 - 1919

❧61❧

AMÉLIE CHOSE a rich white silk taffeta for her wedding dress, and the sumptuous fabric lent her tall rangy figure a regal air. She waited patiently, arms aloft, as the dressmaker pinned the bodice tighter at the waist, enjoying the swirl of the spreading skirts over the rustling frilled petticoats. She had designed the dress herself, poring over sketches and pictures with Xara and Isabelle until she had it exactly right. Double ruffles edged the skirt and ran down the center of each short puffed sleeve and the scooped neckline left her throat bare for the beautiful pearls her mother had given her as a baby.

"Let's try the veil," said Xara, lifting the thirty yards of silk tulle that formed the base for the century-old Brussels lace that Isabelle had worn to her own wedding, as had her mother and grandmother before her. Together she and Senhora Delfina placed the veil on Amélie's carefully poised head, anchoring it for the moment with a circlet of silk flowers, though on her wedding day Amélie would wear orange blossoms.

"Perfect," murmured Xara. "Roberto will fall in love with you all over again."

Amélie's reflected image stared back at her, a stranger—fragile in clouds of silk and tulle and lace—subdued by the significance of the bridal white. In three weeks' time she would be Senhora Amélie Castelo do Santos, a married woman. Roberto's wife. Her whole life would be different. She and Roberto were spending all their time together, every moment he was free he was with her, and Diego seemed to have faded from their lives as though he had never existed. And Roberto was so different now, so tender, so loving. He still teased her, but in a different way, and often their teasing and games ended in kisses and caresses that grew more passionate, more exploratory, as they discovered a new fascination for each other's body and Amélie discovered a new passion in herself.

It was always Roberto who held back, though, she thought guiltily; she wanted more, wanted desperately for him not to stop kissing her, longed for the strange touch of his hands that were yet so familiar. Wait Amélie, he'd whisper, kissing her blushing cheeks, soon we'll be married.

The knock on the door startled her from her dreams.

"Hello," called Sebastião, "can I come in?"

"No, no. Senhorita, he mustn't." Senhora Delfina rushed to the door in panic. "He mustn't see the bride in her dress before the wedding day."

Amélie burst out laughing. "But that isn't the bridegroom," she said, "it's Sebastião."

"Amélie!" She looked so young in her grand wedding dress, a girl on the edge of womanhood, the bride he had always hoped would be his. Sebastião took a deep breath, it was better that he was going away until the wedding, it was too painful to stay and watch her happiness.

"I just came to say good-bye," he said. "I didn't expect to have a preview of the bride in her finery."

"Well," asked Amélie breathlessly, "what do you think?"

"You'll be the most beautiful bride Rio has even seen," he assured her, "and all the men will be jealous of Roberto."

Amélie blushed. "Of course they won't, silly. But Sebastião, you said good-bye? Where are you going?"

"I'm escaping from all these frantic wedding plans. No one can talk of anything else and as hordes of do Santoses are about to descend on us, I'm off to snatch a bit of peace at the *fazenda* while I can. I'll be back for your wedding."

"Sebastião"—her face was still close to his and her eyes were anxious— "Sebastião, you will still be my friend won't you? After I'm married, I mean?"

Poor darling, he thought, she doesn't know that it will never be the same. "Of course I will." He patted her cheek reassuringly. "And wherever I am in the world, I expect to receive those letters complete with the little drawings, though soon, I suppose, you'll be telling me all about your wonderful babies."

"Babies!" cried Amélie, startled by the idea.

"Women do have babies, you know."

"Yes, but not yet—not until I'm grown up."

"Oh, Amélie." Sebastião hugged her, despite the horrified protests of Senhora Delfina hovering in the background. "Little Amélie," he whispered, "you are grown up."

He kissed her on the tip of her nose. "See you in church," he called, stopping to kiss Xara on his way out. She thought his voice was more cheerful than his face. Could Sebastião have hoped for Amélie, too? And mightn't Amélie have been better off with him? She sighed. Those were foolish hypothetical questions. After all, it was for Amélie to decide.

Senhora Delfina folded the dress carefully into its enormous box, and stripped of her silken grandeur, Amélie was her old self again. "Oh, poor

Onça," she cried, rushing to the big double windows that led onto the terrace, "she's been shut out all this time."

"I should think so, too," grumbled Senhora Delfina. "I hate to think what its claws might have done to that veil."

The fluffy jaguar cub sprawled in the shade, her back legs stretched out flat and her head resting on big front paws. The rails of the veranda striped her creamy coat with shadow, hinting of the beautiful tawny amber it would become when she reached maturity, and she gazed up at Amélie with the doleful eyes of a banished kitten.

"You're sulking, Onça," called Amélie, "and I don't blame you . . . you only wanted to see what was going on, didn't you?"

The cat pricked up her ears, a look of hope returning to her eyes. "Come on then, my darling," Amélie murmured, lifting her in her arms and kissing the soft place just above her glossy nose. Onça's clumsy paw came up playfully, but Amélie caught it before it reached her face. "No. No, Onça. Not until you've learned that your claws can hurt me."

The cat lay, belly up in her arms, as relaxed as a baby, while she murmured to her, tickling her chin and stroking her fluffy fur.

"I've never seen anything like it," marveled Xara. "The creature is devoted to you. I don't know what will happen when she grows too big and you have to get rid of her."

"Get rid of Onça! Oh, Xara, I'd never do that."

Xara looked at the cat doubtfully, she hadn't been happy when Edouard had given her to Amélie as a pre-wedding gift. She knew how Amélie felt about all cats and this little jaguar was adorable. But she would grow into a powerful animal.

"I'm training her," said Amélie proudly. "Look, she already walks at heel." The cat followed her feet obediently, stopping when she stopped. "She hasn't learned to sit yet, but she will. You mustn't worry, Xara, lots of people keep jaguars as pets, they're truly faithful to their masters."

Onça rolled over on her back, waving a paw at the ribbon Amélie dangled over her.

"Onça," she said lovingly, "you are the nicest wedding present of all."

Roberto wended his way through the market, busy even at this early hour with traders and porters and customers like himself, buying for their shops, restaurants, and hotels. It was five o'clock in the morning and he was there, as he had been every morning for the past two months, to learn how to buy produce for the Hotel d'Aureville and the Pavillon. It was just one of the aspects of "learning his trade" as Edouard had called it. He pushed his hands in his pockets, watching as the assistant chef from the Pavillon picked over the heaps of shrimp and tested eggplants for ripeness. Roberto had already discussed the quantities with him, learning that waste or overbuying could spell rapid financial ruin for a restaurant. Nothing was ever wasted at the Pavillon and yet everything was superlatively fresh.

"I'll get back to the kitchen now, Senhor Roberto," called the young chef. "They'll be waiting for these."

Roberto stretched wearily. Getting up at four-thirty every day was not easy. Still, it was worth it, he thought, pushing his way back through the throng into the street. You had to know every part of a hotel in order to manage it, from buying the vegetables to supervising the restaurant, from the proper procedure for greeting guests to balancing the books. And since he'd started working at the Hotel d'Aureville, he'd discovered that he was interested in every aspect of it. It would take him two years, he considered, making his way along Rua Ouvidor, and then he'd be able to call himself a hotel manager. He could work anywhere in the world then—France, Switzerland, maybe even England. He remembered with a pang the missed years at Oxford. That had been Diego's fault; no, that wasn't true, it had been his own weaknesses that had caused him to miss the crucial exams. But he had paid for it, working on the *fazenda* all those months.

He glanced at his watch as he pushed open the door of the Café Miltinho. There was just time for a quick cup of coffee before he went back.

The café was surprisingly busy, a mixture of market people breakfasting after their hard day's work, which had begun for some of them at midnight, and the other night people, those for whom the day was not beginning, the night was ending. Glancing at their faces he remembered himself after such nights, the bitter loathing, the regrets. Well, thank God that was all in the past. Amélie was his life now, his lovely simple innocent life.

"Well, hello." The familiar voice was edged with a smile and Roberto knew without looking who it was. "How does it feel being engaged? A bit like being fattened for the kill?"

Roberto swallowed the scalding black coffee in a gulp and crashed the cup into its saucer.

Diego put a hand on his arm. "Mind if I sit down? After all, we are old friends, aren't we?"

He pulled his chair closer to Roberto's. "I've been meaning to come to see you, ever since I saw the announcement, but I've been out of town a lot—Recife, Bahia . . . here and there—you know."

"You're invited to the wedding," said Roberto stiffly, "with your parents. My mother sent the invitation."

Diego's eyes under their thick dark brows were gleaming with amusement. "I know. So how are you going to manage it, Roberto? Marriage, I mean—every night the same woman?"

Roberto's clear blue eyes met Diego's dark gaze and a thousand memories passed through their glance.

"I think you should know," said Roberto hoarsely, "that I'm marrying Amélie because I love her." He averted his eyes, picking up the empty cup and draining it again. Anything to avoid looking at Diego.

"Love!" Diego's voice was contemptuous. "What does love count for someone like you? You know you're different, Roberto, we both are. Get married, but you'll regret it." He leaned closer and Roberto could smell the stale Cachaça on his breath. He knew what his night must have been like; he could almost taste the caresses that must have been lavished on Diego's flesh.

Roberto stood up suddenly, knocking over his chair in his hurry, and people turned to stare as he pushed past them on his way to the door.

Diego followed him. "I'll come to your wedding and I'll behave. I promise. But I've got trouble on the *fazenda* and I need your help."

Roberto kept on walking. Diego hurried by his side, talking as they went.

"It's about my father," he said. "You know how hard it's been for him over the years. God knows why he didn't sell the *fazenda* when he could, but he clung on against all odds and mortgaged it to the hilt—every single hectare. And the house as well. Now he can't pay and the collectors are threatening to come and take over the place."

Roberto stopped. Teo Benavente was his father's oldest friend. Why hadn't he known he was in such trouble? "But that's terrible, we must ask my father to help. You know he'd lend him the money to pay off the mortgage."

Diego stared back at him. "Yes, he would. In fact, Roberto, he already did. It just seems to have ... well ... 'gotten lost' en route."

"What do you mean? Where is the money?"

"Your father gave the check to me as my father's agent in Rio." He shrugged, a faint smile curling the corners of his mouth. "I have his power of attorney. It was easy to have the money paid to me instead. There were a few investments—I thought I would make my fortune—however, it seems I misjudged them ... and you know how quickly money disappears—a little here, a little there."

"That couldn't have been just 'a *little*' money! Jesus, Diego, how could you do that! You've ruined your father!"

Diego smiled, his thin attractive face bland and unblemished by his night's carousing, or any pangs of conscience. "You know me, Roberto, you always said I was no good. But now there's the problem of the mortgage collector. He'll be going out to the *fazenda* in the next few days to take it over. I thought if I could head him off before he got to my father, I could talk to him ... maybe give him a little money now and promise him more later just to stall things for a while. I need your help, Roberto."

Roberto turned away, "No," he said firmly, "I'm not going to help you."

Diego walked beside him. "Yes, you are. After all, you do want to marry Amélie, don't you?"

Roberto's footsteps slackened. "What do you mean?"

They faced each other, unheeding of the pedestrians pushing past them in the now busy street. "I don't want to have to tell her the truth about you, Roberto. I mean, I really want you two to be happy." Diego's smile was as innocent as a child's as he waited, hands in pockets, for Roberto's response.

How could he be that relaxed? wondered Roberto. He's blackmailing me! What am I going to do? What *can* I do?

"It's not for me." Diego changed his tactics. "It's for my father. I know I've been wrong—very wrong. But I've got to help him now. And I need you to help me."

"What do you want me to do?" asked Roberto stiffly.

"I need some money. You'll have to get hold of as much as you can." Diego thought of the safe in the hotel, Roberto had access to that now. "A *substantial* amount, Roberto." He wouldn't put any limit on the figure, he'd let Roberto do that. He waited for Roberto's reaction but there was none. "And I want you to come with me to the *fazenda,"* he added. "I shall need help with this collector, he might not take my word for it. You can tell him you're your father's estate manager and he is acting as guarantor. He'll believe you."

Roberto's mouth tensed. "No! I'll get you the money, but I won't go with you."

"Of course you will." Diego's smile was triumphant; he knew he'd won. "It'll be like old times, Roberto—just the two of us together." And, he thought to himself, you'll never return to Amélie by the time I'm through with you. I've got you, Roberto do Santos.

Diego was charming. He was gentle and soft-spoken; there was none of the old swaggering, confident manipulator about him on the journey down to the *fazenda*. "This has changed me," he told Roberto. "I know I was wrong and I have to make amends to my father. I'll never do anything like this again. I promise you."

His smile was winning, and his eyes gleamed with sincerity, so that Roberto began to wonder if it were true.

"Thank you for coming with me." Diego put his hand on Roberto's arm, touching him lightly, and the shock of the contact ran through Roberto's whole body. He would never lose those memories, no matter how he buried them in the recesses of his mind. "Let's be friends again," pleaded Diego. "We've known each other all our lives, let's forget the past, Roberto, come on." His hand closed more firmly on Roberto's. "Shake hands with me."

The train dropped them at the nearest small town and they hired horses for the last part of their journey so they could ride across country and avoid the long route by road, which Diego knew the collector must have taken. The going was easy, but it was hot and Roberto was thankful when they finally came to the lane that ran along the edge of the Benavente plantation. They were still some fifteen miles from the house but for the first time Diego looked worried. Could they have missed the collector? He kicked his horse into a canter and the dry dust flew from beneath its hooves. It was by the stretch of woods that bordered the *fazenda* that they caught up with the man, just a few miles from the big house. Night was falling and he was obviously preparing to make camp. He had tethered his horse and was collecting wood to feed the small fire he had started. He waved an arm in greeting as they approached.

Diego surveyed him coldly from his horse. "You realize, I suppose, that you are trespassing?"

"I'm on my way to the *fazenda*, senhor, but I didn't want to arrive there late at night. The *patrão* is an old man, I've no wish to disturb him. I'll go in the morning."

Diego struck out savagely with his whip and the collector reeled as the sudden blow caught him on the side of his head. "You'll go nowhere," said Diego contemptuously.

"Jesus, Diego!" Roberto leapt from his horse. "What are you doing?"

"Get away, Roberto, let me deal with this my way." Diego dismounted and approached the man, who cowered behind Roberto.

"I just want to talk to you—about my father," said Diego in a more reasonable tone.

Roberto watched him apprehensively. He seemed cool and rational, as though he'd overcome the initial outburst of rage.

"Your father?" The collector's voice was hoarse with fear.

"The *patrão*, the one you are going to see in the morning." He pulled the wad of money from his pocket—Roberto's money. "I have a plan to pay you what we owe; after all, you only want the money, don't you?"

"That's true, senhor, a *fazenda* isn't much good to anyone these days. If you have the money, we would prefer payment."

Roberto stared at the money in Diego's hand. It was all he'd had in the bank and its total represented a lifetime of family events, birthday gifts, small legacies from deceased aunts, the settlement his grandfather had made on him when he was born. At least, he thought tiredly, it would be put to good use if it helped to save Teo Benavente's *fazenda*.

"Come," Diego was saying reasonably, "let's sit by the fire and talk. I have a flask here, we could all use a drink." He passed the flask to the collector, who drank deeply, wiping his mouth with the back of his hand, coughing as the whiskey burned its way down.

Diego offered it to Roberto, who refused, and then Diego took a large swig himself. "Let's have a look at the documents, senhor," he demanded.

They waited uneasily in the flaring light of the fire while Diego examined the deeds. It was very dark and the humidity pressed heavily on them, forcing small wisps of mist from the cooling earth. The undergrowth rustled with nocturnal activity and in the far distance a dog barked.

Diego took another swig from the flask. "Well, my man," he said, fumbling at his belt, "I have your money for you right here." All at once his arm gripped the man's neck, forcing his head back. A thin knife gleamed at the man's throat.

"I'll have your signature on this, senhor," said Diego holding the paper in front of the man's eyes.

"Diego! What are you doing?" Roberto was on his feet in an instant.

"Stay back," warned Diego, his voice as finely honed as the knife in his hand, the edge of pleasure overlaying the threat in his eyes. Roberto stopped in his tracks, all of a sudden he was afraid. "I told you to let me deal with it in my way." Diego turned back to the man. "It's a receipt to say that you were paid the money. Sign it."

"But you haven't paid me the money, senhor."

"Exactly . . . do you want to sign it or do I kill you?"

The man's voice quavered. "I'll sign it if you give me the money."

Diego laughed and pushed the knife closer. A drop of blood appeared on the man's neck and he quickly seized the paper. His voice was thin with fear. "I'll sign it, senhor."

Diego relaxed his hold and handed the collector a pen. He smiled up at Roberto. "I told you it would be all right."

Roberto felt the rush of relief.

The collector held out the paper in a trembling hand. Diego read it, then folded it carefully and put it in his pocket. He leaned forward and Roberto caught the gleam of the knife in his hand as he neatly and swiftly slit the collector's throat. Blood spurted across the flames as the man sank soundlessly forward into the fire and with a hoarse cry Roberto grabbed him, hauling him back from the flames.

"My God, Diego, what have you done?" he screamed.

"I've killed him, of course." Diego's voice was dispassionate as he held the knife in the flames to clean it. "What else could I do?"

"You told me that you wanted to reason with him, that we would be able to talk to him . . . to make some arrangements."

Diego was icily calm and reasonable. "You can't make arrangements with these bastards, it's pay up or else . . . and for him this time it was the 'or else.' Don't you see Roberto, I have the signed receipt . . . the man just disappears. They'll think he ran off with the money or that he was robbed. It happens all the time. And no one will ever know what we did."

"What *we* did?"

Diego laughed. "Well, you were here, weren't you? It's you and me, Roberto. We saved my father's *fazenda*—that's all that matters. Now all we have to do is to get rid of him."

Roberto looked at the blood-soaked body at his feet. "Get rid of him? You must be mad, Diego." He trembled with shock and he felt ill.

"Of course I'm not mad, I'm merely being practical. He was in my way and he would have caused a lot of trouble. This was the perfect solution. Now come on, you have to help me bury him."

"I can't," whispered Roberto, "I can't do it."

Diego walked around the fire and put his hands on Roberto's shoulders. "Sure you can, Roberto," he said almost paternally. "Come on now, it's not so difficult. We'll dig a hole and give the fellow a decent burial. We can't just leave him here for someone to find or we'll both be in trouble. After all, no one would know who'd done it, would they, whether it were you, Roberto—or me?"

Roberto's eyes widened in horror as Diego took shovels from the saddlebag. "Come on," he commanded, "let's get the job finished."

The reality of the situation unfolded suddenly as Roberto realized what had happened. It wasn't just a spur of the moment violent act: Diego had planned this murder from the beginning—and he had planned to implicate him in it so that there would be no escape. A picture of Amélie's innocent smiling face came into Roberto's mind. Oh, dear God! He had lost Amélie. Diego would never let go of him now.

He picked up the shovel and followed Diego into the underbrush and began to dig at the chosen spot. Together they carried the body and laid it in the shallow grave, covering it with leaves. When it was done they looked at each other in silence.

"We'd better go to your place," said Diego at last, kicking out the remains of the fire. "My father doesn't know I'm here and it's better that he doesn't. That way if they ask him about anything he'll be able to tell the truth: he saw no one and there was only himself and my mother at the house."

The ride to the do Santos *fazenda* was silent and when he finally saw the lighted windows of the big house it seemed to Roberto that nothing had ever looked more welcoming and secure. Yet for me nothing will ever be the same again, he thought in despair. This is the worst moment of my life.

Tia Agostinha was very old now, but she was still queen of her establishment and it was she who bustled forward into the hall to greet them. "Roberto," she beamed, holding open her arms, "this is a surprise for your old aunty. Come here and give me a kiss."

"I'm a bit dirty, Tia Agostinha." Roberto leaned forward to kiss her, avoiding her hug. "It's been a long ride. I'd better get cleaned up."

"Who's that?" she asked, peering into the darkness behind him.

Diego sauntered into the hall. "It's only me, Tia Agostinha." He smiled. "Diego."

"Oh, Diego. Well, come on in, both of you. You certainly look a mess. Look at the mud on the floor . . . and what's this?" Agostinha touched his jacket. "Blood! You're hurt?"

Roberto pushed her hand away. "No, no . . . I'm not hurt. It's nothing, Tia Agostinha, just a scratch. I'll go get cleaned up."

"A scratch? With all this blood?"

Roberto looked down at his shirt, where the mortgage collector's blood had dried to a dark rusty red. A wave of nausea threatened him. *He had to get these clothes off!*

Sebastião pulled open the study door. Who could it be at this time of night? He strode into the hall where Roberto stood, white-faced and disheveled, with Diego right behind him.

"What's happened?" he called anxiously. "What are you two doing here?"

Roberto swayed and his knees began to crumple. "Agostinha, he must be hurt," cried Sebastião, running forward to catch him as he slid to the ground. "My God, look at the state he's in! Diego, what happened?"

"He fell off his horse," lied Diego glibly. "I guess he was tired and didn't see the low branch as we rode through the woods. It knocked him right out of the saddle . . . that's why he's so muddy."

Sebastião ripped open Roberto's shirt and gazed at his unmarked chest. Gently he lifted his arms and examined him. There was no wound. Roberto's eyes opened slowly and he began to struggle upright.

"Help me," Sebastião ordered curtly and Diego hurried to lift Roberto to his feet. Together they half-carried him into the small study and put him in a chair. A fire blazed cheerfully, fending off the chill of the misty night outside, and Tia Agostinha fussed around anxiously.

"Tell me what's the matter, my dear," she said. "Let your old aunty help you."

Roberto leaned forward, his head in his hands. "There's nothing you can do," he said wearily, "there's nothing anyone can do now. It's too late."

"What's all this about?" demanded Sebastião. "You'd better tell me, Diego—and I'll bet whatever it is, you are the cause!"

"What do you mean?" blustered Diego. "Nothing's wrong! Roberto's just tired and overwrought, that's all!"

"He hasn't fallen off any horse tonight—and you know it," Sebastião said menacingly. "I want to know what happened."

"Nothing happened, nothing's wrong. . . ."

"Oh, yes, Diego, something is wrong." Roberto's face was anguished as he looked at him.

Diego's glance was a warning. "Roberto. . . ."

Sebastião put out his hand and touched the stains on Roberto's shirt. "Whose blood is this? My God, what have you two done?"

"Tell him, Diego. We have to tell him what happened." Roberto's gaze was unwavering.

"Nothing happened! You don't know what you're saying, Roberto. He's in shock, can't you see!" Diego's eyes glittered angrily as he looked at Sebastião. "He fell off his horse. He'll be all right after a night's sleep."

Roberto began to laugh. "A night's sleep!" he cried, *"a night's sleep!* I'll never to able to sleep again!"

Diego headed for the door.

"Tell him, Diego—or I will!"

Diego paused, his hand on the door handle. Tia Agostinha watched in bewilderment, sensing evil and violence in the air.

"Diego killed him, Sebastião! He killed the mortgage collector." The words were forced from Roberto's throat in a hoarse rush. "He had him sign the receipt for the money and then he cut his throat. This is *his* blood on me. I helped Diego bury the man in the woods."

The four of them were paralyzed by Roberto's words; even Diego seemed unable to move.

"Ayeee," wailed Agostinha in the silence, throwing her hands in the air. "Murder! It was murder!"

Sebastião was at the door before Diego could turn the handle. "Oh, no," he said angrily. "You'll stay here, Diego. I want to hear what you have to say."

Diego folded his arms and leaned back against the closed door. A smile curved at the corners of his mouth. "It's true," he said softly. "I killed him. I did it for my father . . . he was going to lose the *fazenda,* you see. It meant everything to him—like yours, it has belonged to our family for generations. If he lost it his life would be meaningless. I had to help him, Sebastião." His voice was gentle and persuasive. "How could I see my own father destroyed? I didn't mean to kill the man, it just happened that way."

"It's not true," said Roberto wearily. "He planned the murder. And he hasn't told you that our father gave him the money to give to Senhor Benavente to pay the mortgage arrears. Diego stole it! He stole it from our father—and from his own. And then when he was faced with the result, he planned this murder. He forced me—persuaded me—to come with him, but I didn't know he was going to kill the man. I swear I didn't know! I thought he just needed help to convince the collector to wait a bit longer—I lent him some money."

Sebastião turned to Diego. "But you killed him and kept the money."

Diego pulled the deeds from his pocket. "I have the receipt," he said calmly. "As far as anyone knows, he was paid off."

"But we know he wasn't, don't we, Diego?" Sebastião's voice was full of contempt. He wanted to hit Diego's faintly smiling face. How *could* Roberto have got himself involved in this?

"Of course," said Diego confidently, "you'll do nothing about it."

"What makes you think that?"

"Because Roberto is involved just as deeply as I am. I could always say it was he who stabbed the man, that he just went crazy, that he'd been drinking. He can drink quite well, your nice young brother, you know. . . ."

"They'll never believe you," cried Sebastião, horrified. "You have a bad reputation already in Rio, the police would know it was you. Roberto isn't blameless, but he's no killer!"

Diego sauntered to the fireplace, leaning against it nonchalantly, kicking a log into place with his foot. "But Roberto knows the other reason why he'll say nothing. Shall I tell him, Roberto?" he asked mockingly.

Roberto sat like a condemned man, waiting for the ax to fall, and Sebastião looked at him pityingly, thinking of Amélie happily preparing for her wedding, so lovely in her sumptuous white dress, and of his father and mother. Diego was implying things that none of them must ever know—he wasn't sure what they were, but he had to do something to stop him. He poured a glass of brandy and handed it to Roberto.

"You can tell me nothing that I don't already know, Diego," he lied, "and what you have to say would make no difference to your arrest for murder. Roberto was misled by you and his story has a ring of truth—it would be easy to prove what happened to the money my father gave you."

Diego looked uneasy, his threat had fallen flat. "What about Amélie's future husband? It's only a few weeks to the wedding. And your father—what about him?"

Rage flushed Sebastião's face as he grabbed Diego by the collar. "My father gave you that money in friendship to save your home, your livelihood—*your father!* How dare you threaten him now! And Amélie. It's easy to hurt her, isn't it, but you've got nothing left to gain, Diego. Don't you see that Roberto is finished with you?"

"Is that true?" Diego pulled himself away from Sebastião and confronted Roberto. "Is that true, Roberto?"

"It's true. Say what you like. Do what you like. I never want to see you again." Roberto closed his eyes as if expecting a blow.

"I'll make a deal with you, Diego," said Sebastião suddenly. "I will say nothing about this—on one condition: that you never come near my family again. You have Roberto's money . . . use it to leave the country. If you don't, then I shall go to the police. And I'm warning you now, Diego, don't imagine that this means that in a few months' time you can show up and nothing will be said. You will stay away from Roberto and from Amélie—forever."

Diego's eyes flickered over Roberto, still sitting motionless in the big chair. He couldn't afford an involvement with the law; even if he could talk his way out of it, there were a few other matters hanging over his head in Rio and in Santos. With a final look at Roberto, he headed for the door.

"Very well," he told Sebastião, "I'll leave. I'll be on a ship tomorrow. I'll write to my father and say that the mortgage was paid by Senhor do Santos and that I've decided to try my luck in another country for a while. You never know," he added with a grin, "it might be fun."

Agostinha shrank back against the wall as Diego passed her, superstitiously throwing her apron over her face to protect her from the evil eye.

Roberto stared into the fire, the dancing flames blurred before his eyes as he listened for the click as the door closed. It was finally over.

"I'm not going to ask any more questions," said Sebastião, "because I think you've been through enough tonight. I don't want any explanations or reasons—I don't even want to know what Diego meant. I know that you were not guilty of anything tonight and that's enough for me. But one thing I ask you—no, I *warn* you, Roberto—is that none of this must ever harm Amélie. Whatever has happened in the past must never affect her. Do I make myself clear?"

Roberto nodded miserably. "I would give anything—anything, Sebastião—never to have known Diego. I love Amélie, you know that. I would never do anything to hurt her."

Sebastião nodded, satisfied. "Very well then," he said, helping Roberto to his feet, "let's get you to bed and Agostinha will brew you one of her potions to make you sleep. We'll start afresh tomorrow."

❧62❦

THE WEDDING in the magnificent old church of Nossa Senhora do Gloria was a joyous affair and none of the splendid gold and silver altarpieces gleamed more radiantly than Amélie's face as she pledged her love to Roberto. Vibrations of confident happiness surrounded her like an aura as she walked with her hand on his arm back down the flower-laden aisle to the accompaniment of soaring organ music and the smiling faces of five hundred relatives and friends.

Bells rang out their happiness as the perfect bride and groom, young and strong, blond and beautiful, emerged into the sunlight of a glorious blue day.

Isabelle, on Francisco Castelo do Santos's arm, followed the retinue of six small bridesmaids, all do Santos cousins, down the aisle, smiling her pleasure at the scene. "Nothing," she murmured to Francisco, "could have made me happier than to see these two married. It seems only right that they should—they've always been together."

Francisco looked proudly at his son. "I'm glad he kept Amélie in the family for us, I would have hated to lose her! Now we can share our grandchildren, Isabelle."

They laughed together at the idea of plotting their grandchildren before they'd even left the church, but she knew what he meant. The do Santos and the d'Aureville families would be joined in more than distant kinship now that Amélie had married Roberto.

A vast marquee extended from the terrace of the Pavillon d'Aureville joining the gardens to the restaurant, and guests ringed the wooden floor that covered the lawns, enjoying the best the Pavillon could provide for a wedding feast. Roberto had gone to great pains to find exactly the right musicians to play for them and the strains of happy sambas and carnival songs blended now and then into the waltzes and romantic tunes of Europe and America.

Edouard watched his little girl: a lovely bride, serenely elegant in her rustling dress, greeting her guests, laughing with Roberto at their own private jokes, cutting the cake and responding to toasts and compliments with an easy unaffected charm, and he hoped she might always be as happy as she was that day.

"Will you dance with your old father?" he asked wistfully.

He wrapped his arm around her, smiling into her lovely eyes. "I know it sounds like a cliché," he said, "and I'm probably only behaving like any other father at his daughter's wedding, but it seems like only yesterday I was carrying you on my shoulders and the greatest event of the week was when a new tooth appeared, or we had to patch up another scrape on your knee."

Amélie rested her face against his chest, feeling the crispness of his starched white shirt beneath her warm cheek. "You're the best father any girl could have. Whatever would I have done without you? Remember how jealous I was on your wedding day? How could I have known that you and Xara must have felt just like this?"

"I'll tell you a secret," whispered Edouard. "If it were anyone other than Roberto, I'd be a very jealous man."

Amélie laughed delightedly. "Good, now I don't feel so guilty about you and Xara." A shadow crossed her face. "But I do feel guilty about Léonie."

"Don't," said Edouard quietly. "She could have come, Amélie, but she felt it was better—safer—not to." He thought again of Léonie's letter to him. She would never get over her fear of Monsieur, even though the man was now virtually a cripple and a recluse. He still dominated her life.

"One day we shall go to see her again," said Amélie determinedly. "At least she knows about Roberto, she knows whom I'm marrying. Whom I *married.*" She corrected herself with a laugh. "Edouard, I wish I could love her—I mean, I'm so glad that I met her, it helped me so much. In fact, finally knowing Léonie made me grow up I think. Once she was no longer a mystery, I felt secure. I love you and Grandmère, but I can't say that I love my real mother. Is that terrible of me?"

"Not terrible—understandable." Edouard smiled at her encouragingly. "And who knows, maybe one day you'll know each other better. Meanwhile, this is your wedding day, Amélie do Santos, you shouldn't be thinking of anything but your own happiness."

Poor Léonie, he thought, whirling Amélie around so that her long silk skirts flowed and she leaned back against his arm, laughing. Poor Léonie, how she would have loved to be here. She is always the one whose happiness is sacrificed.

Roberto came to claim his bride. "It's time to change, Amélie, we must be leaving soon."

She slid from Edouard's arms. "I'll find Xara to help," she said, turning back to smile at him. And then she was gone.

Edouard drank his champagne staring gloomily out of the flowery tent to the ocean. Emerald waves curved elegantly, flaunting their white crests before they slid in slow smooth motion to the white beach.

"Don't worry." It was Sebastião's voice behind him. "I'm sure all fathers of the bride feel as you do."

Edouard turned with a rueful grin. "Does it show?"

"Written all over you." Sebastião handed him a fresh glass. "Here, let's drown our sorrows in champagne."

"You, too?" Edouard's glance was curious.

"Me, too." Sebastião leaned his elbows on the parapet of the terrace. "It wasn't to be; in fact, I never stood a chance. She's always loved Roberto. I'm the 'good friend,' " he said, draining his glass. "And that's what I intend to remain."

"Sebastião, I hadn't realized. . . ."

Edouard's voice was kind, and Sebastião held up his hand in protest. "The best man won," he said lightly. "Come on, Edouard, I think it's time to throw the rice and rose petals."

"Amélie," Xara said hesitantly, as she buttoned the pretty blue linen dress and handed Amélie the matching pale blue shoes. "Will you be all right? Tonight, I mean."

Amélie swung round, wide-eyed. "You mean sex?" she asked with a grin. Xara blushed. "Of course I'll be all right, Xara; in fact, I can't wait! Is that a very naughty statement for a brand-new bride to make? I've wanted Roberto to make love to me for months but he insisted that we must wait until we were married." She took Xara's hand impulsively. "Is it wonderful, Xara?" she breathed. "Is it the most marvelous thing that can ever happen to you?"

"When you love someone the way you love Roberto," she replied gently, "then it is."

Amélie suddenly saw Edouard in a new light, as a very attractive man that a lovely woman like Xara was very much in love with. She smiled at Xara with a new complicity as she slipped her feet into the blue shoes. "There, I'm ready." She kissed Xara suddenly. "Thank you—for everything. I'm so very glad that you married Edouard."

"So am I," said Xara with a laugh, "and I'd better collect my babies before they cause too much trouble down there." The twins, Vicente and Jean-Paul, were two years old and the delight of her life.

Roberto was waiting for Amélie at the bottom of the stairs of the Villa d'Aureville and together they walked back through the fragrant gardens to the marquee and their waiting families. Hand in hand, with Amélie still clutching her bouquet of tiny white roses, they distributed last-minute

kisses and then they were off. Amélie turned as she climbed into the beribboned carriage with its perfect pair of white horses, their tails and manes
sporting ribbons to match. She tossed her bouquet lightly toward the
guests, joining in the laughter as it landed neatly in Sebastião's arms. He
passed it on to a tiny bridesmaid. "Here little one," he said, "treasure that. It
means you'll be a happy bride one day."

"Good-bye, good-bye." The happy cries lingered in the air as the carriage drove onto the avenue and bowled along beside the ocean, making for
the pier and the boat that would take them to New York, from where they
would wander down through Florida to Key West and the Villa Encantada.

"Well, Senhora Castelo do Santos?"

"Well, Senhor Castelo do Santos?"

Their smiles linked them to their future. She was his bride and Roberto
was her husband. And he would never let her down.

Amélie hesitated. Should she wear the pale green satin nightie with the
thin straps and the ecru lace, or the white cotton, that fell in fine pleats
from a low square yoke embroidered with tiny flowers? Suddenly nervous of
the sensuous satin, she pulled the white cotton over her head and peeked in
the mirror to see how she looked. Yes, that was all right, she supposed.
Everything was covered anyway. She pulled up her skirts to take off her
panties and stopped, her hands on the waistband. She stared at herself in the
mirror. Were new brides supposed to leave their panties on? What to do?
Oh, Xara, she thought, if only you were here now, these are the questions I
should have asked you. She dropped her skirt, deciding to leave them on.
Her hair crackled with electricity as she brushed it and she smoothed it
down impatiently. Why tonight of all nights did it choose to misbehave
like this, it must be the sea air! Well, that was it. There was no other reason
to delay and Roberto was waiting in the next room. Still she hesitated. This
is ridiculous, she told herself firmly. It's not a stranger out there, it's Roberto. And isn't this what you've been waiting for, longing for? It was just
that now that it was here it all seemed different.

"Amélie? Are you all right?"

Roberto's voice floated to her distantly. She squared her shoulders and
took a deep breath.

"Here I am," she announced, walking barefoot across the bedroom.
Roberto was wearing blue pajamas and his hair was neatly brushed. He
smelled faintly of some citrusy cologne.

"You look very pretty," he said.

"So do you." Her voice was small.

"And scared."

Amélie glanced at him guiltily.

"It's all right," said Roberto gently, "you're just tired and we've both had a little too much champagne. Why don't you just sit here by me—just the way we used to when we were kids, remember? You used to whisper all your secrets to me in bed?"

They lay on the bed together, his arm protectively around her shoulders, staring up at the ceiling. The big ship moved gently beneath them and Amélie felt her tense muscles relax. "Did you enjoy your wedding day, Senhora do Santos?"

"I loved it," she murmured. "I loved the church with all those wonderful white flowers, and the bridesmaids, so sweet in their pink frilly dresses and satin slippers with the ribbons slipping down their fat little legs, and Grandmère was so very elegant in lilac and that wonderful big hat and Luiza and Francisco and Xara—only Xara would wear scarlet to a wedding, she looked like a Goya painting. And Edouard. You know, I felt so sorry for him, Roberto, he looked so sad, as though he was losing me forever. I told him he wasn't. You know he is the *best* father any girl could ever have."

"What else did you love?" asked Roberto, stroking her soft hair.

"What else? Oh, I can't remember . . . just . . . everything."

"How about me?"

Amélie turned in the circle of his arm and kissed him lightly. "You know I love you."

Roberto wrapped his arms about her. "Tell me again," he murmured, kissing her eyelids.

"I love you," Amélie whispered. His skin smelled so good. His tongue brushed across her eyelashes and she lifted her face for his kiss, feeling the delicious awakening response as his mouth closed on hers. This must be what heaven is like, she thought, as his hand caressed her neck. He lifted her heavy hair and buried his face in the warmth of her soft nape, kissing it with exquisite tenderness, holding her next to him. Amélie was almost breathless with anticipation. She loved him so much that the touch of his hand on her breast was the most natural feeling on earth, it was the way God had meant love to be. Nothing mattered anymore, her inhibitions fled and her body responded to his as she wrapped herself closer to him. All the worry about her nightdress and panties might never have existed, she scarcely even noticed their removal and when they were naked, her trembling curious hands sought him instinctively.

It was a first time for Roberto, too, the first time that sex was combined with love. He thrust aside the dark memories of a more brutal passion, and the tenderness and respect he felt for Amélie made him the gentlest and most understanding of lovers. Amélie lay beneath him hardly realizing that she was smiling as she held him close, so close now. It was wonderful, she had always known it would be. She didn't know if she felt

what he did at that final moment when she opened her eyes and saw his face
contorted with passion, but it was beautiful.

❧ 63 ❧

THE NILE WAS STILL the main highway of Egypt, its traffic of graceful
lateen-rigged feluccas looking exactly as they had through centuries and dynasties. Léonie had been up since dawn, sitting on the deck of the pretty
houseboat at Luxor, watching as the first rays of the morning sun gilded the
massive cliffs of Deir al-Bahri and the Valley of the Kings on the west bank
of the river. The fact that the name of the valley was also her name was one
of the reasons she was here—that and Sekhmet.

"Bahri," she'd said to Jim, as they had pored over the map he had discovered in the English bookshop in Nice just one month ago. "Could that
be where my father came from? Surely it's too unusual for it be a coincidence? I may have relatives there . . . maybe my father even went back there
to live?"

"You realize it's unlikely." Jim had been practical as ever.

"Yes, but still . . ."

Léonie's eyes had shone with such hope that he couldn't disappoint
her. She'd been through enough lately. Only he knew how much it had
hurt her to refuse to attend Amélie's wedding, though, of course, even apart
from the danger she still insisted was real, they had both realized that it was
an impossible situation. Léonie had recognized the d'Aurevilles' good intentions in inviting her, but had had the tact and strength to choose to remain in the background. It had hurt her, there was no doubt about that.
Jim had been thankful that her interest had been diverted from brooding on
her daughter to a desire to seek out her own past. And, of course, to see
Sekhmet.

"All right," he'd agreed at last, "let's go to Egypt and see this Temple
of Ptah and the notorious statue of Sekhmet for ourselves. We'll get it out
of your system once and for all, Léonie." It was time Léonie was cured of
her belief that Sekhmet ruled her destiny.

Léonie turned her gaze to the near bank, past the cluster of houseboats
where red-tarbooshed servants were busy washing decks and polishing
already-shining brass rails, to the desert landscape that was finally releasing

its long-buried treasures and the secrets of its gods to an interested world. But not her secrets, not yet. They had been in Luxor for three days and she hadn't yet been able to bring herself to visit the Temple of Ptah and the statue of Sekhmet. Why am I putting it off? she wondered. I keep telling myself it's because I want to find out about my family first, so that I'll feel more Egyptian, closer to my roots and my past. But was that the truth? Or was it fear? And if it is fear, then what am I afraid of?

"Léonie." Jim appeared on deck, a cup of thick black coffee clutched in one hand. He grimaced as he tasted it, and took a seat next to her. "Well, what are our plans for today?"

"I thought we might see the Valley of the Kings—the tombs are supposed to be fascinating."

His glance was skeptical. "No Sekhmet today?"

"Not today, Jim."

He sipped his coffee. At least the tombs would be more interesting than struggling with uncomprehending bureaucrats in crumbling offices, where lethargic ceiling fans did nothing to dispel the overwhelming heat, but merely spread another layer of fine dust over the desiccated papers of centuries. Pyramids of papers heaped in piles on cabinets and floors, lurking in corners like toppling curled-edged towers. Maybe one of those brittle dusty papers contained the births and deaths of a family named Bahri, but he was pretty certain they would never find out.

"I thought we might go to some of the local villages," said Léonie. "We could speak to people, ask them if they knew any families named Bahri."

"I'll get a guide who can interpret for us," said Jim, "but I don't want you to raise your hopes too high, Léonie. Promise me."

Léonie knew it was only a remote possibility. "I promise," she sighed.

Habib Yassin was only twenty-four but he was already an experienced guide. He was, as he told his clients, more at home in the tombs and the temples of the past than he was in his own dwelling. "I was born in the wrong century," he said, polishing his spectacles on his shirt as they made their way toward the Valley of the Kings. "I should have lived in the eighteenth dynasty—and maybe I did."

Léonie looked at him curiously. "What do you mean, Habib?"

Habib placed the gleaming spectacles on his formidable nose. His eyes, round and dark as twin cherries, shone with enthusiasm from behind their thick lenses. "The ancient Egyptians believed that when you died you journeyed through the underworld and if you survived that journey you would be born again. I feel so at home in the ancient culture that sometimes I think that is what happened to me." He grinned at Léonie cheerfully. "You'll understand what I mean when you see the tombs."

Nothing Habib had said, nor any pictures or books, could have prepared them for the immensity of what they saw. The great mortuary temples of King Montuholep II and Queen Hatshepsut loomed from the craggy background of the massive cliffs of Deir al-Bahri, awesome in their colossal scale and antiquity.

Jim held Léonie's hand in his as Habib spun tales of 1100 B.C. as though it were yesterday. It was impossible not to be overwhelmed by the brooding majesty of a place that was at once so ancient and yet so immediate.

Léonie peered through the dusty light of the tombs at the painted friezes. The colors glowed brightly, terra-cotta and coral, turquoise and gold.

"They are not merely stories and legends," murmured Habib next to her. "These people lived. The kings ruled their lands, they had children and palaces and their special gods." His finger pointed out the details of the frieze. "The man you see with oxen: he existed, he farmed that land, he owned those oxen . . . and he looked exactly the way you see him there."

"I feel almost as if I knew them," breathed Léonie.

"History is timeless because it lives on in all men," said Habib. "We are all of us shaped by the events of the past."

"Will you go with us, Habib?" asked Léonie suddenly. "To the villages. I have to find my own past."

"Of course, madame." He hesitated. Jim had explained her mission and he, too, felt it was fruitless. "But the villages are not what they once were. Many people left to find work in the cities. The people are scattered now in Cairo and Alexandria. There is little left here but the dead." His arm encompassed the tombs.

Léonie's eyes met Jim's. He shrugged, but said nothing. "We can at least try," she said stubbornly. "And then tomorrow we'll go to Karnak."

And Sekhmet, thought Jim. At last.

Léonie lay on her bed staring at the ceiling. Only the rhythmic whirr of the ceiling fans and soft slap of the river against the houseboat disturbed the hot afternoon silence. Jim sprawled beside her, sleeping on his stomach, his naked body damp with sweat. She reached out a hand to touch him. It was too hot to lie close together as they usually did, and she missed the physical contact. Why had she brought him on this wild goose chase? She would never find her family, she knew it now. The villages had been depressing, the fly-ridden poverty overwhelming. Instead of bringing her closer to her roots, the images of black-garbed old women in baked-mud houses, now indelibly imprinted on her brain, had made her feel more alien than when it had all been just a vague dream. If that were her past, then she felt no part of it.

Cairo, yes, that she had understood: the city with its hot crowded streets and mysterious lonely alleyways, its souks full of splendors and spices and trashy souvenirs and ancient scarabs, and sinister stores whose narrow fronts led tunnellike into dim shadowy rooms, where they sold who knew what. And the city's smart hennaed ladies whose dresses came from Paris, but whose cosmetics and perfumes were pounded and pressed right here in the souks, and the urbane businessmen, handsome in freshly pressed linen suits and panama hats, buying gold trinkets for fleshy mistresses from artisans who sat cross-legged on their mats fashioning exquisite earrings and necklets in complex ancient patterns.

Léonie sighed. She had felt a part of Cairo, but not this. She knew now what Habib had meant, the Valley of the Kings was more alive than the villages. Perhaps her grandfather had lived in one of those places and run away to escape the stultifying tentacles of the past. Léonie couldn't imagine her father here; it was easier to think of him as a dashing young athlete, charming the star-struck girls in the audience as he rode bareback in some circus ring, or perhaps keeping some assignation in the mysterious alleyways in the souks of Cairo.

And what about Sekhmet? Was that also just a dream? Suddenly she could wait no longer. She would go to the Temple of Ptah now, this afternoon. She glanced at Jim, still fast asleep beside her. It would be better to go alone.

She slid gently off the bed and peered at the clock. It was four-thirty. By five the sun would be losing its strength, and at five she knew that Habib would be in the café near the ferry station.

Habib held the sunshade protectively over Léonie's head as they walked together down the long avenue lined not with trees, but with magnificent ram-headed sphinxes that led to the Temple of Mut. The sun's rays were still hot and she could feel damp beads of sweat forming on her back beneath the fine muslin of her dress. They were going to see the hieroglyphs on the gate of the temple—the same ones that were inscribed on her figure of Sekhmet.

Habib began to explain the convoluted history of the temple. "Often when a great Egyptian king died he was created a god, so that he became a combination of king and god. Thus, on his death, King Amon's name was linked with the sun god Ra and became Amon-Ra. The goddess Mut was his consort and the symbolic mother-goddess. This temple—alas, now just a ruin—was erected by King Amenhotep III to replace an earlier structure on the same site. Mut and Bastet, the sacred cat-goddess beloved of the ancient Egyptians, were closely associated with Sekhmet. Many, many small statues of Sekhmet were found in this temple—some say more than six hundred—and that, madame, is probably where your statue came from."

The temple was a crumbled ruin, only the lower courses remaining to show its previous size and grandeur, and Léonie's hope crumbled with it. The columns of the gates were broken and badly eroded but the flaking stone still showed traces of the hieroglyphs that were the poem.

Habib ran a finger across the powdery surface as he translated:

> Praise to Sekhmet . . .
> She is the mistress of all the gods
> It is she who gives the breath of life
> to the nose of her beloved
> She is the one who is great of strength
> Who protects the lands.
> Protector of those she loves.
>
> Sekhmet with fearful eyes
> The mistress of carnage
> The messenger who brings pestilence and death
> Sekhmet the great mistress of power
> Who sends her flame against her enemies.
> Her enemies have been destroyed.

The rest of the poem had disappeared as dust on the desert wind, and Léonie stared at the mysterious symbols carved here by some long-dead craftsman, their mute message unraveled from the centuries for her by the gentle young Egyptian at her side. This was where her statue had come from, though how it came into her father's possession she would never know. She ran her fingers over the carvings and the stone felt warm and alive under her hand.

Now she was ready for Sekhmet.

The Temple of Amon was vast and its columned magnificence had suffered less from the eroding dry desert winds. Léonie caught her breath as they walked through its courtyards, marveling at its beauty.

Habib led her through the series of six magnificent columned gateways, until at last they stood in the courtyard of the Temple of Ptah. Léonie felt a chill run down her spine. The sun was sliding down toward the horizon, but its amber rays gave a bright normality to the scene. Why, then, should she feel afraid? It was just a temple, it was a long time since people had worshiped here.

Nervously she followed Habib into the northernmost room, shivering in the sudden chill of the thick stone walls.

"This is the sanctuary of Ptah—alas, without the splendors it once contained." Habib led her through to the next chamber. "And this is the chamber dedicated to Hathor, the flamboyant goddess of love."

The stone walls of the chambers were dry and crumbling, but still seemed to emit a dankness that was only partly eliminated by the rays of thin sunlight filtering through the small apertures in the walls and roof. Léonie suddenly wished that Jim were with her. Reluctantly she turned to the third chamber.

"In there, madame, you will find the great statue of Sekhmet. It is carved from granite and was erected in the eighteenth dynasty by King Thutmose. . . ."

Léonie hardly heard Habib's explanations. She was suddenly overcome by the feeling that this was all a mistake. She wanted to leave, to run from here. But she couldn't. She *had* to see her.

She stepped toward the shadowy doorway, resting her hand on the dank wall.

"Wait, madame, I'll come with you," called Habib.

"No. No, please. I want to go in alone."

Léonie closed her eyes to accustom them to the darkness, and the dank air pressed against her closed eyelids. Something rustled nearby and her eyes flew open in panic. Immediately in front of her the massive statue of Sekhmet loomed like some startling apparition from another world. Instinctively, she stepped back a pace, fighting the choking feeling of terror that threatened her.

A thin shaft of light pierced the darkness, filtering its single beam onto the leonine head of Sekhmet. The solar disc that symbolized her connection with the god of the sun glowed like a dusty corona above the beautiful face with its stylized mane. The body was carved strongly yet it was infinitely female with high rounded breasts and slender shoulders. As the deity who granted life, Sekhmet held in her right hand its symbol, the ankh, and in her left was a papyrus scroll indicating her power to allow life to flourish.

Léonie stepped forward again, the peculiar fascination of the statue holding her in its spell. There was nothing to be afraid of, she was sure of it now. It was just the darkness and the unexpected size of the statue that had made her uneasy. She lifted her eyes to Sekhmet's face. The granite looked smooth and cool. "I'm here," she whispered at last. "I don't know what I expect from you, but I came—finally."

The sightless lion face was unmoving and Léonie took a step closer.

She was within touching distance, all she had to do was to reach out. Do it, she told herself. All these years you've wondered about Sekhmet, more than wondered, you've believed that Sekhmet had power over you, that your fate was predestined. Touch her.

She stroked the smooth granite hand. The stone was icily cold to her touch and yet her fingers were burning. She cried out in pain, stumbling as she tried to pull back. *She couldn't move!* The shadows swirled around her and she sank to her knees, clinging to the outstretched hand of Sekhmet. Her mind was alive with strange noises and colors and heat. Then all at once a sense of peace came over her, there was no pain in her fingers now, just the soothing warmth from the granite hand in hers. Léonie raised her head and gazed at the face of Sekhmet illuminated by the final ray of the sun. She hadn't been wrong all these years; she knew it now. There was no way to know how or why, maybe in some past life she had been bound with Sekhmet—whatever it was she must accept it.

The granite grew icily cold as before. Léonie pulled her hand back and rose from her knees. If she had come here to purge herself of the burden of the past she hadn't succeeded, but she had reconciled herself to accept her future, whatever it might bring.

Backing away from the statue, she reached the doorway and, with a last look over her shoulder, emerged into the warm evening air. She glanced at her hand. It was swollen and the fingers were bruised.

"Madame, are you all right?" Habib was looking at her anxiously.

"Yes, yes, I'm all right."

He looked relieved. "There are strange stories about that statue and I was getting worried about you, you were such a long time."

"Strange stories?"

"Sekhmet was a powerful goddess and her influence is still felt—there have been attacks on the statue by people who thought that she was evil. There are even those who swore that the statue reached out her arms and touched them and who felt faint in her presence." Habib's spectacles gleamed in the last thread of sunlight, hiding his eyes. "Who knows," he said, "whether it is for good or for evil, but whichever way Sekhmet affects lives, she is powerful."

Léonie was silent, drained by her experience. Habib looked down at her sitting on the stone. "Sekhmet was the perfect mistress," he added softly. "She allowed each man to see in her what he himself sought."

"You should have let me go with you," said Jim for the tenth time.

"I *had* to go alone, Jim. Don't ask me why, but I knew I had to."

"And now you come back with this crazy story."

Léonie looked at her hand. Purplish bruises ringed the outer edges.

Was she mistaken? Could it just be that she had fainted and put out a hand to save herself as she fell? Jim was convinced of it.

"I'm taking you back there," he said determinedly. "We'll go together and then we'll see what Sekhmet does!"

Léonie stared out of the window. It was eight o'clock in the morning and the sun was shining brightly. It would be another hot day. Suddenly she was filled with an overwhelming longing for the familiar landscape of the inn at Cap Ferrat. She wanted no more of this harsh, sun-baked, desert world and its ancient dreams.

"No, no more." She sighed. "Take me home, Jim. Please."

He searched her face for a clue to her true feelings. She seemed calm, clear-headed, even content.

"Right, Mrs. Jamieson," he said, relieved. "Pack your jewels and let's go home."

≫64≪

THE HOTEL on the rue Delambres was seedy and Diego looked around the greasy hallway angrily. What the hell was he doing in a place like this? The unsmiling old woman behind the grubby desk passed him a key and he handed over the few francs it cost for a single night. He hated Paris—and the French! The patterned carpet on the stairs was worn by the continual traffic of many feet, its once cheerful reds ground down to a thin rusty brown. A woman in a flowered dress hurried past him, her cigarette leaving a trail of pungent blue smoke in the air. Diego's eyes followed her as she sauntered through the open door and into the street, turning her head to look first right and then left before strolling off down the hill. He knew what sort of hotel this was. His gaze tracked the woman's progress—perhaps there was a way to make a little money here? Goddamn it, those pimps he'd seen in the bars would kill him! Anyway, there wasn't enough money in it. He wanted *real* money, the sort that bought you dinner at the Ritz not drinks in a cheap bar.

The flimsy lock slid open easily and Diego surveyed his room: a battered chest held a pink-flowered washbasin, a jug, and a small once-white towel. A single chair stood beneath the grimy window, whose thin curtains concealed the depressing view of the back of another building. Diego turned on the light and the sudden glare from the unshaded bulb swinging from the ceiling illuminated the bed. The brown wooden headboard was scratched and scarred and its pink chenille spread held ominous-looking stains. Diego flung his fine leather suitcase onto the chair and pushed aside the bedspread. He was exhausted—how many nights was it since he had slept? He lay down on the bed wearily; he should have known better than to go on gambling when he was tired, he must have had four or five hours' sleep over the past three days. The bed sagged in the middle, worn from countless ten-minute passions, and Diego wriggled uncomfortably. The naked bulb swung directly in his line of vision and he turned his head irritably. On the white cotton pillow next to him lay a single long black hair.

"Jesus Christ!" he exclaimed, leaping from the bed. "What the fuck are you doing here, Diego Benavente?"

Hands in pockets he surveyed the tired room. "Okay, Diego," he said to himself, a grin lighting his attractive face, "there's no future here. You know your old policy: when in trouble start again—at the top!" Picking up the suitcase, he strode purposefully from the room, leaving the door ajar and the light still on.

He ran lightly down the stairs and went directly to the desk, placing his case carefully on the floor beside him. "The room is not suitable," he told the old woman. "I want my money back."

Her red-rimmed eyes peered from the gloom. "We don't give money back," she said, adjusting her black shawl. "You wanted a room and you paid for it."

Diego leaned across the counter. "Give me the money," he said quietly. His face was close to hers and his low voice held a threat. The old woman swallowed nervously, there was no one around, not even on the street.

Diego's hand reached out and gripped her shawl, tightening it around her neck. "I said . . . give it to me. . . ."

"Here, here you are—take it." She pulled open the drawer and handed him the few francs.

Diego looked into the drawer. There were a few other bills there—not much, but then every little bit would help. He picked them up and stuffed them in his pocket without letting go of the old woman. Leaning forward again, he smiled at her, a charming gentle smile, but his voice, though soft, was menacing.

"If you tell anyone about this, I shall kill you," he said, still smiling. "Remember that."

Diego picked up his suitcase and walked to the door and the old woman stared after him. She smoothed down her shawl with trembling hands. He was crazy, he might have killed her. As he stepped through the door and out into the street her gutter-bred courage returned, it wasn't the first time she'd been threatened. "Don't come back here," she screamed at his departing back. "Try the Ritz—see how they like your sort there!"

Diego threw back his head and laughed. He'd walk as far as the Opéra and take a cab for the last couple of blocks, that way he could arrive in style. The Ritz was exactly the right place to begin.

Diego shrugged on his freshly-pressed dinner jacket and examined his reflection in the ornate gilded mirror, adjusting his black silk bow tie so that it lay perfectly against the crisp white shirt collar. He smiled at his attractive reflection with satisfaction as he lit a cigarette—it was a pity he had to hock Edouard's gold cigarette case, as well as the Cartier lighter and the emerald cuff links from Colombia. Diego shrugged; he'd have to do without them for the time being. No doubt he'd be able to recover them from the friendly pawnbroker in Montparnasse in a day or two.

The long velvet-curtained windows showed a rapidly darkening evening sky and the lights of the place Vendôme glimmered through the summer rain. A faint sound of traffic filtered through the glass as Paris geared itself for another evening's entertainment, and Diego smiled in anticipation as he took in the pretty room with its rose-shaded lamps and soft carpets. The walnut bed was solid and discreet and the heavy-ribbed silk bedspread immaculate. Later that night it would be folded carefully by some courteous little chambermaid and the crisp white sheets would be turned back invitingly, ready for its tired occupant.

Diego picked up the soft burgundy leather wallet with the gold corners and counted the meager stained notes. It should have been filled with clean crisp bills of large denominations but, he thought philosophically as he stowed it in his pocket, beggars can't be choosers. On the desk near the window lay his only other asset: the return half of a first-class round-trip ticket to Rio de Janeiro. He picked it up and looked at it. There was always Roberto, of course. It had been two years, after all, wasn't it about time to make contact again? One thing was certain, knowing Roberto, after two years he must surely be bored with Amélie!

The bar at the Ritz had a very strange rule: no women were allowed unescorted and Amanda St. Clair found that very annoying. After all, how was a girl to meet a man if she couldn't go where the men were? It wasn't like this in New York. If a girl were attractive and well-dressed she could go anywhere—or almost anywhere. Amanda didn't count those society balls and things, she meant the cafés and restaurants and bars more usually frequented by members of the theatrical profession, the playwrights, the producers, the entrepreneurs, the stage door dandies—and the members of the chorus, like herself.

Amanda dithered at the entrance to the bar. When the show had closed suddenly in London it had seemed like a good idea to use all her accumulated savings to take in Paris for a few days before returning home, but now she wasn't so sure.

"Is anything the matter?"

The question was phrased in English and she looked around in surprise. The man was young and very attractive, thin and dark—he looked sort of foreign.

"But how did you know?"

"That something was the matter?"

"No, that I was American?"

Diego laughed. "French women don't look like you," he told her. "American girls are so much more attractive."

Amanda smiled back at him, pleased. "They wouldn't let me into the bar," she pouted, "even though I told them it was unfair."

Diego bowed to her. "Would you permit me to escort you Miss . . . ?"

Amanda beamed at him. "St. Clair," she said. "Amanda St. Clair from Morristown, Pennsylvania—although now, of course, I live in New York."

Diego held out an arm and she slid her smooth-skinned white one through his, still talking. "I'm in show business," she said as they walked into the bar. "I'm a dancer, you know—of course, I sing, too. In fact, I sing very well. Mr. Van Gelen the big producer says I definitely deserve a featured solo part in his next show."

"Really? I'm very impressed, Miss St. Clair. I know so little about the theater and it always sounds so fascinating to an outsider like myself." Diego assessed her rapidly as he spoke: in her early twenties; smartly dressed, but he'd bet she spent every penny she had on her clothes; ambitious and possibly on the way up; with some money in her purse for her first trip to Paris. Was she worth a bottle of champagne? His glance flickered over her eager face, the pale blue eyes were wide and naive. And she was alone in Paris.

"Waiter," he called. "Champagne, please."

Amanda smiled happily. Champagne! Well, hadn't she gotten lucky? And he was attractive, too. "I don't even know your name," she realized suddenly.

"Diego Benavente." He lifted her hand to his lips. "And I'm a stranger in Paris, too. It's very lucky that we met, Miss St. Clair."

"Oh, Amanda, please," she breathed, her eyes widening in delight as his lips brushed her hand. Paris was going to be all right after all.

"Your champagne, sir." The waiter placed the tall silver cooler beside them and uncorked the bottle expertly, filling the crystal glasses. He placed the bill in its saucer, discreetly at Diego's elbow, and Diego glanced at it casually. "Charge it, would you," he said. "And by the way would you book a table for dinner in the restaurant—a table for two," he added with a smile at Amanda, "in an hour's time."

"Certainly, sir. Of course. What room number shall I charge it to, sir?"

"Room three-two-five," said Diego, placing a lavish tip on the saucer.

"Yes, sir. Thank you, sir."

"Three-two-five," gasped Amanda. "Well, that's an odd coincidence, I'm in three-two-six."

Diego smiled into her wide blue eyes. This was almost too easy. He handed her the glass of champagne. "To a very happy coincidence, Amanda," he murmured in her pretty ear.

"Of course our coffee plantation is vast," he told her expansively over dinner in the candlelit intimacy of the dining room of the elegant hotel. "But I've always had a taste for adventure. It's taken me halfway around the world by now and the last place I was in turned out to be the most profitable."

Amanda was impressed. "And where was that?"

"Colombia, mining for emeralds." It was almost true, he had been in Colombia and he had been to the emerald mining areas, but he certainly had never set foot in a mine—there were easier ways to get your hands on emeralds then digging them out of rocks! And he'd come away with a glittering green pocketful—regrettably all gambled away now except for the two cabachon stones he'd had set in gold to make the cuff links that were at the pawnbroker's.

Amanda's gaze became even wider. "Oh, Diego, emeralds! How exciting. Do you own the mine?"

"Of course." Diego shrugged modestly. "But I rarely go there anymore. Colombia is such a boring country. Now, New York . . . that's the place to be. I'd like to be there with you, Amanda."

Amanda patted the fluffy fringe of blond hair, smiling at him from beneath darker eyelashes. What a lucky girl she was to have met such a perfect man on her first night in Paris, he was handsome, charming—and rich.

Courting Amanda St. Clair was getting to be not only boring, but expensive, thought Diego, studying the hotel's account, which had been discreetly left on his desk. Not only that, he had to pretend to be elsewhere on business during the day because he didn't have the money to take her out, and then he had to insist on eating at the expensive Ritz restaurant every night—it was more romantic, he had told her when she wanted to go to Chez Martine because that was where all the show people went. He tossed the bill onto the desk. He had to make a move soon or the hotel would begin to put the pressure on—and before Amanda spent all her money on new dresses to make herself more beautiful and tempting for her rich suitor. Tonight would have to be it.

Diego was the most handsome man in Paris, decided Amanda, sitting opposite him at their table in the Ritz dining room. But he wasn't his usual entertaining self tonight, he was quieter and seemed to have his mind on other things. Was it something *she* had done? she wondered guiltily. Had she upset him in some way? Or worse: was he bored with her? The pang of doubt turned into one of fear. She didn't want to lose him, he was too good a catch.

"What's the matter, Diego?" Her wide blue eyes were concerned and Diego patted her hand kindly.

"Of course you would notice that something was wrong," he said with a rueful smile. "You're so sensitive."

Amanda relaxed, it wasn't her fault then. "Tell me," she coaxed, "maybe I can help."

Diego stared moodily at the tablecloth. "Help? No, you can't help." He looked up and smiled at her suddenly. "Let's forget it," he said, determinedly cheerful. "Why don't you tell me what you were doing today?"

Amanda remembered what had happened that afternoon. "You'll never guess who I saw today shopping in Poiret's salon!"

Jesus, thought Diego, she's spending her money at Poiret's now!

"No." He smiled. "Who?"

"Léonie!" Amanda sat back in her chair triumphantly, "the famous singing star. I saw her perform once years ago in New York and she was fabulous—of course, she doesn't appear in public anymore now that she's married, but she's just as beautiful."

Léonie—the name triggered a nerve of response in Diego: the corridor of the Pavillon and Edouard's voice speaking to Isabelle. Léonie—that was the name of Amélie's famous French mother. Could it be the same woman? It must be—and what was the rest? Something about a man. Monsieur! That was it, a man called "Monsieur" was some kind of threat to Amélie. "Tell me," he asked with sudden interest, "what did Léonie look like?"

"Don't you *know?*" Amanda was astonished. "She's very tall and elegant. Her eyes are this most marvelous amber color, and when she smiled at me she looked really pleased that I had spoken to her. And, of course, she has that great mane of blond hair—only it was swept back today because she was in town shopping—she's still so beautiful." Amanda smiled, showing her pretty little teeth. "It was the most exciting thing that's happened to me in Paris ... apart from meeting you, of course."

Diego took her hand and kissed it. There was something in all this, if only he could find out what it was—and how to use it. How much did Amélie know—and Roberto?

"Wasn't there once some terrible scandal about her?" he asked casually. "I seem to remember something."

"Oh, you mean the child. That was years ago, right at the beginning of her career. Some rich guy claimed that he was the father of her daughter and tried to take the child from her. Of course he didn't succeed, I don't know why. Someone told me the story once, apparently it was headlines in all the newspapers here."

The newspapers! That was it. Tomorrow he'd find out exactly what the story was. And then he'd know what to do about it.

"Amanda, I don't know what I'll do without you," he said, brushing his lips on her naked arm.

A thrill shot up Amanda's spine at his caress. "Without me?"

Diego dropped small kisses on her arm. "I didn't want to tell you, but I've had bad news from home ... it's my father."

Her eyes flew open in concern. "He's not ... dead?"

"No, but he's very ill, Amanda, and I have to return right away." Diego hesitated. "It's not what I had planned."

"What had you planned?" The candle glimmered on the table between them and the red-walled intimacy of the alcove, screened by a flowering plant, hid them from view. Only their waiter lingered nearby and the hum of conversation in the room mingled with the strains of the small orchestra in the salon.

Diego looked her in the eyes. "I wanted to ask you to marry me, to take you back to Brazil with me as my wife, but now ..."

"Oh, Diego," Amanda melted toward him. "Oh, Diego, but you can still ask me."

"Would you marry me, Amanda? I love you so very much, you're the most perfect woman I've ever met. You're so beautiful and sensitive ... and so talented. I wanted to invest in your shows so that my lovely wife could be a star—like Léonie."

Amanda caught her breath. "Yes," she breathed, "yes, I'll marry you."

"The trouble is," said Diego, kissing her cheek as she glowed with happiness, "that at the moment I have very little money in France. I'm expecting a banker's draft from my father, but there's no time now to wait for the money to arrive from Brazil." He shrugged apologetically and slumped back in his chair. "I can't even afford to pay the passage of my future bride to take her home to Brazil with me."

"But that's all right, I have money, Diego. I can pay for myself."

Diego sat stiffly in his chair. "As a gentleman I can't possibly let you do that, Amanda."

"But why ever not? We're going to be married, aren't we?"

His gaze met hers. "Would you really do that?" he murmured. "How lucky I am to find you. I didn't know that any woman could be this perfect, this wonderful."

Amanda wanted so badly to kiss him. He'd been such a gentleman and he thought her such a lady, he had never done more than just kiss her—yet. She imagined what it would be like, the two of them, naked in bed together.

"There is just the one other thing," said Diego worriedly. "I have money tied up as a deposit in this business deal. If I leave now, without paying the balance, I'll lose it. It's only a small thing, but I hate to lose."

"I told you not to worry," said Amanda happily, snuggling her head into his shoulder. "I have some money, maybe it will be enough to help you."

Diego slid his arm around her shoulder. "I love you, Amanda," he whispered, "and I want very much to kiss you, to hold you next to me."

Her pretty face turned up to his and her parted lips waited.

"Not here," he murmured, "it's too public, my darling. Can we go to your room?"

He helped her on with her pretty lace jacket and picked up her purse, smiling goodnight to the waiter as they walked arm in arm through the restaurant to the foyer and the elevator.

It had been a busy day, but a satisfying one. His suitcase waited by the door and Diego cast a final glance around the room. He'd called Chez Martine, where Amanda was waiting for him, and left a message that he would be late and that she was to wait there for him. It made sure that he wouldn't run into her on the way out of the hotel—after all he'd been through, he thought with a grin, it would be a pity to spoil it!

The porter came to take his luggage and Diego followed the man down the spacious corridor. This was a good hotel, he thought appreciatively; he'd use it next time he was in Paris. He pulled out the thin gold cigarette case and lit one of the strong French cigarettes he had acquired a taste for. The slender Cartier lighter felt good in his hands, and the emerald links gleamed again in his cuffs.

At the door he tipped the porter from a pleasantly stuffed wallet and climbed into the taxi that was to take him to the station. He would sail from Cherbourg that night.

Yes, he thought, settling back in the cab, it had been a very satisfying day. The newspaper office had been very cooperative in letting a Brazilian newspaperman look through their old files—and more than happy to translate for him. So now he knew. Amélie was illegitimate; not only that, it seemed doubtful that Charles d'Aureville was her father. "Monsieur" was. And Monsieur was the Duc de Courmont!

Well, well, well. It was a pity there was no way to get to the duc, he might have been able to make a little something there, but no one could see him. And besides, he was such a powerful personage that it was just a little intimidating. No, this information was best used against Amélie. He was back in the game again with Roberto. Diego laughed out loud suddenly and the taxi driver looked around, startled.

"It's all right," called Diego. "It's just been a very good trip."

❧ 65 ❦

ROBERTO PICKED UP his jacket, patting the pocket to check that the letter was still there. It crackled reassuringly and he smiled as he flung the jacket over his shoulder, thinking how pleased Amélie was going to be. Or was she? He strolled along the path from the hotel to the villa. Maybe now that she was pregnant she might not be so pleased with the news. His footsteps slowed as he contemplated the possible problem. A pebble lay on the path in front of him and he kicked it aside impatiently. It had been a very long day and he needed a shower and a quick bite, and then he had some more work to do. Running the successful Hotel d'Aureville was a seven-day-a-week job, and he often worked late to catch up on paperwork. He simply had to get those figures checked tonight.

"Roberto?"

Diego's familiar mocking voice stopped him in his tracks. Roberto drew his eyes slowly from the path. Diego was smiling at him, every line of his face was imprinted on his memory, the strong green eyes, the dark brows, the wide full lips, and the thin spare body. Diego was smartly dressed: an immaculate shirt, a light linen jacket. He looked older.

"Aren't you going to greet an old friend?" Diego stepped toward him, hands outstretched. "Let bygones be bygones?"

"What are you doing here?" The words seemed forced from Roberto's harsh throat.

"I couldn't stay away forever, Roberto. This is my home, too, you know."

His heart seemed to be beating in double-time. "Sebastião warned you. . . ."

"Roberto, listen to me, please." Diego held his arms open in supplication. "It's been a long time. I can't change what happened in the past, but I'm deeply ashamed of it. I was a young fool, Roberto, and I did things, terrible things, but I've changed, I swear I have. I'll never forgive myself for what happened, but I'm hoping you will."

"I don't want you here. I don't want to see you . . . stay out of my life." Roberto hunched his shoulders, feeling the sweat dripping down his chest. He wanted to pass Diego, but his old friend blocked the path, it would mean touching him.

"Roberto, I promise you I'm different. Sending me away like that was the best thing Sebastião could have done for me. I was away from all the old bad influences, out in the world on my own. I had to make good. I went to Colombia. I got a job there mining for emeralds. It was bloody hard work, Roberto, but I stuck with it, living like a pig in some remote frontier mining town—I was working out my prison sentence. I had to do it. I owed it to you for what I'd done. I came out of that experience a new man; I felt cleansed of the past."

Roberto moved toward him, brushing aside Diego's outstretched hand, flinching at the contact. "Stay away from me," he muttered. "I don't care where you've been, or how you've reformed." He strode down the path, turning as he reached the corner. "And stay away from Amélie," he warned. "If you go near her, Diego, I'll kill you."

Their gaze met along the length of the pathway. Diego flung his arms wide. "Roberto! How can you be like this! We were like brothers—more than brothers." His smile held a thousand implications.

Roberto turned away and Diego watched him striding down the path. He shrugged. Well, if that was the way it was going to be, then he'd have to take a different line.

Onça lay in the corner of Amélie's room, her head resting on her wide paws. The muscles of her sleek back twitched lazily as a fly bothered her; her amber eyes, almost the color of Amélie's own, were half-closed as she watched her sleeping mistress.

Amélie stirred and Onça's head lifted immediately. Her eyes waited to see what would happen and as Amélie swung her legs off the bed the cat rose to her feet and stretched.

"Hello, Onça." Amélie yawned. "It's time to get up. Roberto will be home soon." She stroked the sleek tawny fur. "I'll take you for a walk later," she promised, "when it's cooler."

She dressed quickly and brushed her hair. It was later than she had thought. She seemed to sleep so much better in the afternoons, it was the nights that gave her trouble. Not trouble really, she thought, patting her round belly, it was just that the baby chose the night to wake up. We'll have to straighten that out once you're born, she told it affectionately.

Onça padded down the stairs in Amélie's wake and out onto the terrace. Her ears pricked up as the door opened and Roberto came in. He flung his jacket across a chair, poured himself a neat whiskey at the sideboard, and tossed it back quickly. God, that felt better. His hand was shaking as he put down the glass. He needed another.

"Roberto." Amélie came in from the terrace. "I didn't hear you come in, but Onça did—she doesn't miss a thing." She looked in surprise at the whiskey in his hand. Roberto rarely drank anything but wine. "Is something wrong?"

He forced a smile as he bent and kissed her. "Of course not, in fact, quite the opposite. If you look in my jacket pocket you'll find a letter from Edouard."

"From Edouard?" She picked up the jacket, rummaging eagerly through the pockets. It had been a few weeks since they'd heard from Xara and Edouard in Key West.

"I've been offered the job as assistant manager of the Palaçio d'Aureville in Miami when it opens next month," said Roberto casually.

Amélie shrieked with delight. "But that's *fantastic*—when do we leave?" She scanned the letter rapidly: the twins were wonderful, Xara was fine, Edouard was fine, the hotel was just about ready—at last—and it was superb, a credit to the d'Aurevilles. And they wanted Roberto to have the job—with a view ultimately to becoming manager. It was the best news in the world and Roberto was ready for it, she knew he was. He had worked so hard, he deserved the opportunity.

Roberto tossed back the second whiskey. "You don't mind leaving Rio?"

Amélie looked thoughtful, it meant that her baby would be born in America. She grinned at him. "I don't mind, Roberto, our baby will be a little American."

"I'm glad to hear it." He dropped a kiss on her hair. "Look, I have a lot of work to do this evening, Amélie. I don't really feel like any dinner. I'm going to shut myself in the study and get on with it. Why don't you go over to the hotel and have dinner with Grandmère?"

Amélie was disappointed. "Shouldn't we be celebrating or something?" she asked, putting her arms around his neck. He smelled unfamiliarly of the whiskey. "I love you, Senhor do Santos, assistant manager of the fabulous Palaçio d'Aureville."

Roberto smiled. "And I love you, Senhora do Santos, but I'm far too busy to celebrate—maybe tomorrow night."

"Promise?" Amélie kissed him lingeringly on the lips.

"I promise." Roberto's voice was abstracted as he picked up his jacket and made for the stairs.

Amélie watched him with a pleased smile; he was so attractive, she thought, the way his body tapered into narrow hips and the way his blue shirt looked with his blond hair—neatly trimmed now, but still quite long.

"Come on, Onça," she said, slipping a chain through the animal's collar. "Let's go see Grandmère."

There was a sound from downstairs and Roberto glanced at his watch. Could Amélie be back already? No, it was too early, it was probably just Ofelia tidying up. He went back to his figures.

The d'Aureville villa on Copacabana was just the same, thought Diego, helping himself to whiskey from the decanter on the sideboard. He took a gulp, savoring the thin aromatic spirit. He preferred Cachaça, nothing could top a good *batida,* and he'd already had several of those. He took a seat on the white couch, propping his feet on the low marble table in front of him, sipping the whiskey. He'd always liked this house, it had a modernistic, elegantly casual style that suited him perfectly—far more than the *fazenda.* He recalled the enormous chests and cupboards in dark woods, the studded leather chairs and ponderous heavy-legged tables. No, he felt much more at home here, the d'Aurevilles certainly had a knack for combining the old and the new. He walked to the sideboard and poured himself a second drink, returning to the couch, carrying the decanter with him, letting it slide through his suddenly uncertain hands onto the marble table. The decanter split cleanly into two pieces and the smell of whiskey mingled with the scent of flowers. "Pity," murmured Diego, lounging back against the cushions, "pity about all that whiskey."

Roberto was at the doorway and Diego turned his mocking green-eyed smile on him. "Well, hello, old friend. Here I am again."

"I warned you to stay away." Roberto's tone was icy.

"Come on in, Roberto, make yourself at home. *Come on!"* Diego's voice grew impatient. "I need to talk to you."

Roberto hesitated by the door. "There's nothing to say."

"Oh, yes, there bloody well is—and you know it, Roberto!" Diego's face was ugly in its anger. "Now get over here, there's too much gone down between you and me for you to be so cockily casual about it now. *Get over here, Roberto!"*

Roberto walked slowly across the room and took a seat opposite Diego. His eyes took in the broken decanter and the whiskey spilled over the creamy marble table.

"Very well," he said distantly, "say what you have to say."

Diego smiled again, that was better—things were more his style now. "I need money," he said abruptly. *"A lot of money*—and *right now!* I want you to give it to me, Roberto, and when you do I shall go away and leave you in peace. I'll go back to Paris again, I liked it there. I found it a very . . . interesting city. Expensive, of course, for a man of my tastes."

Roberto was silent. It was blackmail again. What could he do? he wondered helplessly. Even if he got hold of some money and gave it to Diego, he would come back again—and again. He wouldn't do it, he decided suddenly, he couldn't; he would just have to face up to the consequences. A vision of Amélie's happy trusting face came into his mind, and her newly rounded body, filling with their unborn child.

"Of course, the bordellos in Paris aren't as good as some of the ones we know, Roberto," continued Diego smoothly, "not quite the same techniques, the same finesse. . . ." He swung his feet from the table and sauntered back to the sideboard in search of more drink. There was a bottle of brandy—that would do. He placed the bottle carefully on the marble table. "You see," he said blandly, "I'm being careful—that was just an accident, Roberto, a simple accident, it slipped out of my hand!"

Diego's laughter filled the room and Amélie stiffened in surprise as she closed the front door behind her. Onça pricked up her ears, growling softly, and she put a hand on her head to silence her, listening.

"Come on, Roberto, relax . . . have a drink. For old times' sake?" Diego slopped brandy into a glass and pushed it toward him.

Amélie's eyes widened. It couldn't be Diego? A frown creased her brow. It had been years. Roberto had told her that Diego had run away from home because he was in trouble with the police, that he'd gone abroad and would never come back, that his bad ways had finally caught up with him.

Tightening her grip on Onça's chain, she walked into the salon.

"Well, well, it's Amélie. The mistress of the house—and future mother, I see." Diego's eyes flickered familiarly across her body and Amélie felt the blush rise in her cheeks.

"Diego! What are you doing here?"

"I just dropped by to see old friends. What, no friendly hello kiss, Amélie?" His laughter was mocking.

"I've never kissed you, Diego Benavente, and I never will." Amélie went to stand by Roberto, taking in the broken decanter. Onça backed away from the table, avoiding the strong whiskey fumes.

Diego grinned. With Amélie here, the situation was perfect. Roberto

wouldn't dare refuse him now. He strolled across to the grand piano, set-tling himself on the stool. His glass formed a sticky ring on the glossy ebony wood of the piano as he ran his hands across the keys. "I thought I might entertain you"—he smiled—"with a song or two from Paris—maybe one that your mother used to sing, Amélie."

Her face was blank with astonishment and Diego laughed, this was going to be easy.

Roberto took Amélie's arm and escorted her to the door. Onça walked beside them, glancing back nervously, feeling the atmosphere charged with tension. "Go on upstairs, Amélie," said Roberto quietly. "Let me deal with this."

Her eyes met his. "What is it, Roberto, what's happening?"

"I'll tell you later," he said firmly. "Go on upstairs, Amélie, please."

Holding Onça's chain tightly, she walked slowly up the stairs, hearing the door click as Roberto closed it behind her.

Their bedroom was peaceful, its windows open to the warm night air, and she sat uneasily on the bed, stroking Onça's smooth head, straining her ears for any sound from downstairs. She could hear nothing and with a sigh she lay back against the pillows, wondering what was going on.

The sound of raised voices erupted into the quiet night and the sudden splintering crash of broken glass—and then silence. Amélie jolted upright. The sudden silence was unnerving. She grabbed Onça's chain and hurried down the stairs.

The two men sat opposite each other. Diego was drinking from the bottle of brandy and Roberto held his hand to his head where blood trickled from a cut. Broken glass littered the floor. Their eyes turned toward her as she strode into the room, Onça by her side.

"I think you had better go, Diego," she said quietly. "You have done enough damage for one night."

"I haven't finished." Diego's smile was innocent. "I still haven't talked to you, Amélie—and I think we have a lot of things to discuss."

Amélie's voice sounded a pitch higher than normal and Onça lifted her head inquiringly. "There is nothing I want to discuss with you—and noth-ing I ever want to hear from you."

"Then perhaps I should talk *about* you. There are one or two things Roberto might care to hear about his lovely aristocratic wife."

Amélie stared at him, puzzled. What could he mean?

"And there again," continued Diego, "there are one or two things Amélie might like to hear about you, eh Roberto?" Placing the bottle on the table with exaggerated care, Diego began to pace the room. Putting his hands in his pockets, he turned to his prey, sensing his power.

Onça sat quietly beside Amélie, observing every move.

"Don't you want to know about your lovely husband, then, Amélie?

Might such raw details be too upsetting for a woman of such refined background as yourself? Well, I'll tell you now, Amélie d'Aureville: Roberto belongs to me, we're bound together by ties stronger than any you understand, ties of blood, Amélie—and flesh."

Roberto leapt toward him, a heavy alabaster ashtray clutched in his hand. "I'll kill you, Diego, if you say one more word, I'll kill you."

Diego threw back his head and laughed. "Kill me? You'll not kill me, Roberto, you can't live without me. You know what we're like together. Come on, Roberto, it's Amélie you should get rid of."

"Enough," shouted Roberto, "that's enough." He raised the ashtray threateningly and Onça's low growl rumbled through the room.

"Do you know who she is?" Diego said with a laugh. "She's the daughter of a whore—a cabaret girl picked by a rich man to be his mistress. She's no d'Aureville. Léonie was never married to Charles, her father is 'Monsieur.'" He turned to Amélie. "You've been living a lie, my dear," he said smoothly, "a lifetime of a lie . . . you are no more a d'Aureville than I am."

Amélie's hand trembled and Onça tugged at her chain, straining forward nervously. Tears pricked Amélie's eyes. What did he mean, she wasn't a d'Aureville? She could hear Roberto shouting threateningly and Diego's mocking laughter; it all seemed to come from such a distance, it was so far away—happening somewhere else, not there, not to her. Violence crackled in the air as Roberto rushed toward Diego. She could sense his anger. He was going to kill Diego for her; she couldn't let him do that. Onça was on her feet, claws scrabbling on the polished boards as she lunged forward, snarling. "Onça," Amélie whispered as the animal lunged again. The muscles of her shoulder flashed with pain, and automatically her hand relaxed. The chain slid through her open fingers as the big cat launched herself through the air and at Diego's throat. In the split-second before she was on him, a knife flicked into his hand and as he fell to the ground beneath the force of her body, her powerful fangs already at his neck, he thrust the knife upward into her belly.

The man and the animal lay motionless on the floor. The beautiful salon, littered with broken glass and stained with whiskey—and blood—was silent.

Amélie knew they were dead even before Roberto knelt over them. A man lay dead because of her and she felt nothing. Why was that? she wondered distantly. She had let go of Onça's chain and now Onça was dead, too. Roberto's face was ashen and his voice shook. He put a protective arm around her. "Amélie, let me take you upstairs."

"What will happen to me, Roberto?" She walked by his side obediently. "Will the police take me away?"

Roberto stared at her, horrified. "It was an accident, Amélie. Onça killed him. There was nothing you could do about it."

Amélie could hear the tremor in Roberto's voice, he was staying calm for her sake, she knew it. He was so good to her, so sweet. But it hadn't been an accident, had it?

Roberto lay her down on the bed. "I'm going to call the doctor," he said, "and Grandmère. And then I must call the police. Everything will be all right, Amélie, I promise you."

"Roberto," she said urgently, "what did he mean, Roberto, that I wasn't a d'Aureville?"

"It was nonsense, Amélie, all nonsense, he just wanted to cause trouble," said Roberto wearily. "Forget it now, my darling, just forget it. I'll take care of everything."

Roberto walked back down the stairs. Violence still trembled in the silent night air and he stood at the door of the salon staring at the bodies. Diego's hand still clutched the knife that was in Onça's belly and his green sightless eyes gazed at the ceiling. Blood from his ripped throat had washed over his white shirt and mingled with that of the animal on the rug.

Roberto's face contorted with pain and tears flowed down his cheeks. Oh, God, he thought, I loved him. Despite it all, I loved him.

The police had been anxious not to upset poor Senhora do Santos any more than necessary. "Such a terrible thing to happen to the senhora," the captain had said soothingly. "It's not the first time, though. These big cats can turn nasty without any warning."

The police had removed the bodies quickly and the salon had been sponged clean of their blood.

"What have they done with Diego?" she asked Roberto, staring at the spot on the floor where he had lain.

"They took him to the hospital." He added after a pause, "He'll be buried tomorrow."

"And will you go to the funeral?"

"Amélie," said Roberto simply, "I must."

Tears began to roll down her face. "Don't cry, Amélie, it wasn't your fault, truly it wasn't."

"I'm not crying for Diego," she sobbed. "I'm crying for you and me. Don't you see, Roberto, things will never be the same again?"

"Yes, yes, they will," he soothed her. "You'll see, Amélie, everything will be just like it was. Come and lie down again, you mustn't excite yourself like this—think of the baby."

The baby! She'd forgotten about the baby! Amélie shuddered. Thank

God her child would know nothing of this, he would never know his mother had killed!

"Dr. Valdez will give you something to make you sleep," said Roberto, stroking her hair back from her hot forehead. "You'll feel better in the morning. And remember, Amélie, we'll be leaving for Florida in a few weeks, we have our new life ahead of us."

She lay in the darkened room with her eyes closed, thinking. Yes, thank God there was a new life ahead of them—a life without Diego, and without Onça, her beautiful, beloved Onça. Tears seeped from beneath her closed eyelids onto the pillow as she cried for Onça, and for her own lost innocence.

≽66≼

LÉONIE LIT THE CANDLES and stepped back to admire the table. The robin's egg blue country plates sprinkled with tiny deeper blue and yellow blossoms waited at five places, flanked by graceful long-stemmed crystal goblets. The tablecloth was the very palest shade of blue, and butter yellow napkins were set by each plate. Two squat silver candle-holders, complete with pointed snuffers, that had once lighted Georgian maidens to bed, held fat honey-colored candles, and freshly picked marigolds and cornflowers brimmed from the round crackle-glazed yellow bowl.

It was perfect, she decided, turning to inspect the bottles of rosé wine waiting in the silver coolers, a perfect table for a midsummer evening dinner with old friends, and a dual celebration: her fifth wedding anniversary and the birth of her twin granddaughters—Lais and Leonore do Santos.

"Lais and Leonore," she said the names out loud with satisfaction. Leonore had been born half an hour after Lais, and Amélie had said in her letter that there had been something about her expression that had reminded her of Léonie. It was then that she had decided on the name, Leonore.

Maybe she was just being kind, thought Léonie with a smile, but if she was, it was a double kindness to name one child after the mother she hardly knew. Amélie had begun to write to her in the last months of her pregnancy and Léonie had found herself unable either to resist the pleasure it brought her, or to deny the reassurance it seemed to bring Amélie. Surely after all these years it was safe to correspond. At first they were just short notes, telling of her progress and how much she liked being in Florida, but gradually, as she received Léonie's replies, unburdened with excess emotion, their correspondence developed into that of two friends, with Léonie as a sounding board for Amélie's new feelings about her life in America and approaching motherhood.

She had definitely grown up, thought Léonie, remembering the volatile young girl who had appeared in her dressing room that memorable night, and there was something else, an undertone of something that bothered her. It wasn't sadness, it was more an awareness that life wasn't all roses and happiness and effortless love.

She heard the sound of a car on the road above the villa and hurried to the door. As always it stood wide open to the summer air, its flanking pots of geraniums providing a splash of color against the white walls.

"Léonie, there you are. It's been ages." Caro looked delicious in a nubby raw-silk yellow skirt and wide-necked blouse, with her hair for once flowing loose, pinned at the sides with pearl and tortoise combs.

"You look wonderful," they exclaimed simultaneously, examining each other for new marks of time.

"Not a day older," said Léonie firmly.

"Nor you," agreed Caro. They laughed at their foolishness. "Anyone would think we were seventy," said Caro, "and anyway, you look exactly the same as you did fifteen years ago. Except you look happier."

Léonie's mouth widened into a grin. "That's a very astute observation, and it's probably because that's what I am—happy."

"And Jim?"

"Oh, Jim would be even happier if I allowed him to work eighteen hours a day. Now he's buying land along the coast that he's convinced is going to be valuable some day. He spends all his time planning how to develop it—or else he's dashing off to New York or San Francisco. Sometimes I go with him, more often I stay here and look after my garden. I'm getting lazy, Caro, I'm too attached to this place ever to want to leave."

"That was what you always wanted, though, wasn't it?" said Caro. "You needed the security of owning land. He's buying it for you, Léonie, he knows it means more to you than diamonds."

Léonie considered this. "Yes, I suppose he is . . . in a way. Except now I have Jim, I don't need anything else. With him I feel secure."

Their eyes met in a smile. "I'm glad," said Caro.

Alphonse and Maroc had paused with Jim to admire the view of the bay from the path, shading their eyes against the setting sun to take in the sweep of the headland and the chalky paths that led across the Point.

"Oh, I can't wait," cried Léonie, running up the path to meet them and throwing her arms around Maroc. "You deserter," she laughed, kissing him soundly. "I haven't seen you in almost six months."

Her face was just as eager as when he had first seen her lurking nervously in the alley behind Serrat, thought Maroc, and just as beautiful. "I'm a working man," he apologized, handing her an enormous box of her favorite truffles from Tanrades in Paris. "Hotel life is a busy one—all consuming, in fact. I never seem to have time for myself."

"You should run one of the hotels down here," Léonie said firmly, "then at least we would see more of you. And if you can't do that then I shall have to visit Zurich more often." Maroc's return to the hotel business had been successful but the distances were no good for close friendship.

"I hear we have a double celebration." He took Léonie's arm as they strolled down the path to the house. "Are we permitted to know what it is?"

"Not until after dinner," she said firmly, "then I'll tell you." She led the way to the terrace, where Jim was distributing tall glasses of the local vermouth laced with sprigs of fresh thyme from the hillside and delicious berry-flavored cassis.

"This is heaven!" exclaimed Caro. "Why does anyone live anywhere else but right here?"

"Exactly what I was thinking," agreed Alphonse.

"Tell me," said Caro, sniffing the air, "what's for dinner? It smells wonderful."

"Stuffed eggplant, baked lamb ... and before that, shrimp fresh from the bay to eat with your fingers in Madame Frenard's fresh mayonnaise, and asparagus. And later all the raspberries and strawberries you can eat." Léonie laughed at their dazzled anticipating faces.

"I'll drink to that," said Maroc cheerfully. "And here's a toast to you two. Happy anniversary."

"Happy anniversary," echoed Caro and Alphonse.

Jim put his arm around Léonie's shoulders. "You wouldn't believe how I had to pursue her," he said with a grin, "but I told her I was the only man for her."

They were so obviously completely happy that their guests basked in their reflected glow. Who would have imagined that Léonie would *ever* be this happy, thought Caro, remembering Monsieur. Léonie rarely mentioned him now—not since it was announced that he had suffered such a crippling stroke, and it was even rumored that it had affected his vocal cords and that he was unable to speak. Knowing Monsieur's vital energy and forceful personality, the rumors were hard to believe, but it seemed to be true. Most of the year he was living in an enormous apartment in the Hôtel de Paris in

Monte Carlo, venturing out on his yacht occasionally, though it was said that he left the hotel only in the middle of the night so that no one would see him in his wheelchair. Caro shuddered and took a sip of her drink. If only his passion for Léonie had been a sane one, it might have been him standing here tonight with his arm around her, celebrating their anniversary.

"Come on everyone," called Léonie, "dinner is served. Maroc, you sit here on my right, and Alphonse on my left. That leaves Jim for you, Caro."

"Good," said Jim, "I've been trying to get her alone for years."

"You see! We're married five years and he's already chasing my best friend," she cried as they arranged themselves at the table. Then Léonie lifted her glass. "I can't wait any longer to tell you," she said, her face lit with a smile. "I want you to drink a toast to Lais and Leonore do Santos— Amélie's twin daughters. My grandchildren."

"Léonie," gasped Caro. "Oh, Léonie. How wonderful! How *exciting!*"

Maroc and Alphonse smiled at her obvious happiness.

"What's more," said Léonie, "I may have been deprived of my own daughter, but she's promised that I will see my grandchildren. When they are old enough, she'll bring them to visit me."

Caro thought of all the normal happy grandmothers with their daily or weekly contact with their children and their offspring. It's amazing, she thought, lifting her glass to toast the health of the new babies, how Léonie has learned to be happy with so little: a tenuous promise of a visit in the future is enough to fill her cup to the brim.

Dinner had been leisurely, filled with a mixture of discussion and gossip, and they lounged on the terrace once more, sipping coffee and thinking of making their way home to bed.

"I don't know why you won't stay here at the villa," complained Léonie as Caro finally made a move to leave.

"You don't have a closet big enough to hold her clothes," said Alphonse dryly. "As it is, we have to take a suite with two bedrooms so that she can get everything in. And we're only here for four days!"

Léonie hugged her. "It's good to hear you haven't changed since the day I met you," she said, remembering the armoires full of silks and satins, and the boxes of jewels.

"What's a woman without her adornments?" cried Caro airily as they walked up the path. "We'll see you tomorrow then, and I'm planning on a little gambling in the evening."

Alphonse groaned. "She'll ruin me yet," he said, helping her into the car.

"Never," teased Caro. "I always win."

Maroc was to take the wheel. "Thank you for a very happy evening," he said quietly. "I miss you, Léonie." His eyes were tender.

"And I miss you, my old friend." Léonie's arms were warm around his neck.

Jim took her hand and they strolled back in the moonlight down the little paved path whose stones she had laid herself, years ago. "I haven't given you your present yet," he said. "I wanted to wait until I could show you, but now it's almost too late." He looked at the sky; the moon was high, illuminating the landscape in a whitish glow. The Point looked like a painted backdrop to the silently rippling sea.

"Wait here," he said, placing Léonie on a chair on the terrace, "I'll be right back."

She sank back against the cushions, gazing out at the magical scene. In all the time she'd lived there, no two nights had ever been the same—the sea and sky were always different. She sighed with pleasure. Her home was the most wonderful place in the world.

"Close your eyes," commanded Jim, "and see what you'll get."

Léonie closed her eyes obediently, feeling the crisp rustle of paper as he thrust a packet into her hands. She fingered it wonderingly. "Can I open my eyes now?" she asked.

"Open them," he said.

She had seen papers like these before, the long legal documents with the pink tape and scarlet sealing wax. Title Deeds, she read with a sense of déjà vu. Monsieur had given her a present just like this once—the title deeds to this very house. She took a deep breath and read on. They were the deeds to all the land on the east of the villa as far as the Point, the land in the back up to the brow of the hill beyond the road, and several hectares to the west. Her eyes met Jim's in amazement.

"You are mistress of all you survey, Léonie Jamieson," he said with a cocky grin. "It's all yours."

She stood beside him, looking out across the moonlit landscape. It was truly all hers, those trees, those hills, those chalky pathways—all hers. She slid her hand into his and leaned her head against his shoulder. Most wonderful of all, it was given not with strings, like Monsieur gave, but with love. "How can I thank you?" she murmured. "It's the most wonderful present you could ever have given me."

"I know," he said, gripping her hand in his, "I always know what you need."

Léonie didn't say anything, she didn't have to. Jim did know what she needed, he knew how to make her feel secure. And he had given her all this land. He had made her again what she had always wanted to be, a woman of property.

❧ 67 ❧

LAIS AND LEONORE dozed peacefully in the shuttered afternoon twilight of the nursery at the Villa Encantada in Key West and Amélie's face held a tender smile as she closed the door softly behind her. Further along the corridor she peeked into Vicente and Jean-Paul's room. The six-year-old boys were sprawled across their beds in identical positions on their stomachs, heads turned to the right, eyes tightly shut. It had been a turbulent morning, the heat was getting to everyone, but finally they were all sleeping and maybe by the time they woke the heat would have lessened and they would be less irritable.

Amélie wandered out onto the terrace and flung herself into a low hammock strung between two posts. Xara was resting in her room and the house was quiet. In fact, the whole hillside seemed quiet today, for once the birds were subdued and only the insects continued their normal buzzing.

Pushing her heavy hair back from her forehead, she gazed at the sky. The sun shone brassily against a cloudless bright blue and Amélie sighed, they could expect no relief from the heat, she was sure of it. Why did it seem so much hotter this year than usual? Still, it was better here than in Miami, she had been right to escape that enervating humidity. Just one more week and the hotel would close for the three-month out-of-season break and Roberto and Edouard would join them. And then, when the weather cooled from high summer and the new season began, Roberto would be the new manager.

Sole charge of such a magnificent hotel was an all-consuming job. Roberto would be working all hours, spending more time at the Palaçio than in their neat little house on the grounds—even less than he did now.

A frown furrowed her brow. Roberto seemed happy, he loved his work, he adored the children, he loved her—*but it wasn't the same.* A picture of the salon at the Villa d'Aureville with the blood-stained bodies lying on the floor sprang unbidden into her mind and her eyes flew open in an attempt to dispel the memory. Had a single day passed in two years when she hadn't thought of it? And she knew Roberto did, too, although he had never— ever—mentioned it again after Diego's funeral. It's finished, he had told her then, and we must forget it and go on. We have our baby to think of and our lives together. Her mind had seethed with questions, but perhaps he had been right, they were better left unanswered. Yet she had known it would never be the same. Diego had succeeded in the end, as he always had, in coming between them.

The heat was intolerable, there wasn't a scrap of breeze as she swung herself from the hammock and wandered, barefoot, indoors. Her room was cooler and in the dimness she shed her clothes and lay down on the bed. It was vast, white-sheeted, and comfortable. It was meant for siesta-time lovers, she thought, on afternoons like this when the heat of their passions would match the heat outside.

And what do you know about passion, Amélie do Santos? she wondered. She knew about love because she loved Roberto, and he loved her and their lovemaking took its tone from that. But it wasn't an all-consuming *passion*. She had never felt that sort of passion—would she ever? She was the Senhora do Santos, whose very busy husband loved her, and she had her children to fill in any gaps that might have appeared in her life.

Amélie turned over and closed her eyes. Wasn't that enough for any woman?

Hilliard Watkins sauntered through the graceful columned inner courtyard of the Palaço d'Aureville, a book tucked under his arm, searching for a shady place with a bit of breeze to take the edge off the unwavering heat of the day. He nodded a polite good morning to the two old ladies, neat in crisp linen with upright Boston backs and sensible New England shoes. They seemed completely unaffected by the heat, their only concession being shady straw hats that they always wore, indoors as well as out. Their brother was a different matter: the old man had a twinkle in his eye behind the gold-rimmed spectacles and there was a rakish tilt to the brim of his panama. Hilliard bet *he'd* been a bit of a boy in his time, though the old girls had him under their thumb now; still, Hilliard had seen him in the bar alone at night when the ladies had gone to bed, enjoying a couple of brandies and a chat with Jordan, the barman.

The Peabodys were his only fellow guests in this grand hotel in the last week of its season.

Hilliard paced the long shady marble terrace that faced the sea. Deep awnings protected the rows of plate-glass windows from the direct rays of the sun, but even in their shade there was no breeze. He leaned on the rail and stared at the sea, heaving sullenly under the brassy sky. The heat was relentless. There was nothing for it, his room would be the coolest place for a quiet read.

* * *

"Mr. do Santos?"

The old lady stood straight-backed in front of Roberto, her straw hat squarely on her head, immaculately shod feet planted firmly apart. Behind her lurked her brother, more stooped than his sisters, a blue-veinedness to the nose giving a clue to his fondness for after-dinner brandies.

"Mr. do Santos, my brother believes there is going to be a storm."

Roberto offered her a chair. "I'm afraid it's to be expected at this time of year, Miss Peabody. It's the end of the season you know."

"You misunderstand me," she replied crisply, "not a regular storm . . . a hurricane."

Roberto looked at her in surprise. What could this stiff Boston lady know about hurricanes?

"All the signs point to it," Miss Peabody continued firmly. "My brother says that he can feel it in the air. He's had experience of these storms."

"Yes, yes," the old man dithered behind her. "The South China Seas, you know, I was there for many years—"

"Quiet, Henry, when I'm speaking." His sister cut him off in midsentence and taking off his gold-rimmed spectacles Henry began to polish them agitatedly on an immaculate white handkerchief.

"We would like to know what precautions you intend to take against the storm, Mr. do Santos."

"I'm afraid I hadn't thought about it, Miss Peabody, there has been no warning of any hurricane activity heading this way. However, the hotel has storm shutters and sandbags are prepared for the windows, and, of course, all portable pieces—furniture, flower tubs, and suchlike—would be brought indoors. I feel the hotel would be reasonably secure in those circumstances. But as I said, we've had no hurricane warning."

"It's coming," said Henry suddenly. "It always starts like this. Take my word for it, Mr. do Santos, and make your preparations now. We'll be in for it by nightfall." He beamed at them from behind the spectacles. "It'll be like old times," he said excitedly. "I remember in 'seventy-nine when old Cooper and I were exploring the islands—"

"My brother used to be in the Foreign Service," Miss Peabody cut him off again smoothly. "We shall leave you to take care of things then, Mr. do Santos."

Despite her authoritative manner she was a lady in her seventies and Roberto felt responsible for her. "If you are concerned, Miss Peabody, you could leave now for the north; there is a train leaving in an hour's time for St. Augustine."

"We have booked for a further week and we intend to stay, thank you, Mr. do Santos."

Henry followed his sister out of the room. "It'll be a bit of fun, won't it," he whispered conspiratorially. "I think I shall quite enjoy a hurricane."

Edouard lugged a final sandbag into place in front of the big windows that led onto the seafront terrace, wiping the sweat from his brow with his handkerchief. It would have been a hell of a lot easier if they weren't down to a skeleton staff with the hotel closing next week. On the other hand, imagine the panic if the hotel had been filled with guests. He shuddered at the thought.

Raising his head from the pile of sandbags, he glanced along the terrace. All the white wicker furniture had been carried indoors and every flowerpot and tub that could be moved had been locked away in the storage rooms. The awnings had been folded back and clipped firmly into place, though he supposed they would be the first to go in a storm. He shrugged philosophically, hoping that that was the worst they could expect.

Although it was only four in the afternoon, it was twilight. There was still not a hint of wind and in the breathless silence, no birds sang. He thought of Xara and Amélie in Key West and hoped they were all right. Roberto had assured him that the coast watch had said that there was no danger for them that far south, and that even Miami would only catch the tail of the storm. Looking at the sky, Edouard wondered how accurate that forecast could be.

Inside, the hotel lights blazed, sparkling on the black-and-white marble floor of the lofty hall, but the hotel was shuttered and silent. Roberto roamed the empty halls. He had sent the daily maids home and the only other live-in staff who hadn't already left for the seasonal break were Michel, the chef, and the two underchefs, and Jordan, the barman. And, of course, their four last guests of the season.

He closed the big doors firmly, dropping the iron bar into place. That was that, everyone was inside now. There was nothing more they could do.

The Misses Peabody sailed down the grand stairway, Henry following, his panama tilted at an even more rakish angle than usual.

"It's almost five o'clock," announced Miss Peabody. "We shall take tea, if you don't mind, in the small salon."

Roberto smiled. "Of course, madame." No hurricane was going to upset Miss Peabody's routine.

By six o'clock the wind was howling and the rain could be heard lashing at the shutters. In the background was the booming noise of the sea, hurling itself in great curling waves against the shore. At exactly six-thirty the electricity failed and three immense candelabra were placed in the hall.

By their flickering light the two Misses Peabody and Henry, with Hilliard Watkins as a fourth, played interminable rounds of bridge, sipping the champagne Edouard had provided to boost morale and nibbling sandwiches as though on some elegant picnic. The wind had risen from a low rough gusting growl to a high keening whine, slashed with rain, and Roberto prowled the hotel uneasily. It was unnerving only to be able to hear what was going on and not to see it.

By nine o'clock it seemed that the wind could surely get no higher; shutters and doors rattled, and over the top of the wind they could hear crashing noises as trees, planters, fountains, and, for all they knew, even the garages and outbuildings were ripped apart and hurled into the storm. Every now and again a stronger gust rattled the heavy wooden doors like a warrior demanding entry.

Roberto knew what Edouard was worried about. At eleven o'clock it would be high tide. There was no way to know how high the sea was, but by the sound of it, it must have already covered the beach and be washing over the long sloping lawns that stood between it and the terrace. If the wind were still blowing like this with a strong incoming tide . . .

Henry Peabody lay full length on a couch in the hall, snoring gently. Six glasses of champagne had made him sleepy, and two each for the sisters had had the same effect. They dozed, upright in twin chairs on either side of their brother.

Roberto became aware of the silence as he had never before in his life been aware of it. His eardrums almost ached from it. There had been no slackening of the force of the wind, no lessening of its pitch—it had simply stopped.

Henry Peabody sat up yawning, and taking out his handkerchief, began to polish his spectacles. "We're in what's known as the eye of the storm: the vortex. The wind will be raging all around us a few miles away. Of course, it will return, blowing from the opposite direction this time, but it would be quite safe to take a look outside and see what the damage is."

Edouard and Roberto stared at him in amazement. Henry Peabody was turning out to be a mine of information.

The indigo sky was calm and starlit. There was no trace of even a breeze and the air was warm and heavily humid. Flickers of blue lightning played soundlessly across the sky and hundreds of birds twittered noisily, whirling and swooping, huddling along the edges of rooftops and on the now leafless trees.

"The poor things have been swept along for hundreds of miles," said Henry, picking his way down the marble steps, "from wherever the hurricane last crossed land."

A scene of devastation met their eyes. Trees had been uprooted and flung into the overflowing pools. Heavy stone urns had been hurled along the pathways and smashed. The terrace was littered with broken tiles and was awash with a river of rainwater that the sodden earth and overflowing drains had been unable to absorb.

The ocean hurled itself toward the shore with a continuing frightening roar. Huge waves surged onto the lawn less than a hundred yards away, running fast as the tide gained momentum. Even without the wind the ocean was a force to be reckoned with and Edouard's eyes met Roberto's worriedly. "We'll need more sandbags on the seaward windows," said Edouard, "and we'd better be quick."

Helped by Hilliard Watkins and the chef, the two underchefs, and the barman, they lugged the heavy bags into place. "That's the lot," panted Roberto, sweating from the effort. He accepted gratefully the cigarette Hilliard offered and leaned against the rail of the terrace, staring out at the white-foamed sea.

"All we can do now," sighed Edouard, "is wait."

The sudden gust of wind hit them with tremendous force, sending them reeling in front of it, running helplessly, throwing them to the ground.

Roberto lay there stunned. The wind snatched the breath from his mouth and he gasped, hiding his head in his arms. Peering through his fingers he could see Hilliard on all fours, crawling toward the corner of the hotel, and Edouard clinging to the terrace rail at his side.

"Grab the rail," shouted Edouard over the wind, "until we get to the corner, then crouch down and make a run for it."

They inched their way clutching the rail as the wind hurled itself at them from the sea and the rain began, slashing horizontally, blinding them. The pounding waves sounded ominously nearer.

"Go on!" yelled Edouard. "Run now." He watched Roberto disappear into the rain and prayed he'd make the shelter of the corner. He could see the white edges of the waves as they poured across the lawns below him. "My God," he gasped, "it'll be over the terrace in another few minutes." He launched himself after Roberto, gasping for breath, running sideways like a crab, pushed by the wind. Bending his head and doubling into a crouch, he forced his way to the corner where Roberto and Hilliard were huddled together in the comparative calm of the lee of an archway. They waited, panting, in their temporary shelter, deciding what to do next.

"Do you think we can make it to the main door?" asked Roberto.

"We have no choice," replied Edouard grimly. "If we stay here we'll drown."

Keeping their backs against the wall, they edged sideways along the east wing of the hotel, floundering and slipping in the mud, until they came to the wreck of the once pretty formal garden that lay between them and the hotel door.

"There's nothing for it but to crouch as low as we can and push forward," called Roberto, heading out into the night.

They *could* do it, thought Edouard, head down and shoulders bent. He could still make out Roberto in front of him and slightly to his left, but there was no sign of Hilliard.

The uprooted palm tree came at them with the force of an express train, catching them unawares as they struggled, blinded by the rain and the dark. Roberto saw it first, a looming dark shape heading at them from the darker night. With a cry he thrust up his arms in a futile gesture as though to catch it. It struck Edouard and Roberto simultaneously and they went down like dominoes under the blow.

The wind tossed the voices around him and Edouard gradually made out figures crouching over him in the rain.

"We're trying to lift the tree, you'll be all right," yelled Hilliard. "Don't try to move yet." Edouard was suddenly aware of water surging around them and realized that the sea had already swept over the terrace. His shoulder hurt and blood was trickling into his eyes from a wound on his head.

Heaving and straining, they freed Edouard first. He had been pinned by the upper part of the tree and had taken a glancing blow to the head, but most of the weight had hit his right shoulder. His arm hung limply from the broken bones. It was Roberto who had taken the full brunt of the heavier part of the tree, and he was still trapped.

"You must help Roberto," cried Edouard. "For God's sake, help him. . . ." The wind gusted his words into the black night.

"We'll bring him next," shouted Hilliard. "You must get back before the sea gets us all."

With a man on either side for support they stumbled, half-crouched, toward the door, every step an agony for Edouard. Wrenching it open, they pushed Edouard inside and disappeared back into the storm. Edouard leaned against the door, panting. Sweat and rain mingled with his blood and dripped onto the elegant marble tiles. The old ladies dozed on in the flickering candlelight.

The pain in his shoulder was intolerable and Edouard bit his lip to keep from crying out. Oh, God, what about Roberto? If they didn't hurry it would be too late. They would all drown. Even as he thought it there was a crash and the tinkle of broken glass as the sea hurled itself at the shuttered, sandbagged windows.

The door burst open once more as rain and wind swept through the hall, extinguishing the candles, rattling the chandeliers, and sending glasses and small objects crashing to the floor, before it was forced shut under the combined weight of four men. Miss Peabody's voice sounded calm and un-faltering in the darkness. "Is anyone there? What's going on?"

Edouard groped his way across to the candelabra. "It's all right, Miss Peabody," he called, his voice sounding strange even to himself. "We'll have the candles lit in a moment."

In the candles' fitful light he watched as Roberto was carried across the hall and placed carefully on a couch. The men stood back respectfully avoiding his eyes and Edouard stared at them puzzled. *It couldn't be true!* He didn't want to believe it was true. *Please God,* let it *not* be that. But Roberto was dead.

"Would you please take Mr. do Santos upstairs?" asked Miss Peabody quietly. "Lay him on one of the beds. And bring Monsieur Edouard a glass of brandy, Henry. My sister has had nursing experience," she said to Edouard. "She will see to your shoulder."

There was another sudden gust and the sound of more broken glass. "I think I'd better take a look at that," she said calmly, "and see what can be done."

Edouard watched numbly as she disappeared in the direction of the grand salon. Miss Peabody was in charge and she was indomitable. He leaned his head against the chair and closed his eyes as they carried Roberto's body upstairs. He could recall with complete clarity the blond little boy with Zeze, his pet ram; the young Roberto, a golden-limbed athlete playing polo for his team; kindhearted Roberto, always the peacekeeper between Amélie and his friends. Amélie's husband, the boy and the man she had always loved, father of her children. And he wept for the boy he had known and for the sorrow Amélie would have to face.

The nightmare was not yet over. The sea surged along the terrace and into the gardens and the waves hurled themselves at the shutters. They could feel the building shudder as though it were a sinking ship and they stood around, nervous and apprehensive, sipping Scotch as the night wore on and the wind and sea showed no sign of abating. The sisters sat side by side on the sofa, knitting calmly and, for once, voicing no complaint as their brother joined the whiskey drinkers.

Although Edouard's watch said seven in the morning, there was no glimpse of any dawn through the cracks in the shutters, night and day were the same, and it wasn't until noon that the first lessening in the wind came and the sky began to brighten. The hurricane had passed. Only the dead and the damage remained in its wake.

❧ 68 ❦

AMÉLIE COULDN'T REMEMBER which was worse, the moment when Edouard had told her that Roberto was dead, or his funeral, when his poor broken body had been laid to rest beneath the golden blue skies of a clear Florida day. Anyway, it didn't matter, she thought wearily, nothing mattered anymore. She pulled her chair close to the window and sat gazing at the blue bay down below.

The Villa Encantada was silent. Grandmère had returned to Rio, and Xara and Edouard were in Miami with the children, their own and hers. A pang of guilt ran through Amélie as she thought about her little daughters. It had been a month since she had come to Key West with just Grandmère for company, a month since she had seen her children. And it was two months since Roberto had died. Even just thinking the word made her feel cold inside. She closed her eyes against the pain as if she could see him with the palm tree pinning his beautiful strong body into the mud. It was too much to bear, she couldn't take it! There's nothing left to live for, she moaned softly to the empty room. Nothing! But there was, Grandmère had told her, there were Lais and Leonore—Roberto's children—she should thank God she had that legacy. How could Grandmère possibly know how remote those two sweet blond babies seemed at this moment? They were too young and too innocent to know anything other than that they missed that nice man they had just learned to call Papa. Maybe Grandmère was right and they should be a comfort, but they *weren't* and it must be *her* fault. She was an unfeeling mother, neglecting her babies, wallowing in her own grief!

Amélie felt helpless; there was nothing she could do to fight against her feelings, she was swamped by them, overwhelmed by pain. She wanted to sit in this darkened room forever and never have to talk to anyone. It was easier that way.

Edouard strolled from the ferry along the pier, head bent, lost in thought. He was here because of Xara, it was her idea and he hoped fervently that it would work. The keys jingled in his pocket as he walked along the main street to the ice-cream parlor, where he bought a quart of chocolate and a quart of peach, Amélie's favorites, smiling at his foolishness—as if a childish thing like her favorite ice cream could help her! Isabelle had warned him that Amélie wasn't eating, that she wasn't doing anything. She stayed indoors, she barely ate, she would see no one. They must do something about her. It was then that Xara had come up with the idea. Edouard sighed as he climbed into the taxi, he surely hoped it was going to work.

Who could that be? wondered Amélie, startled by the sound of footsteps in the hall. She glanced at her watch. Four o'clock, she must have been dozing. It was probably only Zita, the maid. But no, it couldn't be—she'd given the maids the week off, she'd wanted to be quite alone. Her ears strained for the sound again as she tiptoed to the bedroom door and stood listening. There was a noise in the kitchen!

"Who's there?" she called, flinging open the door and walking along the gallery at the top of the stairs.

"Amélie. It's me—Edouard."

She sagged against the rail in relief, gazing down at him. "Edouard! What are you doing here?"

Edouard hurried up the steps toward her. "I came to see you, of course." She felt weightless as he put his arms around her, holding her close. Her bones were like those of a bird under his hands. Edouard held her back from him, assessing her. "I thought so," he said accusingly. "You're not eating."

"I eat enough," said Amélie defensively. "I'm all right, Edouard, really I am. There was no need to come rushing over here just because Grandmère has left. I'm quite happy being alone."

"I'm sure you are," said Edouard grimly, "but your daughters are not."

Amélie's eyes widened in alarm. "There's nothing wrong is there?"

"No. There's nothing *wrong* with Lais and Leonore, it's just that it will be their second birthday next week and it would be nice if their mother was there to celebrate it with them. Especially now that they have no father," he added deliberately. Shock her, Xara had told him, you must jolt her out of the awful apathy, put the responsibility on her shoulders, make her face up to it, Edouard. She must, for the children's sake—and her own.

Amélie stepped back a pace. What was he saying, didn't he know she couldn't bear to talk about it? "I . . . I was just lying down in my room," she whispered, edging away down the corridor.

Edouard grabbed her hand. "Come downstairs with me," he said pulling her along. "I've got something for you."

"Edouard, I . . . I don't feel very well, I think I'd rather just go back to

440

my room and lie down. Oh, I forgot, I've given the maids the week off, you will have to go to the St. James for dinner."

"And what were you proposing to eat for dinner?" Her silent face answered Edouard's question. "Come with me," he said, walking her down the stairs.

The two cartons of ice cream were already melting onto the kitchen table, and Edouard sat Amélie in a chair and scooped a spoonful of each flavor into a bowl. "There," he said with a grin, "your favorites."

Doesn't he know, wondered Amélie, that nothing is any good anymore? Doesn't he understand that? Her eyes met Edouard's piteously across the table as the ice cream sat untouched in front of her.

"Not eating isn't going to resolve anything, Amélie. It won't bring Roberto back."

Her eyes fell, the long curling lashes making shadows on her pale cheeks. Her once-lustrous hair lay limp, its golden strands dull and lifeless. Edouard's hand trembled on the spoon, how he hated hurting her like this, but it had to be done for her own sake.

"Lais and Leonore are wonderful," he said. "They're toddling all over the place, there's no holding them. They remind me so much of when you were that age, Amélie, it's wonderful to see. Of course, they look like their father, too; Roberto was as blond as you. Lais has his eyes, that nice clear blue—"

"Stop it!" Anger throbbed in Amélie's voice beneath the pain. "Why are you doing this ... stop it, Edouard. *Please.*"

"Then you think it's fair never to speak of Roberto now that he's dead? Are we all to pretend that he never existed? What kind of foolishness is that, Amélie? Roberto has the right to be remembered, to be spoken of ... to be *loved.* Don't you see, Amélie, his death has to become a part of our lives so that we can all live with it!"

Amélie stared at him, stony-faced, and Edouard hesitated. Had he gone too far? If he had, there was no going back now. "There are two children in Miami who need their mother. More than that, Amélie, they have a *right* to their mother. Their father was killed and their future is in your hands. They are dependent on *you,* Amélie do Santos."

Amélie lifted her chin as though she were taking a blow. Edouard was right, the children were her responsibility. But she didn't want to go back to Miami, she didn't want to go anywhere, she just wanted to stay in the safety of that room upstairs. How could she return and be laughing and playful with the children the way they would expect her to be, the way she had always been? It was all different now. Life was empty.

Edouard took the keys from his pocket and held them up in front of her. "These are the keys to the Palaço d'Aureville," he said calmly. "They are the keys that I would have handed to Roberto when he took up the position of manager of the hotel next month, a job he had worked hard for and one that I had no hesitation in offering him. He deserved it." He put the keys on the table between them and pushed back his chair. The tiled floor echoed to his footfalls as he paced the kitchen. "The damage to the hotel has been repaired and the grounds are being relandscaped. We expect to be able to open on time and the hotel will be at least half-full for the first two weeks—after that it is fully booked for the season. We're installing two swimming pools and a gymnasium and Michel, the chef, is already dreaming up new menus to tempt our guests. The staff is ready and waiting. All we need now is a manager."

Amélie sat stiffly at the table, wondering why she had to know all this, what did it matter?

Edouard's eyes bored into her. "We have put a lot of time into the Palaçio d'Aureville—myself, Xara, Grandmère, Roberto—and a hell of a lot of money. The job of manager is yours, Amélie." Her head lifted and her shocked eyes gazed into his. "Roberto would have wanted it this way," Edouard continued. "You ran the Rio hotel for Grandmère, and you helped Roberto with the Palaçio, there's no reason why you shouldn't be capable of this task." He held up his hand as she started to protest. "I won't take no for an answer, Amélie, there will be no other manager. If you don't take the job, then the Palaçio d'Aureville will close before it even reopens."

Edouard walked to the table and pushed the keys toward her. "There are the keys. The Palaçio d'Aureville is waiting for you. It's a challenge, Amélie, but I know you can do it."

He strolled to the door, turning to look at her still sitting there silently, her back to him. "You'd better eat your ice cream," he called. "It's melting."

A half-smile played around Amélie's mouth. It had taken a lot of nerve to make a grandstand play like that and she admired him for it. Not only that, she knew that having said it he would stick by his word: if she refused the job as manager he would let the Palaçio close. He had left her no choice. She picked up the heavy bunch of keys, hefting their weight in her hand as Roberto must have done many times. The chair scraped on the tiles as she pushed it back and walked to the door to find Edouard. "A challenge," he said; it would be more then a mere challenge, it would be an uphill struggle of sheer hard work, but she welcomed the idea. My God, how she welcomed it.

❧ 69 ❦

IN JUNE 1914 Léonie had dismissed the threat of war in Europe as ridiculous. Who could imagine war when the sun shone, the Mediterranean seemed bluer than ever, and soft breezes cooled exquisite summer nights? Who, she wondered, could want to disturb such perfection?

And how could there be war when in July the streets of Paris were alive with beautiful young people, dressed in the chic city's latest fashions, always seeming to be going to, or coming from some wild, extravagant party? Music hung like a haze over Paris's terraces and pavements, and the delicious smell of coffee and freshly baked breads tantalized early morning strollers. But in the cafés, Frenchmen read their newspapers in worried silence, and the gossip turned from women to war, from vacations in Deauville to problems in the Balkans.

"It has to come, Léonie," Jim told her, flipping the black-headlined newspaper onto the table between them.

Léonie sipped her coffee, gazing at the crowded terrace of La Coupole, avoiding his eyes. She didn't want to spoil this perfect morning with talk of war.

"It's no use avoiding the subject or hoping for miracles, Léonie, the situation is grave."

"But everyone says that the newspapers are exaggerating, that it will all be worked out."

"It's too late, darling, the machinery is already in motion. We must make the decision."

"Decision?"

"Do I take you back to America? Or do we stay here and face it?"

Leave France when there was to be a war? Leave the inn? Damn it, she had struggled and suffered to achieve her home, and now he was suggesting she simply up and leave it for the enemy! "Never," she cried passionately, "I'll never leave France. I'll kill anyone who tries to take the inn from me!"

Jim grinned, he had known what she would say. "Okay. That resolves that! We stay. The next question is, how will they feel about having an American in the French army?"

* * *

Selfishly Léonie half-hoped that the army wouldn't accept him. The thought of being without Jim, and worse, of him probably being in battle, terrified her. Jim was made a member of the intelligence service and suddenly Léonie perceived another side to the carefree, easygoing man who had pursued and won her. His always cheerful smile could no longer hide the concern in his eyes, his confident plans for their future covered an increasing feeling of futility as world events charged headlong to the only conclusion, and his love for her carried the passion of a man unsure of how many more days they might spend together.

Even though it was anticipated, it seemed to happen all of a sudden. Armies were on the march across Europe, troops were massing on borders, and the young men of France were swept rapidly into uniform and off to the front.

Léonie was alone at the inn. Jim had left that morning for Paris and their good-byes had been calm and tearless, though for once Jim's optimism had almost failed him. "I don't know how long it's going to be, Léonie," he had whispered, holding her close, "and I don't know when I'll see you again, but remember I love you ... will you ever know how much I love you?"

"Nothing will happen to you," Léonie had said fiercely, "I'm sure of it. No war can destroy us!"

The little cat, sensing that something was wrong, had leapt into her arms and lay trembling, her high-pitched meow becoming a hoarse wail as Jim's car disappeared into the distance.

It was almost anticlimactic when he called her from Paris the next day, and every subsequent night for a month. And then nothing for weeks. Then, suddenly, he was home—just for a few days—and they pretended life was normal again, until the dreaded time came for him to leave again.

After a few months Léonie could bear the waiting and inaction no longer. The war was being fought in the north, on hills and in trenches far away from her lovely blue and golden Provence, but the effects showed in the pinched faces of the women in the market worried about sons and husbands, in the *boules* game in the square with only tired old men for players, and in the lack of young people on the streets.

It took her two days to get through by telephone to Caro in Paris, but the call accomplished exactly what she wanted. Within an hour clothes were packed, Chocolat was stashed in her basket in the back of the car, petrol was begged from an old friend at the garage, and she was on her way to Paris—and then to the war.

"They won't let us fight," Caro had stated, glittery-eyed with emotion, "but there are other ways we can help."

"I want to be *there*," Léonie insisted, "at the front, not hiding back here, rolling bandages. Can't we at least help the wounded? They need ambulances, don't they? Then let's give them ambulances, Caro!"

Together they raised funds for a fleet of a dozen ambulances, driving them to the front with their troupe of once-glamorous Parisienne ladies, garbed in smart but serviceable gray-and-red uniforms designed by Caro's favorite couturier. Nothing could have prepared them for the horror left by the aftermath of battle, but they drove their cargo of wounded men, hardening themselves to ignore the piteous cries, the screams, the sounds, and the smells of war. Edging ever closer to the front, inspired by a hatred of an enemy so implacably brutal, they rescued the shattered, bleeding remnants of what had once been the youth of France and Britain. "The Winged Victories," the men dubbed them because of the way they drove—like bats out of hell—ignoring shells and fire, flying over rough muddy fields as though their vehicles had wings. And for Léonie the irony was that the ambulances they drove were de Courmont vehicles, the rifles the soldiers carried were made in de Courmont's vast armaments works at Valenciennes, and the heavy guns whose ceaseless shelling left them deaf for days on end were fashioned from de Courmont steel.

Every now and again when it all became too much, when Léonie felt she could bear to see no more bloody gaping wounds, no more agonized frightened eyes, light no more cigarettes and place them trembling between dying lips, she and Caro would pack their vehicles with a dozen of the vacant-eyed young men, unwounded but shocked, seeming always to look into a hell too private to be mentioned and never to be forgotten. They would drive them to the south, to the ever-welcoming inn and the tender care of Monsieur and Madame Frenard, in the hope that its peace might make them feel human again. And sometimes, when it succeeded, they would feel that there was hope once again.

Occasionally, on these visits, Jim appeared out of the blue and they had an ecstatic few days together, made painful by his imminent departure. He never spoke of what he did and on the surface he was the same cheerful, sardonic man, but she sensed the new bitterness that ran as deep as hers.

Alphonse, whose pride had suffered a bitter blow when they had told him he was too old for military service, had remained in Paris, deeply involved in negotiations for international loans to fuel the war effort. His work for France was invaluable, but it failed to compensate for his physical separation from the place he felt he should be: on the front line, fighting for his country.

It was Jim who brought the news of his death. Caro, newly returned from a long stint of ambulance duty, held her chin high as he told her what she already sensed he was going to tell her. Alphonse was a victim not of enemy bullets but of the influenza that was sweeping the country.

"I never married him," said Caro quietly, shocked tears raining down her cheeks, "and I'll never forgive myself for that—and for not being there with him. He never had his uniform, but he died for his country. I know he would expect me to behave like the wife of an officer and a brave man. I hope he knew, Léonie. I just hope he knew that I loved him."

She had gone back to the front the next morning, dry-eyed and resolved that if she could not kill the enemy then at least she would save as many Frenchmen as she could.

Occasionally a letter would filter through from Amélie in Florida, as though from some other planet where the world was still full of colors instead of everlasting gray. Léonie delighted in the news of her twin granddaughters. They filled her with hope for a future whose problems had suddenly become greater than Monsieur's personal threats had ever been. But the sadness of Roberto's death, as savage and unearned as any on the battlefield, conveyed to her months after the event in a scrawled note from Amélie, added to her bitterness at her separation from her daughter, in whose joy of life she had never been able to participate and for whose sorrows she was never there to lend comfort.

As suddenly as it had begun, the tide turned. And in the summer of 1918, with the progress of the Allied armies toward victory, the skies of France lightened, too, and hope returned to all their hearts. In November of that year, Paris and London celebrated the armistice with music and wine, with dancing in the streets and fireworks. For Jim and Léonie it was enough to be together, looking out over the dark sea from that great white bed in the simple room in the old inn.

There was one postscript to the war that for Léonie underlined "The End." The report took several paragraphs in the newspapers because of the prominence of the man's family—in particular his association by marriage to one of Germany's biggest steel and armaments manufacturers, the Krummers. It was the day after the armistice had been declared, and Rupert von Hollensmark had been on his way to the Krummer factory at Essen when his car had gone off the road in dense fog. He had been killed instantly.

Walking alone along the beach, Léonie tried to recall their time together, how young they had been, so frighteningly young, how she had loved him so. All the important events of her life were shaped here at the inn where he had brought her, all the tangled relationships and loves: Monsieur, who had bought the inn for her; Charles, who had given her Amélie; and now her life here with Jim. Lost love leaves bittersweet regrets and she was saddened for Rupert and for Puschi.

❧70❧

AMÉLIE MADE HER WAY back through the grounds of the Palaçio d'Aureville toward the little white house with its private walled garden that was
home to her and her little family. She checked the big sensible watch on her
wrist, time was an important element in her life these days. Six o'clock. She
had exactly an hour to bathe and play with the girls before their bedtime,
and then she must return to the hotel and go over the bookings. They
couldn't afford a repetition of the overbooking that had happened last
month, and she still hadn't found out how that mistake had occurred. It
was inexcusable and the fact that it had never happened before in the three
years she had been in charge didn't matter. It should never have happened at
all and it was up to her to make sure it didn't happen again. There was always something, she thought with a wry smile, as she pushed open the gate
and strode up the path to the ever-open front door.

"Mama, Mama," the children's voices shrieked in unison as the girls
burst through the front door—two blond heads haloed in curls, plump
sun-bronzed legs running, arms pushing. Lais would be the one who pushed
ahead, of course, while Leonore just smiled and let her get away with it.

"Me first," panted Lais, throwing her arms around her mother's knees.
"Sebastião is here," she announced as Amélie bent to kiss her.

"Here I am, Mama." Leonore lifted her face for her kiss. "Sebastião is
here."

"What fun!" Amélie took their hands and walked back up the path
with them. "I bet he brought you presents."

Lais looked at her with Roberto's blue eyes. "The biggest—the *biggest*—doll you ever saw." Her hands described the size and Amélie laughed,
she knew her daughter's powers of exaggeration.

"No, it's this big." Leonore's hands formed a more modest size.

"That still looks very big to me," said Amélie cheerfully. "Let's take a
look at these dolls."

"How's the working woman?" Sebastião's good looks never failed to
remind her of Roberto. "Charming and beautiful as ever, I see," he said,
kissing her.

Amélie flung herself into a chair. "I don't feel so charming." She smiled. "But it's nice of you to say so. And I feel a lot better for seeing you."

"Those words are music to my ears," he said, handing her a parcel. "I couldn't leave you out, could I?"

"A present? Oh, Sebastião, you shouldn't have bothered . . . you're too kind, you're always bringing us presents." What would she do without him? she wondered. He'd been the rock she had leaned against these past couple of years. He heard all her problems, discussed all her worries, lived through all her self-doubts. He comforted her, encouraged her, and, when necessary, bullied her, and she loved him for it.

The white box was tied with a silver ribbon and bore the name of a smart New York shop. Inside was the prettiest lace blouse.

"They told me it was the latest thing," he said anxiously, waiting to see if she approved.

Amélie held the fragile lace against her, beaming at him. "It's quite the loveliest thing in my wardrobe," she said. "How clever of you to choose it, Sebastião." She laughed at the idea of him going into a women's shop. "And brave!" she added. Amélie glanced at the dress she was wearing. It had been ages since she had bought anything new, there simply was never enough free time for shopping. There was no time for anything—just the hotel and the children—and she ticked between the two like the hand on a metronome, each minute allocated. There just wasn't any time left over for *her!*

"It's really a bribe, so you'll be sure to have dinner with me."

"Oh, but Sebastião, I have to go back. I must check next month's bookings and there's Mr. and Mrs. Freeland's wedding anniversary dinner and dance in the ballroom tonight. I really must be there to make sure there's no disaster."

"Amélie, didn't anyone ever tell you that the secret of success is knowing how to delegate? Delegate, my dear, put part of the burden on your staff, that's what they're there for!"

Amélie smiled ruefully. "I know, I know. It's just that . . . well . . . you know, Sebastião, ultimately the responsibility is mine and I don't want anything to go wrong. Edouard trusts me."

"I should think he trusts you after the job you've done. In three years this place is the most successful hotel in Florida. Why shouldn't he trust you? And why shouldn't you trust your staff? After all, you chose them."

"You're right, I should let them get on with it, I suppose. The trouble is, Sebastião, that I'm just so damned interested in it that I can't bear not to be involved. I love every bit of it." Amélie laughed, scooping Leonore onto her knee. "But this is *your* time, isn't it, my darling?" she said, kissing her. "How about that bath?"

Leonore's eyes were the same tawny amber as Amélie's and as Léonie's.

"It's my turn to sit at the end without the plug," she said, tugging at Amélie's arm. "Tell *her*, tell Lais *now*, Mama. You're not to sit at my end," she warned her sister.

Lais leapt to her feet and ran across the room to the door. "If I get in first, I'll sit where I like," she called, casting off her clothes as she ran.

Amélie and Sebastião laughed. "Don't worry, Leonore, I'll make sure you get the end without the plug." Sebastião picked up the little girl and swung her onto his shoulders.

"Come on," he called, "let's see how you can swim." He glanced at Amélie as they mounted the stairs together. "What about that dinner—or do I come all the way from New York to see you and then dine alone?"

"Ah, such pathos." Amélie grinned at him. It really was so good to see him. "Will ten o'clock be too late?"

"Ten o'clock it is."

Amélie wore the lace blouse with a swinging white skirt. Her hair was pinned up with pearl-studded combs, pearl drops dangled from her ears, and a silver belt sashed her waist tightly. She felt pretty. It wasn't something she'd given much thought to lately, but it was definitely time to start. She wondered what Sebastião would think of her idea.

Sebastião was waiting for her at her special table in the restaurant of the Palaçio. It was ten minutes past ten and the room was crowded with guests enjoying Michel's superb food and the elegant surroundings. Amélie's touch was everywhere, in the palest mint green tablecloths and the heavy plain silverware, the Limoges plates and the exquisite flowers. Her taste had been formed and guided by Isabelle and it was flawless. And so was she, thought Sebastião, pushing back his chair as Amélie came toward him. He wondered what she would think when he asked her. The time was right now, he felt it. They were so close already.

"Sebastião, I have an idea. I want you to tell me what you think of it."

She looked so earnest that Sebastião wondered what it could be now. Was she planning a fifty room extension? Or adding extra tennis courts and a polo field? He wouldn't put anything past her imagination, or her flair, she seemed to have a real sense for what would succeed.

"All right, tell me," he said, thinking how pretty she looked in the white lace blouse.

"The war in France is finally over. I want to take the children to see their grandmother."

The only thing that would have surprised him more would have been if she'd said she was retiring and leaving the hotel for someone else to manage. He knew that Amélie wrote to Léonie, though she rarely mentioned her, yet obviously this had been brewing in her mind for some time.

"It sounds like a good idea," he said carefully, "as long as Léonie agrees." He remembered their flight from France the last time when Léonie had been convinced that Amélie was in some sort of danger.

"I'm not going to tell her," she announced. "I shall just go there and find her."

"Like the last time?" Sebastião raised his eyebrows.

"Not like the last time. This time I won't run away. Whatever trouble there was when I was a child must surely be over now, Sebastião. I'm twenty-four years old—and a widow with two children of my own." Amélie shrugged. "There's no danger except in Léonie's head, and I think my children have the right to know their grandmother."

Sebastião took her hand. "You're right, it's a good idea, good for you and for Lais and Leonore. And for Léonie."

Amélie smiled her relief; Sebastião was so level-headed, if he'd tried to dissuade her she would have been forced to reconsider her decision—or at least to listen to his arguments against it. "Oh, good," she breathed, "I'm glad you approve. It'll make it easier when I tell Edouard." The old animation lit her face and for a moment he had a glimpse of the vivid, eager young girl she used to be. "Oh, Sebastião, I'm so excited!"

Sebastião's eyes met hers. "Amélie, why go alone? Can't I go with you?"

"You don't want to be dragging around Europe with a widow and her brood! You have that architectural practice in New York to think of—and no doubt a dozen beautiful and maddeningly smart girlfriends!"

Amélie dismissed the idea lightly, as she could with an old friend, but Sebastião wasn't to be put off.

"Amélie, I didn't mean it like that. . . . I'd like you to be my wife." Her long, dark-tipped lashes fluttered to her cheeks. He continued, "I've always loved you—we could be happy together, like we are now. The best days of my life are when I'm here with you and the children."

He was her dearest friend in the world, he'd always been that—and it was true they were happy when they were together. Marriage to Sebastião would be calm and reasonable and always comfortably loving. Memories of Roberto flitted through her head; it had been full of youth and gentle and wonderful. But now she was different. She was a woman, and she wanted to feel like a woman. Maybe somewhere, someday there would be someone who aroused the passion in her that she felt sure existed.

"Sebastião." Amélie's amber eyes met his, pleadingly. "I can't—not now anyway. I'm not ready for marriage, but I do love you, too, really I do." Her hands squeezed his anxiously. "It's just that I have to go to France alone. I need more time to sort out my feelings."

Maybe he acted too hastily; it had only been three years, after all. "I'll be here, when you get back then," he said with a smile, "if you need me."

Amélie breathed a sigh of relief. "I'll always need you, in fact, I need you right now. I want to take the children to Paris for a few days before we go down to the Côte d'Azur. Don't you have some friends there? I'd like to know there was someone I could turn to in case anything went wrong."

Sebastião thought of Gérard de Courmont—here was a chance for him at last to meet Amélie. "Of course, a *very good* friend. I'll write to him at once and let him know you're coming. He'd be more than happy to show you Paris."

"Wonderful," said Amélie as the waiter arrived bearing their supper. "I can't wait to meet him."

☙ 71 ❧

GÉRARD DROVE the big dark blue car through the night; every mile that clicked onto the gauge on the dashboard in front of him put more distance between him and his father in Monte Carlo. It was never easy spending time with him, though now that Gilles was able to speak again, the terrible sense of isolation Gérard had felt around his father had lessened. Give him his due, Gérard thought as the dawn light filtered across the outskirts of Paris, the old man's a fighter and he's got courage. He needed it to get through what he did. The bitterest blow was his inability to walk. Gilles de Courmont did not take to the life of a cripple easily, he despised his wheelchair, hated his useless legs. For the second time in his life he battled with daily exercises that would have defeated a man half his age, and the greatest triumph of the past years had been the day he had stood unaided by the side of his chair—upright on his own two feet for the first time in five years. At sixty-four he was still a handsome man, thought Gérard critically. Normally a man of his looks and position would have been enjoying life with some pretty woman on his arm, though probably not his father; he'd probably still be clinging to the past and to the one love of his life: Léonie. Nothing was ever mentioned about her—there were no intimate conversations between father and son—but he suspected that she was still there, in his father's convoluted mind.

He swung the car across the bridge and along the Quai d'Orléans to the big house. Since his father had taken to living permanently in Monte

Carlo, Marie-France had taken over the family townhouse, throwing open its windows to the fresh air and livening its dimmed surfaces with fresh paint, new upholstery, and beautiful new curtains. For the first time in years and despite its size and grandeur, the place felt like a home.

It was just six-thirty as Gérard strode into the hall. There was time for some breakfast and about a half gallon of coffee before he went to the office. The plans for that new extension to the art gallery presented some fascinating problems as far as lighting.

A pile of letters awaited on his desk and he leafed through them quickly. There was one from Sebastião—good, it had been a long time. What could he be up to? Well, well, so little Amélie d'Aureville was coming to Paris. He remembered the letters Sebastião used to show him with the funny drawings: Amélie with the round face and the curly hair, the big upturned grin when she was happy and the downturned mouth when she wasn't.

Gérard tossed the letter onto the desk. He wondered how happy she could be now, a young widow with two small children. Well, he was going to be pretty busy, but he'd make time to see her, for Sebastião's sake.

Paris was unfolding itself for them like a flower, thought Amélie, as they sailed sedately along the river Seine, dipping under ancient bridges and floating through the city, marveling that it had placed so many glorious buildings by its river to be admired by visitors like herself. Lais and Leonore hung over the side of the barge with their nurse keeping a firm grip on them—just in case they leaned too far.

Amélie relaxed against the wooden seat. It was pleasant just gliding along like this, listening to the monotone discourse of the guide as he named names and recounted dates, and it was pleasant being in Paris again. This time she really wanted to get to know it, the last visit had been so quick. It was odd really, she thought, that now she was here in France there seemed no great urgency to rush down to the south, it felt good just being with the children, and they loved having her to themselves. In fact, they blossomed under her attention and maybe they were becoming just a little bit spoiled? And why not, she thought indulgently, though they really should take a nap this afternoon or they'd never last through supper.

The pretty barge nudged its way back to the pier and the children leapt out, darting up the gray stone steps with their nurse in pursuit. Yes, it was definitely time for a quiet lunch and then bed for those little girls!

The suite at the Hôtel Crillon was sunlit and quiet as Amélie reread the note from Gérard de Courmont. This was the friend Sebastião had told her about—his *"very good"* friend, he'd said. She had been enjoying her solitude and her daughters so much that for a moment she almost regretted that Gérard had asked her to lunch the next day, but still, she supposed it would do her good to get away from the children for an hour or two. And, after all, mightn't it be fun to have lunch with a Frenchman in Paris?

Amélie went to her closet and glanced through the array of dresses hanging there. Why was it that Paris always managed to make her feel dowdy and out of style? She didn't have a thing to wear for a lunch engagement with a man. A little shopping was definitely called for. And perhaps she should also have her hair done, try something new, something a little more stylish?

Gérard looked at the tall blond woman in the summery yellow dress walking toward him across the lobby of the Crillon with a jolt of recognition. Sebastião's words from years before flashed into his head: Amélie looks like Léonie, he had said, *exactly* like her. And she did! Hadn't Sebastião said she must be some long-lost relative?

"Madame do Santos?"

Amélie smiled at him, a wide-curving coral smile that sparkled her tawny eyes and seemed to Gérard to light the Hôtel Crillon better than any of its multilustered chandeliers.

"You must be Gérard de Courmont," this vision said to him in perfectly accented French. "I would have recognized you anywhere from Sebastião's description—and it was a flattering one, Monsieur de Courmont. He said you would be the handsomest man in sight." Amélie's laugh rang through the muted hallways of the Crillon as Gérard took her hand.

"And, of course, you could only be Amélie," he said, a smile lighting his own face. "I would have known you anywhere."

"Then I'm glad Sebastião didn't let either of us down. It could have been very embarrassing if there had been two handsome men in this lobby being importuned by a strange foreign female!"

Gérard felt his spirits rise as they eyed each other with mutual appreciation. Taking Amélie's arm, he walked with her to the door, mentally canceling the plans he had had for the elegant formal restaurant. He was with a beautiful and intriguing woman on a wonderful summer's day and there was only one place to take her: the Bois.

Lemony beams of sunlight filtered through the trees as they drove through the park, dappling Amélie's champagne hair with greenish lights and shading her clear peach-skinned face like tiny clouds. Her mouth was curved in an expression of delight as she gazed around her, and the yellow dress reflected its color beneath her delicately boned chin like the petals of a buttercup.

She was, thought Gérard, the most beautiful, the most desirable woman he had ever met. Sebastião had always claimed to be in love with her and now he knew why.

The restaurant's tables were set beneath the shade of a vast sweeping chestnut tree and surrounded by flowers. "It's quite the most perfect place for lunch on a beautiful day," remarked Amélie, feeling suddenly a little shy now that they were sitting opposite each other. He really was very good-looking, tall and broad-shouldered, and his face, though he was smiling at her, was that of a serious man. His eyes were an indigo blue, deep like the darkest part of the ocean, and his black hair was swept back, waving slightly, from a broad intelligent brow. There was a sort of intensity about him, a feeling of leashed power that made her a little uneasy, but it was very attractive.

"Sebastião told me that you were recently widowed," he said, the words dropping shockingly into the soft afternoon air. "I wanted to offer my sympathy."

Amélie was startled—it wasn't anything she had expected him to say. Why wasn't he just making trivial lunchtime conversation with her? "Thank you," she replied stiffly. "It has been three years now."

"Amélie, if we are to get to know each other, it had to be said. Otherwise we would just have a pleasant lunch. We could chat about Paris and about your journey and that would be that, but I would like to know you better."

For once in her life Amélie was at a loss for words and she stared at this forceful stranger who wanted to know her better, her eyes round with surprise.

"Though," Gérard went on, "I feel that I already know you. Sebastião used to show me your letters—the ones with the little drawings."

"I remember, I used to draw maps of the rides we'd been on, or pictures of my cats."

"And there were pictures of you—a little round face and a mass of frizzy hair—not all that accurate judging by what I see now."

His face lit up as Amélie laughed. "There, that's better, now you're relaxed and we can talk like old friends instead of new acquaintances." He held her gaze for a long moment.

"You're very direct, Gérard de Courmont," said Amélie, turning her gaze down to the menu in front of her.

"I simply felt we could be friends, you and I. Paris can be a lonely city for a visitor—I'd like to show it to you, if you'd let me."

Their eyes met again, and Amélie's heart skipped a beat as a blush of happiness colored her cheeks. "I think I'd like that," she murmured.

For a man she thought so serious-looking when she had walked across the lobby of the Crillon to meet him, Gérard proved highly entertaining, recounting stories of his student days with Sebastião so that she suddenly saw both of them in a whole new light, as carefree architectural students involved in the silly escapades of youth. And Gérard was so *easy* to talk to that stories just spilled from her, childhood memories of the Villa d'Aureville on Copacabana with Sebastião, Roberto, Edouard, and Grandmère. She found herself remembering things they had done that must have been buried in the recesses of her mind, and her laughter rang out as she shared them with Gérard de Courmont.

"You know, it's odd," he said finally, "but I always thought somehow Sebastião meant to marry you."

Amélie looked down at the bowl of *fraises des bois* in front of her. Their sugared scarlet juices stained the silver bowl and their fragrance was that of summer. This dark blue-eyed man knew almost too much about her—he even knew about Sebastião. It was an unfair advantage when she knew so little about him. For some reason she didn't want him to know that Sebastião had asked her to marry him, not now.

"No, it was always Roberto. Sebastião knew that."

Gérard spooned a berry from the bowl and offered it to her, smiling as she took it in her delicate pink mouth.

"Tell me, Amélie, why did you come to Paris? And alone?"

"But I'm not alone, I have my children with me."

Gérard wanted to kiss her, she was like a child herself in her guilelessness; she didn't know how to flirt with him.

"I plan to spend a week here and then I'm going to the south—to the Côte d'Azur." The name sounded exotic on her lips, full of the mystery of the glamorous unknown.

"That, too, is not a place to go alone."

Amélie blushed. What was he getting at? "I'm not alone, I'm going to visit someone . . . an old friend there." She couldn't tell him about Léonie. She barely knew him.

"You know," said Gérard suddenly, "there's a puppet theater in the Jardins du Luxembourg and there's a marvelous toy shop on the Faubourg Saint-Honoré and I know just the place your children would love to go for lunch."

Amélie sat back in her chair; he was full of surprises. "Where? For lunch, I mean?"

"A picnic, right here in the Bois. And then there's the circus—"

Amélie burst out laughing, he was clever, too! The certain way to her heart was through her children.

"Tomorrow?" His eyebrows were raised in a question.

"Tomorrow," she agreed, still laughing. "I shall look forward to it."

* * *

It was late afternoon when Gérard returned her to the hotel. "Let me take you out to dinner," he said as he walked with her through the lobby.

"I can't do that—the children will be waiting for me."

"Then I'll have dinner with you *and* your children."

Amélie shook her head. "No, really, they'll be tired and I'd like them to eat early in the suite."

The elegant little scrolled and gilded elevator stopped and its gates swung open. Gérard put out his hand. "Don't say no," he pleaded. "Surely the children must go to bed at some point! If you can't have dinner, perhaps we can go to the theater, or even for a stroll—Paris by night?"

Amélie succumbed to his persuasive charm with a smile. "Very well, why don't you come and meet my daughters this evening before they go to bed? And then I'd like to take a walk, I haven't seen anything of Paris by night."

"Then I shall be the one to show you," he exclaimed, pleased with himself.

I shall remember this walk forever, thought Amélie, as she strolled hand in hand with Gérard by the Seine. Paris was overlaid with the blue glaze of a summer-night sky, and yellow lamps dotted their progress, illuminating couples like themselves enjoying the balmy evening air and each other. Only they are probably lovers, thought Amélie, aware of their intertwined arms and languorous looks, and we are not. We're just friends. Or were they? Didn't her hand feel every inch of its contact with his? Wasn't she aware of the way his fingers laced with hers? And of his height and his powerful shoulders. She glanced at his profile, silhouetted against the sky; it was pleasingly arrogant, in fact there was a strength about him that attracted her. He looked like a man who knew what he wanted.

Gérard led her through his city, seeing it with new eyes himself. It all looks different when you're falling in love, he thought, and now I know I've never been in love before.

The café tables were sprawled across the pavement beneath the trees and they sat like other couples, sipping licorice-tasting little drinks and gazing into each other's eyes, saying little. This is happening too fast, thought Amélie, it can't be real, it's just that I'm alone in Paris and this is the first man I've met in a long time—and he is so very attractive.

"I must go back," she said, picking up her purse. "It's getting late."

"Please stay with me."

His eyes were intense, they seemed to see into her most private thoughts.

"I can't, the children—"

"Please, Amélie?"

She pushed back her chair determinedly. "No, I must go."

He sat close beside her in the cab but he didn't attempt to kiss her. Her hand rested in his as they walked back through the hotel.

"Until tomorrow, then," he said, raising her hand to his lips.

Gérard's deep blue eyes were the last thing she saw as the elevator whisked her away from him, and Amélie stared down at her hand, where his lips had rested so lightly just a moment before. Like a schoolgirl, she didn't want to wash her hand because she'd wash away his kiss.

Leonore and Lais walked hand in hand with Gérard, looking, in their smocked flower-print dresses, one pink and one blue, like untidy angels. Socks were slipping into their white shoes, and every few steps Leonore skipped a little in an effort to hitch them up. Not Lais; life was too busy for her to worry about socks, and her head was too full of bareback riders on white prancing ponies and trapeze ladies in spangled suits dangling over their heads. Excitement spilled from her in short bursts of laughter and memories as she danced along clutching Gérard's hand.

"I hated the clowns, Gérard," said Leonore, holding his hand tighter. "They were scary."

"Scary, Leonore? I thought they would have made you laugh?"

"Sometimes, when they were falling down, but not the sad one with the white face and the pointed cap . . . he was *really* scary."

"She's afraid," said Lais scornfully. " 'Course they weren't scary, you ninny!"

Leonore's lower lip trembled and Gérard squeezed her hand sympathetically. "Sometimes they are," he assured her. "I think it's because the Pierrot always looks so sad. But he's not really, he's just a person—probably with little girls of his own."

"Really?" Leonore's worried face lit with relief. It was good to be with Gérard, he understood things. She began to skip along, jumping over the cracks in the path.

Amélie waved as they appeared around the corner. Judging by their disheveled appearance they must have had a very good time. It had been sweet of Gérard to want to take them to the circus by himself, though she had had her doubts about it. I want to get to know them, he'd told her, just the way I'm getting to know you. With a blush, she remembered his gaze when he'd said that. There was no doubt they were getting to know each other rather well; the few days in Paris had already drifted into almost two weeks. Gérard had spent every afternoon with her and the children, and they adored him already. He was the charming uncle who took them to the puppet show and the pony rides, who rowed them splashily on the lake in the park and provided wonderful picnic baskets of goodies he knew would appeal to children, and he never seemed to mind their sticky fingers on his elegant jackets.

Amélie watched as they hurried toward her, swinging on his hands and laughing at some shared joke. Lais and Leonore had adopted Gérard into the family as casually as if they'd known him all their lives. It was she who was holding back. She who had kept their progressively intimate friendship to just that. She hadn't even kissed him yet. If I do, thought Amélie as she smiled into his eyes, it might change everything, it might not be what I hoped it would be.

The children's excited voices clamored for attention with stories of the circus.

"Well, it sounds as though you had a good time." Amélie smoothed back their hair and kissed them, retying their sashes, and pulling up their socks. "There, that's better. Now, how about a glass of milk, and this café has the best chocolate cake in the world."

Their eyes grew round at the sight of the many-tiered cake, oozing chocolate, and Lais's finger hovered over her slice.

"Don't you dare, Lais do Santos," Amélie said with a frown. "Use your fork!"

Gérard laughed at Lais's disappointed face; the gooeyness was very tempting to little fingers.

"I'm a very lucky man to have fallen in love with a woman with two such delightful children. Like their mother, they are easy to love."

Amélie caught her breath. "You shouldn't say things like that," she murmured as the children's eyes rose from their cake to her blushing face.

"Does that mean that he loves us all, Mama?" asked Leonore. Her amber eyes were serious above her chocolate-covered mouth.

"It certainly does," said Gérard emphatically. "Now eat your cake and let me talk to your mother. Will you have dinner with me tonight?"

"Of course." She had dinner with him every night and he seemed to know every small intimate bistro in Paris that was candlelit and frequented by lovers. They would hold hands and talk and he'd kiss her cheek. She knew the smell of his cologne as if it were her own, she knew the way his serious face could break into a sudden charming smile, the way his firm mouth moved when he spoke. The contact of his hand on hers exhilarated and frightened her, she was aware of each separate bone, even the slight ridges in his fingernails.

Leonore leaned against her sleepily. "We must get back," said Amélie, scooping up her daughter from the chair.

Gérard picked up Lais. "Come on, then," he said gently to the little girl, "it's time for a bath."

* * *

The formidable lady at the cash register in the center of the bistro watched them with an indulgent eye. They had been here three nights in a row and they were such an attractive couple and so very much in love. They hung on to each other's every word, tucked away in the booth in the corner, their hands only unclasping for the mundane task of eating the food placed before them. With a sigh of envy she accepted the money held out to her by a departing diner. It must be good to be young and carefree and in love like that.

"I really must leave Paris soon," said Amélie, pushing aside her plate. She felt too breathless to eat, too tense.

"Don't go. Please." Gérard's dark eyes were pleading. "Stay here with me."

"I must go, it's the reason I'm here."

"Are your friends expecting you so soon? Can't you tell them you'll go later? Please, Amélie, I don't want to lose you now ... we've scarcely begun."

She didn't ask him what he meant by that, she knew what the answer would be and she wasn't sure she was ready for it. She'd only known him two weeks; was it possible to be in love in just two weeks? With Roberto it had been a lifetime. Yes, but this was different—wasn't it?

"But I must go soon."

Her voice was reluctant and Gérard breathed a sigh of relief. It was a small victory, but at least she wouldn't disappear tomorrow.

"Let's go," he said, collecting her up. "I want to take you somewhere where I can dance with you." At least that way he could hold her in his arms.

The cashier sighed again as she accepted his payment, her eyes following them out into the warm summer night. Yes, life was good when you loved like that.

Gérard kissed her in the place de la Concorde at three o'clock in the morning as they strolled home together after dancing, bodies close and arms wrapped around each other, for hours. Passion rose in her like the sap in a spring tree as she clung to his warm mouth. At last Gérard released her and they gazed into each other's eyes, looking for the answers to the secret questions lovers ask.

"I want to make love to you," he murmured in her ear. "I want to hold you and stroke you and kiss you. I don't ever want to leave you, Amélie. I want you by my side when I wake up in the morning. Stay with me, please stay with me."

Amélie's knees felt shaky; if it weren't for his arms around her, she felt she might fall. Her children were asleep in the hotel, she should be there, what was she doing kissing Gérard in the middle of the place de la Concorde? And worse, what was she doing feeling like this? She barely knew him.

"I must go home." Even to herself the words sounded foolish, what she really wanted to say was that she loved him, that she wanted him, too.

Gérard's arm circled her waist as they walked, and the soft undulations of her hips sent pulses through his head.

"Tomorrow," he whispered, "I want to take you somewhere special."

"Yes," she breathed. Anywhere, she would go anywhere with him—tomorrow.

Gérard kissed her on the tip of her nose as he left her at the hotel. "Tea," he said, "with my mother. I want her to meet the girl I'm going to marry."

Amélie watched his retreating back bemusedly. What had he said? Could she have heard right? She whirled into the elevator, leaning against its padded moiré walls. A smile lit her face and as the elevator stopped, she leapt out and danced down the corridor, laughter bubbling from her. Life was wonderful, *wonderful!* She had know a man for only two weeks, she was madly in love, and he had *almost* asked her to marry him. What more did any girl need to make her happy?

The house was *very* grand and Amélie stared at the soaring frescoed ceiling as the butler led her across the marble hall to the small salon where the Duchesse de Courmont awaited them.

"I didn't know your family was quite as grand as this," she whispered to Gérard, hearing her footsteps echoing on the tiles.

"It's not," he whispered back. "We all hate this house, but it's convenient when we're in Paris."

Marie-France de Courmont was small and smiling and pretty, and if her smile seemed a little hesitant, Amélie was unaware of it as Gérard introduced her to his mother.

It was with a sense of déjà vu that Marie-France took Amélie's hand in hers. The girl standing in front of her could have been Léonie twenty years ago. Perhaps she was a shade taller, a little more slender, the chin a fraction less wide, but she was Léonie. She glanced at her son; could he not have noticed? But then, he had never known Léonie—as far as she knew he had never even met her, though he had seen her on stage.

Controlling her feelings, she made polite conversation. She passed the girl a cup of tea. "Gérard tells me your home is in Brazil, Madame do Santos?"

"Yes, madame, or at least it used to be. Now I live in Florida."

ful beauty; she would see Léonie soon. She would know; her mother would have to tell her the truth.

❧72❧

THE SUN BLAZED from a cloudless sky as Léonie strolled the chalky path around the Point Saint-Hospice with Chocolat trailing at her heels. It was five o'clock, soon the sun would begin to lose its power and the evening would be soft and scented, time for drinks on the terrace with Jim. Life was almost perfect, even Jim's absences in America only made them happier when he returned and they were together again. All her other lives seemed so long ago and what was left was solid and real, her work with her children at the Château d'Aureville, her good friends, her home, and her land—and, most of all, her love for Jim. He was the laughter in her life, the sharer of pleasures whether it was a plate of langoustines fresh from the bay, a journey to a foreign country, or a starry night on the terrace of the inn listening to the sound of the sea. Even Monsieur had faded into the background, though his yacht was often in the bay. And with the lessening of his threat, Sekhmet had relaxed her grip on Léonie's imagination. Léonie picked up Chocolat, carrying the tired little cat across her shoulder and hearing the grateful purr.

Was it her imagination? Had she convinced herself all these years that Sekhmet governed her destiny? With a shrug she quickened her step, she wasn't going to think of that now. It was remote, far away—a long-dead past; this was real, the sun sparkling off the points of tiny waves in the blue bay, the groves of olive trees, and the scent of flowers and wild herbs. She climbed light-footed up the broad steps leading from the beach to the house, pausing halfway to listen. What was that? It had sounded like children laughing. Yes, there it was again. Two identical smiling faces peered at her from over the rail of the terrace as Lais and Leonore clung to the rail, waving.

"Hello, hello, Grandmère," called Leonore. "We've come to visit you."

For a moment Léonie couldn't take it in and then with a joyful hello she ran up the stairs to her grandchildren.

Their beaming upturned faces waited for her kisses, and their arms were eager to give her hugs. There were no inhibitions in these children, she thought, fighting back the tears of joy as she clasped them to her. "Let me see you," she said with a shaky laugh, holding them at arms' length. "Now you are Leonore because you have your mother's amber eyes, and you are Lais with your father's blue eyes."

"And you look just like Mama," said Lais.

"Only prettier," added Leonore, clinging to Léonie's hand. "Mama said you were very beautiful and that you had been waiting a long time to see us."

"Ever since you were born," confirmed Léonie, holding their small warm hands tightly in hers.

"Didn't you see us then, when we were born?" asked Lais.

"No. This is the first time . . . and I'm so happy to find you here on my terrace. But where is your mother?"

"She's inside talking to Jim." Lais dashed into the house. "I'll get her."

Leonore stroked Chocolat's soft brown fur and the cat rubbed against her legs and then rolled over, head tucked to one side and paws curled, waiting for her caress. "Oh, how lovely she is." Leonore's hand was gentle as she stroked the soft furry underbelly.

"Mother!"

Léonie's eyes met those of her daughter and the years of separation fell away like the closed pages of an already-finished book. "Mother, I had to see you."

Amélie flung her arms about Léonie, and tears slid down her cheeks. "I need you," she whispered.

"Of course, of course, darling." Léonie's hand fluttered soothingly over Amélie's soft hair. "You're here now, everything will be all right."

Taking Amélie by the hand, she led her into the coolness of the salon. She had thought that life was almost perfect only an hour ago—and now it was. Her daughter was with her at last. She needed her. And she had called her "Mother."

Jim was waiting when they returned to the salon, the two small children trailing behind them. Léonie's face was soft with a smiling contentment as she sat Amélie on the sofa beside her, but the girl was crying. Jim had sensed Amélie's tension as she had waited with him for Léonie to return, she had seemed tired and distracted though the children had been lively enough after their journey. They stood now in the doorway, Leonore with a thumb in her mouth and Lais jumping from one foot to the other.

Thank God Léonie had taken it in her stride; this should be one of the happiest days of her life, and if he had anything to do with it, it would be. He'd leave them alone, let them say to each other whatever needed saying.

"Come on, you two," he called, grabbing the children by the hand, "let's see what Madame Frenard has for us in the kitchen—she bakes terrific cookies—and then how'd you like to go down to the beach?"

Amélie brushed the tears from her lashes with the back of her hand. "He's such a nice man, your husband," she said. "He's so understanding."

Léonie wondered what had caused the tears; it was more than just the reunion, she felt sure of it. Amélie didn't seem to be the sort of person who cried easily.

"I can't tell you how happy I am that you're here, Amélie—and with the children. They're so pretty and so amazingly alike. I hope you're here to stay for a while?" She was suddenly afraid that she might lose them as quickly as she had found them.

Amélie took a deep breath. "We've been in Paris. I was on my way to see you, but ... I met someone there. Oh, it's all so mixed up, Mother." The tears came to her eyes again and she sniffed angrily. "I'm sorry, I didn't mean to cry. This was meant to be a happy visit—I was bringing my children to meet you—oh, but you see, Mother, I met someone in Paris and I fell in love."

The tears flowed unheeded down her cheeks and Léonie handed her a handkerchief. "Well, darling, that sounds like a very natural and very pleasant thing to do. Why so many tears?"

Amélie dabbed at her eyes. "I don't want to hurt you by asking ... I don't want to pry into your life, Mother." She took a deep breath. "The name of the man I'm in love with is Gérard de Courmont."

Léonie fought back a burst of hysterical laughter. Only a short while ago she'd been congratulating herself that the past was finally the past, and that Monsieur had disappeared from her life. *Gérard de Courmont!* The elder son, the young boy in the café all those years ago; he looked like Monsieur, she remembered, dark blue eyes, dark hair, the same arrogant profile. She leaned back against the sofa cushions wearily. Amélie had fallen in love with Monsieur's son!

Amélie watched her mother anxiously for her reaction. There was weariness in Léonie's eyes, and sadness, but not the horror she would have expected if—

"Mother"—her hand reached out and clasped Léonie's—"I only know parts of the story, just the surface, and I'm not prying into your life or criticizing, but you see *I must know the truth.*" She took another deep breath. "Am I truly a d'Aureville ... or ... or am I, too, a de Courmont?"

Her mother's eyes regarded her with surprise; there was no hesitation, no hiding of any secrets. "Why, of course you are Charles d'Aureville's daughter. Why else would I have given you to his family to bring up?" The implication of Amélie's question hit her suddenly. "Oh, you poor girl, my poor darling, let me tell you what happened, you should know."

"No." Amélie's relief was so great that she needed no more explanations. "No, it doesn't matter. That's all I needed to know." Her eyes brimmed with happier tears. "It would have been too terrible. Mother, Gérard wants me to marry him—he took me home to meet his mother. . . . That's how I found out."

Léonie was filled with sudden suspicions. Monsieur's son claimed to be in love with Amélie, but was he? Perhaps it was just a game he was playing, maybe he was in league with his father, perhaps Monsieur finally had Amélie in his grasp. Oh, my God, but she couldn't let Amélie know of these suspicions, the girl had been through enough already. What must she do?

"Gérard wants you to marry him?"

"Yes, oh, he's so wonderful, Mother, I can't tell you. . . . I've never felt like this before. I loved Roberto all my life, but it wasn't like this. I know that you and Gérard's father . . . well, that you hate each other, but isn't it over now? So many years have passed, does it really matter anymore?"

Poor Amélie, poor, poor girl. She doesn't know that Monsieur was responsible for the death of her own father, for his *murder!* And Gérard—was he like Gilles, was he ruthless and seeking the revenge Monsieur had wanted? Amélie's eyes were waiting trustfully for her answer; how could she tell her these terrible truths? And if she did, wouldn't she lose her daughter again—this time forever? It was a risk she wasn't prepared to take. Léonie took a deep breath, she would have to deal with this herself, though she didn't know quite how.

"I was only thinking when I was out walking just now, that it all seemed so far away, lost in the past. The present is what counts now, Amélie, you're quite right. Now, when do I meet Gérard de Courmont?"

Amélie looked downcast. "I don't know. You see, I just ran away—I mean, I couldn't stay in Paris, I couldn't be with him—until I knew. Oh, dear, Mother, he must think I hate him, what shall I do? Perhaps I should telephone him and explain."

Léonie managed a wry smile. "If Gérard is anything like his father, he'll have figured out exactly where you are and he's already on his way."

Something was wrong. Jim watched Léonie as she smiled around the supper table at her family, together for the very first time. There was a dimming of her natural exuberance, something lurked at the back of her eyes, a faint worry. Surely she couldn't still be concerned about Gilles de Courmont, the man was a cripple, powerless, and probably still living in fear that his blackmailing assassin would return to threaten him again.

"Well, this is a true celebration." Jim patted the hand of the little girl next to him. "Are you Lais or Leonore?" he asked with a grin.

The child giggled. "Lais."

"All right, Lais, here's some lemonade for you—and some for Leonore." Jim filled their glasses from the big crystal jug with the gleaming slices of lemon. "And we'll all drink a toast. To your mother and your grandmother—together at last."

He clinked glasses with the children, laughing as lemonade slopped onto the table. "This must be the happiest day of your mother's life," he told Amélie. "She's waited years for this to happen."

Amélie relaxed, it was as though she had known them forever, she felt so at ease with them, so comfortable.

"You'll probably be seeing a lot more of us, now that I'm going to marry a Frenchman. At least I think I am . . . if he still wants me."

"A Frenchman?"

Amélie looked so like Léonie when she smiled; the smile lit up her whole face. "Gérard de Courmont. Didn't Mother tell you?"

Jim's eyes met Léonie's. So that was it. My God, the girl was thinking of marrying Monsieur's son!

"I'm happy to hear it, Amélie," he said, helping the children to the roast chicken. How was Léonie going to handle this? He glanced at her as she sipped her wine, gripping the glass a little too tightly. Well, this was one they hadn't counted on. What next?

The story his mother had finally told him kept running through Gérard's mind as he drove his big blue de Courmont car through the night. No wonder Amélie had run away, and there was only one person she would run to: Léonie. He hadn't known the terrible fear that was in her mind until Marie-France had told him everything, but she swore that Léonie had told her the truth—she knew it. Monsieur had been Léonie's lover, but he was not the father of her child. Gérard pressed his foot on the accelerator angrily. Nothing was going to stand in his way: not his father, not Léonie. He and Amélie were the future and they had a right to their happiness. The car slowed as he turned into the outskirts of Nice and headed for the coast road, almost there, just a few more miles and he would be with Amélie.

The sun was warming the hillside as he finally swung the car to a halt outside La Vieille Auberge. Gérard glanced at the clock on the dashboard: it was just seven o'clock, very early for such a visit. What if Amélie weren't there? He dismissed the idea as he leapt from the car, slamming the door behind him. Of course she was there, where else would she go? The front door stood open and he could hear the soft slap of a mop on a wet floor as he hesitated with his hand on the bell.

"Hello," he called softly.

A face appeared around the edge of the door at the far end of the hall.

"Hello," called Gérard, "I'm sorry to disturb you so early but I've traveled all the way from Paris. Is anyone up?"

Madame Frenard nodded. "You'll be Gérard de Courmont. Madame Léonie is expecting you, I'll tell her you're here."

Gérard stared after her in surprise. She was expecting him?

Madame Frenard returned. "Madame says will you wait, sir, in the salon. I'll bring you some coffee and madame will be with you in a few minutes."

She showed him into the salon and disappeared again. Gérard sat down on the sofa and then stood up again, prowling the charming room nervously. It was going to be strange meeting for the first time the woman whose shadowy presence had dominated his whole life.

Léonie stood in the doorway with Jim behind her. He had refused to let her see this through alone. You're not on your own anymore, he'd argued. This affects me as well as you and, anyway, I feel as though you need someone in your corner. She'd given in gratefully, she wasn't at all sure what was going to happen. Jim's opinion of Gérard's honesty would be the deciding factor.

"Good morning." Léonie's voice was low and Gérard swung round in surprise.

"Madame." He stepped forward holding out his hand. He had the looks of Monsieur when she had first met him, thought Léonie, and she sensed the same forceful nature, the same strength of will, that had made Monsieur so successful in business. But his eyes had a more gentle gaze, and there were cheerful crinkles at the corners. He smiled at her now, an open grin that belied the anxiety and fatigue in his face.

"This is my husband, Mr. Jamieson."

"Well, now," said Jim, pouring coffee, "let's hear what you have to say, Monsieur de Courmont. Amélie's here with her mother, but I think there is a little explaining to do before you see her."

He looked at Gérard inquiringly, stirring his coffee, like a father surveying the prospective suitor for his daughter's hand, thought Léonie gratefully.

Gérard hesitated. "It's not easy. . . ."

"You can speak freely, Gérard," Léonie said quietly. "There are no secrets in this household."

"Very well, madame, though there's very little for me to say. I love Amélie. We met in Paris a few weeks ago, though you might say I've known of her for years, through my friendship with her cousin, Sebastião do Santos. I had no idea that she was your daughter until my mother met Amélie, and then, of course, she realized. It was she who told me of the court case my father brought against you and how you hid your daughter from him. *Your* daughter, madame, not *his.*" Gérard paused to emphasize his point.

Léonie nodded slowly. "Go on."

"I'm here to ask Amélie to marry me—and to ask you not to allow the past to harm our future together. It was your past, madame, and my father's. I beg you not to let his errors—his sins—influence your judgment. I'm here only because I love Amélie; maybe the way my father loved you once."

"Your father never loved me." The words sprang from her lips as though they'd been trembling there waiting to be spoken for years.

"Forgive me, madame, but I think you are wrong. My father's tragedy was that he cared too much, and because of some twist in his nature he was unable to show it."

Léonie avoided Jim's eyes. Why was her heart pounding like this?

"And how do you think your father will react to the fact that you want to marry my daughter—the girl he once claimed was his own?"

Gérard's shrug was expressive. "I have never known what my father felt, but whatever it is, it will not affect my intention to marry Amélie. My life is my own."

Léonie believed him, his face was earnest and anxious. He was a young man desperately in love. She didn't want to say it, but it had to be said.

"There's something else you should know about your father, and then you will understand why I am anxious for your reassurances and for Amélie's safety. It's difficult for me to say this, Gérard, but your father was . . . concerned in the death of Charles d'Aureville."

Gérard's gaze sharpened. "His death?"

"There was an accident, nothing was ever proven, but I have reason to believe that he was . . . involved."

Was there no end to this? Gérard's head sank into his hands. He could hear Léonie speaking, as though from afar. "Your father made me fear for Amélie's safety. It was because of him I had to hide her in Brazil with the d'Aureville family . . . because of him that I was unable to have my child with me."

Gérard stared miserably at the floor. This was worse than he could ever have imagined. He knew his father well enough to know how he must have tortured her, but "involved" in the death of Charles d'Aureville?

"Did my father kill him?" he demanded hoarsely.

"No . . . no, he didn't kill him. He was involved." Léonie couldn't hurt him any further; it wasn't his fault. How could she tell him his father was a murderer?

"Madame Léonie, my father is an old man—older even than his years. He is crippled. For years he couldn't even speak and only with the bitterest struggle has he managed to conquer his disability a little. Whatever happened in the past, I can assure you that he is unable even to look after himself now, he needs constant care. I can't say that he has forgotten the past, because I don't know. I was never close to him, no one ever was, except perhaps you. But I can promise you this: no harm will ever come to Amélie. She is safe now, madame, I am sure of it. I can't ask you to forgive my father's sins, but I do beg of you not to let them affect us. Don't let this battle go on, madame, with Amélie and myself as the only victims!"

Jim walked across to Léonie and put his arm around her shoulder. "Gérard is right, the past is the past. If he and Amélie love each other, that's all that matters."

Gérard's eyes met his gratefully; if ever he needed an ally, the time was now.

Léonie gripped Jim's hand; she wanted to believe him, she really wanted to believe him.

"Gérard!" Amélie stood in the doorway, the children peeking from behind the long skirts of her robe. Sleep vanished from their eyes as they recognized him.

"Gérard, it's Gérard!" they shrieked, dancing forward into his open arms.

Léonie saw the love in her daughter's radiant face. She looked at Gérard with her grandchildren climbing on his knee, while he smiled at Amélie over the tops of their heads. Of course he loved her. They belonged to each other and she had no right to keep them apart. The past was the past—hers and Monsieur's. Gérard swore he was helpless now. She glanced up at Jim and he met her eyes reassuringly.

"Well," he announced cheerily, "it's a little early for champagne, but I vote we celebrate with breakfast. Come on, Léonie, let's leave these two alone. Lais, Leonore, let's see what's cooking for breakfast."

Gérard and Amélie gazed into each other's eyes from across the room. "You've heard the story, then?"

He nodded. "It's their story, not ours." Gérard strode across the room and took her in his arms, where she belonged.

"I love you, Amélie," he whispered. "Don't ever run away from me again."

"Never." Her face was buried against his shoulder and her hair smelled sweet.

"Amélie, my father is the man your mother was afraid of all these years, the one she felt wanted to harm you." She stirred in his arms and looked at him in bewilderment. "It's hard for us to understand such emotions, but I have no doubt they were real—then. It's all in the past, Amélie. He's an old man, he's crippled and helpless. I want to rid us of this burden once and for all. Will you come with me after lunch to meet him—as his future daughter-in-law? Please, Amélie, for my sake?"

"Of course." Amélie didn't hesitate. If Gérard said it would be all right, then it would be.

Gérard heaved a sigh of relief. The past would be buried and finished with today.

Gilles de Courmont's apartment in the Hôtel de Paris occupied half an entire floor. Its big balconied windows overlooking the tropical gardens and the bay were shaded against the strong afternoon sun that left the room in an almost too-cool twilight. Gérard led Amélie to a chair by the window and opened the shutter so that the sun flowed in, while his manservant went to inform Monsieur le Duc that they had arrived.

"It's all right," Gérard reassured her. "When I saw him this morning he was in fine form. He said it was the best news he'd heard in years and that he would be happy to meet you. He just hopes you'll not be upset by his infirmity—and by the troubles of the past."

Though she smiled at him he could see she was very nervous, there was no doubt about it. After all, his father was the reason she had never been able to be with her mother, never been able to return to France.

"Monsieur le Duc will see you now, sir, madame."

Gilles was waiting behind a vast leather-topped desk. Its surface was covered with books and papers and a pair of reading glasses served as a marker in the open volume in front of him. One shutter had been thrown back and light streamed in from behind him so that it was hard at first to make out his face and Amélie stood in front of the desk uncertainly.

"Forgive me for not being able to greet you properly, but you are most welcome, my dear. I have waited a long time for this moment."

His voice was low and slightly hoarse and the sentences were broken up into sections where he drew breaths. The effort he must have made was immense and Amélie's sympathy went out to him.

"I'm happy to meet you, too, Monsieur."

Unconsciously she had called him by Léonie's old name and Gilles flinched. She looked so like her mother it was painful, her hair had that same blondness—the color of good champagne, he remembered thinking that all those years ago on the yacht, that first time. He forced his thoughts back to the present, to Gérard's voice.

"You'll love the children, Father, two ready-made grandchildren. What more can any man ask for?"

Léonie's granddaughters! Of course! Gilles sat back with a smile, contemplating his good fortune. Here was the girl he had been searching for for more than twenty years and she was his at last—marriage to Gérard would ensure that. And not only that, her children would be his, too, in his power, his to mold as he wished. A smile of satisfaction played around his mouth and observing it Gérard felt pleased. The old man was looking happy for the first time in years. This might be the best thing that could have happened.

A waiter arrived with iced tea and Gérard handed his father a glass, noting the involuntary tremble of his hands. He hoped they weren't overexciting him; after all, it was a lot for him to accept in one day. "We shall leave soon, Father," he said, sipping the tea, "we don't want to tire you."

"Nonsense." Gilles's tone was brusque. "I'm not tired. Perhaps I could meet my grandchildren soon. Bring them out on the yacht for the day tomorrow, I think they'd enjoy it."

"I'm sure they would." Amélie moved her chair slightly closer so that she could see him better. Her mother's lover met her glance coolly. His eyes were like Gérard's only darker and the gaze more intense, but that might be because of poor eyesight. He was still a handsome man but with the air of fragility that denotes a longtime invalid. Yet his shoulders were broad and she could see the powerful man he had once been. "Forceful and ruthless" was how Léonie had described him and perhaps he had been with her. But now he was just a man growing old alone, the victim of a crippling stroke.

"We'll leave you now, Father; this has been enough for one day. We'll be back tomorrow with the children."

"Early," said Gilles eagerly, "come early."

"We'll be here for breakfast," said Amélie laughingly. "The children will look forward to it."

She walked around the desk this time to shake his hand, averting her eyes from the wheelchair, which he obviously hadn't wanted her to see.

Amélie's hand was cool in his; Monsieur looked into her eyes and was swept back into a world of memories by her glance—the same as Léonie's.

"Until tomorrow then," she said, bending impulsively to plant a kiss on his cheek.

Gilles watched the two of them walk hand in hand across the study, turning to wave to him from the door. So his son had won where he had lost! His fingers moved softly across the place where Amélie had kissed him. But he wasn't finished yet. Oh, no! He hadn't lost yet; in fact, the game was just beginning.

Hoskins delivered the note personally, driving from Monte Carlo to the inn and waiting for the reply. Léonie was alone. She could see Jim from the terrace in a little boat out off the Point, fishing, and Gérard and Amélie had taken the children into Nice for the rest of the afternoon.

The big blue car with the crest on its door was parked in the lane and Hoskins waited impatiently for her answer.

She glanced again at the heavy plain white card with the simple engraved "de Courmont" across the top. His writing was a little less firm but nonetheless familiar and it still sent a stab of fear through her heart.

"Léonie," it said, "I think we must meet and talk over this situation. I'm sure you will agree that there is much to be said. Would you do me the honor of having a drink with me on the yacht this evening, say at 6:30? Gilles."

She paced the terrace agitatedly. There was a terrible fascination in the idea of meeting him again. She put a hand to her hair—would he still think her beautiful? *What was she thinking?* She couldn't meet him. *She wouldn't!* Yet he was right. Of course they must meet and discuss the situation— weren't their children planning to marry? She looked at the words again, they were innocuous enough, but she didn't trust them. Gilles was clever; there had never been a time when he hadn't been plotting. And she was sure he hadn't finished with her yet.

She turned off the terrace and into her bedroom. A beam of sunlight bounced off the statue of Sekhmet and Léonie paused in front of it for a moment, gazing into its sightless eyes. She put out a tentative hand and touched the familiar figure; the stone was warm from the sun, as warm as flesh.

Chocolat rolled over sleepily on the bed where she was taking a nap, but for once Léonie ignored her. Taking out a sheet of notepaper she wrote quickly. "I will be there—Léonie." And before she could change her mind she hurried up the path and handed it to Hoskins.

He touched his cap and thanked her. "Monsieur said I should come back at six o'clock to pick you up, madame," he said as he climbed into the car. "I shall be here promptly."

Léonie stared after the car as it drove off down the lane followed by a cloud of dust. Monsieur had known she would come.

❧ 73 ❦

LÉONIE WOUND the soft belt around her waist and smoothed the skirt of the simple apricot linen dress. Her reflection in the mirror showed a slender woman, casually chic, with smoothly brushed blond hair and a wide-boned, alert face, sleekly golden from the sun. It was in this same room that she had prepared to meet Monsieur as a young girl. She had gone to meet Monsieur on the yacht, just as she was doing now. Only then he'd made love to her. She picked up the small white leather purse and looked inside. The revolver looked delicate, nestled in the white lining of the purse, only its blackness seemed lethal. She snapped the bag shut and put it under her arm. She was ready.

The yacht lay at the far end of the small pier, isolated from other smaller boats in its deep-water mooring. It was exactly six-thirty as Léonie stepped onto the gangway and walked along the familiar deck. Memories flooded back to her and she stood for a moment looking around. Up there was where, in that first summer together, they had sunbathed naked and she had fed him fruit for lunch, and they had dived from the platform into the bluest of seas. They had paced these decks many a starlit night after a long languorous dinner sparked with champagne and before he had carried her off into that spartan bedroom where they had devoured each other in an excess of passion.

Fear gnawed at her stomach, a tiny irritating scratching that at first forced her to press her hand against her middle to try to stop it, but then flooded through her so that she leaned against the deck rail, trembling. No one was around and she knew that she was alone on the boat with Monsieur. He was waiting for her in the saloon. What was he going to say? What was he going to do?

Léonie pulled herself together. Maybe she was wrong and he wasn't plotting anything at all, perhaps he was just a tired, sick man. But if he weren't? She tucked the small white bag more firmly under her arm and squared her shoulders. Flinging back her head and raising her chin, she strode toward the study.

Monsieur was standing by the table and on the wall behind him hung Alain Valmont's portrait of her. She might have known, she thought bitterly. He leaned heavily on the silver-topped cane in his right hand; a wheelchair waited—ominously—by his side. Apart from the cane and his new thinness, the clock might have been swept back almost thirty years and, standing by the doorway, Léonie caught her breath. It wasn't fear she felt, it was the old magic. As her eyes adjusted to the shadowy room she saw the new lines of illness and pain on his face, the faint trembling of his hand gripping his cane. But his eyes were the same unreadable deep dark blue, gazing into hers with the old intensity. Monsieur's physical distress had not affected his mind—or his emotions.

"Léonie." His voice was cool and courteous, but hoarser than of old. "I'm glad you came."

She waited for him to catch his breath before continuing.

"You look as lovely as ever, of course. That color was always my favorite on you."

Léonie still stood by the door, half-in and half-out. "Won't you come in? As you can see I have the champagne waiting."

The bottle of Roederer Cristal sat in a silver cooler, filmed with chilly droplets. His cigar smoldered in the ashtray and a thin line of rich blue smoke pierced the air. Leaning heavily on his cane, Monsieur held out a hand to her. "Please, Léonie, you've come this far. . . ."

Hesitantly Léonie moved into the room, walking carefully, as if she were on a tightrope. She could see the strain on his face as he waited for her and she realized that he must have made a supreme effort to be standing when she arrived. Avoiding his hand, she took a seat opposite him, watching without any sense of triumph at his helplessness as he lowered himself into the big green leather chair—the same one she had chosen for his study in the house on the place Saint-Georges.

"So," said Monsieur, pouring champagne into the waiting crystal flutes, "the tables are turned since your first visit to this yacht, Léonie. Do you remember that day? You were a poor and desperate young girl abandoned by her lover. *You* were helpless and *I* was the strong one. Well, look at me now. Some would say it's God's revenge, I suppose—if you believe in God."

"I'm not here to talk about the past, Monsieur, or about us."

Gilles lifted the glass and held it toward her. "I'm sorry, I can't get up again to bring it to you." Her hand brushed his as she took the glass and the small contact sent a response through each of them.

Léonie sat down quickly. She sipped the delicate champagne and watched him over the rim of the glass.

"Léonie, if you would come back to me, everything would be all right again, you know. You've got strength enough for two—with you I would be my old self."

His gaze was almost fanatical in its intensity and he leaned forward in his eagerness, gripping the top of the cane with a faintly trembling hand.

"Don't you see, Léonie, I need you now, and you need me—although you pretend you don't. I know you feel what I feel, you always have."

Léonie's voice was firm and icily calm. "You're talking nonsense, Monsieur. And as I said before, I'm not here to discuss our lives, I'm here to talk about our children."

"Léonie, forget the past, forget everything except you and me. I'm asking you to come back to me . . . we'll be together again, you'll live like a queen. I'll give you anything you want. Just say you'll come back to me. I need you, Léonie."

Now he needed her. *Now* he'd do anything to make her stay. Anger swelled inside her, exploding into trembling points that shook her physically.

"Don't you understand, Monsieur, I hate you for what you've done to me. I will never come back to you. I'm a happy woman, I have a husband who loves me—really loves me, Monsieur, not just someone who wants me with some obsessive madness. And I love him. My life is full and now that I have my daughter and my granddaughters, I could wish for nothing more."

Léonie's voice was low, her rage controlled, and Monsieur recoiled from her words as though she had struck him.

"I'm here for only one purpose, to discuss my daughter and your son."

"*Your* daughter?" The words were spat from his mouth venomously. "Only *your* daughter, Léonie? Aren't you forgetting something?"

Did he really believe that Amélie was his child, or was he just tormenting her? There was no way to tell, as usual his face was unreadable.

"Amélie is Charles d'Aureville's daughter . . . and let's not forget about Charles d'Aureville."

Monsieur shrugged away the vague threat. "That's a long time ago, forgotten in the past. Amélie is the present, very much the present. Only you know whose child she is, but by all that's logical, she's mine."

"Logic never played any part in our lives, Monsieur, and it's too late to use it now. Am I to understand then that you are not going to allow Gérard and Amélie to marry because of this—this ridiculous claim?" The champagne slopped from her glass onto her skirt as she placed the glass on the table with a trembling hand.

"Not at all, Léonie. I'm delighted that they are to marry. Just think, Amélie will be a member of my family . . . at last. I daresay we'll be seeing a lot of each other once she marries Gérard. Think of it, after all these years of waiting, she'll be mine."

Léonie stiffened. His expression was so triumphant that she knew he was plotting something. It was the look he had always had when he was winning.

"Of course," he went on, "it would be so much nicer if you were with me, too. We could be one big happy family. There are those nice children—they'll be my grandchildren, too, now. Yes, I've learned a lot since Charles d'Aureville, I was younger and more impetuous then. . . . There are other ways to achieve one's ends besides killing. I've learned—the hard way—to bide my time. There are infinite ways to torture people . . . a word here, a suspicion there. . . . It would be easy to turn such young minds against their mother—poor little things, neglected by her. And poor Gérard, his wife is always so busy when he is away on business, she's seen here, there, and everywhere, perhaps with a certain man. It's all so easy, Léonie. I can arrange everything. Unless, of course, you come back to me."

He watched her face, waiting for a reaction, but her expression was remote, her eyes looked unseeingly beyond him, as though peering into the future he presented.

"Those poor little girls," he murmured, "those poor, poor little grand-children." His smile told her that he knew he was winning.

The small gun was very black in her capable soft-skinned hand and Monsieur stared at it in surprise. She couldn't be serious, not his Léonie. She was using it to scare him.

Monsieur's laugh rang across the room, a joyless expression of contempt. "You'd never get away with it," he said mockingly, "and anyway, you'd never do it. Just think of the headlines: 'Léonie murders lover—daughter to marry his son.'" It was so funny, so terribly funny. How could she point the gun at him like that, she was so close to him now.

"You can't manipulate my life any longer," she whispered, her face next to his. "It's enough, I can't take it anymore."

Monsieur's laughter ceased abruptly. Her face was calm and purposeful as she lifted the gun and placed it at his temple. It felt cold against his skin and fear flashed through him.

My God, she meant to do it, she was going to kill him. Thrusting out his arm, he gripped her by the wrist. Léonie pulled back her hand, and he lurched forward clumsily. He almost had it though, almost. His grip tightened—even crippled he was still stronger than she. His heart fluttered and skipped a beat and he gasped as his hand fell numbly back into his lap. His heart was vibrating, it was pushing agonizingly against his chest, he couldn't move! Oh, God, not again, not again. His whole chest was banded with burning steel. Why didn't she help him, why? His lips tried to frame the words but couldn't, he couldn't say it now, she would never hear it. Léonie, Léonie don't you know I love you? Help me.

The gun fell from her nerveless hand and lay, gleaming and forgotten, on the soft rug. His body was contorted in agony, his face mottled, and he was gasping for breath. She leaned closer, straining for the words that never came. Oh, God, what was happening? Wouldn't there be pills somewhere? Léonie looked down at the gun. Only moments ago she had been prepared to pull the trigger. She looked back at him. His dark blue eyes waited for whatever she was about to do.

The wind was blowing more strongly now, the smoke from the cigar stung her eyes, and Léonie lifted her hand to brush the sudden tears brought on by the acrid fumes. She should find the pills, she must, he was in agony; she couldn't bear his pain. "The pills," she whispered, clutching his hands in hers, "the pills, oh, my darling, tell me where. Where?"

His dark eyes, almost black with pain, locked into hers. She'd called him her "darling"—God, it made him so happy. Monsieur gasped as the pain hit him anew, she must do what he wanted, she must, she must; didn't she know, couldn't she read his soul? No pills could save him now, but he couldn't die without her in his arms, without her lips on his . . . her kiss . . . her love.

"Tell me," begged Léonie, "please, please, Monsieur." She couldn't bear it, she couldn't let him die, not Monsieur, so strong, so indomitable. All the things she'd fought against in him were the same qualities she had loved. She took his hands in hers, pressing kisses on them. "I've got to get help, Monsieur," she whispered. "Let me find a doctor. . . ."

He couldn't bear it if she went, he'd be left alone again with only the pain. She was holding his hands but he couldn't feel them, couldn't feel the velvet texture of her skin, but there was the fresh summer scent of her hair, and the jasmine. Kiss me, Léonie, just kiss me; give me your strength, for you are stronger than us all. . . .

Léonie put her hands behind his head, tugging the cushion into place, desperately trying to make him more comfortable so that he might breathe easier. His eyes gazed upward into hers, so blue, so dark, so demanding. Bending her head she placed her lips on his, holding his face in her hands.

Pulling herself away from him, she walked back toward the door. "I'm going, Monsieur," she whispered, "I'm going to get help for you. I'll be back as soon as I can, wait for me."

She spun around and disappeared through the door. He heard her footsteps on the polished teak deck—running away from him. He sat, motionless, his eyes fixed on the door, praying that she would reappear, that she would come back, that she would be unable to leave him. He closed his eyes, recalling the way it had felt when she kissed him. Her lips on his, her hands on his face, her breath on his cheek. Wait, she had said, wait for me. Didn't she know he had spent his whole life waiting for her—even when they were living together and he went to his office, he was just waiting, waiting until he could be with her again. He couldn't remember now the pleasure he had taken in the pain of going away and leaving her, forcing himself to be without her so that he could have the passion of his return and their reunion. Léonie, Léonie, come back, come back to me.

A sudden breeze roamed through the cabin, rustling the curtains, brushing his cheek like her warm breath. He could smell the smoke of his cigar, rich, and strong. With an effort, he opened his eyes, glancing sideways at the table beneath the window. The silver bucket that held the bottle of their special champagne glistened with moisture, the two glasses, still full, beside it. Beyond sat the heavy crystal ashtray where he had left his cigar, but it was empty. The cigar lay smoldering on the polished wooden surface of the table. As he watched, blisters bloomed under the smooth veneer. The thin azure curtain wafted in the breeze as the cigar rolled toward it and came to rest beneath its folds. He watched, mesmerized, as the pretty curtain fluttered gently, hiding its secret—for how long, how long? There, he could see the brown scorch mark, spreading. Then the first small flame tonguing the blue linen, crumpling it into gray ash. And then the great spear of orange flame. It was quite beautiful, the way it licked along the table toward him.

The wheelchair waited just two paces from where he sat. It might as well have been a mile. He'd been too proud to let her see him in that wheelchair, hadn't wanted her to know he was a cripple. And now he would never see her again. The pain in his chest gripped him harder; he closed his eyes against it and saw her face. Léonie, oh, Léonie, I love you. He was fighting for breath; the flames were creeping closer and the smoke was acrid, choking him, as his own heart was choking him, casting him into blackness.

Léonie's room was dark, the shutters closed against the warm, still sunlit evening. Chocolat lay beside her, comfortingly, on the big bed as she relived for the thousandth time the sight of the beautiful white yacht, a leaping mass of flame, the splintering sounds of glass, the twisting scream of metal, the crackle and hiss of giant timbers as they crashed into the sea— and then nothing. Just a charred gray hulk. She forced her thoughts away from the image of Monsieur, trapped in the flames, alone. "I tried," she whispered, "I tried to save him. I didn't want him to die, not like that. But why? Why, when I went there to kill him?" Was it pity? Or did she still love him? When she'd kissed him, for a moment it was as though they had never parted, all those terrible years had disappeared. What was he feeling when she kissed him? Was it pleasure because he thought he had won? Or did he really love her? She would never know.

She glanced at the statue of Sekhmet, lit with the lamp that was never turned out. The lion face was serene, arrogant, cold. It was just a statue. Carved from stone. She didn't have to read the inscription—she knew it by heart. "Sekhmet . . . mistress of all the gods . . . protector of those she loves . . . sends her flame against her enemies."

Getting up, she walked across to the statue and touched it. It felt cool under her hand, remote. Impersonal. It was over. There would be no more dark corners in her life, no more hiding, no more secrets.

Rushing to the window, she flung open the shutters, letting in the last rays of the sun, devouring the beautiful view with new eyes, her white terraces, her jade and emerald garden, the infinite blueness of the bay and the sky. She was free.

ABOUT THE AUTHOR

Elizabeth Adler was born in Yorkshire. She is married to an American designer, and they lived in Spain, Los Angeles, and Rio de Janeiro before settling in Oxfordshire. They have one daughter, Anabelle.